❧ *Hidden in a Whisper* ❧

TRACIE PETERSON

∽ *Hidden in a Whisper* ∽

BETHANY HOUSE PUBLISHERS

Minneapolis, Minnesota

Hidden in a Whisper
Copyright © 1999
Tracie Peterson

Cover design by Melinda Schumacher

Published by Bethany House Publishers
11400 Hampshire Avenue South
Bloomington, Minnesota 55438

Bethany House Publishers is a division of
Baker Publishing Group, Grand Rapids, Michigan.

Printed in the United States of America

ISBN 0-7642-0049-6 (2005 edition)

Library of Congress Cataloging has catalogued the original edition as follows:

Peterson, Tracie.
    Hidden in a whisper / by Tracie Peterson.
        p.   cm. — (Westward chronicles ; 2)
    ISBN 0-7642-2113-2
    I. Title.   II. Series: Peterson, Tracie. Westward chronicles ; 2.
PS3566.E7717   H53   1999
813'.54—dc21
                                                                99–6413
                                                                CIP

Dedicated to

෨ *Ramona* ෧

With thanks for the years of friendship—
for walking through dark valleys with me—
for celebrating in the sun.

You are truly a gift from God.

Books by Tracie Peterson

www.traciepeterson.com

The Long-Awaited Child • *Silent Star*
A Slender Thread • *Tidings of Peace*
What She Left for Me

BELLS OF LOWELL*
Daughter of the Loom • *A Fragile Design*
These Tangled Threads

LIGHTS OF LOWELL*
A Tapestry of Hope • *A Love Woven True*

DESERT ROSES
Shadows of the Canyon • *Across the Years*
Beneath a Harvest Sky

HEIRS OF MONTANA
Land of My Heart • *The Coming Storm*
To Dream Anew • *The Hope Within*

WESTWARD CHRONICLES
A Shelter of Hope • *Hidden in a Whisper*
A Veiled Reflection

RIBBONS OF STEEL†
Distant Dreams • *A Promise for Tomorrow*

RIBBONS WEST†
Westward the Dream • *Ties That Bind*

SHANNON SAGA‡
City of Angels • *Angels Flight*
Angel of Mercy

YUKON QUEST
Treasures of the North • *Ashes and Ice*
Rivers of Gold

*with Judith Miller   †with Judith Pella   ‡with James Scott Bell

TRACIE PETERSON is a popular speaker and bestselling author who has written more than sixty books, both historical and contemporary fiction. Tracie and her family make their home in Montana.

Chicago, February 1885

INEVITABLE. HER MOTHER HAD SAID it was inevitable.

Rachel Taylor stared at her gloved hands and tried to imagine what she would say when Braeden made his appearance at the park gazebo. They had met here every Sunday afternoon for the past two months, defying the cold, bitter winds that blew off Lake Michigan. Defying the gossip that surrounded any lady who met a man unaccompanied.

But today would be the last time they would meet.

Her mother had said it was inevitable that a dashingly handsome man of means such as Braeden Parker would find himself attracted to women of more physical beauty and social standing than Rachel could boast. And so it had happened—at least according to the women who boarded in her mother's house. The esteemed Mr. Parker was seen to have been in the company of a rather wealthy and beautiful blond socialite. Not only in her company, but in her arms—maybe even her bed, as some suggested.

It hardly seemed to matter that Braeden also inhabited Rachel's heart and would for as long as she lived. But fate seemed cruel and God rather distant on the matter.

Rachel considered herself plain and at times even unpleasant with her curly auburn hair and green eyes, but Braeden had pledged to her his love and showered her with words of admiration and praise. He had likened her ruddy complexion to the blush of a rose. Her green eyes,

9

he had said, were like twin emeralds burning with the fire of adventure and love of life. He saw in her the epitome of perfection. At least that was what he had told her.

Rachel rose and walked to the gazebo railing. Pieces of white paint were chipping away, evidence that the winter had been unduly harsh. Life was unduly harsh, she decided.

She sighed, trying to pretend that this wasn't the most difficult day of her life. Her head ached with a dull pounding that seemed to permeate her every thought. The pulsating beat was driving her mad. *Fool! Fool! Fool!* It seemed to beat in a driving rhythm. Rubbing her temple with gloved fingers, Rachel closed her eyes, hoping, even praying that when she opened them again she would find it was nothing more than a nightmare.

But opening her eyes revealed the culmination of her pain. Even now she could see Braeden making his way down the cobblestone path. He whistled a tune and it carried on the chilly, damp breeze, reaching Rachel's ear as a painful reminder of what she was about to lose.

It seemed destiny had mapped for her a future that did not include her beloved Braeden.

He waved from the distant walk, then grabbed hold of his bowler just as the wind caught hold of the edge. He smiled as though all was right with the world. Perhaps he had hoped she would never find out about his secret—certainly he had never figured on her putting an end to their romance. But then, ending their romance had been the furthest thing from Rachel's mind as well.

Only a year ago Rachel lost her father, a rail yard worker, in a tragic accident. Crushed between two freight cars, he had died within moments of the impact, love for his wife and daughter the final things he had spoken of. Rachel still found it difficult to believe he was gone. He had doted upon her as his precious little princess, and Rachel had found herself rather accustomed to his spoiling.

Her mother, now widowed and forced to turn her home into a boardinghouse, busied herself with her friends, listening to one tale of woe or another, encouraging news from the neighborhood, and reveling in the information. Always given to seeking out the latest tidbits on the community, the boardinghouse made this lifestyle even more productive, and Elvira Taylor always knew what was happening well before anyone else. That's why Rachel couldn't doubt her now. As much as it grieved her, Rachel knew her mother was seldom wrong when it came to telling tales on other folks. She didn't share this latest information with Rachel to be mean or malicious; in her mind she was simply looking out for her only daughter. Her hope was to keep a young and vulnerable Rachel from falling in love with a man who would only use her and then discard her for someone else.

Her mother believed there was nothing wrong with sharing the news of one person's mishap or another's triumph. The neighborhood was her personal domain, and everything that took place was of the utmost importance. It didn't matter that the preacher spoke out against gossip on Sunday mornings. As far as Elvira Taylor was concerned, it was her civic duty to know the lives of her neighbors. After her husband's death, this duty only became more prominent and essential. Her mother clung to her friends while Rachel had turned to Braeden for comfort. But no more.

Braeden had nearly crossed the park, and Rachel turned her attention back to the water of Lake Michigan—fearful that if she did otherwise, she might betray her misery.

God help me, she prayed. At twenty-one, the last thing she wanted was to turn down the prospect of marriage to the man she loved. But at twenty-one she was also old enough to understand that emotions counted for very little when it came to committing your life to another person. Her mother constantly reminded her of her gullible nature— her willingness to believe the best about everyone. Rachel had thought it was Christian charity that allowed for this, but her mother said it was immaturity and lack of life experience. She supposed, given the most recent events of her life, that this fact was well proven.

"You must be half frozen," Braeden said, ascending the steps to the gazebo. "I shall have to warm you up."

She could hear the teasing in his voice without even turning to greet him. She bit her lip for courage. What should she say? How could she explain? Once she turned to face him, he would see the redness of her eyes and guess that she had been crying.

As if understanding something was wrong, Braeden's voice

changed. "Rachel? What is it?" He turned her gently to face him and his voice became more pleading. "Has something happened? Is it your mother?"

Rachel shook her head and forced herself to meet his gaze. Her heart seemed to shatter. She had thought it already broken, but it wasn't until just now, seeing him face-to-face, that she knew her heart was completely destroyed. She would never love again.

"Then what is it?" he asked, the compassion evident in his voice.

Rachel studied him for a moment in silence. She wanted to memorize everything about him—his blue eyes, fringes of golden hair at the base of his bowler. She wanted to remember the squareness of his jaw, the prominent nose, and thick blond moustache. She wanted to take these things with her—to hide them in her heart for those long, lonely nights when the memories came to haunt her and her conscience taunted her that perhaps she had not made the right choice.

"I'm afraid this is good-bye," she said, her voice barely a whisper. Funny, she thought. In a whisper of hearsay her future had been destroyed. Now in a whisper she would bid her love farewell.

His expression changed from compassion to confusion. "What are you saying?"

"I'm saying that I cannot marry you."

"Am I entitled to a reason?" he asked gently yet urgently.

Rachel shook her head. "I believe you know the reason, and speaking of it would only give me pain."

Braeden's brows raised. "No, I don't know the reason, and as much as I am loath to cause you pain, I must know what divides us."

Rachel turned back to the railing. "I have been given some information."

"Do you mean gossip?" he questioned sarcastically. He pulled her around and forced her to look at him. "What has your mother told you this time?"

"Leave her out of this!" Rachel demanded.

"Why? Is she not the reason you are breaking our engagement?"

"We are not yet formally engaged."

"We are enough so that our hearts are one. Or so I thought."

"I thought so too," Rachel said, her voice quivering. She was desperately close to tears. "Apparently you have different plans. Would you have kept your other friend on as a mistress once we were married? Or would I have suffered the fate of mistress while you married her?"

"I have no idea what you are speaking of," Braeden replied.

"You were seen with another woman. A lovely blond-haired woman of means."

Braeden shook his head in confusion. "I don't know what you're talking about."

"Oh?" Rachel replied, moving away from him and pulling her cloak tight. "You were seen in her arms at the Tourey Hotel as you made your way up the stairs to . . ." Her voice broke off.

"What?" Braeden paused, as if trying to remember the scene. "You can't believe for one moment—"

"I didn't want to believe," Rachel interjected. "But my mother's best friend saw you with her own eyes. She was at Tourey with a group of women from the church to meet the choir director and his wife. They all saw you, Braeden."

"It isn't what you think. It's nothing more than a misunderstanding. I swear to you." He came to her and reached out to take hold of her.

"There have been other times," Rachel replied. "It isn't the first time someone has come to me about you being in the company of other women."

"Of course I've been in the company of other women. I move about in many circles of friends, family, and business acquaintances. How can I help but be in the company of women?"

"You know it is more than that."

"No, I don't. Why don't you explain it to me."

Rachel twisted away. "I know I'm not a wealthy woman, nor am I beautiful and endowed with elegance and graceful charm. But I am a woman of my word, and I expect to be treated with honesty. If you had found another woman more suitable to your interests, you could have simply told me. I would have been hurt, but not like I am now."

Braeden's expression changed yet again, and this time Rachel recognized the anger in his eyes. "You would believe those ninny-headed women who live to tell tales and spread all matter of story over me?"

"My mother wouldn't lie to me," Rachel protested.

"Your mother wasn't there, according to you. She simply took the observation of her friend."

"You weren't at the Tourey Hotel last Friday?" she asked, seriously considering that he might be telling the truth.

Braeden's face paled. "I was there, but it was on business." He sounded guilty to Rachel, even as he spoke the words.

"You are a prosperous accountant," Rachel said softly. "You are handsome and easily hold the attention of most any woman who comes into your presence. I do not blame you for finding someone more beautiful, more fitting to your status." Tears filled her eyes as she moved toward the steps of the gazebo. "But I do blame you for the deceit."

"And I blame you for destroying our love with mistrust!" Braeden declared. "How dare you come to me on a matter of such grave importance and base your entire decision on nothing more than the words of hearsay! Love requires trust. Have you not learned that in your twenty-one years?"

"I've learned a great deal in my twenty-one years," Rachel replied sarcastically. "My father was a good teacher, even if my mother tended toward gossip, as you are so good to point out. Perhaps the most important thing my father taught me was that men often deceive innocent young women in order to get something that should never have been theirs to begin with."

"Are you accusing me of less than proper behavior?" Braeden questioned.

Rachel quickly walked down the stairs and started up the cobblestone walkway. Braeden was at her side before she had taken five full steps. He grabbed hold of her arm and turned her to face him.

"Answer me," he said, his face only inches from her own. "Has my behavior not spoken for itself? I have treated you with nothing but gentleness and respect. I didn't even kiss you until you agreed to become my wife."

Rachel trembled from his touch. She was so under his power that it became imperative to get away from him before she changed her mind and agreed to believe him over her mother. "You stole that kiss, along with my heart," she murmured. "But you'll get no other part of me. Now leave me to go in peace."

He dropped his hold. "Then go," he said, his voice edged with pain and regret. "Go and listen to your stories and lies and let them keep you warm on a cold winter's night. Let them speak to your heart when you are lonely and sad."

Rachel said nothing more. She pushed up the walkway, praying he would not come after her. If only he had denied being at the Tourey, she might have believed it a case of mistaken identity. But he hadn't denied it, and something in that helped her to believe that she was justified in ending their engagement.

A light snow began to fall as the sun was swallowed up by heavy gray clouds. Tomorrow she would board a train for Topeka, Kansas. She would accept the position offered her by a friend of the family, becoming a trainee for the Harvey Company restaurants along the Santa Fe Railroad. And she would forget that Chicago and Braeden Parker ever existed.

✑ ONE ✑

August 1891
Morita, New Mexico Territory

RACHEL STARED AT THE GATHERING of twenty-five black-and-white-clad Harvey Girls and smiled. In six years of service she had reached what many considered the unobtainable position of house manager for the Harvey House Restaurant at Casa Grande Resort. It hadn't been that long since she'd sat where these frightened, fresh-faced girls now sat. She could remember her early days of training in Topeka, Kansas, as if it were yesterday. Standards and decorum, Harvey rules and regulations . . . all of these were drilled and enforced until she could recite them in her sleep. And now it was her job to instruct others.

"If everyone will quiet down," she said rather sternly, "we will begin."

Those who weren't already seated made their way to one of the empty dining room chairs as a hush embraced the room.

"My name is Miss Taylor, and I am the manager of this Harvey House dining room. Casa Grande, as you probably already know, will have its grand opening in three weeks, and we need to be ready." Rachel moved around the room, inspecting the girls.

"All of you have had training in Topeka, and most of you have worked at least six months or more elsewhere on the line. There are a couple of less-experienced girls joining us, however, and I want to make it clear that these employees are no less valuable in my eyes and should be treated with the same respect afforded someone who has been with the company for years." The girls nodded and continued to watch Rachel with expressions that betrayed their curiosity and excitement.

Rachel enjoyed getting to know her girls in a collective group, as well as interacting with them one at a time on a more personal level. People reacted differently depending on the audience, and Rachel had learned to recognize troublemakers and those who would refuse to take the job seriously by watching them respond in a group setting.

"In a few moments," Rachel continued, "you will each be issued a numbered badge. The badges will be used to identify your employment status in this particular Harvey resort. The initial issuance will be based on your time served in Fred Harvey's company. However, as you progress and perform at levels of extreme competence, you will work your way up and take a higher number."

"Who decides if your work merits a higher position?" a petite blond-haired girl questioned.

"I will," Rachel replied, recognizing Ivy Brooks, the niece of the town's matriarch, Esmeralda Needlemeier. Ivy had already shown herself to be a troublemaker of sorts. She had complained about the uniform, argued about not being allowed to fashion her hair in a more appealing style, and generally made everyone around her disgruntled. Rachel tried to have compassion on the girl, for she was an orphan. Life had dealt her a heavy blow, and Rachel knew full well how that could harden a person's heart. Nevertheless, Ivy would have to comply with the rules, just like everyone else. It was imperative for the running of Mr. Harvey's restaurants.

"Miss Brooks, you will come to realize that everything that has to do with you and your position here will pass through my review. Very soon I will appoint a head waitress who will be your immediate supervisor in matters taking place on the dining room floor. She will also help me to determine who might qualify for a step up in the ranks."

"And who will that be?" Ivy challenged.

"I've not yet decided," Rachel countered, steadily losing her patience. At twenty-seven, Rachel found herself rather intolerant of sassy teenagers. Ivy was barely eighteen and had been allowed to accelerate her training in Topeka and take a coveted position at Casa Grande only because her aunt owned the town and had sold Fred Harvey and the Santa Fe Railroad the land on which the resort had been built. The old woman was to be esteemed and coddled at every turn because of some undone business dealings with the Santa Fe. Ivy knew this and counted on it, but Rachel was undaunted. She would fire the presumptuous teen without remorse or outside influence if she refused to pull her weight. This issue was clearly addressed in one of her many meetings with Esmeralda Needlemeier.

"Miss Taylor?" a dark-headed girl spoke up.

"Yes, Miss Whitehurst?" Rachel questioned, trying hard to keep the correct name with the right girl.

"What type of things will merit a promotion? And, if you go up a number or two, what happens to the girl whose number you take? Will she assume your number?"

Rachel again came to stand directly in front of the girls. "Each girl will be judged according to her service, attitude, and even her reputation and actions away from the dining room. Your ranking will be determined by your actions. If the girl wearing the number four badge does her job but conducts herself in an improper manner off duty, she will no doubt slide down several notches and others will rise to take her place. And if the girl at number twenty performs in an exemplary manner, while those above her merely squeak by doing what little they can, she will be promoted and they will lose their standing.

"Mr. Harvey is very concerned that we represent ourselves in the utmost of propriety. You are hired here and paid the generous sum of nearly twenty dollars a month and given your clothing, room, and board. And you will generally receive tips from the patrons you service. Your laundry will be collected and done for you, and you will be given one day a week to do with as you please. At the end of your contract, you will receive a pass to go anywhere the Santa Fe Railroad can take you and given time to visit your family or friends.

"In return, Mr. Harvey asks that every customer who comes to dine at Casa Grande, or any other Harvey House for that matter, be treated with the utmost respect and consideration. He demands complete attention be given the rules he has set up, and the design of training for service must be strictly followed."

She watched each of the young women carefully as she continued to explain their duties. "You will report to your station in the dining room by five o'clock each morning. You will be properly attired in your uniform, your hair neatly contained in a hairnet, and your face void of any powder or paint to enhance your beauty. If I have reason to believe you are wearing cosmetics upon your face, I will not hesitate to take a wet towel to your face and confirm my suspicions. You will then be sent back to your room to repair yourself, and you will be issued demerits for your behavior. It is this type of thing, a blatant disregard for the rules, which will see you lose your standing."

In spite of how she tried, Rachel couldn't help but refocus her attention on Ivy Brooks. "No one will be given special favor for any reason other than meriting it for themselves through their work. If I find that you have done a good job on your assigned tasks, you will continue to be valued as an employee. If I find that you have done an excellent job, I will so note and merit your performance. If you should perform in a manner that goes far above and beyond those tasks for which you are responsible, your actions will also be noted and remembered for consideration during such times when promotions are available or bonuses of extra time off are issued."

She then explained Fred Harvey's concept of treating each customer as though they were in the finest restaurant in New York City instead of a small resort in a New Mexico town. Several of the girls asked questions regarding the resort and the hours of the dining room, and as Rachel concluded her talk and began handing out the numbered badges, she answered their concerns. She noted the frown on Ivy's face as she issued her the number twenty-five.

"To begin with, we will assign your work based on hotel occupation. If the resort is full, we will need to maintain a larger staff and therefore your shift may well run twelve hours. If the hotel is less than half full, you will probably be assigned to work one of two shifts. The first shift lasting from five o'clock in the morning until one o'clock, the second shift running from noon until nine that evening. If there should be a special party or festivity such as a dance or a banquet, then you will be assigned according to need. Now, I'd like everyone to go to your stations and acquaint yourself with the duties at each place. I have assigned you based on your experience. After this, we will do a run-down on serving procedures and hotel etiquette."

Rachel gave an inaudible sigh of relief as most of the girls went quietly to their proper stations. Some would be responsible for serving drinks, others for taking orders for meals, and there would be linens to care for and silver to polish, along with a dozen other jobs both great and small. It was no easy feat to run a restaurant to Fred Harvey's demands. Of course, the biggest responsibility given the girls would be their service of the customers. There was additional kitchen staff to help with the odd jobs, but the art of greeting, serving, and seeing to the needs of the resort visitors would fall upon the shoulders of these soberly dressed young women.

Rachel watched them silently for a few moments. Her memories took her back to her arrival in Topeka and the training she'd endured to become a Harvey Girl. The training had been rigorous and demanding, but the work was very satisfying, and Rachel always made wonderful tips in addition to her regular pay. She often found herself the envy of other girls in her house because the regular customers went out of their way to wait for Rachel's service, and the visiting customers always seemed to tip more generously at her tables than at any other. To Rachel, it was nothing more than taking an interest in their needs. She listened to them talk, as much as time would permit. And given the fact that they served four-course meals in thirty minutes or less, it didn't allow for much in the way of idle conversation. Casa Grande, however, would be different. There would be more of an atmosphere of relaxation, although there would be the occasional rush to catch a train. Most of the train traffic would wait until Albuquerque before putting their customers through the paces of the routine Harvey service, but Casa Grande was a resort for relaxation and restoration. Rachel shook her head at this thought, knowing that personally it would probably not afford her either pleasure.

But I took this job on knowing it would be a challenge. I am the first woman to be allowed to manage the restaurant of a resort hotel, and as such,

*I must keep my wits about me and show them they've not been mistaken to take
such a risk with me.*

Rachel knew the hardest part wouldn't be keeping up with the job.
The hardest part would be the long, lonely nights of isolation. Ever
since her first promotion to head waitress, Rachel had known the pain
of being separated from the crowd. She made friends easily, but as the
waitress in charge, she often had to rebuke those friends. This in turn
inevitably created hard feelings and conflicts. There were exceptions
and a few friends had remained, but Rachel had never known it to be
enough. She knew the emptiness of a life unfulfilled. A life lacking
what she most desired—a husband and family. Refusing to let her emotions get carried away, Rachel refocused her attention on the girls.
There were some very promising young women in her group, and she
had little doubt that the affairs of the dining room would run smoothly
in no time at all.

After allowing the girls to acquaint themselves with their duties,
Rachel put them into teams, with one of the more experienced girls
heading up each group. They practiced being customers and servers in
order that they might have an understanding of the days to come.

With the girls duly occupied, Rachel made her way into the
kitchen and found Reginald Worthington reorganizing his new kitchen.
A refined gentleman in his forties, Worthington cut a striking figure in
the sterile kitchen. Rachel had thought him a handsome man upon the
occasion of their introduction, and seeing him now only confirmed her
assessment. His brown hair, parted down the middle and slicked back
with tonic water, was no less orderly than his kitchen, and his eyes,
dark brown and quite appealing, seemed to take in everything around
him in a manner that suggested he might well be taking inventory.

"Ah, Mr. Worthington," Rachel announced with a smile, "I'd like
to introduce you to the girls when you have a chance."

The tall, slender Englishman glanced up from where he sorted
through his knives and returned her smile. "Miss Taylor, I would be
delighted."

He put the knives away in exacting order while Rachel watched
him in fascination. He knew precisely where he wanted each instru-

ment and assigned it a proper place in no less detail than Rachel had used to assign her girls.

"Well, then," he said, coming from around the massive preparation table. "Let us be about our business."

Rachel nodded. "The girls, as you know, will report to the head waitress and ultimately to me. Should you have trouble with any of them, I would appreciate it if you would bring the issue to me rather than try to deal with it yourself. As chef, you will have a free hand with the kitchen staff, but the girls are strictly my responsibility."

Worthington laughed. "And happy is the man who knows his place."

"I beg your pardon?" Rachel questioned before opening the door to the dining room.

"I'm very glad they are your responsibility," he replied soberly. "I would no more know how to deal with their tears and tempers than I would know how to construct a building. Women are a peculiarity to me, and save a quiet relationship with my dearly departed mother, I am at quite a loss to determine exactly how to conduct myself with them."

Rachel nodded. "I wouldn't worry overmuch about it. We often feel the same way about men."

"Do tell," Worthington replied, his thin moustache quivering ever so slightly at the tips as a hint of a smile played upon his lips. "I can't imagine you suffering from that feeling."

Rachel looked away, not willing for him to see that the same words that amused him caused her to feel a sharp pang of regret and pain. "I assure you, Mr. Worthington, the enigma regarding men and women is mutually acknowledged and endured."

She moved through the swinging kitchen doors into the dining room, where her girls were still working amicably together.

"Ladies!" she called, and all heads turned to her. "I would like to introduce the chef for Casa Grande. This is Mr. Worthington. He comes to us from a very prestigious New York hotel at the insistence of the Santa Fe management. His culinary skills are highly regarded, and he will no doubt bring to Casa Grande a flavor of the European continent as he has trained in Paris, Milan, Madrid, and his own native

London. You will heed his instruction regarding the serving and preparation of food; however, should any problems arise regarding your conduct, Mr. Worthington will not hesitate to bring the matter to my attention."

"I'm delighted to make your acquaintance," the Englishman said, his accent clearly marking his origins. "I shall endeavor to better know each of you as our duties require."

Rachel thanked Worthington, then turned to address her girls as he returned to the kitchen. "I believe it is necessary to restate something for your benefit as well as for mine. There is to be absolutely no fraternizing of Harvey Girls with male staff members. You are under contract to Mr. Harvey, and in being so, you agree to refrain from marrying before your contract is up. Those of you who have been with the Harvey system for longer than the initial contract realize the importance of these rules. They are for your own good," Rachel told them, but her mind was taken back to a time when she had been young and in love. Who could have possibly convinced her that such rules were wise and necessary?

It was hard to convince the heart that some matters were better left unexplored. She would, if she could, advise each and every woman before her to avoid romantic entanglements at all costs. Nothing was quite as hard on the spirit as realizing that the only dream you had dared to allow yourself would never come true. And, as far as Rachel was concerned, nothing lasted longer or hurt more than a broken heart. Which was the case with Braeden Parker. Even the mention of his name—the single thought of his smile—caused Rachel to tear up, even as she was just now. Coughing, she excused herself and appointed Gwen Carson, a young woman she'd trained several years earlier in Topeka and the one to whom she'd given the number one badge, to take over supervising the girls in their duties.

Back in the silence of her office, Rachel took several deep breaths and forced her emotions to reorder themselves to their proper places. She would not allow Braeden's memory to destroy her happiness. She couldn't. He was in the past and that was where he would stay. No matter the cost.

✺ TWO ✺

TWO DAYS LATER, as the girls finished cleaning the dining room after practicing a supper service on area railroad men and hotel staff, Ivy Brooks watched as Rachel took Gwen Carson aside to discuss some matter in private.

This has to stop, Ivy thought. *It's bad enough Gwen gets the number one badge while I have twenty-five. I won't be able to stand it if Miss Taylor assigns head waitress to her as well.*

She finished washing down the last table in her assigned area, then turned to see what her newest follower, Faith Bradford, was doing. Faith, a short, skinny nineteen-year-old whose immaturity irritated Ivy, stood listening to two of the other more experienced Harvey Girls explain their way of clearing a table. Faith, being the rather mindless twit that she was, would be the perfect victim to Ivy's plots and schemes. Manipulating such a creature would hardly be a challenge at all, but then, it was better that way. Faith would do as she was told without question, and Ivy would never have to worry about informing Faith of her comings and goings, especially when those activities kept her out past the ten-o'clock curfew.

Ivy smiled to herself. *I might be the most inexperienced Harvey Girl on staff at Casa Grande, but if I have my way, it soon won't matter.*

When Rachel finished with Gwen, she made another boring speech about the details of Fred Harvey's beloved system. Ivy found the entire matter unimportant. Her only reason for demanding that her aunt Esmeralda allow her to work as a Harvey waitress was in order to set herself up to acquire a wealthy eastern husband. The railroad restaurants owned by Harvey were, as she had noted in the local paper, notorious for bringing couples together. Ivy would have seen this as an answer to prayer—if she'd been the type to issue such requests. A husband would be the answer to all of her problems. He would be rich enough to see her kept in a fashionable style, with all the comforts she could possibly desire, and he would live somewhere other than Morita, New Mexico. These were the most important requisites for the man she would marry.

Rachel concluded with some sort of nonsense about the Harvey Girls keeping themselves spotless at all times. As if a person working in and around food and sloppy diners could be responsible for such a matter. She further enraged Ivy by instructing that should their uniforms become stained or spotted, they were to immediately retire to their bedrooms and quickly change their clothes. The idea was ludicrous, but Ivy kept her mouth closed on the matter. She wanted and intended to have the head waitress job in spite of her inexperience. She might be new to the system, but her aunt was wealthy and influential, and Ivy intended to use that to her benefit. Already she'd penned her aunt a letter and sent it by way of one of the hotel maids. Esmeralda might have stupid notions about making Morita into some sort of desert oasis, but Ivy knew she was capable of even more impossible feats and intended to enlist her aunt's help in the matter. Until then, Ivy planned to bide her time, doing what she could to ease her discomfort while plotting to change the Harvey system.

When Rachel dismissed them with high praise for a job well done, Ivy grabbed hold of Faith's arm and fairly dragged her back to their room.

"We need to talk," she told Faith, and the easily influenced girl simply nodded her head enthusiastically and followed after her new mentor.

Once inside the small bedroom, Ivy began stripping off the hated white apron and black skirt and shirtwaist. "I am embarrassed to have to be seen this way," she said, unbuttoning her skirt. "I believe Mr.

Harvey to be unusually cruel to dress us as nuns in a church."

"At least we don't have to pay for the uniforms," Faith offered in a singsong voice. She plopped down on her bed and smiled.

Ivy cut her with a glance. She knew the power of a look and had spent many an hour crafting her expressions to be just right. "You fool. It certainly doesn't excuse the fact that I must go about looking ridiculous while handsome men of influence and fortune make their way about the resort grounds."

"I don't understand," Faith replied, her tone more modest and sober.

Ivy pulled the net from her hair and unpinned her thick blond hair. Shaking it out, she reached for her hairbrush and began to stroke through the lengthy mane. "I couldn't care less about Mr. Harvey or his rules and his resort," she explained. "I'm simply here to get a husband of means and to leave this sad excuse for a town behind me."

"Oh," stated Faith as though such an idea made no sense whatsoever. The puzzled look on her face made Ivy frown.

"Why did you come to this job, Faith?"

The girl brightened a bit. "Because my family thought it would do me good."

"And has it?" Ivy asked, halting her brush long enough to consider Faith's response.

The girl shrugged. "I don't know."

Ivy wondered if the girl had a single thought in her head that hadn't been previously placed there by someone else.

"Well, I wouldn't count on it doing you much good, unless you're looking for a husband. I certainly don't intend to wait on people and serve meals the rest of my life, and frankly, polishing silver is something the servants will do when I have a home of my own." She resumed her brushing, stroking the cornsilk-colored hair until it crackled. "And I will never again wear black and white, at least not in this capacity."

She put the brush down and finished undressing until she stood in nothing but her lace-edged chemise, silk corset, and drawers. Positioning her hands on her tiny waist, Ivy gave a twirl.

"I won't grow old in this town. I won't be an ugly spinster and boss other girls around like Miss Taylor does. *I* shall have a beautiful mansion in St. Louis or Chicago and fifty servants to wait on me hand and foot'."

Faith giggled. "And beautiful clothes of taffeta and silk."

Ivy stopped and smiled. "Yes, and jewels and lavish finery enough to make all of my friends green with envy. But first I have to find a proper husband, and I must have a position of merit at this resort."

"A position of merit?" Faith asked, reaching up to take her own hairnet off.

"Yes. I want to be the head waitress, and with my aunt's help, I will be just that."

"But Miss Taylor said——"

"I don't much care what Miss Taylor said," Ivy retorted. "She may believe that plain little mouse Gwendolyn Carson is entitled to the position by right of her three years with the Harvey Company, but I shall see how she reacts when my aunt Esmeralda instructs her to give the position to me. My aunt is a powerful woman, and she will see things my way."

"How exciting!" Faith declared. "When will you talk to her?"

"As soon as we manage to set up a little bit of a complication in the life of Gwendolyn Carson," Ivy said, going to the closet to thumb through her regular clothes. She chose a pale pink dressing gown and slipped into it without saying another word.

She would devise a plan—a plan that would put Gwen on poor terms with those around her. But how? Ivy mused over the problem for several minutes before coming up with a plan.

"Of course," she said with a smile. "Faith, I shall need your help."

"My help?" the girl questioned, a stunned look on her face.

Ivy rolled her eyes. "Yes. Your help. We need to make Gwen look bad, and I have the perfect solution. She will steal your hairbrush."

"*My* hairbrush? But it's right here in my drawer," Faith said, getting up to open the drawer of her tiny dresser. She reached in and held it up for Ivy to see.

"Yes, I know it is," Ivy replied in irritation. "But we shall hide it among Gwen's things, then declare it missing. When Miss Taylor searches the rooms, she will find it, and Gwen will no longer be quite so favored." Ivy knit her brows together as she continued to consider this. "Of course, that might not be enough. We might have to do this several times. Maybe we could find something really valuable and hide it in Gwen's room. Maybe some jewelry from one of the guests."

Faith's expression revealed her confusion. "Steal from the guests?"

"If we need to," Ivy replied, finishing up the buttons on her gown. "Look, give me your brush and I'll sneak across the hall and hide it under Gwen's pillow."

"But it's my only brush," Faith protested.

"You shall have it back before an hour's time," Ivy countered, snatching the thing from her roommate's hand. "You'll see. Just go along with me in this, and I'll remember you fondly when I'm the head waitress."

Faith smiled. "Truly?"

"Absolutely," Ivy replied. "You shall be second only to me."

"Oh, how wonderful!"

Ivy smiled. "Yes," she murmured.

Going to the door, Ivy opened it just a crack and listened. Faith watched her and looked about to speak, but Ivy put her finger to her lips. She couldn't believe how dim-witted the girl really was. But then, a smart girl might not have agreed so willingly to Ivy's schemes. Sometimes a person simply had to utilize whatever was at hand in order to accomplish what they desired.

"Oh bother!" Ivy said, leaning back against the wall. "Gwen and several other girls are talking at the other end of the hall."

With their room positioned at one end of the hall and Gwen's room directly across from theirs, Ivy had only worried about the fact that Rachel's office and suite were positioned between the two rooms capping the hallway that served as one of two entrances into the Harvey Girls' dormitory. Now, with the girls gathered to chat at the other end, Ivy knew she would have no chance to slip into the hallway without being seen.

She tried to think about what she should do, but anger was overrunning rational thought. She simply had to put herself into a position of control. Her entire life had been mastered by others, but no more. The past might stand as witness to her previous mistakes—even regrets—but she wouldn't allow it to rule over her. She had made mistakes, but then, everyone did. No, she wouldn't remember the past or bathe herself in sorrows from her losses. She had suffered enough at the hands of those around her. First by her aunt deciding to stay in Morita to find a way to make the town prosper, then at the hands of the Harvey establishment and their personnel.

She peeked again and, seeing things basically the same, sighed and started to close the door.

"Why not just give the thing a quiet shove?" Faith asked. "Just nudge it into the hall and maybe Gwen will pick it up."

Ivy stared at the slightly older girl. "That's a positively brilliant idea."

Faith's face lit up. "Truly! Do you think so?"

Ivy nodded and opened the door enough to slide the hairbrush across the highly polished hall floor. "Perfect!" she exclaimed in a hushed whisper. She waited to see if anyone down the hall noticed her action and when nothing was said, she breathed a sigh of relief. "Now we wait a few moments and see if Gwen picks up the brush when she comes to her room. And if she does, then you must kick up a storm and holler your head off about your missing brush. Make it look good, or Miss Taylor will never believe you."

Faith, still standing on her laurels of having thought up the idea of sliding the brush into the hall, nodded enthusiastically. "I'll do it."

Ivy grinned. This was going to be simple. She narrowed the door opening to a crack and waited.

In a few moments, Gwen appeared outside her room. At first Ivy didn't think she would see the brush in the dimly lit hall, but then, just before she opened her door, Gwen glanced down and noticed the object lying at her feet.

She reached down and picked it up and while she stood observing it, Ivy clued Faith to begin her rantings.

"My brush! My brush!" Faith squealed.

Ivy threw open the door and loudly protested that someone had stolen Faith's hairbrush. The commotion instantly brought Rachel and several of the other Harvey Girls to see what was going on. Gwen stood speechless in the midst of the ruckus, almost as if the suddenness of it all had stunned her.

"What is going on?" Rachel questioned.

"Someone has stolen Faith's hairbrush," Ivy announced.

"Stolen it?" asked Rachel.

"Yes. It was in her drawer here in our room and now it is missing. In order for it to be so, someone would have had to have taken it."

Gwen held up the brush. "Is this it? I just found it here in the hallway."

Ivy scowled and Faith expressed glee. "Yes!" Faith exclaimed. "That's it!"

"Why do you have it?" Ivy asked suspiciously.

"As I said, I just found it here on the floor when I came to my room."

"That makes no sense," Ivy said, hands on hips. "I believe you took it."

"But I didn't!" Gwen protested.

"Now, wait just a minute," Rachel interceded. "There is no sense in accusing someone falsely."

"How can it be falsely?" Ivy asked. "She's holding the object in her hands."

"Yes, but she said it was found on the floor. Isn't it possible that Faith simply dropped it?"

"In the hall?" Ivy's voice held a tone of complete disbelief. "Why in the world would Faith carry her brush to the hall?"

"Well, given that the bathroom is at the end of the hall, perhaps she carried it with her when she took her bath this morning," Rachel offered. The other girls nodded, as this seemed quite reasonable.

"You'll have to be more careful in the future," Rachel told Faith as Gwen handed her the brush. "Now everyone go on about your business and leave off with this nonsense about stealing. We are a family here, and families do not steal from one another. If I should find it to be otherwise, that person would be immediately discharged."

The girls went back to their separate quarters, and Ivy smiled to herself as she closed her bedroom door. She had set the stage and placed Gwen at the center. Now she would simply have to look for other ways to draw attention to her dishonest actions. . . . Perhaps another theft.

"Perhaps a rather large theft," Ivy murmured softly. "One that can't be chalked off to a misplacement on the way to the bathroom."

❧ THREE ❧

THE HARVEY DINING ROOM for Casa Grande bore an air of elegance and refinement that rather startled the senses. Of course, all of Casa Grande was that way. From the artfully crafted brick exterior, complete with sun porches that faced masterfully landscaped gardens, to the rich walnut wood floors and chandelier-lit interiors, Casa Grande was something created from the ancient imaginations of European architects and designers. There was an air of Spanish flavor to the styling of the archways and porches, a presence of French palaces in the lobby and ballroom, and a homey warmth of English manor houses in the fire-warmed library.

For the dining room, Fred Harvey insisted on the very best furnishings. There were elegant sideboards and dining room chairs along with numerous oak tables that could easily seat ten people, sometimes more. The tablecloths were of the finest Irish linen, as were the napkins, which were nearly four times the size that would be found at any other restaurant. The dishes were china, the place settings silver, and the goblets were crystal. But Casa Grande was nothing special in this area. Fred Harvey insisted that his dining rooms bear the same charm and warmth of welcome no matter where they were located along the line.

Charmed completely by this elegance, Rachel enjoyed walking through Casa Grande whenever time allowed. The lobby itself declared an opulent wealth that dazzled the eye. No expense had been spared—from the marble colonnades and tiling to the brass fixtures on the walls and cappings on the marble stair railings. There were oriental rugs on the cream-colored floors with rich, dark walnut furniture upholstered in a golden raw silk. Blended with the red and gold accents of the carpet and furniture, heavy brocade draperies complemented the enormous floor-to-ceiling windows. Rachel knew from experience that the scene transported the person who walked through the doors of Casa Grande from a quaint, dusty village to a wealthy resort.

In spite of the grand opening still being a couple of weeks off, Casa Grande was, even now, aflutter with activity as the girls worked to feed breakfast to a bevy of railroad workers. Rachel felt pleased, in general, with the way things had progressed. She had heard that it might be difficult to pull together a staff of twenty-five girls, especially given that they were experienced in working elsewhere along the line and might expect to do things their own way. The uniform training and regulatory operations of each dining room along the Santa Fe made it easier, however. Every girl knew what was expected of her under the Harvey rules, and because of this, Rachel felt confident that the transition would be fairly simple.

Now if she could just eliminate the pesky problems that seemed to frustrate her efforts. Problems like Ivy Brooks's insistence to stir up strife and problems like . . .

"Miss Taylor!" an elderly voice boomed out, causing all heads to turn toward the main entry doors.

Rachel sighed. Problems like Esmeralda Needlemeier.

Crossing the dining room, Rachel smiled. "Good morning, Mrs. Needlemeier. What may I do for you today?"

"I have come to observe your operations," the older woman replied, tapping her cane on the hardwood floor.

"We are nearly finished with the morning meal. It was only a trial run for the railroad staff, but if you would like to partake of breakfast, I could check with the chef."

"Mercy, no!" the woman exclaimed. "I've already taken my morning meal. I've merely come to watch you work and to speak to my niece."

"Very well," Rachel replied. "You may take any seat you like."

She watched the elderly woman move across the room to position herself in one of the far corners. Sitting very primly on the edge of the oak dining room chair, Esmeralda Needlemeier observed the room with a critical eye.

Rachel tried to be unaffected by her presence, but the icy blue of Esmeralda's eyes chilled her. The old woman was difficult at best to relate to, but she was nearly impossible to understand. Rachel had tried to extend a warm welcome on many occasions, but inevitably Esmeralda held her at arm's length. *No,* Rachel smiled to herself, *she keeps me at a far greater distance than an arm's length.*

Jeffery O'Donnell, stationmaster for the Santa Fe in Morita and a very dear friend from Rachel's past, had told her that the old woman was key to the success of Casa Grande. She owned most of the land upon which the town surrounding the resort sat, and she appeared to be highly esteemed by the board of directors for the Santa Fe Railroad—especially given that additional negotiations were still in the works. Jeffery had explained that the Santa Fe was dependent upon her good graces since she owned the passageway from the depot to the resort. She also owned the omnibus company that would transport passengers along that same passage.

Rachel thought it rather amusing that one tiny old woman could cause the mighty Santa Fe Railroad to come to its knees. She glanced up and found Esmeralda frowning in her scrutiny of the operations. She was dressed in black bombazine from the tip of her high-collared jacket to the hem of her skirt. Her snowy white hair had been pulled back in a tight bun, its severity only altered by the application of a rigid black felt hat and veil. Her widow's weeds were reverent attire in the memory of her dearly departed Hezekiah, or so Rachel had been told.

Jeffery explained to Rachel that if they should harbor any ill feelings at all, it should be toward that stately gentleman. Having never sired a child, the man turned his attention instead to siring a town. Morita was that town, and in spite of being located along the Santa Fe Railroad, its close proximity to Albuquerque seemed to keep it from becoming a major stopping place. It was only after Hezekiah Needlemeier's death that Esmeralda took up the issue and went to work to bolster the fledgling town.

When the last of the railroad workers left the dining room, Esmeralda called once again for Rachel.

"What are those girls doing?" she questioned.

Rachel turned to see Gwen and two of the other girls stripping the tablecloths from the tables. "They're taking away the soiled cloths and will wipe down the tables and put on new ones."

"Seems wasteful," Esmeralda declared.

Rachel smiled. "Mr. Harvey says that each guest is to arrive to a freshly set table. The Irish linen tablecloths are to be in pristine order."

"I should speak to this Mr. Harvey about his waste. I have seen the portions of food served by this organization, and it is clearly in excess. Why, one of the steaks took up an entire plate! The man can't make a profit that way."

"I don't believe Mr. Harvey is overly worried about making a profit, Mrs. Needlemeier."

"Ivy! Ivy, come here at once," Esmeralda called out upon seeing her niece. She didn't seem to care about the disruption, nor did she apparently worry about leaving off with her previous conversation.

Ivy approached and kissed her aunt on the cheek. "Why, Aunt Esmeralda, what a surprise!"

Rachel watched their reaction to each other before deciding to slip away and see to the remaining work. Esmeralda, however, would have nothing to do with that.

"I have not finished speaking with you, Miss Taylor," she stated firmly.

"I apologize," Rachel replied. "It's just that I do have responsibilities here and it affords me little time to stand about in discussion." She wanted to make it clear to the old woman that she might have bullied the Santa Fe Railroad into submission, but she wouldn't find it quite so easy to control Rachel Taylor.

"I want to speak to you about my niece. I find it abominable that she should live here in such small quarters. In my home, she has a suite of rooms at her disposal and would no doubt be far more comfortable there."

"No doubt," Rachel countered. "However, I find it is good for the spirit of the group if they live and work together. There are areas along the Santa Fe where some girls live at home while working for Mr. Harvey, but because Ivy is the only one who comes from this area, I thought it might make her feel isolated to suggest such an arrangement. Together, they come to better understand what it is to be a family, and Fred Harvey wants them to act like sisters."

"Poppycock!" the woman replied, tapping her cane on the floor. "My niece is not a farmhand, nor is she a soldier. There seems little to be gained by forcing her to bed herself down as one."

Rachel saw Ivy smile smugly at this declaration. She wondered if the girl had put her aunt up to the task of insisting Ivy be allowed to move back to the Needlemeier mansion. On the other hand, Rachel thought, it just might solve a great many problems. If Ivy were housed elsewhere and merely availed herself for work as her schedule demanded, perhaps she would have less influence over the others.

"Mrs. Needlemeier, I completely agree with your thoughts that the girls are neither farmhands nor soldiers. They are quality workers for Mr. Harvey's dining rooms, and they are expertly trained to act in accordance with his wishes." She smiled at Ivy, feeling the girl's disdain radiate from her dark blue eyes.

"But I see no harm in allowing Ivy to move back home. She would, of course, have to maintain her duties and adhere to the schedule in the strictest manner, but I see no other problem. After all, your estate adjoins the resort gardens, and it is merely a short walk across the footbridge. I see no reason to force Ivy to remain here." Rachel turned her attention completely to Ivy and added, "If that is what she wants."

"No doubt," Ivy whispered none too quietly, "I would be made to suffer for a decision such as that. Perhaps Miss Taylor says it would meet with her approval, but I seriously doubt it does."

Rachel clenched her teeth and refused to be goaded by the younger girl. Ivy maintained a pose of angelic indifference, while Esmeralda considered her words.

"I would not have you treat my niece with hostility."

"I wouldn't dream of it," Rachel countered. "And I would seriously reprimand any girl who would try. As I told my girls when they first arrived, Ivy is not to be treated any differently, neither because of her inexperience with the Harvey system nor because she is your niece. Partiality would only lead to conflict."

Esmeralda seemed to consider this for a moment before nodding. "Yes. Yes, you are correct. Ivy, I believe it would cause a threat of conflict between you and the other workers. However, you may always resign your position. You don't have to work here, and you know it better than anyone."

Ivy frowned, seeming to sense that the tables were starting to turn against her. Rachel smiled pleasantly and leaned closer to Esmeralda. "I'll leave the decision to you and Ivy. After all, we want our girls happy. Now, if you'll excuse me, I must see to my work."

Rachel took herself away from the ordeal, a smile still playing on her lips as she walked into the solid form of Jeffery O'Donnell.

"Jeffery!" she exclaimed, then glanced around her. "I mean, Mr. O'Donnell. Please excuse me, I wasn't paying attention."

Jeffery laughed. "It's quite all right, Miss Taylor." He emphasized her title and gave her a wink. They had been on very informal terms in Topeka, and would be again in moments of privacy, but for now they carried the formalities for the sake of the organization.

Rachel smiled. "How is your wife?"

"Bearing up as well as she can. These first few months are said to be the most trying."

Rachel nodded, a twinge of jealousy coursing through her heart. Simone O'Donnell had become a dear friend during her training in Topeka as a Harvey Girl. Her marriage to Jeffery and their move to Morita had seemed to coincide nicely with Rachel's promotion to house manager for the resort's restaurant. She had even intended for Simone to be her head waitress. That is, until Simone had become pregnant shortly after their wedding. Jeffery wouldn't hear of her working in her condition.

"So what brings you here today?" Rachel questioned.

"I have brought the new hotel manager. You two will work closely together to control every aspect of this resort, so I want you to get to know the man well. You should both have a clear understanding of each other's jobs and responsibilities."

"I see," Rachel replied, looking behind Jeffery but seeing no one. "And where is he?"

"He'll be right along," Jeffery replied, turning to look outside the dining room doors. "Looks like he's been stopped by Mr. Smith, one of the top men from the Santa Fe offices in Topeka. He happens to be here to see to some of the details of the grand opening. He had several things to share with our new hotel manager. Ah, here he comes now."

Rachel couldn't yet see the man, but she immediately smoothed down the lines of her black serge skirt. *No sense in making a bad impression*, she thought. She looked down to make certain she had no food stains upon her clothes and, feeling confident of her appearance, raised her gaze to meet that of the new hotel manager.

"Braeden." She whispered the name almost reverently, but the shock sent a ripple through her body that nearly knocked her backward. Their eyes met, and Rachel found it impossible to draw breath.

"Do you know Mr. Parker?" Jeffery questioned, turning back in surprise.

Her heart felt as though it had come to a complete stop. For all of her pretenses that the past held no power over her, seeing Braeden Parker standing before her now quickly dispelled that hope.

"I . . . I . . ." She could only stammer. There were no words.

She lost herself in his gaze. He appeared unaffected. Calm, self-assured, not at all surprised by her appearance. His tanned face was more handsome than she'd allowed herself to remember, and when he smiled in greeting, his thick blond moustache moved ever so slightly at the corners.

"Miss Taylor, it's so nice to see you again."

RACHEL FELT IMMEDIATELY PUT OFF by the smug expression on Braeden's face. She tensed and looked at Jeffery, as if expecting some form of explanation.

"I had no idea you two knew each other," Jeffery said, grinning from ear to ear.

Braeden chuckled, breaking the spell for Rachel. Emotions and longings from the past blended with fears and worries. Why was he here? What could it mean?

"Well, I imagine this will make things much simpler," Jeffery added.

"Don't count on it," Rachel muttered, crossing her arms against her breasts. Her reaction caused everyone in the room to immediately take note. Seeing Braeden here, his countenance suggesting that he knew he'd find her here, as well, caused a spark of anger to ignite within her. She clung to it in hope of ignoring the longing stirred deep within her.

"No," Braeden said matter-of-factly. "As I recall, nothing with Miss Taylor is ever simple."

"Perhaps that was due to the company I kept," Rachel countered. Her anger gave her strength. She refused to back down, even as the Harvey Girls gathered a little closer. "Mr. Parker has proved difficult to work with in the past. I'm uncertain as to why you would bring him on for something as important as Casa Grande."

Jeffery's confusion was evident in his expression. "Mr. Parker came with the highest of references. His reputation in Chicago precedes him."

"That's putting it mildly," Rachel said sarcastically. "Though I'm certain there are plenty from that wonderful city to vouch for his, shall we say, many talents. It seems to me that people were always willing to share news of Mr. Parker."

Braeden, too, stood his ground. "Yes, indeed, Miss Taylor. And it seemed not to matter much whether those opinions were stated out of fact or fiction."

Rachel smiled a tight, fixed smile. "Ultimately we are judged by the fruit which we bear," she stated.

By this time even Esmeralda had gotten to her feet to edge her way closer to the trio. Rachel glanced up to see all gazes turned toward them. Jeffery apparently saw this, too, for he reached out and took hold of Rachel's elbow.

"I would like for us to adjourn to your office, Miss Taylor. There is much to be discussed regarding the resort and the grand opening."

Rachel nodded. "That would be perfectly acceptable, Mr. O'Donnell. Allow me to meet you both there. I need to see to my girls and make certain they know their duties."

Jeffery dropped his hold. "Very well. Mr. Parker and I will meet you in your office."

Rachel refused to look at the men as they departed. Instead, she went immediately to Gwen. "You shall be in charge, Miss Carson. I will expect each station to be spotless when I return."

Gwen nodded and her gaze seemed to express sympathy. Perhaps she had some instinctive idea what Rachel was about to face.

"Ladies, I will expect you to give Miss Carson your utmost respect and attention. I will be inspecting your stations upon the conclusion of my meeting."

With that, she left them to talk amongst themselves about what they'd just witnessed. She hated being the subject of gossip and spec- ulation. Hadn't she suffered enough from the suppositions of others?

She thought to follow Jeffery and Braeden's path by exiting the dining room into the lobby, then changed her mind. Her office actually contained three doors. One entrance from the lobby, one exiting door into her private living quarters, and one door that entered in from the dormitory hall. It was the latter that she chose to make her entrance. It afforded her a few more moments of calming distance. Plus, she reasoned that Jeffery and Braeden would be expecting her to appear from the lobby entrance. She smiled, thinking that this arrangement would allow her the upper hand. She would keep Braeden off-center by taking unexpected actions, and in doing so, she would safeguard herself against his plans—whatever they might be.

She hurried through the kitchen, ignoring Reginald Worthington as she passed. He appeared somewhat concerned, as if someone might have explained the scene to him, but she refused to stop and tell him of her situation. Reginald was just one more Harvey employee as far as she was concerned. They'd certainly not had enough time to become the kind of friends who shared confidences.

She entered the parlor and closed the door behind her, leaning against it heavily for a moment. Seeing Braeden had robbed her of all strength.

Dear Lord, she prayed, *why in the world has he come back into my life?* She looked to the ceiling, as if expecting God to be there smiling down. For as long as she could remember, she'd looked upward in anticipation of some visible sign of God. And for just as long, she'd not received anything to bless her sight . . . but much to bless her heart.

"Weren't things difficult enough here?" she questioned aloud. "I don't know how to deal with this. The man is to be my partner here at the hotel. How in the world am I suppose to manage this?"

She tried to regulate her breathing before pushing on toward the hallway. She stared down the long, well-lit corridor at her closed office door. The glow from electric lights, a real novelty in rural New Mexico and a feature that was bound to attract eastern visitors for the sense of convenience, reflected on the polished wood floors. They seemed to beckon Rachel forward. He was there. Just beyond that closed door sat the object of her longing and affection. Her heart ached at the thought.

"I can do this," she told herself. "It's been six years, and everything is settled between us. I can simply deal with this as a business arrangement."

But in her heart she understood the irony of her statement. Who was she trying to fool? If she couldn't be honest with herself, then she might as well pack up her things and leave now.

She still loved him. That had never changed.

The tightness in her chest seemed to increase. How could she look into his eyes again and not tell him everything? How could she sit there calmly discussing Casa Grande affairs and not beg him to understand that she had never stopped caring for him—that every day her thoughts somehow always found their way back to him?

She reached out for the handle of her office door and bit her lip. Six years. It should have been enough time to prepare her for this moment. But somehow it had failed miserably, and Rachel knew that if it had been twenty years instead of six, she'd still feel the same way.

She opened the door without any announcement or regard for where Jeffery and Braeden had positioned themselves. She refused to even look at the men until she had taken a seat at her desk.

"Gentlemen," she said, finally glancing up to where they had risen to their feet. "Shall we continue?"

Jeffery nodded and closed the lobby door, while Braeden took his seat. He looked at her as though he wished he could say something. Rachel thought it might be her imagination, but she would have sworn his expression was almost apologetic. The look softened her resolve.

"I'm sorry, Mr. O'Donnell," she began, deciding that directing her apology to Jeffery would be easier than dealing with Braeden. "Your actions took me by surprise. I realize that's no excuse, however—"

"Rachel," Jeffery said rather sternly, "would you please explain what's going on here? Apparently you both know each other well enough to share a feeling of animosity, and I would very much like to know what it's all about. Mr. Parker refuses to speak on the matter, suggesting that I consult you."

Rachel bowed her head. "It isn't important, Jeffery. I assure you it won't affect the affairs of Casa Grande. It simply startled me." She looked back up, giving Jeffery a pleading glance. At least she hoped her expression appeared pleading, for she sincerely wanted him to drop this subject.

To her absolute horror, Braeden seemed to take up a protective response. "Miss Taylor was once a dear friend. We were unable to keep up correspondence with one another and had no idea where the other had taken themselves off to. I do apologize for my part in this."

Jeffery studied them both for a moment, as if trying to decide whether to pursue the matter or leave it be. He ran a hand back through his brown hair, pursed his lips together for a moment, then nodded. "Very well." He took his seat and waited for a moment before continuing. "Since you two know each other, I suppose we can do away with the formalities of detailed introductions. Mr. Parker came to us highly recommended by another railroad company in Chicago, and with his accounting background, I believe he will be the perfect man to run the hotel portion of this resort."

Rachel nodded, forcing herself to listen and say nothing. She felt almost sick to her stomach and wondered if she'd end up making a scene before it was all said and done. She glanced quickly at the door to her living quarters, grateful that she'd remembered to close it this morning before heading out to oversee the dining room progress.

"Casa Grande, as you know, is only one of two resorts of this type. The other, located near Las Vegas, has been hindered by many problems, including the fact that the place has burned down twice. Some folks believe it to be cursed, but of course we don't hold with that theory. Financially speaking, we believe it to be simply based on logical conclusions. Namely, there is very little to entice a person to stay more than one night in Las Vegas, unless they are there to take advantage of the curative waters and hospital facilities available. So while the place does quite well for itself at times, we hoped for better.

"Casa Grande, however, is positioned closer to Santa Fe and Albuquerque. Also, the scenery is more enchanting with the mountains in the background, and our own hot springs and baths offer the same advantage and curative features."

"I understand that nearly every type of diversion is offered here for the entertainment of our guests," Braeden interjected.

Rachel heard the rich timbre of his voice and immediately felt light-headed. *This is ridiculous*, she told herself. *I'm not a schoolgirl, all swooney and silly.* But it did little good to argue with her heart.

"Casa Grande will offer it all. Later, during our tour of the grounds, you will see for yourself," Jeffery replied. "But for now, let me tell you some of what you can expect. We have a theatre room with seating for two hundred. This will be available for concerts, operas, plays, or even lectures. There is a ballroom more grand and glorious than any New York has ever seen. The chandeliers were shipped from Tiffany's, and the decor will enchant even the most hardened heart."

Rachel thought this a rather poignant expression. Against her will she glanced at Braeden and felt a small amount of relief to find his gaze fixed upon Jeffery.

"There are also sun porches and gardens," Jeffery continued. "You will find because of Mrs. Needlemeier's meticulous attention that the gardens on the east side are as much an oasis as any desert could boast."

"Mrs. Needlemeier?" Braeden questioned.

"She was the elderly woman in the dining room," Jeffery replied. "The one who maneuvered herself closer in order to better understand your reunion with Rachel."

Rachel felt the wind catch in her throat. Why couldn't this meeting just be over with so that she could go to her room and rest? She desperately needed to think about all that had happened, but Jeffery didn't seem at all concerned.

Braeden was smiling and nodding, while it was all she could do to remain seated. "I do recall her. Done up in widow's garb and armed with that silver-headed cane."

Jeffery laughed. "Yes, armed is a good way to think of it. The woman is fanatical about this town and about issuing her opinion. Nevertheless, she has maintained a lovely ten-acre garden and is graciously allowing us to share it for the benefit of our guests. Her mansion adjoins the gardens on the other side."

"I see."

"The hot springs and bathing pools and houses are to the north of the hotel. There are separate facilities for men and women, as well as

a lovely common pool for all to enjoy. The resort maintains very con-
servative bathing apparel for the guests, and as a staff member, you are
also welcome to enjoy this refreshment when duty does not require
you to be elsewhere. Besides this, we have stables for riding, croquet,
lawn bowling, badminton, and a bandstand where musicians will perform periodically throughout the day and evening hours. Indoors we
have a wonderful library with writing desks and quiet nooks for those
who would rather remain inside, and as you were already told, we are
fortunate enough to have electricity. The powerhouse is just across the
front drive, positioned at the base of Morita Falls."

"I must say, I'm impressed," Braeden said, considering all he'd
been told. "And how many rooms are available for hotel guests?"

"At this point, seventy. There are ways to allow for additional
rooms, but for now this seems sufficient." Jeffery passed his gaze to
Rachel. "As you've already been told, Miss Taylor is house manager
over the Harvey House Restaurant. She has absolute charge of twenty-
five girls, most of whom you saw there in the dining room. She also
has final authority over the kitchen staff, including the chef. She will
be responsible for ordering all food items and arranging with the local
citizens to provide what Fred Harvey does not ship in."

"She was always very capable," Braeden stated matter-of-factly.

"She has proven so for the Santa Fe as well," Jeffery confirmed.
"Rachel has been a longtime favorite of mine. She was responsible for
training other Harvey Girls during her time in Topeka and has worked
her way up the ranks over the last—" he paused and looked at Rachel.
"What has it been? Five . . . six years?"

"Six." The words came from Braeden before Rachel could even
open her mouth.

She could only nod.

"Well, for what it's worth," Jeffery continued, "it is hoped Casa
Grande will offer the Santa Fe a bit of salvation from its economic
woes. Kansas farmers suffered a horrible crop last year, and that, along
with poor investments, has brought problems upon the railroad. Casa
Grande is seen as a true oasis for the line, as well as for its passengers.
And with Mrs. Needlemeier's enthusiastic support and promotion, we
perceive the possibility of something very, very big here."

"And my duties will be to oversee the hotel portion of the resort, while Miss Taylor operates the restaurant and other food services for the guests?"

Rachel felt her mouth grow increasingly dry. She twisted her hands together in her lap, grateful that the desktop hid them from view.

"That's exactly right. You will have a hotel staff," Jeffery replied. "Many of the staff are native to the area. They were chosen because they had good reputations with Mrs. Needlemeier or other impeccable references. Positions that could not be filled with local people were advertised back East, and people were brought in from elsewhere. Your head housekeeper, in fact, was hired from Kansas City. You'll have a chance to get together with your staff later tomorrow. I'll give you a brief tour of the grounds today—show you where your office and living quarters are—then tomorrow we will arrange for your job to begin in earnest."

Braeden shifted in his seat and looked quite seriously at Jeffery. "What might we expect from the grand opening? I understand it will be mostly dignitaries and Santa Fe board officials."

Jeffery smiled. "Rumors do fly when you're about new business. But to answer your question, yes. The grand opening will be in just under two weeks, and there are all manner of activities planned for the celebration. Besides the band hired to perform here full time, there will be two other musical ensembles on the train to Morita. Miss Lucretia Collins, the renowned opera singer, will perform opening night, and a grand ball of such enormous proportions that even my head tends to spin a bit at the thought, is to be held on the third night. Both you and Miss Taylor will find yourselves very busy, and working together will be of the utmost importance. I want to know that I can count on you both to organize and maintain this resort in perfect order."

"I assure you, on my account," Braeden began, "that your trust will not be misplaced."

Trust. Rachel cringed inwardly at the word. Was Braeden trying to twist the knife that was already firmly implanted in her heart? Trust had been the reason for the demise of their love. Trust was now the issue that would stand between them to help create a new relationship—or divide them hopelessly.

A knock sounded on the door before Rachel could speak her answer. Jeffery got to his feet and opened it to find a young messenger.

"Mr. O'Donnell, you're needed back at the depot as soon as possible," the boy relayed.

Jeffery turned to Rachel. "Would you be so kind as to show Mr. Parker the grounds and the living quarters and office we've secured for him?"

Rachel wanted to refuse, saying that she'd have no part in it. She feared being left alone with Braeden, yet she could find no reasonable excuse for denying Jeffrey's request.

"Of course," she managed to say without sounding totally dumbfounded.

"Wonderful!" Jeffery exclaimed with a broad smile. "It will help me a great deal if you will see to this matter." He bid Braeden goodday with the promise that he would see him early the next morning, and then he was gone. Thoughtfully, he had closed the door behind him, leaving Rachel once again feeling completely trapped.

Allowing her eyes to meet Braeden's, Rachel was at a loss as to what to do or say. So with a deep breath, she said the only thing she could think of.

"What in the world are you doing in Morita?"

∽ FIVE ∾

BRAEDEN KNEW THE SITUATION was extremely trying for Rachel. After all, he was suffering on his own account and he had known she was here. Of course, he could hardly tell her that. It wasn't like he accepted the job because of her, for he'd already applied and been chosen for the position before being told that Rachel Taylor was a part of Casa Grande's staff. He could have bowed out at that point, but his heart bid him to stay.

His mind raced with the possibilities of what he could say to put her at ease. She looked quite angry and frightened, but even more so, she looked beautiful. He had often thought of her, wondering where she was and if she had married.

"I'm here to do a job," he finally said, realizing he couldn't very well go on studying her indefinitely.

Rachel pushed back a wispy auburn curl and squared her shoulders. "Did you know I was here?"

Braeden nearly choked. The very thing that he had sworn he'd keep secret he would now have to lie about or admit. "Why do you ask?"

Rachel shrugged. "I suppose I am curious. It hardly seems logical to accept that fate has thrown us together."

"What about God?"

"What about Him?"

Braeden shifted slightly. "I think it's possible that He brought us together for a reason."

Rachel tensed. "Yes, I suppose it is possible. The Bible is full of stories where people were tested."

Braeden couldn't help but laugh. "So you believe working with me is a test?"

"Without a doubt."

Seeing they were getting nowhere, Braeden tried another approach. "I tried to find out where you'd gone, but your mother wouldn't divulge the information."

"She was following my instructions," Rachel countered. Her green eyes narrowed ever so slightly. "I told her there was no purpose in you knowing my whereabouts. I had no desire for deceit and lies to follow me into my new life."

Braeden couldn't help but react. "I'm surprised she managed to keep the information to herself." He felt his anger mounting. In his thirty-six years of life, he'd never found a woman who affected him more than Rachel. Be it in anger or love, Braeden knew her to consume him. "So did you ever marry?" he asked, his voice tinged with sarcasm.

"No." Rachel spoke the word simply, as if daring him to pry for a more detailed answer.

"Couldn't find a man perfect enough to meet your standards?" Braeden questioned, regretting the words the minute they were out of his mouth. *I didn't have to say that*, he chided himself. *I can't let my anger get the best of me*. He looked into her green eyes and saw her wince.

"I suppose not," she finally answered. "And what of you? Did you ever marry that woman whom you were dallying with?"

Braeden clenched his teeth together. He angered at her insistence that he had somehow wronged her by being unfaithful. He had a perfectly logical explanation for his actions that day, but up until now, no one had even asked him for such an answer. And being the stubborn, prideful man he was, Braeden wasn't about to offer it.

"I've never married."

For several moments neither one spoke. Rachel appeared completely drained of energy, Braeden thought. Her normally rosy cheeks were pale and her eyes averted meeting his, as if the action might cause her too much pain. He hated seeing her like this, and for the first time since realizing that the Rachel Taylor of Casa Grande was *his* Rachel Taylor, Braeden wondered at the sanity of accepting the position. After all, he would be working with Rachel on a daily basis. And not only that, but they would be housed under the same roof and live their lives in a tiny little town where neither one could avoid the other.

He eased back in his chair and wondered what to do next. He glanced up at her as she studied her lap. The anger and sarcasm that tainted their words was getting them nowhere. He would have to swallow his pride and find a way to make this arrangement less consuming.

But consuming was the only word for it. She had consumed his thoughts and dreams for the last six years, and now that he was here, sitting not two feet away, Braeden longed to take her in his arms. She hadn't changed much, he decided. Her ruddy complexion and auburn hair stood out in contrast against her high-collared white blouse. She had fashioned her hair in a popular style of the day, with the bulk of her dark red curls pulled back and rolled into a knot atop her head. Wisps of hair curled down gently, softening the effect and framing her face. She was just as lovely and enchanting as Braeden had remembered.

"It seems we are in a bit of a fix here," Braeden said softly.

"I suppose that's putting it mildly," Rachel said, folding her hands on top of the desk.

"Look, I don't want to spend the next months snapping at each other and creating scenes."

"I have no intention of creating a scene with you, Mr. Parker," Rachel said stiffly. She pushed back her shoulders and lifted her chin ever so slightly.

"I think the folks in the dining room would tell it another way."

Rachel narrowed her eyes once again. "I was shocked by your sudden appearance. I feel my actions were justified."

"You've always felt your actions were justified."

"I try to base my actions on the facts at hand."

"We're playing games here, Rachel," he said, leaning toward her. He hadn't intended to use her first name, but it had come out without hesitation, as if their separation had never occurred.

"I'm not playing at anything, Mr. Parker."

"Don't!" he said, getting to his feet. "Don't try to pretend with me. I know you too well."

"You don't know me at all!" Rachel retorted and jumped to her feet. "If you knew me as you suppose you do, you would understand why I've reacted the way I have today."

"As well as how you reacted six years ago?" Braeden questioned, putting his hands on her desk. Leaning forward, ever closer to those wonderful red lips, he pressed his point home. "You acted out of mistrust then . . . just as you are now."

"I have no reason to trust you," she said rather lamely. Her bravado was fading as fast as it had come.

He thought she looked rather lost and vulnerable. Like a child who had turned down the wrong street and found himself separated from all that was familiar. He wanted to comfort her—wanted to tell her that the past didn't matter. But pride stood in his way. He would not yield on this matter. He could not.

"I have never lied to you," he said simply. "Trust is earned through actions, that much we agree upon. My actions were never out of line, but your trust was fleeting and given only on whim."

"You're wrong about that," she replied, her voice barely a whisper. "My . . ." She halted awkwardly.

Braeden wanted her to continue. In fact, his desire was so great that he felt something akin to rage when she refused. He had never been able to justify himself to her—had never been allowed to explain his actions at the hotel the day her mother's friends had witnessed him there. And he had never, ever gotten over her walking away from him. Ending their engagement. Destroying his dreams.

"I suppose it might be better if we saved this for another day," he said, trying hard to keep his temper under control. "Mr. O'Donnell expects you to tour me around the grounds, and it might be wise to do that before the sun sets and we have to go about in lantern light."

Rachel took her cue from him and drew a deep breath. "I have to take care of my girls and tend to their needs first. If I had my way about it, I wouldn't have to deal with you at all."

"Well, that is too bad," Braeden replied, "because you do have to *deal* with me. I'm not going anywhere. Casa Grande is a fine resort in a beautiful location. I intend to be here for as long as there is a job available for me. At thirty-six, I have a good number of years to look forward to life and employment, and just because you intend to treat me poorly is no reason for me to retire my position. Unlike you, I'm not the type to run away."

He watched Rachel's hands ball into fists. She kept her hands tightly at her side, but her gaze never left his face. "I do what I must to survive," she stated, then moved toward the door. "I would like for you to wait by the fireplace in the front lobby. I will see to my girls, and then I will show you where things are."

He reluctantly followed her into the lobby. He didn't like the fact that he was so angry. Neither did he like that she was upset with him. He had known she would be surprised to see him, but he had rather hoped that she would put the past behind them and give him another chance. He had never stopped caring for her or desperately wondering where she was. And now that he knew, he was hard-pressed to decide exactly how to handle it. Should he go back to Chicago and make her life less miserable? Or should he stay and hope for a miracle?

"Wait here," she told him.

"Yes, ma'am," he said with a stiff little bow.

She stopped in midstep and looked at him with a frown. "You needn't be so tiresome."

"Perhaps you would rather I had called you Rachel?" he asked, a bit of a grin forming on his lips. She was just so incredibly beautiful, and he loved that she was so obviously affected by his appearance in her life. Perhaps behind her anger he would find tolerance . . . and eventually love.

"No," she replied, and he saw the pain flash across her expression. "Miss Taylor will do."

He took a hesitant step forward and extended his hand as if to ease her sorrow. "Please understand—" he began.

She backed away, shaking her head. "I have work to do. Wait here and I'll come back to show you the grounds."

He watched her go, feeling a conflict within his soul. On one hand, he questioned his own sanity in coming to Casa Grande. On the other hand, he wondered quite seriously how he had lived the past six years without Rachel at his side. The future promised to be more than he'd bargained for, yet for the life of him, Braeden couldn't force himself to simply turn and walk away before it was too late.

"It's already too late," he whispered, knowing that his appearance here at Casa Grande had changed everything for both of them.

Rachel moved through the dining room, instructing her charges in a methodical, mechanical manner. She could scarcely draw breath, much less think rationally. He was here—and he was staying! She had often wondered what she would do if he reappeared in her life. She had pictured herself happily married with children at her side, meeting him on the street in passing. She would have loved for him to have seen her happy and content without him in her life.

Shaking her head, she knew that wasn't true. A tear came to her eye as she walked into the kitchen. Without thought to who might see her, Rachel paused, leaning heavily against the immaculate counter top. Somehow, she had to get a tight rein on her emotions.

"Miss Taylor, are you all right?" Reginald Worthington's soft British accent broke through her overwhelming misery.

"I'm perfectly fine, Mr. Worthington."

"I say," he continued, as if buying into her reply. "Would it be possible for us to work on a first-name basis? I realize it implies an intimacy and closeness that you might otherwise not feel, but I would rather enjoy the refreshing simplicity. It seems most folks out here in the West are less inclined to use such titles."

Rachel looked up and found his compassionate gaze fixed upon her. She wasn't sure at that moment that she could have denied him anything. He appeared so completely concerned for her well-being that it seemed only natural to grant him this request.

"Why, yes. We generally do business in a less formal manner in the Harvey House. Of course, when customers are present . . ."

"I will address you quite properly in sight of others. I simply hoped that in private we might form a friendship. If I've overstepped my bounds, then forgive me."

Rachel offered him a brief smile. "No, Reginald—"

"Please, call me Reg," he interrupted. "Reginald still seems too formal."

"Very well," she replied. "I don't believe you have done anything out of line. You asked my permission for less formality; you didn't impose it as a demand. I appreciate that very much."

"I would like for us to be friends," he said softly.

"It does make for smoother operations," Rachel answered, feeling her anger and emotional state lessen. "I would be honored to be your friend."

He shook his head and boldly took hold of her hand. "No, the honor would be all mine. I would happily do anything I could to ease your burden."

Rachel felt strange standing there in the kitchen while Reg held her hand. Fred Harvey had strict rules about any Harvey staff members dating, and while Reg was asking for nothing more than friendship, she couldn't help but wonder what else he might expect.

"You seemed quite distressed when you arrived here moments ago," Reg stated. "I wonder if there is something else I might assist you with?"

Rachel shook her head. "It's just that there is so much to do in preparation for the grand opening. Now Mr. O'Donnell brings me the new hotel manager, and I'm supposed to show him around the grounds and help him become familiar with his new surroundings." *But unfortunately*, she thought, *he's only managing to become more familiar with me.*

"I could show him around," Reg offered. "I have everything under control here."

Rachel brightened. "You wouldn't mind?"

"Not at all," he said, giving her hand a squeeze before letting go. "I would consider it a privilege to relieve you of this added burden."

"It would help me a great deal," she answered, her mind focused on how Braeden would take this form of rejection. She smiled. "Yes, I believe I would like it very much. He's waiting now in the lobby. Come and I'll introduce you."

She led Reg to where Braeden stood cooling his heels. "Mr. Parker, I would like to introduce our chef, Reginald Worthington. Mr.

Worthington has graciously agreed to tour you about the grounds." She smiled smugly and met Braeden's quizzical stare with great pleasure. She could see in his expression that he hadn't planned on this turn of events.

"Mr. Worthington, I'm pleased to meet you. I will be the hotel manager here at Casa Grande."

"Ah, Mr. Parker, it is an honor," Reg said, giving a slight bow. "Miss Taylor's schedule is already overburdened, and I offered to assist her in this matter. I hope you do not mind."

Braeden shook his head. "Of course, the company of a beautiful young woman is hard to pass by, but I shall enjoy getting a chance to better know you, Mr. Worthington."

"Likewise, Mr. Parker."

Rachel watched them go off together, and for the life of her she couldn't understand the disappointment that crept into her heart. *I should feel relieved*, she thought. But she didn't. Instead, she felt divided. The future and the past had just collided, and now she was hard-pressed to know which direction to take.

ESMERALDA HATED OLD AGE. She hated feeling less capable of doing the things she had to do. She detested looking in the mirror to see yet another wrinkle mar her once beautiful skin. And she loathed knowing that death was not far away.

Dying had never frightened her, and it certainly wasn't an issue of eternity and what would happen in the afterlife—it was more the inconvenience of it all. She had great plans for the future and aspired to do it all properly and in full control. Dying would definitely put a halt to those plans.

It was both troublesome and a blessing to be classified as old. Troublesome because your body no longer cooperated with you as it did in youth, and people often considered it necessary to shield you from shocking events and scandalous thoughts. But being old could also be a blessing. People recognized that you had come this far by knowing something more than the count of chickens in the hen house. You were generally respected and often deferred to. But then there was that whole pesky issue of death. As far as Esmeralda could see, the only good thing about dying was the idea of joining her beloved Hezekiah. He had been gone for five years now and it seemed like an eternity.

Hezekiah had known her better than anyone. He had shared his hopes and dreams with her, and in turn they had become her own hopes and dreams. Now that he was gone, she was a lonely old woman, although she would never have allowed anyone to know that fact. Instead, she created a façade of strength and dignity that set her apart from others.

The Needlemeier mansion, a two-story native stone Queen Anne house, stood as an oddity against the adobe and clapboard buildings of Morita. Until Casa Grande had been erected in its wealthy beaux arts eclectic styling, Esmeralda's home had commanded the attention of everyone in the community. Now, standing in the shadow of Casa Grande, Esmeralda wondered if she'd made a mistake allowing the resort to be built so close to her own home. There was no doubt that Casa Grande was beautiful—she wouldn't have had it any other way— but having it steal away the attention her home had otherwise enjoyed was a bit like being passed over at the dance for a more beautiful belle.

Staring down at the collection of letters on her desk, Esmeralda sorted through the replies to her advertisements. She had taken up the cause of her dear husband's dream and had worked to create a town that would flourish and grow with the ages. Hezekiah had wanted to be remembered for something, and Morita embodied that memorial. Now, with Esmeralda hard-pressed to let go of his desires, Morita was slowly but surely taking shape.

It hadn't been easy to convince investors to consider the small whistle-stop as a possible location for development. After all, Albuquerque wasn't that far away. It wasn't until she had convinced the Santa Fe and Fred Harvey to come to Morita with the idea of creating a resort hotel that Esmeralda had found any real portion of success. She had spent a fortune cultivating acres of gardens and creating bridges over the hot springs and falls. She'd given up equally large amounts of money to support the development of a proper town and to entice businesses to fill the buildings once completed. Her fortune was completely tied up in Morita, and now more than ever she intended to see it succeed.

Some said she was a bit touched in the head. She had no family except for her uppity niece, Ivy Brooks. But she was working to create a legacy that perhaps no one but those left behind could appreciate. She felt her emotions stir. The years had left a void inside her that couldn't be denied. Sometimes the loneliness of carrying on Hezekiah's dream herself was more than she could bear.

Stiffening her resolve, Esmeralda refused to allow her feelings merit. She would simply give her attention to the job at hand. There was no sense in allowing her heartbreak to interfere with that which demanded completion.

Picking up an envelope, Esmeralda considered the reply of a Baltimore storekeeper. He stated that he would be happy to take her up on the offer of free rent for the first six months and to consider signing papers pledging himself to a full five years of service in Morita. He went on to list the type of store he'd owned in Baltimore, and Esmeralda placed his letter in the stack of acceptable businesses.

The next letter had been penned by a banker who offered to bring his knowledge to the West. He wrote in a most condescending manner, saying that while he understood the desire to strengthen the town economically and to bring in business, he believed Esmeralda's methods to be a bit addlepated. His letter went immediately into the trash. Esmeralda would brook no criticism of her plan.

An interruption to her day came as it always did at two-thirty every Tuesday afternoon. Lettie Johnson, the plump and rather plain-faced pastor's wife, was led into the parlor where Esmeralda formally received her company. Lettie called this her Christian visitation and, as the pastor's wife, considered it a solemn duty. Esmeralda called it her Tuesday gossip session and would have refused the woman altogether had she not always brought with her valuable information related to the attitudes and current thoughts of the townsfolk.

"Good afternoon, Mrs. Needlemeier," Lettie said, removing her simple brown bonnet. "My, but it's a beautiful day out there. Have you managed to take a walk today?"

"No," Esmeralda said, tapping her cane upon the hardwood floor as she moved to take her position in a red velvet chair. "I've been much too busy with the affairs of the town."

"Mr. Johnson tells me we're going to elect a mayor," Lettie said, her full face breaking into a grin. "Word has it that there are several who would qualify for such a position of importance. I wonder whom you might consider acceptable for such a position."

Esmeralda hated the woman's prying, knowing that her utmost

concern was to find out whether her husband would receive the backing and support of the town's matriarch.

"I don't suppose I've had much time to think about it," Esmeralda stated rather severely. "Politics has its place, but there are matters of far greater concern."

Lettie nodded, her expression showing her disappointment. "I suppose so."

Esmeralda refused to be goaded. "The affairs of the new resort have kept me quite consumed. Have you managed to take a tour of the grounds?"

"No," Lettie replied. "We do plan to attend the festivities, however. I'm quite looking forward to it, and I even received my husband's permission to make myself a new dress. Won't that be wonderful!"

"I suppose all of the women of the church sewing circle shall consume their days with fashioning new creations to show off at the grand opening of Casa Grande," Esmeralda replied dryly. She could imagine the insufferable ninnies running about in their homespun gowns, each boasting the smartness of the other's design. They would all be put to shame by the dignitaries' wives who would come with their collection of Worth gowns and expensive jewelry.

Lettie giggled as though she were a young girl instead of a woman quickly approaching her fifties. "We're having a sewing circle tomorrow morning, and you would certainly be welcome to attend."

"I hardly think so," Esmeralda replied, looking down her nose at the woman. She had worked hard to establish a position of aloofness and reserve. Sometimes it served her well, and other times the loneliness it caused consumed her. However, sewing circles were hardly the type of socializing Esmeralda would bend to attend. Instead, she looked forward to the class of clientele that would be drawn to Casa Grande. The resort was expensive, and that in and of itself would help to keep the riffraff out. And given the diversity of Morita, Esmeralda was a firm believer in keeping society properly divided.

"Well, you'd be welcome just the same," Lettie continued. "We all think it's just wonderful the way Morita is coming to life. I walked down Main Street yesterday and thought I'd bust a button when I saw the new apothecary. You know how I suffer with my headaches and that strange little pain I get in my back. It'll be nice to have remedies so close at hand."

Esmeralda harumphed this breech of etiquette. Lettie would have discussed her physical ailments with total strangers if given a chance. But instead of rebuking, Esmeralda picked up a bell to ring for tea. "I'm certain the town will continue to grow and meet the additional needs of its citizens," she finally replied. "Ah, here is Eliza with our tea."

Esmeralda hired only a few workers for her home. She cherished her privacy, and a large house staff would hardly fit with this need. Servants tended to put their noses where they oughtn't. With only a few trusted people—a cook, a butler, and a housemaid—Esmeralda was more certain of keeping them under control.

The young, dark-headed woman poured their tea and offered a selection of cakes before replacing the tray on the cart and bobbing a curtsy. Esmeralda waved her off before sipping the lightly creamed tea.

"I presume Mr. Johnson is busy at work on the church budget," Esmeralda said as she placed her cup and saucer on a nearby table.

Lettie took a bite of her rich dessert, spilling powdered sugar on the front of her brown dress. She laughed and nodded, working to brush off the crumbs. "That he is," she managed to say in between chewing. She didn't appear to notice that her manners were atrocious. "He's real excited about the improvements you want to make. Just imagine, real pews in the church! Those benches have been so uncomfortable that it's hard to concentrate."

Esmeralda rolled her eyes, grateful that Lettie's attention was focused on the dessert tray. "Would you care for another?"

Lettie grinned. "Well, I shouldn't, but you know you have the best cook in town. Perhaps you should have her start up a bakery. I'll bet folks would come from miles around."

Esmeralda nodded. "I'll keep that in mind. Please help yourself."

Lettie did so, as Esmeralda knew she would. She could hardly abide the woman's manners, but there was something about these Tuesday afternoon visits that Esmeralda refused to let go of. Perhaps it was because Lettie was one of the few to come calling. Esmeralda ranked herself clearly above the other women in the community, and she could hardly expect them to worship at the heels of their matriarch and include her in daily activities.

"So what else do you have planned for Morita?" Lettie asked.

Knowing the woman to be unable to keep a secret, Esmeralda smiled stiffly. She had long since learned that this was the easiest way to get information out and about the town. "We are to have a new dentist and another dry goods store," she told the woman. "We have a new saloon, which of course I was not a bit happy about, but it is on property that did not belong to me. I suppose they shall make a rowdy time for themselves," Esmeralda relayed, "but with them positioned near the river, it is my hope that they will not be a problem to proper society."

Lettie laughed. "Saloons and soiled doves seem to be a natural fact of life for towns out here. Why, the mining town we left in Colorado had twenty saloons in a four-block setting. We didn't even have a school or proper church building, but those saloons were never empty."

Esmeralda nodded, knowing that the woman spoke the truth. Until the Santa Fe had agreed to purchase her land for Casa Grande resort, she could easily say that the saloon was probably the most productive business in her town.

"Speaking of saloons," Lettie said, leaning forward, "did you hear that Mrs. Mills' husband was locked up again?" She didn't wait for Esmeralda to respond. "He shot a hole in the floor of the Mad House Saloon and threatened the bartender when he refused to pour Mr. Mills another drink. The poor woman was beside herself when she learned the news. It practically broke her heart. You know they have five children and barely make ends meet with his profits from the mercantile. Not only that, she's going to have another baby, and I figure it was this that sent Mr. Mills to the saloon."

"Another child is far from what they need," Esmeralda admitted.

"Well, they aren't the only ones making additions to the town," Lettie replied. "We have at least three women in the congregation who will give birth next year. Of course, I can't mention them by name, but one of them just married two weeks ago. I'd imagine we'll see that baby arriving just a little sooner than the date on their marriage license would indicate proper."

Esmeralda nodded and listened as the woman continued to chatter about the matters of the townsfolk. One child had a broken arm, another had nearly drowned in the river but was saved by a kindly passerby. The town marshal believed he would seek out a deputy, and the butcher was to have fresh lamb available on the day after tomorrow.

Eventually the conversation lagged, and as it did, Esmeralda followed routine and glanced up at the ornate mantel clock. "My, but the afternoon is getting away from us."

"Oh, indeed," Lettie replied, wiping her mouth with her linen napkin. "I still have several calls to make so I mustn't tarry here. I do wish you would reconsider the sewing circle. We would be pleased to have you join us." She brushed off her crumbs, mindless of where they fell, and placed her teacup on the serving cart. "It's always so nice to chat with you."

Esmeralda walked her to the door, ignoring the way Lettie gaped at the furnishings of the house.

"You simply must take me on a tour of the house when I have more time," Lettie said.

This, too, was a part of the routine. Lettie always pushed for an invitation to see beyond the front parlor, and Esmeralda always managed to put her off with a simple, "We shall see." Lettie never seemed to understand that she had once again overstepped the bounds of propriety. Nor did she worry overmuch about what Esmeralda thought. She seemed quite happy just to make her rounds and visit—sharing tidbits of information Esmeralda might otherwise never hear. Lettie Johnson was better than any town newspaper.

"Give my regards to the pastor," Esmeralda told the woman as she pulled on her bonnet.

"I will do that. See you Sunday," Lettie replied, taking herself down the stone steps. "Oh, and don't forget there's to be a potluck dinner after church. I sure hope you'll come."

"I seriously doubt that I will," Esmeralda replied. She offered neither explanation nor excuse, and Lettie didn't press for one.

Esmeralda sighed in relief after the woman had gone, but even as she closed the door, she realized the sensation of emptiness that flooded the house. It was bad enough that Ivy had chosen to stay on at the resort. She had thought to bring the girl home and still allow her to maintain her ludicrous idea of waiting tables for the Harvey House, but that failed to work out.

She remembered their fierce argument when Ivy had learned of Esmeralda's decision to remain in Morita. It hadn't been a pretty sight because Ivy had felt certain they would return to her own native St. Louis or maybe even Chicago. But when Esmeralda had announced the coming of the resort and her decision to help Morita flourish, Ivy had been livid.

The girl had even refused to speak to her for days, but because she was underage, there was little she could do. Esmeralda was in charge, and without her approval, Ivy had little or no funds with which to make a move. She had hoped to guide the child into understanding how one could easily invest money and, if done properly, see a nice return for their efforts. But Ivy couldn't care less. She wanted nothing more than a wealthy husband and a home of her own.

Esmeralda looked up the long staircase to the second floor. Ivy's empty room stood just to the left of the top of the landing. The door was closed, reserved for that time when Ivy should choose to come home. Esmeralda didn't waste time worrying about when that might be. The child was stubborn and headstrong. Her willful nature had destroyed much of her life, and though Esmeralda had tried to mold her into a responsible adult, Ivy missed the mark in many ways.

Walking back to the parlor, Esmeralda stared at an oil painting of her now departed brother, Carl. "I fear I've failed you. Ivy is hardly the child you would have taken pride in." She drew a heavy breath and realized the futility of talking to the image. She was totally on her own in the matter of trying to rear Ivy in a responsible manner. That the child had no moral values and no interest in godly matters was alarming enough. But that she put her own aspirations and desires ahead of everyone else's, even to the point of hurting those around her, was too much for Esmeralda to comprehend. Perhaps it was better to give her over to Rachel Taylor and the Harvey system. At least that redheaded manager seemed not to be intimidated by Ivy's cunning and conniving ways.

"Perhaps this will help the child to change," Esmeralda muttered to herself, having little faith in the thought.

❧ SEVEN ❧

AFTER IMMERSING HIMSELF in his new duties for over a week, Braeden realized the job of managing Casa Grande was going to entail a great deal more than he'd originally understood. He was not only in charge of keeping the hotel books and records, arranging for the supplies and staff, and seeing to the reservations for special events, but he was also responsible for bringing in entertainers, scheduling resort appearances, and continuing to improve the grounds. Dealing with entertainment, he quickly learned, was guaranteed to be enough to drive him positively insane.

Making his way back from the telegraph office at the depot, he felt only a moderate amount of relief from the two telegrams in his pocket. Both confirmed acceptance of performances for future dates, one by a well-known acting troupe and another by a renowned European opera singer who would divert from Denver to join them in Casa Grande on the twenty-first of October. He supposed he should feel happy about the news, but he found he couldn't take pleasure in the matter when his thoughts were consumed with Rachel.

A mountain breeze blew across the valley, causing Braeden to raise his head. The dry warmth of the air felt good against his skin. The past few days had been unseasonably warm, and in spite of the modern convenience of electric lights and fans, Braeden knew Casa Grande would be rather stifling by midday. He speculated that once they were actually up and running with guests, most folks would take afternoon naps or spend quiet moments in the shaded gardens. For himself, he knew there would be more than enough work to occupy him through the heat of the day and didn't relish the idea at all. Chicago could have its own blistering summers, but generally they were mild and easily tolerated. He had no idea what to expect from New Mexico. Nor did he know what to expect from Rachel.

The walk from the depot to the resort wasn't all that far, but Braeden slowed his approach to the two-story hotel when his thoughts rested on Rachel. She'd been avoiding him as if he were the Grim Reaper. Many times he'd seen her in the dining room and had thought to approach her, only to have her duck out through the kitchen and into the private parlor for the Harvey Girls. Men were simply not allowed in that portion of the hotel, and infringing upon this rule would mean instantaneous dismissal. Braeden had little desire to be fired, but he had an overwhelming need to set the record clear with the only woman he'd ever really cared for.

He smiled, thinking of the months to come and how closely they would be expected to work together. Already there were a number of staff meetings scheduled, and he would have the opportunity to co-head the meetings with Rachel at his side. It promised to be entertaining, if not advantageous to his situation—if he played his cards right.

He paused on the bridge that spanned Morita Falls. Fed by the abundant hot springs and two other streams, the falls cascaded in a series of steps, dancing over rocky passages and splaying out in a churning pool some twenty feet below. Someone had thoughtfully placed park benches in the grassy area at the bottom of the falls for scenic enjoyment. No doubt it would also make for a lovely romantic interlude.

The picturesque scene drew him to reflect on how he might woo Rachel into agreeing to give their love a second chance. Moonlight, waterfalls, and the flowery gardens just might create the needed atmosphere. The hardest part would be setting the stage that would put them together in such a place. If Rachel had her way, she would never again be alone in his company.

Sighing, he turned away from the enchanting little falls and made his way up the drive and past the white marble fountain to Casa Grande. On his desk he had a stack of original inventory sheets to compare to the inventory recently taken by his housekeeper, and there was no telling how long it would actually take to reconcile the two. With this business in mind, he raced up the steps and plowed through the doorway just as Rachel was exiting the hotel.

He had to take hold of her arms to keep from knocking her to the ground, but the look on her face was his reason for maintaining his hold. She was surprised, to say the least, but there was a longing in her eyes that matched the emotion in his heart. She trembled at his touch, and Braeden felt encouraged by the fact that he was the reason for her reaction. *She must have feelings for me; otherwise this wouldn't affect her at all.*

"Rachel," he whispered, refusing to call her anything else.

For a moment, neither one of them moved. Braeden was afraid to move for fear of what might happen afterward. No doubt she would rush off and hide herself away from him, and that was the last thing he wanted.

"I have to . . ." she tried to speak, then stopped.

She appeared to be battling within herself, and Braeden was even more certain her feelings for him hadn't died. What could he do to help her realize that they could overlook the past and move forward?

"I've tried several times to talk to you," Braeden finally offered.

"I've been busy," she replied.

Gently, he rubbed her upper arms with his thumbs. "Too busy for a simple conversation?"

Rachel's resistance returned and she stiffened. "With you, there is never a simple conversation. Now, if you'll excuse me, I have business to attend to at the depot."

Braeden dropped his hold, seeing the hostility return to her expression. "You'll have to talk to me sooner or later."

Rachel smiled rather snidely. "I think you underestimate me, Mr. Parker."

"You can't avoid me forever."

"Watch me," she replied and hurried past him and down the steps.

Braeden said nothing more. It was hard to let her go, but he had no desire to force her to remain, only to have an argument. Instead, he returned to his office and buried himself in paper work. He felt more frustration now than in the six years since they'd separated. He tried to pray, but in truth his frustration extended to God. Why would God bring them back together if humiliation and anguish were to be Braeden's only reward?

Finding no consolation in thought, prayer, or duty, Braeden finally gave up on his work. Glancing at his watch, he saw that two hours had passed since he'd encountered Rachel. Was time to be forever gauged by his last moment with her?

Slamming his ledger closed, Braeden realized he could just as easily mope over lunch. Hotel staff were allowed to take part in the Harvey dining room and were, in fact, an intricate part of the preparations. All of the girls had received their month-long training in Topeka, and most of the girls had worked for months elsewhere on the line, but Casa Grande was a new layout for everyone, and it was imperative that the operation run smoothly. Especially once they were dealing with hundreds of guests.

Grabbing his suit coat of worsted navy blue, Braeden made his way to the dining room. He had a chance of seeing Rachel here, but it was a slim one. She often saw him coming and would quickly exit to busy herself elsewhere. But sometimes he managed to catch her in the act of instructing one or more of the girls, and even watching her from afar made his meal more enjoyable.

Braeden slipped into the coat, hating the added burden as the day warmed considerably. Fred Harvey kept a hard, fast rule that all men dining in his restaurants would wear suit coats, and staff members for the resort were no different. Stopping at the door, Braeden could see that the black-and-white-clad girls were already bustling around the room, and in the corner Rachel spoke intently with two of the waitresses.

Smiling to himself, Braeden took a seat at one of the empty tables and watched as Rachel continued her instruction. She intrigued him as she always had—partly because she didn't see herself as pretty and therefore it only seemed to add to her beauty, and partly because she was an extremely intelligent yet tenderhearted woman. She had a way about her that bespoke of her confidence, but in managing this group of girls, he saw an almost motherly side to her.

He could see, however, that this moment appeared to present a confrontation of wills. The petite blonde on her left appeared anything but gracious in receiving direction. He could tell by the stance she took and the tilt of her chin that she was in complete disagreement with Rachel. The girl on Rachel's right seemed far more interested in what the blonde had to say, and Braeden instantly felt sorry for Rachel.

As if she could feel his gaze upon her, Rachel glanced up. She stiffened notably and squared her shoulders as if preparing herself to do battle. She refocused her attention on the job at hand, but it wasn't another minute before the blonde was pointing out that Braeden was going unserved.

Rachel nodded and instructed both girls to follow her to the table. Fixing her gaze somewhere above Braeden's head, she said, "Welcome to the Harvey House."

"Thank you," Braeden replied, trying hard to keep a straight face. "I see today I will have three lovely ladies to wait upon me."

"We're in training," the blonde replied with a flirtatious smile. "Miss Taylor says I need to improve my serving skills in order to better please everyone."

"Hmm, that is a lofty task," Braeden said, lifting his gaze to Rachel.

"The degree of difficulty depends on the customer," Rachel replied curtly.

"But we have only the nicest customers," the blonde interjected.

"There will be times, however," Rachel said, turning her full attention on the young women, "when the customers will not be so nice. You must be prepared to deal with them in an open, friendly manner. That does not mean, Miss Brooks, that you mistake acting in a flirtatious manner for a courteous one."

"I hardly see that the girl did anything wrong," Braeden said, undermining Rachel's instructions.

She turned to glare at him. "No doubt you see her actions as acceptable, but Mr. Harvey sets the rules in this house, and he expects his girls to act in a dignified manner."

"I'm sure even Mr. Harvey enjoys the smile of a beautiful young woman. Miss Brooks, is it?" he asked, knowing he was infuriating Rachel further. Something inside him couldn't resist agitating her in this manner. Perhaps if he continued, she would take him aside and speak to him about his actions, and then he could force her to listen to him.

"Yes," Ivy said, beaming him another smile. She lowered her lashes coyly and added, "I'm glad someone can appreciate my charm."

"You are here to serve meals," Rachel countered while the other girl giggled. The blonde seemed unmoved.

Braeden thought they made a most unlikely trio and grinned. "Yes, serve me a meal, I'm nigh on to starving." He grabbed the oversized napkin and snapped it out.

Rachel frowned and looked at Ivy. "Your service should be pleasant and friendly, but not improperly so."

"I haven't been given friendly or pleasant service by you, Miss Taylor," Braeden interjected. "I wonder, is the rule only for your girls or must you follow it as well?" The Harvey Girls giggled while Rachel turned crimson.

Through clenched teeth she managed to say, "Forgive me."

"Now, there is an admirable suggestion. Forgive me," Braeden said thoughtfully. "Forgiveness is an important aspect of a happy life. Wouldn't you agree, Miss Taylor?"

"Mr. Parker, we haven't time to dally here. What would you like to drink with your meal?" Rachel questioned sternly.

"First, I want that friendly service," he answered. "I think this is the perfect opportunity to show your young ladies here how to interact when you feel less than friendly."

Braeden watched the curious expressions of the two waitresses while Rachel seemed to deliberate within herself as to how to continue.

"There will always be days when you feel less than friendly, and there will always be irritating people who make you want to act less than cordial," Rachel finally said.

"Yes," Braeden added, "but everyone deserves kindness and consideration."

"Sometimes that is true," Rachel replied, seeming to forget the girls. "But sometimes people act in a way that causes you to feel less inclined to put yourself in harm's way."

"Sometimes people are simply misjudged—misunderstood," Braeden answered flatly. He looked hard into Rachel's eyes. "Sometimes people don't bother to get all the facts."

"I take the word of those I trust, and that trust allows me to believe in them regardless of circumstances."

"Oh, and what would it take to build this trust?"

Rachel paled. "We're getting off the subject."

"We've never quite been on the subject," Braeden retorted rather sarcastically. "Not unless Mr. Harvey has somehow included the subtleties of how to deal with your customers' painful past experiences and disappointments."

"Only if it interferes with the future."

"Mr. Harvey's future or yours?" Braeden asked seriously.

For just a moment, Braeden saw a flash of something akin to sorrow pass through Rachel's eyes. She quickly recovered, however, and smiled.

"Mr. Braeden likes coffee with his meals," she said, then turning to the Harvey Girls, she added, "I'll let you continue to serve him while I attend to other matters."

Braeden watched her walk away, wishing he could go after her or at least call to her and force her to deal with the issues between them. No matter what happened, he had to find a way to get her to open up to him.

I still love you, Rachel, he thought. *I love you more now than I did then. If only you would listen to reason—forget the past—forget the lies that destroyed us.*

"So where did you live before coming to Casa Grande, Mr. Parker?" Ivy Brooks asked, smiling sweetly.

Braeden looked up to see her face, wishing it were Rachel instead. "I hail from Chicago originally," he replied. "But Morita is now my home."

"Surely you don't intend to stay on here forever?" Ivy questioned.

"It all depends," Braeden replied.

"On what?"

"If there's something worth staying for."

Ivy watched as Braeden finished the last of his coffee and bid Faith good-bye. Faith giggled all the way back to where Ivy stood. Her eyes fairly shone in admiration.

"That man is so handsome," Faith whispered.

Ivy nodded. "Yes, he is."

"Miss Taylor doesn't seem to like him much," Faith continued, "and I don't know why. He was perfectly charming the entire time we waited on him. And I thought him especially gallant when he admonished us to pay him no mind and to heed Miss Taylor at all times."

"Heed Miss Taylor, indeed. I'd rather heed a rattlesnake. There's something going on between those two," Ivy replied. "It's more than the simple fact that they knew each other before now. I'd bet my best petticoat that there is some reason why Miss Taylor treats him the way she does. And," Ivy said with a smug smile, "when I find out what it is, I'll use it to my advantage."

❧ EIGHT ❧

"RACHEL, ARE YOU RECEIVING VISITORS?"

Rachel looked up from her desk and a smile immediately came to her lips. "Simone! Come in."

The exotic-looking Simone O'Donnell entered the room attired in a very comfortable calico afternoon dress. The coral-colored flowers set against the cream background complemented Simone's lightly tanned skin and black hair. Rachel envied the simplicity of her beauty.

"I've always heard that expectant mothers are radiant, but you are fairly glowing," Rachel declared. "Close that door and we shall retire to my living quarters and make ourselves more comfortable. That way no one will be inclined to interrupt us."

Simone did as she was instructed and joined Rachel in her private suite. "This is lovely," Simone said upon seeing Rachel's small sitting room.

"Yes, Fred Harvey has been most generous with me. I have all the privacy in the world back here."

"I should say so."

Rachel gave her a short tour. "I have my bedroom set up on this side in order to buffer myself from the noise of the lobby. It's a snug fit, as you see, but by putting the dresser at the end of the bed, I'm able to give the bedroom a little bit of separation from the sitting room."

"This is a wonderful quilt," Simone commented, running her hand along the top of the bed.

"I purchased it from the ladies' sewing circle at the church. They call the pattern Crown of Thorns, and I think it is absolutely marvelous. However, Reginald calls it English Wedding Ring."

"Reginald? Who's that?" Simone questioned, her perfectly arched brow raising ever so slightly.

Rachel laughed. "He's the chef for Casa Grande."

"And he's seen your bedroom?"

Rachel felt her face grow hot. "Certainly not. He caught me walking home from the church sale. As I came in through the back door, he saw me and commented on the quilt. That's all."

"But you must be good friends. I mean, I've never heard you refer to any man, save my Jeffery, by his first name."

Rachel bit at her lower lip. She had hoped for a quiet moment to share her heart in regards to Braeden. "Well, Reginald insisted, and I didn't see any harm in it. I mean, you remember how I felt about maintaining a closeness among staff members when we were back in Topeka."

"Of course I do," Simone replied, watching Rachel very carefully, "but you seem awfully preoccupied, and Jeffery told me there was a man here at the hotel who was upsetting you. Someone from your past."

Rachel nodded. "Come sit with me and I'll explain." She moved away from the bed to her sitting area and offered Simone one of the two high-backed, thickly cushioned chairs. Once they were seated, she continued. "Jeffery was right about there being a man from my past here at the hotel. But it isn't Reginald. The man is Braeden Parker. He's the manager for the hotel."

"I see," Simone replied with a grin. "And is he the reason you suddenly seem so nervous and pale?"

Rachel laughed, but not with her usual enthusiasm. "No, that's caused from trying to straighten out my girls and make certain they work in perfect order."

Simone smiled. "I should be here with you."

"Yes, you should. How dare you go and get pregnant on your

wedding night?" Rachel teased. "Have you seen the doctor yet?"

"I have. He says that I am the picture of health. Of course, he hasn't seen me in the morning with my head bent over the washbasin."

"Have you been terribly sick?"

"No, not really," Simone replied. "I'm fine so long as no one mentions food before eleven-thirty. Poor Jeffery. He's had to start taking his morning meal down at the café or up here. I can't even stand the smell of food cooking. But after the morning passes, I feel much better."

"I suppose that's why they call it morning sickness," Rachel commented.

"I think it's pretty normal," Simone answered, "but one of my neighbors informed me that she was never sick in the mornings but suffered terribly at night. So apparently there's nothing routine or regulated about having a baby."

Rachel nodded. "I would imagine each case is pretty much unique—like the babies involved." She reached out and took hold of Simone's hand. "I'm so very happy for you, Simone—and for Jeffery too. I know you'll be a wonderful mother." She felt the words stick in her throat as tears filled her eyes. She dropped Simone's hand and looked away.

"What is it, Rachel?" It was now Simone's turn to voice concern. She reached for Rachel's hand and squeezed it gently. "Please tell me. Jeffery said you are hardly yourself, and I can see that now for myself."

Rachel forced her emotions under control. "It all has to do with Braeden Parker." She looked up at Simone and tried to smile. "We . . . that is to say, I . . . oh, I don't know what to say." Rachel shook her head in exasperation. Simone was her dearest friend, and if she should be able to speak to anyone about this mess, it should be her.

"You two were once very close?" Simone questioned.

Rachel nodded.

"You loved him?"

Again Rachel nodded, fighting back tears.

"You're still in love with him?"

Simone's words hit Rachel like a slap in the face. Rachel had argued over and over with herself about her feelings. She knew she would never love anyone save Braeden, but she had tried desperately to convince herself that she was no longer "in love" with him.

She looked up and met Simone's compassionate expression. That was her undoing. With a sob, Rachel answered, "Yes."

"Is he married?" Simone questioned quietly.

"No." Rachel pulled a handkerchief from her deep apron pocket. "No, it's nothing like that."

"Then what is it?"

"We were once engaged," Rachel said with a heavy sigh. "I broke off the engagement because of something someone told me. Something that condemned Braeden as being unfaithful to me."

"And were the allegations true?"

"I thought they were, but now I'm not so sure." It was the first time Rachel had ever admitted her doubts on the matter. "I took the word of my mother and her friends. They told me Braeden was seeing someone else. My mother was well-known for having knowledge of the neighborhood and those around her. It seemed logical to believe them—especially her . . . because . . . well, I'm not a beautiful woman and I had no fortune to speak of. Braeden had plenty of money and a good job. He was well liked and dashingly handsome. I knew it was a wonder that he would even look at me."

"Rachel, you are a lovely woman. You have a beautiful face and your figure, well, I've heard the girls comment on wishing they were so well proportioned."

Rachel sniffed and smiled. "My hips are too wide and my bosom equally full."

"Yes, but your waist is small. You have the perfect hourglass figure."

"You're sweet to say so, but even if I could take pride in my looks, it wouldn't change the past. I had no confidence in anything about myself then. I was the daughter of a railroad worker. After he died, we were even poorer and my mother had to seek financial support by running a boardinghouse. I'd only managed to meet Braeden because we attended the same church."

"Ah, so he's a believer?"

"Yes," Rachel admitted. "Or he was. I haven't talked to him lately about his feelings on the matter."

"Have you talked to him about any of his other feelings?" Simone asked seriously.

"No. I can't. Every time he's near me, I know I can't speak to him about anything important. I've hidden behind a façade of anger and snobbery, and I hate myself more each time I walk away and leave the matter unresolved."

"So tell him this."

Laughing, Rachel dabbed her eyes. "You make it sound so simple."

"Why does it have to be hard? You obviously still care for this man. He isn't married, and you will be working closely together under the same roof. I'd say this isn't likely to be a situation that will go unquestioned for long."

"I know you're right. I've seen him go out of his way to talk to me."

"What happened?"

"I went out of my way not to be talked to," Rachel replied with a hint of a grin. "I just keep thinking that I'll accidently open my mouth and out will pour all manner of thought that I've kept buried and would like to keep hidden for good. I mean, what if I suddenly declare my feelings and he laughs at me? What if he despises me for my weakness?"

Simone shook her head and let go of Rachel's hand. Easing back into her chair, she crossed her arms. "You must stop this nonsense of worrying 'what if?' and talk to him. Take him aside on the pretense of business and force him to listen to what you have to say. Just be honest. If he won't listen to you, then you will have at least tried."

"I'm afraid it isn't Braeden who refuses to listen. It's me. I suppose I'm just as afraid of what he might say."

"Like what?"

"Like it was a good idea for us to part company and how he's glad we never married. I could just see myself baring my heart, then having to watch as he devours it."

Simone nodded. "Or you can say nothing and always wonder."

Silence filled the room for several moments as the two women simply looked at each other. Rachel wished the answer were that easy, but she knew deep inside that the entire matter of Braeden Parker was anything but.

"I let hearsay destroy my life. Even knowing what the Bible says about avoiding idle talk, I allowed it to influence my choices in life. I refused to trust my heart on the matter because I was young and figured my naïveté had led me to this place. I never gave Braeden a chance to defend himself because I'd always known my mother to be right about the things going on around us." Rachel sighed. "I don't know if we can go back to what we had."

"Then don't," Simone replied matter-of-factly. "Go forward to something better."

"I just don't know." Rachel felt overwhelmed and frightened by the feelings raging within her. One minute she was convinced that Simone was right and she was ready to march across the lobby and plant herself in Braeden's office and tell him everything. The next minute she was certain that as soon as she admitted to having feelings for him, Braeden would mock her and cause her further pain.

"A wise woman once told me that God does nothing by chance. He has a perfect order for everything. Do you still stand by that philosophy, or was that just a flowery speech for my benefit?"

"I still believe that," Rachel finally admitted.

"Then God must have brought you two together for a reason. And if not for love, then for reconciliation," Simone said softly. "Either way, you win."

"But if he doesn't return my feelings—"

"You'll be in no worse a state than you are right now."

"But he'll know how I feel."

"So your pride gets a little singed," Simone replied. "At least you'll know, and you'll have this matter behind you. Either way, I'm figuring that God is big enough for the job."

Rachel considered Simone's words long after she'd gone. She had very nearly convinced herself that leveling with Braeden was the right thing to do when Reginald approached, declaring that it was time to finish interviewing the last of the kitchen staff.

"I have two men who should do nicely for the baking," he told her. "And there's a local boy, Tomas Sanchez, who is in desperate need of employment. I thought he might work out well as a general errand boy and stocker. He's only sixteen, but he's now the man of his family."

Rachel thought of the awesome responsibility. "Are there many in his family?"

"I should say so. He has eight brothers and sisters, a sickly mother, and an ancient grandmother. He's the only one old enough to seek employment."

"Give him the job," Rachel quickly agreed and dabbed at her forehead. The afternoon heat was quite taxing, making everyone irritable.

"Would you rather I take responsibility for hiring the bakers? That is to say, I see no reason you should have to add to your labors when they will be under my direct supervision."

Rachel smiled. Reginald was always looking for ways to ease her burden. "That would be wonderful, Reginald."

"Call me Reg. Reginald always sounds so formal. You Americans are good about putting aside formalities and ceremony—let it be so between us."

"All right, Reg," Rachel replied and smiled. "As hot as it is, I'm not about to argue with you or anyone else."

"September is said to be a cooler month. I believe we shall enjoy an enchanting Indian summer, with less severity in temperature."

"Who told you this?" she questioned, knowing that Reg was as foreign to this part of the country as she was.

"Mrs. Needlemeier. The woman is a vast source of information. She informed me where I might find fresh mint. Her gardener planted an abundance, and she has given me leave to harvest it whenever I have need."

Rachel smiled. "Nothing seems to escape Mrs. Needlemeier's attention."

"She has a bevy of other herbs in her private garden and has also made these available to the Harvey House. I told her we could pay, but she said that was nonsense and shooed me away."

Rachel could well imagine the scene. She dabbed her forehead again and silently wished she could go lie down and cool off as many of her girls were doing. Reg must have sensed her exhaustion because in the next moment, he turned her away from the kitchen.

"I am perfectly capable of handling this job. You go rest. You are very much like our beloved Queen Victoria. Her majesty is well-known for her hard work. You are like her in that way and in many others," Reginald said, guiding Rachel gently to the door of the Harvey Girl's parlor. "I will bid you good-afternoon and leave you to rest. I wouldn't want anything to happen to one so lovely and delicate as you, Rachel."

Rachel thought his concern to be quite refreshing. She wondered why Braeden couldn't respond to her in such a tender way. It seemed that whenever they met up, he was always sarcastic and forceful, and Rachel, angry and scared.

"Thank you, Reg," she finally said, noticing that he seemed to be awaiting her decision. "I think I will go rest for a little while. I'm sure to be a new person once the sun goes down."

"That's the spirit," Reg replied. "Then off with you, and I will return to my duties."

Rachel nodded and left him there in the kitchen. The parlor was empty as she moved through it to the adjoining hall. She smiled to think of Reg comparing her to Queen Victoria. Rachel had once seen a picture of the woman in a newspaper. It was her golden jubilee or some other sort of celebration. The woman was not at all a pleasant-looking sort, but instead wore her authority in her very expression. She could certainly not be called a beauty, although Rachel recalled having heard that in her youth she had been quite lovely.

"But youth fades," Rachel sighed, bringing her hand to her cheek, as if feeling her own face wrinkle and wither. "Time is passing by quickly for me. It won't be that many years before I'm thirty, and then my life will be half over and I'll still have nothing more to show for it than this."

She looked down the hallway of doors and polished wood floors and sighed. For all her responsibility and the admiration of her superiors, it would never compensate for the lack of love and family in her life. For although she loved her job and even loved her girls, at least most of them, they would never fill the need inside her nor satisfy her hunger for marriage and children.

"If you have a purpose, Lord," she said, glancing upward, "I certainly pray you reveal it soon. Otherwise I shall end up as old and wrinkled as Queen Victoria, without the country and family to show for it."

❧ NINE ❧

SET AMIDST AN ARCHED GROTTO, the hot springs at Casa Grande generated an invigorating flow of warm mineral waters that made it a particularly welcome attraction. Even in the heat of summer, the hot springs were sought out by the staff of Casa Grande for entertainment and restoration. With her work completed, Rachel thought a dip in the springs would be just the thing to help her sleep better.

She donned a bathing suit supplied by the hotel and laughed at the shortness of the skirt. It barely came to the middle of her stocking-and-bloomer-covered legs. The top, with short, fitted sleeves, buttoned up the middle to her neck. Rachel had never worn anything so daring and still had trouble believing it acceptable to be seen in such a condition—especially without a corset. She pulled on her robe, took up a book of poems and a towel, and steadied her nerves. The hour was well past the time when most of the staff went to the pool, so she kept her confidence and hoped she might be the only one there. She had no desire to share small talk with any of the girls—most were considerably younger and chattered away about the handsome men they'd known or had seen. Such talk was boring at best, and at worst it depressed Rachel.

It wasn't for a lack of understanding, because Rachel knew what it was to daydream about such things. But the pain it stirred deep inside made her miserable, and therefore it seemed senseless to occupy herself with such idle conversation. Besides, she was their supervisor. A motherly, matronly figure who told them what to do and when. And although she enjoyed a closeness with the girls, Rachel knew it didn't compare to the camaraderie that they shared with one another as peers. They might come to her with their problems, hoping for solutions and an understanding ear, but they were not likely to share their dreams or invite her to partake in their entertainment.

At least there was Simone, and that was a great comfort to Rachel. Perhaps God had perfectly interceded on Rachel's behalf by having Simone be unable to work at Casa Grande. Now they could just be friends and not worry after the incidentals of running a business.

Rachel slipped out the back door and made her way around the side of the resort to where a stone walkway led to a lighted path to the pools. Once the guests actually arrived at Casa Grande, Rachel would wait to change her clothes at the bathhouses that extended off the stone grotto, but for now it was far more convenient to do things this way. She hummed as she made her way in the darkness. Somehow it helped her feel less self-conscious about her appearance. She tried to believe what Simone had told her about having a fine figure, but it was difficult at best. Rachel had always believed that beauty came from within a person, and right now she didn't feel at all beautiful.

A frown came to her face. *No, I feel hard and frustrated. I have so much misery inside of me, it would be difficult for anything lovely to coexist.*

Opening the wrought-iron gate at the grotto's central arch, Rachel felt a small sigh escape her as she found the main pool completely deserted. She put her book and robe aside and hurried to get into the pool before anyone else could appear. At least the water afforded her a bit of coverage.

The warmth penetrated her aching muscles and brought a smile to her face. Her feet hurt from the long hours she'd spent working, and her neck and shoulder muscles seemed to be bound in cords that refused to relax. For a moment she floated lazily on her back and tried to concentrate on nothing but the starry sky overhead. It was a little more difficult to see the stars because of the soft glow coming from electric light posts, but they were there. This was the reason she chose the main pool rather than the more secluded women's bathing pool.

The latter had a lattice-styled wall connecting with the rose stone arches to completely surround the bathing area. Overhead, another series of vine-covered lattices helped to shield the harshness of the sun. The lattice allowed the mountain breezes to blow through, while shielding the women from view. It was a lovely setting, but you couldn't gaze upward into the night skies and see the diamond-like sprinkling of stars. Here, so near the mountains in the dry, crisp air, the stars often looked close enough to touch. Even now the skies spread out like a masterpiece unlike anything Rachel had ever seen. Reaching her hand to the sky, Rachel pretended she could touch the stars. The idea made her smile. When she was a little girl, her father had often put her on his shoulders so she could "reach" the sky. She liked to imagine that even now, as she reached upward, her beloved papa was reaching down to touch her from heaven.

Feeling her body begin to relax, Rachel rolled over on her stomach and dove under the water. She felt the rush of warmth hit her face. What a marvelous sensation. It caused her nose to tingle and tickle as she pushed toward the bottom of the pool. She continued to dive underwater for several moments, desiring only to stay there forever and let the water continue to drain away her miseries. But soon she found herself short of breath and forced herself to return to the surface. As her face emerged above the water, Rachel instantly became aware of a presence. Smoothing her wet hair out of her face, Rachel gazed up to find Braeden quietly watching her.

"You shouldn't come here by yourself," he said, leaning back casually against the stone entry arch. "Don't you know it's dangerous to swim alone?"

Rachel felt her pulse quicken. "It's not proper for you to be here. Leave at once!"

"I've as much a right to come for a swim as do you," he answered with a grin. "After all, this is the common pool for both men and women."

Rachel realized that she would have to do something. She couldn't just remain in the pool and allow Braeden to join her. It simply wouldn't be proper for them to swim together—alone. Knowing that she would have to expose herself to his view, she very calmly swam

over to the stone steps and climbed out of the pool. She quickly tow-
eled off and pulled on her robe without another word. What she had
hoped would be a quiet, leisurely swim and a chance to read a few
pages of poetry under the twinkling stars quickly faded into a confrontation.

"Have your swim, Mr. Parker. I wouldn't dream of interfering.
However, I see that you, too, are very much alone. Are you not worried about such evils?"

"But I'm not alone," he replied softly. "For you are here."

Rachel shook her head, then squeezed out the water from her
long, curly hair. "But I shall not linger."

She tried not to notice the look of disappointment on his face, nor
how marvelous he looked in the dim lamplight. He stood fully clothed
but more casual than she was used to seeing him. His shirt, usually
buttoned and secured with a necktie, was daringly open, while his
sleeves were turned up. She glanced around him and noticed there was
no sign of a suit coat anywhere.

"You hardly look ready for a swim," she finally managed.

"It doesn't take that much time to disrobe," he said, grinning.

Rachel felt her cheeks grow warm. "I shall bid you good-evening
and give you over to your own preparations."

"Rachel, don't go."

She ignored him and turned to walk away, but he called after her
in such a pleading tone that she had to stop.

"Please."

The richness of his voice and the desperation in that simple word
forced her to turn back around. She looked at him for a moment,
unable to find words to berate him with for delaying her departure.
His sandy hair fell forward across his brow, leaving her with a strong
desire to push it back into place. But it was the intensity and pleading
of his stare that fixed her to the spot. How could she not stay? How
could she not remember the time they'd shared so long ago? She could
almost remember what it was like to be in his arms—to laugh at his
stories—to tremble at his spoken words of love.

"Rachel, I know you've been avoiding me," he said softly. "I know
it was a shock to see me turn up here after so many years. But now

that it's happened, now that we're both here, couldn't we at least discuss the matter?"

"I don't know," she answered plainly. Trepidation coursed through her like white-hot fire.

"Why?" he asked, taking a couple of steps toward her.

Rachel clutched the lapel of her robe. "I don't think it would be wise."

"Again, I must ask—why?"

Rachel swallowed hard. "There's no sense in dredging up the past."

"In our case, I would beg to differ. Our past has never been resolved. You never allowed me a chance to defend myself, and I'm asking for that chance now."

Rachel considered his words for a moment. She supposed it was only fair to allow the man to speak his mind after six years. It was true enough that she'd denied him any real chance to counter her accusations. But if she let him talk now, she might have to face her fears. Fears that suggested she had been wrong six years ago and that by her own hand she had ended any chance she had for happiness.

"All I'm asking is that you give me a chance to speak," Braeden said, stopping directly in front of her.

Rachel nodded. "Very well. Speak."

"Thank you. I know you're afraid of what I have to say, but I honestly think it will be better for both of us in the long run."

She had no idea how that could possibly be the case, but she nodded and tried to steel herself inside for whatever declaration was to come.

"You never let me defend myself six years ago. You refused my proposal based on the inaccuracies you'd been told, and you never allowed yourself to trust in me. I suppose our love was rather immature to have to weather such an intense storm, but I believed in you and I thought you believed in me."

She said nothing. How could she? It was so hard to admit that she had given up her trust in him with a few well-intended words of warning.

"I was at the hotel that day, as your mother's friends revealed. I was even in the company of a beautiful young woman, and yes, I was headed up the grand staircase with my arm around her. But she wasn't my mistress or my new lady love. She was, however, the daughter of a dear friend whom I was scheduled to meet that afternoon at the hotel. She had just given me the news of her impending wedding and . . ." He paused, seeming to search for the right words. "I told her of our own plans—of the ring I'd just purchased for you. We were congratulating each other, and she was accompanying me to meet her father."

Rachel felt the blood drain from her head. Hadn't she already presumed it to be something innocent and misunderstood? Hadn't she already condemned herself for allowing hearsay to be the final word on a matter of such importance? But she had loved her mother dearly and had been confident that her mother would never do anything to harm her. Even given Elvira Taylor's penchant toward gossip, Rachel couldn't believe her mother would ever pass judgment on something so important without anything more than the supposition of her friends.

Braeden reached out to touch her cheek. "I did nothing wrong. I couldn't have betrayed you."

Rachel found it impossible to admit that she knew of his innocence. She could hardly stand the thought of what she'd done. She had lost six years of happiness with the only man whom she would ever love. And perhaps she had lost future years, as well, for why should he find any reason to believe in her now?

She bit nervously at her lip and looked away. "So how have you been all these years? Did you . . . that is to say . . . you said you never married?"

When he didn't answer her right away, Rachel forced herself to look back at him. His expression seemed pained, and he appeared to be considering her words with great thought.

"No, I didn't marry," he finally replied, as if deciding she deserved an answer after all.

"Oh," she said, trying desperately to sound neutral on the matter. He smiled ever so slightly. "Don't you want to know why?"

Rachel did indeed want to know the answer to that question, but she wasn't about to ask it. "I suppose," she said slowly, "that is a rather private matter. It's really none of my business."

Braeden took hold of her hand. "It is very much your business, Rachel. I never married because I have loved only one woman." He paused and looked deep into her eyes. "And that woman is you. It's always been you. It will always be only you."

Rachel felt her knees begin to tremble. Shaking from head to toe, she pulled away and walked to the archway. She couldn't think. Her mind flooded with the wonder of the declaration he'd just made, but she couldn't force herself to form a coherent thought.

"Rachel, you must believe me," Braeden said, coming up behind her.

"Yoo-hoo!" The voice of Ivy Brooks carried lyrically on the night air.

Rachel felt herself tense. It didn't look good to be seen here alone with Braeden, much less to have him standing so close to her.

"Oh, there you are, Mr. Parker," Ivy declared.

Rachel whirled on her heel. Ivy approached them wearing a scandalously short bathing suit with bloomers but no stockings.

"I received your note," Ivy fairly purred the words as she batted her eyelashes.

Her sultry words and scandalous apparel were enough to cause Rachel to believe the worst. Had it all been a lie? A carefully plotted and contrived scene for her benefit? Had Braeden decided to hurt her as badly as she'd hurt him by pretending to still care? Then, once she gave in to her feelings for him, he'd have Ivy appear poolside at just the right moment to plunge the knife into her dream of reconciliation?

She shuddered and moved past Braeden and Ivy and headed up the walkway. *I have to get away from here*, she thought. No matter what the real reason was for Ivy's appearance, Rachel felt extremely vulnerable. *I can't believe I almost admitted my love for him*. The image of him laughing in her face caused tears to come to Rachel's eyes. Simone might have thought injured pride was a nominal price to pay, but at this moment Rachel felt it unbearable.

"Rachel, wait!" Braeden called after her while Ivy's lyrical laughter filled the night air. "Rachel, it's not what you think!"

It pained her to think he might have duped her. The thought of him setting her up in order to crush her once and for all was enough to cause tears to wet her cheeks. Just then she remembered her towel and book. Only it wasn't her book—it belonged to the resort, and she couldn't just leave it outside exposed to the elements. She would have to stop and retrieve it, but that meant going back and dealing with Braeden and Ivy.

She stopped midstep and realized that she had to go back for more reasons than the book and towel. If she allowed them to drive her away, she would never have any control over Ivy and she'd never, ever be able to face Braeden again. She wiped her face and drew a deep breath. *God, give me the strength to face them.*

Slowly she marched back to the pool just as Ivy let out a shriek while Braeden wrapped his arms around her. Rachel stopped for a moment and watched them. She tried to make herself believe that it didn't affect her. That it meant nothing. But in truth, it cut her to the core.

Braeden's gaze locked with hers. "She lost her footing," he tried to explain, setting Ivy upright on the walk.

"A girl could certainly lose a great many things around you, Mr. Parker," Ivy said seductively before glancing over her shoulder at Rachel and adding, "Her heart for one."

"I forgot my book and towel," Rachel stated very calmly. Her façade of strength was back in place, and she refused to allow either of them to know the true emotion of her heart. She gingerly moved across the now wet stones, retrieved her book, and made her way back to the open archway. "Do not forget your curfew, Miss Brooks," she stated stiffly.

She looked briefly at Braeden, saw his expression of pleading, but refused to say anything more. She felt overwhelmed by confusion and anguish. There was nothing she could say.

Blinded by tears, Rachel made her way back to her quarters. She clutched the book to her damp robe as though it could somehow offer her strength to deal with the pain inside her. She wanted to believe Braeden's words—believe that he still loved her. But why should he? After the way she had acted, why should he care?

Once inside her room, she quickly changed her clothes, then fell across her bed, sobbing. *I've ruined it all now. He'll never want to see me again. He'll believe me unworthy of his trust, and perhaps he is right. I am so fickle and silly. How could I have acted like that?*

Such thoughts only made her cry harder. All of her life she had only been made to feel special by two people. One was Braeden, the other was her father. Now both were lost to her.

Her words tainted with pain and regret, she looked up and asked, "God, what have I done? Why did I act like such a child?"

∞ TEN ∞

"WELL, AS I SEE IT," Rachel said, beginning the meeting, "we're right on schedule. There are some minor problems, but I feel confident we can deal with these issues before the grand opening." She watched as Braeden eased back in his desk chair, grateful that the management meeting had been held in his office instead of hers. This way, when all was said and done, she could quickly exit before anything became too personal.

"I've simply had marvelous luck obtaining help from the locals," Reg declared. "Fresh produce, fish, lamb—not to mention spices and herbs."

Rachel looked to Reg with a smile. He created the perfect buffer between her and Braeden. There could be no talk of the past with Reginald Worthington situated neatly between them. Rachel felt no small amount of relief in realizing this benefit. She would simply stay close to Reg in all matters pertaining to the dining room, and when she exited the company of her girls, she would do so through the private parlor and hallway. That way, she wouldn't allow herself to be caught unaware of Braeden's presence. Furthermore, she would insist that Reg be present at every management meeting. He was, after all, in charge of managing the kitchen, and she had already delegated a great deal of responsibility to the man. He should, by all rights, be included in their meetings.

"I have a problem with my inventory," Braeden said, glancing over the papers in his hand to meet Rachel's gaze. "The originals do not match the tallies made by my housekeeper and her staff."

"We have the same problem," Rachel declared. "Reginald—" She felt her face grow hot as she corrected herself. "That is to say, Mr. Worthington has taken an inventory of our supplies, as well, and they do not match my original paper work."

Braeden put the papers down. "What do you suppose it means?"

Rachel shrugged. "Why must it mean anything? I would imagine the manifest listing of what was originally shipped here was inaccurate."

"Seems unlikely that they would be so remiss in their inventory," Braeden countered. "After all, the Santa Fe is suffering from some poor investments, and they are no doubt counting their pennies carefully as they bring this new resort to life."

"But people make mistakes," Rachel said softly. She realized he might believe her words to hold a double meaning and quickly moved her attention to Reg. "Have you been able to figure anything out from our inventory?"

"Personally, I believe it to be a simple case of miscounting," Reginald replied. "I presumed the mistake to be my own, but I had Tomas redo the count and he came up with the same thing. There are various articles missing: silver services, pots and pans, utensils, linens, napkins, even food. With such a wide variety of articles in dispute, it seems unlikely that it would be a mere case of thievery."

"Why?" Braeden asked seriously.

Reg ran his fingers along his pencil-thin moustache. "An intelligent thief would have purloined only those articles of value. The silver services, for instance. Our inventory counts show a discrepancy of two; however, neither of those services were of the highest quality. The very best of our silver has been untouched."

"Perhaps the thief is untrained as to the value of silver."

Rachel listened as the two men reasoned the situation. Finally she interjected a question. "What exactly are you missing, Mr. Parker?"

Braeden allowed his gaze to linger on her for a moment before picking his papers back up. "Many of the bed linens are off count.

There are soap dishes, books, lounging chairs, towels, and bathing suits," he said, glancing back up. "Along with a variety of other odds and ends."

"None of which sound like the kind of thing to make a thief rich," Rachel replied.

Braeden shrugged. "I don't know. It depends on what the thief is looking to gain. Money or possessions. You might well have a very poor thief who is simply supplying his family with needed linens and table service."

"Linens obviously marked for the Harvey Company?"

"A lot of folks wouldn't care about such a thing."

"I still believe it's possible the inventory sheets were simply wrong," Rachel replied. "After all, we're still receiving supplies daily from the trains. Perhaps some of the goods are still en route."

"I suppose it's possible," Braeden finally conceded. "However, I'd like to call the town marshal in on the matter."

"I hardly think that's necessary," Rachel said sternly. "It would make us look incompetent. No, I suggest we wait and see what happens as we go. Let us do an inventory daily and see if anything else turns up missing."

"Daily? I don't have time for daily inventories. Not if I'm going to have this resort ready for a grand opening in little more than a week."

"Then assign someone to help you," Rachel replied impatiently. "I've done that very thing with Reginald, and it's working out very nicely. Put your housekeeper in charge of the matter. That is, if you trust her." She knew her words were cutting, but she didn't care. The tension in the room grew stronger and even Reginald was starting to look uncomfortable. Rachel grimaced and tried hard not to let her emotions control her actions.

"I trust her," Braeden said, staring hard at Rachel. "She's proven herself to be worthy of my faith."

His eyes narrowed and seemed to deepen in hue. To Rachel they were the most beautiful shade of blue she'd ever known. Why did he have to be so handsome? Why couldn't she just forget what they had shared and leave the past well enough alone?

"I . . . ah . . . quite agree with Rachel," Reginald said hesitantly.

Obviously he didn't really want to get in the middle of their affair.

At the usage of her given name, Braeden visibly clenched his teeth together. The ticking in his cheek told Rachel he was quite irritated at this new-found friendship she shared with the resort's chef. It bothered her to have him angry, but at the same time it infuriated her to think he would perhaps consider her undeserving of friends.

"Thank you, Reginald," she replied, feeling only the tiniest bit of comfort to have him take her side in the matter. "If the inventory continues to disappear, then perhaps we could call in the law."

Braeden shrugged. "Have it your way."

"Good, now moving on to other business," Rachel said, trying hard not to notice his agitation. "I plan to appoint Gwen Carson as head waitress. She will be in charge of everything whenever I am off duty or otherwise occupied. Gwen has just over three years with the Harvey system, and I find her to be the best candidate for the job. However, there is a slight problem."

"What kind of problem?" Braeden questioned.

"Esmeralda Needlemeier."

"Ah," he replied, nodding.

"The old woman is quite a fearsome creature, if I do say so," Reg offered.

"Still, the railroad and Mr. Harvey have asked us to treat her with the utmost of respect," Braeden interjected. "She owns over half the town, and what she doesn't own, she seems to have little trouble controlling. She could easily make life for us here at Casa Grande most difficult if we don't allow her a say in some of the issues."

"Well, this is one decision I cannot heed her advice or desires on," Rachel replied. "She expects for me to put Ivy Brooks in the position of head waitress, but the request is completely out of line. Ivy has barely made it through her training and has no experience, at least not in being a Harvey Girl." She knew her words sounded sarcastic, but she didn't care.

Braeden took her words for what they were, a reminder of that evening by the pool. "I wonder if Miss Carson knows how to trust people and not jump to conclusions?"

"She appears very level-headed," Rachel answered, tensing at his words. She'd known better than to goad him that way, but the truth of the matter was that Ivy was inexperienced and unacceptable as head waitress. And before Braeden could further cause her pain and suggest she appoint Ivy to the head waitress job, Rachel wanted to dismiss the idea once and for all.

Trying hard to ignore the scowl on Braeden's face, Rachel continued. "Gwen Carson is the most reliable person I have on staff. She is always willing to do additional jobs when need demands, and she never complains about the extra work. There isn't an aspect of the job she doesn't know, and we get along very nicely."

"I should speak to her and learn her secrets," Braeden muttered.

Rachel ignored him and looked away to Reg. "You've worked with her. I presume you have some thought on this matter."

"I believe she would make an excellent leader for her peers," Reginald replied. "She seems quite willing to follow orders and to adhere to the suggestions of her superiors."

"Then it's settled." Rachel gave him a broad smile.

"I didn't know you needed our approval in order to make the decision," Braeden said seriously.

"I didn't, Mr. Parker, but I wanted you to understand the situation. Mrs. Needlemeier will no doubt raise quite a ruckus. She may even feel as though I have slighted her on purpose—which is not the case. Miss Brooks is often insolent and uncooperative, and her attitude toward those she deems to be her inferiors is generally harsh and demeaning. With this spirit and clash of wills, I could not have promoted her to the position even if she had more experience than all of the girls put together. Mr. Harvey firmly believes that attitude is just as important as experience."

"I agree," Braeden replied. "A good attitude can get you through the worst of times. How one deals with bad times has much to do with what lies in the heart."

Rachel drew a deep breath and got to her feet. "The time is getting away from us. I must join my girls for a staff meeting in the dining room. I believe we've resolved all of our issues for the day." She tried to smile, but when she caught sight of Braeden's expression, she knew of at least one issue that had not been dealt with—maybe never would.

Why, God? Why can't I let this matter be? Why does my heart have to be so consumed? Help me to get beyond this, to live my life without this burden. She sought solace in her prayer but found nothing but unanswered questions.

Saying nothing more, Rachel made her way from Braeden's office. She couldn't help but think of Braeden's reaction to her obvious openness with Reginald Worthington. He appeared not only irritated by her first-name basis with the chef, but if she didn't know better, she'd have believed him jealous of the friendship they shared.

She smiled. Maybe it would do him good to be jealous of Reg. After all, he treated Rachel with more respect and tenderness than Braeden did these days. Not that she had allowed Braeden much leeway in that area.

The meeting with the girls passed quickly and without too much ado. Rachel saved the announcement of Gwen's promotion for the very last. She knew in some ways she had done this to save herself from having to deal with Ivy's negative response, but she also saved it in order to leave the meeting on a higher note than the one she'd had with Braeden and Reg.

"Most of you know that the position of head waitress is appointed based on several issues. The most important being length of service and your work record during that time period. Secondly, personality and interaction with your fellow workers is considered. Head waitress is hardly a popularity contest, but how you work and get along with others is an important consideration. Lastly, I consider the way you have worked with me. The head waitress will be my eyes and ears during times when I am away or otherwise occupied. She will need to be someone I can rely upon and feel open to discuss problems related to our dining room. However, I don't want anyone here getting the wrong idea. My choice for this position is not based on whether I like one young woman more than I like another."

She looked out to meet the expression on each girl's face before continuing. With the exception of Ivy and Faith, everyone seemed happy and content and eager to hear her announcement.

"So without further delay, I would like to present our new head waitress, Gwen Carson." Most of the girls clapped, including Faith, who seemed content just to be a part of the group when Ivy wasn't forcing her attentions elsewhere. Ivy quickly jabbed her in the ribs, however, putting a stop to her revelry.

Gwen joined Rachel at the front of the group and beamed a proud smile as Rachel shook her hand. "I shall come to rely heavily upon you, Gwen."

"Thank you, Rachel. I won't let you down."

Over the last few days she had allowed the girls to start calling her by her first name, although it was clearly understood that this was only to be done when there were no customers or officials present. Rachel dismissed the meeting and watched as everyone but Ivy and Faith hurried to surround Gwen and congratulate her. Rachel felt a small amount of satisfaction in seeing Gwen's joy. She'd made the right decision, there was no doubt about that, but she sighed heavily as she saw Ivy slip out the side door. No doubt she would get word to her aunt as soon as possible, and then Rachel would have to face the music.

Nearly an hour later, Rachel was still considering the arrival of Esmeralda Needlemeier when the old woman appeared at her door. Her pinched expression made her intent quite clear.

"Miss Taylor, I believe a mistake has been made," Esmeralda said, tapping her cane loudly on the floor.

"Won't you have a chair," Rachel offered graciously.

Esmeralda tilted her chin slightly and took a seat. "I suppose you know why I've come."

"Yes. Ivy told you that I've appointed Gwen Carson as head waitress for the dining room."

"I thought we had an understanding that my niece was to receive that position."

"No, you had that understanding. I am under the instructions of Fred Harvey, however, and his understanding is considerably different."

"Miss Taylor, your Mr. Harvey and the Santa Fe Railroad assured me that I would have their utmost consideration in matters related to Morita and this resort hotel."

"And so you have. I considered your request for Ivy," Rachel admitted, even though she'd not considered it very seriously. "She is hardly qualified when compared to Miss Carson's experience. I personally trained Miss Carson in Topeka and have continued to receive letters from her since she was sent to Emporia to work for the Harvey dining room there. She was quickly promoted and attained the position of head waitress in little over a year. So not only does she have experience as a Harvey employee, she has already performed the duties of a head waitress. She is well versed in the rules and regulations, which your niece seems wont to ignore, and she is well liked by most of the girls on my staff."

"I see there will be no convincing you to change your mind," Esmeralda stated severely. "I suppose I shall have to take the matter up with the officials of your railroad."

Rachel felt frustrated by the woman's inability or refusal to see the reason behind her decision. "Mrs. Needlemeier, are you a Christian woman?"

The black-draped woman gasped. "I should say so! What kind of question is that?"

"I ask about your faith in order to ascertain if we value the same things. I seek my direction in prayer and God's guidance. If you held no value for that, then I would be wasting my breath in trying to justify my choice. But since you are a God-fearing woman, I can speak to you as a sister in the Lord."

Mrs. Needlemeier harrumphed at this thought but said nothing. She leaned both hands on her silver-capped cane and awaited Rachel's explanation.

"I prayed about the choice I made," Rachel began. "I prayed about coming to Casa Grande and I prayed about the girls I picked for my staff. Ivy was not one I would have chosen, primarily because a resort of this size and expectation needs to have staff members who are already well trained. Secondly, I have never cared for situations where people with money caused other people—good, faithful, hard-working people—to suffer loss because they were unable to compete with the money others used to buy themselves into a position.

"Your niece would certainly not be at this resort had I had my say in the matter. Not only because she is young but because she is totally new and inexperienced and the pressures that will come to her here are hardly fair to put upon a new employee. Also, there is the matter that this resort is looked upon as a privileged place of employment. Many requests for transfer were received for this house, but of course, only twenty-five could be accepted. To allow Ivy to take one of those positions, as well as Faith Bradford, the granddaughter of one of the board members, kept others who were more deserving from being allowed to serve here." She paused, surprised that the old woman hadn't seen the need to interject her opinion on the matter. Grateful to find Esmeralda listening intently, Rachel continued.

"I prayed about each one of these girls, asking God to direct me in working with them. I continue to pray for each of them. I also asked for divine direction on choosing a head waitress. What few people know is that up until a couple of weeks ago, my head waitress was to be Mrs. Jeffery O'Donnell. She and I had worked together in Topeka, and I have come to consider her a good friend. However, she is expecting her first child and Mr. O'Donnell has requested she not work. That caused me to look elsewhere for a head waitress. After much prayer and contemplation, Gwen Carson seemed the most fitting. In fact, it would have been hard to explain choosing Simone O'Donnell over Gwen, as the latter has at least two years of service over Simone. So there you have it. I felt certain God had led me to make the choice of Gwen Carson. I would ask that you pray about it and see if God doesn't give you the same peace of mind on the matter. Rather than making this an issue of our wills, I propose it be given over to God for *His* supreme will on the matter."

Esmeralda rose to her feet. "You make a logical argument and a wonderful speech. I suppose, given your reasoning, it makes sense to appoint this Carson woman to the position of head waitress. However, I'm used to getting what I want."

Rachel stood and smiled. "I assure you, my choice was not made in order to deny you. You are an intelligent businesswoman; your dealings with the Santa Fe and Harvey Company are proof of that. Your creation of Morita is another. I would hope you might see the logic of my choice in that light, if in no other."

Esmeralda tapped her cane to the door, then turned. "I am an intelligent woman, Miss Taylor. Intelligent enough to deal with your kind and any other who crosses my path. I will yield in this matter, but do not think to push me in any other. Regardless of your faith and religious convictions, God does not sit on the board of the Santa Fe, nor does He run the Harvey Company, although there are those who would argue that point. I am God-fearing and a Christian, but I am also a businesswoman as you pointed out. Therefore, the decisions I make will be based on what will benefit my business, and my business is Morita and this resort—despite any thought you might have to the contrary. Good day!"

She left in the same stormy mood by which she had appeared, and when she had gone, Rachel fell back into her chair in a rather exhausted state of mind. The woman was simply more trying than any person Rachel had ever known. With a sigh, she picked up her paper work and tried to refocus her attention, but it was almost impossible. Between Ivy's conniving and hatred, Esmeralda's bossiness, and Braeden's presence, managing Casa Grande's dining room had ceased to be any fun. In fact, the stress of the whole operation was beginning to take its toll.

Then a frightening thought came to Rachel—one she tried very hard to ignore.

Perhaps she should resign her position and put in for a transfer elsewhere on the line.

๑ ELEVEN ๑

THE NIGHT AIR WAS COOL, almost chilly, as the shadowy figure slipped into Rachel Taylor's office. Quietly, the marauder closed the door, then lighted a candle. The dim amber light illuminated the office in an eerie manner, and this, coupled with the wind as it howled down from the mountains, set the stage for the covert scene. The wind would actually benefit the thief, throwing out noises and moanings as it whistled through the junipers, coyote willows, and jaboncillos to play itself out against the buildings of Casa Grande. That way, should some sound accidentally emanate from the scene of the crime, no one would give it a second thought. At least that was the plan.

Hot wax dripped down the edge of the candle, causing the thief to curse softly before tipping the candle in a different direction. It was always the little details that ruined great plans, and this plan needed very much to succeed. The job should be performed quickly, as well as quietly. Mistakes were not allowed.

Sliding Rachel's desk drawer out, the forager moved rapidly through the stack of papers until finally finding the one sought. Unfolding the bound copy, it was quickly scanned, deemed to be the necessary article, then refolded. The search continued until all of the drawers had been examined for content. Two other papers were confiscated, and finally the robbery was concluded.

The looter gave a momentary glance toward Rachel's bedroom.

That door was securely closed—probably locked, but it didn't matter. Patience needed to be practiced. Patience and wisdom. There would be time to see to her later.

Blowing out the candle, the thief quietly opened the door and stared out into the dimly lit lobby. The front desk was deserted and would continue as such until the grand opening brought in tourists and other celebrating fools. Pulling the door closed without a single sound, the marauder slipped the candle into a pocket and hurried away into the night. The first act of deception had played itself out rather nicely, but part two now needed to be planned.

———

Yawning, Rachel opened the door and stepped into her office. Though dressed to Mr. Harvey's standards and fully groomed for the day, Rachel couldn't seem to shake her weariness. She would have loved nothing more than to have remained in bed, but she saw little sense in it. Her mind simply wouldn't let her rest. She couldn't stop worrying about all the new complications to her job at Casa Grande, and with each succeeding thought she desired nothing more than to run away and hide. But she had a job to do—at least for now. She could give serious consideration toward her future while continuing to maintain her post.

She reminded herself that it was important to ensure that her girls were at their stations and performing. It didn't matter that she'd slept fitfully through the night, dreaming of Braeden Parker's strong arms and Esmeralda's scowling expression. The work had to be done, and until she resigned her position, the work remained her responsibility.

She heard a commotion down the long hall outside her door. The girls tried to be quiet for the sake of those who had the day off or were serving on a different shift, but nevertheless, it was hard to keep things absolutely still. A gathering of twenty-five girls would never be known for silence, but rather brought to mind giggles, scuffles, and shrieks of dismay, excitement, or protest.

Shaking her head, Rachel went to her desk and opened one of the drawers. It was payday, and she needed to complete some work before Jeffery O'Donnell appeared with the payroll. But before she could so much as find her pencil, a knock sounded on the lobby door.

"Come in," she said, barely managing to stifle a yawn. She looked up and found Reginald peering in through the door. "Oh, good morning, Reg."

"Good morning, milady," he said, throwing back the door to give her a wide, sweeping bow. He looked up and smiled. "And how are we today?"

Rachel laughed. "*We* are tired."

"You are taking far too much upon those delicate shoulders," Reg said from the doorway. "Might I suggest a solution?"

Rachel shrugged. "If you think you have one."

He smiled, came into the office, and closed the door. "Tell me what seems most taxing at this point." He took a seat opposite her desk without waiting to be invited.

Rachel found his actions surprising but made no comment on that fact. "I suppose I'm worried about this inventory problem. Perhaps Mr. Parker was right in thinking that we should involve the local authorities."

"That's possible," Reg admitted. "However, I think your idea has merit."

"It's just that I was hoping this wasn't going to turn into an actual problem. I wanted to believe that the inventory sheets were simply out of order."

"And perhaps they are. You mustn't let it worry you, Rachel. We will do as you suggested and consider the inventory from day to day."

"Yes, but that only adds more work and with the grand opening coming up so quickly, the last thing I needed was yet another job."

Reg nodded. "Let me offer my services, then. I could easily put Tomas on the job to oversee the inventory for the kitchen and food. Perhaps one of your girls could help to keep a tally of the linens."

"That's awfully kind of you to offer," Rachel said, feeling blessed to have such good help. "But won't that put you in a bind?"

"I don't imagine it would be any worse than any other task. The key is to delegate the problem to others whose schedules are not quite so pressed. If not me, then you could always put several of your girls to work on the matter."

"No, I think I would feel better having you take it over. I don't mind you having Tomas assist you, but I don't think it would be wise to share the girls on the task. They need to recognize my authority over them, and to put them into this situation would confuse that authority. You would have say over them working on the inventory, I would have say over them otherwise—and what would happen when the boundaries of one job crossed another? See my point?"

"Of course," Reg replied. "The wisdom of it speaks for itself. I certainly hope you aren't suggesting that I was seeking to usurp your position."

"Absolutely not," Rachel answered, shaking her head. "I wouldn't think that for a moment. I'm grateful for what you're offering."

"Good. I'll get right to it. Do you still have those inventory lists?"

Rachel nodded. "Yes, they're here in my drawer. I'll get them to you after breakfast, but first I have to see to the payroll paper work." She paused and smiled. "I hope you know I truly appreciate your help."

Reg shared her smile and his brown eyes fairly twinkled. "I rather fancy the idea of rescuing a damsel in distress and playing the brave knight."

"Well, I don't know how much bravery is required to work on the inventory, but you are indeed rescuing me," Rachel teased. She liked the camaraderie she shared with Reg. It felt good not to have to worry about guarding her words and actions. Stifling another yawn, she looked at her watch. "I need to get going. I have to make sure every-one is at their stations, then I have to come back here and sort through inventories, food orders, and the payroll."

"I wonder if I might make one other suggestion."

Rachel nodded as she got to her feet. Reg instantly stood and his face seemed to sober a bit. "I'm worried that you are working too hard. Have you taken any time for a leisurely walk or a quiet moment at the pool?"

Rachel felt her face grow hot as she thought of the night Braeden had surprised her at the hot springs. "I've tried once or twice but haven't found it to afford me much in the way of restoration."

"Then why not take a walk with me after breakfast?" Reg ques-tioned softly. He gave her such a sweet look of concern that Rachel couldn't help but be touched. "We could stroll down to the falls and perhaps just sit and talk. They have installed charming benches for just such occasions. I could tell you about England. You always seem to find that of interest. Perhaps the setting would lend itself to something even more special."

"I'm sure we would have a wonderful time," Rachel said, growing suddenly uncomfortable. It was clear that Reg had interests in her other than just friendship. "But I can't."

Reg nodded, seeming to understand, but the words he offered next shocked Rachel.

"Is it because you're still in love with that Parker fellow?"

"I beg your pardon?" Rachel stared intently at Reginald. Meeting his gaze, she was certain that he knew something more than she had ever offered.

"It's fairly obvious that you two share something more than the management of Casa Grande."

Rachel felt as though a band had tightened around her chest. "Why do you say that?"

"Rachel, you don't have to worry. I won't share your secret, although others can probably surmise what I have."

"I see."

Reg came to stand a little closer and his voice lowered to a whisper. "You don't have to talk about this if it makes you uncomfortable. I simply wondered if that was the reason you refused to walk with me or if I somehow repulsed you with such an idea."

Rachel shook her head. "You could never repulse me, Reg. I certainly wouldn't want you to take that idea. No, it's a great many things. We can be good friends, but even Mr. Harvey has rules about us becoming more than that."

"Rules are made to be broken," Reg countered.

"Not when you are trying to live by God's rules," Rachel replied. "As a Christian woman, I should seek His will and not my own, and His will would never be to go against my authority on such a matter as fraternizing with another employee."

"And you aren't just saying this to put me off?"

"Absolutely not," Rachel replied. "I'm glad for our friendship,

Reg, but it cannot be something more than it is."

"Because of him."

Rachel bit her lip and looked away. She didn't feel close enough to Reg to explain her past with Braeden. And she certainly didn't want to discuss the present or even the future, as it seemed most unlikely that she could possibly hope to make sense out of either one.

Reg spoke before she could reply. "I understand you two knew each other prior to coming here to Casa Grande. Were you very close?"

Rachel looked back to Reg and nodded. "But I don't want to talk about it. The past is the past and I'd rather leave it behind me."

"That might prove difficult given Mr. Parker's very real existence in your future."

"Maybe," Rachel replied. "But I don't see any other way to deal with it."

"Well, then," Reg said, moving toward the door. "I shall excuse myself and get to work. The dawn is nearly upon us and I must oversee my staff." He opened the door and started to leave, but Rachel called to him.

"Reg," she said softly, "thank you for caring about me. I consider you a dear friend."

He gave her another bow, then with a mischievous smile replied, "Perhaps one day you will consider me something more."

He was gone before she could reply, but Rachel couldn't help feeling a mixture of emotions at his words. She didn't want to lead the man to believe her capable of something more when she knew her heart was forever bound to Braeden. She tried not to think of the night by the pool—of Braeden's words of love—but she couldn't help herself. She longed with all of her heart to believe them to be true. To imagine that Braeden had spent the last six years just as miserable as she had was not exactly comforting, but it did make her feel better. If he had refused to marry because of his love for her, then perhaps there was hope for them to rekindle their relationship.

But even as these thoughts filled her head, Rachel remembered the pompous attitude of Ivy Brooks and her part in that disastrous night by the pool. She had mentioned receiving Braeden's message, and he certainly hadn't disputed sending her one.

Just then Rachel glanced down and noticed something on her chair. Leaning closer to inspect it, she chipped at the ivory-colored substance and realized it was wax. Why would there be wax drippings on her chair? Studying the area around her desk, Rachel realized there were also wax drippings on the floor. Casa Grande boasted electric lighting in all of their advertisements, and while oil lamps and candles were available in case of crisis, there was no reason to use candles at this point. Unless, of course, someone had come into her office after the electricity had been shut down for the night, as was the routine in Morita.

The wax made a curious presentation to Rachel. Where had it come from? Someone with a lit candle would have had to have been in her office, and since the wax wasn't there the night before, she could only guess that someone had come into her office in the middle of the night. But for what purpose?

A feeling of uneasiness crept over her. If someone had been in her office, that meant they were capable of going through her desk and other properties. She immediately began looking around the room to see if anything was missing. Nothing appeared out of place.

Sitting down, she pulled open her drawers and gave a cursory glance at the contents. Nothing looked disturbed. But—

She startled as she touched the unmistakable hardened wax that edged the top of several sheets of paper. Someone had gone through this drawer. Shaking her head, she couldn't figure it out. Why would someone have come into her office and helped themselves to her desk? What were they looking for? The only paper work she had in this particular drawer dealt with the Harvey House staff, inventory, and other necessary papers. What could the thief have been after? Better yet, did they find what they were after?

The only thing she could do was wait until after she managed to get the girls operating in an orderly fashion. After that, she'd have to come back here and go piece by piece through the contents of her desk.

Rachel shuddered as she closed the drawer and looked around the room. Someone had intruded upon her, and it left her feeling frightened and wary. Not only that, but it added to the complexity of her already complicated life—and that was something Rachel didn't need.

৵ TWELVE ৵

BRAEDEN HAD TAKEN ALL HE was going to take. For nearly a week now, Rachel had managed to avoid him no matter how hard he tried to see her. He had given her a wide berth at first, realizing she appeared to be consumed by her emotions and doubts, but his patience had run out. With new determination he laid a plan and set out to see it through. He would talk to her and she would listen. Whether she liked it or not.

Rachel's routine was nearly the same every evening. She concluded her business in the dining room, and then, if she didn't spy Braeden waiting in the wings, she made her way through the lobby to her office. However, if she saw him, she would hurry through the kitchen and into the private Harvey Girl parlor where no men were allowed. From there, he could only presume that she took the long dormitory hall to her office, where she could lock him and the rest of the world out.

He knew she was hurting. Knew, too, that her fears were running her ragged. He had spoken in brief to Jeffery O'Donnell, finding it easy to confide parts of the past to this old friend of Rachel's. Jeffery had been sympathetic but also very protective. He had told Braeden, in a most determined manner, not to dally with Rachel's heart. But Braeden had assured him that wasn't what he had in mind. He cared deeply for Rachel, but she would have no part of him. He'd tried on many occasions to force her to talk to him, but she always managed to create a scene that would allow for little or no privacy. And now she had managed to completely avoid him. But no more.

Braeden figured that if he waited in the darkness near her office, he could jump out and take hold of her before she had time to run the other way. Then he would drag her back to his office, if need be, and force her to sit down and discuss this whole ugly matter with him. She wouldn't like it, but frankly, it didn't matter. Braeden didn't like what was happening between them now, and no one seemed to care how he felt.

The grandfather clock chimed nine as Braeden took his place in the darkness by her door. He wondered silently what he should say to her when she first came upon him. It wouldn't be an easy scene, but hopefully it would take place quickly and quietly. The last thing he wanted was for Rachel to call out for help from Reginald Worthington or one of her girls.

The minutes ticked by and Braeden shifted uneasily, hoping he hadn't misjudged her routine. Of course, given his position, he would have heard if she'd come into her office through the other door. So far there was only silence on the other side, and certainly no sign of light. He silently prayed that she would follow the normal course and come his way. He prayed, too, that God would give him the words to say when they finally came face-to-face.

The swishing of her skirts brought him instantly to attention. She would stop and close the dining room doors before making her way across the lobby. He had seen her do this for the last three nights and knew she had established the habit over her weeks at Casa Grande. She would reach into her pocket for the key to her office just about now.

Braeden tensed and drew a shallow breath. He hoped he wouldn't frighten her overmuch, so just as he heard her approach, Braeden stepped into the lobby.

"Good evening, Rachel," he said in a low, husky voice.

He watched her stiffen and glance quickly around her as if looking for a means of escape. Her expression was one of pure shock, nearly panic. She moved backward, and he could see that already she was making her way to the dining room doors.

"I want to talk to you," he said, taking three quick strides to where she stood.

"I don't want to talk to you," she countered, turning away.

With a sigh, Braeden reached out and took hold of her. "I don't care at this point what you want. You will hear me out." He dragged her, protesting, to his office, then forced her inside and closed the door behind them. "Now I want you to sit down in that chair," he said, pointing to an ornate wainscot chair. Harvey had elaborately decorated the house in antiques of many varieties. This particular piece was a favorite of Braeden's and dated from the mid–1700s.

He could see Rachel battling against her emotions as she backed away from him. "I don't think this is appropriate," she told him.

"Sit!" he demanded, hating to take such a harsh tone with her, yet knowing there was no other way to get her to listen.

Rachel nodded and backed into the chair. It seemed to swallow her up, only adding to the helplessness of her situation.

Braeden came to stand in front of her, planning only to remain close enough to keep her in the chair. Yet when he came to that point, he naturally followed his instincts and leaned over her, planting both hands on either arm rest. The action imprisoned her, leaving her totally at his mercy.

She looked first to each of his hands, then took a deep breath and looked into his eyes. "Why are you doing this?" she barely managed to whisper.

Braeden had thought he would berate her for her childishness at the pool. He would tell her how silly she had acted all week and how ridiculous she was to go on mistrusting him. Then he would explain the past again and demand that she understand and accept his explanation. It all seemed reasonable and logical. But standing this close to her, Braeden couldn't help but feel the pulsating current that seemed to travel between them. He looked down into her oval face, a face so sweetly fixed in his memories, and all he wanted to do was kiss her full red lips.

"Rachel." The name came out more as a moan than a word as Braeden leaned closer to kiss her.

She didn't fight him, which eased Braeden's guilt for forcing himself upon her. And as his kissed deepened, Rachel seemed to match his enthusiasm by leaning into the kiss. Neither one touched the other, except by the joining of their lips. It was a perfect moment, Braeden thought, losing himself in the stillness of his office. How he had missed her! Six years and not a single word to ease his worried heart. Six years of love stored away for a chance that might never come.

He pulled away just a bit in order to speak of his love, but when he did he watched her squeeze her eyes shut and knew he'd pushed her too hard.

"I'm sorry," he whispered, straightening to stand before her. "I didn't mean to upset you."

"It's all right," she murmured, still refusing to open her eyes.

He thought he understood and watched her for a moment. Did she strive to block out his image, or rather, did she send her memories back in time to a place where she would have enjoyed his actions? Braeden smiled to himself knowing that she had enjoyed his kiss just now. She hadn't even tried to put a stop to his advances.

Pulling up another chair, he sighed and pushed back the errant hair that had fallen across his forehead. He waited until she had regained her composure and opened her eyes. Her expression betrayed her longing, and it was this that caused Braeden to press forward with his explanation.

"I had to see you. I had to make you talk to me, or at least to listen to me," he began. "I've been half crazy working so close to you, yet never being able to be near you—to touch you—talk to you."

She appeared surprised by his words, and Braeden knew instinctively that she was still harboring painful memories from the past.

"Rachel, Ivy Brooks means nothing to me. She's a conniving little child who is searching for a husband and a ticket out of Morita. I'm not that man. What you saw at the pool was pure coincidence and nothing more."

"But she said you'd sent her a note," Rachel murmured, confirming to Braeden where her heart was in the matter.

"I forwarded her a note from her aunt. I had gone to the depot to pick up some telegrams and ran into Mrs. Needlemeier. She gave me a note for Ivy and asked if I would be so kind as to deliver it."

"I see," Rachel said, clearly enlightened by this news.

"As for her being in my arms when you returned for your book, it was just as I tried to explain. Either honestly or dishonestly, Ivy slipped. Instinctively, I reached out to steady her. It was nothing more than this. I left the pool right after you did and thought to come talk to you, but I knew you would need to change out of your wet clothes and figured it would be better if I talked to you the next day. But you wouldn't allow me anywhere near you."

Tears formed in Rachel's green eyes. "I'm sorry," she managed to say before allowing a tiny sob to escape. "This has been very hard on me."

"You aren't the only one," Braeden countered with a smile. But his smile quickly faded as he saw how tormented she was over the entire matter. "Tell me that you no longer love me, and I'll never bother you again," he said suddenly. He knew it was a risk—he wasn't at all sure he wanted to hear the answer but felt confident that the matter had to be discussed.

She looked at him in disbelief, trying hard to rein in her emotions. "What?"

He leaned forward, reaching out to take hold of her hand. "Tell me, Rachel. Tell me that you don't love me."

He could see her breathing quicken and watched as her expression contorted. She was fighting a battle within herself, and he couldn't help her. But her battle gave him the answer he needed and that gave him hope.

"I love you, Rachel. That has never changed. I've never stopped, even when you refused to believe in me. All I ask is that you admit what you're feeling for me. If I'm right, then we can move past this and reclaim our future together. If not, then I'll leave you alone. In fact, I'll leave Casa Grande. You only need to tell me that you no longer care."

A gasping sob broke from Rachel's throat as she pulled her hand away from his. "Don't do this. I can't . . . I . . . ."

Braeden's heart was encouraged. She still loved him, of this he was certain. It gave him all the hope he needed to press her for the truth. "Why not, Rachel? Why can't you tell me that you don't love me?"

Rachel shook her head in misery, giving him no answer but her silence. She began to cry in earnest now. "I've been wrong about so many things, and I just don't trust my judgment where my emotions are concerned. You must see that I can't have my life so disorderly—so disturbed. I feel like I'm constantly running up one hill and down another in some form of endless race. I'm making no progress, but I have to keep running. It's wearing me out."

He opened his mouth to speak, but she was too quick for him. Releasing all the pressures of her life over the last few weeks, Rachel poured out her heart, edging close to hysteria as she did so.

"First I have to deal with the likes of Ivy and her aunt. Esmeralda Needlemeier has interfered in my decisions at nearly every turn. She criticizes my choices, my decisions, and my close observation of Mr. Harvey's instructions. She threatens to have me fired at least once a day, and she considers it her personal business to see me miserable. Then she saddles me with Ivy. Ivy comes along and wreaks havoc with my authority—questioning every order, commenting on every detail of instruction. She's young and beautiful and she knows it, so she works her wiles on every man who comes through the door—including you."

She drew a ragged breath and continued. "It's just too much. Can't you see? The pressure is too great and it's destroying me. You are here as a constant reminder of what I've lost, while Reginald pursues me in hopes of courtship and a future that I cannot give him. I can't go on like this!" She buried her face in her hands and cried in great heart-breaking sobs. "I can't."

Braeden felt momentarily overwhelmed. He had never seen anyone break down so thoroughly. Even when Rachel had bid him good-bye in Chicago, she had been rather stalwart. This time, however, was clearly a different case. It stunned him and left him totally confused as to how he might help. He certainly hadn't anticipated causing her this kind of misery.

Help me, Lord, he prayed as he edged forward on his chair. *I don't want to hurt her anymore. I only want to love her.*

Uncertain that it was the right thing to do, Braeden got to his feet and pulled Rachel up into his arms. She nearly collapsed against him, unable to fight him or to stop her tears. He let her cry, holding her tightly against him, feeling her tears wet the front of his shirt. Her entire body trembled from the force of pain and misery inside of her. Searching desperately for something to say, Braeden found he could only stand there, praying and waiting for her to release the anguish that seemed to consume her.

He lost track of time, knowing that it didn't matter. He would have stood there for years had it taken that long. If it meant that Rachel could leave off with the past and her doubts and give him a second chance at a happy future with her, Braeden would have waited forever. When her sobs seemed to quiet a bit and the trembling and great wracking heaves eased off, Braeden began stroking her hair. His fingers tangled into the rich auburn curls, pulling loose her hairpins. Her hair was soft and it smelled like lilacs and roses.

He loved her so much and he just couldn't lose her again. *Please, God, don't let me lose her.*

She finally quieted against him, her arms wrapped tightly around him, clinging to him as if he were some stronghold in the storm. Finally it seemed right to speak.

"I love you, Rachel. I have always loved you. You must trust me. You must believe in that love, for it will never die."

She pulled away just far enough to look up into his face. She seemed to study him, as if by observing his expression she could tell the truth of his words. He remained quite sober as her green eyes seemed to search him for answers.

"Esmeralda can't hurt you," he continued softly. "She's a lonely, domineering old woman who is used to having things done her way. She doesn't know how to deal with someone who stands her ground against her as you do. But she is not the one in charge of your position here, and Fred Harvey knows what an asset you are to his system. He won't let you go easily, and he certainly won't dismiss you at the grumblings of one old woman.

"And Ivy is nothing to me. She is a spoiled brat who seeks to cause problems. I wouldn't take her too seriously. She's just a child. She has no power over you, unless you give it to her. And as for Reginald Worthington, well . . . let's just say I'll deal with him."

Rachel sniffed and shook her head. "It's not your problem."

"But I want it to be my problem," Braeden countered. "I want it to be my problem because I want *you* to be my problem."

"He's done nothing wrong."

"Nothing but ask to court my lady," Braeden said with a grin. He reached up and touched her tear-stained cheeks with his index finger. "He can't have you, Rachel. You belong to me—just as I belong to you."

Because they were still in each other's arms, it seemed only natural that he kiss her again. He lowered his mouth to hers very slowly, giving her every chance to protest. He might have forced that first kiss, but not this one. This one he wanted to be a symbol of their life to come. He wanted it to be the first of many sweet, passionate kisses they would share by mutual desire.

Rachel closed her eyes, and he knew she wanted this kiss as much as he did. Gently, so as not to startle her, he pressed his lips to hers. He felt her embrace tighten, even as he held her closer to him. His heart rejoiced that he had found her again and that she cared for him. Although she'd not said the words, he knew she still loved him.

But without warning, Rachel pulled away, this time putting several feet of distance between them. "Mr. Harvey doesn't allow for dating between his employees. You mustn't . . . I mean . . . we mustn't—"

"Mustn't what? Love each other?" Braeden asked, stepping closer.

"No!" Rachel exclaimed. She held out her arm as if to ward him off. "You must understand. I have been quite strict with the girls and even with Reg. I told him it was not allowable for Mr. Harvey's employees to court. It's against the rules."

"So we break the rules."

She shook her head again. "That's what Reg said, but you know that isn't what God would want of us."

Braeden smiled. "I don't recall there's any law of Mr. Harvey's against being married to another employee. In fact, as I recall, there were several incidences of that at the Las Vegas resort where I took my training."

"Married?" Rachel questioned, her eyes growing wide with what Braeden could only surmise was a mixture of shock and fear.

"Rachel," he said softly, hoping to alleviate her fright, "would marriage to me be so bad?"

"Marriage?" She seemed stuck on variations of the word.

He smiled. "I don't wish to court you. I've already done that. I want to marry you and make you my wife forever. I don't want there to come another chance for you to slip away from me. Marry me."

"Marry you." She said it rather stoically, as if he'd asked for nothing more than her assistance in sending a telegram. She took a deep breath and let it out before answering. "Braeden, I think we both need to pray about this. We're acting on emotions and the turmoil of the moment. We can't think clearly under the circumstances."

"I'm thinking quite clearly," he said, taking a step toward her.

She shook her head and backed up to the door. "I can't."

He knew he couldn't continue to force the issue and nodded. "Very well. Then I suppose I must wait until that time when you can think this through and see it for the sensible remedy that I know it to be."

She appeared to relax a bit. "Thank you, Braeden." She opened the door but paused as if reconsidering what had just taken place. With the tiniest of smiles she said, "I seem to have made a mess of your shirt."

"No more so than I made of your hair," he offered with a grin. "I'd say we're even."

Her hand went to her hair, and she smiled as she pulled loose the last remaining pins. "I might as well let it all down."

"I've always liked it very much that way."

She shook her head. "You've never seen it this way, as far as I can recall."

His grin broadened. "I have in my dreams."

He watched as her ruddy complexion darkened to crimson in her embarrassment. He thought her the most beautiful woman in the world. "Good night, Rachel. Don't forget."

She looked at him quizzically. "Don't forget what?"

"That I love you." He barely whispered the words, but they seemed to echo loudly in the room. It seemed an inadequate representation of all that he felt for her, but he knew they were the words she would most understand.

She nodded but said nothing more, leaving him there to watch her leave. He went to the doorway and watched her cross the lobby to her own quarters. His arms ached to hold her again, and it was all he could do to keep from running after her. *I have to give her time*, he reasoned. *I have to be patient and steadfast and prove my love to her all over again, if that's what it takes to win her heart.*

SEEING BRAEDEN AND RACHEL greet each other rather amicably that morning at breakfast, Ivy Brooks could only imagine that they had resolved their differences and had agreed to be friends. Such a development didn't fit into Ivy's plans at all.

Finishing the last of her breakfast, Ivy considered how to spend her day off. She had planned to go to her aunt's house and spend a luxurious amount of time in a hot bath where not only would there be no line of giggling girls awaiting a turn, but she would have peace and quiet to think. However, seeing Rachel smile demurely at Braeden's comments caused Ivy to feel a bit riled. She had hoped they would go on being enemies. At least as long as it took to find out from her aunt Esmeralda who Braeden Parker was and what prospects he might afford her as a potential husband. She'd already overheard bits and pieces of information pertaining to his relationship with Rachel, including what she'd overhead that night at the pool.

"Wish I could spend the day with you," Faith said as she cleared away some of Ivy's dishes.

"I'm sure Rachel arranged to keep us separated," Ivy said snidely. "She claims to want us to act and relate as one happy family, but she certainly goes out of her way to see that we are kept from spending too much free time together."

Faith frowned. "I suppose that's true. I simply hadn't considered it."

Ivy nodded, knowing there was a great deal Faith had never bothered to consider. The girl was positively daft, and Ivy wondered quite seriously how she managed to remember how to breathe without someone standing by to instruct her.

Tossing her napkin atop the table, Ivy got to her feet. "Well, I must go and visit my auntie. She pines away for me, you know."

Faith nodded as if fully understanding this to be true. "At least you have somewhere nice to go."

"Don't fret, Faith. One day I shall take you to the mansion with me, and we shall have a lovely tea and you may try on my Worth gowns." Ivy threw this last temptation in to remind Faith just how far beneath Ivy's status she truly was. She might be the granddaughter of one of the Santa Fe board members, but she was still a simple girl from Kansas. Ivy, on the other hand, had been abroad, had shopped in the finest stores in New York, and was more than a little aware of the differences between her life and Faith's.

"Oh, that would be simply divine," Faith said, hugging the plates to her apron.

Just then Rachel walked by. "Miss Bradford, is that a stain I see on your apron?"

Faith looked down rather mortified. "I hadn't noticed."

"Well, now that you have, I would suggest you go change immediately. You know Mr. Harvey's rules."

"Yes, Rachel," Faith replied and hurried off to do as she was instructed.

Ivy looked at Rachel and smiled. "Well, I'm off to enjoy my day. I don't suppose that nice Mr. Parker also has the day off?"

Rachel frowned. "No, I don't suppose he does, and even if he did, you know Mr. Harvey's rules on that issue as well as rules about stained aprons."

Ivy laughed. "Rules are made for those who can otherwise not figure out how to govern themselves. I, Miss Taylor, am certainly not amongst that crowd. I can think for myself, and I can certainly structure my life accordingly. I'm very organized."

"Well, I would keep in mind the time, Miss Brooks," Rachel said, squaring her shoulders. "You were late returning on your last day off. I certainly wouldn't want to assign you extra duty in order to make up for that infraction of the *rules*."

"Don't worry. I'll be back," Ivy said, giving Rachel what she knew would be her haughtiest stare. "So long as this job suits my needs, I'll be here."

She sauntered off toward the lobby, thoroughly enjoying the fact that she'd just made Rachel very uncomfortable. Ivy was one of the few people to stand her ground with the spinster and she enjoyed making it clear that she didn't need the position, but rather was entitled to it if she wanted it. Rachel might be a problem to her immediate plans, but Ivy decided it was a problem she'd soon take care of. The likes of Rachel Taylor was hardly an adversary worth fretting over.

Moving down the hall, Ivy exited the building out the side door. This door opened onto the wide, sweeping sun porch that lined the garden side of Casa Grande. Here guests could sit and study the park-like garden that stretched out for acres between Casa Grande and the Needlemeier estate. It was quite picturesque and said to be some of the loveliest country for miles around. But it could never be lovely enough to entice Ivy to want to stay. She hated Morita. Hated it more than any place else on earth.

She remembered coming here after the death of her parents. The house fire that had taken their lives had left her with little but borrowed clothes and bad memories.

Ivy frowned. Thinking of her parents pricked a spark of conscience that Ivy had long since refused to deal with. It had a way of making a person regret their mistakes, and Ivy had no time for such things. The past was the past and nothing would change it. The future, however, still held great possibilities . . . no thanks to her aunt or this pitiful town.

Ivy had hoped and prayed that Morita would be something exotic and wonderful. Instead, she found a desertlike town with a funny little hot springs oasis and a vast garden that her aunt likened to Eden. But other than this and a few minor business establishments, Morita was as desolate as St. Louis had been exciting.

Leaving the porch to venture along the stream, Ivy tried to take some pleasure in the series of tiny waterfalls. They traveled in rapid succession downward to the greater Morita Falls, allowing for the energy that provided some parts of the town with electricity. Aunt Esmeralda said very soon the entire town would have access to the power source, but it still wouldn't be enough for Ivy. It was hard to get excited about something that had once seemed rather commonplace in her life.

No, Ivy longed for the thrill of the uncommon. She longed to travel again as she had when she'd been a child. She wanted to see the world, at least more of the world than this little stop along the Santa Fe Railroad. Faith had chided her to be patient because after one year of service, Ivy would be entitled to a vacation and a free pass to go anywhere the Santa Fe Railroad went. Ivy thought the idea laughable. There was no destination on this wretched railroad that enticed her to travel. Unless, of course, she considered the possibility of Kansas City or Chicago. Both places would be accessible along the line. But even this idea held little interest. What Ivy really wanted was a wealthy husband—someone who could arrange for her travels and see to it that she never wanted for anything.

Smiling, she made her way across the small footbridge that connected the Casa Grande side of the gardens to the Needlemeier side. It was all open territory for the guests of Casa Grande. Her aunt had even offered to give her gardeners to the resort, and Mr. Harvey and the Santa Fe had eagerly accepted. They reasoned that if this team of workers knew how to create a garden in the middle of the arid, sandy soils of New Mexico, they were well worth any pay to keep on staff.

Of course, the Santa Fe officials had never had to spend a winter in Morita. When winter came, everything seemed rather dried up and dead in spite of the usually mild temperatures. But sometimes the snows came, and then the boredom of sitting in the middle of nowhere with nothing to do was almost maddening. But with or without snow, Morita was sheer misery to Ivy.

Aunt Esmeralda had tried to interest Ivy in everything from needlework to music lessons, but nothing appealed to her. Ivy had pleaded her case to go east, to live in a bigger city where she might truly benefit from the agenda it could offer. Her aunt was nearly convinced until the Santa Fe and Mr. Harvey had taken notice of her oasis. Of course, Ivy hadn't learned until recently that Esmeralda had been issuing a barrage of letters to those officials, enticing and urging their interest in the property. She had made all manner of promises, and with their purchase of the land, Ivy saw her dreams go up in smoke.

"I hate it here," she muttered, cursing the very ground that she walked on. "If I have my way, I won't spend another winter here."

The real trick was to figure out how she might make her dreams come true. She needed a wealthy husband—someone who was already established in one of the eastern cities, or who had a mind to go there once Ivy assured him it was for the best. The grand opening celebration was sure to bring in dignitaries and wealthy investors, and Ivy figured to give them all a lengthy consideration before deciding her true course.

She passed her aunt's beloved roses and stopped to pick a particularly delightful pink blossom. The thorns pricked her finger as she ripped the stem away from the plant. *I'm like this flower*, she thought. *I, too, have my sting. Pluck me if you will, but it comes at a price.* She put her bleeding finger to her lips in order to ease the pain and smelled the sweetness of the rose at the same time. It was exactly as she saw herself. Lovely and sweet to the senses, but deadly and painful if taken the wrong way.

Humming to herself, she went into the house through the kitchen door, snagged one of the cook's cherry tarts, and tossed the rose to the housemaids as she came down the back stairs.

"Put this in water and leave it in my room, Liza."

The girl caught the rose, grimacing as the thorn stuck her thumb. "Yes, miss." She curtsied, and Ivy gave a nod as she left the kitchen.

Ivy nibbled at the tart and made her way through the house. She had planned to take a bath first and change out of her uniform into some of her lovely clothes, but she needed information, and that would only come from her aunt. Ivy was desperate to learn more about Braeden Parker, and if anyone would know his history, it would be Esmeralda Needlemeier.

"Aunt Esmeralda," Ivy said, going into her aunt's favorite sitting room. She could see the old woman was poring over her mail and telegrams. No doubt spending more of Ivy's inheritance trying to further populate the tiresome little town.

"Ivy," the woman said, glancing up momentarily. "I expected you to come home last night."

Ivy shrugged and took another bite of the tart. "I had things to take care of and it wasn't convenient. So what are you doing today?"

"Business as usual," Esmeralda replied. "I have the possibility of luring a New York seamstress here to Morita."

Ivy sunk casually to her favorite rococo-styled chair. This particular chair had been fashioned in Italy, and the arms had been inlaid with mother-of-pearl. The exotic design against the ornately carved walnut wood gave Ivy the feeling of being a queen on her throne. A fitting depiction, in Ivy's mind.

"And what would Morita do with a New York seamstress?" she asked, toying with the last bits of her treat.

"Casa Grande will attract a high class of clientele. A seamstress already well acquainted with the desires of such women will stand ready and able to meet any necessity they might have. Perhaps those staying for lengthy respites will find themselves in need of lightweight but fashionable clothing. A seamstress could provide this and make herself a reasonable living, while also serving the community. You yourself have complained about the quality of the local gowns."

"Yes, but a trip to Denver quickly rectified the situation. Others might find it just as easy to take the train north."

"Not if the goods are readily available. I plan to see that no one desires to leave for any reason. I will install all of the necessary businesses to make Morita a success. It's just as your uncle would have wanted it."

"Would he have wanted you to waste your money—money that is your only hope of survival for the future?" Ivy asked, seriously eyeing the old woman.

"I believe he would have," Esmeralda said. She put down the letter and met her niece's stare. "I suppose you believe it foolish. Youth cares very little for the concerns of making a mark on the world. Your uncle wanted to leave something behind that would cause men to remember his name. He had no son to carry his name, thus he determined to have something else."

"But Morita hardly bears his name," Ivy countered. "You should have at least called it Needlemeier."

"Rubbish. Your uncle liked the way the word sounded and used it accordingly."

Ivy shrugged, ate the last of the tart, and brushed the crumbs from her fingers. "Still, what if this venture refuses to pay out?"

"It will pay out. There's already good money attracted to this town."

"Truly?" Ivy questioned, taking immediate interest in the conversation.

"Yes," Esmeralda replied, nodding. "That rather tolerable Mr. O'Donnell hails from a wealthy Chicago family. I've heard it said they're worth millions. Then Mr. Parker, the hotel manager, has a considerable sum in his bank account, and as I'm told, it is only the tip of his worth."

"Honestly, Auntie, how do you manage to find these things out?"

Esmeralda smiled a tight, reserved little smile. "I ask questions, and I demand answers."

"And you did this in Mr. Parker's case?" The conversation was playing out exactly as Ivy had hoped it might.

"I completely investigate each of the businessmen who come to Morita."

"And Mr. Parker is wealthy?"

"Apparently he is very comfortable," Esmeralda replied. "He, too, comes from Chicago, where his family was heavily involved in banking, the stock market, and other manners of moneymaking. Mr. Parker attended college, chose the field of accounting, then found an interest in hotel management. For whatever reason, I can scarcely imagine. He is unmarried, his parents are now deceased, and he claims to have absolutely no regrets in coming to such a small town after living in the big city all of his life."

"Well, that could change," Ivy said, fingering the mother-of-pearl.

"I wouldn't count on it. Apparently there is some old friendship between him and your Miss Taylor. Of course, this comes to me clearly through the grapevine, but I wonder if it isn't enough of an attraction to keep him here."

"I doubt it," Ivy said, narrowing her eyes ever so slightly. "I have seen them nearly at each other's throats. I don't think they have the slightest liking for each other," she lied, even now wondering how difficult it would be to make this an absolute truth.

Esmeralda harrumphed this news and returned her attention to the letters before her. "I suppose time will tell."

Ivy nodded. "Yes, I suppose it will." Getting to her feet, Ivy could think of nothing more than a hot bath and time to consider all that she'd learned.

"I would imagine that with the changes and elegance provided by Casa Grande, you might well learn to content yourself with this small town of ours."

Ivy paused at the archway and laughed. "Don't imagine that too hard, Auntie. I hate this town as much as I ever have. I don't intend to live here one second longer than it takes me to find a rich husband who lives elsewhere." She could see the brief expression of hurt on her aunt's face. The woman covered it quickly, but it was enough to encourage Ivy to speak further.

"This town will never amount to anything. People will come, but inevitably they will go because there is nothing here to entice them to do otherwise. You can hardly believe that a cheap railroad resort, even one that brings in famous entertainers, could ever hope to hold the attention of the public for long. Once the people have come here and experienced it, what's left? Do you really suppose they would venture to this barren land solely to enjoy your hot springs and pitiful little town? Do you really imagine that the whispered promise of a New York seamstress will bring upper society running to Morita?" She laughed, knowing that she'd just cut her aunt's dream to ribbons.

"It will merely run its course as everything else does," Ivy said, turning on her heel before a satisfied smile crept across her face. *Live with that thought, old woman. You've forced me to live in this desert hole, but don't imagine that I will ever stay here.*

Hours later, Ivy emerged from her bath and wrapped a robe of pink lawn around her still-damp body. She sat herself down in the window seat and let the wind gently blow dry her waist-length blond hair. She knew her appeal to men and smiled to herself as she thought of the handsome Braeden Parker.

"So what if he has a past with Rachel Taylor," she murmured. "It hardly matters, considering the plans I have for him."

She stretched catlike and leaned back against the wall. She needed a plan in order to entice Braeden to see the benefits she could offer him. He had taken off too quickly the night of the mishap at the hot springs, or she might have allowed him to better understand how easy it would be to fall in love with her. But the real dilemma wouldn't be in getting Braeden Parker to lose his heart. No, Ivy had confidence enough in her ability to get her man. The greater problem would be how to convince him to leave Casa Grande and New Mexico and return to the big city.

Thinking on this, Ivy smiled to herself. "Of course, if Casa Grande's reputation were ruined, it might provide an answer. Say, if the guests were constantly taking ill from the food . . ."

The idea intrigued her. How difficult could it be to add a little something here or there to the already prepared meals? After all, it was her job to handle and serve that food. Who would know?

"It might take a bit of time," she reasoned aloud, "but it could be done. If people grow sick dining at the Harvey House Restaurant, they certainly won't be coming back to Casa Grande." Not only that, but by targeting this attack on the restaurant, she would also cause Rachel a tremendous amount of trouble.

She smiled smugly and lifted her chin in an arrogant manner. "If there are no customers for Casa Grande, there can hardly be a reason for Braeden Parker to remain here. And, of course, he would have to take his wife with him wherever he ventured. And that wife . . . will be me."

ᥫ FOURTEEN ᥫ

"REGINALD WORTHINGTON, may I introduce Mr. Marcus Smith of Topeka," Jeffery O'Donnell stated more than asked.

Reg looked up from his labor to create curried rack of lamb and smiled. "How do you do, Mr. Smith? I hope you'll forgive me if I fail to shake your hand."

Smith, a robust man with a thick mass of curly gray hair, nodded. "I completely understand, Mr. Worthington. I have heard great things about your cooking and couldn't resist coming here to sample some of the fine cuisine."

"Very good, sir. We shall offer only an abbreviated menu, but it shall be our very best efforts."

"Mr. Smith is here to make a final inspection of the resort on behalf of the Santa Fe board," Jeffery explained.

Reg nodded and listened as Smith immediately jumped in to explain his position. "I find that taking matters into my own hands often allows me to avoid those pesky complications that become destructive elements at later dates."

"I trust you've found no such complications here at Casa Grande," Reg said, putting the lamb aside. He gave a quick instruction to one of his assistants, then went to wash his hands.

"No, I am very pleased with what I've found," Smith replied. "Why don't you come join us in the dining room for a moment and tell us how you feel about the matters of the kitchen."

Reg hardly felt it necessary to sit about a table and discuss issues of his kitchen. He was very much under control, knew his job, and desired no outside interference. However, he knew what was expected of him and gave the briefest nod of his head.

"I shall be there momentarily," Reg told the men. "Allow me to put together a tray of refreshments."

"What a capital idea!" Smith said enthusiastically. He rubbed his stomach and grinned. "I could go for a bit of refreshment."

Reg nodded, figuring the man would go for much more than a "bit" of Casa Grande's delicacies. He pulled out a silver tray and instructed one of the baking assistants to arrange a selection of pastries and cakes, then ordered another man to bring him a pot of coffee. At just that moment, Gwen Carson appeared. She was in charge of the dining room for the evening meal, and while Reginald liked her well enough, she couldn't compete with the high esteem he held for Rachel.

"I understand there is to be some form of refreshment offered to the gentlemen in the dining room," she said, greeting Reg. "I thought maybe I could help. Would you like me to serve for you?"

Reg smiled. "I say, that would be quite the thing. Show Mr. Smith a bit of our Harvey charm before the evening meal!" He smiled at the soft-spoken girl. "The trays are being prepared even now. We shall await you in the dining room."

Gwen nodded and went to work while Reginald, seeing that everything was under control, exited the kitchen to join Smith and O'Donnell.

"We are to be served in Harvey fashion," he told the men. They looked up at him as if to question his empty hands and he smiled. "The head waitress herself shall look after us."

"Miss Carson is a very amiable person," Jeffery told Smith. "She was originally trained in Topeka and held a position of high regard at the Emporia House."

"I must say, Fred Harvey's idea sounded completely ludicrous to me. He never makes a profit, and in fact, he must be concerned by the Santa Fe losses. However, everywhere I go people talk of his fine food and service," Smith commented.

"I know," Jeffery replied. "It doesn't sound reasonable, but Harvey's restaurants are making the Santa Fe a prosperous rail line. Despite poor showings this year, profits continue to rise where passenger service is concerned, and the hotels and resorts should make even more money. So lavishing the guests with outrageous portions and gourmet cuisine at the dinner table hardly seems to keep Mr. Harvey from success. I believe Harvey's prosperity has crossed over to benefit the Santa Fe as well."

"Well, it won't be beneficial for long if those in power continue to make poor decisions," Smith countered.

"Whatever do you mean, sir?" Reginald questioned.

Just then Gwen appeared holding a silver serving tray. She quickly arranged cups and saucers, dessert plates, and silver before them, then placed the pot of coffee in the middle of the table. Without giving them any chance to comment, she returned to the kitchen and came back with a tray of delectable goodies.

"Oh my," Smith commented as she asked them to make choices. "Such decisions."

"Have no fear," Reginald said, seeing the heavy man lick his lips, "there are more awaiting us in the kitchen."

This seemed to satisfy Smith, who quickly pointed to two cream-filled pastries. Gwen served the men, poured coffee, then returned to the kitchen for cream and sugar.

"If you gentlemen need anything else, don't hesitate to let me know. I'll be over there folding napkins," she told them and pointed to a small counter where even now another Harvey Girl was at work.

Smith nodded and quickly tore into the pastries with his fork. He sampled the éclair first, closing his eyes as the food met his lips. With a broad smile he exclaimed, "Simply superb!"

Reginald smiled at the man. "Thank you." He paused momentarily, worried that he might be overstepping his bounds with the next question. "You mentioned that there were poor decisions being made among your railroad officials."

"Indeed there are," Smith replied in between bites. "The Santa Fe is not as solvent as we would like. Unwise business decisions have proven harmful to the well-being of our industry."

"Is it truly all that bad?" Jeffery questioned.

"I believe it may prove to be so," said Smith, though he appeared far more concerned about his desserts. However, he quickly moved the focus of the conversation back to Reginald's kitchen.

"So how do you find this resort, Mr. Worthington? Is your kitchen everything you need it to be?"

"I'm quite pleased," Reginald replied. "The equipment is of the highest quality, and I am in want of nothing. I would venture that even Her Majesty in England does not have a finer kitchen."

Smith seemed to sober a bit and leaned toward Reginald, almost conspiratorially. "I'd venture to say the queen is missing out on the finest of cooking since you are here among the commoners of the United States." He laughed at this and slapped Reginald on the back.

Reg smiled, although he despised being handled so familiarly. Americans seemed to think nothing of touching each other at the slightest provocation. They slapped each other when they were happy, they punched each other when they were angry, they even hugged and kissed each other—sometimes quite publicly—whenever the mood struck them. It seemed even worse here in the west, where manners and decorum were often overlooked due to the rugged wilderness setting. And while Reg found this sometimes difficult to accept, he also found himself using the freedom to his advantage.

"If they intend it to be a successful investment," Smith said, sampling the coffee with a smile, "they will have to continue drawing the attention of eastern supporters."

Reg had no idea what Smith was talking about now, but neither did he really care. His mind drifted to thoughts of Rachel. She was one of the biggest reasons he could appreciate this American style of liberty. He had little trouble introducing ideas for sharing moments alone or private conversations.

"Mr. Worthington?"

Reg realized he'd apparently missed a question directed to him by Mr. Smith. "Forgive me, my mind was back on the rack of lamb," he lied.

"I merely suggested that towns such as Morita and Las Vegas pale in comparison to New York and Chicago, but that they also provide hidden surprises and new variations for the cuisine. In Las Vegas I had something called an enchilada. The chef used little pancakes called tortillas and stuffed them with chicken and cheese. He topped them with a spicy red sauce, and I tell you, I've not tasted anything like it in the rest of the country."

"Yes, Tomas, my errand boy, has shared several of his mother's recipes with me. I've experimented with some of them, but I cannot say that I would feel comfortable in introducing them to the menu."

Jeffery laughed. "I've had some great cooking here in Morita. Down near the depot and river there's a wonderful little café. I've had enchiladas. They're just as you've described."

They talked on of food and the grand opening of the resort, and when the conversation seemed to wane a bit and Jeffery heard Braeden Parker at the front desk, he excused himself. "Mr. Smith, I believe Mr. Parker has returned. I suggest we make a meeting with him and Miss Taylor while we have a chance."

"You go ahead and see to it, Mr. O'Donnell," Smith replied. "I shall indulge myself with one more of Mr. Worthington's delicacies."

Jeffery patted his midsection and nodded. "I think I'd better quit for now or I'll ruin my appetite for dinner."

Reginald looked up as Jeffery crossed the dining room. Then he glanced to where Gwen was instructing a couple of the girls on inspecting napkins and tablecloths for any sign of wear.

"It's good to finally have a face with the name," he said softly as Smith finished devouring his fourth pastry.

Smith's eyes brightened. "Do you still believe you can accomplish our goal?"

"I see no problem," Reginald replied. "I'm keeping my eyes open for all the right opportunities."

"Keep your ears open as well. There's no telling who might try to thwart our effort, and the plans for this resort absolutely must come together."

"I heartily agree. Especially in light of the money you are paying me," Reginald said, getting to his feet as Jeffery made his way back to their table. Braeden Parker was at his side and Reg immediately stiffened. This man was the only real obstacle that stood between himself and Rachel.

"Here's Mr. Parker," Jeffery announced. "He has time now for us to discuss resort matters." Jeffery glanced at his pocket watch and noted the time. "However, I can see that soon the dining room will afford us little in the way of peace and quiet. Why don't we take this meeting to your office, Mr. Parker."

Braeden smiled and Reg felt his distaste increase. He was much too confident in his position, his looks, and his entire demeanor. Reg figured him to be no more than five years his junior, yet if rumor held true, the man certainly didn't need his position at Casa Grande. He could walk away at any time and live off the money he had in the bank or the dividends paid him through stocks and bonds.

"If you'll come this way," Braeden said to Mr. Smith.

"I'll go find Miss Taylor," Jeffery offered.

"She is in her office," Reg said, reaching up to run his index finger against his thin moustache. "We've been working on the inventory. Trying to clear up those discrepancies. We certainly can't let that get out of hand."

Braeden's eyes narrowed a bit, and the action was not lost on Reg. "No," he agreed, "we don't want anything out of hand."

"Well, we appear to have it under control. Miss Taylor and I seem to work very well together."

"Yes, she's mentioned how hard you've pursued the matter."

Reg got the distinct impression Braeden was hardly talking about matters of inventory. Could Rachel have shared some mention of Reg's interest in her? It hardly seemed likely. She and Mr. Parker, although more amiable toward each other of late, were still at odds over their past . . . weren't they? He realized the matter was beginning to make him most uncomfortable.

"If you'll excuse me," Reg said with the briefest bow, "I must see to my lamb."

He then headed to the kitchen while the men laughed and discussed their dealings. He felt a twinge of anger and pushed it aside. There was nothing to be gained by losing his temper. He had a job to do here—several jobs. He needed to think clearly and focus himself entirely to ensure their success.

He inspected the cooking, chided the cook in charge of the breaded veal cutlets for having cut the pieces too thick, then moved on to taste the salad dressing being prepared by yet another.

But his mind was hardly on cooking. Reg couldn't forget the look in Braeden Parker's eyes. The man assumed him guilty of something, but of what? Reg had done nothing more than voice interest in Rachel, gently suggesting outings that would allow them to grow closer. Perhaps it was nothing more than jealousy, but if that were the case, why bother with the look or the words that seemed to hold a double meaning?

Rachel is all that I have ever wanted in a woman, full of life and joy— when she's not busy pining over that pompous fool. Reg wondered how he might convince Rachel that Braeden Parker was hardly worth her time and energy.

He picked up a sprig of parsley and studied it to ascertain the freshness of the piece. Satisfied, he replaced it on the plate and moved on. There had to be a way to create a wedge between Rachel and her Mr. Parker—a separation that would so completely divide them that there would be no hope of them ever coming back together. It would only be then that Reg would have a chance to win Rachel over.

He stirred a concoction on the stove and frowned. "Idiot! You've curdled it. Now start again and throw this mess out." The dark-skinned man cowered at Reg's anger but nodded obediently.

Finally satisfied that all was moving along as it should, Reg went back to working on the rack of lamb. "It shouldn't be that hard for an Englishman to overcome a dim-witted American," he muttered with some satisfaction. "After all, we've been at the game far longer than they have."

⤜ぐ FIFTEEN ぐ⤛

WITH SOME OF THE DIGNITARIES arriving early for the next day's celebration, Rachel began to feel a bit overwhelmed. Not only were there meals to oversee, but there were also last-minute changes in menus and other arrangements that were nonsensical and frustrating to her sense of order. The last thing she needed was any further interruption. But that was exactly what she got when Ivy Brooks demanded her attention.

"My ruby brooch is missing," she declared, coming into Rachel's office without an invitation.

"I see," Rachel replied, not even bothering to look up from her desk. "And what have I to do with the matter?"

"I want you to look for it. I believe one of the girls came into my room and stole it."

This caused Rachel to glance up. "Stole it? One of my girls? Ivy, I hardly think anyone would consider such a matter."

"Well, they've not only considered it—they've done it, and I demand that you find my brooch and jail the thief."

"Ivy, the resort opens tomorrow. There are already dignitaries here from Topeka and Chicago, and more are due to arrive tomorrow morning. Is it really necessary to cause this kind of disruption?"

"It's hardly my fault!" Ivy wailed. "I'm the one wronged here, and you act as though it were unimportant. The brooch was a gift on my fourteenth birthday from my dear departed mother and father. That piece means a great deal to me."

Rachel could see there would be no living with the girl until she acquiesced to find the pin. "Very well. Where did you last have it?"

"I had it in my dresser drawer. That is why I know it has been stolen. And since no man is allowed in our quarters, it must have been one of the Harvey Girls or you!"

Rachel stood and shook her head. "I have no need for your brooch. Now, tell me what it looks like."

Ivy described the pin as being in the shape of a butterfly with rubies dotting the wings and black onyx for the eyes. "And the entire body is gold," she added.

"All right. Let us go ask among the girls."

Rachel rounded up those who were still in the house. A few extra girls had been given the day off because the following day would require that everyone work around the clock. "Has anyone seen Ivy's brooch?" She described the piece for her girls, then stood back and watched as each one shook her head. She had presumed it would be just this way, but in order to pacify Ivy she had gone the extra mile.

"There you have it," she told the smug-faced girl.

"Surely that's not all you plan to do!" protested Ivy. "That brooch is quite valuable. Of course those ninnies are going to say they didn't take it. The thief could hardly admit to it."

"I didn't ask if they stole the brooch," Rachel reminded her. "I asked if they had seen it. There's a big difference between seeing something and stealing it. Isn't it possible you left the brooch at your aunt's house?"

"No, it isn't possible I left the brooch at my aunt's house," Ivy replied sarcastically. "It was here in my drawer. You may ask Faith if you don't believe me."

Rachel knew better than to take that route. "Very well. What else would you suggest?"

"Search their rooms! I want that piece back, and I want the thief thrown into jail!"

"Ivy, if the brooch has been stolen, do you seriously think it would be left in plain view of anyone who might come along to find it?"

Ivy looked to be fairly seething by this time. Not that Rachel really cared, but she was getting weary of the game. She was supposed to have dinner with the O'Donnells that evening, and she wasn't about to let Ivy's madcap chase alter her plans.

"Everyone search your rooms and see if it is possible that Ivy merely dropped her brooch there by mistake." Rachel turned to Ivy after saying this and added, "I'm sure if the piece is located, the girls will tell you."

She started back to her office and had nearly reached the door when Ivy demanded she stop. "This is outrageous! You plan to bring in wealthy guests from all over the world, yet the brooch of one woman is not safe. I will tell everyone of this incident if you refuse to help me."

Rachel knew the reputation of Casa Grande was at stake. She had no desire for the girl to spread falsehoods and finally nodded. "Very well, Ivy. Let us conduct our search." Glancing at the gathering of girls, she spotted Gwen. "Gwen, I would like your assistance on the matter."

"But perhaps she stole the brooch," Ivy protested. "Remember, she did take Faith's hairbrush."

"I did not. I found it in the hallway," Gwen argued.

"Well, maybe you *found* my brooch there as well."

"Enough!" Rachel declared. "We shall search Gwen's room first, and when we clear her of any suspicion, then she will take this side of the hall and I will take the other."

This surprisingly seemed to satisfy Ivy and should have been Rachel's first clue in the matter. They entered Gwen's room, the only one not shared with another worker. As head waitress, she was given this extra privilege of privacy.

"Gwen, please open your closet and drawers," Rachel instructed.

The young woman did as she was told while Rachel quickly went through each article. When she finally finished with the last drawer, she turned to the nightstand and bed. "Please pull down the covers, and Ivy, you stand on the other side with Gwen and help lift the mattress." Every possible nook was checked. Rachel wanted to leave nothing undisturbed. She'd not have Ivy coming back later to complain of a less than thorough job.

They found nothing under the mattress, but as Rachel replaced the pillow on the bed, something rolled out of the case and made the sound of a dull thud on the floor. Looking down, she discovered the pin.

As she picked it up, Rachel was heartsick to realize that Ivy had planted it there. Rachel's trust in Gwen was complete, but how could she prove that Ivy was to blame instead of Gwen?

"Is this your brooch?" Rachel questioned, knowing full well that it was.

"That's it! See, I told you it had been stolen. Gwen Carson, I hate you!" Ivy declared.

There was much murmuring from the gathering of Harvey Girls outside Gwen's door, and Rachel knew the matter was about to escalate into madness. Calmly she asked, "Gwen, did you take the pin?"

Gwen had tears in her eyes. "Honest, I didn't take it. I don't know how it got there."

"How convenient," Ivy replied snidely. "Of course the thief can't remember how it found its way there. I demand that you fire her immediately and call the marshal!"

"Calm yourself, Ivy," Rachel replied. "No one is getting fired or going to jail."

"She stole my pin. I want her punished."

"Your pin is safely returned to you and shows no mark of harm. Now, I suggest you all forget about this and prepare for the evening meal. Tonight's crowd will be the largest yet." Rachel looked at Gwen, who was silently sobbing into her apron. "Gwen, you need to change that apron and prepare for the evening. You will be in charge, as I will be out until late."

"You can't just leave her in charge. She's a—"

"Miss Brooks, I have very little patience left," Rachel stated firmly. "I believe this matter to be nothing more than a misunderstanding. Unless, of course, you wish for me to make more out of it." She eyed the girl sternly, hoping Ivy would realize her determination in settling the affair.

"Well, fine! It will be a pity, however, when things start disappearing in earnest around the hotel."

Rachel eyed Ivy seriously for a moment. She thought of all the missing articles in her inventory and wondered if that, too, was a part of Ivy's game. Glancing at her watch, she decided she could consider the matter in more depth at a later time.

"I want all of you to get to work," Rachel declared. "Right now!"

The girls scattered, seeming to sense Rachel's frustration and mounting anger. "Ivy," Rachel called as they made their way into the hall, "I want no more of this."

Ivy looked at her, feigning stunned concern. "Why, whatever do you mean?"

Rachel shook her head. "You know exactly what I mean. I won't have it, and that's my final word on the matter. From now on, if so much as a radish disappears, I'm coming to you first."

Ivy's eyes narrowed and her face contorted hatefully. "You'll pay for this. You'll see," she whispered loudly enough for only Rachel to hear.

"And then she stomped off to her room," Rachel told Jeffery and Simone, "and I readied myself for our visit. But other than that, the day was fine."

"It's too bad you can't fire Ivy Brooks," Simone said, getting up from the kitchen table. "Come sit with me in the front room. I'll see to this mess later, and Jeffery can go check on his new pride and joy."

"I thought that wasn't coming until March," Rachel said, eyeing Simone's still-flat stomach.

She laughed. "Oh, it's not the baby. It's a matched pair of carriage horses. They came in on the four-o'clock freight."

"Ah, I see. Well, then," she said, turning to Jeffery, "I quite understand."

"I won't be a moment," he said, kissing Simone on the head. "You ladies make yourselves comfortable."

Rachel nodded and followed Simone into the parlor. "I have quite a bit to tell you before he comes back."

"Oh?"

"Well, it's just that it's not exactly the kind of subject to share in a man's company."

Simone grinned and touched a hand to her ebony hair. "Hmm, I believe this must be a matter of the heart."

Rachel laughed. "Does it show that much?"

Simone nodded. "But then, you figured out my feelings for Jeffery long before I did. So tell me. Have you mended fences with the wonderful Mr. Parker?"

"I suppose I have, in a sense. I mean, he did ask me to marry him."

"What!" Simone exclaimed and clapped her hands. "Why, that's wonderful! When is the happy day?"

"I don't know," Rachel said, sobering rather quickly. "I didn't say yes."

Simone shook her head. "I don't think I understand."

"I'm not sure I do either. I mean, he forced me into his office, made me listen to his speech about loving me, then I started crying because everything at Casa Grande seemed to be overwhelming me. The next thing I knew . . . well . . ." She felt her face grow hot. "Well, the next thing I knew, he was kissing me. And it was as if all the years melted away and we were back in Chicago—happy and engaged."

"But that's what you wanted, isn't it?"

"I don't know," Rachel said, giving a bit of a nervous laugh. "I thought I would never see him again, and even if I did, I presumed him lost to me. But this was the second time he assured me of his love. He chided me for not trusting him, begged me to put the past behind us—and when I reminded him that Harvey employees could not date, he proposed."

"Is that all?"

"He reminded me that plenty of people along the line enjoy both matrimony and Fred Harvey's employment."

Simone smiled again. "Rachel, I think you're finally getting your prayers answered. I mean, why fret over this turn of events? The man obviously adores you."

"Does he?" Rachel questioned. She twisted her hands together. "I don't mean to be such a doubting Thomas, but what if this is just some grandiose scheme to win me back, only to turn around and crush me for having betrayed him in the first place?"

Simone raised a brow and asked, "Does that speak to the character of the man you know?"

"But it's been six years since I felt I honestly knew Braeden, and even now, I see that apparently I didn't know him well at all. He explained away the incident that divided us, chided me for listening to whispered gossip, and has lamented my lack of faith in him. I don't know what to do. I want to trust him, but I'm so afraid."

"Why?"

The question seemed ridiculously simple, but the answer came at great price. "I suppose because I'm afraid of being hurt again. I'm afraid that he truly hates me and has played this like a hand of cards. Well . . . I just don't think I could take it."

"If it were true," Simone pressed, "and he merely wanted to punish you, what's the worst thing that could happen?"

"I think I would die."

Simone smiled. "We both know that isn't true. Your heart might break and you might decide to never again love another, but I doubt seriously you would die."

Rachel knew how silly it sounded, but at the same time she thought of how empty her life had been without Braeden. "It might not happen exactly that way, but—"

"But you'll never know if you don't at least give him a chance. You may well be passing up your last chance for happiness. You've prayed about this, right?"

"Not really," Rachel replied. "I mean, I prayed after we separated. I used to pray God would right the wrong between us and bring us back together, but I never believed it would happen."

"I can't believe *you*, Rachel Taylor—woman of faith—would say such a thing. You're the one who taught me the benefit of believing in miracles. You helped me to come to understand how important it is to have faith—especially when nothing seems possible. And furthermore, you taught me that no decision should be made without first considering it in prayer. Are you telling me now that you doubt God's abilities in the matter?"

Rachel sighed. "I've never doubted God's abilities, but I've certainly doubted mine."

"Show me someone who hasn't."

"But in this case, Simone, I'm doubting not only myself. I'm doubting Braeden as well. And if I continue to doubt, I may ruin my only chance with him. I don't want to lose that."

"Then don't. From what you say, I must believe that he loves you. Why would the man waste his time in grandiose schemes, as you put it? Men hardly think that way in affairs of the heart. That sounds more like the reasoning of a woman."

"Truly? Do you really think so?"

"It doesn't sound like anything Jeffery would ever do. No, if Jeffery wanted to play that role, he would completely snub me. He'd have nothing to do with me. He certainly wouldn't open his heart to me— going out of his way to make sure I listened to him, pleading his case. Mr. Parker may be wounded by the past, but from what you are telling me, he sounds sincere in his desire to put it behind him."

"I hope you're right. I would really love to agree to his request," Rachel replied, feeling happiness at the mere thought of marriage to Braeden.

"I wouldn't fret anymore about this, Rachel. I think after tomorrow's grand opening, you'll be under far less pressure and you'll see for yourself if Braeden is sincere."

"Tomorrow is just the tip of the iceberg," Rachel said with the hint of a laugh. "There are so many other problems to consider that I can't begin to explain."

"Why not try me?"

Rachel looked at Simone in appreciation. "Ivy Brooks is causing me no end of grief."

"Jeffery told me that her aunt forced your hand in accepting Ivy at Casa Grande. Is that true?"

Rachel sighed. "Yes. It's a constant source of frustration, mainly because of how unfair it was to accept Ivy into a position that was considered to be a privileged assignment. Money bought her that position, and money is keeping her in place."

"The old woman bought your cooperation?" Simone asked in disbelief. "That doesn't sound like the Rachel Taylor who trained me to Mr. Harvey's rigorous regimen."

"No one has bought me," Rachel replied. "And that's more than half the problem. Esmeralda Needlemeier haunts my office every other day complaining about one thing or another, and Ivy tries her best to interfere in my life—even where Braeden is concerned. No, I have a feeling tomorrow will just be the beginning of many days of continual conflict and problems."

"Well, to bring back the subject of marrying Mr. Parker, think how much better it will be to spend your time with a husband at your side, rather than a mere managerial partner. It seems ideal to me. The man would be with you to offer strength and support."

They heard the back door open and close, and Rachel immediately put her finger to her lips. Simone nodded conspiratorially and grinned.

"Are they as you left them?" Simone questioned as Jeffery took his place at her side.

"Yes, and just as beautifully matched as two geldings could be. So what did you ladies discuss while I was gone?" Simone grinned broader, while Rachel's face flushed. "Ah," Jeffery continued, "I can see it must have been of an intimate nature. Did it have anything to do with Mr. Worthington?"

"Reginald?" Rachel asked rather surprised.

"Ah, so you are on a first-name basis."

Rachel rolled her eyes. "You know I do that with all of my staff. At least when no one is around."

"Well, Reginald has asked me numerous questions about you and your past. It seems the man can't get enough information when it comes to you. I'd say he has more than a passing interest."

"He's very nice," Rachel admitted, "but that's all. He has asked me out to walk with him or to go riding, but I've always refused. I can't see trifling with him."

"Why would it have to be a trifling?" Jeffery asked.

Rachel looked to Simone for help, but her friend just shrugged her shoulders. Finally Rachel noticed the hour. "Oh my, it's nearly ten o'clock. I really should be getting back. I have a feeling four-thirty is going to come around mighty early. Are you sure I can't help you with the dishes, Simone?"

"Absolutely not," Simone replied. "I'll have them done before you even reach the front steps of Casa Grande."

The trio rose together, and after Rachel hugged Simone good-bye, Jeffery announced that he would walk Rachel back to Casa Grande. "I would take you in my carriage and show off my new horses, but since I've not yet had time to try them out—"

"And since we have scarcely half a mile to walk," Rachel interjected, "it hardly seems worth the trouble of hitching a team."

They walked through the night in a companionable silence. The gentle roar of Morita Falls made for lovely night music as they passed over the bridge. However, as they climbed up the carefully cultivated lawn and passed by the lighted fountain, Rachel noticed a light on in her office.

"That's odd," she said, turning to Jeffery. "Someone's turned on my light."

"Are you certain you didn't do it yourself and left it on when you came to see us?" Jeffery questioned.

"No, I'm certain of it. Furthermore, I'm certain that I locked both doors to my office."

They climbed the front steps and as they reached the front door, they saw a dark form pass before Rachel's window. Jeffery frowned and put out a hand to stop her once they were inside the lobby. "You wait here and let me check this out."

Rachel nodded and waited while Jeffery went to the door. Her breathing quickened as she watched him calmly try the door handle, finding it locked. He gently eased the knob back into place, then quickly came back to Rachel as the glow of light disappeared under the door.

"The light just went off!" she exclaimed.

"Quick! Give me the key!"

She handed the key to Jeffery and watched as he raced back, no longer worried about being quiet. He unlocked the door and stepped into the darkened room.

"Who's there?" he called out.

Rachel bit her lip, wondering if she might at least give Jeffery the assistance of turning on the light. She tiptoed toward the room just as a loud crash sounded.

"Jeffery!"

Without concerning herself over what the consequences might be, Rachel raced into the room and turned on the light just as someone exited the other door, slamming it behind them.

"Jeffery? Is that you?" she called out, uncertain as to who it might have been if not Jeffery. But just as she came to the door, she found the moaning, crumpled body of Jeffery O'Donnell.

For a moment Rachel felt frozen in place. She could see that he was bleeding from a wound on the side of his head, but it all seemed surreal. By the time she opened the other door and glanced down the hallway, the intruder was gone.

"Rachel . . ." Jeffery barely whispered the word as he struggled to sit up.

"Don't move," she ordered, finally back in control. "You're bleed-ing."

"I'll be all . . . all . . ." He gasped and fell back against the floor.

"Dear Lord, help me," Rachel prayed, realizing that Jeffery was now unconscious.

❦ SIXTEEN ❧

KNOWING OF NOWHERE ELSE TO TURN, Rachel ran across the lobby and pounded on Braeden's office door. After several moments of knocking with no answer, she grew even more fearful. She was just about to give up hope when she thought of the entrance to his private quarters.

Maneuvering past the front desk, she turned to her right and made her way into the darkened shadows where Braeden's second door could be found. This door opened, she was told, into his private living quarters. If he were in bed, even asleep, he would surely awaken at the sound of her knocking.

"Please answer me, Braeden," she whispered as she pounded against the door.

It only took a couple of minutes before a very disheveled Braeden appeared. He was struggling to pull up his suspenders and tuck in his shirt with one hand while opening the door with the other, and Rachel couldn't help but be taken aback by the way he looked.

"Oh my," she said in a raspy voice.

At this, Braeden stopped fumbling with his clothes and looked up in surprise. "Rachel?" He reached back behind him to twist on the light. "What in the world are you doing here?" Then he grinned. "Come to give me an answer for my proposal?"

She shook her head. "I wish it were that simple. Look, something has happened in my office, and Jeffery O'Donnell is bleeding."

"What?"

"It's a long story," she said, trying to regather her wits. "Jeffery was walking me back from dinner at the O'Donnell house, and we saw a light on in my office. Then we saw the shadow of a figure pass in front of the window. No one should have been there, but Jeffery went to investigate and someone hit him over the head. I need your help, Braeden. He's bleeding and I have to get him to the doctor."

Without warning, Braeden pulled her into his room. Rachel tried to pull away, but his grip was too tight. "What are you doing?" she demanded. "I can't be in here. I can't be seen in your private rooms."

"I need my shoes," Braeden replied, now fully alert. "It would be foolhardy to leave you alone if there's some madman running around the place hitting people over the head. This will only take a second." He sat down on the edge of his bed and reached for his shoes.

Rachel felt her face grow fiery hot and quickly turned her back to him. There was something so intimate about seeing him there, sitting on the bed. She stared at the closed door and wondered how she'd managed to get herself into this mess. If anyone saw her coming from his room, her reputation would be in shreds.

"You can turn around," Braeden told her.

"That's all right," she managed to say. "I'll just stay right here."

She heard him chuckle and wondered why he thought the matter so funny, but there was little time to further consider it. Braeden came up from behind her and put his hands on her shoulders.

"If you won't move, we cannot open the door."

Rachel felt his warm breath upon her neck and shivered from the sensation. "We need to hurry," she reminded herself aloud. She reached out for the door handle just as Braeden did. His hand closed over the top of hers, causing Rachel to turn and look up into his face. "I'm sorry I had to bother you. I had no place else to turn."

"Reg wouldn't help you?" he asked with a mischievous grin.

"He never entered my mind," she replied flatly. And he hadn't. When the first sign of trouble had come upon them, she immediately thought of Braeden.

"Good. See that it stays that way," he said and opened the door.

They hurried across the lobby and found Jeffery regaining consciousness. "Jeffery, don't move," Rachel told him, kneeling down beside him. "I've brought Braeden to help, but you mustn't move."

Braeden moved Rachel's desk back in order to get closer to Jeffery. "O'Donnell, can you hear me?"

"Yes," Jeffery said. His head wobbled back and forth as he struggled to focus his eyes on Braeden.

"We need to get you to a doctor," Braeden declared. "Rachel, grab one of those linen napkins Mr. Harvey loves so much and wrap it around his head."

Rachel nodded and ran down the hall to the linen closet. She grabbed a handful of napkins and hurried back to her office. Just as she did, Gwen Carson's door opened.

"I heard the noise," the young woman said softly. "Is something wrong?"

"Yes!" Rachel exclaimed. "Mr. O'Donnell has been injured. Would you run and wake Tomas? He should be sleeping in the storage room. Send him to bring up a carriage from the stables. We'll have to drive Mr. O'Donnell back to town." Gwen nodded and, mindless of her robed attire, hurried down the hall to find Tomas.

"Here," Rachel said, coming into the office. She handed the linens over to Braeden. He quickly folded one into a thick bandage, then ripped another in strips and tied the bandage to Jeffery's head. "I had Gwen wake Tomas. He should be able to bring around a carriage."

"Good thinking," Braeden said, giving her a look of approval.

Rachel relished his gaze. He was proud of her actions, and his expression told her without a doubt that she had done the right thing.

Braeden helped Jeffery to his feet but had to fully support him. "Did you get a look at who did this?"

"No," Jeffery managed to say. "In fact, I don't remember anything but opening the door."

Braeden turned to Rachel. "What about you? Didn't you see anything?"

"No," Rachel answered, feeling a deep sense of disappointment. "I wish I could say that I had. I heard the crash, which undoubtedly was Jeffery falling, but when I came in and turned on the light, the other door was just slamming shut. When I opened it and looked down the hall, the intruder was already gone."

Braeden nodded. "Let's get Mr. O'Donnell outside. We can wait on the porch for Tomas, and maybe the cool night air will help clear the haze in his head."

Rachel followed behind the two men, feeling rather helpless in the matter. *Poor Jeffery*, she thought, then realized she would have to be the one to break the news to Simone. She only hoped the shock wouldn't hurt the baby.

"Rachel, you open the door," Braeden instructed.

She hurried to do his bidding, opening not one, but both of the entry doors. Braeden maneuvered Jeffery onto the porch and helped him to a chair, while Rachel closed up the hotel again.

"Where does the doctor live?" he asked Rachel.

"Just down the road," Rachel replied. "His house is actually across the street from Jeffery and Simone's house."

"And the O'Donnell house is the first one on the right after passing over the falls, correct?"

"Yes."

"All right. I'll get Mr. O'Donnell to the doctor and—"

"You aren't going alone. I'm going with you. Simone is a dear friend, and I need to be the one to tell her about her husband."

Braeden looked as though he might argue with her, then nodded. "Sounds reasonable."

Tomas then appeared with the buggy. It would be a tight squeeze, since he'd only thought to hitch the lightweight two-wheeler.

"Thank you, Tomas," Rachel said as the boy climbed down to help Braeden with Jeffery.

"You would like me to drive you, senor?" he asked.

"No," Braeden replied. "You go on back to bed. I'll see to putting the buggy away when we return."

"Sí."

"Rachel, you get in first. That way we can put Jeffery between us. If he passes out again, he can lean against you."

"All right." She climbed quickly into the carriage and scooted to the far side in order to give the men more room.

Braeden helped Jeffery up and followed behind in short order. Tomas handed him the reins and stepped back as Braeden urged the horse forward.

Jeffery moaned and leaned back against the seat, clutching his head. Rachel felt instantly guilty for his misery. "I'm so sorry this happened, Jeffery. I blame myself."

"You didn't hit me," Jeffery muttered, even now trying to keep matters light.

Rachel smiled. He had become such a dear friend. "When we get to the doctor's house, I'll run across the street and get Simone."

"No, don't worry her," Jeffery replied.

"I'm not about to endure her wrath by not telling her that her husband has been hurt and is bleeding from a head wound in the doctor's office, while she sits in the parlor knitting."

Braeden laughed and Jeffery attempted to. "I suppose you're right," he said, seeming a bit more alert. "She has a temper, you know."

"What woman doesn't?" chuckled Braeden.

They pulled up to the doctor's house, and Rachel was grateful to see the warm glow of lamplight in the window. She hurried ahead of the men and knocked on the door.

It took a few minutes, but soon a robe-clad man opened the door. "Yes, what's the emergency?"

Rachel knew the gray-headed Dr. Krier because his daughter Alice was one of her Harvey Girls. "Doctor, Jeffery O'Donnell was hit on the head tonight. He's bleeding pretty badly."

The doctor looked past her to where Braeden was helping Jeffery down from the buggy. "Bring him in. I'll get some more light, and we'll see how bad it is."

Rachel nodded. "Thank you." She stood back to allow Braeden to bring Jeffery into the house.

"Come on back here," Dr. Krier called.

They entered his office, where he instructed Braeden to lay Jeffery down on the table. Rachel decided now would be the best time to go for Simone. "I'll be back in a minute," she told Jeffery and gave his hand a squeeze.

She was nearly to the door when, to her surprise, Braeden caught her by the arm. "Wait up, there. You aren't going out alone."

"I'll be just fine. It's only a few steps," she protested.

"Yes, and it was only a locked office that brought Jeffery a head injury. I'm going with you."

The look of determination on his face told Rachel that Braeden would do just as he said. And actually, she found herself grateful that he cared so much. "All right," she replied.

Rachel hesitated at the O'Donnells' door, not wanting to tell Simone what had happened. But as it was, Simone took the news very well, immediately grabbing up her shawl and heading out the door.

"I knew something was wrong," she told Rachel as they hurried back to the doctor's office. "I just had this feeling."

"He doesn't look all that bad," Braeden told her.

Simone looked up at him as they entered the doctor's home. "Thank you for being there, Mr. Parker. I've heard such nice things about you."

"Oh?" he said quizzically. "I wonder from whom."

Rachel bit her lip as her cheek flamed. She could feel the heat even though the night air was chilly. But Simone saved her from any further embarrassment.

"Why, from my husband, of course."

Braeden grinned and looked at Rachel. "Of course."

Simone walked into the doctor's office without any apparent fear of what she had to face. Rachel admired her strength because she herself had been trembling ever since finding Jeffery. Braeden must have sensed this, as well, for he put his arm around her and pulled her close.

"Jeffery O'Donnell, I suppose you are getting me back for all the worry I've caused you," Simone stated as she went to her husband's side.

"Mrs. O'Donnell, good to see you," the doctor said. He sat at the head of the table threading a needle.

"Yes, Mrs. O'Donnell," Jeffery said with a lopsided grin, "good to see you."

"I'm gonna have to stitch your husband up," the doctor said, turning his attention to Simone. "It's not all that bad, and once I'm done he'll be nearly good as new. However, he's lost a good bit of blood."

Simone paled a bit at the final statement, and Rachel knew it stemmed from Simone's painful memory—one that included Simone hitting an attacker over the head and believing herself to have killed the man because of all the blood.

"Head wounds do that," the doctor continued. "Funny thing, though, usually they aren't all that bad, even when they bleed like they are. It'll make him light-headed, though. You'll need to keep him in bed for the next few hours." Simone nodded but said nothing. The doctor finished preparing the needle, then looked back up at Simone. "Why don't you all wait out there. I'll call you when it's done."

"I want to be with my husband," Simone insisted.

Rachel stepped away from Braeden and put her arm around Simone. "Don't you think it would be better, given your condition? We'll be right here if Jeffery needs you."

Jeffery nodded. "Go. I can't cooperate with the doc if I'm all worried about you passing out on the floor."

Simone reluctantly let go of his hand. "Very well."

She let Rachel lead her into the front room and sat down with a sigh on Doc's very worn sofa. "I don't suppose it would do any good for me to have argued."

Rachel laughed. "Not in this case."

"Why in the world did this happen?" Simone questioned, looking to her friend for answers.

"I don't know," Rachel replied. "Strange things have been happening at the resort. There were some discrepancies in the inventory, and we're pretty sure someone is stealing from the storage rooms. The dining room things seem to be safe now that we have Tomas sleeping in the back room, but Braeden is still losing things from time to time. Then not long ago I found wax on the floor in my office—"

"You what?" Braeden interrupted.

"I found wax on the chair and on the floor," Rachel said, knowing he would be furious that she had kept it from him. "And there were some correspondences missing from my desk." She looked up, feeling rather sheepish about the whole matter. "I meant to tell you."

"I should hope so," Braeden replied, his brow knitting together as he considered this news. "What correspondences?"

"Honestly, it didn't seem like anything important. They were just letters related to the . . . inventory."

"And that didn't seem important?" he asked.

"Well, not as important as the fact that the original inventory list was also missing. I thought Reg had come to get it, but he hasn't seen it either. I sent Tomas with a telegram to Topeka, in hopes of having them send me another list."

"And when do you suppose you were going to get around to telling me about this?" Braeden questioned, crossing his arms and leaning back in the chair opposite her.

Simone laughed. "You two make such a funny couple. I think you're perfect for each other."

Rachel turned to stare at her in absolute horror. "Simone!"

"Mrs. O'Donnell, I couldn't have put it better," Braeden replied.

"Thank you, but if you are to marry my best friend, then you must call me Simone."

"Simone!" Rachel declared again. Now Braeden would not only know that she had discussed everything with her friend, but he had Simone's blessing as well.

"Oh, stop being such a ninny," Simone said, patting Rachel's knee. "I could tell the man loved you from the moment I opened the door. Look at the way he's so attentive to you, the way he worries after you, the possessive way he treats you. For goodness' sake, Rachel, it doesn't take a genius to figure out what's going on."

"Rachel's only put off because it *is* taking her a while to figure out what's going on," Braeden countered with a grin.

"I suppose we women can be that way," Simone replied. "Jeffery says there's a lot of times when I don't know what's good for me."

Braeden nodded as if in complete agreement.

Rachel wanted to get up and run. To be cornered by two of the people who meant more to her than anyone else was almost more than she could stand. Simone seemed to understand, however, and took hold of Rachel's hand.

"Please don't hate me for what I've said. You know how I am about speaking my mind. It's just that when I saw how he looked at you, I was certain of his feelings for you." Then turning to Braeden, Simone added, "However, Mr. Parker, you are not to take advantage of my outburst."

"I will adhere to your request, only if you acquiesce to call me Braeden."

She nodded and craned her neck in the direction of the doctor's office. "I wonder what's taking so long. I've always teased Jeffery about being hardheaded—I guess now I have proof. The doctor probably can't get the needle through his thick skull."

Rachel secretly wished the doctor would hurry up, too, so she could make her way back to Casa Grande and be rid the scrutiny of her good friend. But then a troubling thought came to mind: She'd be making that trip back with Braeden, and what had seemed like such a short distance when walking with Jeffery now loomed ahead of her like a cross-country journey.

"Mrs. O'Donnell, you may come back in," the doctor called out.

Simone jumped to her feet and hurried past, leaving Rachel and Braeden alone.

"So you've been talking about me behind my back, eh?" Braeden questioned.

Rachel swallowed hard. "She's my friend. I come to her for advice."

"And will you heed her thoughts on the matter?"

"I don't know," she whispered, forcing herself to meet Braeden's eyes.

"I like her very much," he said with a grin. "She seems quite sensible."

"I suppose, but—"

"Rachel," Simone said, coming into the room with her arm around Jeffery's waist, "would you mind lending me Braeden just long enough to get Jeffery settled at home?"

Braeden was already at Jeffery's side, much to the other man's protest. "I'm fine," Jeffery said. "I'm not as light-headed as before."

"That's great," Braeden replied. "Then clearer thinking shall prevail and you won't mind the assistance."

"Ah, a man of logic," Simone said with a nod. "Just the one to get this pigheaded husband of mine into bed without an argument."

It barely took ten minutes to get Jeffery settled in. Simone hurried Rachel off, reminding her that the grand opening would take place in the morning whether Rachel had any sleep or not.

"But what if you need help in the night?" Rachel questioned. "I could stay here with you." The thought had just dawned on her, and Rachel realized it would allow her to forego the ride back to Casa Grande with Braeden.

"Nonsense. The doctor lives just across the street. I could probably raise the window and yell for him," Simone said, patting her arm. "Just go. I'm sure Jeffery will be up on his feet in time for the celebration."

Rachel nodded and walked onto the front porch with Simone. Braeden stood waiting for her at the bottom of the steps.

"Take good care of her, Braeden," Simone said smiling. "She's very important to me."

"Me too," Braeden replied. "Do let me know if there's anything else I can do for you or Mr. O'Donnell."

"I will," Simone promised. "Oh, and thank you for what you've already done. I'm sure things would have been much worse if you hadn't been there to help."

Rachel made her way down the steps and nervously allowed Braeden to help her into the carriage. She slid to the far edge of the seat and looked away when Braeden gave her a curious look. Instead of saying anything, however, he slid up against her, trapping her between himself and the edge of seat. The contact was electrifying.

"Braeden," she whispered. She could feel the warmth of his body generating heat to her own. She wanted to tell him that he should move away but couldn't bring herself to say the words. There was great comfort in his closeness. "Thank you for your help," she finally managed to say.

"You're quite welcome. I would have been grieved had you turned to someone else."

Rachel opened her mouth to speak, then closed it tight. Her heart was in turmoil over the gamut of emotions within her.

"Are you cold?" he asked.

Shaking her head, Rachel replied, "No, why do you ask?"

"You're trembling. I can feel you shaking from head to toe."

"Oh," Rachel said, feeling her face flush. She was grateful for the dim moonlight, hoping her embarrassment was less evident in the shadows of night.

He chuckled, however, leaving her little doubt that he knew the real reason for her quaking body. They drove in silence to the resort, and Braeden happily handed the buggy back over to Tomas when the boy appeared.

"I know, senor, you say to go to bed, that you take care of the buggy—but I could no sleep. Is Mr. O'Donnell all right?"

"He's fine, Tomas. Thank you for waiting up. I need to help Miss Taylor with cleaning up her office, so I appreciate you taking the responsibility for the buggy." The boy beamed at this compliment and jumped onto the buggy seat.

"Come along, Rachel, and tell me about the wax you found and the missing papers and why you tremble every time I touch you." He pulled her close and smiled. "Let's start with the last part first."

Rachel stiffened in his arms, but Braeden moved her up the stairs and inside to her office before she could even protest. Someone had thoughtfully left an oil lamp blazing cheerily since the electricity had been shut down at ten.

"I told you everything I know," she finally managed to say. "Someone apparently broke into my office one night. I don't think it's really all that important."

He pulled her into an embrace and shook his head. "That's to be decided. It still doesn't explain why you won't be honest with me— with yourself."

Giggles were heard from the girls' dormitory hall. Rachel glanced over her shoulder to find Ivy and Faith watching the scene. Instantly, Rachel pushed Braeden away and turned to meet the girls head on.

"What are you doing up at this hour?" she questioned, taking the upper hand.

"We might ask the same thing," Ivy said, toying with the ribbon on her robe. She looked seductively at Braeden and smiled. "I don't suppose you're having a meeting over the resort at this time of night."

"Mr. O'Donnell was injured in here earlier," Rachel announced. "He was hit over the head by someone who had broken into my office. We've just come from the doctor's office, and Mr. Parker has come to help me get things back in order."

"Things look just fine to me," Ivy said, her gaze never leaving Braeden.

Rachel glanced down at the floor and noticed that the blood had indeed been cleaned up. "Gwen must have done that. How thoughtful." She looked up at the girls. "Well, then, since you know what's going on, you may go back to bed."

The girls smiled at each other, then turned to leave. Rachel heard them giggling, but she didn't care. She was just surprised to have Ivy leave without a fight. Braeden was already repositioning her desk when Rachel bent down to put the iron doorstop back in place against the wall. But as she picked it up, her hand touched the wet stickiness on the backside. She looked at her hand and saw it stained with blood. Jeffery's blood. A small gasp escaped her and she dropped the doorstop in fright.

"What is it?" Braeden questioned, but he quickly saw the cause of her alarm. Taking out his own handkerchief, he wiped the blood from her hand. "It's all right, Rachel. That's probably what the thief used to hit O'Donnell."

"Yes," she replied. "I'm sure you're right." She was trembling again and couldn't stop, only this time it wasn't Braeden's nearness that caused her to quake. She kept thinking of how Jeffery could have been killed. How would she have ever explained such a thing to Simone?

Braeden pulled her close. "It's all over now. It's all right."

"But it could have been so much worse."

"But it wasn't. God had it all under control."

Rachel pulled away and frowned. "If God had it under control, then why does Jeffery now have six stitches in his head?"

Braeden shrugged. "I don't suppose to have all the answers, but you have to trust God to know what He's doing, Rachel. Trust is very important."

"Trust is hard."

"Yes, it is," Braeden replied. "No one knows that better than I do. Trust is believing God is still in control, even when the woman you love walks away. Trust is believing that God can clear your name of wrongdoing, even when everyone around you believes falsely against you."

"Oh, Braeden," she said, realizing the depths to which she had wronged him. It only served to add to her guilt. "I'm so sorry."

He put a finger to her lips. "I wasn't looking for an apology. I only wanted you to know that after questioning God and wondering why in the world He would allow bad things to happen to good people, I came to realize that it isn't important that I have the answers—it's only important that I trust Him."

She looked into his blue eyes and lost her heart all over again. Trust was the key. She knew it as well as she knew anything, but she also knew that letting go and trusting made her very vulnerable. And that frightened her more than anything.

Braeden was nearly back to his own quarters when Gwen Carson called out to him from the dining room doors. Surprised to find the normally shy young woman calling to him, Braeden stopped immediately and went to see what was wrong.

"You're keeping mighty late hours, Miss Carson."

"I know," she said, glancing over her shoulder as if afraid someone might see her. "But I had to tell you something, and I couldn't do it with Miss Taylor around."

Braeden narrowed his eyes. "What is it?"

"I cleaned up the office—"

"Yes, I saw that. It was a kind act of responsibility."

"I didn't tell you about it in order to receive praise. It's just that . . . well . . . there was something else."

"I don't understand, Miss Carson. What is it you're trying to say?" He could see that she was extremely nervous, and instantly his mind began to conjure all manner of thought. Had she seen something? Had the thief returned? "Please tell me what's the matter."

Gwen nodded. "I cleaned up the blood, then I tried to move Rachel's desk back, but it was too heavy. So I thought if I opened the drawers, I could take them out and lighten up the weight."

She faltered, and Braeden could see that she was clearly shaken. "Go on," he urged.

"I opened the largest of the drawers . . . and . . . and . . . inside it . . . well, inside it was a snake."

"A snake?" Braeden questioned. "How would a snake get inside a desk drawer?"

Gwen shook her head. "I don't know, but it was there and I think somebody put it there to hurt Rachel."

Suddenly Braeden got a bad feeling about the entire matter. "What kind of snake was it?"

Gwen's eyes widened. "It was a rattler."

"What did you do about it?" Braeden was trying desperately to keep his emotions under control.

"I took it out of there."

He smiled at the shy girl. "You?"

"I've had to deal with snakes since we lived in a soddy when I was just a girl. They don't frighten me all that much, but this was different."

Braeden actually reached out and hugged the young woman. "You may well have saved Rachel's life. You should be commended."

"I figured I'd tell you because Miss Taylor might not think it was all that important. She tries hard to take care of herself, you know. She's a very proud woman."

He smiled. "Yes, I know. Look, you did the right thing in telling me. I believe you may well be right about someone trying to hurt Rachel. I'll need you to help me keep an eye on her. Can you do that for me?"

"I'll do whatever I can to keep her from harm. She's been a wonderful friend to me."

Braeden nodded. "Go to bed. Tomorrow is a big day and we'll all need our strength." She turned to go, then Braeden called again. "And thanks for what you did." He watched her until she disappeared into the kitchen. With a calm he didn't feel, Braeden closed the dining room doors and wondered silently how he was going to deal with this latest incident. It would appear, he thought, that this was no theft. This act was more along the lines of a threat, and Rachel was clearly the intended victim.

∽ SEVENTEEN ∾

CASA GRANDE APPEARED TO BE a tremendous success. From the first morning meal until the afternoon luncheon, elegantly dressed people flooded into the resort with no other purpose than to celebrate. Rachel was exhausted by the time the noon meal was finally served, and as customers sat around the tables enjoying their dessert, she finally took a moment to grab a glass of water for herself.

"You are working much too hard," Reg chided her. He seemed genuinely concerned, but he also seemed a little preoccupied, even as he studied her.

"This day is much harder than the others will be," Rachel replied. "I'm not giving anything of myself that everyone else isn't giving."

"I suppose you didn't sleep well last night," he murmured. His expression seemed to almost dare her to deny it.

"Honestly, I'm fine."

"Still, you haven't even eaten."

"I had some breakfast," she protested.

"Here, at least have a bit of fruit," Reg encouraged.

"No, I have to get back on the floor. Ivy Brooks is giving me considerable grief, and I must oversee her constantly. She never listens to Gwen." Reg nodded, as if understanding completely.

Rachel handed Reg the glass, smiled, and squared her shoulders. It was rather like going into battle, she thought. She came into the room just as Ivy's lyrical laughter filled the air. She stood at a table of well-dressed business associates for the Santa Fe. Smiling and batting her eyelashes, Ivy flirted outrageously with one particularly handsome man.

Gritting her teeth, Rachel went to the table and smiled. "Are you gentlemen finding everything to your liking?" she questioned.

Like children caught stealing cookies, the men looked nervously down at their plates, while Ivy sobered and turned on Rachel.

"I have everything under control here," she told Rachel sternly.

"That's wonderful," Rachel replied. "Then if you gentlemen have no other needs at the present, I must have a word with my employee."

They nodded, murmuring their understanding, but Ivy was hardly receptive. She was clearly angry that Rachel would dare disturb her plans. Rachel ignored the look on Ivy's face and instead stopped long enough before leaving the dining room floor to tell Gwen Carson that they were retiring for a few moments to the office.

Once inside the privacy of her quarters, Rachel closed the office door and turned to face Ivy's hostility.

"If someone else takes my tips because of this little escapade," Ivy declared, "I'll tell my aunt and see to it that justice is done."

Rachel folded her hands calmly and stared in silence at Ivy for a moment. She had hoped only to reduce her anger and get her emotions under control, but Ivy took it as some sort of threat and said so.

"If you are trying to intimidate me with that look, you might as well forget it."

"I'm not trying to intimidate," Rachel finally replied. "I brought you here for a long-overdue verbal warning. Fred Harvey has a strict policy regarding the actions of his girls and their service to customers. While some small portion of flirting is to be allowed and expected, outright wantonness is not to be tolerated. It is hard enough to get people to understand and believe that Harvey Girls are not an extension of the lewd women who serve at saloons. However, by your actions in there just now, I would say your charms would be better used at Big Clara's Cathouse down by the river."

"How dare you!" Ivy said, drawing up her full five-foot-four height. "I am the niece of this town's founder, and you have no right to talk to me like that."

"You are my employee. I decide, in spite of what you might otherwise believe, whether you stay or leave Casa Grande. I have given you more leeway than most, allowing for your stubborn willfulness even when I knew it was not the best thing for the welfare of our group. I allowed you to fashion your hair differently, spend nights away from the resort at your aunt's home, and have, in general, overlooked many of your offenses even while taking someone else to task for it. But no more. I sympathize with your plight in life. I am deeply sorry that your parents had to die so young, leaving you an orphan. However, I will not tolerate insolence. Nor will I allow for your lewd behavior on my dining room floor."

"What of your own lewd behavior?" Ivy questioned.

"And what behavior would you be speaking of?" Rachel questioned, knowing she was implying having found Braeden and Rachel alone in her office well after curfew hours.

"I think you know very well what I'm talking about."

"If you are referring to last night, then forget it," Rachel countered, her Irish temper beginning to flare. "Go look at the stitches on Mr. O'Donnell's head if you think to contradict me."

"Rules are rules. You said there was a ten-o'clock curfew for everyone. You said that no men were to be allowed in private quarters and assured us that no men would be allowed in your office after nine o'clock at night when the dining room would be formally closed and business concluded for the day."

"And all of those rules are still in effect," Rachel replied. "I don't have to explain myself to you, but in this case, I will. I took dinner with the O'Donnells, and when I returned, someone was in my office. I could see this because the thief was apparently not smart enough to think about leaving the light off while they came to steal what they would."

"How do you know it was a theft?" Ivy said smugly. "Maybe there was some other reason for someone to be in your office."

"There are no reasons for anyone to be in my office without my permission. The office was locked, which means someone had to find a way into it without notifying me for the key. But that aside, as Mr. O'Donnell attempted to catch the thief red-handed, he was, in fact, hit over the head."

"That might well be," Ivy said smoothly, "but it doesn't explain why you were in Braeden's room earlier in the evening." She laughed at the shocked expression on Rachel's face. "I can see you weren't prepared for me to know about that little escapade."

"I went for help."

Ivy laughed. "That's not what it looked like. Oh, and don't think for one minute that it's just my word against yours. I have witnesses."

"I can't believe this!" Rachel declared. "An innocent man is injured in my office, and you would condemn me for getting him help?"

Ivy crossed her arms and gave Rachel a look of bored indifference. "Rumors have a way of getting around, and the truth isn't always as clear as it should be."

Rachel felt as though a knife had been plunged into her heart. She knew full well the power of rumors. She had seen her own life destroyed by them, and now she feared they could destroy her once again.

"My reputation speaks for itself, Miss Brooks."

"Maybe so, but you still broke the rules. And what about dear Braeden's reputation?" she said, using his first name casually.

Rachel ignored the bait and shook her head. "I'm sure Mr. Parker's reputation is as easily defended as mine."

Ivy laughed. "Not when word gets out that he seduced me at the hot springs. You saw it yourself. He lured me there with a letter saying that he had to talk to me, then grabbed me in his arms at the first possible chance. I was helpless. Had you not returned for your book, who knows what might have happened?"

"Mr. Parker explained that entire situation," Rachel replied. Then, seeing the smug look of satisfaction on Ivy's face, she realized that she'd played right into her hand. Now Ivy knew in no uncertain terms that the event had bothered her enough to require an explanation after the fact.

"Of course he explained it," Ivy replied. "He wouldn't want his reputation compromised, now, would he?"

"This is ridiculous. We're wasting time."

"I quite agree," Ivy said as her eyes narrowed. "Now you will listen to me. Unless you leave me alone and stop badgering me about my actions, I shall have to go to the proper authorities and tell them of Mr. Parker's behavior."

Rachel swallowed hard. She couldn't have cared less for the threats to herself, but that Ivy would actually seek to hurt Braeden in the process was more than she was willing to deal with. Still, she couldn't allow the girl free rein, and that in and of itself created quite a dilemma.

As if sensing Rachel's inability to decide what to do, Ivy uncrossed her arms and walked to the door. "It does make a sticky situation, does it not?" she said, turning to pause. "I mean, if you care about him the way you seem to, then you have to save his reputation from harm. My aunt would never hear of him remaining in charge of Casa Grande if she thought him capable of molesting an innocent young girl."

"You know he did nothing wrong," Rachel protested.

Ivy gave her an ugly smile. "You'd really like to believe that, wouldn't you?" With that, she opened the door and walked away, leaving Rachel to stare in dumbfounded silence. The girl had managed to strike at the very core of Rachel's fears and insecurities.

"What do I do with this one, Lord?" Rachel muttered. She went to her desk and took a seat. Her mind raced with thoughts of running after Ivy and firing her on the spot, but her heart bid her to be less reactionary. What if Ivy was able to get Braeden fired? What if she so ruined his reputation that he couldn't remain in Morita?

"Why can't things be simple?" she questioned, looking to the ceiling as she did on so many occasions. "Why must I continue with this thorn in my side?"

Outside her office, music could be heard as a full orchestra played in the ballroom down the hall. They were featuring a piece with plenty of rhythmic changes and brass fanfare. It was intended to draw people in from all over the resort, and Rachel had little trouble believing it would do just that. The orchestra was to perform at one-thirty for half an hour, then one of the dignitaries would speak to the group and make announcements for the afternoon and evening's events.

Rachel would normally have taken great joy in the celebration, but Ivy's threats, Jeffery's injury, and the violation of her office were all weighing heavy on her heart. Putting her head down on her desk, Rachel prayed for the strength to endure and for the protection of those she loved.

"I wondered where you had gone off to," Braeden said in a soft, low tone.

Rachel immediately came upright. He was leaning casually against the doorjamb, watching her quite intently. The expression on his face betrayed the feelings he held for her. It nearly took Rachel's breath away. "I was . . . well . . . I had to . . ." She stopped and shook her head. "Never mind."

"The crowds are gathering in the ballroom," he said, stepping into her office. "It should afford you a bit of rest. You look completely exhausted."

Rachel smiled. She gladly let the conversation take a turn from anything too personal. "I suppose I am, but there's nothing to be done about it. Have you seen Jeffery?"

"Yes, I talked with him and his lovely wife. He appears no worse for the wear."

She nodded. "Yes, he came to speak with me first thing. I'm so relieved he wasn't hurt more seriously."

"It could have been much worse." Braeden's expression grew very serious, and Rachel couldn't help but wonder why. "I want you to be very careful, Rachel. It might not even be a bad idea to have me look through your office and private quarters before you retire for the night."

Remembering Ivy's threat, Rachel shook her head. "That's hardly necessary, Braeden. I'm sure I'll manage just fine. I'll keep the doors locked."

"You kept the doors locked last night and it did little good."

She knew he was right, but her mind was hardly on that incident as he came nearer to where she sat. She could smell his cologne, and it reminded her of being in his arms. She thought of Ivy and her threats and knew there was no end to the lengths she would go to protect Braeden.

She also thought of Ivy's words about Braeden luring her to the pool. It hurt to imagine that anything like that would ever happen, and she knew that she had to make a decision about trusting Braeden. Maybe trust had to be earned, but no doubt there would always be circumstances that would interfere with the process. In this case, trust would have to be a choice that she made. Either she trusted him or she didn't, and looking up at him now, seeing the love in his worried expression, Rachel knew that she must trust him.

She tried to smile as she got to her feet. "I must return to my girls. But I want you to know that I've thought a great deal about what you said regarding trust. Trusting God is something I've never questioned—not in earnest, anyway. God has always been very faithful, and I've never had a reason to doubt Him. I know trust is important for us as well. I'm sorry that I allowed my mother to so thoroughly ruin our plans. It wasn't my intention—it was just that I couldn't believe that the one person who loved me most in the world would do anything to make me unhappy. I'm still positive that she never meant to unduly hurt me. She actually liked you very much. Anyway, what I'm trying to say is that I know I have a difficult time trusting—you or anyone else. But because I expect trust, I know I must give it."

He took hold of her hand and caressed it very gently. "I know this comes hard to you. But I promise to be faithful and never give you any reason to doubt me again." He raised her hand to his lips and kissed it gently. "I love you, Rachel, and I want you to always trust me."

Rachel nodded and drew her strength from her prayers. "I do trust you, Braeden. I honestly do."

IVY STORMED BACK to the nearly empty dining room, pausing only long enough to collect her tips from the now deserted table. The money was good, but not nearly as good as it might have been.

I'll show Rachel Taylor who she can and can't order around.

She pocketed the money, then, ignoring the other girls, made her way into the kitchen, where Reginald Worthington stood talking to one of his bakers.

The man clearly had a romantic interest in Rachel, although Ivy couldn't figure out why this should be. Rachel's auburn hair and hourglass figure might serve her well enough, but her face was plain and her personality left a great deal to be desired. But perhaps because of Reg's interest in Rachel, Ivy could enlist him as an ally.

"Mr. Worthington," she said rather sweetly, "I wonder if I might have a word with you." She batted her eyelashes and added, "Privately."

Reginald looked up rather surprised, but nodded. "Step into the storage room, Miss Brooks."

Ivy nodded and followed him to the large supply room, where a conveyor belt was laden with crates. Maneuvering around stacks of boxes, a plan began to formulate in Ivy's head. She wondered how she might figure out his response before committing herself to something underhanded. The last thing she needed was for Reginald Worthington to act the part of do-gooder and go blabbing her plans to Rachel.

"Mr. Worthington," she said as he turned with a questioning expression, "I know you are interested in Rachel Taylor."

"Miss Brooks, I hardly see that this discussion is appropriate."

"Just hear me out. I think I might be able to help you."

"Help me what?" Reg questioned, obviously confused.

"Help you get Rachel."

"I'm afraid I don't understand."

Ivy wanted to scream. The man was positively dim-witted. Would she have to draw him a picture? "I know you fancy yourself in love— or at least smitten—with Rachel Taylor. I can see it in your face every time she's around you." The man actually blushed, and it gave Ivy all the fuel she needed to continue. "I believe there's a way for you to get Rachel for yourself. And, if you don't mind a tiny bit of underhand- edness in the process, I believe you could have her in such a position by tomorrow . . . probably even tonight."

Reginald only stared at her for a few moments, and Ivy had nearly figured the issue to be of no interest whatsoever when he stepped closer.

"I hardly believe we can discuss this properly here. Meet me in fifteen minutes down by the falls."

Ivy smiled. "I'll be there."

She continued smiling the entire time it took for her to reach the falls. She thought it a perfect plan to enlist Reginald's help. He would keep Rachel occupied while she went to work on Braeden Parker. It all seemed too simple.

She crossed the lawns and the road and made her way down a narrow path that led to the powerhouse. The waterwheel churned vig- orously from the constant surging of the falls. She had no idea how this all related itself to providing the community with electricity, but she had to agree that it had made life in Morita more endurable.

Pausing at the first park bench, Ivy took a seat and glanced back at the resort. Beautifully clothed people made their way inside to hear the music. Ivy envied the women who wore lavish jewelry and incred- ible creations of taffeta and watered silk. And as if these outfits were not opulent enough, Ivy knew the ball gowns and opera dresses that would be worn in the evening would be feasts for the eyes.

Staring down at her own black skirt and white apron, Ivy knew she couldn't endure the humiliation of continuing along these lines. She had been born to wealth and affluence. How dare her aunt hide her away in Morita when she should be doing the grand tour of Europe and dining with royalty?

She thought of the resort again and of the festivities planned to entertain the wealthy. These were the peers she desired, but dressed as one of Fred Harvey's serving girls, Ivy knew she would never be accepted into their circles. She thought about retiring her position and returning to her aunt's house. Perhaps she would have better luck of it if she merely showed up at the festivities gowned in creations from Worth. Surely she could find a wealthy husband among the visitors to Casa Grande.

She shook her head, however, remembering her angry words with Rachel. No. She would have Braeden Parker for her husband. He might not be the wealthiest man who would grace the steps of Casa Grande, but he would be the one to give her the most satisfaction. Now, if she could just find a way to interrupt his duties during the Casa Grande celebration.

The entire event was planned in detail, and for the next three days the atmosphere would be that of a three-ringed circus. There were to be balls, opera singers, magicians, lecturers, and all manner of banquets and teas. She would be overworked and every moment of her time consumed, except for this evening. This evening, with a celebratory dance to be followed by a solo performance by a famed Denver soprano, Rachel had announced she would only need ten girls to remain on the floor. A huge buffet would be arranged for the dance, and other than keeping the table stocked with all sorts of delicious delicacies, the Harvey Girls would not be needed. Rachel chose her more experienced girls for the duty, and Ivy had been very angry about the circumstance—until now. Now she was more inclined to see the opportunity it afforded her.

She watched Casa Grande's chef make his way across the lawn as she had done only moments before. He was a tall, thin man—not at all bad looking, but he was English and Ivy found Englishmen to be so void of emotion and feeling that she had no interest in pursuing him to see whether he might make a suitable spouse. Besides, he seemed rather content to remain at Casa Grande.

He had shed his white chef's coat and hat and pulled on a brown coat that matched his trousers. Reginald Worthington could have just as easily been one of the dignitaries, Ivy thought. He was refined and well-mannered, but oh, so boring. Not to mention that he'd settled for a position that practically put him on the same level as her aunt's cooking woman.

"Yes, well, I suppose you know why I've come," Reginald said as though he thought himself to be rather witty.

Ivy nodded. "Do sit down. I need to know exactly what your thoughts are when it comes to Miss Taylor."

"I can hardly explain all of my thoughts," he told her plainly. He sat down rather stiffly and continued. "But if you are trying to inquire as to the length I will go to pursue Miss Taylor, then I'm not opposed to a little, as you say, underhandedness."

Ivy smiled. "Good. Because some people can't see what's good for them. Take Rachel, for instance. She's been very hurt by Mr. Parker, and while this was in the past, I've no reason to believe it couldn't happen again." She looked at Reginald and waited a moment before continuing. She didn't want to spill out the information without being certain he wouldn't betray her.

"Pray continue, Miss Brooks. You have me quite intrigued."

Ivy adjusted her skirts and folded her hands. "Mr. Parker has shown an interest in me, and I have a great affection for him. However, Miss Taylor is still under the belief that he cares for her. And while I believe Braeden wouldn't desire to see her hurt, he clearly has placed his heart elsewhere."

Reg gave a bit of a chuckle at this. "Miss Brooks, if we are to help one another, then I believe we should first and foremost be honest. Mr. Parker is clearly smitten with Miss Taylor, as is she with him. If you would like to plot a way to divide them, then I am most assuredly your man. If you desire to sit here and spin fairy tales, then I am much too busy."

Ivy laughed out loud. "And here I thought I would have to pick and choose my phrasing with the utmost of care. Very well, Mr. Worthington, I propose to place a wedge of circumstance and doubt between Rachel and Braeden. I want this to be something so powerful that not only will Rachel walk away from Braeden, but he will be forced to remain with me. I have something in mind, but I will need your help in order to make it work."

"By all means, please proceed." Reg's interest was evident.

"From my own understanding of what I've overheard, Braeden and Rachel were once engaged. There was some manner of betrayal, however, on the part of Braeden. I heard them talking one evening down by the hot springs. Apparently trust is very important to Rachel, and she feels that trusting Braeden will require a good deal of effort on her part. I believe that should she find that trust violated again, she would not hesitate to turn her back on him once and for all."

"Why do you feel so confident of this?"

"Because she was clearly upset by my actions that night. I pretended to be there at Braeden's request and she became pale as a ghost. She stormed off, forgetting her book and towel, which I spied about the same time I heard her reapproaching. I feigned a fall and ended up in Braeden's arms and the look on her face told me everything. He tried to explain, but she wouldn't hear it. If I can manage an even more damaging scene, I believe it will finally dissolve any affection she has for the man."

"And you have such a scene in mind?" Reginald questioned.

"I would hardly ask you here if I didn't," Ivy replied. But in truth, she hadn't really considered the matter in much detail. "I have tonight off and while the festivities are going on, I believe I could arrange for such a circumstance."

"But Parker will, no doubt, be tied up with activities at Casa Grande. It would take the notification of someone other than yourself to drag him away from his post. Rachel, too, will be obligated to the evening."

"Yes, but Rachel will be free after nine o'clock—I heard her say so. Maybe Braeden will also be free after that. Either way, I believe I can work out the details. However, what I will need from you is this. You must make certain that Rachel is occupied this evening. I can't very well make my plan work if she's in Braeden's company or if she follows him around all night."

"What do you really have in mind for me to do?"

"Well," Ivy said, suddenly getting a brilliant thought. "I will send Braeden a note from my aunt Esmeralda. The note will demand he come to the mansion at ten till nine. That way, even if he hoped to spend time with Rachel, she'll be obligated to stay at Casa Grande until nine."

"But won't your aunt be obviously occupied with the festivities? Surely Mr. Parker will see her there."

"Yes, she does plan to come to the dance, but I know for a fact she will not remain for the singing. My aunt has an aversion to remaining away from the house after nine in the evening. She believes it improper to take in too much night air and, being an old woman, she needs her rest. She plans to return when the dance concludes, and that's where you come in. I want you to be with Rachel when that dance concludes. Tell her you need to go over inventory. Tell her you saw someone in her office. Tell her anything, but just keep her occupied and with you."

"I'm quite certain I don't understand how this will resolve anything."

Ivy smiled as the plan took form in her mind. "I'll arrange to meet with my aunt at nine o'clock on the pretense that I will walk her back to the mansion. She'll come looking for me and when she doesn't find me, I'll have Faith inform Rachel that I left for the mansion some time ago. My aunt will be livid, and if I know her the way I think I do, she'll head home immediately. That's where you come in. You offer to walk her home, insisting that Rachel go along to chaperone or give you companionship or whatever. Just make sure she goes with you. The rest will be up to me."

"So you want for me to ensure that Rachel shows up at the Needlemeier mansion at a few minutes after nine."

Purely amused by her own conniving, Ivy nodded. "Exactly."

"But how can I invite myself or Rachel in once we've walked your aunt home?"

"I'll have one of the servants helping me. Eliza will do anything for extra money. She can keep watch, and when she sees you approach the house, she can let me know. Then I'll start screaming, and you will play the gallant gentleman and insist that my aunt accept your help in the matter. Hopefully this will cause all three of you to come upon Braeden and me in the front parlor. I promise the scene will be most compromising."

"And this doesn't alarm you?" Reg questioned seriously. "It will not only be Mr. Parker's reputation that you place on the line."

"I know," Ivy said, undaunted. "And because my reputation is also at stake, Mr. Parker will have to do the honorable thing."

"And if he refuses?"

"He won't," Ivy stated firmly. "He won't or else he'll lose everything. I'll make such a scene that he'll be fired from Casa Grande and publicly humiliated. He won't want to lose his job, and he won't want to be thrown into jail for molesting a young woman." She nodded quite confidently and looked out to the picturesque scene of the waterfalls. "He'll have to sacrifice his freedom one way or another. Either by marrying me or by going to prison."

"You seem particularly confident that this can work," Reginald replied. He stood and jammed his hand into his coat pocket and retrieved a pipe. "I suppose it is my one chance to play the comforter to Rachel. Perhaps her gratitude at my being there in her hour of need will open her heart to something more permanent and intimate." He nodded as if seeing everything fall into place. "I shall do my part, Miss Brooks."

Ivy got to her feet. "I knew you would see it this way. I could tell you were positively daffy for Miss Taylor."

"She is a woman of exquisite beauty and spiritual depth. I enjoy our conversations greatly, and I cannot imagine wanting any other woman for my lifetime companion."

Ivy couldn't imagine feeling anything but loathing for the woman. "Then we shall strike this pact between us, and, Mr. Worthington, I have many resources available to me. Don't even think of crossing me in this matter. I would not at all be adverse to making your Rachel's life a very miserable existence."

"You needn't threaten me, Miss Brooks," Reginald said, lighting his pipe and taking short little draws of breath to ensure the tobacco caught. "I know full well about your scheming, and I wouldn't dream of interfering. A person might well find themselves the victim of . . . well, let's just say something deadly."

Ivy eyed him suspiciously. "What are you saying?"

Reginald shrugged. "I'd like it very much if you would arrange no further attempts on Miss Taylor's life."

Ivy grew nervous. "I'm sure I don't understand."

"And I'm sure you do," Reginald said, his eyes narrowing. "I know about the snake in Rachel's drawer."

Ivy felt the blood drain from her head. How could he possibly know about that?

"I can see by your expression that this was a turn you did not expect. Well, you see, I overheard you pay the man who put the snake in her office. I followed him to see what he was up to and saw him enter Miss Taylor's office. I know, too, that when Mr. O'Donnell surprised him he was forced to attack the man and then make a run for it. You hid him in your room and let him escape through your window. I know, because I was just outside, hidden by the shrubs, when he came from your room."

Ivy knew her mouth had dropped open in stunned amazement. She wanted to say something that would sound completely unconcerned, but nothing came to mind.

"I have no intention of telling anyone about it, unless you have plans to harm Rachel further—other than emotionally, that is."

Ivy knew she would have to go along with Reginald's demands. "I only wanted to scare her so that she would leave. I never intended for her to get hurt."

"Of course not," Reginald said, eyeing her contemptuously. "Just so we understand each other."

"I agree completely," Ivy replied, regaining a bit of her composure. "I want very much for this to work, and I wouldn't have come to you if I didn't believe you capable of being an asset to me."

"Very well, Miss Brooks. We shall strike out this evening to win the hands of those we esteem and, dare I say it, love?"

Ivy watched him walk away and felt a wash of uneasiness settle over her. This evening she would once and for all come between Rachel and Braeden. Whether it worked to her advantage and she was truly able to force his hand in marriage or not, she would at least ensure that Rachel would want nothing more to do with him—and that was a very satisfying thought. What troubled her was Reg's knowledge of her actions. The last thing she wanted was to be under his thumb. What if he blackmailed her? The thought caused her to shudder. Perhaps she would have to think of some way to control Mr. Worthington while she plotted against the woman he loved.

"Marshal Schmidt, I'm glad you could give me a moment of your time," Braeden said, ushering the older man into his office.

"Can't say that I've ever seen anything quite like this place. Lived in Kansas and Texas most of my life, and usually the town was small. That there music is mighty fine," he commented.

Braeden nodded. "I believe that's Mozart."

"He that fellow playing the piano?"

Braeden couldn't help but smile. "No. Mozart is the composer of the music. I'm not certain of the pianist's name."

"Well, it's right purty just the same. Makes a fellow a little sleepy, though."

"At least the heat has subsided," Braeden commented. "I find this cool weather much more to my liking."

"Weather's been acting funny here lately. Usually stays pretty warm clear into November. I don't mean hot like it has been, but real comfortable. The natives are saying there's signs of an early winter with plenty of rain between now and then."

Braeden nodded, growing bored with the idle chat. "Look, I've called you here for a reason. I need your help."

"Problems?"

Braeden nodded. "It appears so. We've been suffering from theft of materials since our arrival. My inventory is reduced by several items on a daily basis, and all of this took place well before the arrival of guests. Miss Taylor is also having problems, and . . ." He let his words trail off as he tried to decide whether to continue. Rachel hadn't wanted the law involved, but then, she didn't realize that someone had made an attempt on her life.

"And what?" Schmidt asked.

"May I tell you something in the strictest confidence?"

The man's eyes narrowed. "I'm no blabbermouth, if that's what you take me for."

"Not at all," Braeden replied. "It's just that this is such a delicate matter, I can scarcely figure out how to handle it by myself. But I wouldn't want word to get out about it."

The man seemed to understand and relaxed a bit. "It'll be just between you and me."

"Good. That's exactly how I want it to be for the time being," Braeden replied. "Last night someone broke into Miss Taylor's office here at the resort."

The man scratched his chin, then hooked his fingers in his dusty leather vest. "Yeah, I heard about that. Jeffery O'Donnell's sportin' stitches in his head."

"That's right. The thing is," Braeden continued, "it wasn't the first time someone broke into her office. I didn't know about it until last night, but apparently someone snooped around in her room some time back."

"You thinkin' the thief came back for something?" the man questioned, seeming to mull the matter over in his mind.

"I can't be sure what the real reason for the first break-in was. Some papers were taken, but nothing else. However, this break-in was different. This time the person clearly wanted to cause Miss Taylor harm."

"In what way?"

"They planted a rattlesnake in her desk drawer."

Marshal Schmidt's eyes widened at this. "Do tell?"

"It's true."

"Then shouldn't she be in here discussin' this matter as well?"

"She doesn't know about it," Braeden replied. "One of the other girls found the snake there and, having had a great deal of experience in dealing with them, simply removed it before Miss Taylor found out about it."

"I see. Sounds like a good little woman to have around." He smiled before asking, "What's her name?"

"Gwen Carson. She's the head waitress in the dining room. She came to me with the information but didn't want to get Miss Taylor upset by it."

"How come she came to you?"

Braeden felt uncomfortable explaining his relationship to Rachel but realized quickly enough it didn't matter. "I suppose she came to me because I'm rather like a partner to Miss Taylor. She manages the restaurant, and I manage the rest of the hotel. But, besides that, I think Miss Carson knows I care very much about Rachel. We've known each other for a long time."

The man nodded. "So you don't want to let this get around in case Miss Taylor might hear it and be upset?"

"That, and I can't help but wonder if by keeping silent, the perpetrator won't show their hand by asking questions that could help them to learn what happened that night. Maybe they think the snake is still in the drawer. I mean, after all, there might not have been an opportunity for Miss Taylor to need anything out of that particular drawer."

"Hmm, I see what you mean. Well, what do you want me to do?"

"I suppose I'd like to have the place watched, at least from the outside. Someone is stealing from the establishment, and while I don't know why or where they are taking the goods, the tally is growing at an alarming rate. It's almost as if they want to get as much as they can right away because it won't be available to them later."

"I can set up some deputies to ride up this way on a regular basis. You want me to start that tonight?"

"I'd appreciate it. And like I said, I'd rather we don't say anything to Miss Taylor or anyone else for that matter."

"Sure thing, Mr. Parker."

RACHEL PUT THE FINISHING TOUCHES on her hair before doing up the final buttons of her new green calico gown. She looked forward to Braeden's promise of a walk in the gardens and wanted to look her very best. The dining room had closed only moments before, and now, with most of the resort celebrators installed in the theatre room to listen to Miss Lucretia Collins sing various operatic selections, Rachel simply needed to wait for Braeden to come to her. She took up her shawl, closed her bedroom door, and locked it. This had become her routine, even if she planned to only be away from her rooms for a few minutes. It was hard to understand what the thief had been after, but Braeden had insisted she be meticulous in her actions.

Glancing across her office, she could recall the image of Jeffery crumpled and bleeding on the floor. She still shuddered every time she saw the doorstop, realizing how much worse the situation might have been.

Opening her lobby door, Rachel quickly checked to make certain the other office door was locked before sitting down to await Braeden.

"Miss Taylor?" a bellboy questioned as he peered into her office from the newly opened door.

"Yes?"

"Mr. Parker asked me to give you this note about a half hour ago. I looked all over for you but couldn't find you until just now."

Rachel nodded and took the folded paper. She thought to thank the boy, but he left just as quickly as he'd come. She glanced at Braeden's handwriting, easily recognizing it from all of the love letters he'd written to her six years ago. She still had those letters, although she kept them tied together and hidden in the bottom of her dresser drawer. Perhaps someday soon she'd take them out and reacquaint herself with their earlier love for each other.

She frowned at the contents of the note as she read, "Mrs. Needlemeier has called me to an emergency meeting at her house. Sorry about our walk. I'll make it up to you. Braeden."

Rachel thought it rather queer. Mrs. Needlemeier had been very visibly in attendance at the opening dance, and while Rachel hadn't seen her during the last hour of the affair, she had figured Mrs. Needlemeier to be partaking of all the festivities.

"My dear Rachel, you are positively glowing," Reginald said from the still-open doorway.

Rachel quickly put the note into the top drawer of her desk. "Thank you, Reg. What can I do for you tonight? I thought you might be listening to Miss Collins' performance."

"I thought it might be best to discuss the inventory situation," he said, suddenly turning quite serious. "There are additional items missing, and I knew you would want to know right away."

Rachel shook her head. "But I thought everything was okay after you put Tomas in the storage room. This just doesn't make any sense. Who could be stealing all of this stuff—and why? And why would anyone want to ransack my office? Surely they know they will get caught. I mean, now I feel like I have to go along with Braeden's suggestion and call in the law."

Reg nodded. "It would probably be wise. Maybe after the grand-opening festivities are over with and things settle down, we could sit down with the marshal and explain everything we know to be true."

Rachel shook her head. "Sometimes it just overwhelms me."

Reg moved closer. "Rachel, let me take you away from here. We can go back to England, and I'll set you up like a queen. You know how much I care about you, and I do detest seeing you overworked and underappreciated."

His words stunned her, but Rachel forced herself to remain calm. She smiled. "I doubt Her Majesty Victoria would appreciate two queens in her country."

"Don't tease me, Rachel." He moved closer and reached out to take hold of her hand. "You know I've come to care a great deal about you."

"Reg, we hardly know each other. Besides, as you pointed out so nicely once before, my heart is otherwise engaged."

"But he doesn't deserve you. The scoundrel can't possibly appreciate—"

"Miss Taylor!" Esmeralda Needlemeier called from the doorway, causing Reg to jump back and drop his hold. She tapped her cane across the floor and, pushing past Reginald, came to a standstill directly in front of Rachel.

"Mrs. Needlemeier," Rachel said, getting to her feet in greeting. She had presumed the old woman to be in her emergency meeting with Braeden. Perhaps she had now decided that it was necessary for Rachel to attend as well. Maybe she knew something about the missing inventory or maybe Ivy had spilled the facts about seeing Rachel in Braeden's room and later in his arms. But Esmeralda's next words shattered that thought altogether.

"I have come to see my niece. She arranged to walk me home this evening and spend the night with me."

Rachel had no idea of this previous arrangement, and it irritated her greatly to think that Ivy had once again taken it upon herself to arrange affairs. "I gave Miss Brooks the evening off. I'm sorry, but I have no knowledge of her plans with you."

"Well, I can't seem to locate her," Esmeralda said sternly. "She told me she would be here, probably in her room. May I have admission to that room?"

"We can go together," Rachel suggested. "Her room is just outside this other door." She went quickly to the door and unlocked it. In the hallway, several girls moved back and forth from room to room, causing Rachel to glance over her shoulder. "Mr. Worthington, I made an agreement with my girls that there would be no men in my office after nine o'clock in the evening. I realize you were concerned about the inventory, but we can further discuss this in the lobby. Would you mind waiting there?"

"Of course not. My apologies." He gave a courteous bow and exited her office without another word.

"Come along, Mrs. Needlemeier," Rachel instructed. She entered the hall and knocked loudly upon Ivy's door.

Faith opened it and smiled. "Yes, Miss Taylor?"

"We've come to see Ivy. Her aunt is expecting her."

Faith looked past Rachel to the foreboding Mrs. Needlemeier and the smile faded from her face. Her brows knit together as she tried to explain. "Ivy went to the mansion earlier this evening. She said someone had asked her to meet them there."

"I know of no such arrangement," Esmeralda declared.

Faith shrugged and seemed to cower back a bit. "All I know is what she told me."

"When did she go?" Rachel questioned.

"Hmm . . . about seven-thirty, I think."

Rachel had a bad feeling about the entire matter. Braeden had made it clear that the Needlemeier mansion was his destination, but he had said that he was to meet Mrs. Needlemeier. Was it possible that it was a ruse to meet Ivy? Shaking her head as if the question had been asked aloud, Rachel reminded herself that she needed to trust Braeden. Ivy was the one who deserved little or no trust.

"I apologize for the inconvenience, Miss Taylor," Esmeralda announced, making her way back to the office without even bothering to verbally dismiss or thank Faith for the information.

Rachel followed her quickly out into the lobby. "I'm sorry, Mrs. Needlemeier."

"Is something wrong?" Reg asked, coming up to the two women as they emerged from Rachel's office.

"It would seem my niece is already gone ahead of me. I shall make my way home before the night air grows too cool."

"You mustn't walk alone," Reginald said in his refined British manner. "Perhaps you would allow me, and perhaps even Miss Taylor, to walk you home?"

Rachel had no real desire to accompany the older woman

anywhere, but she realized Reg was only being kind and considerate.

"Do as you like," Esmeralda countered. "I'm capable of taking care of myself."

"No doubt that is true," Reg said, extending his arm, "but as a gentleman, I could not rest knowing you went unescorted."

Esmeralda nodded and took hold of his arm. "Then let us be on our way. I will find out more about this matter concerning my niece."

Rachel realized she was committed to accompany the two unless she wanted to appear uncaring about Mrs. Needlemeier. "I'll be right with you," she called after them. "I must attend to something first." She quickly went back to her office and locked her doors before catching up with Reg and Esmeralda as they maneuvered down the hall toward the sun porch exit. All she could think about was that perhaps she should say something about Braeden's appointment at the mansion.

"You didn't come in one of your carriages?" Rachel questioned as they walked along the porch. The golden glow of light made the decorated porch quite lovely. Perhaps people would mingle here in the evenings and take a rest while conversing of their days at Casa Grande.

"No need to take a carriage when the walk is so short. It does a body good to walk and take the air—but not this night air. There come all manner of illnesses from breathing too much night air," Esmeralda told them. "Hard on the heart, you know."

Rachel said nothing but walked in silence behind Reginald and Mrs. Needlemeier. She rather enjoyed the crisp night air and seriously doubted that any harm could come from breathing it. Just then a shiver ran through her. Her mother would say someone had just stepped on her grave, but Rachel knew better. This shiver was neither from the cold nor from superstitious sayings. This came from thoughts of what they would find at the Needlemeier mansion. *Please don't be there, Braeden. Please let this be nothing more than a misunderstanding.*

Colorful paper lanterns hung from the porch to the hot springs and along the garden footbridge. Rachel thought again of how she and Braeden had planned to walk out here alone. She had hoped to tell him that she loved him. . . . Her intuition, however, told her that things were not going well. Somehow she knew that as much as she desired Braeden to be elsewhere, they would no doubt find him with

Ivy in the Needlemeier house. She sighed, but no one heard her. She felt terribly alone, despite her company. If only she could be strolling here now with Braeden instead of her over-amorous chef and the cantankerous matriarch of Morita.

Ivy took one last drink of brandy and felt it course through her blood as she ran the brush through her long blond curls one final time. She smiled at her drunken appearance in the mirror. Hours before, she'd discarded her uniform, bathed in scented water, and redressed in a low-cut gown of lavender silk. She had chosen this gown specifically because of the front fasteners. She smiled again and nearly laughed at the lopsided way her mouth appeared. She had only been drunk on one other occasion, but that had been purely for the purpose of forgetting the past. This time she was intoxicated just enough to make a bold and rather daring plan come to life.

"Miss Ivy," Eliza called from the door, "Mr. Parker is waiting downstairs. He wouldn't take a drink, but I poured one like you said and left it on the tray."

Ivy smiled to herself. "Thank you, Liza. You'll find your money in the cookie jar."

"Thank you, miss." Ivy heard her hurry off down the hallway.

"My plans are coming together perfectly," she said and turned to walk to the door. She stumbled a bit and laughed at her condition.

She managed to make her way into the hall and maneuver down the stairway by keeping a hand on the wall. She'd had more to drink than she should have, but not so much that she couldn't see this matter through to completion. She had planned to simply give an illusion of drunkenness to her aunt, rather than the real thing, but once she started it was hard to stop. The brandy gave her false courage and helped her to forget the demons of her past.

She hiked up her skirt, then noticed that she'd forgotten her petticoat. Giggling, she continued down the steps, wondering to herself what else she might have forgotten. She had barely managed to make the final step when the hall clock sounded nine.

Drawing a deep breath, Ivy summoned her wits and threw open

the sliding doors to the front parlor. Sure enough, there sat Braeden Parker—dashingly handsome and apparently stunned.

"Miss Brooks, are you quite all right?" he questioned, getting to his feet.

"I'm fine, Braeden darling," she said softly.

"I beg your pardon?"

"Oh, Braeden, you must know how I feel. I've been waiting so long to get a chance to tell you."

"I don't understand," Braeden replied, his expression confirming his confusion. "I'm supposed to meet your aunt here. There's some emergency business related to Casa Grande."

Ivy laughed. He looked so pathetic standing there. "I know you were expecting my aunt, but in truth, the note you received was sent by me." Her voice lowered. "I had to see you. You must understand."

The reality of the situation was beginning to dawn on Braeden, and Ivy realized she would have to make her case rather quickly or he might leave. Already he was eyeing the open door behind her.

She reached up and began unfastening her gown. "You must know how much I love you. I want to be with you, Braeden."

"Ivy, you're drunk and this is completely uncalled for."

"Please don't leave me," she said, urgently running to him. She threw her full weight against him and Braeden couldn't do anything but take hold of her arms. She hugged him even as he attempted to keep her from him. "We belong together, Braeden. It's our destiny."

Then, just as Ivy had arranged, Liza dropped a heavy metal pan against the stove, signaling that her aunt was approaching. Ivy had carefully seen to it that all the lights in the house were off, with exception to the front porch and the parlor, necessitating their arrival through the main entrance.

"What was that?" Braeden questioned.

"Oh, just my silly maid. Don't worry about her. Think about me. Think about us."

Braeden again pushed against her. "There is no us, Miss Brooks. I appreciate your flattery, but I am not at all inclined to reciprocate your feelings."

"But you must. I'm giving myself to you. Just you," Ivy said, desperate to make him see things her way. Her mind felt rather muddled, but she was sober enough to realize that there was little time to make her plan work. Without thought, she ripped away the final fasteners on her gown just as she heard the front door opening.

Screaming at the top of her lungs, she fell against Braeden as if suffering some sort of fit. He caught her, as she knew he would do. Now, if Mr. Worthington had done his part, Ivy Brooks would put on a better show than Casa Grande could ever hope for.

∽ TWENTY ∾

THE FIRST THING RACHEL HEARD as Reginald unlocked the front door of the Needlemeier mansion was Ivy's imploring cries for Braeden to leave her alone. It sent a despairing chill up her spine and nearly took her breath away. *So he did come here to meet her!*

Another scream tore at the silence, and Rachel wondered if she herself might faint. She didn't want to witness what she instinctively knew was to come. Esmeralda pushed past Reg, but without giving thought to what they were doing, Reg and Rachel followed her into the house. All three halted at the front parlor. As the only room in the house with the lights on, it seemed the proper place to stop.

What they found there, however, was anything put proper. Braeden had Ivy in his arms and was bending down to place her on the sofa. She beat her fists at his chest, moaning over and over one single word: "No."

As Braeden stood up, Rachel, as well as the others, could see that Ivy's bodice had been undone. Her chemise and corset were clearly visible from where the lavender silk fell away. Unable to hide her gasp of surprise, Rachel instantly drew Braeden's attention to her impropriety as Ivy tried to sit up, clutching her bodice.

"Mr. Parker, you have a great deal to explain," Esmeralda said in a low, calculated tone.

"I suppose you might think so," Braeden replied, "but this isn't at all what it looks like."

"I don't want to hear lies," the old woman continued. "I've heard enough lies in my lifetime. You are clearly out of line here, and I want to know what is going on."

At this, Ivy managed to get to her feet and, still grasping her bodice, stumbled to where her aunt stood. "Oh, Auntie, it was terrible. He came here, he said, to see you. I thought it rather silly since you were at the celebration and everyone knew you'd be there." She swayed a bit on her feet. "I told him he could wait here for you, but then he asked for a drink—"

"That's a lie!" Braeden roared.

Ivy looked terribly frightened and backed up a step. "Well, it wasn't for him, as it turned out. He forced me to drink it. In fact, he forced me to drink a great deal. See for yourself. The glass and the brandy decanter are over there."

All four of them looked to where she pointed and sure enough there was a half-filled glass and a decanter with less than two inches of amber liquid still inside.

"That was nearly half full," Esmeralda declared, looking to Braeden for explanation.

"I had nothing to do with her drinking," he replied adamantly. "She came in here drunk and started throwing herself at me."

"Oh really, Mr. Parker? You come here knowing I won't be here, then expect me to believe it was all for decent purposes?"

"I don't care what you believe," Braeden replied, but his glance went to Rachel and his eyes seemed to plead with her to believe him innocent.

Rachel couldn't think clearly, much less determine who was telling the truth. She knew Ivy was prone to deception, but was Ivy capable of pulling off something like this?

"He made me drink," Ivy continued, "and then he became too friendly with me." She let loose a stream of tears. "I'm ruined," she declared, nearly causing Rachel to scream out loud in fear and frustration. She put her hand to her mouth, as if to stop any sound from coming forth, but her action caused Reg to move closer. His protective stance became more personal as he drew her to him supportively. For a moment, Rachel actually welcomed his touch.

Braeden scowled at this but turned his attention back to Ivy and her aunt. "She is hardly ruined. She did nothing but throw herself at me—and it failed. What you saw was my attempt to calm her down and get help. I was merely placing her upon the sofa in order to keep her from falling down. Look at her. She's swaying back and forth as if she were a flag in the wind."

"Liquor has that effect on a person, Mr. Parker," Esmeralda stated severely.

"He's ruined me, Auntie. He doesn't care now that he's done the deed. You have witnesses," Ivy said boldly.

"Whether she's ruined or not," Braeden replied, "has nothing to do with anything I've done or not done. She's angry because I've rejected her for another, and she means to see me pay for it."

"Oh, Braeden, you're just being mean. That's not at all what you told me earlier," Ivy sobbed. "You made me believe you cared. You said we'd always be together and that—"

"It hardly matters what was said earlier," Esmeralda declared. "What I really want to know from you, Mr. Parker, is whether I send for the marshal or the preacher."

Rachel could take no more. She turned on her heel and ran for the front door. She couldn't bear the look on Braeden's face, nor the smug gleam of satisfaction in Ivy's drunken expression. She hurried down the front steps of the mansion, catching the hem of her gown and nearly falling down the final two steps. She righted herself quickly, and as she raised her head, she saw the church just across the street. It seemed to beckon her forward. It offered her comfort and hope. But no doubt it was locked up tight and would afford her no refuge. And right now, in her deepest desperation, she didn't want to take the chance that someone would follow after her, allowing no means of escape. Especially if that someone turned out to be Braeden.

Without giving another thought to what she was doing, Rachel cut across the well-kept lawn of the Needlemeier estate and made her way deep into the gardens. There were quiet spots of refuge along the pathway, stone benches and wooden swings, any one of which could afford her privacy and silence. But Rachel needed something more than this. She needed solace. She needed to hear the voice of God speak comfort to her heart.

Moving deeper into the gardens, away from the hot springs and the laughter of lingering resort guests, Rachel found a secluded bench and sat down to weep. Here, far from the festive lighting of Casa Grande, the blackness seemed to enfold her like a mother's arms. The junipers and mesquites shielded her from the brunt of the chilling breeze, but the coolness of the night seemed unimportant compared to the icy foreboding that stabbed at her heart. Suddenly she felt more weary than she had ever felt in her life. It was all too much to deal with, and down deep in her heart, all she longed for was a long, silent sleep.

"*Come unto me, all ye that labor and are heavy laden, and I will give you rest.*" She remembered the verse from Matthew. "I need that rest, Lord." She sighed and gazed into the trees.

For several moments she did nothing but draw strength from her surroundings. The heavy scent of juniper and pine assaulted her senses, and the canopy they formed made her feel rather secure and hidden from the world. A glorious aroma of flowering shrubs and meticulously tended flower beds blended with that of the trees, painting a picture in scents more wondrous than the human eye could imagine. But as lovely as this was, Rachel could hardly appreciate the majesty.

Her ear caught the melodious rippling of the hot spring as it flowed down a series of falls. The sound soothed her nerves and helped her to relax. Pulling her shawl tighter, Rachel leaned back against the bench.

"I'm so tired," she said aloud. "I'm tired of fighting against the feelings I have inside of me. Feelings of love for Braeden, anger toward Ivy, frustration with Mrs. Needlemeier, and confusion over Reginald. I'm tired of the whining and complaining of the girls on my staff and the sinister turn of our unknown thief. I'm just worn out from it all. I get up in the morning more tired than the night before, and when I do make it to bed, I toss and turn for hours. God, what's wrong with me? Why can't I seem to find rest and peace?"

She thought of her father, a railroad man in Chicago. He had died only the year before she'd left to join the Harvey House system. He had been everything to her. While her mother was absorbed in the goings-on of her neighbors, her father had taken time to talk to Rachel, share stories, and encourage her.

"I wish you wouldn't have died," she murmured, remembering his joyful smile. "I wish you were here now to advise me. You could always help me to see the brighter side of my circumstances."

Sighing, Rachel hugged her body. It was as much to comfort herself as to ward off the cold. "There seems to be so much going on in my life. So much that is out of my control. I thought I had faith enough to get through those times, but maybe I've only been fooling myself. I honestly thought nothing could move me. Maybe I've never understood faith."

Rachel remembered the scene at the mansion and felt hot tears course down her cheeks. The world seemed suddenly turned upside down, and with it she had been tossed to and fro like a lifeless doll. She had come to Morita with one expectation—to serve and make life more easy for the guests of the resort and, in the process, maybe find an easier way for herself. But her life here had resulted in stress and heartache.

Rachel continued to speak aloud, hoping the sound of her voice would help clear the confusion within her. "It seems I've always anticipated something better than what I found. I come to expect things a certain way—believe I understand them perfectly—and then something happens to destroy my way of thinking. Sometimes it's simply because I believed the words of someone who knew far less about a matter than they were willing to let on. I'd step out in faith that those words were true, only to find they were lies. I've wasted a great deal of time giving myself over to such matters—trusting people who did not deserve my trust."

But your trust should be fixed first in the Lord, a voice seemed to say.

How often had she heard her mother say that people often fail you? Hadn't those been her mother's words of comfort when she had gone home completely devastated after her confrontation with Braeden?

Of course, there were different ways of looking at trust, and with exception to the trust she placed in God, Rachel had been otherwise disappointed. *Maybe I expect too much*, she thought. *Maybe I expect a perfection that only exists in heaven. People will always be motivated by hundreds of different reasons, and it isn't my place to judge them.* She knew her own thoughts were wise counsel, but it was hard to find strength in them.

Feeling completely spent, her limbs leaden and useless, Rachel contemplated what she should do. Perhaps she would just doze here in the gardens and when she awoke in the morning, all of her problems would be resolved and the burdens would be lifted.

"In prayer you are responsible to let go of your burdens," she remembered Pastor Johnson preaching. *"Remember, God cannot take them—if you will not give them."* She smiled. It seemed to be very sound reasoning.

"This will not be easy," she said, remembering the events of the evening. Ivy was a meticulous liar; of this Rachel had no doubt. She had caught the girl conniving against Gwen and others, and it should come as no surprise that she would scheme to get back at Rachel through Braeden.

Haven't I heard her state that she's only looking for a husband of means and then she will leave Casa Grande? She felt a wash of peace come over her. She stated as a confirmation, "Braeden is innocent. He's merely a victim of her manipulation."

It seemed so right to believe this, and Rachel took a deep breath and sighed. "I give you this burden, Lord. I give you my sorrow, my worry, my fears, and my doubt. I give all of this to you, but I give something more as well." She paused and again looked upward. "I give you my trust, my hope, my faith, and my love. I know that you are able to take all of this madness and turn it into calm and peace. I will rest in you."

Just then voices sounded from somewhere beyond her refuge. Rachel perked up and looked around her in the darkness. Had Braeden come to find her? Or Reginald? She drew a deep breath and realized she would have to face them sooner or later. Reginald had been supportive and kind, and she appreciated the way he looked after her. And Braeden—Braeden deserved her support in this trial. He had suffered by her hand because of her choice to believe in gossip and hearsay. He shouldn't be punished now by the manipulated circumstances fashioned by Ivy's hand. And Rachel was certain that was all the matter amounted to.

Getting to her feet, Rachel picked her way through the brush and vegetation and was surprised to find herself standing not ten feet away from the empty bandstand. The massive structure had been positioned about twenty yards from the hot spring pools and was large enough to contain a full-sized band or orchestra. But the gazebo itself didn't hold her attention for long—rather, the activity at the base of the structure urged her curiosity. Two men had taken off a piece of the latticework and one was now crawling inside, under the bandstand, while the other handed him something. It seemed most peculiar, and Rachel couldn't help but move closer.

When she was nearly upon them, Rachel could see a wooden crate with articles taken from the resort. "What are you doing?" she questioned without thinking of her isolated position.

The nearest man turned around and grinned a gapped-tooth smile at her. "Buenos noches, senorita," he said, moving toward her.

Rachel backed up several steps, realizing her mistake. She thought to scream but the man was too quick for her. He was upon her in a flash, clapping a filthy hand over her mouth and dragging her backward toward the cover of darkness.

✒ TWENTY-ONE ✑

STILL REELING FROM THE EVENTS of the last few minutes, Brae-den stared in disbelief as Reginald Worthington rushed out of the Needlemeier mansion after Rachel. Esmeralda seemed not to notice the departures as she stood staring at him, as though she expected something—perhaps a confession. But there was nothing to confess.

Ivy teetered back and forth, seeming rather pleased with herself and the events that had just taken place. Braeden was then certain beyond all doubt that he'd been set up.

"Ivy, you are positively drunk on your feet," Esmeralda declared. She rang for the maid and when the young girl appeared, she seemed rather frightened.

"She can vouch for the fact that I didn't ask for a drink. She told me upon instruction she was to leave a drink on the serving tray," Braeden told the older woman.

Liza seemed to cower as Braeden stepped toward her. Esmeralda looked at the girl for a moment, then questioned, "Is that true? And if it is, exactly who instructed you to leave the drink on the tray?"

Liza glanced to Ivy, then lowered her head. "Mr. Parker told me to pour the drink."

"That's a lie," Braeden said, his voice low and accusing.

The girl raised her head and met his eyes. Braeden refused to go easy on her. She was clearly Ivy's accomplice, and he'd have no part of their games. Because of her and her mistress, he might have lost Rachel.

"Tell her the truth," Braeden stated in an even tone.

"Lizzz-a al-waysss tellsss-a truth," Ivy said, slurring her words badly. It was evident that the liquor had taken a progressive hold on the girl.

"Liza, take Miss Ivy upstairs to her room. Help her to prepare for bed and get some coffee on to boil." Esmeralda waited sternly while the housemaid scurried to Ivy's side.

"Braeden." Ivy murmured the name as she passed by him.

Braeden held his arms tightly to his sides, afraid that if he moved even an inch, he might throttle Ivy Brooks and force the truth from her own mouth. But once Ivy and Liza had gone from the room, Braeden shoved his hands in his pockets and turned to Esmeralda Needle-meier.

"I don't know what kind of game your niece is playing, but I assure you nothing improper took place here tonight—at least not improper on my part. I received a note telling me to meet you here for some emergency meeting. I thought it rather strange, but given the nature of your demands of late," he said in a terse manner, "I figured it was probably legitimate."

"I sent no such note," Esmeralda declared, unmoved by his insult.

"Well, someone did," Braeden replied, pulling the paper from his pocket. "I have it here. It appears to be on your stationery. You will note the scrolled initials *E N* in the center."

The old woman's face contorted. "Let me see that." She snatched the paper from his hand as he extended it to her.

Esmeralda studied the note for several moments, then folded it and held it tightly in her gloved hand. "What happened here tonight was witnessed by two of the resort employees. Tongues will wag, no doubt, and my niece's reputation will be ruined. Despite how this event came to pass, it would be the honorable thing for you to act the part of gentleman and marry the girl."

"It would be a false honor," Braeden countered. "I do not love your niece, neither do I feel at all inclined to spend my life with her. She is a manipulating liar. You know it and so do I. She staged this entire thing, and if she has to suffer the consequences of not getting her way in the matter, then that is her problem."

"If it is a matter of money . . ."

"It is hardly that, madam," Braeden said, feeling his anger build. "I will not pay the price for something I had no part in. I suggest you take your niece to task for this event, perhaps even send her to some proper finishing school where she might be taught decorum and manners. No doubt she'll just try this again with some other unsuspecting fool. Now, if you'll excuse me." He stormed out the room, barely remembering to take his hat from the table in the hallway.

"Mr. Parker, this matter is far from being settled. I will speak to my niece, but if I am not convinced of her guilt in this situation, I will send the law to speak to you on my behalf," Esmeralda called out from behind him.

"Send anyone you choose, Mrs. Needlemeier," Braeden said, turning to address her face-to-face. "It will not make this any more my fault than it already is, neither will it force me to marry your unruly niece. I believe you know the truth in what I'm saying. I see it in your eyes. For whatever reason you choose to maintain this stance of believing me guilty, it will not change the facts of the matter—and you know that very well." He put his hat on his head and gave her a short bow. "Good night, Mrs. Needlemeier."

He left the stunned old woman speechless as he raced down the porch steps, driven by the notion that somewhere Rachel was dwelling on the scene she'd just witnessed. And possibly, Reginald Worthington was offering her comfort in his arms.

Braeden slammed his fist into his hand and let out a growl of protest at this thought. The nerve of Worthington to act as Rachel's defender! Braeden had nearly knocked the man aside when he'd dared to put himself between Braeden and Rachel. As if she needed to be shielded—protected from Braeden. But when the man put his arm around Rachel, as though they were both very comfortable in such an action, Braeden had desired nothing more than to put his fist into Worthington's smug face.

He moved through the gardens and across the footbridge, knowing that if Rachel was sensible and thinking with marginal clarity, she would have made her way to the privacy of her quarters. At least he prayed that's where she might have gone. He desperately wanted to talk to her, to reassure her that he wasn't unfaithful to their love. He knew how very tender her heart was in this area, and he knew that her trust in him had cost her everything.

"It won't be her fault this time," he muttered aloud. "If she initially believes the scene staged this night, well, who could blame her?" He knew the evidence was very damaging. He could easily imagine how the entire setup had looked to Rachel.

Grinding his teeth together, Braeden stifled the urge to ring Ivy Brooks's neck. He could still see her seductive little smile as she toyed with the bodice of her gown. She had planned it out in meticulous order. She knew when her aunt would return, and she somehow seemed to know that Rachel would return with her.

He entered Casa Grande through the back entryway, grateful that most of the hotel guests were listening to the conclusion of Miss Collins' singing program. He passed by the theatre room, where the crowd was congregated, and heard the thunderous applause as the soprano hit her final note. Picking up speed, Braeden moved down the corridor, past the intersecting hallway and the entrances to the library and dining room. All was ominously silent.

Reaching Rachel's office, he called for her first, then knocked loudly on the door. There was no response. He repeated the process two more times before deciding to go outside to see if there was any light shining in the windows of her private quarters. But when the windows only yielded darkness, Braeden found himself at yet another dead end. Glancing around the front lawns, he wondered if perhaps she had taken herself to the pools or to a quiet place to think. The gardens were full of benches for just such a purpose, and Morita Falls boasted a scenic walking path with tables for picnic luncheons.

Moving out across the lawn to where the illuminated fountain glowed in the darkness, Braeden prayed to find her—prayed that she'd be unharmed and at peace with the events of the evening. If she could only find a way to hold on to her fragile trust in him, she would recognize that he had no feelings whatsoever for Ivy Brooks—at least not feelings that entailed any warmth.

He paused beside the fountain, his reflection in the water catching his eye. He looked hard and long at himself for several moments. His anger was evident, and his eyes were dark in their fury. Forcing himself to calm down, Braeden took a deep breath and tried to formulate a plan. He couldn't just run from one end of the grounds to the other without any real purpose in mind. He should make a mental list and meticulously search from one end of the estate to the other. Time was of the utmost importance. While the days were still pleasantly warm, the nights bore a chill that could easily strike one down with illness.

Staring back at Casa Grande, Braeden watched as upper floor lights came on to indicate that the resort guests were retiring for the evening. Soon the front lobby doors would be locked tight, and while Rachel had a key to the resort, Braeden was uncertain that it would be upon her person.

"I have to find her," he whispered. "Please, God, help me find her."

However, despite his avid search, Rachel was nowhere to be found. No one had seen her. No one had any idea where she had gone.

Finally, with the upper floor lights now winking off for the night, Braeden went into his office and closed the door. He needed to concentrate. Rachel had to be somewhere nearby. But where? He contemplated the matter for some time. Then, breaking Fred Harvey's most important rule, he took himself into the dining room, back through the kitchen, and into the private parlor and dormitory hallway of the Harvey Girls. Curfew was ten o'clock, and since the hour was nearly midnight, all of the girls should be safely locked in their rooms. With this in mind, Braeden felt some confidence that he'd not have to be further accused of molesting yet another Harvey employee. His reputation was already suffering, and with Fred Harvey's strict rules on propriety and honor, Braeden wondered if he'd even have a job once Esmeralda spoke out against him. After all, Harvey himself had arrived that evening by train to share in the celebration. He would no doubt preside over any dispute of such a grand nature. For the first time, Braeden realized he might lose his job or even find himself jailed. He shook his head. All of that was immaterial to finding Rachel.

He knew where Gwen Carson's room was and made his way there

as quietly as possible. Knocking lightly on the door, he continued to glance over his shoulder to make certain no one else had appeared in the hallway.

"Yes?" Gwen asked, opening the door wide. When she saw it was Braeden, she shrieked and pushed the door closed all but a couple of inches. "Mr. Parker, what in the world do you want? You aren't supposed to be here!"

"I know, Miss Carson, and I do apologize. It's just that Rachel is missing, and I wondered if you knew of some favorite place she might go."

Gwen opened the door a few more inches. "Rachel is missing? What do you mean?"

"It's a long story," Braeden replied in complete exasperation. "Something happened tonight that upset her. I need to find her and explain."

Completely taken in by this development, Gwen let the door fall open. "The only place I know she goes is the O'Donnell house. Mrs. O'Donnell is probably her best friend."

Braeden felt relief wash over him. "Of course! Why didn't I think of that! Thank you, Miss Carson."

He hurried back the way he'd come and ran out the front door of the lobby, mindless of the bellboy who stared at him in curiosity.

The O'Donnells lived just over the main bridge, and they were less than three blocks away from the Needlemeier mansion. It made perfect sense that Rachel would have gone here. Braeden knew of her love for Simone O'Donnell and of Jeffery's deep abiding friendship for the woman he'd worked with. Braeden felt a small amount of relief in believing her to be there. She would be safe, and Simone would calm her down and help her to see reason. At least he prayed she would.

But when he arrived, the small clapboard house was dark and it wasn't until then that he remembered Jeffery and Simone had been at the resort celebration. Knocking loudly, Braeden felt his anxiety mount. They were probably already in bed and completely exhausted from their evening. After all, Jeffery was still recovering from his incident from the night before. If Rachel would have come to them, they probably wouldn't have even been here. Now his mind tried to logically conclude where she might have gone upon finding the O'Donnell house empty.

While he contemplated this, the door opened and Jeffery stood looking in questionable silence at Braeden. Without waiting for him to speak, Braeden apologized. "I know it's late, but I'm looking for Rachel."

"Rachel's not at Casa Grande?" Jeffery asked, concern edging his tone.

"No," Braeden said with a sigh. "Look, something happened tonight. Something awful—and Rachel thinks the worst of me. I have to find her."

"Why don't you come in and explain while I get dressed. Then I can help you look for her."

Not knowing what else to do, Braeden nodded and followed Jeffery into the house just as Simone O'Donnell appeared. She had wrapped herself up in a dark blue dressing gown and was fussing with her hair as she came into the room.

"What's happened?" she asked. Her gaze rested on Braeden as though she were trying to read his mind. "It's Rachel, isn't it?"

"Yes," Braeden said. "She's missing."

"I'm going to get dressed and help him look for her," Jeffery stated, as though that would answer all of Simone's questions.

"I'll get dressed too," she said. "Maybe I can help."

"No, someone should stay in case Rachel comes here," Braeden replied.

"Why would Rachel come here?" Simone asked, eyeing him sternly.

Braeden swallowed hard and tried to think of a delicate way to explain. In exasperation he ran his hand through his sandy hair, then plunged it deep into his pocket. His nerves were getting the best of him. "I was called to meet Mrs. Needlemeier at her house this evening. Only it turns out she didn't send the note—her niece, Ivy Brooks, did the deed. Ivy, as you may well know, has been a thorn in Rachel's side since the beginning."

"I do know that much," Simone replied, her expression revealing nothing but calm and the reassurance that she wasn't jumping to conclusions.

To Braeden, she seemed to be weighing all the facts and not reacting at all in a condemning fashion. It gave him the courage to proceed. "Ivy arranged for a seduction scene. It seems she wants—or maybe even needs—a rich husband, and she picked me for her victim. When I came to the house, she was as drunk as anyone could be and proceeded to disrobe. Rachel came in at a most inopportune moment, to say the least."

"Why would Rachel be there?" asked Simone softly.

"That was exactly my thought," Braeden replied. "I mean, Mrs. Needlemeier coming in was no surprise at all. It is, after all, her home. But Rachel and Reginald Worthington had no reason to be there. It made me realize Ivy had set up the entire affair to come between Rachel and me." Braeden felt a tightness in his chest. He hated feeling so out of control—so hopeless. "Look, I know she's talked to you, but I don't know how much she's said. You know I love her, but this may well have destroyed any hope for our future, and I can't let that happen. Trust comes hard for her—at least where I'm involved."

"Rachel is a good woman," Jeffery replied, hopping into the room as he struggled to pull on his boots. "She doesn't seem the type to just jump to conclusions."

"She is a good woman," Braeden agreed, "but even good women have their limits."

"Where could she have gone?" The question came from Simone, as though no one else might have thought of it.

"I had hoped she'd come here, but then I realized the ordeal took place earlier in the evening when you both would have been at the celebration. Rachel might have thought to come here but most likely would have found the place deserted. From there, I have no idea what she would have done. Has she spoken to you of someplace special to her? Someplace she might go for safety or solace?"

"The church might be a logical choice," Simone replied.

"That's a good idea!" Braeden replied. "And it's just across the street from the Needlemeier mansion."

"Come on," Jeffery told him. "We can walk up there and check it out. If she's not there we might need to wait until morning to do a more thorough search. Maybe the extra time will allow her to calm down and think things through."

"Maybe," Braeden replied, but he didn't feel convinced. "But I can't bear to think of her spending the night outside. The chill could be harmful."

"Possibly," Jeffery agreed. "But we don't need to jump to conclusions. Maybe she's safely spending the night with someone else. Maybe she went to pray at the church and the pastor and his wife urged her to stay with them. If she was as upset as you think she might have been, she might not have been capable of reasonable thought. Maybe the pastor just took charge and let his wife put Rachel to bed in their guest room."

"Maybe," Braeden replied, hoping that Jeffery was right.

However, when Rachel could not be found at the church, the parsonage, or anywhere in between there and the O'Donnell home, Braeden felt the bottom fall out of his world. Hope eluded him as he reluctantly agreed to wait until morning to begin searching in earnest.

Simone touched his arm gently as Braeden turned to go back to Casa Grande. "Rachel will consider the situation, and I believe she will know the truth."

Braeden nodded in resignation. Maybe upon reflection, Rachel would realize his innocence. There was a chance it could work out that way, though Braeden feared it was slim.

"I'm sorry to have bothered you," Braeden finally said. "If she's still not back in the morning, I'll be heading out to search for her at first light."

"I'll be there," Jeffery replied.

"What about your head?" Simone questioned her husband. "You probably shouldn't be anywhere near a horse for another few days."

Jeffery lightly touched his wife's cheek, but his gaze went to Braeden. "I'll be there."

When Braeden returned to Casa Grande, it was two in the morning. With no sign of Rachel anywhere, Braeden's frustration and misery mounted. It was only then that it dawned on Braeden that he might question Reginald Worthington about where Rachel had gone. Perhaps

Worthington held the key to the whole matter if she had confided in him.

Braeden tried not to think of Rachel finding solace in Worthington's arms. He couldn't dare to react illogically in this matter—too much was at risk. Instead, he would simply go upstairs and speak to Worthington and state his case, plain and simple. With this in mind, he had reached the third step on the grand staircase when the lobby door opened behind him and in walked the very man he was going in search of.

"Worthington!" Braeden called out, going back down the stairs. "Where's Rachel?"

"I have no idea, Mr. Parker. I've been searching for her ever since the fiasco earlier this evening." He paused, and the look of contempt on Worthington's face matched the feelings Braeden held in his own heart. "Besides, even if I knew where she was," he added, "I wouldn't tell you."

Braeden balled his hands into fists but stopped short of raising them to Worthington's face. "I did nothing wrong," he managed to say, his jaws clenched tight. "That whole scene was Ivy's concoction."

"I suppose you might see it that way, but I think it probably appears otherwise to Miss Taylor. Now, instead of standing around arguing about it, I suggest we put together some sort of search party. It'll be light in a couple of hours, and while I have to oversee the kitchens, I'm certain you can be spared from your post," Reginald replied rather snidely.

Braeden grabbed Worthington by his lapels, and with his face only inches away from the Englishman's, he whispered low and menacingly, "If you are lying to me, I'll personally see to it that you never work again."

"I say," the startled man replied, "you needn't take your anger out on me. You've brought these problems upon yourself."

Braeden thought long and hard about punching the man squarely in the nose but instead tossed him backward so that he lost his balance and landed on the floor. "Just remember, Worthington, Rachel is my concern and my problem—not yours. Leave her alone."

Worthington watched him for a moment before getting to his feet and dusting off his trousers. "You, Mr. Parker, are a ruffian of the worst kind, and if Rachel so desires it, I will do my utmost to protect her from you. Good-bye."

Braeden watched him go, wondering when he'd ever felt this angry. There was nothing to be gained by losing his head, however. And as much as Braeden hated to yield to Worthington on any matter, this was one of those few times he would do exactly that. Dawn would arrive in a few hours, and when it did, Braeden needed to be ready.

He decided the first order of business would be a change of clothes. He was still wearing his best suit on behalf of the grand opening, and it would never do to go traipsing around the countryside dressed in such formal attire. Opening the door to his office, Braeden turned on the lights, grateful that because of the resort activities the electricity had been left on instead of shut down at ten as was the routine. But no sooner had the light illuminated the room than Braeden found himself staring dumbfounded at the scene. Someone had ransacked his office—and from the looks of it, they'd done a pretty thorough job.

Papers were strewn all over the floor, his chair overturned and left in the corner, and every drawer of his desk had been pulled out and emptied. It didn't make sense. He had nothing of value here. There were papers related to the hotel's management, inventory, purchase orders, and payroll information, but all of the important things like actual payroll money, storage room keys, and anything of value were locked up tight in the hotel safe. What could the intruder have been looking for?

He squatted down and began picking up the papers. They were hopelessly mingled and would take hours to sort through. Braeden stood amid the disarray, trying to imagine what it all meant. As he thought of the note given to him by Ivy and of the scene she'd managed to set up, he couldn't help but wonder if she was also responsible for this mess. Then again, someone had broken into Rachel's office on more than one occasion. Perhaps whatever was searched for there was never found and the thief thought to find it in Braeden's office.

"It doesn't make sense," he said as he set his chair upright. Beneath the leather chair, Braeden's gaze fell upon a square piece of stationery.

He picked it up and realized instantly that it was a program from the opera singer's performance. How had that managed to get into his office? Had the thief left it there? It seemed logical to think they might have. Shaking his head, Braeden felt a growing sense of frustration. It was like having all the pieces to a puzzle but being unable to figure out where they all went.

After beginning to clean his office, Braeden realized there was no time for putting the papers in order. It would have to wait until after he found Rachel. Rachel's safety was more important than anything else. He couldn't allow himself to be distracted.

Distracted.

The word seemed to echo in his head. Maybe he was meant to be distracted. Maybe the mess he'd found in his office was created to slow him down. But slow him down from what? Finding Rachel? The intruder couldn't have known about Ivy's arrangements—or could they? He thought of the evening's events and realized that Ivy could very well have had many accomplices. She had incorporated the help of her maid at the mansion—why not additional help from her Harvey friends or other staff members of Casa Grande? Perhaps she had promised them money or something else.

He ripped off his tie and threw it on the bed in the adjoining room. Changing into jeans and a more serviceable shirt and coat, Braeden tried to figure out what it all meant. He uttered a prayer for guidance but felt no nearer to the truth. He recalled a verse in the Bible about seeing things through a glass darkly and thought it perfectly depicted his feelings just now. The images were distorted and unclear—the answers evaded his reach.

"I don't know what's going on," he murmured as he took up his hat, "but I'm going to find out."

ஆ TWENTY-TWO ஒ

AS IVY SOBERED UP, the first thing she became aware of was her aunt's imposing glare. The old woman glowered at her in such a way that it would have given her a headache—had she not already had one from the effects of the liquor.

Still, the fact that she'd managed to pull off her charade from the night before made the pain worthwhile, as far as Ivy was concerned. She had sketchy memories in places where the brandy had overpowered her senses, but for the most part she remembered everything—especially the look on Rachel Taylor's face when she found Ivy and Braeden together.

"You needn't smile," Esmeralda declared in such a no-nonsense manner that Ivy couldn't help but wonder if there was something more than the events of the evening that disturbed her now.

"I'm sorry, but considering all that has happened, I believe I am entitled to think of this entire affair in the best of possible ways. If I had to be ruined by someone, it's at least beneficial that he was handsome and rich."

"Stop it now. Stop this nonsense and finish your coffee. I want you good and sober in order to discuss this matter properly," Esmeralda told her niece.

Ivy stared at her aunt for a moment, then shrugged and downed the contents of the delicate china cup. The strong, hot liquid scorched her throat as she gulped it down, but Ivy hardly felt the pain. Soon she would leave this hideous place and the painful memories it harbored. She was going to marry Braeden Parker and move back east and live in a fine house for the rest of her life. She'd already planned it all out in her mind.

Putting the cup back on the saucer, she looked to her aunt as if to invite her to speak. When Esmeralda only continued to frown, Ivy realized she'd have to be the one to start the conversation.

"I'm quite myself now," she told Esmeralda. "Although my head hurts and there are other parts of my body that feel rather misused. But I'm ready to discuss this matter, if that is what you desire." She'd play the part with sweetness and consideration, especially since she knew it would take her aunt's power in the community to force Braeden Parker to marry her.

"I'd like an explanation, Ivy." The words were matter-of-fact and issued without emotion.

"An explanation for last night?" Ivy questioned. "Don't you think that would better be asked of Mr. Parker?"

"No, I do not. Mr. Parker hardly seems the one to question when you were the one to plan the entire event."

"I don't understand. A man comes into our home, tries to—no, succeeds at molesting me, and you want my explanation?" Ivy questioned indignantly. She reached for the ties of her pale pink robe and tightened them for lack of something else to turn her attention to. She was going to have to play this very carefully. Apparently her aunt had reason to doubt the scene she'd witnessed. "I think you are being very hard on me," Ivy continued. "But then again, you always have been. You've always treated me poorly."

"That's not true, but neither is it relevant to this discussion," Esmeralda replied calmly. "I know that you wrote the note that brought Mr. Parker to this house."

Ivy's head snapped up at this declaration. "What in the world are you talking about? I wrote no such note."

"Oh no?" Esmeralda said, pulling the piece of paper from her pocket. "Then suppose you explain this. The writing is clearly yours, not mine as the note implies."

Ivy knew what the piece of paper was without having to look at it. But for the sake of her story, she took the offering and looked it over. "I didn't write this."

"Well, neither did I, and whoever did has a remarkable ability to forge your handwriting to perfection," Esmeralda said rather sarcastically.

Ivy shrugged and handed her back the note. "I'm not responsible for this."

"Say what you will," Esmeralda replied, shaking her head. "We both know the truth. What I don't understand is why you were so desperate for a husband that you felt you had to stoop to such levels. Why, there isn't a decent man in Morita who would have you now, and you certainly cannot believe that Mr. Parker will marry you simply because of that little charade."

"Charade!" Ivy said angrily. "The man completely destroys my reputation and you call it a charade? There were witnesses—or have you forgotten?"

"I haven't forgotten anything." Esmeralda carved out a pattern in the floor as she paced, appearing to consider what she might say next. "I haven't forgotten the request you had for me to seek you out after the ball. I haven't forgotten that you expected me to return home at precisely nine o'clock, and I haven't forgotten your hatred of Miss Rachel Taylor. And because of this," she said, halting in front of Ivy, "I believe I am absolutely correct in saying that you planned the entire ordeal in order to take your revenge on Miss Taylor and force the issue of marriage with Mr. Parker."

Ivy regained her composure and bowed her head to appear devastated. "Then you are wrong. I may have been angry with Miss Taylor, but I do not hate her. I would never plan my own ruin in order to get back at her. You may accuse me of many things, Auntie, but pettiness has never been one of my flaws. Nor is stupidity. I wouldn't risk my future in order to have my own way for now."

Esmeralda sighed and began to pace again. "At fifteen, you came to me with no one else in the world to see you through. You had lost your mother and father and the only home you had ever known. You were a child then, your actions and attitudes excusable. However, I had hoped you would outgrow this selfishness. I had hoped that you had learned the painful cost of your conniving and would have chosen a better way."

"I don't understand you," Ivy said, looking up to meet her aunt's mournful expression. What was the old woman talking about now? Ivy could hardly stand to listen to her aunt's useless blather. There were plans to be laid. She needed to find Braeden and declare the need for an immediate wedding. Instead, she had to sit here and listen to her aunt go on and on about something Ivy had no understanding of. "What conniving and painful cost are you speaking of?" she finally asked in complete exasperation.

Esmeralda held a look of immense pain. "You know very well where your conniving has brought you. After all, it brought you here to live with me."

Ivy felt a chill run up her spine. Could her long-buried secrets be known? She shook her head in denial. "I came here to live with you because, as you pointed out, I had no one else."

"No, not after your plans had gone awry."

Ivy remained seated but her heart began a frantic pace and her chest grew tight. "My plans? I don't know what you're talking about."

Esmeralda leaned against the cane and scowled. "I know you caused the fire, Ivy. I know it was your hand that took the lives of your parents—of my beloved brother, Carl. I've had reports from the insurance inspector and a statement from the one maid who survived a short time after the fire."

Ivy felt her skin tingle. There was an almost unexplainable stimulation in having the truth be voiced aloud. "It was an accident," she replied, her voice barely audible.

"No," Esmeralda countered, this time her voice taking on an angry edge. "You planned that fire, just as meticulously as you planned to have us find Mr. Parker in this house last night."

"How can you say that?" Ivy questioned in disbelief.

"You thought I would never find out about the fire. You thought it would be perceived as an innocent accident by a clumsy housemaid," Esmeralda said evenly. "You spilled an oil lamp and let the parlor catch fire, and you did it in the middle of the night so that the fire would be well out of control by the time anyone noticed. The only thing I don't understand is why? Why, when you had everything an only child could possibly desire, did you burn down your own house and take the lives of your parents?"

"You're crazy! You've gone completely mad," Ivy declared.

Esmeralda refused to back down. "Have I? There were times after the fire when I wondered if I might go mad. Times when, burdened with the memories of having lost Carl so shortly after losing Hezekiah, that I wanted to go mad." She paused. "Madness would have been merciful. Instead, I was forced to live a lie with you."

"You are crazy," Ivy said quite seriously. That unwelcome feeling of her conscience was threatening to surface. She knew better than to admit to the truth, so she intended to force her aunt to question the facts she'd been given. "I loved my mother and father. I would never have done them harm. It sounds to me that the people in charge of investigating the fire simply didn't want to pay out on Papa's insurance. It was just an accident—nothing more."

"That's not what the fire itself proved. The inspector and the witness explained the deliberate actions taken by you on that night. You may call them liars, especially since the maid is now dead from her burns, but I've spent a fortune—actually, your fortune—to ensure that the facts of those events remain forever hidden from the record."

"What are you saying?"

"I'm saying that I had to buy the favor of the inspector. I couldn't see you put on trial for three murders. You are, after all . . . family." The word was said rather snidely, and Ivy knew her aunt's wrath was mounting. "Your housemaid saw what you had done. But she was too late to sound the alarm, and the fire spread much too quickly. The inspector found her dying words to be convincing enough, and he was set to prosecute you for your actions. That's when I interceded to convince him otherwise. When all was settled and the inheritance your father had left you had been established with me as your guardian and trust keeper, I found it necessary to use that money to ensure that you would never be blamed for the deaths and destruction." Her aunt smiled as Ivy's mouth dropped open. "You had no idea, did you?"

"You took my money? All of it?" Ivy asked in disbelief.

"Yes. All of it. You have nothing, Ivy. Nothing but your life and that which I give you."

Ivy could no longer contain her anger. She had always presumed upon a fortune that would add to that of her husband. In fact, the only reason she really pushed to marry early was because her own fortune was out of her hands until the age of twenty-one, and she had hated the idea of waiting.

"You've left me without anything?" she questioned, getting to her feet. She fixed her gaze on the elderly woman and felt her anger rise. She stalked toward Esmeralda while the old woman stood her ground.

"You left yourself without means," said Esmeralda without feeling. "You took the lives of your parents and destroyed the future your father had built for you. You killed my only brother because of your senseless, childish ways."

"All right, old woman," Ivy said, realizing she had nothing left to lose. "I did start that fire, but it was an accident that they died. I would never have wanted them harmed. My father spoiled me and my mother doted upon me. Why would I set out to kill them?"

Esmeralda appeared to understand her rage and took a step backward. "Then why burn the house?"

Ivy laughed cynically. "Because I wanted a better house. Father wouldn't listen to me. He didn't listen to me that night, either. I told him not to go back inside. But mother had gone after some photographs. Father saw me safely outside and went after her." Ivy remembered the scene as if it were yesterday: the three-story house ablaze, the sounds of the roaring fire greedily consuming the frame, people yelling and crying for help. The entire thing was permanently frozen in her mind like a bizarre, nightmarish costume party. The pain of the memory she had neatly buried within her now seared her deadened emotions, as if she herself were being consumed by flames.

Ivy looked at her aunt and shook her head. "He should never have gone back inside. Neither of them should have gone inside. We were safe. We could have gone on, moved to a better home. Papa had insurance on the house—I know because I saw the policy."

"But the policy never paid out. Not for a deliberately set fire. Do you not yet understand, Ivy? They would have sent you to prison. It's just that simple."

"I don't believe you. No one will believe you. I was just a little girl, and all I wanted was a better house." She paused, feeling the weight of truth fall upon her shoulders. "I loved them."

As Ivy continued to advance toward her, Esmeralda glanced over her shoulder, appearing more and more nervous. She obviously felt threatened, and for this Ivy knew a sense of power. She purposefully kept her voice low, refusing to allow any of the servants to overhear them argue. But she made certain her expression left little doubt in Esmeralda's mind that Ivy couldn't allow her to ruin her plans.

"You loved them? You risked losing everything for a better house, and you excuse your actions by saying you loved them. You don't know what love is, Ivy."

Ivy paused, feeling momentarily confused in her memories. "Our neighborhood was becoming increasingly common," she said softly. "I told Father we needed a bigger, more affluent estate, but he wouldn't hear of moving. Mother loved our little house and couldn't bear to think of going elsewhere. So I took matters into my own hands. I decided the house had to go."

As Ivy focused on the form before her, she suddenly realized she would have to deal with her aunt, for the old woman would never understand her plight. She'd never see things her way, which meant she would never keep her mouth closed or cooperate with Ivy's plans. She continued. "I know how to eliminate obstacles in my life. The house was an obstacle, and it had to go," she said, shrugging nonchalantly. "Just as I've decided that you have to go. You can't be allowed to stand in my way." She watched the old woman pale and stumble back another few feet.

Advancing on her aunt, Ivy forced her backward again, smiling as the old woman teetered at the top of the staircase. "I will marry Braeden Parker, and you won't interfere. I may have forced his hand last night, but I didn't go to all that trouble just to let you expose me to ridicule."

"Ivy, you're mad," Esmeralda said softly.

"No, not really. Not when you consider that after you are dead, all of this and most of Morita will be mine. I know you arranged your will to leave it all to me. You told me so."

Esmeralda shook her head. "I told you that I'd left you what you deserved."

Ivy stopped in her tracks. "What are you saying?"

"I'm saying that I left everything to the support and promotion of Morita. And a moderate amount of money will be used to erect a monument to my dear husband."

"You've left me nothing?" Ivy said, her eyes narrowing. "Me, your only living relation?" Confusion set in and she felt her ability to reason slip away. What was happening to her—to her plans?

"You, who killed my brother and his wife, and now plot the same demise for me," Esmeralda said matter-of-factly. "You will have nothing. Not even this roof over your head. It all goes to the town."

"Fool!" Ivy said under her breath. "You fool!" She reached out to strike the old woman, but Esmeralda moved backward once again. Only this time she stepped beyond the top of the stairs. As she fell, Ivy watched in stunned silence, her mind refusing to put the pieces together. "No!" she cried, reaching out at the thin air. "Don't go!" In her mind she saw her father dashing back into the burning house. She closed her eyes and tried to force the images out of her mind. When she opened them again, Esmeralda lay at the foot of the stairs.

Realizing the noise would draw the servants, Ivy screamed at the top of her lungs.

"Someone help! Auntie has fallen down the stairs!"

Liza came running, along with the cook and the butler. They all came running from different directions of the house, but all three stopped abruptly at the crumpled form of their mistress. The aging butler knelt down beside Esmeralda's pale, still form. He shook his head and stood once again.

"I'm afraid she has expired."

Ivy saw all three servants look up to her as if she might offer some explanation. In an act of instinct, Ivy collapsed to the floor. Her aunt was dead, another accident that Ivy couldn't avoid responsibility in. Thinking of it would only cause her grief and frustration. She had to think of her plans—of her future, especially now that she knew the truth. Now that she was without funds.

She heard the rush of footsteps on the stairs and focused on her purpose. Her obstacles were slowly but surely being removed. They would believe her to be the grieving niece, totally devastated by her aunt's passing, and because she didn't stand to inherit a cent, no one would believe Ivy to have done anything out of line.

"Here, miss," Liza said, reaching her side first. She fanned Ivy's face with her hand and struggled to raise her to a sitting position. "It'll be all right. Let's get you back to bed."

Ivy moaned softly and let the trio assist her to her bed. She mumbled something about getting help before closing her eyes and falling back against her pillow.

"Best get the doctor for them both," Liza said.

"Madam is quite beyond the doctor's help," the butler replied, "but I'll send for him on behalf of Miss Ivy."

Ivy lay silent, with her eyes closed tight. This entire thing might just work out to her benefit after all. Braeden might even take pity upon her, but even if he didn't, she knew she could depend on Reginald for support in what had happened the night before. She'd simply tell everyone of Braeden's actions and explain that the shock had been so great upon her aunt that while they were going downstairs, the woman had simply succumbed to the news.

With any luck at all, she'd find herself in a wedding by nightfall. Now there remained only one question on Ivy's mind. *What should I wear for my marriage to Braeden?*

⊰ TWENTY-THREE ⊱

BRAEDEN NOTED THE PINK HUES of dawn against the eastern skies. He had hoped to be off with a search party by first light, but since he couldn't locate the marshal, it seemed Braeden would simply have to put together his own group or go off by himself to look for Rachel. Neither choice would probably be anywhere nearly as productive as if he had professional help.

Remounting the horse he'd borrowed from Casa Grande's stables, Braeden made his way back to the resort. He couldn't help but think about the events of the past few days. Casa Grande had begun to hold promise for him, and now with Ivy's manipulation, he wondered if it could represent anything but frustration and regret. People would no doubt think of him differently now. They might even mistrust him and his motives, and that could do nothing but bring misery on everyone. Then, too, if Rachel remained at Casa Grande and refused to listen to his explanation or believe his innocence, he might as well load up and go back to Chicago. There just didn't seem to be any easy answer, and the future was hazy.

Tomas greeted him as he arrived at the stable. The boy looked worried, even fearful. "Have you found her yet, senor?"

"No," Braeden replied, dismounting. He tossed Tomas the reins. "I'll need your help, Tomas. You know the local people. Can you round up about five or six men to help me search the area for Rachel?"

"Sí, I can do this." Tomas appeared relieved to have something to do.

"I'll go inside and get some provisions. There's no telling how long we'll be at this." Braeden said the cautious words, but in his heart he prayed he was overexaggerating the situation. Rachel had probably taken herself to some quiet point of refuge. After all, he didn't know her so well as to predict her every move. Perhaps she had other friends in Morita besides the O'Donnells. It was possible that she had made the acquaintance of someone else and had sought comfort from them when Simone and Jeffery proved to be elsewhere.

He took the side delivery entrance into Casa Grande and made his way through the kitchen. He saw Reginald frown at his intrusion but remained silent. Out in the dining room there were at least twelve Harvey Girls busying themselves with the morning chores. Spying Gwen Carson, Braeden saw the concern in her eyes. She came to him, even as he made his way to her.

"Have you found Rachel?" she questioned.

"No. I suppose you've had no word from her either?"

Gwen shook her head. "Nothing. Ivy Brooks is missing as well."

Braeden frowned. "Ivy probably won't be in this morning. She was rather unwell last night, and if my guess is correct, she won't feel like putting in an appearance."

"Is that part of what happened to Rachel?" Gwen asked softly.

"Yes." Braeden hated to admit it, but there was no sense in denying the truth.

"Ivy hates Rachel. She'd do anything to see her leave Casa Grande."

"Yes, and had I not been sure of Ivy's whereabouts, I'd wonder quite seriously if she knew anything about Rachel's disappearance."

"Did you talk to the marshal?" Gwen questioned.

By this time several of the girls had apparently overheard their conversation and had moved closer to learn the truth of what was going on. Braeden sighed. He might as well make some form of public announcement. "Ladies, if you'll join us for a moment, there's something I need to share."

The girls quickly left their stations and tasks and came to stand beside Gwen and Braeden. "Miss Taylor is missing," Braeden announced matter-of-factly. "She disappeared last night and no one has seen anything of her since. That is, not unless someone here knows something about it." The girls shook their heads, their expressions showing their surprise.

"I didn't think so," Braeden said, continuing. "I'm getting ready to ride out to search for her. In the meantime, Miss Carson is in charge of the dining room. I'd appreciate it if you would keep an eye open for Miss Taylor. If you think of anything that might explain where she could be, or if you overhear something that could help us in our search, then by all means, please come to Miss Carson and give her the information."

"Ivy Brooks is missing too," Faith declared. "She was supposed to be here by now, but she never showed up."

"I wouldn't count on Ivy to show up this morning," Braeden replied, barely keeping the sarcasm from his voice. "She was a bit preoccupied last night."

"Oh, Braeden darling!"

Ivy's voice sounded from behind him, causing Braeden to turn in disbelief. He found it unbelievable that she would show her face after such a wanton display the night before. Had she no shame—no shred of embarrassment for her actions?

All of the Harvey Girls were staring at Ivy in disbelief. She was dressed in her uniform, but her hair was down and rather disheveled from what appeared to have been an early morning walk. But even this wasn't as shocking as her approach to Braeden.

Ivy reached out to touch Braeden's arm. "Something awful has happened. Something so very terrible." She pouted and batted her blue eyes at him, appearing to will the tears that formed there.

Braeden frowned. "Yes, I know." He despised her touch and moved away a pace to separate from her.

"No," she practically wailed, grabbing him again. "You don't know."

Braeden shook her off and raised a brow in question. "Then suppose you tell us what's happened now?"

"Aunt Esmeralda is dead!" she said, tears spilling from her eyes to her cheeks.

Braeden thought her to be a most consummate actress. He doubted the truth in what she said, but even if it were true, Ivy certainly would shed no tears of loss. Not if her actions from the past few days were any indication. He thought her rather hardhearted and callous—too callous to care whether Esmeralda lived or died.

"If Mrs. Needlemeier is dead, then why are you here?" Braeden asked rather coolly. "Shouldn't you be home planning out the funeral? You certainly aren't expected to work so soon after losing a loved one."

Just as the words were out of his mouth, Mr. Smith and several other Santa Fe officials, including Fred Harvey himself, appeared in the doorway of the dining room. Their stunned expressions indicated that they had overheard the latter portion of the conversation.

"Mrs. Needlemeier is dead?" Smith and Harvey questioned at the same time.

"Oh yes!" Ivy declared. "It's simply awful. She couldn't take the shock."

"What shock was that?" Harvey questioned.

Ivy stunned them all by throwing herself into Braeden's arms. "She came home and found us together. I knew it was wrong, but Braeden was most persuasive. I simply couldn't resist his superior strength and ardor."

Braeden realized she had him exactly where she wanted him. The entire room seemed to turn in unison to him for explanation. "She's lying," he said, trying to pry Ivy from his body.

"No, she's not!" Reginald Worthington declared. Everyone turned to acknowledge his statement. Seeing he held a captive audience, he continued. "I witnessed the scene myself. A more shameful display of forced attention I have never seen. Your Mr. Parker apparently is quite the rogue. He arranged to meet Miss Brooks when he knew she would be alone and unprotected, and now he scorns her."

Smith eyed Braeden in contempt. "You dallied with this young lady and now deny it?"

"I deny the entire matter. This young *lady*, as you call her, set up a scene of seduction to rival them all." Braeden realized how preposterous it all sounded even as he spoke the words. Ivy stood looking wide-eyed and stunned, tears glistening against her pale cheeks. Even

Gwen looked at him with a questioning expression that suggested disbelief. "It was entirely her doing, not mine. She has it in her mind that the Harvey establishment is her ticket to finding a wealthy husband. She knew I had no interest in her, but she pursued the matter with a vengeance."

"Is this true?" Fred Harvey asked Ivy, giving Braeden the briefest bit of hope that she would come to terms with his anger toward her and admit the truth.

Ivy sobbed. "No, it's not true. What woman of proper breeding would allow her reputation to be put into jeopardy in such a manner? After all, such events do bring about consequences."

Fred Harvey stepped forward, a scowl on his bearded face. "Young woman, are you telling me this man dishonored you?"

Ivy again reached for Braeden. "It wasn't all his fault. I should have known better—I did know better—but I've loved him since I first laid eyes upon him. But I knew about the rules, Mr. Harvey. I remembered meeting you in Topeka, and you said we weren't to date other Harvey employees." She dabbed her eyes most effectively and gave the slightest hint of a smile. "I know I dishonored my auntie, but Mr. Parker made me forget myself. I'm sorry, but my heart wouldn't listen."

Harvey and Smith both smiled. "It's understandable," Harvey replied. "But apparently now that this man has taken some sort of advantage of you, he seems reluctant to own up to his part in the matter."

"I had no part in the matter," Braeden declared angrily. This time he pushed Ivy away from him, nearly causing her to fall. Had a couple of the Harvey Girls not stepped forward to help Ivy regain her balance, she would have done just that.

"Oh, Braeden," Ivy said, tears streaming down her face. "Don't be like this. You know I love you, and I promise to be a good wife. I don't care what happened last night. I don't even care if I'm carrying your child right now." There were notable gasps from around the gathered audience. "I simply need you now more than ever. Auntie is dead and I'm all alone."

Smith moved forward. "Is this true? Mrs. Needlemeier is really dead?"

Ivy sobbed and brought the edge of her apron to her face. "Yes. We were discussing my behavior and the need for Mr. Parker to save my reputation and marry me when she succumbed to some sort of apoplexy and collapsed on the staircase."

"Then why are you here?" Braeden questioned. "Dressed for a day of work, no less."

"I couldn't bear to be there alone," Ivy said, meeting the sympathetic nods of Mr. Smith and Mr. Harvey. "I wanted to be with the one person I knew could offer me comfort. The man I love."

Braeden felt everyone turn their attention to him, as if he held the key to the entire puzzle. With a sense of animosity and irritation that he'd never known, Braeden shook his head. "I've had about all I'm going to stand of this. She's lying about there being anything between us," he said aloud, directing his gaze to Fred Harvey's doubtful expression. "She was jealous of the friendship I shared with Miss Taylor—a friendship developed long before I ever came to Casa Grande. I'm deeply ashamed to have fallen for such a manipulation, but in truth, I didn't know to what degree this young woman would stoop in order to eliminate her competition." Just then the thought of the rattlesnake came to mind. He frowned. The situation was beginning to clear, and he could see and understand more of what had once been clouded and obscured. "I think I'm starting to realize it now," he muttered.

Ivy once again moved to embrace him but stopped directly in front of him. "I'm not ashamed of my actions. I love you and no matter what, I'm not ashamed." She looked to Mr. Harvey. "I don't even mind bearing a child because of it. As long as it's *his* child."

"There is no child!" Braeden raged, unable to contain his anger. "Because there was nothing more than your errant plan to seduce me." He reached out as if to shake her, then stopped and stepped away. "I wouldn't marry you if you were the last available woman on earth. You are corrupt and conniving and you may lie all you like, but it won't change the matter."

"I say," Reginald stated, stepping closer to Ivy, "I witnessed the entire matter. There seemed to be no error on Miss Brooks's part. She was intoxicated, but that, too, came at the forced will of Mr. Parker."

"She came to me drunk!" Braeden declared.

Reginald's brow furrowed ever so slightly. "He was carrying her, half clothed, to a fainting couch. It was quite clear what had taken place, and what would have continued to take place."

"Is this true?" Fred Harvey asked Braeden seriously.

"No," Braeden replied, gritting his teeth together. "It's not true. Miss Brooks staged the entire thing in order to force herself upon me. She knows my interest lies elsewhere. Now the real crisis of the morning is not whether or not Miss Brooks's reputation has been ruined. It's not even that Mrs. Needlemeier has passed on to her eternal reward. The problem is that Rachel Taylor is missing and has been ever since she witnessed Miss Brooks's little charade last night."

"Missing? What do you mean?" Harvey questioned.

"I mean, no one has seen her since she fled the Needlemeier mansion. Worthington, here, went after her, but he claims to have had no luck in discovering her whereabouts."

Reginald shrugged. "I tried to follow her, but she was apparently running. She was completely gone from sight when I came out of the mansion, but I can't say I blame her. Mr. Parker had made suggestive promises to her as well. I think it simply devastated her to know that she had been duped into believing him honorable."

Braeden scowled and seethed at the suggestion that he had led Rachel astray. Supposition and lies had destroyed his life six years ago, and he would not stand for it to happen again.

Fred Harvey rubbed his bearded face. "This appears to be quite a disturbing situation. However, we can discuss this at length in private. Right now it would seem the dining room should be readied for breakfast. Who's in charge?"

Gwen stepped forward. "I am, sir. I'm the head waitress, Miss Carson."

Harvey nodded. "Very well, Miss Carson, I suggest you get your girls to their stations and ready yourself for the day. Miss Brooks, I believe you should return home and see to your aunt's funeral arrangements, and Mr. Parker—"

"I'm going to look for Rachel," Braeden interjected. "Fire me if you must, but that's what I'm going to do."

He turned without waiting for any other word on the matter and stalked across the lobby feeling nothing but anger blended with fear. Fear for Rachel—fear for himself. There was an entire audience of people who appeared to believe every word Ivy Brooks said. He would either be forced to leave his position or encouraged to marry Ivy, and neither option was one he wanted. He wanted Rachel, and he wanted to continue at Casa Grande with her at his side.

Tomas waited in the stable yard with four other mounted men. They were all dark skinned and filthy looking, but Tomas had supplied them with Casa Grande horses, and they appeared quite willing to help with the search.

"Tomas, you know this land better than I do, so I'd like for you to stay with me and act as a guide. The rest of you spread out and see what you can find. Miss Taylor has dark red hair and she stands about as tall as Tomas. She might be injured, so if you find her, fire off your gun once and the rest of us will come to you. Do you understand?"

Tomas relayed the information in Spanish just to make certain no one misunderstood the situation. When the four men nodded, Braeden mounted his horse and headed toward the open valley behind the stables.

"Wait up!" a voice called out from behind them.

Braeden turned to find Jeffery O'Donnell coming up fast from First Street.

"Glad you could make it," Braeden stated, trying hard to give the man a welcoming smile.

Jeffery brought his horse to a halt, kicking up a cloud of dust. "I couldn't sleep anyway. I would have been here sooner, but I wanted to check in at the depot and make sure she hadn't caught a train out of Morita. No one there has seen anything of her. What about here? Still no word?"

"None. No one has seen anything of her since yesterday evening. I've looked all around Casa Grande, but she just isn't here. Now we're going to head out and explore the countryside around the resort. She could have wandered off, not paying any attention to where she was going. Maybe she got lost."

Jeffery nodded. "I don't know my way around here very well, but I'll do what I can."

"I'm going out with Tomas. Why don't you go with one of the other men? They're all familiar with the area."

Jeffery looked to the four riders and questioned the man who appeared to be the oldest in the bunch. "May I ride with you?"

"Sí," the man said without further acknowledgment.

"Then let's get to it," Braeden said. "Let's plan to meet back here around noon." They all nodded and headed off in different directions, while Braeden watched them go. He felt a squeezing tightness in his chest as his mind asked a hundred questions he couldn't answer. What if they didn't find her? What if she had somehow left the area altogether? What if . . .

"Help me to find her, Lord," Braeden finally prayed. He pushed aside his worry and urged the horse forward. "Keep her safe and don't let harm come to her. Let her know the truth about me and what happened. Let her trust the love she has for me—the love I have for her." The prayer was barely whispered aloud, but Braeden wanted to shout it to the skies. He wanted to plead over and over for the life of this woman—but he knew he had to keep an eye on the trail. He had to remain alert and concentrate on anything that might give him a sign to Rachel's whereabouts.

They rendezvoused at noon without anyone having seen any sign of Rachel, and hours later, with a storm brewing on the horizon and the temperature dropping from the breezes off the thunderstorm, Braeden was growing increasingly worried. He studied the landscape around him as Tomas tested an obscure little trail that led up into the foothills. The sandy soil seemed stark and lifeless. An occasional flash of life came in the form of a jackrabbit or mouse, but that was it. Even the skies overhead seemed unusually empty.

His throat felt parched from the long day on the dusty trail, and tipping up his canteen, he was alarmed to find it nearly empty. They would have to find water or return to town.

"No one has passed this way, senor," Tomas told Braeden as he led his horse back down to where Braeden rested.

"Is there water nearby?" he questioned. "My canteen is nearly dry."

"We could go back to the river," Tomas suggested.

"If we do that, we might as well go back to Casa Grande."

"That might be best, senor. The storm is still coming this way, and it won't be long before we lose the light."

Braeden looked toward the mountains and then at the rapidly approaching weather. Reluctantly he nodded. "I know you're right. I just hate leaving her out here . . . wherever she is."

Tomas nodded, then turned his horse to head back in the direction they'd just come. "Maybe she's already gone back to Casa Grande."

Braeden tried to be encouraged by the thought but knew it was probably far from the truth. Rachel was gone—maybe forever. Braeden had never known anything that hurt so much as acknowledging this possibility.

IVY IGNORED MR. HARVEY'S SUGGESTION that she return home and instead took off to the room she shared with Faith and sequestered herself away to think. The turn of events over the last twenty-four hours left her rather breathless. And in light of her aunt's dying declaration that Ivy would be left penniless, Ivy knew she had to quickly secure herself in marriage to Braeden Parker.

The scene in the dining room had been an added bonus that Ivy had not counted on. She felt especially comforted by the fact that Fred Harvey himself seemed to completely believe her statements regarding Braeden. Surely she could count on the kindly man to force Braeden's hand. She could only hope that once faced with the idea of losing his job and his honorable name, he would succumb and marry her. *And why not?* Ivy reasoned. *It's not like I'm some pudgy farm girl with brown skin and freckles. I'm beautiful and cultured, and I would do him honor by becoming his wife.* She reclined on the bed and punched at her pillow.

"He doesn't have to know that I'm penniless," she said, stifling a yawn.

For several hours she slept, dreaming of life in a big city with a lovely house of her own and a bevy of servants to wait on her every need. She was exhausted from the night before—exhausted, too, from having to carefully consider her problem from every angle.

Faith appeared shortly after one o'clock, waking Ivy with her noisy movements around the room. After allowing the girl to change out of her uniform, Ivy ordered her to spend the day elsewhere and Faith quickly complied. There was no way Ivy wanted the addlebrained girl interfering with her plans. When Faith was present, Ivy found it hard to think with any clarity for all the questions the girl threw at her.

After Faith departed, Ivy got out of bed and began to systematically pace the room, pausing only long enough to grab up her hairbrush. Stroking her long blond hair, Ivy considered the gravity of her situation.

She grimaced as she thought of the scene in the dining room. It wasn't that it hadn't gone her way, because in truth it had seemed to leave everyone in a sympathetic mood toward her. Still, she saw the way Braeden looked at her. There was no compassion, no feeling except anger. He would fight her on this if it took everything in his power. And if she did manage to force him to the altar, he would despise her for the rest of her life, and maybe even punish her by remaining in Morita or moving them to some equally horrid little community.

Perhaps she could find a way to somehow sweeten the matter for him. Perhaps there was a way to entice him to see things in a new light, to make him see that this would be monetarily beneficial to him in the long run. But remembering her aunt's rejection, Ivy knew that wouldn't be possible. Then a thought came to mind. Maybe she could contact her aunt's lawyer. Perhaps she could work out an arrangement with him that would benefit them both if he would be willing to change the will. It could work! There wasn't anyone in the world who couldn't be bought. Hadn't her aunt taught her that by explaining her deal with the fire inspector?

She put down the hairbrush and went to her window. Directly outside her room were the stables. She'd be able to see and hear when Braeden returned, and when he did return, she would be waiting.

She'd force him to talk to her, to make plans for their future. If he didn't show up with Rachel, she might even lie and tell him that Rachel had returned only long enough to confront Ivy and relinquish any hold she had on Braeden. The thought held some intrigue for Ivy. Maybe she could talk Reg into helping her once again. Maybe with the knowledge that Rachel was gone for good, Braeden would give up holding out for her and marry Ivy.

But Ivy was smart enough to realize the empty promise of that thought and of all the others she'd had. Braeden would rot in jail before he married her. Especially now. Especially after her public humiliation of him.

Muttering a curse, Ivy dropped her hold on the curtain and moved back to sit on the bed. There had to be an answer to the problem, a way to fix the situation. Maybe she could force Braeden to marry her by enlisting the help of Fred Harvey. Perhaps Mr. Harvey could offer him a job elsewhere if he promised to treat Ivy with respect and love. She thought of the thin, well-dressed man and decided it was surely worth consideration. Fred Harvey seemed to run his affairs in a completely honorable manner. He would surely not desire a scandal for this, his newest of resorts. Perhaps Braeden, in turn, would value his job more than making Ivy pay for coming between him and Rachel.

The idea seemed plausible in Ivy's mind.

The wind picked up outside, causing Ivy to return to the window. Clouds were moving overhead, shadowing the land below. Ivy knew from her three years of living in Morita that this was a sure sign of a storm. Perhaps it would drive the searchers back sooner than expected. After all, it was now afternoon, and they wouldn't want to get caught out in the weather and the darkness.

I still have no set plan, she thought. *I must decide what is to be done in order to be prepared when he returns.*

She glanced at the clock. It wasn't yet two. Perhaps she should seek out Mr. Harvey and discuss the situation with him. She could better tell from his reaction how to handle Braeden when he returned.

Slipping out of her room, Ivy ignored the chattering girls in the parlor and quickly entered the kitchen. Seeing Reginald working at the far end, she decided to question him on the matter of Rachel before going to Fred Harvey. It was always possible that he would have a better idea how to carry out her plans. After all, he'd come through admirably for her the night before.

"Mr. Worthington," she spoke softly. "Might I have a moment of your time?"

Reg eyed her suspiciously for a moment, then nodded. "What is it?"

"I thought perhaps you could offer me some counsel."

"You've never seemed to need advice from anyone before now," Reg replied, rather disinterested.

"It would benefit us both if you would give me just a few moments of your time," Ivy insisted.

"And how do you suppose that?" he asked, finally stopping to give her his full attention.

"You seem more than a little interested in making a financial profit from your days at Casa Grande," Ivy stated, loudly enough so only Reg could hear. After having Reg explain his understanding of her involvement with the attempt on Rachel's life, Ivy had sent her own spies out to learn anything they could about Reg. It appeared he had more than one job at Casa Grande.

His expression never changed as he considered her words. "I'm sure I don't know what you mean, but if you are of a mind to seek my opinion—or as you say, counsel—then be my guest."

She smiled, feeling rather herself again as the control clearly passed to her hand. "I wondered that you were not out looking for Miss Taylor. After all, I know of your affection for her. Is this lack of interest because you already know of her whereabouts?" She hoped to completely throw him off base by suggesting something so out of line that he would forget her earlier words. She wasn't ready yet to tell him what she knew about his actions and hoped to use her knowledge as a final trump card should the occasion necessitate.

Reg remained stoic. "I wondered that you were not home mourning the loss of your aunt. Is it because you feel nothing in her passing? Unless, of course, what you feel is relief."

Ivy tried not to react to his piercing gaze. "That's nonsense. There's nothing I can do there. Aunt Esmeralda is in the hands of the mortician."

"So it is with Rachel. There is nothing I can do to aid her search. My job requires me here, and Mr. Parker seems completely capable."

"But you don't want *him* to find her, do you?" Ivy questioned quietly, glancing over her shoulder to make certain no one else overheard.

"After all, if he finds her, he might well convince her that what she saw was completely my fault."

"Which, of course, it was," Reginald replied. He gave his sauce a quick stir, then moved down the line to where he had arranged several platters. This put even more distance between the conspirators and the other kitchen staff members.

"Look, all I want is for Braeden to return so that I can discuss this matter with him in private. I figure once we do that, he'll come around to seeing things my way."

Reg smiled. "Oh, you think so?"

"And you do not?" Ivy questioned.

Focusing on the filleted chicken breasts, Reg shrugged. "All things are possible, or so they say. I simply believe you have given Mr. Parker an even more urgent desire to solidify his relationship with Miss Taylor. He is a desperate man at this point. And, Miss Brooks, desperation makes men do what they ordinarily wouldn't even consider."

"You talk as one who knows," Ivy said, eyeing him suspiciously.

Reginald smiled patiently. "I know a great many things, as you are well aware. My suggestion to you is to bide your time and your tongue. In Rachel's absence there are bound to be opportunities to speak to Mr. Parker, and in doing so, perhaps you can win him over to your way of thinking."

Ivy nodded. "Maybe. If Rachel isn't around to interfere, maybe I can convince him to——"

"Settle for you?" Reg asked with a sly grin.

Ivy felt her face flush. "No one settles for me. I chose Mr. Parker, and he'll soon see the merit in my choice. Otherwise, he'll find himself unemployed with no hope of ever securing another job on the Santa Fe."

She stormed off through the kitchen and out across the dining room, ignoring the soft comments of condolences people offered. Her only thought was to formulate a plan before Braeden returned from his search.

———

The wind picked up, blowing bits of sand and grit, stinging

Braeden's eyes. He'd managed to pull up the bandana from his neck and tie it around his face, but it did little to help shield his eyes.

"We go back," Tomas shouted above the wind. Lightning flashed in the distance, followed by a rumbling of thunder that unnerved the horses. As they danced around and pawed at the earth, Tomas added, "Storms here very bad."

Braeden realized his search was hopeless. "All right, let's go."

Frustration and misery coursed through his body. He felt as though he were deserting Rachel by returning to the resort. She was out there somewhere. But where? Urging their horses to pick up speed, Braeden couldn't help but issue another prayer for her safety. He felt so completely helpless, and the misery of it all left him defeated and drained of energy.

Back at the resort, Tomas took the horses and led them to the stable just as the first drops of rain started to fall.

"Braeden!" Jeffery called out as he came from the stable leading his horse. "I wondered if you'd make it back before the storm hit. Any luck?"

"No," Braeden replied, shaking his head. "You?"

"Nothing. No tracks—no sign of anyone having passed through in days."

"Same for us," Braeden said, his heart overwhelmed with grief. "I wish I knew where she was. I'm afraid for her."

Jeffery patted him on the back. "We'll have to keep praying. Look, I need to get home before this storm gets ugly. I'll ride over again tomorrow morning and we can try some different places."

"Thanks for your help. By the way," Braeden said, remembering Jeffery's injury, "how's the head?"

Jeffery shrugged. "Feels like I have an army marching through it, but I'd endure worse if it meant getting Rachel back safely. She's a good friend." He mounted his horse and secured the reins. "At this point, we have no choice but to wait it out. I know it would be foolish to say don't worry, because I know that this will be on my mind until it's settled. Still, try to get some rest. You look worse than I feel."

Braeden nodded, not at all enthused by the idea. He waited to go inside until Jeffery had left. With slow, heavy steps he mounted the stairs to Casa Grande, turned, then stared out past the fountains and circular drive, down across the lawn to the falls and powerhouse. Although he couldn't see the falls from where he stood, he could hear them and see the fine mist that rose up. The rain began coming down lightly at first, gradually increasing until he could scarcely see past the fountain. Lightning pierced the sky with light and thunder shook the ground as the storm came closer.

"Rachel, where are you!" Braeden yelled out against the fury of the storm. And even though the wind blew the rain up across the porch, drenching Braeden in the process, he felt a grave reluctance to go inside. It was as if by doing so, he was somehow further separating himself from Rachel.

Ivy watched as Braeden came wearily through the lobby door. Because he'd grown dusty from his ride, muddy rivulets were streaming down the side of his face and down his neck and arms. Still, he was handsome. He took off his hat and shook the water from it, then moved across the lobby to the front desk. Ivy watched him speak momentarily to the clerk, but the man only shook his head. *No doubt he's asking about her*, Ivy thought. Moving quietly from her vantage point just inside the empty dining room, Ivy waited until Braeden slipped behind the front desk to go into his office. He closed the door and Ivy hurried to approach the clerk.

"Mr. Worthington asked if you could come quickly to the kitchen. He only needs your help for a moment, and I'll watch the front desk while you're away," she told the man. She needed to get rid of him in order to gain entry into Braeden's office without interference.

The man looked at her for a moment. "What does he want with me?"

"He needs your help moving something. It'll just take a minute."

The man sighed and nodded. "Very well." He raised the gate to the front desk, then eyed Ivy rather sternly. "If someone needs help, just keep them here until I get back."

She smiled and nodded. "I promise I won't do anything more."

He left his post and crossed the lobby to the dining room, while Ivy waited until he was out of sight before entering Braeden's office.

She slipped inside quickly and closed the door just as Braeden came into his office from the bedroom. He was drying his hair with a towel and hadn't even seen that it was Ivy before issuing an angry retort.

"Don't you know how to knock, Wilson?"

"I do know how to knock, but I figured you wouldn't let me in if you knew it was me," Ivy replied softly.

Braeden drew the towel away from his head. "Well, you're right on that account. Now get out!"

"No." Ivy took a seat and stared at him intently. "We need to talk."

"There's nothing to be said," Braeden said, his voice low.

Ivy could see the anger flash in his eyes. His jaw clamped tight and his expression grew gradually more threatening. "Just hear me out and then I'll leave. You could certainly do that much. After all, I want to explain a few things."

"You've explained quite enough. Your lies this morning have probably cost me my job—not that it matters anymore. What does matter is Rachel. You've driven her away from safety and into harm's way. That's all I care about."

"If Rachel cared about you the way you claim to care about her, she'd be here defending you. Instead, she's taken off to who knows where," Ivy said defiantly. "I don't think she cares as much as you'd like to believe. She saw the scene in my parlor and believed what her heart told her to be true. If she loved you, she would believe in you. And if she believed in you, she'd be here now."

Braeden let the towel fall around his neck as he leaned over to place both hands on his desk. "I don't want to discuss this with you."

"Well, I think you'd better reconsider," Ivy replied. She twirled a strand of hair and smiled. "There are worse things than losing employment with Mr. Harvey. This decision could affect the rest of your life."

"You can't threaten me, Ivy," Braeden answered angrily. "You've already driven away the only thing I care about. But mark my words. I will find her."

"You don't need her. She doesn't love you."

"Oh, and you do, I suppose?"

"No, not yet," Ivy admitted.

"I think that's the only truth I've ever heard come out of your mouth."

"You are handsome, however. With a pleasant face to look at and a comfortable amount of money to live on, I could learn to love anyone. What *is* important is that I want you. You represent freedom from this miserable hole of a town."

"How can I possibly represent that to you?" Braeden questioned in surprise.

"Because after we are married I want to move east to St. Louis." She suddenly remembered her aunt's words about the fire inspector knowing she'd started the fatal fire that killed her parents. "No, not St. Louis. Chicago. Or New York. I want a big house and beautiful things and lavish clothes. You can give me all of that. My aunt said you are wealthy and—"

Braeden began to laugh. He sat down at his desk and shook his head. "You are quite insane, Ivy. I will never marry you. Go have your talk with Fred Harvey. Talk to the president of the United States. It won't change a thing. You are right; I have enough money to live comfortably without this job. My father was a wise investor and his investments continue to pay off. I chose to continue working because I enjoy the challenge of using my mind for something more than sitting around the house or going on grand tours of Europe. I chose this particular job because I knew Rachel was here." He eyed her distastefully and shook his head. "You are nothing to me. You will never be anything more than the adversary you have set yourself up to be."

"But why not?" Ivy asked, suddenly sounding very much like a little girl. "I'm a beautiful woman. Far more beautiful than Rachel Taylor. I have grace and charm and know how to conduct myself in proper circles."

"And you're a liar," Braeden replied. "An unfeeling deceiver who acts without remorse for the hideous things you've done. Believe me, Ivy, your looks could never hold a candle to Rachel's beauty. Not only is she beautiful in appearance, but her heart is pure and good and that makes her even more lovely.

"You, however, are selfish and self-motivated. You choose the path that will give you the most satisfaction. There is nothing of goodness in you. The woman I marry will love God and will seek to conduct herself in a Christian manner for all of her days. Rachel is that woman. Not some devious little harlot who has no remorse for her actions."

Ivy took a sharp breath, taken aback. She thought of her parents and the servants who perished in the fire. She thought of her aunt's crumpled form at the bottom of the stairs. She even thought for the briefest moment of Rachel's stunned and pain-filled expression. It wasn't that she had set out to inflict pain . . . not really. She simply wanted what was important to her. No one could possibly understand that she'd never intended for anyone to die in the fire. Neither would they believe her if she said she was sorry. And she was sorry. At least where her parents were concerned.

"I've done what I had to do," Ivy finally said. "You don't belong with someone like Rachel. She's much too common and plain. I can be much more to you. I can attend church as you wish, and I can be the docile wife you desire. In the years to come, you'll see that this was the wisest thing and you'll thank me for saving you."

"In the years to come, I will look back on this time as my darkest hours—those hours spent without Rachel." Braeden narrowed his eyes. "I don't suppose you have any idea of her whereabouts."

Ivy smiled. "If I did, do you think I would ruin all that I've planned and tell you?"

Braeden clenched his teeth and a rumble from deep in his throat sounded very much like a suppressed growl. Ivy refused to be concerned by it, however.

"We can marry tomorrow," she said firmly. "I'll talk to the preacher after I leave here."

Slamming his fists down on the desk, Braeden raged. "I won't marry you tomorrow or any day. I don't love you, Miss Brooks. I love Rachel Taylor. You are nothing to me but trouble. You have deeply wounded the woman I love, and while I shall forgive you, I won't ever forget."

Deeply shaken, Ivy fought hard to remain stoic. "You will learn to love me. I'm beautiful, and I'm sure we will find ways to—"

"Your outward appearance may be pleasing, but inside you are frightfully hideous," Braeden interrupted. "Marriage is about more than physical attraction. It's about commitment."

"We could be committed to each other."

"Maybe you could be committed to an asylum," Braeden said sarcastically.

"I'll ruin you if you refuse me."

Braeden shook his head. "Don't you understand? Without Rachel, none of this matters. Ruin me. Take my job. Turn them all against me. It doesn't matter, because *you* don't matter. Not to me, anyway."

Ivy suddenly realized he meant what he said. He found her abhorrent. No one had ever treated her in such a manner. She felt sick inside, unable to shake off the sense of dread. If she couldn't have him by choice, she'd take him by force. She could do this. She only had to think her plans through in a clear and concise manner. "You'll be condemned," she muttered.

"Not by those who matter. Not by Rachel, and not by God."

"You're already condemned by Rachel," Ivy retorted. She had to make him see the truth of the situation. "As for God, who knows what He thinks?"

"He hates lies," Braeden countered.

Ivy shook her head. "He understands why I did what I did."

"Yes, you're right. He does. He knows your motives and He knows exactly why and what you have done," Braeden replied ominously.

Ivy got to her feet, feeling rather unnerved by Braeden's certainty regarding God. "Don't think to threaten me, Braeden Parker. Everyone in that dining room this morning perceives you as a ruthless molester of helpless young women. If you don't marry me, you'll be stripped of everything, including your reputation and self-worth."

Braeden smiled and seemed to calm in the wake of their harshly spoken words. "You can't destroy my self-worth, Miss Brooks. God has given me a sense of self-worth through His love for me. I find my identity in Him—not in this place, this job."

"I thought you found all of that through Miss Taylor," Ivy said snidely. She was confused by his calm and thought feverishly for something more to say. She was losing him—losing her chance for a new start.

"Rachel gives from her heart. She loves me and I love her,"

Braeden replied. "But even if Rachel were gone for good, I would still find my hope and my future in God. That's something you can't understand, Miss Brooks. And it's something I can't explain. So go say what you will. Tell all the lies you think will serve your cause. But you won't win me over, and you won't be my consolation in Rachel's absence."

Braeden got up and walked around his desk. Ivy felt threatened by the action, even though he was much calmer than when she'd first come into his office. She backed up a step, but still he came forward.

"I want you out of my office. Now."

She backed up to the door and shook her head. "You don't know what you're saying. You don't know what might happen. What has already happened."

Braeden eyed her seriously. "If you know something about Rachel, you'd better tell me."

Ivy realized the power she could hold and felt a bit of her confidence return. "You weren't the only man to love Rachel," she said, standing her ground. "Rachel will seek protection and safety with someone she can trust. After what happened last night, you can't possibly believe that she would come to you."

"Where is she, Ivy?" he asked, moving in even closer.

Ivy felt excitement course through her body. She held the answers and now controlled the outcome. Even though she'd have to lie, she could weave a web of deceit that would permanently put an end to Braeden's illusions that Rachel loved him.

"I'm not the one to ask," she finally told him. "Rachel's been spending a great deal of time with Mr. Worthington, as you probably already know. She finds solace with him—comfort and maybe even that love you speak of so freely. Reg is really a wonderful man, and he is fiercely protective of Rachel. You can't deny the way he watched over her last night, and he left right after she did."

Ivy toyed with the doorknob. "If Rachel wanted you to know where she was, Braeden, she would have told you by now. She hasn't left Morita; she's merely taking refuge where you cannot harm her."

Turning the knob, Ivy was surprised when Braeden's hand slammed down on top of hers. "I mean it, Ivy. If you know where she is, tell me." He pressed down hard on her hand as if to emphasize the threat.

Ivy refused to be frightened, however. "Half-truths and rumors destroyed your lives long ago. I heard her telling this to Reg," she lied, for in fact she had overhead Rachel explaining the matter to Braeden. "So take this as you like," Ivy said, opening the door in spite of the pressure to her hand. "Rachel won't be turning to you this time around. She has someone else who is only too happy to fill in where you left off. If you don't believe me, just ask Reginald how he feels about Rachel."

She smiled and walked through the door, coming face-to-face with a very put-out Mr. Wilson. Turning, she saw the discomfort in Braeden's expression and couldn't help but play on his fears. "Oh, and you might also ask him why he's not been overly worried or eager to go chasing about the countryside looking for Rachel. Seems to me that, given his feelings for her, if he thought she were really missing he'd move heaven and earth to find her." She saw the look in Braeden's eyes and knew she'd hit her mark. Striving to drive in the final blow, she shrugged nonchalantly. "I've no doubt she's safe, Braeden. Reg wouldn't let harm come to her."

THE NEXT MORNING Reginald had just completed explaining to his staff the process for stripping the meat from a lobster shell when a bleary-eyed Braeden Parker came into the kitchen. In spite of his exhaustion, he looked like a man with a determined purpose, and Reg had little doubt he was there to confront him about Rachel.

"You must collect all of the meat from the shells," Reg told his assistants. "But leave the brain for later. We will mix that with soft butter and add to the mixture later. Be very careful, as we will need every bit of lobster we can lay our hands on." The shipment of fresh lobsters had been shorted by thirty of the little beasts, and Reginald knew he would have to perform a minor miracle to make the food stretch for the huge banquet and party planned that night. Tonight would be the final celebration of the grand opening, and besides the banquet, there were refreshments for the formal ball that was to be given later that night.

"Mr. Worthington, I would like a moment of your time," Braeden said, coming to stand directly in front of the chef.

Reginald looked up and nodded. "Very well. Shall we go to the storage room or perhaps your office?"

"Given that the dining room is already full to capacity," Braeden began, "I suggest we stay here or step outside. I really don't want to have to walk through that crowd again."

"As you wish," Reginald replied. "Since the morning temperatures are rather cool, let us move to the storage room, where we might have less interference."

Braeden followed after him, and Reginald couldn't help but wonder how he would handle the big man if he decided to turn loose with a bout of temper. If Parker chose to use his fists instead of his mouth, Reg knew he'd be in trouble. Still, Parker seemed capable of controlling his anger—at least up until now. Perhaps he was worried over nothing.

But upon meeting Braeden's harsh glare, Reg wondered if he'd done something very stupid by isolating himself with Casa Grande's co-manager. Backing up against the delivery conveyor, Reg felt his pulse quicken. The man's eyes positively burned with a fire that suggested he would stop at nothing—nothing at all, in order to learn the truth.

"I want some answers and I want them now," Braeden said in a no-nonsense sort of fashion.

"I will tell you whatever I can," Reg replied calmly.

"Do you know where Rachel is?"

Reg raised a questioning brow. "Why would you ask me that? I already spoke to you on the matter the other night. I'm the one who suggested a search party."

"I'm asking you because Ivy Brooks implied that you are hiding Rachel away from me, that Rachel sought her solace with you, and that my searches will prove futile."

Reg smiled. So that conniving little idiot had put Parker on him, after all. She'd implied to know things about Reg's activities at Casa Grande, and while he had no idea what she actually knew, he wasn't about to allow her the upper hand. "Parker, I care a great deal about Rachel, but Ivy Brooks means her nothing but harm. She would tell you anything in order to get you on her side. She set her sights on winning you over, and Rachel was an interference in her plans. Knowing Ivy even as little as I do, I realize she would do or say whatever she had to in order to eliminate her competition."

"What is your point?"

"I'm saying that Ivy has the ability to accomplish pretty much whatever she wants. As you guessed, she planned that little seduction scene at the Needlemeier mansion. She told me her plans."

"She told you the truth and you lied? You let everyone out there believe me to have harmed her—destroyed her reputation. Why?"

"Because I love Rachel," he replied simply. "And I knew so long as Rachel was deceived into believing you deserved her love, she would go on believing in you and loving you."

"Why, I ought to—"

"Tut, tut, Mr. Parker," Reg said, pressing hard against the rollers on the conveyor belt as Braeden advanced. "If you refuse to contain your temper, I will not continue to explain."

Braeden's face contorted in anger, but he held back and nodded. "Then explain."

Reg nodded. "Ivy told me of her desire to have you for her husband, and given the fact that I wanted very much for Rachel to think of me as a prospect for her lifelong mate, I agreed to help her with her arrangement. But I also did it out of fear for Rachel."

"Fear for Rachel? I don't understand."

"Ivy will stop at no length to harm Rachel. If she can't scare her off and force Rachel to leave on her own accord, I feared Ivy might actually try to eliminate the dear woman."

"Why would you say that? Do you have reason to believe Ivy would do physical harm to Rachel?"

"Not only do I think she would, I know she would. I know about the rattlesnake." Braeden paled and Reg nodded. "That's right—the one Gwen told you about. Ivy planted it there. Well, not exactly Ivy. She paid to have it done and then hid the man in her room after he hit Mr. O'Donnell over the head. She simply slipped him out her window and no one was the wiser for her actions."

"No one but you," Braeden said flatly. "If you knew about this, why didn't you go to the proper authorities?"

Reginald smiled. "Because it gave me power over Miss Brooks. And, as you have witnessed her vengeance and her conniving ways, I believe you understand what it might mean to hold at least a marginal amount of influence over that young woman."

"That snake could have killed whomever opened the drawer," Braeden said angrily.

"Yes, but I knew it was somewhere in the office, and when you all left to help Mr. O'Donnell, I planned to take the matter into my own hands."

"Only you didn't have to because Gwen Carson handled the situation."

"Yes," Reg said, nodding. "Quite a woman there."

"Yes, she is quite a woman, and she wouldn't have deserved to have been bitten by that snake either. You should have come forward before it went that far."

"Until I saw the situation being arranged and followed the man, I had no real idea as to what he was about. But that aside, you must understand that I went along with Ivy for Rachel's sake. I couldn't have another attempt on her life. She's too precious. I think even you would have to admit that protecting her was far more important than worrying about your reputation. Ivy told me that if I didn't help her, she would see to it that Rachel suffered. I didn't want to see Rachel in further danger."

"But she may be in danger at this very minute," Braeden said, eyeing Reg suspiciously. "That is, unless you know otherwise. In which case, I demand to know the truth."

Reg crossed his arms and tried his best to appear completely at ease. "Mr. Parker, I do not trust you, neither do I like you. You epitomize that typical American male mentality of taking what you want and worrying about the consequences at a later time. If in fact you have to suffer those consequences at all. But my feelings are unimportant. I believe, however, that after spending time with me, Rachel has come to see the difference in how men of proper breeding conduct themselves. I believe she cherishes the more gentile nature she finds in me, and I doubt very much that she cares for you anymore. Especially given your indiscretions with Ivy Brooks."

"Did she tell you that?"

"She didn't have to say it with words—her face told me everything I needed to know. I believe it told you the truth as well. I saw the exchange between you two. You know she believes the worst. You know she believes you to have taken up a dalliance with Miss Brooks. And because her trust was fixed on such fragile ground with you, you must also realize that such a blow would surely destroy any remaining love she held for you."

Braeden took two steps forward and stopped directly in front of Reginald. "If you know where she is," he said in a low, menacing voice, "you'd be wise to tell me."

"I don't know where she is," Reginald replied. "I wish I did. I certainly wouldn't be here if I had the opportunity to take her away from this mess. I have abhorred this place from the moment I arrived and had very nearly made up my mind to go back to New York when I met Rachel. I only stayed because of her. I only stay now because of her."

Braeden shook his head. "She loves me. I know she still loves me."

"Then you are a fool, Mr. Parker." Reg moved to the side and slipped past Braeden while he appeared to contemplate that final statement. "Now, if you'll excuse me, I have a party to prepare for."

"If you love her so much, then why aren't you out there looking for her instead of sitting here planning for a party?" Braeden suddenly asked. "I think you know where she is, and because you know her to be safe and out of danger, you are merely going about your business."

Reg turned at the door. "Think what you like, Mr. Parker. But remember this, I am a man with connections. I needn't do my own dirty work when there are so many people desperate for a job. I might not be out looking for her, but that doesn't mean I haven't hired others to be doing just that. Just ask around. Ask Tomas. He went with you yesterday, but today he's already gone, working for me. He was, in fact, under my pay yesterday. So don't judge my appearance here to be a sign of indifference. I know I am hardly cut out for the physical demands of searching the wilderness for Rachel, but I would never stand by idly while she's missing."

With that, he left Parker to consider his words. It irritated him that the man would question him when it came to Rachel, but he quickly dismissed it. Even more irritating was Ivy Brooks. He couldn't help but wonder what she might mean to his plans. He had a job to do, and the last thing he needed was the interference of that child.

Still, by sharing what he knew with Braeden, he had turned the tables on Ivy Brooks. He had explained his participation in her little charade, and Braeden couldn't argue that he had been perfectly justified in the choices he'd made. Smiling to himself, Reg felt a deep sense of satisfaction. Now, if only he could convince Rachel that Braeden's loyalty lay elsewhere.

Reg waited an hour after Braeden had taken off to search for Rachel before getting down to business. He had watched Braeden load up his supplies, speak to Fred Harvey and the marshal, and then take his leave. One thing Reg had to say for the man, he was driven and he was persistent.

Making certain that the kitchen staff and Harvey Girls were busy with preparations for the noon meal, Reginald picked up a small box and headed out of the kitchen. He paused at the delivery entrance to make certain no one was observing him, then removed his white chef's coat and hat and donned his tweed jacket before making his way down the road.

Taking a seat on one of the park benches, Reg waited for several minutes before he opened the box and began nibbling at the brunch he'd packed for himself. He needed the quiet moments to better organize his ideas, and looking back up at Casa Grande, he knew his plans would have to come together soon. Smith was counting on him, and so far things had run in a smooth and orderly course. Reginald needed to ensure that nothing disturb their undertaking.

Movement down below on the lower portion of the fall's pathway caused Reg to sit up and take notice. He continued eating, pretending to be unconcerned with the approach of two dark-skinned natives.

"Senor," the first of the two men said as they approached the bench where Reg sat.

"Yes, how can I help you?"

"You are the cook, are you not?" the man questioned.

Reg stiffened. "I am the head chef of Casa Grande."

"Good," the man said, smiling. "Pablo said you would very much like some extra help."

Reg relaxed a bit and nodded. "I'm always looking for good help. Come see me later in the kitchen. Let's say around eight o'clock."

The men nodded and continued toward Casa Grande as if the

conversation had never taken place. Smiling to himself, Reg felt a sense of accomplishment.

After half an hour of mental contemplation, Reg finally repacked the remaining food and made his way back to the kitchen. His mind was consumed with what he had to do tonight, for both the banquet and the initiation of his well-thought-out task. Yet he was also consumed with Rachel.

When night fell and there was still no sign of Parker, Reginald decided the time had arrived for him to make his move. After meeting the two men he'd spoken to earlier in the day, where he handed them a great deal of money and whispered instructions, he waited until both men slipped out of the room before doing likewise.

Now he felt a sense of elation and excitement. It wouldn't be much longer, he reasoned. He would soon be on a train bound for Chicago and then New York, and from there he would take a steamer home to England. And Rachel would be at his side.

He pulled on his coat and stepped outside. He cursed the electrical lighting, which added illumination from the various streetlights in front of Casa Grande. Complete darkness would have suited his purposes much better, but with a sigh he realized he would simply have to make do. He stole across the open lawn and let the shadows swallow him as he neared the falls. The gentle roar offered him comfort as he maneuvered down the narrow walk to the powerhouse. The noise, like the shadowy darkness, offered him more in the way of coverage, and Reg was no fool. He knew he needed to remain completely hidden throughout his mission. Smith had stressed over and over that no one could know of the matter, and though Reginald had hired the two men to help him, he had no doubts that the men would not survive the ordeal once everything was in motion.

Quietly, he opened the powerhouse door and, with one last backward glance, slipped inside. The room was dimly illuminated from one single light in the corner. The power was generally shut off after a certain time of night, but with the grand opening and the long nightly celebrations, arrangements had been made to leave the power on throughout the night. The situation would either serve Reg's purpose or oppose it—he hadn't really decided which way it would be.

Moving to the back of the room, Reg picked his way through the maze of buzzing belts and humming machinery. He knew very little about power stations, but it was of no concern. Nothing mattered now—nothing but the success of accomplishing what Smith had sent him here to do.

Lifting a trapdoor, Reg gingerly made his way down the ladder. He reached up to his right and felt for the light cord. Finding it, he gave it a yank and light flooded the lower level of the powerhouse. Here the noise of the waterwheel and belts were marginally diminished, but not by much. He glanced around and found to his satisfaction that stacks of linens and silver were securely stored away for future sale. He smiled as he thought of the ingenious plan to sell off the most valuable pieces of Casa Grande. He thought of how he manipulated the inventory and how pleased Smith would be with his share of the money.

Hearing a noise, his smile broadened. The most valuable treasure of all awaited just around the final stack of crates. Rachel Taylor.

"I came to make sure you were all right," he said softly. She was bound and gagged and could in no way communicate with words, but her eyes flashed anger and fear that made him feel the need to explain.

"You are quite right to be put out with me," he said, coming to sit beside the small cot where she lay. "I don't suppose you'll believe this, but I've done this for your own good. You have to understand. There is about to be a tragedy, and I don't want you anywhere near harm's way."

Her eyes widened and she muttered something from beneath the gag. Realizing that no one would ever hear her above the roar of the power station and the waterfalls, Reg pulled the cloth from her mouth and smiled. "Better?"

"I want you to let me go," she managed to say before a spell of coughing hit her. "Water, please," she pleaded.

Reg got up quickly and walked to where the Casa Grande goods were stacked. He pulled out one of the crates and searched until he found a small silver sugar bowl. It would have to do, he decided. He went to the far end of the station, to the place where the waterwheel was partially exposed and water splashed over the edges of the paddles. Carefully, so as not to get his arm caught by the wheel, he extended the bowl and collected the water for Rachel. It wasn't exactly cold, having come from the hot springs, but it had cooled considerably as it had blended with other streams that joined to form Morita Falls.

"Here," he said as he made his way back to her. He helped to lift her to a sitting position and held the bowl to her lips. "I'll bring you something to eat later."

Rachel drank the entire contents before pulling away to look Reg in the eye. "Why are you doing this to me? I trusted you and thought we were friends."

Reg felt the sting of her accusation. "I did what I did in order to protect you. You have to understand that. I know what Parker is and why he's done what he has. He sees Ivy as his ticket to wealth and power. He can run Morita and lack for nothing."

"I don't believe you. Braeden didn't do anything wrong. I'm sure what we saw was all Ivy's doing. She thinks if she can convince her aunt that Braeden has dishonored her, Mrs. Needlemeier will force him to marry her. But that will never happen."

Reg shook his head and reached his hand up to gently touch Rachel's cheek. "You're wrong. They are already married."

"What?" Rachel asked, jerking away from his touch. "What are you saying?"

Her voice rang of desperation, and Reginald instantly felt sorry for having grieved her. "I say, I know this comes as a shock. But you have me. I won't allow Parker's actions to further hurt you."

"They're married?"

"Yes. In fact, they've already taken the train east."

"I don't believe you," Rachel said, recoiling against the wall. With her feet tied to the end of the cot and her arms tied behind her back, it was difficult to maneuver, but she was accomplishing the job nevertheless.

Reg shrugged. "I'm so sorry to be the one to give you bad news. I never wanted to see you hurt. I know you loved Parker, but I hope that with this turn of events, you might come in time to love me. I want to take care of you, Rachel. I want to take you away from this hurt and pain you've suffered because of Parker's indiscretion."

"That was Ivy's doing. I know it was." She sounded even more desperate, almost pleading.

Reg knew she wanted him to confirm her suspicions and because it caused her such pain, he decided to give her that much. "Yes, it was Ivy's plan. She told me all about it and enlisted my help."

"You?" Rachel said, shaking her head. "But why would you help her? I thought you were my friend."

"It was because of our friendship that I agreed to help her," he said softly. "I wanted to prove to you once and for all that Parker was not what he seemed. He didn't deserve your heart or your trust. Ivy told me she could help prove this to you by setting a scene where Parker would come to her and behave in a less than honorable way. She would get what she wanted, and I would get what I wanted."

"And what was it you wanted?" Rachel questioned, her expression still betraying her disbelief.

"I wanted you. I want you to love me," Reginald admitted.

"I can't love you, Reg," Rachel replied flatly. "I have loved Braeden for so long that I don't know how to love anyone else in that way. I had resigned myself to spend the rest of my life alone, and then he reappeared in my life. I'm sorry, but he has my heart and always will. Now, won't you please let me go? I promise not to tell anyone that you've been keeping me here. I just need to see him."

Reg leaned back against the beat-up chair on which he sat. He eyed her seriously for several moments and shook his head. "He's not there. I've already told you. They were married yesterday, and Mr. Harvey demanded they pack their things and go. You know his rules. The man was positively livid. Mr. Parker had no choice."

Rachel blanched and Reg realized he'd finally hit upon a truth she had no doubt of. "Ivy made a big scene yesterday morning. You don't know this, but her aunt is dead. She succumbed to the shock of seeing Ivy and Braeden together."

"No!" Rachel gasped.

"It's true," Reg replied. "Ivy showed up at the hotel and announced this. Mr. Smith and Mr. Harvey were both on hand to receive the news and, well . . . one thing led to another and the truth about the night before came pouring out. Ivy was distraught because of her aunt's death, and Braeden was sympathetic and concerned for her. I suppose no one thought much of the matter until she mentioned the possibility of being with child. That was when Braeden decided they should be married."

Tears came to Rachel's eyes as she shook her head. "I don't believe you, Reg. Why are you lying to me?"

"Listen," he said, reaching out to touch her again. She pulled away, but he didn't let it stop him. He wanted to feel the softness of her cheek, the silky curls of her hair. He wanted to breathe in the scent of her perfume. Without warning, he grabbed her and pulled her across the cot and into his arms. "I don't want you hurt," he murmured against her ear. He tightened his grip as she struggled against him. "I want to take care of you. I love you, Rachel."

"No," Rachel said, fighting his hold.

"Shhh," he whispered. "You must understand. There are things that will happen tonight. Things I can't explain. You must stay here and be safe, and when it is over I will come for you."

"No! Let me go! I won't go away with you. I won't!" she declared.

Reg frowned, realizing she might not be the grateful, fragile being that he had earlier presumed. He might have to resort to other means in order to get her out of Casa Grande without having to answer a lot of questions or deal with an unpleasant scene.

"I need your cooperation, Rachel. You know about the missing inventory now. But it's only a part of my scheme. If you hadn't found my men hiding the materials, you might not be here now. But since you are, I can better protect you from harm. In the long run, after we're in England and married, you'll understand that my love has kept you safe tonight."

Rachel became still in his arms. She looked up, shaking her head. "Reg, you've gone mad. You mustn't think that you can steal me away like this. I won't go willingly, and how will you explain that? No minister will marry us without my permission, and I will never give it. You are a sick man and you need help."

"I assure you that I am quite sane," Reg said, thinking how pleasant it would be to kiss her lips. He had nearly convinced himself to do just that but decided against it. No, he would preserve her purity and innocence until they were married. It was only right.

Lowering her back onto the cot, he tossed aside the gag. "I don't suppose this much matters," he said, looking at the piece of cloth. "The machinery is loud enough to keep your screams from carrying, and if not that, then the waterwheel. Besides, in a few hours I'll be back to take you away and there will be enough commotion that no one will even remember that you're missing."

"Braeden will remember," she said, sniffing loudly as tears streamed from her eyes.

"He might remember you, but I doubt Ivy will allow him little more than his memories," Reg said. He pulled out his watch and got to his feet. "I have to go. There are plans to set in motion." He smiled down at her. "Don't be afraid, my beautiful Rachel. I'll come back for you."

He left her there crying. He felt horrible that he could not offer her comfort. She had called him mad, and maybe he was. The lure of money had driven him to do this job. And when it was all said and done, he would have enough money to retire quietly to England and reclaim the family holdings that had been sold to cover his mother's debts. He would spend a quiet life with Rachel, and maybe they would even have children. Little curly-headed children like their mother.

Stepping into the darkness of the night, Reg was nearly knocked over by a powerful gust of wind. The air chilled him to the bone and made him pull his coat tighter. Crossing to the resort, he was nearly startled out of his wits when Tomas called his name.

"Senor Worthington," the boy said, coming quietly out of the shadows. "I have your money."

Reg smiled. The boy had been an excellent help in moving the stolen goods and selling them in Santa Fe and elsewhere. "You've done a good job by me, Tomas," Reginald said as he took the cash. He handed a portion over to the boy and added, "This is your share." He glanced upward toward the mountains as another gale whipped down and moaned through the trees, chilling them both. "It would probably be best if you slept at home tonight."

Tomas looked at him with a questioning expression. He opened his mouth as if to speak, then nodded and pocketed the money.

"It has been good to work with you, Tomas. Why don't you come into the kitchen and take what food you would like for your family?"

"Truly, senor?"

"We won't be needing it," Reg said flatly, slipping the money into his jacket pocket. He looked at the boy and smiled again. "We won't be needing any of it."

❦ TWENTY-SIX ❧

REG MADE HIS WAY UPSTAIRS to his room after the revelry of the ball died down. He was confident of his plans and in having had no contact with Braeden Parker since morning. Perhaps this entire matter would be easier than he'd previously thought.

Once inside his room, he pulled out his suitcases and began to pack. There was much to consider and much to remember. Tonight's plans would have to run in perfect order or innocent people would suffer, and while he had no problem in watching the guilty endure such trauma, he would have no part in creating undeserving victims.

He threw his clothes into the cases in a haphazard manner and went to retrieve his toiletry articles. Forcing himself to slow down and breathe deeply, Reg tried to pace his actions. There was no hurry, no need to rush. Everything would come about in its proper time. His superiors would be pleased and proud to have him as an associate, and he, in turn, would be rich.

As if conjuring up Mr. Smith with that thought, Reg opened the door to find the jittery man on the other side. "Is everything ready?" Smith tenuously questioned.

Reg smiled. "Of course it is. Did you doubt me?"

Smith took a hesitant step inside the room. He leaned against the open door and pulled out a handkerchief to wipe his sweaty forehead.

"It's just so important that this matter be resolved. I have to have that money."

Nodding, Reg went to his suitcase and pulled out an envelope. "Here's your share of money from the sale of the stolen goods. I think you'll be rather pleased."

Smith nodded and moved forward to lessen the distance between them, without thinking to close the door behind him. Somewhere down the lighted corridor a door slammed, causing Smith to jump. Panic-stricken, he looked over his shoulder, then snatched the cash. "It will help, but it won't come near to being the hundreds of thousands I need."

"Well, then," Reg said, straightening up, "it will only be a matter of time until the insurance money comes through and you have all that you need. As for me, I plan to make my way to England immediately. You may forward my share there. I'll leave you my address."

Smith nodded. "You're that certain this is going to work?"

"I am very confident of the matter. I've kept everyone in the dark about this plan. Even the two men I hired to do some of the dirty work only know a small part. You'll see. This will come together in such perfect order that no one will be the wiser for it."

"How will you set the fire?" Smith asked softly.

"It's better you don't know all the details. You can't be condemned for what you don't know," Reg replied. "Oh, and here are those papers I took from Miss Taylor's office. Rather useless in their content, but they served the purpose of creating a minor distraction, just as ransacking Parker's office set that poor man off on a wild chase."

"I don't think it was the mess you made of his office that set him off on the chase," Smith replied. "He's bent on finding Miss Taylor, and I can't say I blame him. She seems like a very nice young woman. I only pray she remains unharmed."

Reginald frowned and retrieved the last of his clothing from the closet. "She is a wonderful woman—a woman whom I intend to make my wife."

"Your wife? But I thought her interest was in Parker."

"It was. But that is in the past. She loves me now and plans to share a life with me in England."

"I see. Then I suppose you know where she is," Smith said, wiping his forehead again. When Reginald refused to acknowledge this statement one way or another, Smith continued. "Well, after you burn this place to the ground, I don't much care *whom* you hitch yourself up with."

"Well, I do," Braeden said, casually leaning against the doorjamb. "I think the marshal here would probably care as well."

Marshal Schmidt came to stand in the middle of the doorway but said nothing. Braeden eyed Reg with a look that demanded the truth. Reg knew the man would not leave without answers to his questions.

"It seemed rather strange that you and Tomas should spend so much time pouring over inventory sheets when there was so much else necessary to ready this place for the grand opening," Braeden began. "It also seemed strange that Rachel's inventory stopped disappearing, at least according to your tallies, while mine continued to show discrepancies."

He walked toward Smith and Worthington, appearing for all the world as though they were about to discuss the weather. "Of course, Tomas was really rather good at giving us the slip on more than one occasion. Weren't you, Tomas?" he called out, and the boy sheepishly appeared to stand beside the marshal.

"You see," Braeden continued, watching Reg carefully, "Tomas has just given us a full confession. He explained how you approached him to help you steal valuable articles from Casa Grande and how he's used the money to help his family. Tomas had a very honorable reason for his thievery, but I wonder what your reason might have been, Mr. Worthington."

Reg shrugged and nervously twisted his hands. "The boy is lying, and you don't frighten me with your bullying ways."

"The boy isn't lying. I just heard more than a simple confession of stealing silver from your little conversation with Smith. You plan to destroy Casa Grande. I suppose the one question I have for you both is why?"

Smith seemed to understand that the matter needed to be taken quickly into hand. "Look here, Parker, you seem like a reasonable man, and while I don't know the marshal here, I would imagine he's intelligent enough to realize when something can benefit him."

Parker exchanged glances with the marshal and smiled. "He's a very intelligent man. He managed to lead us here tonight."

Smith bit his lip and nodded. "Yes, well, then you will understand when I explain the dilemma the railroad finds itself in. The Santa Fe has made some poor investments and, in the course of this last year, has suffered a financial setback. Their investment in Casa Grande alone has cost them hundreds of thousands of dollars."

"So how does it figure that you would benefit from destroying the resort? I thought the Santa Fe and Harvey Company were hoping this would be their best joint effort to date," Braeden said seriously.

Smith nodded. "They do. However, I've found a way to make it pay off in much quicker order. Fire insurance will more than cover the expense put into this place and leave money in addition to those expenses."

"Fire insurance? You figure to burn the place down and collect on the insurance?" the marshal asked after taking a wooden toothpick from his mouth. He looked for all intents and purposes to be rather bored with the entire affair.

"Yes," Smith said flatly. "The idea to sell off the inventory was Worthington's idea, but I went along with it. It wasn't like the stuff would be useful to anyone after the fire. Worthington pointed out that we could take what we wanted and sell it off. No matter how much we received for the articles, it would still be a profit to both of us."

Smith moved closer to the men. "Look, I can make it worthwhile to both of you. I will control that insurance money when it comes in. Tonight is perfect for burning the place down because there's a storm brewing off in the distance, and once it hits here, we can plead a lightning strike or the wind knocking over a lantern. Then the wind will whip up a fury and hopefully—"

"Threaten the life of every man, woman, and child in residence," Braeden said sarcastically. "You really haven't thought this through, Smith. Are you ready to be a murderer as well as a wealthy man?"

"I don't stand to be wealthy from this," Smith replied. "There are some matters that have made this situation necessary. The money will help to keep me out of trouble in Topeka. You can't possibly understand."

"Try me."

Smith took a deep breath and blew it out. As he did that, thunder rumbled off in the distance. "We're losing time. The storm is moving in fast."

"The way I figure it," Braeden said, "you have all the time in the world to explain. You'll have even more time in your jail cell."

"You needn't threaten us, Parker. We know what we're doing," Reginald replied. Parker could threaten and rage all he wanted, but Reg held the winning card. He would have things his way. He would be the top man for once in his life. "We have a plan, and we mean to carry through with that plan. It's out of your hands, and frankly, it's out of my hands."

"What do you mean?" Braeden asked, his eyes narrowing.

"I mean that soon this place will be in a full blaze. You can't prove anything; it's your word against ours. And while Tomas may have told you a great deal, he'll quickly side with us when he sees that the welfare of his family depends upon it. Your reputation is ruined here, and Mr. Smith and Mr. Harvey are the best of friends. So in spite of your bringing in the marshal, I doubt seriously anyone will listen to your tale of intrigue. They'll remember your rejection of the woman you ruined—of her desire to marry you in spite of your actions. You are known now to be a liar, and frankly, I doubt anyone will give much consideration to what you have to say."

"Marshal, surely you could use the extra money?" Smith said in a questioning tone.

The man grinned. "I reckon I can always use a little extra money."

Smith nodded. "Then you'll help us?"

The marshal shook his head. "Nope. I didn't say that."

"But . . . I thought from what you said about being able to use the extra money," Smith countered, "that you were agreeing to go along with our plan. I know that if you will help us, Tomas will be happy to go back to keeping his mouth shut on the matter and rejoin our effort."

"Tomas isn't going to rejoin you," Braeden said, his voice dropping to a near whisper. "And you can't buy the marshal, so what do you propose to do now?"

"Gentlemen," Smith interjected, "we needn't argue amongst ourselves. I can make your silence quite worthwhile. I'm prepared to offer both you and the marshal two thousand dollars in order to simply escort Tomas to jail and forget everything else. I'm sure that by the time you remove the boy and process him for his crimes, that the destruction of this fine resort will already be well underway. So what do you say? Two thousand dollars is a lot of money to turn your back on."

Braeden smiled, but it was a hard, unfeeling smile. Reg felt the hairs on the back of his neck prickle at the cool, unemotional expression on the man's face. "I have more than enough money to see to my needs, Mr. Smith. I hardly need your blood money."

"It's not blood money, Mr. Parker. No one has to be injured. We'll sound the alarm well in advance and everyone should make it to safety before the fire gets out of control." Smith stepped forward, his face pale, his skin sweaty. "I need this money, Mr. Parker. I'm afraid I did something rather foolish and gambled a good deal of money away. It wasn't even mine, but rather money the Santa Fe entrusted me with. If I can successfully obtain the Santa Fe share of the hotel insurance, which of course has to be shared with Mr. Harvey, I can manage things a bit longer. At least until I'm able to make back the money I borrowed."

"Stole, don't you mean?" questioned Braeden.

Reg saw a brilliant flash of lightning and smiled. The thought of the storm made him feel as if everything would be all right. He hadn't dared to hope they would be fortunate enough to have a lightning storm in the area, but now it seemed as if the destruction of Casa Grande was preordained.

If only they could force Parker to cooperate. They were too close now to lose everything they'd worked for. If Parker and the marshal wouldn't agree, Reg would have little trouble in seeing them both killed. And with Parker dead, there would be no further obstacle to Rachel's love. At this thought, Reg chuckled, causing all heads to turn toward him.

"What's so funny, Mr. Worthington?" Braeden questioned.

"You are," Reg said with a smile. "You stand here worrying about your precious hotel, when Rachel is still far from your reach. But it isn't important because she's within my care and that is all that matters. I shall take her to England with me, and we will live rather happily there. I would imagine she might mourn you for a time, but only in the sense of regretting her naïveté."

Braeden practically flew at him, grabbing Reginald by his coat. "Tell me where she is!" he demanded.

Reg thought it all rather amusing. It seemed ironic that he would be standing here in Parker's grip, while Smith begged the man to come in on their scheme. The marshal just stood there not saying a word, while Tomas trembled in the doorway, too frightened to run away and too unnerved to speak. To Reg it seemed like a poorly acted stage play. The final act, perhaps. The scene just before the ultimate climax, where all the pertinent players were gathered and the truth was finally told. He laughed out loud even as Parker shook him hard enough to rattle his teeth.

"Where is Rachel?"

"She's safe," Reg replied, still laughing. "She's with me and she's safe."

Outside, the wind picked up and lightning once again flashed to pierce the pitch-black darkness of the night. Braeden dropped his hold on Reg and turned to the marshal. "We need to get this trio over to your jail. I don't know what they have planned, but I'm determined to bring it to a halt. I'll——"

"Just a minute, Parker," the marshal cut in, tilting his head in the air. "I smell smoke."

Braeden looked at Reginald, as did Smith. But it was Smith who spoke. "Is this your work?"

Reg tried to rationalize what they were asking, for his mind had already drifted to thoughts of Rachel Taylor in his arms. The storm outside and affairs of the hotel no longer seemed important. He looked up with a blank stare. "I've done nothing. The fire will start at two."

Braeden looked at his watch. "That's hours away."

"Maybe lightning did strike," the marshal said, moving toward the door. "Whatever the reason, I smell smoke."

Braeden moved to follow the marshal into the hallway when the lights flickered and then went off. "What's going on?" he muttered.

"Storm must have blown the lines down," the marshal called out. He struck a match against the wall and looked to Braeden for help. "You have any candles or maybe a kerosene lamp?"

"We have them downstairs, but if there is a fire, we've no time to be running all over the place. Tomas, you go downstairs and get us a couple of lamps out of the storage room. If you cooperate with us now, maybe the marshal can see to reducing the charges against you." Tomas looked at Braeden hopefully before tearing off in the direction of the stairs.

The match burned out and the marshal quickly lit another one. "You take the west side and I'll take the east," he told Braeden. "We'll get the folks to safety and then figure out what to do with these two."

"It's too soon," Reg muttered over and over. He could smell the smoke now and felt his heart racing out of control. His plans had been altered and someone had taken matters into their own hands.

Pushing his way into the hall, Reginald was unprepared when Braeden slammed him against the wall, growling low and refusing to release him even as he struggled. "Tell me where she is!" Parker demanded.

Reg shook his head. "She's mine. She doesn't love you anymore. I told her you'd left with Ivy. I told her you were already married. She never wants to see you again." Reg laughed at the look on Braeden's face. Doubt mingled with fear as Braeden realized the potential such statements could have had on the already defeated Rachel.

"Senor Parker!" Tomas called as he brought the lamps. "There is a fire downstairs in the theatre. The stage curtains are already burning."

"That's under the west side rooms," the marshal called. "Come on, Parker, we have to get these people to safety."

Braeden glared at Reginald with contempt, then slowly eased his grip on Reg's shirt. Without a word, he turned and ran after the marshal.

What followed next was like a macabre carnival. People poured from every corner of the second floor. Some were already in their bedclothes, others struggled to dress as they made their way to the stairs. A few of the older women sobbed fearfully, while some were in hysterics. Children, frantic in the wake of their disturbed sleep, seemed to sense the urgency and fear of their parents. This caused them to begin crying as they clung tightly to hands, arms, or even legs. Whatever they could manage to hold on to became their lifeline.

Reg stood rather dumbfounded for several moments as people streamed by him, pushing and shoving, all trying to reach the stairs first. He wondered if the fire would be a success, and even though he wasn't responsible for the blaze, he knew he had completed his duty and could go back home.

Thinking only of leaving the hotel and retrieving Rachel, Reg systematically returned to his room, took up his luggage, and made his way to join the hysterical crowd.

Braeden choked on the thick black smoke. Because the hotel lobby was open to the second floor, smoke had no trouble pouring down the hallways and up into the second story. He took out his bandana and tied it around his nose and mouth, but it did little good. Pounding on each chamber door until someone came to answer it, Braeden felt light-headed from the lack of oxygen. He had to get the people to safety, but his mind kept going over and over the words Worthington had just told him.

"She doesn't love you anymore. I told her you'd left with Ivy. I told her you were already married. She never wants to see you again."

Braeden shook his head. He wouldn't believe it was true. God wouldn't let it be true.

BRAEDEN COULD BARELY MAKE OUT the image of Reginald Worthington as he moved toward the staircase. Without thought to anyone else or even his own safety, Braeden pushed through the crowd and grabbed the chef by the back of his coat. Turning him around rather quickly, Braeden drew on every bit of his self-control to keep from hitting the man.

"You're coming with me, Worthington," he said angrily. Dragging Reg down the stairs with him, Braeden was surprised when Tomas appeared at the bottom. "You come with me as well," he told the boy, and Tomas nodded and followed Braeden outside.

Half dragging, half pushing, Braeden forced Worthington to the stables and instructed Tomas to get him a length of rope. "I don't want to worry about either one of you while I'm trying to ensure the safety of our guests," he said. Tying Reg and Tomas together, then securing them to one of the stall posts, Braeden left them and returned to the hotel.

Acrid smoke was now drifting from the open door, and as Braeden entered the lobby, he felt the air thicken and sting his nose and throat. Pulling his bandana close around his mouth, Braeden made his way upstairs to double-check for any guest who might not have found their way downstairs. He grabbed a lamp someone had thought to leave at the top of the stairs and hurriedly passed in and out of every room.

Relief washed over him when he found the second floor completely deserted.

Making his way to the back stairs, Braeden felt a rush of panic. The staircase was engulfed in flames. The fire greedily ate at everything in its path, the carpet on the stairway appearing to be a favorite meal. Realizing he couldn't use the stairs for his escape, Braeden hurried back down the long, carpeted eastern corridor. The fire seemed to have started on the west side, which would suffer the most damage. He could only pray that the east side would remain intact long enough for his escape. Running now to rid his lungs of the caustic fumes, Braeden nearly fell headlong into the figure of a woman. He took hold of her arms and started to comment on getting her to safety when the glow of the fire behind him made it easy to see her features.

"Ivy?" He pushed her toward the stairs, hoping to remove them both out of harm's way. "You need to get out of here. The whole place is about to go up."

"Oh, Braeden, you mustn't be mad at me," she said sweetly. She clung to his arm and didn't seem to notice that he had nearly lifted her off the stairs as he took them two at a time.

"I don't have time to worry about being mad at you," he said, grimacing as they hit the ground floor. "Look, you go on outside, I need to search the place and make certain no one else is inside." He pushed her toward the open front doors.

"No! You can't go back inside," she protested. "My mother did that. My father too. You don't understand. I did what I had to do."

Braeden shook his head and took the one remaining lamp on the front registry desk. "What are you talking about?"

"My parents died," Ivy said in absolute anguish. "I didn't mean for them to die." She wrapped her arms around Braeden's and pulled. "You believe me, don't you? Auntie didn't believe me, but it's true." She pulled at his arm. "You have to come with me. You'll die if you don't."

"People will die if they're still inside," Braeden told her. "I'm going to make a quick check."

"No one's in there. I saw them all leave. I only came back inside to find you. You are free now. Casa Grande won't keep us from marrying. There will be nothing here for you, and you can take me with you to Chicago."

"You're insane, Ivy," he said, trying to push her away. The lamp nearly fell from his hands as she fought him.

"I had to do it. I know it was wrong, but by destroying this place, you would have no other reason to stay."

He stopped at this, and in spite of the building smoke and growing fire, Braeden simply stared at her for a moment. "You set this fire." It was a statement more than a question, and when Ivy nodded, he felt the overwhelming urge to slap her. He didn't, however. "Get out of here, Ivy. I can't help you now."

"I know about fires," she said, refusing to drop her hold on his arm. "My parents died in a fire. They shouldn't have—I didn't mean for them to, but they went back inside. You have to come outside with me." She actually managed to drag him a few steps toward the front door.

"Are you saying you set the fire that killed your parents?" he asked, almost horrified to know the answer. He coughed as his lungs fought to exhale the smoke. They couldn't remain in the resort for much longer.

She nodded, then threw him a pleading look. "Aunt Esmeralda didn't understand, but she's dead now. She can't hurt me. The secret is safe with us."

Braeden's mind reeled from the information. Then a sickening thought came to his mind. Esmeralda had died from a fall down the stairs. He knew because he'd asked. The doctor had been uncertain if the old woman had suffered some sort of seizure prior to the fall but had promised to do a posthumous examination.

For a moment, the smoke seemed to lessen and Braeden actually thought perhaps the fire was playing itself out. But as the wind blew in from the open door, he realized the reason. Ivy pulled at his arm.

"We have to hurry, look behind you!"

Looking down the hall, Braeden saw the unmistakable glow of flames. Casa Grande would soon lay in ashes.

Realizing there was no more time to waste, he pushed Ivy toward the door, acting as if they were both going to exit the lobby. As soon as Ivy crossed the threshold, however, Braeden ripped away from her hold and marched back into the hotel, heading straight for the dining room. He'd just entered the silent room when Ivy caught up with him.

"No, Braeden!" she screamed, coming after him in a fierce lunge.

Unprepared for this, Braeden dropped the lamp, spilling the kerosene. Flames leapt across the wooden floor. With their exit to the lobby cut off, Braeden pulled Ivy into the dining room just as a woman's screams sounded.

"We'll have to go out the side exit," he told Ivy. He would have just as soon left her to suffer on her own, but he couldn't do such an abominable thing with a clear conscience. God would deal with Ivy Brooks. It wasn't up to Braeden to mete out her punishment.

The scream came again, and this time Braeden was certain it came from the kitchen. Pushing Ivy forward, they entered the kitchen and nearly fell back from the heat of the fire. Apparently the flames had crossed over from the theatre and ignited the back of the kitchen—at least from what Braeden surmised.

"Help me!" a woman cried out.

Braeden made out the figure of Gwen Carson. She was stuck in a small alcove of the kitchen. Directly behind her and in front of her the flames engulfed the walls, counters, and everything else in its wake.

"Gwen, you'll have to jump through the fire."

"I can't!" she screamed. "I can't. I fell, and I think my leg is broken."

Ivy stood mesmerized as Braeden pulled off his coat. "Get out of here, Ivy. I can't help you both at the same time."

Still she refused to move, but Braeden was more concerned for Gwen. Pulling his coat over his head, Braeden made a mad run at the growing wall of flames. Ivy screamed from somewhere across the fiery wall, but he was unharmed as he came face-to-face with Gwen.

He assessed the situation quickly as a huge piece of the back wall gave way. Looking through the flames to where Ivy stood, Braeden was mortified to see that the fire had managed to surround her and cut off her escape. There wasn't much time left. They were all going to die if he didn't think of something fast.

The heat from the fire made his skin tingle and the air rapidly grew much too hot to breathe. *God help me*, he prayed, frantic to think of some way to help them survive the situation. Just then he remembered the storage room. There was a conveyance of rollers to slide goods into the room from the delivery platform window. That receiving window would be their means of escape!

"Ivy, you'll have to come this way. I'm going to get Gwen into the storage room. We can escape through the window."

"No! Don't leave me!" Ivy screamed.

Braeden had already lifted Gwen into his arms. "You'll have to do this on your own, Ivy. I'll be back in a minute." He heard her screaming his name over and over, and in spite of all the trouble she had caused him, he felt a horrible sense of inadequacy in leaving her there. Surely she would muster her courage and come after them, he thought. She wouldn't just stand there and let the fire take her without a fight.

Gwen was sobbing softly in his arms as Braeden moved through the storage area. The fire behind them created enough light to see through the smoky shadows—but just barely. "We're almost there," he told her, pushing past crates and bags of flour.

Placing Gwen on the rollers, he admonished her to hold tight. "I'm going to get that window open," he said, maneuvering to unfasten the wooden latches. The window was more of a door, for all practical purposes, with a heavy wooden gate that swung wide to expose the room for delivery.

Braeden had it open in a matter of seconds. "Just ease your weight down the rollers," he told Gwen. "Get yourself outside while I go back for Ivy. Can you do that?"

Gwen nodded, seeming to regain control of her senses. "I'll do it, Mr. Parker. You go ahead."

Braeden left his coat by the window and maneuvered back through the storage room. There was no sign of Ivy, but he heard her screams through the roar of the blaze. He'd no sooner made it to the kitchen when a huge piece of ceiling gave way and crashed down before him to block off any hope of going after Ivy. Sparks flashed up and pieces of debris landed on his left forearm, burning his shirt. He quickly smothered the flaming sleeve, then struggled again to see where Ivy was.

"Ivy! This is the only way out!"

Her screams echoed in his ears, then fell silent as another piece of wall gave way.

He felt sickened at the thought of her dying in the very fire she'd set. It might be poetic justice or proper revenge for all that she had done, but he would never have wished it upon her.

It wasn't until he made his way back to the receiving window, grabbed up his coat, and followed Gwen outside, that Braeden had time to think of Rachel.

Dear God, please keep her from harm. I have no idea where Worthington has put her, but I can only pray it's far from this resort. He again lifted Gwen in his arms. Lightning flashed in the distance, and Braeden felt only a small amount of relief to see that the storm was bypassing them. The rain might actually have put out the flames.

Yet instead of a welcome rain, the downdraft of the thunderstorm served instead to tear apart the delicate electrical lines and to stir up the flames that consumed Casa Grande. Seeing the destruction before him, Braeden wondered silently if the fire would be contained to the resort. After all, there were plenty of other buildings close enough to catch fire, and if they did, it might well spread to the entire town.

Looking down at the woman he carried, Braeden quickly realized Gwen had fainted. She must have suffered great terror at having been trapped by the blaze. He couldn't imagine what had happened to put her in that position, nor how she might have broken her leg. Carrying her away from the building and back around to the front of the resort, Braeden came upon a shocking sight. Half-dressed hotel guests of every age and size stood staring in dumbfounded silence as Casa Grande burned. Mothers tried to comfort children while the men went to help try to control the flames. No one even seemed to notice the storm in the distance or the wind. They were completely mesmerized by the conflagration before them.

A small gathering of volunteer fire fighters were present with their two-horse pump and tank. It wouldn't begin to put a dent in the fire, nor would the bucket brigade lined up between the stream and the resort. The fire was hopelessly out of control. .

Searching for a place to take Gwen, Braeden noticed Dr. Krier was already attending several people by the fountain. Someone had thoughtfully brought several lanterns and blankets to aid him in the process, and several of the townswomen were helping him deal with the injured. Braeden moved through the people to take Gwen to where the doctor worked.

"She may have a broken leg," he told Dr. Krier as the man's expression silently inquired.

"I don't know if she's received any burns," Braeden continued as Gwen moaned softly, "but she's definitely in pain."

"I'll see to her," Krier replied. "Are there any others? Anyone else inside?"

Braeden felt bile in his throat and pushed it down. "Ivy Brooks was trapped in the kitchen. I couldn't get to her."

The doctor nodded and turned his attention to Gwen just as someone shouted that sparks had apparently set the stables on fire. Braeden quickly remembered Worthington and Tomas and made a mad dash, along with several of Casa Grande's stable hands, for the building. If they were to die, it would be his fault for tying them there without hope of escape.

He found them just where he'd left them. Tomas was wide-eyed and fearful, but Worthington seemed to have slipped into his own world. He was muttering something about a ship and wondering what time they would dock.

"I have to move you," Braeden said, quickly mastering the knots he'd tied. "The wind has carried sparks to the stable. I wouldn't be surprised if the whole town burned down!"

He yanked them to their feet and pushed them toward the door. "If I had time, I'd just move you on to the jail, but there are still others to consider."

"You have no right to keep me here," Worthington said in a strangely calm manner. "My ship is awaiting my arrival."

Braeden knew the man was either losing his mind or the shock of the fire had confused him. Either way, he didn't care. He only wanted to know where Rachel was, and if he had to beat it out of the man, he would get his answer.

﹌ TWENTY-EIGHT ﹌

"IT'S TOO SOON," Reg muttered over and over. He asked Braeden for the time, but before Braeden could respond he continued ranting. "I didn't have time to see to everything. It's too soon. I didn't do it."

Braeden directed him, along with Tomas, toward the bridge at Morita Falls. He thought this to be as safe a place as any to position the men. Here he could secure them to the structure and keep them out of harm's way, and then he would be free to go in search of Rachel.

"The power station," Reg said and muttered the phrase over and over. He looked at the sad little building beside the falls, the water-wheel still churning. "Mine . . . the power station."

"What is he talking about?" Braeden questioned Tomas.

"I don't know, senor. He's been talking loco ever since you tied us up."

Braeden reached the bridge and pushed Worthington back against the railing. "Where is Rachel? You must tell me now."

Reg looked at him with a blank stare. "It's all mine," he said. "All mine."

Braeden shook him. "Look, Worthington, I'm giving you just one chance to tell me the truth. That fire is going to destroy everything in its path. You have to tell me where Rachel is so that I can keep her from dying in the fire."

"I will miss my ship," Reg firmly stated as if his senses had suddenly returned to him. Then he began mumbling. "Water . . . the fire . . . power station."

"What's with the power station?" Braeden questioned, looking at Tomas. "Is there something that interests him?"

Tomas nodded. "We put some of the stolen goods there. He had me choose three places. We put some of the stuff under the bandstand. Then some of it went to the power station and some to a cave down below the falls."

Braeden began to think about the things Reg had said. It didn't make sense, but what did was that Reginald Worthington knew where Rachel was. He had put her somewhere. Somewhere for safekeeping— just like the stolen goods.

"Tomas, do you think it's possible that Mr. Worthington took Rachel to one of those places? I mean, were the areas big enough to hide a woman and keep her from being discovered?"

"Sí," Tomas replied. "The bandstand is not very big, but the power station has much room underground and the cave is far away and very big."

Braeden felt the first bit of encouragement. "Where is the cave? I'll check it out."

"The cave is that way," Tomas pointed down the side of the stream, "But, señor, I can find it in the dark. You can trust me. I promise I no run away. I may be a thief, but I would not do anything to hurt Miss Taylor. She was very good to me. Please let me help you."

Braeden nodded and began untying the boy. "You go to the cave and I'll take the powerhouse. How do I get to this underground room?"

"There is a trapdoor on the far side. A ladder will take you down there."

"All right. You go to the cave and if Rachel is there, bring her back. If she's hurt, stay with her, and I'll come looking for you. Do you understand?"

"Sí," Tomas replied and took off running down the path that ran parallel to the powerhouse. It took only a moment for the boy to disappear from sight.

Braeden took one last glance at Reg, who seemed completely

enthralled with the fire. Turning back around to face Casa Grande, Braeden could see that the entire front section of the hotel had flames fanning out from every window. He looked quickly to the stables, which were now also engulfed in the blaze.

"The pool house and sheds are on fire!" someone shouted. "Looks like the wind might carry it to the entire town."

This caused shrieks of alarm and sent a rush of people toward the bridge. Braeden backed up as the townspeople hurried back to their own homes to save what they could and be prepared to fight the fire as it spread through the town.

"The powerhouse is on fire!" the station manager yelled, running up from the path.

This announcement sent a rippling shock through Braeden. If Rachel was there, she was now in serious peril. He left Reg tied to the bridge and pushed his way through the onslaught of townsfolk.

He opened the door to the station, grateful that the electricity still illuminated the small building. Not seeing any visible signs of fire, Braeden took no chance on the manager having been given over to a case of nerves. He moved quickly to the back of the room, searching through the mechanisms of belts, pulleys, gears, and machinery.

"It has to be here!" he said aloud.

Growing more and more frantic as the smell of smoke seemed to permeate everything around him, Braeden ripped at any object in his way and thrust it aside. Finally he spied the trapdoor and threw it open. He started down the ladder, then felt the tickle of something against his face. Reaching up to swat aside what he presumed to be a cobweb, Braeden's hand fell on the light cord. He pulled at it, silently thanking God when light flooded the room.

He jumped the final few rungs just as Rachel's cries reached his ears.

"Help me! Please get me out of here!"

"I'm here, Rachel!" he called, searching through the maze of goods and stored materials to find her tied to a small cot. Seeing her there, so pale and frightened, Braeden lost no time in working the ropes.

"I knew you would come for me," she said softly, her face taking on an expression of relief. "I knew you hadn't gone away as Reg told me."

"No," Braeden answered, freeing her feet. "I would never leave you."

"I know that now," she said.

He looked deep into her eyes. "You finally trust me, don't you?"

She nodded. "I will always trust you."

He pulled her up off the bed and turned her around to untie her hands. "Look, Casa Grande is burning to the ground, and this power-house is on fire. We have to hurry or we might not make it."

She gripped him tightly. "I love you, Braeden. I've never stopped."

He smiled and pressed a quick kiss upon her lips. "I know that. Why do you think I came here in the first place? Once I knew you were here, my only thought was of winning you back. But right now we have to get out of this building."

He pushed her ahead of him and maneuvered them back to the ladder. He worried that Rachel might not have the strength after her ordeal to climb the rungs, but she surprised him by hiking her skirts and scurrying up them in no time at all. He followed behind, anxious to be out in the open and away from what was no doubt about to become another inferno.

He had no sooner emerged through the trapdoor when he noticed that Rachel had come to a dead stop. He found himself following her gaze to where the entire west wall seemed to instantly burst into flames.

"Come on!" he yelled, dragging her with him to the front door.

They burst out into the cool, damp air and raced up the path away from the station house. Panting for breath and fearful of what could have happened, Rachel collapsed into Braeden's arms, weeping softly and clinging to him as though she might well perish if she let go.

"Shh, it's all right now," he told her. "You're safe."

"I was so afraid. I kept thinking that Reg was actually going to get away with taking me to England. He said we would be married and that I . . ."

Braeden pulled her away and shook his head. "You don't have to talk about it. It's not important. He can't hurt you anymore."

"Where is he?" she asked, glancing over her shoulder and seeing Casa Grande for the first time. "Did he get out of the fire?"

"Yes," Braeden assured her. "I have him tied to the Morita Falls bridge."

"You do? But why?"

"It's a long, long story, one that I will tell you some long winter's night when we are curled up in front of a fireplace instead of a burning hotel. Suffice it to say, the man will be going to jail for more than kidnapping you."

Rachel shook her head and watched the resort scene in fascination. "All of that money—all that potential. And now it's gone, just that quick." She turned back to Braeden. "I don't understand. What happened? I thought I heard thunder. Did lightning strike the hotel?"

"No," Braeden replied, pulling her close and walking her farther away from the power station, which by now was completely ablaze. "Ivy Brooks set the fire, although Reg had plans to do the same. It's part of that long story, and it has to do with fire insurance money and some swindle that Worthington managed to get in the middle of."

"He told me you were already married to Ivy. He said that Mrs. Needlemeier was dead and that Ivy needed you and you complied."

Braeden rubbed her shoulder, letting his touch trail down her arms until he took hold of her hands. "But you didn't believe him."

"No," Rachel replied.

"Not even after what you witnessed at the Needlemeier mansion?"

Rachel gave him the briefest smile. "I knew it was all Ivy. I knew it even when I ran from the house. Still, I couldn't bear what had happened. Then after I calmed down, I realized that you needed my support, my trust. I knew you were not to blame, and I vowed not to let the circumstances destroy our love."

"But you never came back. I suppose Worthington caught up with you."

"No, actually, I found some men working to put stolen goods under the bandstand. I confronted them," she said, smiling sheepishly. "I realize now that was incredibly foolish."

He chuckled. "To say the least."

"Anyway, they gagged and carried me down here to the power

station. They tied me up and, I figured, left me to die. Next thing I know, Reg appears. I hoped he was there to rescue me, but he quickly made it clear that he had other plans. He . . . he . . ." she shuddered and lowered her gaze to the ground.

Braeden lifted her chin gently. "It doesn't matter anymore what he did to you. No matter what he did. Do you understand?"

Rachel's expression instantly changed, but before she could speak, cries rose up from the crowd.

"The Needlemeier mansion is on fire!"

"So's the school!"

"We should go see what we can do to help," Braeden said, pulling Rachel with him. "I doubt there's anything anyone can do, but it's worth a try."

"What about Jeffery and Simone? What about my girls? Are they safe?" she asked, holding tightly to his arm as they joined the mass of resort guests.

"They're all safe, as far as I know," Braeden replied. "I pulled Gwen from the fire myself. She may have a broken leg and some burns, but I think she'll be fine." He paused, then answered flatly, "Ivy didn't make it."

"Oh," Rachel said and nodded. Her sense of purpose seemed to be resurfacing. "You do what you must. I should see to my girls and make sure they are safe."

Braeden refused to let her go. "I'll help you. We'll move them down the road, and if Jeffery and Simone's place is safe from the fire, maybe they can stay there until we see what else there is to do."

"Dr. Krier probably needs help," Rachel said, letting Braeden lead the way. "My girls and I could help with those needs."

"I think most everyone got out safely," Braeden told her, "but I'm sure the good doctor could always use a spare set of hands."

They came to the pallet where Gwen lay. She was conscious now and the pain that filled her eyes caused Braeden and Rachel to exchange a glance of worry.

"Gwen, I'm so glad you're safe," Rachel said, kneeling down beside the younger woman.

"Mr. Parker saved my life. I was trapped by the fire. He tried to save Ivy, but she wouldn't come with us."

"He saved my life too," Rachel told her. "Has the doctor taken care of you?"

Gwen nodded. "He says that my leg doesn't look to be broken, just badly sprained. I have to stay off of it, but otherwise I'll be fine."

"No burns?" Rachel asked softly.

"No," Gwen answered. "Mr. Parker got to me in time. He couldn't save Ivy," she repeated as if it was necessary to make certain Rachel understood. "She wouldn't listen to him. She wouldn't come with us. It's not Mr. Parker's fault."

Rachel nodded. "I know. Look, we're going to get the girls rounded up and moved down to the O'Donnell house. That is, if the fire isn't headed that direction." She straightened and looked at Braeden. "Can we get a carriage to transport the injured?"

"I'll see to it," Braeden replied, proud of Rachel's ability to forget her own ordeal in order to help her girls. "You stay here and I'll talk to the doctor."

Rachel watched Braeden disappear into the crowd before kneeling back down beside Gwen. "I'm going to see to the others, but I'll be right back. We'll not leave you here, so don't be afraid that we'll forget you." Gwen smiled weakly and nodded.

Rachel spied a couple of the girls standing not five feet away. Calling to them, she instructed them to find the other Harvey Girls and bring them to her. The girls seemed relieved for something to do and quickly set out to fulfill Rachel's request. Within a few moments twenty-three girls stood in front of Rachel. Some were dressed in their uniforms, others were wrapped in their robes. All of them wore expressions of fear and confusion.

"We're going to help Dr. Krier with any wounded, and if he doesn't need our help, then we'll set up in the depot and try to offer whatever assistance we can to the townspeople." One by one the girls nodded. This information seemed to give them new purpose. "Gwen has been injured and cannot walk. Mr. Parker has gone for a carriage and to speak with the doctor. I'm sure we'll have our hands full, and

I'll require each of you to do your duty as if you were serving Mr. Harvey himself."

"That won't be necessary," a voice sounded from behind Rachel.

She turned and smiled to find Fred Harvey standing there, dressed impeccably as usual. "Hello, Mr. Harvey. I was just rounding my girls up to offer community assistance."

"An admirable idea and one I wholeheartedly support. There are supplies at the depot and more due in with the morning freight. If the fire doesn't destroy it, we should be in good order."

Rachel nodded and looked past him toward town. "Do you suppose the fire will spread that far?"

"I have no way of knowing. With the direction of the wind, we may find it contained to the southern part of town. And if the storm would move out or die down altogether, then the wind might ease as well. Only time will tell."

She nodded and caught sight of Casa Grande. "Such a waste."

"Yes, indeed," Harvey replied. "But it could have been much worse. The loss of life appears minimal and instead of hundreds being burned, we have only a handful of injuries. It seems Mr. Parker and the marshal were able to spread the alarm quickly and efficiently."

"It's so sad to see the dream die," Rachel said, meeting his compassionate gaze.

"The dreams never die so long as the dreamer still lives," Harvey said, smiling. "We will dream another dream and rebuild, or we'll go elsewhere. It's not the end of anything, just a postponement."

She admired his positive spirit and decided then and there that if Mr. Harvey, who had so much time and energy devoted to Casa Grande, could face the disaster with a hopeful attitude, she could certainly do no less.

Turning from the man, she rallied her girls. "You've all heard what Mr. Harvey just said. We have a job to do, and a Harvey Girl must always be prepared to serve the public with a smile and an encouraging word. Let us be to our tasks."

ᥱᨏ TWENTY-NINE ᥱᨎ

THE RAINS FINALLY CAME, but they were too late to save most of
Morita. The southern portions of town, including the church, the
school, many businesses, and even the fire department, all fell victim
to the blaze. The depot remained intact, as did several other buildings
that were quickly converted into temporary housing for the resort
guests. Those who were left in their bedclothes were found something
to wear, and before the morning train moved in from Lamy, near Santa
Fe, and farther up the line, a telegraphed plea went out from Fred
Harvey. Informing the telegraph operator in Lamy and Albuquerque
that the resort had burned down, he asked for extra blankets, clothes,
and anything else that might help aid the residents of Morita.

With the morning freight came a substantial amount of food and
other goods, and only a few hours later a special Santa Fe passenger
service was brought in to move the victims of the resort fire to Albuquerque, where they could recover from their shock before moving on
to other destinations.

Rachel took up residence with Simone and Jeffery while her girls
were disbursed, at Fred Harvey's discretion, throughout the town.
Braeden took his leave of Rachel once he'd seen her safely to the
O'Donnells, since he needed to deliver Reginald Worthington and
Tomas to the marshal. Rachel understood, but she hated to see him
go. She had worried about ever seeing him again when Reg had refused

to free her. Now she didn't worry about whether or not he'd come back, but rather, how things would be for them now that this tragedy had taken place in their lives.

"You are awfully deep in thought," Simone said, coming into the front room.

Rachel stood at the window, staring out at the only part of town that remained. "I can't help but wonder about my future."

"I know what you mean," Simone replied. "I don't know what we'll do. I mean, Jeffery still has his job with the Santa Fe, but there may be no need for someone of his caliber to remain here in Morita. Especially if Mr. Harvey and the railroad decide against rebuilding."

"Is that what they're thinking?" Rachel questioned, moving away from the window with a slight limp.

"I think the doctor should look at your leg," Simone stated. "In fact, I insist. Now, are you going to make me drag you over there or do I need to run Jeffery down and get his help?"

"I just twisted it," Rachel said. "Reg had me tied by the ankles. I tried to get free and during the process I made matters worse. I didn't even notice it until after all of the excitement died down, so it can't be all that bad."

"Nevertheless, you aren't a doctor and neither am I. Dr. Krier is just across the street, so let's have you hobble over there and have him look at it."

Rachel looked at her friend and laughed at the look of sheer determination on her face. "All right. I'll go see the doctor, but you needn't accompany me. You have to take care of yourself and that baby. Whether or not we have a job to go back to in Morita or a place to live, you and Jeffery have a wonderful future to look forward to." She hoped the words didn't sound envious. She couldn't have been happier for Simone, but at the same time, she couldn't help longing for her own life to come into proper order.

"Don't forget your shawl," Simone admonished. "It's very chilly this morning. Jeffery wonders if there won't be an early winter this year."

"Could be," Rachel said, retrieving a navy blue shawl her mother had crocheted for her. "If Braeden comes back . . ." she said, opening the door and glancing with a hopeful eye down the road.

"If Braeden comes back, I'll tell him what he wants to hear. That you finally went to the doctor and that he's invited to stay for lunch."

Rachel smiled. "Thank you, Simone. You're a good friend."

Half an hour later, Dr. Krier finally had a chance to look at Rachel's ankle. He gave her some ointment to help with the rope burns and advised her to stay off her feet for a day or two and keep her foot propped up. She came out of his examination office telling him that she would do what she could to rest, while reminding him that as the woman in charge of the Harvey Girls, she had certain responsibilities that needed to be attended to.

"She'll rest," Braeden said quite seriously.

Rachel looked up, surprised to see him standing near the front door. She smiled and felt a rush of warmth come to her cheeks as he winked at her and came to help her.

"I'll see to it that she goes to bed and stays there, if I have to sit on her."

Dr. Krier chuckled. "I'd hardly think that necessary, but then again, I don't know her as well as you obviously do."

"She's a stubborn one," Braeden said, reaching out to Rachel.

Rachel took hold of his arm and was surprised to see him grimace. "What's wrong?"

"It's nothing," he said.

"Oh really." She put more pressure on his arm and watched his face pale. "I don't believe this. You're hurt and you didn't even tell me."

"Come on in here," Dr. Krier instructed.

Braeden rolled his eyes. "I'll be fine. There are a great many more folks who need your treatments. I'm not that bad off."

Rachel put her hands on her hips. "Braeden Parker, do you mean to disobey the doctor's direct order?"

"It's just that—"

"It's just nothing," Rachel said, pushing him in the direction of the examination room. "You have no excuse that I want to hear. Now get in there."

Dr. Krier laughed at the confrontation between them while

Braeden rolled his eyes and gave up the fight. He let Rachel hobble in behind him and help him take off his coat. Once this was done, Rachel could see for herself where the sleeve had been burned. Braeden tried not to grimace as he rolled up what was left of the sleeve, revealing a rather nasty-looking burn.

Shrugging, he smiled sheepishly at Rachel. "I didn't even know it was there until this morning."

Rachel nodded. "And you were worried about my ankle."

He grinned and lowered his voice. "From now on, I intend to worry about every part of you, Miss Taylor. Not just the ankles."

She felt her cheeks grow warm again. Looking away, Rachel hoped to regain a portion of her dignity by changing the subject. "So what will happen to Reg and Tomas?"

"The marshal's going to see about getting Tomas off easy. He figures the boy was easily persuaded given the crisis at—hey, that hurts!" he declared, forgetting how his words might affect Rachel.

She hurried to his side. "Is it all that bad?"

Dr. Krier grunted and continued working. "It might not have been so troublesome if you'd taken care of it first thing. You've got all sorts of dirt and bits of cloth imbedded here. It's going to smart as I clean it out, but if I don't, it'll probably get infected."

"Do what you have to, Doc. I'll be a good patient," Braeden told him.

Rachel tried not to look worried as Dr. Krier continued working on the ugly wound. Braeden seemed to sense her concern and reached out to touch her hand.

"It'll be all right. You'll see."

She swallowed hard and nodded. "I know."

"Look, if you don't have the stomach for this, you can wait in the other room. I'll walk you back to the O'Donnells' when Doc finishes up."

"No, I'm fine. I guess I just keep thinking how much worse it could have been."

"It's amazing that more folks weren't killed in the blaze. That thing went up like kindling. It didn't even seem to matter that the exterior was made of brick," the doctor said as he finished picking at the oozing burn. He went to a cabinet and brought back a bottle of solution, which he promptly poured onto the wound.

Braeden's hand tightened painfully hard around Rachel's hand, but she refused to even so much as wince. He seemed to realize quickly what he was doing and, even though his face grew white and perspiration formed on his brow, he loosened his grip and apologized.

"Sorry. I wasn't expecting that."

"That's the worst of it," Dr. Krier said, replacing the bottle in the cabinet and opening a drawer below. "I'll bandage it up and you can be on your way."

Rachel sighed with relief when the job was finally completed. Braeden asked about the bill, and it was only then that Rachel remembered she'd not paid the doctor either.

"I'll need the tally for mine as well," she told the doctor.

"I'll see to hers," Braeden replied. "She's my responsibility now."

The doctor raised a brow and leaned in close to Braeden. "So you've asked her to be your wife, eh?"

"Not yet, but I'm working on it. I would have probably taken care of the matter had you not waylaid me here."

Rachel looked at them both in disbelief. What was Braeden thinking, discussing their future in such a casual manner?

The doctor just laughed, told Braeden the total, and waited while he counted the money into his hand. Rachel stood speechless as Braeden pulled on his singed and sooty coat and escorted her to the door.

"Come along, Miss Taylor, there are some matters that we need to discuss." He looped his good arm around her waist and pulled her close. "Lean on me rather than putting your weight on that ankle."

"You tend to your arm, and I'll tend to my ankle," Rachel countered.

"I rather hoped you'd take care of my arm," he said as they stepped onto the front porch. "Along with the rest of me. And while you were doing that, I'd take care of you."

Rachel looked up at him rather hesitantly. "Are you sure that's what you want?"

He grew very serious. "I'm positive. What about you?"

Rachel felt her heart flutter. Marriage to Braeden Parker was what she'd dreamed of for over six years. Marriage, children, a life lived with love.

"Hey there, Braeden!" Marshal Schmidt called from the street.

Rachel felt a sense of frustration wash over her, but instead of showing it, she turned to greet the lawman with a smile.

"What's up, Larry?" Braeden questioned.

"Just thought you'd like to know I found Smith. He was hightailing it off to Albuquerque on horseback, but I caught up to him. Seems he doesn't know much about horses and managed to team himself up with an ornery critter that didn't cotton to the saddle."

"Probably got one of the carriage horses," Braeden said with a smile. "So what about the others?"

"I let Tomas go on his pledge to show up for the trial. I have your Englishman ranting and babbling on one side of the cell, while Smith is muttering and cursing on the other side. Guess if we're going to have this kind of activity, I'm going to have to build a bigger jail."

Braeden shook his head. "From the looks of this mess, I'm not so sure it'd be worth the effort."

"Yeah, I kind of figured that myself," the marshal said, glancing back over the town. "I might just be out of a job once everything is said and done." He seemed to consider this for a moment, then tipped his hat. "Well, just thought you'd like to know about Smith. I've had Mr. O'Donnell wire the necessary folks, and now it's just a matter of getting all the facts in place. Oh, and I talked with Miss Carson. She told me how you tried your best to save Miss Brooks. I don't think there'll be any problem with folks assuming otherwise."

Braeden nodded. "That's good news."

"I'll be seein' you around," Schmidt said, moving off in the direction of the depot.

"Do you suppose anyone would have actually thought you capable of leaving Ivy in that fire?" Rachel asked.

Braeden shrugged. "Sometimes folks believe whatever they want to—whatever seems to fit their logic at the time. Facts don't always matter."

Rachel felt the full weight of his words. "Of course, you're right.

I guess no one knows that better than I do, especially after what I did to you—to us."

Braeden held her close and maneuvered her down the steps. They walked in silence as they made their way back to the O'Donnell house. Pausing on the back steps, Braeden turned Rachel in his arms. "That's all in the past. I want us to start fresh. I want us to share a complete trust in each other, no matter what the circumstances."

Rachel nodded, losing herself in his steely blue eyes. "I want that too. I'm so sorry for the way I wronged you. I'm so sorry for the wasted years. I put myself into a self-imposed prison, then prayed to find a key to let myself out. I was very foolish, and I can only hope that you will forgive me."

Braeden raised her hands to his lips and kissed her fingers. "You could never do anything so bad that I would refuse to forgive you. I love you, Rachel. I always have and I always will. Nothing about the past matters anymore. Only the future. I want us to be together always, and I'm hoping you want the same thing."

Rachel's heart felt as though it might pound right through her chest. Touching his cheek gently, she saw all the longing in her soul reflected in his eyes. She drew a deep breath and opened her mouth to answer, when Braeden's proposal was interrupted for a second time.

"Braeden! Rachel!"

It was Jeffery O'Donnell, and Rachel could only sigh, letting her breath out in an anticlimactic way. "Hello, Jeffery," she said, wishing she could say good-bye instead. .

"Jeffery," Braeden said, his voice edged with the slightest hint of irritation.

Jeffery looked at them both for a moment. "Am I interrupting?"

"Yes," Rachel replied quickly. "Yes, you are, Mr. O'Donnell, and I'd appreciate it if you would go inside and keep your wife company. I don't need her to come out here as well."

Jeffery seemed a bit taken aback by Rachel's instruction and Braeden just laughed.

Leaning over to Jeffery, Braeden whispered loudly enough for everyone to hear, "I've asked her a rather important question twice now, and if I don't get an answer the third time, I'm not going to ask again."

Jeffery couldn't contain his smile. "I see."

"So unless you want to be in very big trouble with me—and with Simone," Rachel stated flatly, "you'll do as I asked."

Just then the back door opened and Simone stared openmouthed at the trio. "What's going on?"

Jeffery pushed his way past Rachel and Braeden and opened the screen door. Taking Simone in hand he said, "I'll tell you later."

"But—" Simone protested as Jeffery pulled her inside and promptly closed the door behind them.

Rachel looked up at Braeden and met his amused expression. "Now, before any more interruptions come . . ." Inside the house Simone let out a shriek, causing them both to laugh out loud.

"Well, now you have to say yes," Braeden teased, pulling Rachel back into his arms. "No doubt Mrs. O'Donnell is already making plans."

She carefully tried to avoid hurting his arm and maneuvered to wrap her arms around Braeden's neck. "So you were going to ask me something for the third time."

He grinned. "Okay, but this is it."

She nodded. "Absolutely."

"Marry me, Rachel. Promise to love me forever, as I will love you."

She sighed and answered in a whisper, "I will marry you, Braeden Parker, and I will love you forever, with all my heart."

He lowered his mouth to hers, touching her lips gently. She felt his hands in her hair and thought that nothing had ever felt so right or so good. Melting against him, reveling in the very strength he emitted, Rachel felt as though she had finally come home. The passion she had buried within her for six long years surfaced in that kiss. She wanted nothing more in life than to marry Braeden Parker and be his wife. And she wanted it very soon because she had already wasted a good portion of her life running from the love she felt.

Pulling away, Braeden looked at her very seriously. "Can we get married soon? Like maybe even tomorrow?"

Rachel shook her head. "No, Mr. Parker. I will not marry you tomorrow." She laughed at the stunned look on his face. "Unless, of course, Pastor Johnson can't do the job today."

Braeden grinned from ear to ear. "You're supposed to be off of that ankle, but I'll hit the road and find Johnson, wherever he may be. And whether he has the time or not—I guarantee you, he'll marry us."

Rachel watched him jump over the side of the steps and hurry off in the direction of town. Smiling to herself she looked heavenward. "Thank you," she whispered. "Thank you for making my dreams come true, even in the wake of such devastation."

Opening the door, Rachel hobbled inside to find Jeffery and Simone waiting rather impatiently.

"So what happened?" Simone asked, looking behind Rachel. "Where's Braeden?"

"I sent him away."

"You what?!" Jeffery and Simone questioned at once.

Rachel laughed. "You two are worse than a couple of mother hens. I sent him off to get the preacher. We're going to have a wedding."

"Now?" Simone questioned. "Here?"

"Well, seeing how the church burned down, and how I have no desire to get married at the saloon or the depot, or even Doc's house, I figured this would be the best place."

Simone instantly flew into action. "Well, come on, then. We have to get you ready. You'll need a dress and we have to fix your hair."

Rachel laughed and let Simone lead her away.

﹡ EPILOGUE ﹡

TWO HOURS AFTER their impromptu wedding beside Morita Falls, Rachel and Braeden found themselves in a private railroad car, courtesy of Fred Harvey.

"It seems the least I can do after all you've done for us, Miss Taylor—Mrs. Parker," Fred Harvey said as the conductor called the final "all aboard."

Rachel threw a small bouquet of wild flowers from the platform and laughed with joy as Gwen Carson, seated on the back of a two-wheeled cart, caught them.

The train gave a lurch forward and then another. The jerky movement caused Rachel to grab hold of the railing as Braeden took a possessive hold of her waist. They waved good-bye as the train pulled out of the station and headed north toward Lamy.

Rachel couldn't help but notice the blackened destruction of the town as they passed by. In the background she could barely make out the charred remains of Casa Grande. Shaking her head, she turned away from it and let Braeden draw her into their home on the rails.

"I'd say we made out pretty well, Mrs. Parker," Braeden declared, motioning to the room.

"It was kind of Mr. Harvey to offer us this car," she said, suddenly feeling very shy. It was the first time they had been alone, truly alone.

Sensing her change of mood, Braeden drew her into his arms.

"You look absolutely terrified, Mrs. Parker. Our future isn't that bleak. We may be temporarily unemployed and without a home or wardrobe, but it could be much worse."

She shook her head. "Yes," she whispered, reaching her hand up to his face. "I could have lost you in the fire."

"Or I could have lost you to Worthington."

She laughed. "No. There was never a real chance of that. Once he had me, he didn't seem to know what he wanted to do with me anyway. He never even touched me."

Something akin to relief seemed to wash over Braeden's expression. "I'm so glad. I would have hated for him to have hurt you." He put his hand over hers and pressed both to his cheek.

The uneven rocking of the tracks seemed to ease with a rhythmic flow as the train moved up to full speed. Rachel reached up to pull Braeden's face closer to her own.

"He only inconvenienced me," Rachel said seriously. "But losing you would have devastated me."

"You'll never lose me, Rachel," Braeden said before his lips caressed her mouth.

The future held many questions for them, but their love was the one thing that Rachel knew she could count on. Never again would whispered lies come between them. She would turn to truth and trust, and she would count on God's direction for their happiness. A long-awaited and hoped-for happiness that had come like an unexpected gift.

As Braeden lifted her in his arms, Rachel buried her face against his neck and sighed contentedly. She remembered a verse in the Bible about perfect love casting out fear and thought it very true. God had given her a perfect love through His Son, a love so sure and so complete that her spirit could never want for more. And then God blessed her with a perfect love in the form of a man named Braeden Parker.

Explore the World of Plain People Whose Lives Are *Not* So Simple

"*Lewis is a master of eliciting empathy for characters caught in troubles of their own making.... The tension between [the Plain people] and the encroaching English world is palpable.*"
—Library Journal

New York Times bestselling author Beverly Lewis brings to life the stories of ABRAM'S DAUGHTERS in this series about a quaint Old Order community, whose way of life and faith in God are as enduring as their signature horse and buggy. Or so it seems....

Join the hundreds of thousands of readers who have made every book in this series a #1 Christian fiction bestseller and discover for yourself the captivating charm of this Amish family.

ABRAM'S
DAUGHTERS
by Beverly Lewis

The Covenant
The Betrayal
The Sacrifice
The Prodigal
The Revelation

Whisper

Chris Struyk-Bonn

ORCA BOOK PUBLISHERS

Library and Archives Canada Cataloguing in Publication

Struyk-Bonn, Christina, author
Whisper / Chris Struyk-Bonn.

Issued in print and electronic formats.
ISBN 978-1-4598-0475-3 (pbk.).--ISBN 978-1-4598-0476-0 (pdf).--
ISBN 978-1-4598-0477-7 (epub)

I. Title.
PZ7.S9135wh 2014   j813'.6   C2013-906683-7
C2013-906684-5

First published in the United States, 2014
Library of Congress Control Number: 2013954148

Summary: Whisper, a teen girl with a cleft palate, is forced to survive in a world
that is hostile to those with disfigurements or disabilities.

*Orca Book Publishers is dedicated to preserving the environment and has printed this book on
Forest Stewardship Council® certified paper.*

Orca Book Publishers gratefully acknowledges the support for its publishing
programs provided by the following agencies: the Government of Canada through
the Canada Book Fund and the Canada Council for the Arts, and the Province of British
Columbia through the BC Arts Council and the Book Publishing Tax Credit.

Design by Chantal Gabriell
Cover image by Juliana Kolesova

ORCA BOOK PUBLISHERS   ORCA BOOK PUBLISHERS
PO Box 5626, Stn. B   PO Box 468
Victoria, BC Canada   CUSTER, WA USA
V8R 6S4   98240-0468

www.orcabook.com
Printed and bound in Canada.

17 16 15 14 • 4 3 2 1

For Eric, Quinten and Eli.

On the very first day of my existence, hands pushed me into the cold water and held me down, waiting for me to drown, but even then I was quiet and knew how to hold my breath.

Part One

One

It was my job to catch the crayfish for dinner. I didn't mind. I tried not to let Jeremia and Eva know that I actually liked it. They saw it as punishment, standing in the cold water, waiting and watching for the pinchers to appear from beneath the slippery rocks. Jeremia thought that he should catch them as a man would—leap high, pounce, grab anything he could get hold of. He emerged from the stream wetter than the crayfish, frustrated with work that produced so little and took so long.

Eva quickly lost interest in the task. She gazed up into the branches of the trees and then hummed to herself, distracted by zooming dragonflies or the light fractured by the leaves. She would swim with the fish, paddle with the ducks and become part of nature rather than try to capture it. We would starve if we had to depend on her ability to gather food.

I was quiet and still, like a leaf floating in the stream. The crayfish became accustomed to my clammy feet occupying space beside their favorite rock, and they started to trust me. I could almost hear them, even beneath the water, as they crept across the bottom of the creek. Everything else became background noise—the screech of the crickets, the gurgle of the water, the rustle of rubbing leaves. Then I eased my hand through the water and grabbed them just behind the pinchers, swift and sure.

But that day, just as I was about to grab a crayfish with only one pincher, the warning call interrupted me, and I missed.

The warning call meant a visitor. I crouched, twisting my head in a frantic search for a hiding place that would protect not me from them, but them from me. My breath came in short bursts, and the pounding of my heart drowned out all other sounds. I'd dropped too low and the seat of my shorts had soaked up the water, clinging to my skin. The silence of the woods felt unnerving, like the heavy air before a storm.

We only ever received two visitors at our secret forest hideaway where the leaves of the oaks, strangler figs and sky-reaching pines shaded us from sight. The nearest village, a tiny place with four more huts than ours, was a day's walk through the trees, and the villagers didn't like to come upon our camp of outcast children by surprise. The messenger came once a month, and we prepared for his appearance by hiding. The only other visitor was my mother, who always came on my birthday, but my birthday was still four weeks away.

I hid low in the bushes and inched forward, pushing aside branches, crushing the forest debris, silent as breath. The sudden buzz of a cicada vibrated the air around me.

I approached the back of my log-and-mud hut and crept around it until I was huddled between Jeremia's dwelling and mine. Our camp, so tiny and cloistered, consisted of four huts: mine, Jeremia and Eva's, Nathanael's and the storage hut. They squatted in a rough circle, with our fire pit and sitting logs creating the hub. Trees darkened the sky around our camp, leaving only a small round opening above us where we could see the stars at night, the sun during the heat of the day and the silver flash of an airplane as it drew lines across the sky. We knew about airplanes, refrigerators, trucks, toilets—Nathanael had educated us about the world beyond our camp—but knowledge and experience are two different things.

Jeremia crouched in the shadow of his hut, five-year-old Eva beside him. Both stared at me with wide eyes. Jeremia had his good arm around Eva, stilling her motions and calming them both. They had less than I did—they didn't even have mothers who visited them—but they also didn't have fathers who had tried to drown them. Nathanael had told them of my history so their jealousy wouldn't consume them when my mother came to visit.

I flattened myself against the rough log wall of my hut and peeked around the side. Nathanael stood by the fire pit in the middle of our camp. The sun behind the trees cast dappled shadows over his face. He waited, and while he waited he seemed to shrink. His clothes, which used to fit him, now flapped, loose and baggy, about his body. Even his shoes looked long and awkward. We didn't know what would happen to us when Nathanael, now sixty-nine, became too old to care for the unwanted. Where would we go? What would we do?

"Who are you?" Nathanael said, his voice wavering with age and perhaps fear. "What do you want?"

The messenger, who had never come mid-month, trampled the leaves and sticks of the woods, pushed through the hanging branches that shielded our huts from view and stepped out from the shadows. He wore the bill of his hat sideways, his pants so yellow they glowed, his shirt so red it flashed like a cardinal through the trees. His colors alerted all the creatures of the woods, including ourselves. I didn't understand why he had come; usually he carried the heavy load of our supplies. This time, all he had was his own food pack, a bundle under his shirt and something black strapped to his back. And then I heard the peep.

It sounded like a kitten—its high mewl made my hands flutter. I put my palm against my chest, afraid that my heart would respond to the cry and reveal my hiding spot. The messenger sat on the log and opened his shirt. Nathanael sat beside him. The messenger took out a small bundle wrapped in cloth and laid it on his knees. Both Nathanael and the messenger looked down at it. I stopped breathing. Nathanael grunted.

"They come so often now, one every three years. Before, it was one every ten or twenty," Nathanael said.

I glanced toward the graveyard. Low-hanging limbs, vines and shrubs obscured the space between me and the four graves, but I knew they were there. One had died after I came, before Eva arrived, before I understood that some babies lived.

"How old?" Nathanael asked.

"Three days."

"Eaten anything?"

The messenger shook his head and said, "Clemente and Maximo's fourth. They don't want it."

Nathanael nodded. He reached down and picked up the tiny bundle. He placed it on his own knee, his broad brown hands stretching beyond the cloth.

"I'm too old for this," he said. "Someday I may need to consider finding a replacement." He didn't look at the messenger.

The messenger's laugh sounded like the bark of a coyote. "No one else wants this job," he said. "Can't one of the rejects do it?" His hand waved outward. I crouched in the shadow of the hut, ten feet away from where they sat. I could see sweat trickle down the messenger's face.

"They won't want the job either," Nathanael said. One of his hands pulled back the cloth around the bundle, and a brown nose peeked through the blanket's opening.

"You want me to...you know"—the messenger leaned in toward Nathanael and spoke lower—"get rid of it?"

My body betrayed me then. My hands clutched at each other, gripping and wringing. Earlier I had been holding my breath; now it came fast, hard and shallow. I felt light-headed, and before I thought about revealing myself (and the possible consequences), I pushed off from the wall, heard my feet hitting the packed earth of the camp's meeting place and listened to the wind whistle past my ears. I grabbed the bundle off Nathanael's knees and leaped into the forest. I was jaguar, I was puma, I was hidden behind the nearest tree before they could react.

I peeked around the trunk. The messenger faced the forest, his eyes focused on the woods but not seeing me.

He crouched low, next to the log where Nathanael still sat, and spread his hands out, as if warding off evil. The sun beamed down on him, his nose creating a shadow that stretched across his mouth, down his chin and onto his neck. The black oblong object on his back, attached with a strap across his chest, banged against him a couple of times. He was clearly braced for an attack, and I smiled. His head turned back and forth. I hid only ten feet away from where he stood, but he didn't see me, he couldn't hear my heart hammering, he couldn't hear the breath I sucked in through my nose. He had seen too much already.

"What was that?" he asked. His eyes were wide, the whites showing all around his dark irises.

Nathanael turned his head and glanced into the woods.

"That was Whisper. She doesn't want you to get rid of it."

"That was Belen's child? Belen and Teresa's? She's an animal—and her face is…" His hands touched his own face, his unsplit lips and undamaged nose. "Is she dangerous?" The messenger backed away from the woods and stood near the fire pit. From his pocket he pulled a cell phone, and he held it up in the air, turning it this way and that. He pushed some buttons and shook the object.

"What, will you call for help?" Nathanael asked. "Ask for a helicopter to lift you out of this dangerous place? You'll have to climb the tree to get even the weakest of signals."

I snuggled the bundle against my chest and rocked my body back and forth. No movement came from it, nothing but a faint touch of breath. I gently flipped up the edge of the blanket and examined the round face. How anyone could think her ugly was astonishing to me, but I'd seen my own face in the creek on a clear day, and someday she would look exactly like me. I touched the tip of her nose against mine and breathed in her freshness.

Nathanael brushed a fly away from his ear. "What do you have on your back?"

The messenger pulled the black strap over his head and handed the oblong object—I could see now that it was some kind of case—to Nathanael. His eyes continued to look into the trees, trying to find me. I moved through the underbrush a few steps closer so I could see better.

Nathanael unlatched the locks on the case and removed something made of wood, with strings stretched from the narrow end to the rounded end.

"It's from Whisper's mother. She won't be coming on her birthday."

The wind howled in my head, and I sat down hard on the forest floor. I didn't care that twigs snapped beneath me and leaves rustled. When I slumped to the ground, the smell of moss, earth and crushed scorpion flower wafted into the air, making my head feel insubstantial. I didn't care that the messenger might have seen me, could have come through the trees and found me crouched with the baby in my arms.

My mother wasn't coming.

She was abandoning me too. I had known it would happen. I had known that eventually she'd want to avoid the inconvenient trek to our home, like the parents of the others in our camp. For fifteen years she had walked the three days to the camp, loved me, sung to me, talked to me like a normal human being, called me Lydia, the name I'd been born with, and then walked the three days back.

And because she had come for so many years, I'd grown weak, hopeful, accepting that this was the pattern of my life. I believed that she still loved me and that maybe someday she would take me home.

I clutched the bundle close to my chest and felt the rhythm of the baby's breathing against my neck. I leaned against the rough bark of a pine tree and tilted my head back. I gazed up, taking in the branches that arched over my head, obscuring the blue of the sky. The comfort of loving arms was gone. My own arms would have to do now.

Lose a mother, gain a sister.

"They won't attack me when I'm in the woods, will they?" asked the messenger as he slung his food pack over his shoulder and adjusted the brim of his cap. He looked around as if the woods were full of rejects, huffing and grunting, waiting to consume him. Nathanael said nothing.

He went to his hut and returned with one of Jeremia's sculptures, about the size of Eva, wrapped in palm leaves. He held it up while the messenger turned, bent over and held out his hands behind his back while Nathanael leaned the object into his hands. The messenger supported the weight, and Nathanael wrapped a thick cord around and under the sculpture, securing it to the man's back. This was how we paid our expenses. The messenger sold Jeremia's sculptures in the village or in the city and bought our supplies with the profits. Nathanael believed the messenger was pocketing any extra money. We had no idea how much Jeremia's sculptures sold for, but he carved more than enough to sustain our modest lifestyle.

The messenger grunted and began his plodding retreat from our forest home. His eyes shifted from side to side, as if waiting for us, the rejects, to ambush him.

When we were alone again, Nathanael sat on one of the logs by the fire pit and waited. I crept out from behind the tree. Jeremia and Eva tiptoed out from beside their hut. We stole forward on silent feet to Nathanael. I gently lowered the bundle to Nathanael's knees and then sat on the very edge of the log. Jeremia and Eva crouched at Nathanael's feet and touched the baby's head.

Nathanael told Eva to get a bowl of water and she ran nimbly to our creek, returning with a cup sloshing liquid over the edge. Nathanael dipped his pinky into the water. He slipped droplets onto the baby's mouth until the lips parted and she squeaked. Nathanael placed more water into her throat where it was sure to go down. If the water touched the slices in the skin between her nose and mouth, nothing would go down her throat and into her stomach. The baby swallowed again and again and then opened her eyes.

We looked at each other. She was beautiful, with her brown eyes and fresh smell. I didn't understand why her parents didn't want her, why Jeremia's didn't want him, why Eva's didn't want her, why my father had tried to kill me.

Nathanael held the baby with one hand and slid my birthday present onto my knees with the other. The case was cold, hard, unfeeling, so different from a mother's touch. I unlatched the clasps and opened the case.

"A violin," Nathanael said. He had grown up in the village, traveled to the city and then chosen to come to our camp—on purpose, not because he had to. "What use is that to us? Maybe we can start the fire with it," he said.

The instrument was warm to the touch, chestnut brown with streaks like golden sunlight radiating through it. I plucked each string with my first finger and listened to the sound. Twangy. High-pitched. Nasal. Like my voice.

"Here," Nathanael said. He slid the baby into my lap and then pulled the violin out of my hand. He set the cup of water by my foot, and I began dipping my finger into it and dropping the water into her mouth. She swallowed, blinked, swallowed again. Jeremia slid his finger into her pink tight-fisted palm, and her tiny hand hugged his narrow finger. Eva laughed.

Nathanael shuffled to his hut and threw aside the deer-skin door. After a minute I heard the voices from the radio, one of two stations we could hear clearly. Usually, to save the batteries, we only listened to the news station and tried to understand what was happening in a world we'd never seen and would never be accepted into. But now Nathanael adjusted the knobs and I heard static, more static, and then—music. Nathanael turned up the volume and shuffled back out of his hut.

The music fit with the sounds around us—the wind, the birds, the crickets. Jeremia put his chin on my knee. He was in an affectionate mood, but his moods changed with the wind, and I'd learned to be cautious.

I'd never heard music like this before. It was the sound of the blue-black grosbeak, only sweeter and more painful.

It was the sound of my loneliness, clear and nerve-tingling. As I listened to the music, my heart squeezed itself small, flattened into a straight line and compressed into nothingness: a tick, a flea, the point of a pencil.

"That's the sound a violin can make," Nathanael said.

I looked down at the instrument in Nathanael's hand. He lifted it up, fit it beneath his chin and drew the long stick with hairs across the strings. His fingers pushed against the strings in various places and different notes emerged. His hands were stretched out long, the muscles taut, and when I looked at his face, I saw a tear make a snail's trail down his cheek. He abruptly placed the violin in the case and walked to his hut. The goat, Naya, bleated and followed him.

I understood why my mother had given it to me. The violin *was* me, nasal and foreign, but somewhere within its depths something beautiful resided. I looked at Jeremia. He looked at me. And on my lap, the new reject, the beautiful baby, closed her eyes, smiled and passed gas.

"You two must be related," Jeremia said, squeezing my calf muscle.

Two

In the morning, Jeremia was gone. His time had been approaching. He disappeared in cycles, like the moon, and then reappeared. I knew that in two years, when he turned nineteen, he wouldn't come back. He would vanish like the four rejects before him, not one of them returning to our little camp in the woods. They went to more civilized places where the trees grew crooked in their search for sun and where the crickets couldn't be heard. They journeyed through the forest, traversed the creeks and joined hundreds, thousands, of people gathered in places with no birds. Nathanael said the city was an unforgiving concrete slab, full of so much noise that it was hard to hear yourself. He said the air was toxic and a smell—dark and evil—caused sickness like the tendrils of ivy, touching and choking everything.

I didn't understand what, in that cold world of square buildings, unnatural light and illness, was so wonderful and so precious that the other rejects would abandon the only home they'd ever known. I couldn't imagine that I would ever make that choice. It wasn't bad, living in our camp, just isolated.

That first morning after the baby arrived, Nathanael and Eva were sitting together on the log when I stumbled from my hut, the sun already above my head. The baby, strapped to my chest, had woken me every time I fell asleep, and during the night when I had looked through my window, the moon had seemed not to move at all. Old cloth diapers, yellowed and worn with age—saved from when I first came to the camp, from when Jeremia first came to the camp and even from those before Jeremia—had been tossed haphazardly in front of my hut and required washing. The baby needed something more substantial than water. She slept and woke, slept and woke.

Eva hiccupped and sniffled through tears. At first I thought it was because Jeremia was gone, but then I saw her hand. Porcupine barbs were thrust deep into her palm. Nathanael shakily twisted them out with his thumb and first finger. When he saw me, he moved over, and I sat next to Eva. She was trying so hard to be brave, her chubby cheeks red and mottled from tears and held breath. She bit down on her lower lip and looked at me through watery eyes. Her webbed hands were red and swollen.

I twisted each barb and then removed it with a quick yank. She jerked every time I pulled one out, but she didn't run away nor did she hide her hand.

"Jeremia left because of me," she said.

"No."

"Yes. He told me only stupid people touch porcupines, and I'm the stupidest person he's ever met." Eva was a creature of the forest. She sang with the birds, jumped with the grasshoppers, fed squirrels from her hands. It made sense that she would try to touch a porcupine. Nathanael sat on the other side of Eva and put his arm around her shoulders.

I pulled the last barb from her hand and then poured water over the wounds. The blood and water mingled, dripping from the webbing between her fingers in dark-red rivulets.

"Jeremia is like a cat, Eva," Nathanael said. "He is moody and angry. He needs to be alone for a while."

"Why is he so angry?" Eva asked.

"Jeremia is the only boy ever rejected. Even disfigured boys aren't rejected, but his parents already had four sons, and when he was born with only one arm and couldn't do the same amount of farmwork as his brothers, they decided they didn't need him."

"My parents didn't want me either," Eva said, her sore hand held in her good one. "And Whisper's dad tried to drown her. We're all the same...aren't we? That's what you always told us."

"Yes," Nathanael said, "and no. You two are girls. Jeremia is the only boy. He feels it more—this abandonment. Boys are precious and respected—to be rejected means—"

"That the boy is like a girl," Eva said, smearing the water around on her face, leaving smudges of mud. "I don't see what's so special about being a boy. They smell worse than girls. They fart and burp."

Nathanael looked to the sky and laughed. It was a good sound, but he woke the baby, who wailed that nasal, throaty cry that made my throat tighten. I wondered if a mixture of goat's milk and water would help her sleep.

I fed the baby a bit of water, strapped her to my chest with the cloth and walked around the fire pit. Her eyes drooped, her mouth opened, her breath slowed. Nathanael took her from me, laid her in the camping chair and handed me the violin. I held it to my shoulder and Nathanael's fingers pushed against my own, showing me how to create a different note by applying pressure to the strings. I moved the bow with my right hand and changed the positioning of my left-hand fingers. I could do this. It was tricky, but I could do it.

My fingers fluttered over the strings, pushed here, pushed there. At first a nasal twang screeched from the instrument, but if I pulled the bow just so and held it down, a sweetness rolled from the strings, and I could feel the music pouring out of me. I smiled at Nathanael.

"Yes," he said and looked at me with eyes narrowed, weighing and assessing. I put down the violin, picked up the baby and sang her a simple lullaby, one my mother had sung to me. Soon I would play it for her on the violin.

The goat's milk didn't work. When I first gave it to her, she gulped it greedily, swallowed and demanded more, but when it settled into her stomach, she started to cry and then cried for hours. I burped her against my shoulder, walked her back and forth, felt my own tears joining hers, and then remembered my mother's lullaby.

Nathanael was asleep in our only camping chair. His head rested against the flimsy fabric; his mouth was wide open, and he emitted a loud, rumbling snore every few seconds. Mornings in our camp were for lessons. Nathanael, who had lived in the village until he was twenty, taught us how to read, how to do math, how to utilize the plants around us. He had lived in the city for three years. When we asked him why, he told us he had been "searching."

I set the baby on a bed of layered blankets in my hut and propped her up like a warm sack of flour so that she could still burp if she needed to. Then I opened the violin case. Her crying came in hiccups and shivers, her face a deep, bruised red. I fit the instrument against my shoulder and under my chin as Nathanael had shown me. I held the bow in my right hand and eased it over the strings. I listened for the notes Nathanael had taught me. The sound was so harsh and creaky, the baby hiccupped her crying to a stop and opened her eyes. I tried again.

The noise the violin made was no better than my own voice, but I had heard the music from the radio. I knew what the violin was capable of creating. I slowed down, took a deep breath, tried not to let the baby's renewed cries make me so shaky. I whispered the lyrics in my mind and fumbled my way through the tune, pressing my left fingers to the strings and drawing the bow with my right. After a few minutes of fumbling, the song became recognizable.

Corinna, Corinna
time for the baby to eat.
Milk in the morning
at noon ripened wheat

at night soft dates,
acorns from the trees,
dandelion fluff
on the quiet evening breeze.

I listened to the notes and pictured my mother holding me, rocking me, caressing my head with her hand. She would tuck my black hair behind my ears and smooth the strands over my head. I remembered the feel of her palms, rough and calloused but also beautiful and loving. I remembered the sound of her voice, so deep, full and true. The violin began to take on those tones as I played the simple tune over and over. When I felt the warm notes winging around the hut, I opened my eyes.

The baby was asleep. So was Eva. She had crept in while I was playing and now lay in front of the door, her left hand under her cheek, her swollen right hand wrapped in a white cloth and clutched against her chest.

I played the lullaby again.

The baby's sharp, desperate cries startled me awake four times in the night, my hands trembling from lack of sleep.

I dripped more water into her mouth; I held her against my shoulder and patted the gas from her stomach. This child would not be another mound in the graveyard, not if I could find something to fill her, something that could replace mother's milk.

The third time she woke me up, when the moon had already crossed the opening between the trees above our huts, I heard a keening so sad and mournful I wanted to cry along with the baby. I wrapped her tightly against my chest and walked silently through the woods, down the path to the creek, the sad song pushing against my nose, making it drip.

He didn't hear me when I padded up behind him. The baby was quiet now, satisfied with the sound of my heart, and I squatted on my heels where I could see him, a shadow on the branch over the swimming hole. Nathanael was like a grasshopper, his arms bent at the elbows, his knees angled out, his feet hooked around each other under the branch.

He played a song as lonely and sad as an owl at night. My throat tightened, and I sat in the mud of the path. This was the song of a broken heart, and I suddenly understood Nathanael a little better. I'd always thought that he hated the village we were from, hated the city, and chose to live with us because it was his best option. But Nathanael had had other options, and they must have vanished.

When he pulled the bow over the strings one last time, the lingering notes floating across the water like the dragonflies, I opened my eyes, stood and slipped back down the path. I knew now that Nathanael had known love and it had disappeared like dew on the grass. Nathanael had told us so little about himself that I'd always thought of him as our father, single, satisfied.

I heard him creep into my hut, replace the violin in its case and drop the deerskin door back into place. I slept after that, for a few hours anyway, until the baby's piercing cries woke me again. I slept with an ache now, an ache that food could not fill.

In the morning, Eva climbed up the great pine by our camp. There was a large macaw's nest in an open cavity halfway up the trunk. Eva believed there were babies in that opening. Jeremia refused to let her climb the tree because he remembered me at seven, when I'd climbed up for no reason other than because I could and had become stuck. I'd stayed up in that tree all day long. Rosa, my mentor at the time, had stood below the pine, her arms across her chest, refusing to let anyone help me down.

"You got up there, you get down. You won't always have someone to rescue you, you know."

She'd gone to bed at dark, and Jeremia had climbed the tree, showing me the best places to put my feet and how to slide down the trunk when branches were scarce.

But Eva was not me. She was loud, courageous, willing to touch porcupines with her bare hands. She acted while I preferred to listen. When I woke up in the morning, tired from a broken night of shuddering cries, Eva already held tightly to the trunk of the tree, her webbed feet clutched against either side, a towel in one of her hands. The opening with the nest was inches above her head.

Nathanael had explained to Eva that baby birds weren't born in late summer; they're born in the spring and should be out of the nest, flying on their own, by this time, but Eva, hands clenched into stubborn fists, didn't believe him.

"What about the fox?" she said. "Look at her puppies."

We didn't know what to say to that. We didn't understand why the puppies were still running about, half the size of their mother, and why they followed her, not daring to hunt on their own.

"There is a baby bird in that nest that can't get out. I'm going to rescue it."

I stood below the tree, my thoughts muddled from lack of sleep, the baby quiet against my chest, smudges of black beneath her eyes where healthy brown skin should have been. Nathanael milked the goat by his hut and turned the radio on. Sometimes the stations came through clearly, and sometimes they came through garbled. Today was a mix; I caught much of what was said but didn't understand the words. "Due to high interest rates, high unemployment and a low economic report, both the Dow Jones Industrial Average and the NASDAQ dropped last night. A recovery is hoped..." Nathanael hummed along as though it were music, but I focused on Eva up in the branches.

She was cautious and inched her way up the trunk with the ease and confidence of a sloth. She reached her hand into the hole, the towel draped over her shoulder. When she began to remove her hand from the opening, peeps and squawks filtered down from the nest, and I saw the mother macaw hovering above Eva, shrieking and nervously flapping her wings.

Eva began to sing, a sweet, light call. She crept forward again, the mother bird squawking and fluttering near her head. Eva ignored the mother, ignored the wings that flapped in panic, and pulled a green splash of color from the nest, wrapping it quickly in the towel. She tucked the towel into her shirt and began her retreat. The mother macaw, green and red against the sky, a flower in motion, screamed and cried. Her shrill call reminded me of the baby's, so desperate and scared. Mothers should protect their babies, threaten those who would take them away and cry in desperation. Why had all of our mothers surrendered us, given us away to this forest home instead of flapping their wings and calling for help?

The sun was high in the sky by the time Eva reached the ground. Her short black hair clung in sweaty clumps to the back of her neck, and her limbs trembled. She set the towel down and shook out her arms and legs, wiping the sweat from her eyes. Huddled in the brown cloth was a macaw, hardly a baby anymore, green and pink with a red tuft above its beak. The bird looked perfect, its beak thick, gray and pointed, its eyes pink and wary.

Eva placed both hands around the bird so it could not flutter or peck. The macaw squawked, and the mother answered in shrill fear from a branch near our heads.

"Look," Eva said. She held the bird with only one hand and slid a finger under the bird's wing. The feathers opened, puffed, ready for flight, but the wing was miniature, a tiny, perfect replica that had failed to grow along with the bird. Eva lifted the wing on the other side, also miniature.

"I'm keeping her."

Eva carried the baby against her chest and walked with jutted chin to her hut, closed the deerskin door and shut the mother out. The terrified mother perched on the roof of Eva's hut and called to her baby all day. I watched that mother and wondered what she would have done when her new babies came the next year. Would she have kept the older baby or pushed it out of the nest to make room for the perfectly formed new ones?

Three

Jeremia returned after a few days. He went to the city sometimes, to crouch in alleyways, to understand what people did
who lived outside our little camp and were an accepted part
of the world. Sometimes he watched the people in our old
village. He saw his father, observed his family. He loved and
hated them with a fierceness that scared me. He never spoke
to them or revealed himself, but he referred to them by name.

He ran into my hut while I played the violin, shimmied
over the dirt floor, leaped across the blankets that made up
my bed and danced in front of the stack of books on my rock
and wood shelf, all the while wagging his butt and waving
his one hand in the air. He opened his mouth and pretended
to sing. He grabbed me around the waist and twirled me
around. Then he was out the door. No one asked him where
he went or why, and no one accused him of abandoning us
and shirking his chores. Abandonment was nothing new

and we all knew that it was better for Jeremia to understand himself—understand the rest of the world—than for him to stay and torment us with his moodiness.

Nathanael cooked rice for supper. He mashed some of the rice until it was mush and then added water. He stirred the pale substance, and when I looked at it, I could almost believe it was milk. I sat on a log by the fire and dripped bits of rice milk into the baby's throat. She gulped eagerly.

I waited for the gas to start, her stomach to clench, her crying to begin. Already I was prepared for a sleepless night of shrieks, shuddering and fussiness. Even though we'd fed her goat's milk for days, she'd never become accustomed to it.

Instead, she watched me, her eyes round and dark, her face solemn, as if examining my distorted features was the key to understanding herself. She was content and calm, not squirming and crying, so I unwrapped her from her cotton clothing and cleaned her with warm water.

Jeremia and Eva laughed. They laughed until tears dripped muddy streaks down their cheeks because the baby's tummy was so full and round, her limbs so thin and small, that she looked like a frog, a *rana*, and that is how she got her name. Ranita. Little Frog. I liked it. It fit her.

We gathered on the logs around the fire, the baby calm and still, Eva's head resting on Jeremia's knee, Jeremia's eyes bloodshot from lack of sleep, his face smudged with dirt from the trip. He was always so happy when he returned that

I wondered why he did it, why he tortured himself by watching a bruised world he couldn't heal.

There were others from our camp who had never returned. Rosa, my roommate, camp sister and mentor, left when she was fourteen and never came back. Jeremia's mentor, Telise, never returned either. Every time Jeremia disappeared, Eva fidgeted, worried and slept in the hut with me. She was always sure Jeremia wouldn't come back.

"It's worse now," Jeremia said. "Many, many of us."

Ranita's eyelids began to close. Her tiny hands relaxed and she breathed softly through her open mouth. I lifted her from my legs and held her beneath my nose, breathing her in, sweet and fresh.

"Tell us," Nathanael said. He leaned forward in the camping chair, his knobby hands on his knees. He looked into the fire.

"It was the same as before. I came through the oaks, through the stunted bushes, over the reeking creek to the place with roads. I followed the road back to the mountains, to the city, until I came to the hill of rocks and slept there, watching travelers on the road, coming and going."

We'd heard this part of the story before. Jeremia often found a cave or a rock overhang for shelter and watched from his safe perch. Other people lived in these rocks, many like us, he said, and they sometimes lived together in camps like ours, where they shared a fire, food, company. But he also said they sometimes stole from each other or rolled among the rocks kicking and hitting or attacking the weakest.

This time he had slept near a camp with four boys in it, beside a train track, over which trains roared every few hours.

Two of the boys looked a bit like me, he said, with openings in their faces that shouldn't have been there, but the other two boys were different. One had no arms or legs and had to be carried from place to place. The other had no nose or ears, only openings where the cartilage should have been. I tried to imagine this, having a face with no nose. Even though my face is open in odd places, I have cartilage. I wondered if he could smell—what life would be like if you never knew the aroma of honeysuckle in the spring.

"They were a tribe," Jeremia said. "They'd built a platform on wheels for the boy, a rolling platform with a strap that held him in place. In the morning, they rolled to the city, and they came back at dusk, when the sweeping lights search the sky. They would have food, money, bottles of drink. They sat around their fire and talked to each other, their voices growing louder and louder as the moon moved across the sky, until one boy became very sick and the other three fell asleep. They did not hear the other tribe coming."

I held Ranita tightly against my chest and listened to her breathing. Jeremia had stopped speaking, his hand curled into a fist. A pulse appeared in his left cheek, as though his jaw was clamped so tight it begged for release.

"The other tribe was normal, without blemish, like Nathanael."

We all looked at Nathanael as though we had forgotten his face. He had little hair now—a few thin strands that grew against the sides of his head—and his face had grooves in it like a walnut shell, but he did not have extra openings in his face where water sometimes trickled out, he did not have webbed feet like the ducks, and he was not missing an arm.

"While the first tribe slept, the other tribe took everything. They took the food, the money, the drinks. They took the radio and headphones, they took the rolling platform for the boy with no legs, they took the plastic covering that sheltered the first tribe from the rain. And then they woke up the first tribe."

Eva covered her eyes with her hands. Jeremia watched Nathanael now, the muscles in his arm tensed. Jeremia looked like an adult with his black eyes, the fire dancing shadows across his face. He was almost eighteen, much older than the other rejects had been when they left, but he still returned. I hoped it was because of me.

"Why are they like that, Nathanael?" Jeremia said.

I thought Nathanael had not heard. He didn't move or blink. He stared into the fire while I listened to the sounds of the wolf on the hill, the crickets in the grasses, the bats in the sky. Slowly he turned his head. His eyes were old, creased below, above, to the sides.

"People are cruel," Nathanael said. "Here we are unnoticed, isolated, maybe even a bit lonely, but it is better to be unnoticed than to be in civilization where cruelty will find you."

Jeremia nodded as though he understood Nathanael's comments.

"It found that first tribe, cruelty. Those other boys used boards, they used rocks. I heard the first tribe screaming, running, trying to get away to hide in the hills or between the boulders. I'd never heard screams like that, so terrified, like animals in pain. I thought of the screaming rabbit that woke us one night with its head caught beneath the root. These boys screamed like that, like death would be welcome."

I remembered the scream of the rabbit. I'd been about eight, still living in the hut with Rosa, and the scream cut through our dreams and woke us. She'd held me that time, held me close, covering my ears, adding her own screams to that of the rabbit until Nathanael had freed the creature and it had run, unhurt, into the trees. We'd slept together then, her arm around me, her body warm and protecting. The night of the screaming rabbit is my best memory of Rosa.

"They got away, the two who looked like Whisper, and the one without ears. The fourth rolled on the ground, twisted below their legs while they laughed and hit him with the board. He begged once, prayed that they would stop, but after they laughed and spit on him, he was silent. He waited for the board to come down again. I couldn't watch anymore, so I ran at the cruel boy whose back was to me. I knocked him to the ground, grabbed the board from his hand and stood over the armless boy on the ground. There were three surrounding us, three whose bodies appeared perfect, but they backed away when their friend did not rise. I snarled, and they ran."

I wasn't breathing. I held Ranita tightly against my chest and thought of violent boys chasing me through the night. I thought of how my heart would have pounded, how I would have run like a puma, fear chasing me. I would never go to the city.

"I dragged the boy into the space between the rocks, went down the hill and filled a bottle with water from the creek. The water had a film over the top like the skin of dead leaves after winter, and he drank from the water. He drank for two days, but he could not speak. He never told me his name, and the wound on his head would not stop bleeding even when I pressed a cloth against it. On the third day, he died. I covered the opening with rocks and walked through the forest, the wolf howling on the hill. I never saw his tribe again—they never returned to look for him.

"And then I went to see my family." Jeremia was silent for a moment, his hand skillfully flipping a knife between his fingers. He had been working on a large maple sculpture, and in it I could see leaves from the trees, falling, falling, never touching the ground. We were Jeremia's family.

"I watched my brother, my oldest one, Calen. He hunted the wolf."

Jeremia's wolf followed him everywhere, but always at a distance. Jeremia had never smoothed the coarse fur of the wolf's mane and the wolf had never brushed his rough tongue along Jeremia's hand, and yet they watched each other, predicted each other's moods, followed in each other's footsteps.

Calen couldn't catch the wolf, of course. He followed it up into the hills, tracked the footprints in the soft mud of the creek bank, but he was so loud and clumsy in his movements, the animals stayed miles away.

"My brother returned to the village with nothing and Jun, my father, hit him on the side of the head with the gun Calen carried. My mother came out of their square house, pressed a cloth against Calen's head, but Calen pushed her away so roughly she fell to the ground."

Four boys his mother had raised, four rough boys who beat each other blue and purple for saying the wrong word, breathing too loudly, giving the wrong look. Only Calen, the oldest, lived at home anymore. Jeremia wasn't sure why his brother chose not to get married and have his own family. He was like Jeremia, though, taking aimless walks that were not intended for food gathering. Such walks produced ideas, claimed Jeremia, and understanding.

In our village, parents abandoned us, older sisters left for the city and we never heard from them again. Would I do the same when I got older? Would I someday leave Eva, Ranita and old Nathanael? I swore I would not do this. I would not abandon the people who had become my tribe.

All night I held Ranita against my chest. I heard the creek trickling its song through the night, I heard the coyotes snuffling by the fire, I heard the soft barks of the fox puppies, I heard the distant whine of an airplane, and I heard Eva's macaw, Emerald, chirping in her hut, but I did not hear boys with boards running through the woods, even though I listened until the sun reached its fingers into the hut.

Since returning from his last excursion, Jeremia had changed. His actions seemed desperate now, more frantic and intense. While I warmed water on the fire, preparing to wash Ranita, he came up behind me, silent as a moth. I felt his nervousness, his fluttering hand, and when I looked at him, I saw his mouth moving, his lips whispering to himself. If I remained calm, gave him his space, maybe he would relax, stop fidgeting. Instead, he picked Ranita up from where I had laid her on the grasses and held her against his cheek. He closed his eyes and breathed deeply. He brought Ranita to Nathanael, who sat in the camping chair in front of the fire, and rested her on the old man's knees. Nathanael picked up the baby, rocked back and forth, hummed.

Jeremia grabbed me around the upper arm with his long, muscled fingers, pulling me away from the water and toward the creek. He let go and began to walk up the path. He didn't turn to watch me, didn't check to make sure my steps followed his—he knew I would come. We'd walked this path many times, day and night, sun and wind, but usually Eva was with us, running ahead, shrieking and hopping over the branches in our path. Often Nathanael came along with his fishing pole, wishing to catch the trout in the water hole.

It was early in the day to swim, but the water was always warm in late summer. The trees above the hole stretched their branches to the sun, leaving an opening above the water that sucked in heat. Jeremia sat on the branch of the pine that reached out over the water, took off his shirt and swung his feet. His body reminded me of the willow tree, limber and thin, his muscles moving beneath the skin, his ribs gently raised bumps. His second arm was a rounded limb that reached to where his elbow would have been. I was so accustomed to seeing his arm without fingers that it didn't seem strange to me.

I sat beside him and waited.

Our feet were almost the same color, darkened by the sun, but his toes were long and bumpy while mine were short and curled. I tilted my head back, felt the warmth of the sun and looked up into the sky. A solitary vulture, with its bald head and shaggy wings, flapped across the opening between the trees, and I saw the smoky trail of an airplane as it cruised through the sky in its carefully plotted path. I heard the hum of the mosquitoes just awakening. I saw the stirring of the water bugs skimming the surface of the pool. A leaf lazily drifted to the opening where the stream trickled from the pool.

Jeremia's hand touched mine. I looked down at our hands, his fingers over mine, warm and dry against my skin. That small touch, so light and delicate, sent tingles through my wrist and up my arm. I had been touched by Jeremia many times, but lately his touch had changed. When we were younger, we'd wrestled like kittens. We'd tumbled over each other, fought with each other, scratched, pinched, hit, but now every contact meant something more. I wanted him to touch me all the time.

I looked at him. His eyes were pinched around the edges, as though he couldn't see me clearly without squinting. Something needed to be said, but I didn't know what. None of us talked much—except for Eva, who chattered like the squirrels. Nathanael was quiet, and Rosa had been moody and spoke almost always in caustic bites. Jeremia and I had never needed to speak; we understood each other. But sitting beside him wasn't enough right now because I didn't know what he saw when he visited the city, and I didn't have the words to speak to him about it.

A groan came from his lips. Then he dropped from the branch, his body straight, and slid like an otter into the water. I could see his legs frog-kick and move him just beneath the surface. His black hair spread behind him, straight and streaming. When his head surfaced, the sun glistened off the drops on his skin and made him beautiful. He pulled his arm back and dragged it along the surface of the water, sending a plume into the air that hit my legs. I pushed off from the branch and dropped without a splash, my legs straight. This was a language I understood. I dropped down, down, until my feet hit the muck of the bottom, and then I pushed up right below Jeremia. I found his ankle and pulled hard.

He came down too easily and put his hand on my shoulder, pushing me back into the mud. I flipped my body around and dug my fingers into the sludge of the bottom. I grasped a handful and rose to the surface. I waited for his head to come back up. The dappled shadow of his form moved away from me, toward the bank where the otter's slide muddied the hill.

The ooze in my hand began to slip through my fingers and trickle down my arm. When Jeremia's head came to the surface, I threw the muck, but his hand came up, stopping the muddy assault. He smiled at me, a grin that darkened his eyes. He took a handful of muck from the otter slide and pelted me with it. I ducked below the surface, laughing as I went and choking on the water that flowed through the slits in my face and into my nose. He would come for me now, so I turned and swam to the opposite side of the hole, the side where the wild rose hung over the water. I surfaced beneath the branches, hoping they were thick enough to cover me, and waited.

I couldn't see him, didn't know where he would emerge. I held my breath. His head pushed the water up, a rising bubble, and he looked at me from only inches away. I could see the gold flecks in his brown eyes. Water dripped from his perfect nose and mouth. My feet dug into the ooze of the hole.

"This is the best life we'll ever have," he said, "here, with just our tribe."

I looked at the banks of the pool, trying to understand what he meant. This pool was good. We ate well, except for during the late winter when supplies ran low. But my mother was not returning and I now had a baby to care for. Life could be better.

"Out there, no one cares. We have to stay together."

His hand gripped my arm, squeezed and tightened. His mouth was pulled straight and his eyes did not shift. Where had this Jeremia come from? What had happened to the playful Jeremia who swung me about and danced against the light of the fire, who carved such beautiful sculptures that I wanted to crawl inside them and let their cascading water-falls forever slide over my body? The Jeremia gripping my arm knew about a world I'd never seen and didn't care to understand. My heart pounded beneath his fingers.

"Only us, Whisper."

He pulled me to him, our chests meeting. I could feel his heart beating, speaking to my own, and his mouth against mine was like the first bite of a fresh mango. My lips parted, the slit opening and spreading against the solid skin of his own lips. He didn't seem to mind. My hands slid across the skin of his back and tightened, pressing him against me so the length of his body met my own. He lifted my feet out of the mud and his arm held me close, so close, but not close enough.

And then he let go. I sank back into the mud and we looked at each other. I held my hand against my chest, trying to still my heart, to cover its almost visible pounding.

Jeremia swam to the bank where the pine tree hung over the pool and pulled himself out. He reached for his shirt, glanced at me one last time and then walked back down the path.

I wanted him back. We weren't children anymore, couldn't roll in the grasses, wrestle in the mud, rest our backs against each other for warmth in the night when the chill seeped through our blankets. Something had changed, and even though I was almost sixteen, my birthday only days away, I was not a woman. I had not yet grown breasts, and I had not yet had my period. I knew I was late—Rosa had gotten hers when she was fourteen. But I did know that my feelings were true, and my blood pounded when Jeremia touched me. I wanted that feeling again, his body pressed against mine as snug as bones.

Four

Our job—Eva's and mine—was to dry blueberries, wild raspberries and blackberries for the winter months. We picked them in great quantities and laid them on the plastic sheet near the fire. Eva's job was to scoot away the bugs that liked the berries as much as we did. Eva always forgot and chased after a dragonfly or played her games of pretend. I went through the berries again later in the day and removed what bugs I could find.

When fruit was growing all around us in the summer, it was hard to imagine how little we'd have in the winter. The air was thick with the smell of sweet berries and oncoming fall. I used to love this time of year because it meant my mother was coming. The air itself breathed her presence, a delicious promise.

Rosa had hated my mother. I used to dance in anticipation of her coming, and Rosa would swat at my legs, smack me on the side of the head and huff. "Your mother doesn't deserve your love. She abandoned you. She deserves hate."

I had thought about that. I had considered hating my mother, but she had saved me as best she could. When I was born and my father saw my disfigured face, he said, "Devil, witch, stealer of lives" and ran with me to the stream. He held me below the surface of the water, but my mother had chased after him. She pulled me from him, held me tightly against her chest and refused to let my father touch me. I was their first child. Then she gave me to Nathanael, who told me the story when he thought I was old enough to understand. He had wanted to make it clear that I belonged here and not with my family.

"I see my mother one day a year," I had whispered to Rosa. "Why would I spend that day hating her?" Every time my mother came for a visit, I asked her, begged her, pleaded with her to take me with her, to take me back to the village. She'd tuck my hair behind my ears, smile a half smile, call me Lydia and shake her head. For many years, all I dreamed about, all I wanted, was to go home with my mother, but Rosa told me such dreams were stupid.

When my mother came, Rosa would stay only long enough to glare at her, snarl a few times and stomp around. Then she'd leave and return when my mother was gone.

Rosa was still young when she left our camp. Only fourteen. I thought about her sometimes and wondered what had happened to her. She had lashed out at life, and I often got in the way. But sometimes she'd comb my hair until it glowed black and glossy. She'd braid it for me, tenderly and carefully, and I would forget that she'd slapped me the hour before. When she left, I was lonely but also secretly happy.

I promised to be a better sister to Ranita than Rosa had been to me. I would never hit. I would never torment or ridicule. Rosa had made fun of my whispering all the time. She said it was stupid. "You have a voice—use it," she'd shriek at me. I hadn't wanted to sound like her. Ever. My own voice was nasal, airy and distorted.

My mother never made fun of me. I had her for one day a year, one short day, from early afternoon, when she arrived, to the morning, when she had to leave, and I spent every moment touching her hair, holding her hand, resting the skin of my arm against hers. Did she miss me when she left? Did she miss me as much as I missed her?

"Your father is a very important man in the village," she told me while combing my hair, preparing it for a braid. "He sits on the council with many other important men like Jeremia's father, Jun. They make the decisions for our village."

Her hands, so gentle in my hair, so different from Rosa's, almost lulled me to sleep. My head rocked in motion with her fingers.

"Someday you will meet a man, Whisper. A man you can love because only you know how to reach him. Your father is such a man for me."

How could anyone love a man who had tried to drown their first child? My mother's hands soothed, combed and brushed my tangled hair, making it shine like a raven's wing. But I knew now what she meant. Jeremia, whose dancing anger whirled and burned, was such a man for me. I understood him. Better than anyone else.

"He needs me, and sometimes need and love become tangled," she said.

At the time, I didn't know what she meant, but I remembered every word. I remembered her stories about my brothers, Mateo and David, who looked like my father but were as different from each other as the vulture is from the hummingbird. I remembered her descriptions of life in the village where the council decided everything—what work each person did, what rules the town would follow, what food the town would eat. My father was on this council— my father, who had decided that I could not live with them in the village.

I couldn't hate my mother, who visited every year and whose gentle hands reminded me that someone cared about me, but I could hate my father.

Three days before my birthday, as I sat by the fire and coaxed songs out of the violin, and Ranita breathed against my chest, Jeremia's wolf visited us.

Jeremia sat beside me, carving a long twisted branch of maple in which I could see raccoons, otters, me with my broken lips, Eva with her webbed feet and Jeremia with his half arm. Jeremia heard the soft snuffling, the coughing bark, and put his knife down on the log beside me. Our legs had been touching just at the knee, but he pulled away and walked beyond the circle of firelight.

The breathy bark came again, and Jeremia followed the wolf into the woods. Their padding feet left no marks and no sounds.

Nathanael sat up in the chair. I put down the violin, and Eva, with Emerald on her shoulder, walked to where Jeremia had disappeared into the trees. None of us spoke. We jumped every time the fire popped. We waited. I fed Ranita more rice milk, which she pushed about with her tongue, half of the mixture coming out again through her nose. Eating the food was enough to tire her, and she soon slept.

I rocked back and forth on the log and listened so hard, every noise became the wolf. Eva shuffled her feet in the dirt by the trees. The quiet must have been too much for Nathanael, because he stood suddenly, walked into his hut and returned with the radio. When he turned it on, the loud static crackle made Ranita's eyelids flutter, but she soon went back to sleep. Nathanael adjusted the dial. An eerie shriek came from the machine, and then he found the usual station with the news.

A woman spoke of things I knew nothing about. Hearing another voice, though, using clean, clear words without the nasal quality that I was so used to in my own voice, was enough to make me listen. I tried to remember the names, but they meant nothing to me and moved through me like air. And then Nathanael turned it up.

"…and we will now join the opera, *El Fuego del Mano*, already in progress. Mezzo-soprano Alicia Fabila is singing the part of Barbara…"

We listened to the opera for a few minutes, the music jarring in the silence of the night, and then Nathanael flicked the switch and the voice stopped. Instead, we heard loud panting and the trudging of feet, as though someone with a heavy load was lumbering through the trees. The goat scurried around the campfire and disappeared into Nathanael's hut. I stood up from the log and held Ranita against me. I tensed my muscles and readied myself to run, but when Jeremia emerged from the forest, I relaxed again.

The wolf padded along behind Jeremia. I had never seen it so close and marveled at the beauty of its silver fur. Eva backed away from it and stood by the fire next to Nathanael and me, the silent macaw on her shoulder watching warily. The wolf's long tongue hung from its mouth, and its yellow eyes glinted in the fire.

Jeremia carried another wolf slung over his shoulders and laid it down beside the fire. It was a much older wolf, with tufted black fur that had become tinged with gray. A smell rose from the wolf, a smell so strong that I pushed my hand against my nose, trying to stop the odor from drifting into my mouth. The wolf's muzzle was completely white except where sores had formed around its mouth. Always be wary around hurt animals, I had been told, but this creature's eyes rolled about in its head, and it panted loud foamy breaths flecked with blood. I couldn't imagine it harming anyone.

I took a bowl to the creek and filled it with water. I placed the bowl by the hurt wolf's head. Jeremia's wolf looked at me, licked its lips once and then panted, its tongue again hanging from its mouth. Nathanael knelt beside the hurt wolf and spoke in a low voice. He hummed, murmured and laid a wrinkled hand on the wolf's abdomen. The creature whimpered and panted, more froth spilling from its sore-infested mouth.

"Something it ate or drank," Nathanael said. He turned his head to the side, away from the stench of the wolf. Jeremia held the bowl up to the wolf's mouth, pouring a bit of the water onto the sore lips. The wolf lapped at it eagerly, its tongue searching for more, but its eyes rolled again, and the whimper was so painful to hear, I held Ranita tighter. Eva pushed her hands against her eyes and cried, her voice one continuous wail. Emerald fluttered to the ground on her stunted wings and ran to Eva and Jeremia's hut, where she slid behind the door flap.

Now even the healthy creatures in our woods were becoming sick and maimed like us. How were we to escape whatever it was that had caused all this disease?

Nathanael hummed to the sick wolf and stroked its head and back. The animal's side heaved up and down with each breath, the panting beginning to slow, to lose its panicked quality. As Nathanael rubbed the wolf's back, clumps of hair slid from its body and fell in patches. I put my arm around Eva's shoulders and pressed her against my hip even though I wanted to wail with her and cry through my fingers. Instead, the tears dripped from my nose and pooled in the slits above my lip.

When the wolf's breathing stopped, I felt like mine started. I sucked air in deeply, listening to the shuddering of Eva's breath as she tried to calm herself. I sat down on the log again and looked at the sick wolf. Jeremia's wolf, its coat silver and tan next to the other wolf's dark pelt, lay down by the dead one and put its muzzle on its paws.

We went to our huts then. I curled around Ranita, her light breath a promise of life after the death we had seen. And even though Ranita slept that night, her stomach full, her body warm against mine, I listened to the low barks of the living wolf by the fire as it said goodbye to its friend.

In the morning Jeremia's wolf was gone, and the dead wolf was stiff. Jeremia dug a hole in our graveyard, where the babies had been buried, and the two of us wrapped the body in a sheet of plastic and hefted the wolf up, bringing it to the grave. In the daylight we could see the damage to the black wolf, and we marveled that it had lived as long as it had. Great red sores covered its body, not only its mouth, and it smelled as though it had been dying for a very long time. It was best dead—even Eva understood that.

The night before my birthday, I sat by the fire pit and played the violin. I could play about five songs, none of them screechy or high-pitched. Nathanael pulled on my fingers sometimes, correcting my movements. He wouldn't tell me how he had learned the violin; he wouldn't tell me why he refused to play anymore or why he watched me now with eyes so narrow and dark, I wondered what I was doing wrong. I had lived with Nathanael all of my life, but I knew more about the village he came from, the one I'd never seen, than I knew about him.

Jeremia sat beside me, carving a piece of wood, his hand never still, his short arm holding the wood in place. I slid farther down the log, closer and closer, so I could smell his nearness, breathe in the darkness of his scent. He reminded me of a hummingbird, fluttering here, hovering there, and then gone. We balanced each other—solid, dependable, quiet me and fast, whirling, dancing Jeremia. Sometimes he would leap about the fire, crazed, intense and full of monkey antics.

I would watch him then, quietly and carefully, because his beauty—his supple, lithe beauty—burned with the intensity of a firefly, so wonderful to watch but dangerous to arrest. If I could have, I would have captured him, held him close, but that would have killed him.

The new object Jeremia carved was for my birthday, although he hadn't said so and hadn't given it to me yet. It was a miniature violin, no longer than my middle finger but with details as curved and precise as the larger version. I knew what I would do with it: I'd wear it around my neck, close to my voice box, where it would represent the promise of what my voice could be.

Jeremia put down his tools and looked up into the night. It was too dark to carve—bats flitted against the sky and owls swooped to catch them. I played my mother's lullaby once more and felt the sting in my nose and the glassing over of my eyes. Jeremia grunted.

I set the violin in my lap and brushed the sleeve of my shirt against my eyes. Ranita snored softly. Jeremia looked down into the fire. His shoulders hunched, and I felt his arm tense as it brushed against mine.

"You had fifteen years, fifteen times that she came to visit you." His voice was low, gravelly. "My parents haven't visited me once."

He turned his head to look at me. His face, shadowed and blurred, carried a glint from the fire. "You shouldn't cry."

He stood up, brushed against my knees with his legs and picked up Eva, who had fallen asleep on a mat in front of the fire. I placed my hand on Ranita and felt her warm breath seeping into my shirt. I rocked her back and forth.

He was right. I knew he was right, but I still missed my mother. Is it better to never have known your parents, like Rosa or Eva, or better to have had one brief day a year in which to place all of your hopes?

I woke up and looked out the window. Clouds billowed across the sky. Ranita slept on my chest, her favorite spot. Since we had discovered the rice milk, she awoke only occasionally during the night.

It was my birthday. I wasn't sure I'd get out of bed.

And then I heard the warning—three short whistles and a long one. Someone was coming. My mother. Before I thought that it couldn't possibly be true, I reacted to the pounding of my heart, the shaking of my hands, the rush of my blood. I jumped up, holding Ranita to me, and ran out the door of my hut. I was so happy, even my fingertips tingled.

It was not my mother who stood in the center of our camp. It was a man and two boys. When I emerged from my hut, the man stepped back, narrowed his eyes and put his left hand on his belt where a knife glinted.

My heart began to slow, and my shoulders started to droop. Now I felt twitchy, like lightning was about to flicker from the sky and set my hair on end.

Both of the boys stepped back and the smaller one crouched, his hands clenched into fists. All three of them made the sign of the cross over their chests. Nathanael stood in front of the man. His arms were crossed and his chin jutted forward. He was standing tall, and his clothes seemed to fit him better than before. He had strength that belied his sixty-nine years. I waited at the door of my hut and tried not to let my fluttering heart and hands wake Ranita.

"That her?" the man asked.

Nathanael said nothing.

"You Whisper?" the man shouted. "Lydia?"

I looked at Nathanael.

"We have come for you. We came to get you," the man said. He had a prominent forehead and heavy eyebrows that made him look angry. "It was your mother's dying wish."

I had to take that in for a minute, weigh what his comment meant. My mother's dying wish. She was dead.

I felt the air rush out of my mouth and nose. My stomach clenched. I took a step back and leaned against the door frame of my hut. I closed my eyes and tried not to breathe so hard and fast. I'd thought I'd given up hope, but it had been there all along, and now it burst, shooting shards of glass through my body. I slid down the wall of my hut and sat hard on the ground.

When I opened my eyes, the scene in front of me had not changed. I felt old, trodden upon, worn, and yet no time had passed.

"Does she understand what I'm saying?" The man spoke to Nathanael but looked at me.

"Yes. But I'm not sure I do," Nathanael said. "What do you want with her?"

"She'll come home with us, help in the house, take her mother's place." The man peered at me, the corners of his mouth turned up in a slight smile. I thought he was cunning, although he spoke to me as if I were stupid.

"You have shown no interest in her for sixteen years, Belen, and now suddenly when it suits you, you want her back. She's not going." Nathanael's mouth was pulled straight, tight, and his eyes squinted. The man heard Nathanael's words and turned to look at him.

"I have every right to claim her, which you do not. I want her now, that's what matters, and she'll come home with us."

The two boys stepped forward and flanked their father. The three of them had the same hair—thin and limp. They had hunched shoulders and rounded limbs. I thought all men were like Nathanael, Jeremia and the messenger, with muscles rippling beneath the skin and flat bellies. These three looked weak in body, but there was a strength to them that resided somewhere other than in their muscles.

I didn't want to go.

"Come, girl. Get your things," the man said.

Panic started to rise in me and forced me to my feet. My breath came fast, and the beat of my heart matched Ranita's. My father walked toward me. His head was lowered and his upper lip twitched into a snarl. He reminded me of the coyote who snooped around our camp, always wanting, always hungry. I held Ranita tight against my chest.

"You will come with me," he said. He was two feet in front of me. He looked up and down my body. "Even though I don't want to claim you as blood, you are mine, and you've had sixteen years of freedom, living wild like the animals. Now you will come with me and do your duty."

Ranita stirred. The man's nose wrinkled.

"That your child?" His mouth turned up in a sneer. "You're sixteen and already a mother. I can see what living here in the wild has done for you. Who's the father? The old man?"

Nathanael coughed, and then he spoke low and slow, as if he were speaking to Eva when she was having a temper tantrum.

"The messenger told me this is Clemente and Maximo's child, although I thought they were too old to have children."

Belen looked hard at Ranita, raised his upper lip into a snarl and then reached out, grabbing my arm. I wondered why I had ever thought him weak. His grip cut into my upper arm and I tried to yank it from his grasp, but he had become a rock, unyielding and impenetrable. The older boy grabbed the arm of the younger and pointed at Ranita. The younger boy, Mateo, gasped, his hand over his mouth.

"I said get your things. I don't want this other child, this monster and murderer. You come alone. Now."

I heard rustlings at the side of my hut. *Oh no, please don't.* I felt Jeremia's anger, like low-lying fog slithering along the ground and wrapping itself around us. Jeremia had not yet felt the power of this man. An encounter between the two wouldn't end well. I closed my eyes and prepared for the impact. Belen was taken by surprise when Jeremia flew through the air and landed with his foot against the man's chest. Jeremia was on top of him, pinning him to the ground, snarling into his face.

When Belen screamed, we heard twigs snapping, leaves rustling, and another man emerged from the woods. He held a knife and crouched low. He ran at Jeremia, grabbed him by the back of his hair and yanked his head up while holding a knife to his throat. He pulled Jeremia's good arm behind his back and forced him to his feet. Jeremia's eyes were red, wild. He growled.

Belen sat up, steadied himself with his hand against the ground and stood. His face was red and puffy. He panted. The two young boys didn't know what to do—they ran to their father, then back to the woods, then crept forward again.

"Kill him," Belen said, his voice rough and jumpy. He nodded to the man with the knife against Jeremia's throat. Pounding fear pumped through my veins. The very air itself seemed to throb.

I saw the man with the knife to Jeremia's neck look at Belen. I saw him tighten his grip on the knife; I saw the knife press against the skin of Jeremia's throat. Nathanael slid behind the man holding the knife, gripped the man's arm and pulled the knife away from Jeremia's exposed neck. Jeremia whirled around, facing the man with the knife.

Jeremia had no weapon and only one arm. That would not stop him. When Nathanael released the man's wrist and jumped back to avoid the downward slash of the knife, I saw Jeremia tense his muscles and prepare to leap.

I screamed. I hadn't used my voice in so long, it sounded as though it came from the trees, from the sky, squeezed from the sun. Everyone looked at me.

"I'll go with them," I said.

Jeremia rocked back and forth, his eyes still red, the tendons in his neck standing out like the strings on the violin. When he heard my words, he shook his head.

"You can't leave."

"Please," I said, "take care of Eva and Ranita for me."

In Jeremia's eyes I saw something I had not seen before. It was dark, twisting and filled with yellow swirls. Fear.

"Don't," he said.

"No one will be hurt because of me."

Nathanael and the man with the knife swayed opposite each other, their arms out, their legs wide apart. The man with the knife swung it forward, slicing at Nathanael. Nathanael backed up against one of the sitting logs. I saw what would happen, how this would all end, with old Nathanael cut open. With icy hands I touched Belen's arm, and he jerked away from me, rubbing at the spot as though I'd burned him.

"Stop," I said.

Belen pointed a finger at me and muttered, "Don't you ever touch me, girl." He glared and then yelled, "Celso, enough."

Celso twitched his head, but his eyes never left Nathanael, and with a powerful lunge he lurched toward him, pushing him hard with both hands and slicing the top of his arm with the knife. Nathanael sat heavily on the log and held his hand over the cut. Blood seeped between his fingers, and I ran to him, pulling his hand away, examining the wound. It didn't appear deep, but it would leave a scar, no doubt. Jeremia stood beside me, his hand out to the side, his jaw set with an anger that went into his neck. We were not used to such blatant cheating. We were not used to people who didn't stop fighting when we'd already surrendered.

Nathanael accepted Ranita in his bloody hands when I handed her to him. My fingers, as they laid Ranita in his lap, shook and fluttered. Nathanael gripped my wrist, pulled me down and spoke into my ear.

"Come back, Whisper. As soon as you can. You, of all the rejects, were never meant for the life out there." While he spoke, he slipped something around my neck. I looked down and saw the violin that Jeremia had carved for me—the miniature instrument. Nathanael had fitted it with a string through a tiny hole at the end of the long neck—a little piece of warmth and wood with smears of Nathanael's blood on the edge. I slipped it under my shirt, where it soothed my skin.

I stood, held my head high once more and bit down on my tongue. I would not cry in front of these men. I would not let them have that power over me. I reached into myself and pulled on a small thread of anger. I held on to it, squeezed it, felt how delicate it was.

My belongings were quickly collected; I had very little. Everything my mother had given me fit into a scarf she had worn around her neck. I held the scarf up to my nose and breathed deeply. It still smelled of baking bread and molasses. I wrapped my cloth doll, a silver spoon and three ribbons for my hair inside the material. The violin fit against my back. I left the blankets, pillows, Jeremia's life-size carving that reminded me of waterfalls, and my books—the three encyclopedia volumes I'd read from cover to cover, learning about the world. I pulled on my sweater, flipped aside the deer-skin door and walked out of the hut. I wished I could pack Jeremia, Eva, Ranita and Nathanael into the violin case.

When I emerged, Jeremia stood by the fire pit, holding Eva. The two of them watched me with big, glassy eyes. I wanted to run to them, feel Eva's arms around my neck, feel the tingling that started when Jeremia's body was pressed against mine. Instead, I jerked my head away and tried to hold on to my thread of anger.

Celso and Belen stood by the path into the woods, and my brothers peered out at me from behind Belen. I turned to look at our camp—the log huts, the fire pit, the sitting logs surrounded by huge trees that stretched and strained toward the sun—and I thought of how small my world had been for sixteen years. How small and yet how huge.

When we walked into the woods, I did not look back, but as we moved away I heard nothing from the world behind me as the two men and two boys in my company lumbered through the trees, drowning out any sign of beauty that might have been there.

My mother was dead. And with that thought, my thread of anger disintegrated and I felt my lower lip begin to shake. I bit down on it until I couldn't tell if the tears in my eyes were from my mother's death or the pain in my lip.

Five

The two boys looked at me as we walked. The farther we got from the camp, the braver they became, as if distance gave them strength. The younger one, who looked to be about eight years old, had sturdy legs and a protruding stomach. He waited for me to pass and then followed me. I walked between the tromping men, my feet so silent it was as if I wasn't there. We trod beneath the oak trees with their majestic branches, and I listened to every move the boy behind me made. The other brother walked in front of me but glanced back often, looking at my face, examining my features. Belen led the way along the narrow path through the woods. Tree branches and bushes almost covered the slim trail we followed. Celso brought up the rear. No one smiled at me, attempted to talk to me, softened their gaze when they looked at me. I had no friends among these men and boys with their unblemished faces. There was no one to trust here.

About three hours into our march, I felt the first acorn hit the back of my neck. If Jeremia had taken out his slingshot and pelted me, I would have slipped away, run on silent feet through the woods, sneaked up behind him and thrown a handful of nuts at him, bombarding him with multiples in return for his individual missiles. I glanced at the man behind my brother and understood that if I slipped away, he would come and find me and perhaps return to the camp to take out his anger on Jeremia or old Nathanael.

As I continued to walk, I felt heat from my chest creep up my neck and into my face. The helplessness of fear and anger stung my eyes. I would not give in to this feeling.

Zing! An acorn flew by me.

Zing! Another hit me on the back of the head.

The littlest brother giggled, and the man behind me started to laugh. The brother in front of me looked around, as if trying to understand what was so funny.

I slowed down just a bit. Littlest brother sneaked closer, became braver and hit me on the cheek. It stung, but I said nothing. *Try it again, little brother, try it again.*

Zing! Another hit the back of my neck.

He was very close, and as we crept along, prey and aggressor, I thought of my mother's description of Mateo: loving but mischievous. This little boy was about as sweet as an unripe lemon.

Celso's laughter encouraged him, and he became braver. He stepped up right behind me, and I felt how close he was by the sharp sting on my shoulder blade. When the acorn hit the violin case, Mateo laughed at the hollow sound it made and then forgot to watch where he was going.

I stopped, whirled around and snatched the slingshot out of his hand before he'd noticed how close we were.

"Hey," he said, "give that back."

"Stop hitting me or I'll snap this in half." I held the slingshot over his head.

"Dad and Uncle Celso will make you give it back. You can't feel those hits—look at you. You're a monster."

I weighed that comment, considered taking offense and then laughed. I was still laughing when his face contorted, and his eyes stretched wide as he screamed. He screamed again and again, backing away from me, his hands in front of him. Belen ran back, pushed past me through the thick leaves of the trees and held Mateo against him.

"What did she do to you, son?" He kneeled at Mateo's side, his arm around him. "Did she hurt you?"

I no longer laughed. I lowered the slingshot and held it at my side.

"She made a face at me. She snarled at me. Sh…Sh…She was going to hurt me."

And then I remembered Nathanael's warning. *Never smile,* he had said. *Never laugh or grin at someone who isn't used to your face. When you smile, your teeth are bared, your face splits open, and you become an animal, with teeth and gums exposed.* I was careful not to smile as my father looked at me. His face became a burnt red color, the underside of a cardinal's wing, and he spoke low, his lips tight.

"If you ever threaten this boy again, I will finish the job I began when you were born."

I clenched my jaw. When I felt a tug, I looked down and saw my other brother, David, pulling the slingshot out of my hand. Even though he looked like the other two, his eyes were gentler, more searching, more willing to crinkle and laugh. He held the slingshot up for his father to see.

"Mateo shot seeds at her."

Belen yanked the slingshot out of David's hand and gave it back to Mateo.

"He may do what he likes to her. She's not like us."

David narrowed his eyes. Mateo gloated and fit another acorn into his slingshot, but rather than walking behind me, he joined his father and the two marched on, leading the way.

David walked between me and his father as we continued our passage through the woods. I pushed fern leaves aside, felt the scratch of thorny branches against my legs, tugged my feet through vines. As we walked, I wrapped a shield around myself and prepared for my new life.

On the first day of our journey, we met no other people, and I marveled that my mother had walked this distance all by herself for fifteen years. I understood the dedication she'd shown, the sacrifice she'd made. She truly had loved me. We slept in the vines and bushes, under the arching trees. My stomach rumbled with hunger. I tried to silence the sound by sleeping on my side, but the noise of emptiness reverberated against the ground. Because we had left the camp in such a hurry, I'd packed no food, and they offered me none during our travels. As my stomach continued to groan, I felt something pressed into my hand. My fingers closed around the object, and I brought it up to my nose. It was a piece of flatbread. I ate it in three bites.

On the second day, we passed a small village. About ten huts were grouped together in a rough circle, and children, barking dogs and smiling villagers appeared and disappeared between the huts. I hoped that this village was ours, because I could feel the acceptance.

Children ran out of the woods to greet us. They looked at my face curiously but were not afraid of me. They took our hands and pulled us into the center of the village, where sitting logs circled the fire pit. We were given bowls of rice, cooked vegetables and bits of meat. I ate the food while turned to the side so they could not see me placing the food at the back of my throat, away from my mouth, away from the openings that would make it spill out again.

When I looked around the village, I saw another woman like me, with slits in her face, openings between her nose and mouth, but also with one eye that looked always down. She smiled at me and raised her hand. I raised my hand in response, but Belen moved in front of me, blocking my view. While I ate my dinner, I saw two boys playing together by the fire pit. One of the boys had only one arm, and the other had a sore at the back of his head.

I wanted to stay in this little village where the disfigured children played around the fire pit with the other children and where the parents could watch them. But after we ate the meal in the early evening, we continued on our way.

The path we followed started to widen, and I noticed now the difference in the trees. My legs and hands were no longer stung by the thorns and brambles, and spaces appeared over our heads. More and more people passed us, people with markings and symbols on their arms and faces, people with their hair cut into strips on their heads or braided in long lines down their backs. They looked at me with the same curiosity with which I looked at them. Sometimes Belen and Celso stopped to talk with these people and sometimes we passed them without a word.

On the third day, we stopped in another village and were given a meal, but I did not want to stay in this village. The children hid behind the huts or trees when they saw my face, and one little boy stood in front of me, pointing and screaming.

I was offered rice here, but there were no vegetables and there was no meat, although I could smell something roasted coming from Belen's bowl. I did not sit on the log beside my little brothers but on the ground at their feet, dipping my fingers into the rice, eating as fast as I could in case they decided to take away what little food I had. Here I felt like an animal, squatting, skulking, shoveling, while they watched me as though I might eat their children.

The night before we reached our village, Belen and Celso built a fire in a small clearing. They sat near the warmth with the two boys while I sat behind them, just beyond the fire's reach, trying to see clues to my mother in the shapes of the boys' heads. They said little, but I did hear my name and saw Belen glance back at me.

Celso stood from his place by the fire and walked to me. I kept my chin on my knees, my arms wrapped around my legs. "Your place is with us now," he said. I looked at his brown boots, thick and durable, perfect for the walk through the woods. "You'll not go back."

I barely felt the edge of the fire's warmth. My place might have been with them, but it was not equal to them.

"And if you run, I'll hunt you down. Your father may be weak, but I'm not."

I looked up. The sky was dark, the trees shadowed and black around the outside of the fire. I could see nothing of his face.

He returned to the campfire and sat down beside Belen. The boys glanced back at me. I turned on my side, lay down on the ground and rested my cheek on my hands. Hot tears dampened the fingers under my cheek, but the tears made no more sound than snowflakes might.

This was my life now.

We reached my family's village, Astatla, in the afternoon of the fourth day. As we progressed through the forest, the pine trees thinned and disappeared, replaced by stunted magnolias that were more spread out, less dense. A thick, rotten smell filled the air. My head hurt from the reek, and my hand moved to cover my nose. Death. Decay. A world filled with rot. My eyes stung. I was hungry, but this smell made me queasy.

I heard the village long before we came to it: dogs barking, children yelling, an occasional shout—and absolute silence from the insects and birds. I had never experienced it before, that silence. It was peculiar and indescribable. The emptiness made my heart feel hollow, lonely, even though there were people everywhere.

We walked along a road now, and as we neared the first houses of the village, I noticed many smells. Some were good smells, like the cooking of soups, but behind those good smells always lay the heavy reek of filth, latrines and unwashed bodies. I could feel my nostrils flare. How could people live under this haze of stench? My hands felt unsteady and continually flew to my throat or clutched at my clothes. I tried to control them.

The wide dirt road was lined with houses constructed of flat pieces of wood that fit together snugly. They had metal roofs. For a minute I felt some excitement—maybe I would be warm, dry and protected. Our huts in the woods, made of sticks, logs and mud, always developed cracks in the winter that let the cold air creep into our blankets and bones.

I'd never seen so many people before and couldn't believe how long the dirt street seemed to be. Children took breaks from playing with balls to stare at me. Women paused as they carried heavy loads of water, wood or clothing and watched as I walked by. I stared also.

Everyone was beautiful, with smooth faces, sealed mouths and unsplit noses. No wonder they thought me a monster. I wanted to cover my face, hide it behind my hand, but instead I looked ahead and met their eyes.

When a beautiful man glanced at me and then glared with narrow eyes, I felt a moment of panic. I'd seen him before—but I knew that wasn't possible. His hair hung to his shoulders in graying black waves, his eyes watched me from beneath dark lashes, and his muscles twisted just beneath his skin. It was Jeremia—Jeremia without a missing arm. Jeremia older. When I walked past him, he hissed. Jeremia released his anger by disappearing for days at a time. I didn't want to know how this man released his anger.

My father's house was near the end of the long street. As we walked, we gathered an audience. I trailed behind Belen, Mateo and David, my shoulders tense, my hands sweaty around the scarf that held my mother's gifts. I followed them to the house but stopped outside the door.

This was where I had been born. This was where my mother had lived. This was where she had baked the bread, cared for the boys, loved, lived, died. The outside of the house was brown. Two steps led up to a faded yellow door, the color of fall leaves. Two glass windows gave the dwelling a face, but I saw no friendliness in its expression. No flowers grew around the house, only straggly clumps of brown grass and a few withered plants, which might have bloomed at one time but were so ragged now that I couldn't recognize them.

Mateo prodded me in the back. When I turned to look, I saw a pack of children gathered behind him.

"Snarl," he said. "Make that face again. Show them that face."

My head was so filled with the stink in the town that I couldn't concentrate. I shook my head to clear it and then wrinkled my nose. I felt my mouth pull up, split open from nose to lip, and the children gasped. Mateo pointed a shaky finger at me and shrieked, "See, I told you. I told you."

Belen stood with his arms crossed while Celso pushed me aside.

"You don't go in the house," Celso said. He continued to push me, and I submitted to his hands. He was forceful, and as I saw the other men gathered around, I understood why.

He was in charge here and must prove this to the onlookers. The house faced the dirt-packed road, and a line of people stood along the edge of the street, watching. There were no trees to hide me. My shield had dissolved, and tears tickled my nose.

"This is where you will stay." Celso pointed to a structure next to the house.

I didn't understand what it was. This miniature house was low to the ground, with a large opening. A hard black flap fit over the hole in the front. If I curled into a ball, perhaps I could squeeze myself between the walls. I heard laughter ripple like heat through the crowd.

"Doghouse," someone said.

Doghouse. Warmth crept across my chest, up my neck and into my cheeks.

I crossed my arms and planted my feet. Never in my life had I felt this hungry, this insubstantial. I looked at Celso and then glanced at Belen, standing behind him. I shook my head. My tears would fall any minute, but I would not crawl into a house constructed for animals.

"You'll do as I say, girl," he said. His hand flew through the air and slapped my cheek. My head snapped back. I felt a burning in my cheeks, but I swallowed the need to crouch low, hold my face, cry and ram my head into Celso's stomach. I had learned that Belen would not stand up for me, so I stood on my own, holding my arms closer to my chest, letting my eyes fill.

"Get in the doghouse," Celso said through gritted teeth.

I glanced at the line of people watching us. They smirked, their mouths drawn up into petty smiles. I saw no kindness, no mercy, no forgiveness.

Celso was wearing a plaid shirt with shiny snaps down the front and at the cuffs of the sleeves. He opened up the snaps on the cuffs, rolled the sleeves up to his elbows and waited. Maybe I should have gotten into the doghouse. I knew that if I submitted, though, that would be my accommodation forever. I'd had better shelter in the woods.

The blow hit me so hard, I gasped. The world spun around me and tipped; I clutched at my stomach. I couldn't breathe. I couldn't see straight. A kick from his boot landed against my side. Flashes of light twirled around my head.

As the world spun and I hit the ground, I wondered what had happened to the dog, why its home was empty.

When I awoke, it was dark. The line of people had disappeared. Artificial lights shone from the windows of the houses, and I heard the welcome sounds of the forest. Birds screeched, crickets chirped rhythmically, and bats flitted against the sky. I breathed in as deeply as I could without choking on the smell. This, at least, was a world I knew.

I sat up and inched my fingers across my chest and stomach, feeling for wounds. My right leg rebelled. I tried to straighten it, tried to pull my foot forward where I could see it, but it was stuck to the ground. I rolled onto my hands and knees and crept backward. I groped down the side of my leg and yanked my hand back when I touched the cold unforgivingness of metal.

Nathanael, Jeremia, Eva and I used to joke about being trapped in the camp, locked away in our forest jail, but

Nathanael had told us as we sat around the fire and played games or listened to stories of the civilized world that he would always choose this forest jail over the town we'd been banned from. Why? we'd asked him. Why choose this seclusion?

"People can be cruel," he'd said. Perhaps Belen had allowed Celso to chain me to the ground because it was expected, because he was on the town council and had to set an example—even if that example was his own daughter.

I lifted the flap covering the opening to the doghouse and felt inside. A worn, fur-covered blanket that smelled of urine and worms lay crusted and stiff on the ground. The blanket was beginning to disintegrate, becoming one with the dirt, but I pulled it out and shook it. As I wrapped it around my body, I remembered the violin lashed to my back. I pulled the strap over my head and held the case in my hands, weighing it, considering. There was nothing to do, no one to talk to, no baby to care for, no little sister or big brother to tease. Do I feel sorry for myself? I wondered. Do I crawl into the doghouse, curl around myself and weep?

I opened the violin case, fit the violin against my shoulder and began to play. Light and clean, the notes lifted into the air and spoke of me staked to the ground. I didn't play my mother's lullaby or any of the other tunes I'd pieced together. I played a song all my own, and it came to me on the soft wings of bats.

The door to the house opened and a rectangle of light stretched into the street, illuminating the rough, bumpy ground. David stepped out of the house and sat in the doorway, his shadow long and lean. My music mingled with the darkness and brought a bit of beauty back into my life. I don't know when I finished playing, but David was gone from the doorstep by the time I put down the violin, and the moon was hidden behind the houses to the west.

Six

"Get up," said the voice as a boot nudged my side.

I lay on the ground in front of the doghouse, the disintegrating blanket twisted tightly around me. I turned my head and looked up, squinting into the sky. The sun shone behind Belen's head.

"Get up."

My body felt cold and stiff. I'd slept on the ground all my life, but it had been layered with blankets. We'd collected them from the messenger's supplies over the years, using them as mattresses and sometimes as coats. Here, on this ground, tentacles of cold had crept into my bones and I was stiff. My chest and stomach hurt where I had been hit. I stood, knees bent, my leg staked to the ground.

"You'll make our meals, do the laundry, clean the house and bake bread to sell. You understand me?" He spoke loudly, as though my distorted features might somehow affect my hearing.

I held tight to the blanket around my shoulders. A rumbling, which rose in pitch and shook the ground, started in the distance and seemed to come straight for me. A large rectangular machine turned onto the street where Belen and I stood and made its way toward us, relentless in its approach, as though coming to squash us flat. I stepped back toward the house and as far as the chain on my leg would allow me to go. I held my breath as it approached, but it rumbled by and drove down the street, past many more houses, until it turned left and its roar rattled to a stop. It was, I realized, a truck, with the letters *SWINC* in black on the side. I had no idea automobiles could be so big. Belen continued as though nothing had happened.

"And if you run, the neighbor will shoot you."

Belen nodded to the house next door, where a woman with a puckered mouth rocked back and forth. She wore a polka-dot top with a flared skirt, and a long gun rested on her legs, a threat that lay dormant and cold. When I looked at her, she smiled at me; she had no teeth.

Belen leaned down to my feet and unlocked the chain around my ankle. The metal fell away, leaving a red indentation in my skin. I fought the urge to bend and rub my leg. He pulled the ratty blanket off me, tossing it back into the doghouse. When I tried to walk, I wobbled, my ankle threatening to give out, but somehow I made it to the front steps, using the railing to pull myself up, and then limped through the front door. Belen walked behind me.

The smell in the house pulled on my memories and made me sway. It was my mother, everywhere. Molasses, cinnamon and lemon. I thought for a minute that I might throw up.

I held my stomach and breathed deeply, then stumbled farther into the house when I was pushed.

Mateo and David sat at the kitchen table. They both had plates in front of them, ready to receive food. A third place was set at the table, but I knew better than to think it might be for me. I tried to remember the last time I'd eaten.

"Eggs and bacon in the fridge. Only six people in this town with a stove and fridge, you know. We're out of bread," Belen said.

David sucked in his breath. Bread meant a mother—a mother lost and gone. They'd lost a mother too, whom they'd known much better than I had. I knew nothing of Belen that endeared him to me, but my mother had stayed with him, maybe even loved him, and had loved her two boys. When I heard both boys sniff and watched them wipe the backs of their hands under their noses, I knew they'd loved her too.

I grasped the metal handle and opened the refrigerator. The gush of cold air against my arms, face and neck shocked me, making me think of fresh morning breezes by the creek, where rancid smells didn't clog the senses. In the summer, we had eaten nothing cold—not the goat's milk or the mangoes. Everything we'd eaten was as warm as the day, but here, the milk stayed cold and didn't curdle in the heat.

Eggs, bacon, milk. I removed these items from the refrigerator after searching for their unfamiliar packaging and turned to the stove. If I was able to cook these things over an open flame, I could certainly cook them on this luxurious device. Nathanael had told me that stoves cooked food so evenly, you didn't have to continuously move the pot to the best spot.

Belen stood beside me and pointed to knobs and corre-
sponding spirals. On the back of the white stove, in black
script, was the word *SWINC*. It was on the refrigerator too,
dark letters against a white background, just like the lettering
on the rumbling truck.

"Don't think you're staying in the house just because
you're cooking and cleaning in it. You'll go back to the
doghouse tonight."

I looked down at the pan on the stove. The eggs bubbled
gently, the bacon sizzled, and I felt stirring in my chest, as if
ants or fleas had crept into my clothing and started to bite.
The nibbles fluttered beneath my collarbone, twitched in my
cheeks. My face burned and my breath came fast. I flipped
the eggs, turned the bacon, opened the cap on the milk.
My hands were shaking.

I refused to return to the doghouse—to be chained and
kept. That would not happen. I was so angry, I couldn't
even cry.

I flipped the food onto their plates and watched them
shovel great forkfuls into their mouths. I felt my lips tighten
over my teeth. I glowered at them—hungry, angry, imprisoned—trying to control the moisture that threatened to drip
from the corners of my mouth.

"Stop staring at us," Belen said. He put his fork down.
"I can't eat with you watching and with that face..."

He stood up, pushed his chair back from the table and
marched into another room. David had stopped eating and was
watching me. Mateo didn't bother to look up. Belen walked
back into the room, the floorboards shaking with his weight,
and tossed something over my head.

"You'll wear that from now on." Belen sat back at the table and focused his eyes on his plate.

The black fabric was soft, and it fell just past my shoulders. The weight of it felt right, the material heavy enough to stay in place, the weave loose enough to see through. It smelled of nutmeg and cumin. It must have been my mother's, a shawl to warm her neck and shoulders rather than hide her face. I should have been enraged, angry that my face had to be covered, that I was so hideous they couldn't eat while my face was visible, but I was not angry. Instead, all that rage leaked out like smoke from beneath the black veil, and I allowed myself to smile. This was my mother's. And now when people stared at me, I could curl my lips into a snarl, I could cry, I could laugh, I could wrinkle my nose and glare. They couldn't see me.

When David and Mateo left for school and Belen left to do his work for the town council, I ate the remains of the breakfast. I didn't remove the veil but rolled up the edge and slipped my fork carefully beneath it. It made me feel hazy, vaporous, as if maybe I didn't really exist and all of this was someone else's life. With my face covered, the world became less substantial, and the life in my head, as I wished it to be, became almost real.

My life might have been despicable right then, but I also walked the path my mother had walked before me. I cleaned the dishes and put them away, I picked up clothes from the floor in the main room, found a cloth and ran it over the meager furniture: a couch, a round table in the middle of the room. Some puzzles and a few books sat on the table. I looked at the books. *Holy Bread: The Art of Bread Making.* I silently thanked Nathanael for teaching me to read, to do math, to study life. I would learn to make the bread. My mother had told me that she loved smoothing and kneading the bread until it became a stretchy, soft dough that would expand into a perfect loaf. She had begun to add nuts, bits of fruit, seeds and wild grains, making the recipes her own and selling the special breads at the grocery store. They'd become dependent on the income from that bread, as it supplemented the limited amount of money Belen received from sitting on the town council.

I cleaned in David and Mateo's room first—made a stack of the dirty clothes, pulled the bedding off their beds, picked up their toys and tossed them onto the shelves made of boards and bricks. When I opened a thin door that covered a miniature room, I sighed and began to pull out the piles of clothes. Why did they need so many clothes? So many shirts, pants, socks. In our camp in the woods, we had received our supplies once a month, ordering new clothes through the messenger twice a year. I owned one set of clothing that fit: a pair of brown pants, a white T-shirt with a faded picture of a large-eared mouse, a black sweater with a hole at the right elbow and a pair of brown shoes. These children had ten pairs of pants each, fifteen shirts, short pants, sweaters and coats. They only had one body each—why did they need so many pieces of clothing?

A mouse had been nibbling on something in the corner, a wad of chewed paper that crumbled like snow when I picked it up. I began to realize the extent of the mess and wondered how long my mother had been gone. Maybe she had died the day she sent the violin. That was weeks ago. And then my father had waited until my birthday to come and get me?

With no looming father, no staring brothers, I could explore as I wished. I found a washbasin behind the house. I looked around me, trying to determine how people washed clothes in this village, and saw a woman walking through the brush of the neighboring backyards to some taller grasses. The forest began just past those taller grasses. Perhaps a creek lay in that direction. I placed the clothes in the washbasin and balanced it against my hip as I'd done for years in our camp. I walked parallel to the woman down a narrow path lined with browning weeds and found myself at a creek where women and children lined the banks. The water was dark—brown and murky. I couldn't see the bottom of the creek. This may have been the same stream that ran through our camp in the woods, but somewhere along the way it had become filthy and rotten, the crayfish so camouflaged by the brown waters that I couldn't see them skittering along the creek bed.

The children and mothers quieted for a minute when they saw me approach, but it didn't take long for the little ones to go back to their play and the mothers to resume their talking. I hesitated before lowering my basket to the filthy water, but the other women scrubbed their clothes in the stream, and the children splashed and played in it, so I settled myself and began the work.

I liked the chatter around me. It reminded me of Eva and Jeremia—of having friends. My throat felt tight and raw.

I should have let myself cry—why not? But I didn't cry. Not then, anyway.

When the first pile of clothes was washed, I returned to the house, hung the clothes to dry on the outside line that ran between my father's house and the neighbor's, where the woman with the gun waved at me and grinned her toothless grin, and then took the next stack to the creek. Many of the other women were gone when I returned. There was one family there, a mother with two wee ones, and she also left after a few minutes. I didn't know if she left because I was there or because her toddler had grown sleepy and cranky.

The sun was high in the sky, beaming its rays onto my head, onto the dark veil that covered me. Usually I welcomed the sun—I didn't even mind the heat, the enclosing warmth of humidity, but because my hair had fallen forward over my shoulders, the veil was sticking to the back of my neck. It became itchy, scratchy and annoying. I glanced up and down the creek, saw that I was the only one there and took off the veil.

I folded it carefully and placed it behind me. I closed my eyes, tilted my face to the sun and felt the touch of a breeze against my sweaty neck. My shoulders were beginning to ache, my hands were raw and sore, my upper back stiff from bending. I turned to my work and pulled out a cream-colored slip—the color of a perfect egg. I stopped for a minute with the material in my hand. The thumping of my heart told me what I had, what treasure I had found, and I stood shakily, clutching the slip to my chest, afraid that it might not be real, that it might disappear.

When the material stayed in my hands, solidifying and becoming permanent, I pulled it away from my body and shook it loose in front of me. It was long and straight, and its smell was wrong—it should have smelled of yeast and cinnamon, but from the depths of the cloth I smelled something dark and decayed. I turned the skirt around, and in the back, right in the center, was an almost perfect maroon-brown sphere. Blood. Dried blood.

No.

I pushed the material down into the water, swirled it back and forth, back and forth again. I rubbed the material between my hands and scrubbed the spot between my knuckles. I didn't even look to see if the spot was gone. I ground and rubbed, twisted and scrubbed, until my arms ached and my shoulders burned. Then I stood and shook out the slip.

I could still see discoloration—a darker patch on the lightness of the material—but now at least I could look at it. I would always know what had been there, but I could pretend it was something else, like a water mark or dirt from a log she had once sat on.

The sound of swishing grass whistled on the wind. I stuffed the slip under the other clothes in the washtub and pulled out a different garment. Guilt tickled my nose, making me sneeze, but I tried to reassure myself that I'd done nothing wrong.

When Belen stepped out of the grasses and stood beside me, I scrubbed the garment in my hands with shaky fingers and with sweat dripping off the end of my nose.

"You didn't bake the bread," he said.

The article of clothing between my hands softened, but I didn't exchange it for another.

Belen placed his foot against my back. I crouched on the dirt bank over the water, and when he pushed, I stretched out my hand to catch myself. My hand and face felt the cool shock of water—the rest of my body followed. The water was not deep. I stood easily, dripping and sodden, but now fear took the place of guilt, making me shake even more.

The sun shone over Belen's shoulder, turning him into a blackened shape with no discernible face. The clothes had taken me all day to clean.

"Why didn't you bake the bread?" His voice was so low, it sounded like the cough Jeremia's wolf had made in our camp. I put my hand over my eyes to shield them from the sun. When a slight breeze danced over me, the cool creek water tingled on my skin.

"Answer me," he said.

"I don't know how," I whispered.

Belen picked up the black veil and threw it at me.

"Put it on. The clothes don't matter," he said. My stack of clean clothes sat on a large rock. Belen bent low, shoved with both hands and toppled it into the creek. "The bread pays for the stove, for the refrigerator, for the electricity in our home. We could lose these things without the money, do you understand? I want a washing machine next, which the bread should pay for. You will bake the bread," he said, spit from his lips flying past the edge of the creek and landing on the front of my mother's black veil, "or you will not eat."

Then he turned and swished back through the grasses along the creek.

I gathered the clothes that he had thrown into the water. I wrung them out once again and wrapped the cream slip around my waist, wet and cool against my skin. In our camp in the woods, we'd never needed money. Although Nathanael had shown us the coins, I'd never taken much interest and didn't remember what the different sizes and metals represented. Nathanael had paid for our supplies by selling Jeremia's sculptures, and we had never considered buying more than the absolute necessities.

I didn't understand why Belen couldn't bake the bread himself. Maybe he didn't know how either. I was still standing in the creek, the clothes in my hands, when a thought nudged me. I tried to push it back, tried to submerge it with my mother's blood, but it popped up again.

Power. If I was to bake the bread and help support the family, I would have power. As I gathered the clothes and balanced the washbasin against my hip, I thought about that. It was Jeremia refusing to split the wood until I brought fresh water for him from the creek. It was Nathanael refusing to tell us stories of the city until we had cleaned the evening dishes. It was Whisper trying to find a place for herself in a different world. Was it such a terrible thing to want a little bit of power?

When I returned to the house and hung up the wet clothes to dry, I noticed a door I hadn't seen before. A lean-to was tilted against the back of the house like an ungainly wooden box. I undid the latch, pulled the door open and peered inside. It was empty except for slivers of wood, mouse droppings and cobwebs. The boards didn't fit together well, but it still offered more shelter than our huts back in the woods. I knew, as I examined the rough shack, how I would use my power.

When I walked between the houses to the street, I saw David and Mateo playing there with some other children. They kicked a can and then ran to hide. Belen stood by the clothesline between our house and our next-door neighbor's, his fists curled into his jean pockets, talking to my jailor. When she saw me standing by the front steps, she held up the gun and pointed it at me. I walked up the steps, feeling that gun aimed at my back, opened the door and went inside.

My stomach felt knotted and tight when I heard footsteps following me into the house. If I was wrong, if I did not have power, then this would not work, and I would again be chained to the doghouse. Sweat began to gather in my armpits.

"Make dinner," Belen said.

I leaned my hip against the stove in the kitchen and crossed my arms over my chest. He couldn't see my eyes behind the veil, but he glared as though he could.

"I said, make dinner." His voice was low and dangerous, his eyes almost disappearing beneath his heavy brows.

I didn't move. I bit down on my tongue to control my shaking. He could hurt me—I knew that—and he probably would. I still didn't move.

Faster than I thought possible, Belen crossed the floor between us and slapped me across the face. My head whipped to the side and my crossed arms uncrossed, my hands grabbing the edge of the stove behind me. I closed my eyes for a minute to still the stars that flashed in my head. I adjusted the veil so that it was balanced over my head and draped like a shroud to my shoulders. Belen breathed heavily through his nose, and the vein in his neck bulged. He lifted his hand to slap me again but stopped when I whispered, "Is this how you treated my mother?"

"What? Are you comparing yourself to her?" He dropped his arm, and a barking laugh erupted from him. "Your mother was a saint. You look like the devil. I told you to make dinner."

"No," I said. It was a small word, low, strong, surprising.

A flush started in Belen's neck and flowed up into his cheeks. The vein in his neck throbbed, and he clenched his hands into fists. His anger leaked up into his eyes and made the whites red. Suddenly he roared, "You will do as I say, girl."

My voice was so quiet, I wondered if I'd actually spoken out loud. Everything about me was shaking—even the veil rustled from my trembling.

"I want to stay in the lean-to. If I am chained, I will not bake bread. If I am hit, I will not cook the meals. You may break as many bones as you like, but you will not get anything from me."

Again Belen's speed surprised me. He grabbed my arm, yanked me to the front door, opened the door and threw me down the front steps. I fell with my hands out, my wrists taking most of the impact, but I rolled quickly so that I could see his next move. Belen stood on the top step, panting and sweating, looking down at me on the ground.

The children in the street stopped playing and clustered together in a protective circle, staring at Belen, staring at me. I heard the lady next door creak out of her chair and take a few steps across her porch. I imagined the gun pointed at me—at me, like I was the wild animal about to rip and tear. Belen retreated inside, slamming the door behind him.

My veil had slipped from my head and lay a few feet away, like someone's discarded shadow. David walked to it, picked it up and handed it to me. I stood up shakily and accepted the veil. Then I hunched down on the front step, my chin on my knees, and waited. The children waited with me, shuffling their feet in the dust, looking at me sideways. The woman next door waited as well, her polka-dot shirt like spots at the corner of my eye. I looked down at the ground and listened to my heart beating alone, no Ranita tied to my chest to regulate the beats. I had now been in this town for about twenty-four hours, and an ache the size of Jeremia, Eva, Nathanael and Ranita had made its way into my core. I wanted friends, a world I understood. I wanted peace.

I felt a tap on my shoulder. David stood beside me, holding my violin. My body ached, too hollowed out to play any music, but I understood his gesture—his proffered token of friendship. I fit the violin under my chin and began to play.

Darkness pushed against me. The sounds of the forest crept back into the town to swallow my loneliness, and the song of the cicada joined my own song when I finally stopped playing. David and Mateo had sneaked behind me into the house long ago, and I smelled potatoes baking. When I put the violin down on the step beside me and rested my chin on my bent knees, the door opened a crack. The strands of a broom appeared, and David's voice whispered, like he was trying to squeeze his voice into a bubble and not out into the night. I looked up to see the tip of his nose and chin lit by the stars.

"Here is a blanket and a baked potato and a broom to clean the shed."

I accepted the broom, blanket and potato and carried them around the side of the house. The moon was low, only a sliver, and I could see nothing inside the shack, but I swept anyway, tipped the debris out the door and laid the blanket on the ground. It would do for now. When the cooler night temperatures of winter came, I would need more, but maybe David would truly be my friend by then and would help me survive, help me stave off the inevitable earaches and sore throats that the colder weather brought. I made one more trip to the front of the house, collected the violin, my few belongings and the gifts from my mother. I returned to the lean-to, consumed the potato, which at least filled the hole in my stomach, and flattened my mother's slip underneath the blanket. It cushioned me from the hard ground and reminded me of yeast, cinnamon and blood.

When I lay down on the blanket, I smiled. There would be more battles to come, but for now I was sheltered and not on display. As I lay in my tiny house, a sliver of fear worked its way beneath my breastbone, a slippery tickle that made me wonder if perhaps there was more of my father in me than I cared to admit. I felt the tiny violin on the string around my neck. I ran my hands along its edges, felt the smoothness of its back. With the touch of the wood, I floated to my life in the forest, and when I thought about that life, my throat tightened and my eyes hurt. I missed who I had been in that place.

I rose before the sun the next day, minutes before the rumbling began and the huge white truck rolled down our street and stopped around the corner. My urge to follow the truck and understand its business would have to be fulfilled another time, when Belen wasn't watching every movement I made and when trust had been established.

Breakfast was ready by the time David, Mateo and Belen got up. While they ate, I collected their dirty clothes. Then I stood at the stove, reading *The Art of Bread Making*.

Today I would finish the laundry on time, return home and bake my first batch of bread. Belen would find nothing to complain about.

Seven

The creek was busy in the morning. I joined the other women and we scrubbed the clothes clean, or at least as clean as possible in filthy water that smelled of chemicals and latrines. I didn't mind washing the clothes, scrubbing them rhythmically while the sun shone on my back and the soft shush of grasses hummed beside me. There was beauty here, if I could ignore the smell of the water.

The same woman as before worked closest to me, the woman with the two little ones. I listened to the chatter of her oldest child, a toddler who busily ran about the bank of the creek, and suddenly I missed Eva with a pain as big as the sun. Eva had been like my little sister, just a baby when she came, and full of talk and energy like this child. She had brought so much life to our little camp. Rosa had recently left, and Jeremia and I were eleven and ten. Sometimes I would hide from him, just because I could, and sometimes he would throw acorns at me because there was no one else. Eva's entrance had offered us a distraction—we were responsible for her, and Jeremia, as the oldest, was especially in charge of her care.

And then Ranita. She had been my responsibility. And I'd abandoned her. I'd abandoned them all.

I ground a shirt between my hands, scrubbing and twisting, burning the energy that would otherwise become tears. This was my life now—my new life—and these people needed me too. Somehow I had to reconcile myself to where I lived and how my days would pass.

I'd done enough laundry the day before that I had little left to do. The woman beside me slowly progressed through her stack of diapers, the toddler constantly distracting her. He waddled too deep into the creek and she pulled him back. He wandered too far into the grasses and she retrieved him. He put his hand on a thistle and she comforted him.

I stepped into the grasses by the side of the creek and tugged out a clump. Using single strands of dried grass to tie the clump together in bunches—a round bunch for the head, individual bunches for arms and legs—I fashioned a roughly hewn doll. I had made these grass dolls for Eva—they never lasted long, but they were diverting for a while.

I stepped over clumps of weeds toward the woman with the baby strapped to her chest. She glanced up at me, and I immediately stopped. She looked fearful, her eyes big and her mouth pulled straight. I held out the doll to her, gestured to the toddler and said in a whisper, "May I give this to him?"

She looked at the doll in my hands and the expression on her face changed. She raised her eyebrows and let the corners of her mouth lift into a small smile. She nodded.

I gave the doll to the toddler and he laughed. He hugged it, held it out to look at again and then marched the doll on its feet across the ground. He sang a song as he squeezed the doll to him, hugging until the grasses squeaked.

"Thank you," she said around wisps of hair that fluttered like dandelion fluff against her face.

I gathered the washbasin with its dripping contents and balanced it against my hip. When I glanced at the woman, she was still watching me, her head turned to the side. She wasn't much older than me, perhaps two or three years, and she had a softness to her that I liked. Her round cheeks had a bright rosiness, and her arms were plump and healthy. She was the type of person who would feel good to hug—not all angles and sinew like Nathanael and Jeremia. The babies, with their pudgy cheeks, were obviously hers. I could like her, if only she could like me.

As I read through the instructions for baking the bread, I felt doubt. There was so much waiting: for the fermented yogurt to begin its work, for me to knead the dough just right, for the dough to rise again. I came to a specific recipe that looked the most basic—and beside this first recipe I found notes scribbled in the margin. When I saw them, my heart fluttered, and my fingertips pulled the veil from my head and laid it on the counter.

Honest hands are the key to perfect bread.

I had never seen my mother's handwriting before. I could barely make out the scribble, but seeing her words on the paper felt like a small gift, like a glimpse into her secret thoughts. I continued to read.

Make the yogurt culture a day ahead.

I felt sweat on my back. The yogurt culture was necessary for making the bread rise, and I had failed to prepare the ingredients in time. The bread would not be made that day, which meant Belen would once again be dissatisfied with my work. Quickly, my hands shaking and throat tight, I made the yogurt culture according to the recipe and set it to warm on the back of the stove. Then I scrubbed the indoor bathroom from floor to ceiling.

I cleaned around the base of the toilet—an indoor latrine was a luxury I had heard of but never seen—and then scrubbed again. With the first washing, the water added to the scent of urine, releasing it into the air and making me gag. The floor had to be scrubbed twice. It was made of a shiny material I had never seen before, and after the first cleaning a sticky residue still remained. After I cleaned the sink below the mirror, I lifted my eyes and saw myself. My hair, black and glossy, had a sheen to it that looked like raven feathers. My deep brown eyes were lined with black lashes and stared out at me, solemn, large. I lifted my chin and observed my nose, mouth, lips.

I had seen myself before. The creek on a still day reflected honestly, and I had studied my features on its surface. But the depth of water offered a darkness and obscurity that softened the effect. Here in the bathroom, with the lights glowing against my skin, nothing was softened. Where lips should stretch in a gentle curve across my face, I had instead an X, a crossed opening that exposed lip, gum and twisted front teeth. I looked at the roof of my mouth and saw the opening, the two halves of my mouth split down the center. When I lifted the veil from around my neck and covered my nose and mouth so that only my eyes and hair were reflected back at me, I saw a normal face. As I lowered the veil, I wondered why some people reacted to me the way they did. If everyone had been born with nose and lips like mine, I would be normal and those with smooth faces would look odd—too simple and erased. These irreverent thoughts felt shameful and dangerous, and I jumped when I heard the door to the house open. Silently, I slid the veil over my head and took two deep breaths, preparing to face my family, breadless yet again.

"She escape?" said a voice.

"No. Djala would have shot her."

"Djala can't see three feet in front of her."

"She's not to be trusted, you know, not with two young boys in the house." This last voice was abrupt and quick, like squirrel chatter in the trees.

"Lydia. Whisper," Belen said. The curtness in his voice was obvious, and I didn't dare hide from him. I opened the door to the bathroom and walked down the short hallway until I stood in the front room, behind the couch.

Three men stood in the doorway. One was very old, older than Nathanael, with curved shoulders and an enormous nose that did not fit his face, having continued to grow while his face did not. The other man beside Belen was very tall and younger than the others. He twitched his hands as he stood in the doorway, unable to still his restless body.

"Take off the veil," Belen said.

I slid the veil off my head and looked again at the men without the blurring of the fabric. In return, they examined me, the older man looking at me with one eye as though his vision were blocked by his nose, and the younger one looking once, then quickly looking away. The pause while they examined me lasted as long as it takes a turtle to cross the log over our pond.

The older man spoke. "You've been on the council for many years, Belen, and you would not lose your position, but having a reject in the house does not improve your reputation among the villagers."

"I'd keep her hidden if I were you." The younger man spoke so quickly, biting off the words, that I had to think about what he'd said after he'd finished.

"She's cleaned the house"—Belen swept his arm through the air, indicating all I'd picked up and polished—"and if she's able to make the bread for the store, she provides us with income. Both of these are useful to me right now. If she works elsewhere, who will cook for us, wash the clothing, keep the house in order? This is why I need her."

"If she works in the city, she'll make more money. You'd be able to afford a housecleaner."

The older man took a step forward, peering under his hooded eyes, hovering in front of me like a vulture. His bony hand reached out as though he would grab my arm, but instead he pointed at my face and then made the sign of a cross in the air.

"She can't stay, Belen—it doesn't look good. As a leader in this town, you must set the example, and contaminating your home and your reputation with this girl will hurt your standing. You were right to get rid of her. Speak with Celso when he returns. Send her away. Have her earn money in other ways, where she isn't visible as a presence in your house."

Belen said nothing but looked at me as though he'd never observed my features before. I felt heat rising to my cheeks. I stood in front of them, a human being with feelings, intelligence and ideas, yet they treated me as though I weren't even there. Belen was no better than the strangers, speaking to them instead of to me. Would he have acted differently had my mother been around?

The two men left the house. Belen watched me after they'd left, then went into the kitchen, where he sniffed the yogurt culture on the back of the stove. He didn't ask about the bread, he didn't become angry that I'd been unable to make it, he didn't speak to me and ask for my feelings on their discussion. He simply walked out the front door and stood in front of the neighbor's house, talking with the woman holding the rifle.

I didn't know where Celso had gone or when he would return, but I knew that when he came back, my life could change yet again.

That night I worked on my mother's slip. I made a slit right up through the middle, front and back, slicing the brown stain in half. I sewed the loose pieces together into pant legs using a needle and thread I'd found in the house. I slipped the pants on and then pulled my brown pants over them.

From now on, my mother's slip would fit against my body, an extra layer against the oncoming cold of winter.

As I lay in my lean-to, trying to find a soft piece of ground, feeling my mother's clothing against my skin, I heard rustling outside. I sat up, held my breath, listened with the pores of my body.

"She's in there," a voice said.

"Just open the door and throw it in. She won't hurt you."

"I heard she's a witch. What if she turns me into a crow?"

I crawled on my hands and knees to the door and peered through cracks between the slats of wood. Four little boys, armed with slingshots and a dead skunk impaled on the end of a stick, stood outside my door, silhouetted by the light of the moon. I didn't see David.

A surprise attack was needed. The tension made my shoulders hunch, my neck tighten and my mouth stretch up into a smile. Jeremia, the prince of pranks, had once pretended to be a crocodile, slashing and snapping through the overhanging bushes by the side of the creek. Eva and I had stood in the water, her arms wrapped around my leg as tightly as if she were a spider monkey baby, and we shook in fear until Jeremia lifted his head and howled. Eva and I got him back. We caught ten grass snakes and tucked them into his bed blankets.

Never sneak up on someone with a deformed face in the black of night when the moon is out. Should I show them my face? Yes, decidedly so.

I flipped up the catch on the door. The boy with the skunk on the stick reached for the handle. As his fingers touched the wood and he leaned forward to pull it open, I pushed it hard.

He jumped back, tripped and sprawled on the ground. The dead skunk flew behind him and hit another child in the chest. The three standing boys started to scream, bumping into each other like frightened chickens and screaming again.

I laughed. The boy on the ground scrambled to get away from me and join his terrified friends, but they did not wait. Already they were turning the corner of the house and disappearing from sight. I chased after them, snarling lightly, and as I came around the corner, a light blinded me.

I stood still, leaning from one foot to the other, and stared at the dark blankness behind the light. I felt the corners of my mouth straighten as I sucked in the smile.

David lowered the lantern. The hand holding the lantern shook, the light bobbing like a firefly. We turned away from each other at the same time. The light drifted to the front of the house while I blinked away the spots still suspended in the air and returned to the lean-to. How delicate was our web of friendship? Had I just lost him because he saw me smile? I tried not to think of the fragile friendship I may have sacrificed.

In the morning I checked the yogurt culture on the stove. It needed to stay warm, to grow the bacteria that would cause the bread to rise. I lifted the lid from the pan and then turned my head away, the reek from the yogurt stinging my nose. I had burned the milk onto the bottom of the pan, and a thick layer of blackened scum rose to the top of the culture when I stirred it. Biting my lower lip to keep it from trembling,

I poured the ingredients into the sink, scrubbed the pan and dried it. I would try to make the culture again when I returned from the creek.

I washed the few dirty clothes we had collected. The woman and her children were already there, a stack of dirty diapers beside them. When the toddler saw me, he waddled over on chubby legs and held out his doll, which had disintegrated and lost its suppleness. I stepped into the weeds at the side of the creek and pulled up a new handful. I shaped the head, wrapped a stem around the neck, maneuvered the arms, coordinated the legs and handed the new doll to the toddler. He clutched the new doll to his chest with pudgy hands but didn't let go of the old one. He didn't stare at my veil, wondering what was underneath—he accepted me as I was and touched my fingers, unafraid.

The mother nodded at me, smiled and tilted her head. I stepped to my tub of washing and tried to ignore them, tried to pretend that I was there alone. She didn't have to be nice to me. She didn't have to talk to me because I had made a weed doll for her child. When she spoke, I startled, my hands losing their grip on the pants I was washing.

"I knew your mother," she said.

I retrieved Mateo's pants and scrubbed them between my knuckles, rubbed and ground them against themselves, but I felt as though my hands were separate from the rest of me. My ears burned from strain, my neck ached from control, my desire to turn and stare at this woman was painful.

"I liked her very much," she said. Her voice reminded me of Rosa's, deep and rich with a bit of hoarseness. I tried to open my ears even more.

"She was quiet, like you," she said, "but she listened always and laughed easily. She laughed at Benny all the time." The woman meant the toddler, who was trying to construct a stick hut for his dolls.

Other women around us chatted, laughed, rolled their eyes, but they didn't listen to the conversation between a girl beneath a veil and a young mother with two distracting little ones. More, I thought, give me more.

I realized that I had been rubbing the same spot on Mateo's pants again and again. If I wasn't careful, I'd rub a hole right through the material.

"She talked about you sometimes," the woman said. Her voice was softer now, gentler. I could tell that she wasn't looking at me—she was examining whatever she was scrubbing between her hands. "She said giving you up, her first-born, was the worst experience of her life. She said it hurt more than childbirth ever could."

I stopped scrubbing the pants and gave in to my need to look at her, to absorb as much as possible about my mother. She felt my eyes on her and looked up. We stared at each other across the few clumps of grass and straggly weeds, our hands wrapped in dripping articles of clothing, the stench of the water lifting hazily around us. I wondered what I looked like through her eyes. A witch? A ghost? A vast emptiness?

"It's because of the council that they had to give you up. You know that, right? Your father couldn't be elected to the council with a deformed girl child—who would vote for him? When he saw you, he thought you'd ruined his life. And then, of course, your mother died, and your father blamed..."

Her cheeks reddened and she looked down.

"I've said too much," she whispered.

"No," I whispered back. I jumped slightly and put out my hand to steady myself. "Thank you for telling me."

"He's been on the council for sixteen years and will be there for life. He doesn't fear losing the people's vote now as much as he did before." Her arms wrapped around the baby strapped to her chest, and she held her face up to the sun. I would never be able to do that, openly lift my face to the sun. Not in this village—not in a public setting.

He thought I would ruin his life. So instead he ruined mine.

Eight

The next day, as I scrubbed the front steps leading to the house, pulled the weeds that grew against the boards and swept the debris into a pile, I watched the passersby in the street. I saw women with children, elders with canes and people my age who looked carefully away down the emptiness of the road, as though it was far more interesting and worthy of their time than I was. But then I saw something that made me stop and drop my handful of weeds onto the cement steps.

A boy a few years younger than me walked by. His eyes were dark, his hair black, and two openings appeared between his nose and his mouth. The lady with the rifle across her knees snored loudly on the porch next door, her head to the side and her toothless mouth wide open.

I followed the boy. He didn't seem to notice my quiet feet plodding along behind his as he walked down the road with one hand in the pocket of his pants. I adjusted the veil over my face, hiding my deformity, while he carelessly showed his to the public. He turned left, followed a narrow path that had been worn hard by constant walking and then continued between two houses, moving away from the creek.

He wound his way through long grasses, which spread behind the houses on the other side of the street for almost half a mile. In these grasses a solitary building made of gray stones stood square and brusque against the blue sky. Wide-open windows permitted the sounds of children to filter out into the air. A large sign on the front said *SWINC Elementary School*. As I walked past, I sneaked a quick glance through the window and saw a man barely older than me standing at the front of the room, writing words on the board and asking the students to recite the words in unison. I did not see David and Mateo, but I assumed they chanted along with the other students.

The grasses swished and sang their rustling song as I followed the boy into the field. A grass snake slithered by my feet, its bright green color a surprise beside the browns of the grasses, like an emerald macaw wrapped in a brown towel. The grasses tickled the undersides of my arms, and as I walked, grasshoppers jumped around me, landing on my shirt. The boy ahead of me walked out of the grasses and to a canopy of trees. To keep up with him, I swished more quickly, cutting the underside of my arms and rattling the grasshoppers into sporadic jumps. He went to the biggest tree, a gnarled oak that grew old and crooked. The trees surrounding the oak on all sides were stunted and dwarfed, while the bushes sprouted a few gray and brown leaves when they should have been covered by green ones.

The boy pulled himself up the tree, stepping onto boards that had been nailed to the trunk, and disappeared through a hole in a wooden platform that had been constructed on the lowest branches. I stood under these branches and looked up. I wanted to follow him, mount those steps and knock on the door to his tree house, but I feared that I would be rejected there as well.

I circled the bottom of the tree, walking around and around, sliding my fingers against the rough bark of its trunk. I considered what I should do—return to Belen's house, where the woman with the rifle snored on the porch next door, and attempt to bake bread, or climb the steps and knock on the wood, willing myself to speak to this boy who lived in the village, not rejected.

"Well, what are you waiting for?"

I sucked in my breath so fast, and stepped backward so quickly, that I stumbled over a root and went down, the veil slipping off my head. I looked up at the platform surrounding the tree and saw a face in the opening. It was like looking into a mirror.

Brushing myself off and tying the veil around my neck, I took hold of the boards nailed to the tree and pulled myself up. When I stuck my head through the opening, my eyes took a minute to adjust to the darkness of the tree house. Four boys sat around the small room. Two of them played chess on a board balanced over a bucket, one of them read a book, and the other boy, the one I had followed, crouched in front of me, a wooden recorder in his hands. All of them had deformities. The boy who held the recorder looked like me, the two playing chess looked like reflections of each other, with large purple splotches covering half their faces, and the last boy had crutches that leaned against the wall beside him.

I stepped onto the platform, bending my neck so my head wouldn't hit the roof of the tiny house, and brushed my sweaty palms on my pants. The boys playing chess glanced at me and then went back to their game, the boy reading the book never even looked up, and the boy with the recorder sat down against the wall of the house and grinned so hugely, so unabashedly, even though his face turned into a snarl, that I smiled back.

"Don't get many girls up here," he said.

He stretched his legs out in front of him and crossed them at the ankles. I sat next to him. He fit the recorder into his mouth, his teeth gripping the top of it, and played a breathy tune. His lips did not close over the top of the instrument, so the sound that came out was not clean, but airy and gasping.

"Wish you'd shut up with that thing," the boy with the book said. "You can't play it."

"*Can't* is a matter of interpretation," the boy with the recorder said. "Besides, wouldn't want our visiting musician to think she was the only one with any musical talent."

One of the chess-playing boys played his knight, took his opponent's bishop and then went back to his former position—legs crossed, elbows on knees, chin in hand.

"Welcome to the hideout of the hideous," said the boy beside me. "My name is Jafet. The grouch reading the book is Fabio. Nacio and Adan are the ones playing chess. We are the fabulous foursome, and we spend more time here than anywhere else."

He stuck the recorder back into his mouth and sprayed a spluttery tune. Nacio and Adan both covered their ears, and one of them moved a pawn. Fabio slammed his book on the floor and sighed.

"You can't play that thing. Would you put it away and stop tormenting us? She doesn't want to hear it either."

I liked them immediately. It was like being home with Eva, Jeremia and Nathanael.

"Hey, we don't want her to see all our faults on the first visit, do we? Where are your manners?"

Fabio picked up his book and tucked it under his arm. He adjusted his crutches and hobbled to the opening in the platform. He dropped his crutches through the opening and then climbed down the tree while holding on to the wooden steps.

"See you tomorrow, Fabio. Don't get ambushed," Jafet yelled through a square window cut into the side of the house. He looked back at me. "He's just jealous because I found you first, and you look like me."

Jafet resumed his seated position and put the recorder to his lips. I looked through the window and watched as Fabio moved surprisingly fast through the weeds that grew past his waist. He left a trail in the field, one of many that formed a pattern, as though someone had combed the field, leaving a row of parallel paths from one side to the other. The boys playing chess continued to be engrossed in their game, and Jafet played a tune I didn't recognize and could never repeat.

"Why are you guys here?" I whispered.

"'Cause they don't like us out there," Jafet said, waving his recorder toward the window and the field beyond.

"I mean, why are you allowed to stay?"

"I don't mean to be insulting," Jafet said while studying the mouse on my T-shirt, "but you're a girl. If you hadn't gone to the camp in the woods, you'd probably be dead. I happen to be an only child, and a boy. Like they were going to kill me."

The two boys playing chess looked up. The dark patches of maroon pigment made their faces look blotchy, diseased.

"We're twins."

"Not many twins around." Their mouths opened and closed at almost the same time.

"But girls, they're not so valuable. They can't sit on the council, they don't have jobs that pay much—all they're good for is reproduction, and right now too many messed-up babies are being born. If the girls come out disfigured, might as well get rid of them." Jafet tapped his fingers against the floor and hummed a quick tune. He twitched, hummed and tapped constantly.

I thought he was joking or being sarcastic, but I had a hard time reading him. He didn't look me in the eyes, but I didn't know if it was because of my femaleness or because he never looked people in the eyes.

Low chimes, spaced out and eerie like the call of the loon, filtered through the window. Jafet stood and so did the twins.

"Council's adjourned. Time to go."

My hands became sweaty and a flush crept up my neck into my cheeks. Belen would be home soon, and all I'd accomplished was the washing of a few clothes and the scrubbing of the top step. The yogurt culture still sat on the back of the stove, unused.

Without waiting for an invitation to go first, I climbed down the steps of the tree and began to run through the field.

The dried grasses brushed against my skin and I knew I would be itchy later, but I had to get back to Belen's house and hope that my lean-to hadn't been destroyed and the chain reattached to the doghouse. I didn't bother to silence my movement through the field but ran until my breath came from my mouth in rhythmic exhalations and my side began to ache. When I emerged from the grasses behind a house with sunflowers, I gasped and held my chest when someone spoke.

"Not so fast, miss. Thought you could slip away while I was taking a snooze, did you? We'll see what Belen has to say about this."

Her polka-dot shirt looked so bright and merry next to the browns of the grasses and against her bronzed, craggy skin that she could have been an illusion, a butterfly against a dead field. She stepped closer to me and examined my face.

"Well, you're as ugly as they say. I could barely see you from my place on the porch, but now that you're right up next to me, I can see why they kept you hid. Your mom, you know, said you were beautiful. I knew that weren't true or Belen would've kept you around. Your mom liked everyone, sainted creature that she was, even me."

Her face was so close to mine now that I could see the color of her eyes. They were green, a faded green with flecks of white. I thought about this woman, holding her rifle across her legs while sitting on her porch, watching my movements and considering when to point her weapon in my direction, and realized that she was probably a bit like the macaw. That mother macaw had screamed and screeched, mourned the loss of her baby like it was her left wing, but she hadn't hurt

Eva and never did do more than bluster. Perhaps this woman also made loud noises but little else.

"You ain't gonna cry, are you?"

I shook my head.

"Don't talk much, huh. That's probably smart. Talking always seems to get me into trouble. My husband doesn't even hear me anymore. Don't get yourself a husband, girl, if you don't need one. They're nothing but trouble. If I'da been able to sit on that council myself, I never woulda married him, but women can't do much around here but hold rifles and boss their husbands. Let's get going or Belen is gonna have my hide. Give me your arm."

The woman grabbed my arm and hobbled along beside me. She used the rifle for a walking stick on the other side. Her flared skirt brushed against my leg as we walked—it sounded like the dry grasses in the field.

We crossed the road and I walked her to the front of her house. She let go of my arm and grabbed the railing. Climbing slowly onto each step, and still using her rifle as a cane, she made her way up to the porch and sat heavily in her rocking chair. She waved her gun in the air and called loudly.

"Over here, Belen. I caught her trying to escape."

My mouth went dry when I heard Belen's footsteps on the hard dirt of the yard. He stood near me, next to me, but not close.

"Where you been, girl?" he said.

I untied the veil from around my neck and draped it over my head. The fabric softened my view of Djala's porch, blurring the spots on her shirt and turning the world hazy.

"She visited them freaks over at the tree house. She sneaked by me on the way down, but I caught her on the way back."

Belen grabbed me by the hair and dragged me over the bumpy grass to the back of the house, where he threw me into the lean-to with such force that I tripped and went down hard. I sprawled over the blanket and held my hands over my ears, waiting for the next blow, but instead the light narrowed and disappeared as Belen slammed the door shut.

I stayed on the floor for many minutes, willing myself not to cry, and escaping in my head to a place beside our creek where I liked to sit when I needed to be alone. In that place, the sun shone on my shoulders, the frogs grumped in the reeds by my feet, the dragonflies hovered over the pond, and my balance was restored. As I lay in the lean-to, I willed myself to find that balance, to return to a place that was warm and safe, but it took me many minutes to build that calm. When I finally felt as though I wouldn't cry, scream or bang my fists against the wood slats of my shelter, the sun had disappeared and I had, once again, failed to bake any bread or to please Belen.

The next day, Djala again held my arm with one hand and the rifle as a cane with the other. We hobbled down the street, following the roaring truck, to the store where I was to purchase more milk for the yogurt culture and more eggs for breakfast. I didn't have the money, Djala did, and even if they had given it to me, I wouldn't have known how to use it. Were three big coins a lot for a loaf of bread or a little?

We joined students on their way to school, mothers on their way to various chores and men on their way to work. As we hobbled along, many said hello to Djala, but they acted as if I were nothing more than a crutch. I had been nervous around Belen in the morning, but he'd looked over my left shoulder and told me about the items I needed to purchase at the store.

"The bread," he said. "Today."

I had never been in a store before. We entered through a door that had thick metal bars running from the top to the ground. Inside, a woman stood behind a counter and tapped loudly on a machine in front of her. She watched us as we walked beside shelves full of foods in boxes, foods in packages, foods in cans. I had never heard of half of these foods. What was chili? What were energy drinks and fruit roll-ups? We shuffled to an enormous refrigerator with jugs of milk, eggs and cheese lining its shelves. Such plenty and choice in one place. There was a shelf with packaged loaves of bread, which Djala pointed out to me, but she said in a low voice, "Don't eat that crap—nothing to it. Your mother's bread had taste and texture. Bake something with substance, not this tasteless garbage."

At the counter we placed our items next to the machine, and the woman punched in numbers and told us what we owed. Djala handed over the money while I looked at the sign on the wall.

SWINC Market.

Djala took my arm, I took the sack, and we hobbled home again. I did not go to the creek but stayed home, determined to bake this bread.

I fumbled with the ingredients, first adding too much water, which made the dough sticky, and then adding more flour, which made the dough too crumbly. It was after an hour of kneading and fiddling that I deciphered the note in the margin: *Add a touch of oil*. When I did this, the dough became smooth like baby skin beneath my hands.

I set the dough in a patch of sun on the front porch. Then I scrubbed the refrigerator, pulling out rotten potatoes, moldy sour cream, limp lettuce and four packages of bacon that were slick with age. *SWINC*, it said on the refrigerator door. *SWINC*, it said on the front of the stove. I wondered what this word meant and why it seemed to be the emblem of this town.

The dough was supposed to rise for about an hour and a half. Between removing moldy food from the refrigerator and wiping the insides of the cupboards in the kitchen, I checked on the dough. It wasn't rising. I didn't understand what I had done wrong. I reread the directions again and again. I had done everything I was supposed to do—everything. I had warmed the water, added the yogurt culture and allowed it to foam with a bit of sugar, but the dough sat heavy and solid in the bowl.

After reading the book yet again, I found a small passage, an insignificant detail in miniature print under the picture of a perfect loaf of bread. *Make sure the dough is allowed to rise in an area without a breeze.*

I stood on the front stoop, glanced at Djala snoring on her porch and removed my veil. Wind cooled the sweat on my forehead and lifted the hair from around my face. I brought the dough into the house, shaped it into two thick loaves and put them in the oven, even though I knew they would bake hard and dense.

The house did smell like bread when Belen walked in later that afternoon, but when I pulled the loaves from the oven and set them on top of the stove, I felt my cheeks turn red beneath the veil. With my hands covered by towels, I tipped the pans upside down and felt the hard impact of the loaves of bread hitting the stove top with a *thunk*. I sliced through the dense mass and laid the pieces out. They were as solid and impenetrable as one of Jeremia's wood sculptures. Belen walked back outside.

Nine

That night I sat on the ground outside the lean-to, the patchy straggles of grass poking through to my skin. I tucked the violin under my chin and began to play. I let a new song trickle from me in low, slow notes. The violin sang of my missed life, of my failed bread, of my loneliness. I became so engrossed in the song that I failed to hear the sound of footsteps, and I didn't notice the heat emanating from the body until the man stood right in front of me and nudged my knee with his boot. The shock of the touch ended my song, the finishing note harsh. I held my breath.

Jeremia stood in front of me. At least, with the veil over my face I could believe that this truly was Jeremia—tall, confident, beautiful and seething.

"Is he alive?" asked Jun, Jeremia's father.

He spit the words at me with lips that were stretched taut and pulled down in the corners. His eyes, black and narrow, glinted at me with flashes of the sun that hung low in the sky. He thrust his hands deep into the pockets of his pants, and his knuckles bulged under the material in crocodile ridges. He had two whole arms.

"Is he alive?" he said again, lower, slower.

"Yes," I whispered.

His eyes were so narrow, they became slits as thin as butterfly wings. "When he dies, our shame will be gone."

The man walked through the weeds toward the creek. As he walked, his shoulders rolled with unreleased anger. I hoped he never saw Jeremia again.

As Jeremia's father walked away, I stood. Sometimes Jeremia watched this village. He would come from our home and observe his family. What if he were here now?

My breath came in quick gasps, and I laid my violin in its case, quickly snapping the latches and leaving it in the lean-to. On feet as silent as snow, I slipped through the grasses, waded across the creek and walked into the stunted trees. Jun tromped through the woods on heavy feet that left cracked sticks, bruised bushes and crushed leaves behind. He was easy to follow, and I did so carefully, keeping trees and under-growth between us.

He walked north through the trees until I heard a chorus of chattering, squeaking and chirping. We came to a clearing. In the clearing stood a house like the others, with flat boards and an angled metal roof, but the expanse around the house was open, with large patches of green grass broken by sheds. From these sheds came the sound of birds, hundreds and hundreds of birds. I had heard a similar din before from a flock of crows nesting in the top of an oak or from a group of starlings pecking at seeds. The smell around these sheds reminded me of the heavy air in the village, the oppressive reek that hung on me now and saturated my clothes.

Jeremia had never told me about the bird sheds. Jun walked around the house to the back. I saw no one else, so I slunk across the grassy expanse to the first shed and unlatched the door. The sound inside was like a thousand macaw babies clucking and chirping in an enclosed space. Rows and rows of metal cages stretched from one end of the shed to the other and were stacked on top of each other from the dirt floor to just beneath the roof. The smell, when I opened the door, made me turn my head away and press my hand to my nose. Even my eyes stung.

The chickens were kept in cages so small they could barely move, and some of them needed their straw changed so badly it clung to their feathers in clumps. I held my hand to my nose, breathed through my fingers and wished I was wearing my veil. I couldn't imagine anyone doing this to a living creature, to a fellow dweller on this earth, and I thought of Eva's strutting macaw with its jutting head, quick beak and insistent cry. These were proud birds, but there was nothing to be proud of here.

A woman and a man worked in the back of the shed, walking from cage to cage, opening them and removing the eggs. When I saw the workers, I ducked down where they couldn't see me. I looked into the cage nearest me, right into the pebbly eye of a chicken. She made a low, squawking sound deep in her throat and stood to back away from me, but one of her legs was short, stunted, like the wings of the macaw, so the chicken leaned unsteadily to the side and continued her unbroken screech.

"I won't hurt you," I whispered. "Don't be afraid."

The bird watched me with one eye, her head cocked to the side, but the squawking stopped. Someday I would return and free these creatures—let them peck and run in the weeds, pulling worms from the ground and reestablishing the natural order of things.

I left the shed. My vision was blurred from the smell and the sight, but I crept around the house to where I had seen Jun disappear. I saw no one now, but as the din from the chickens died, another sound drifted from the forest. I didn't understand this noise any better than I had understood the din of a thousand chickens clucking, but this sound made me tense my shoulders and curl my hands into fists.

I crouched in back of the woodpile behind their house, then ran quickly over the packed dirt to the edge of the trees. Someone had been chopping wood, and the smell of the maple reminded me of Jeremia. The sound continued, a whimpering howl. It came from the trees past the woodpile, and I crept between the trees, hoping whatever it was wouldn't leap at me in fear. A square box, nestled like a squatting trap beneath the trees, housed the animal. The sound, I realized, was not whimpering but panicked breathing. My own breathing matched that of the creature's.

I crept closer and peered between the slats of the box. When it saw my face, it screamed, snarled and hurled itself at the side of the box. I jumped back.

"Shh," I said and began to hum.

It was a badger, either hurt or starved. After breathing deeply for a minute, I stood and examined the latch on top of the cage. If I flipped the latch up, allowing the creature to escape, it would leap at me with its claws and teeth, but if it didn't see me, perhaps it would run into the woods. I'd seen badger attacks before, and it was a rare fight when the badger lost. But I couldn't leave it trapped.

With a long stick, I pushed at the latch, knocked it through the hook and then wondered how I would open the door without being seen. The door opened upward, like a hinged roof, and if I stood behind the hinges, perhaps I could flip up the door and hide behind it.

After three attempts, the stick became wedged under the hook and I pulled, lifting the door first an inch and then a bit more. Before I was able to pull the door all the way up, the creature inside threw itself at the opening door, came hurtling out of the cage and stood in front of it, looking me in the eyes. Its mouth foamed, its eyes were crusted and red, its sides heaved, and the fur hung off it as though made for a much larger creature. We looked at each other, that animal and I, and then a gunshot sent me to the ground and the creature to the woods. I held my hands over my ears and squeezed my eyes shut. I didn't open them again until a boot nudged me in the side. When I looked up, I saw a wider, thicker Jeremia with two whole arms and straight hair that hung in his eyes and over his ears.

He said something, and I took my hands away from my ears.

"Two years—that's how long I've been keeping that badger." The man had pulled up the pants on his right leg and was showing me a round wound that had healed flat and red, the muscle and tissue gone. "Been starving it good and mean so we could turn it loose on a dog and watch it fight.

You just lost me a whole lot of…you that girl from the camp in the woods?"

I sat up and then stood, brushing the dirt from my clothes. He'd already seen my face, so I left my veil around my neck and looked at him as hard as he looked at me. I'd never heard of badgers and dogs fighting, but I'd seen a badger scare off a wolf before. Eva and I had watched from the top of a rock, and we'd had to wait half an hour after the fight ended to come down—both of us were shaking so much our teeth chattered. Those creatures had snarled, barked and torn chunks of fur and skin from each other, and Eva and I didn't even know what the fight had been about.

"You live with Jeremia. I'm his big brother, Calen."

He looked me up and down. I didn't know if I liked this man or not, but his eyes weren't as flat and mean as his father's, and he had a way of wiping his hand under his nose that reminded me of Eva.

"Sometimes I think he watches me." We both glanced into the trees. "He follows me into the woods. He don't talk to me, but I like the company." He shifted his weight back and forth from foot to foot. His face was different from Jeremia's—there was a softness to his jaw—and there was a curve to his shoulders. I was surprised that he wasn't angrier about the badger. When he looked at me, he glanced away often—to the trees, the ground, the sky.

"You tell him when you see him that I might not be the smartest, but I know when something's not right. Sending him away wasn't right." He squinted at me when he said this.

"Locking up a badger isn't right," I said.

"That badger bit me."

"It's an animal. It shouldn't be punished for behaving like one."

Calen looked up, as if the darkening sky might help him respond. We stood quietly for a long time and then he looked at me and crossed his arms over his chest.

"But a badger ain't human. This is my gun."

He smiled then, shyly, like a five-year-old, as he held the rifle out in front of him. That was when I understood who Calen was, why he still lived with his parents even though he had been a man for years. He wasn't married, didn't have children and probably wouldn't. Maybe his father and mother, when they'd seen Jeremia's missing limb at birth, had thought he would be like Calen—simple—or maybe it was acceptable in this town to have deformities as long as they were invisible. Maybe they hadn't understood their child's simplicity until they'd become attached to him and then hadn't been willing to let him go.

Calen wiped his hand under his nose again and began to mumble. His lower lip pushed forward, and he put a hand on his hip. I put my hands on my hips and he copied me, leaning his rifle against his body. What had Jeremia said about this brother? He had tried to track the wolf, followed it for miles, but was too loud and clumsy to ever sneak up on anything.

"Calen." A call came from the house. I bent my knees and put my hands against the ground. Calen dropped beside me in a similar stance and bit his bottom lip. I smiled at him, held a finger to my lips and then slipped into the trees the way I had seen the badger go. When I looked back, Calen was still crouched by the badger cage, looking into the trees where I had disappeared. I ran quietly, hunched over, skirting the edge of Jun's property, and came again to the back of the chicken shed. As I turned the corner to head through the woods and back to where I'd come from, a hand grabbed my shoulder, and I gasped.

I spun around, ready to lunge at whoever had grabbed me, but instead a whimper came from my mouth, and I threw my arms around my attacker's neck. Jeremia had come for me.

He held me tightly, his arm wrapped around my back, and I pushed my face against his neck. I shook against him, but he held me still and close until my hot tears stopped dripping and my whimper finally stilled.

"Have they hurt you?" he whispered into my ear.

Of course they had—kicked me, pushed me, slapped me, humiliated me. How could I tell Jeremia that and then watch him be pulled apart in this town? I shook my head.

"Come home with me."

The heat from his body seeped into mine. He lowered his arm on my back so that his hand pressed into the small of my back and our bodies fit together. I breathed in his deep scent—earth and sweat that masked the smells from the shed behind us. His lips kissed the side of my head, and I turned my face so our mouths could meet. He pushed his mouth against my lips, his tongue searching for mine. Everything tingled—my lips, my hands, my insides—but suddenly the image of Jun came into my head, his eyes narrow and his fists tight. He could not find Jeremia here. I pushed away.

"You have to leave," I said.

Jeremia held my hand, and I tried to look away from the confusion on his face.

"He wants you dead," I said.

"Who?"

"Your father." I knew I should run, force Jeremia to leave, but instead I threw my arms around his neck one more time, breathed his scent in deep so that it would cling to me, my clothing, the inside of my mouth, and then I turned to go. "You mustn't come back, Jeremia. They will hurt you." I ran into the woods without looking back.

By the time I returned to the house, it was dark, and Belen stood in front of my lean-to, his arms across his chest, his face a red so dark it looked blackened.

He opened the door when he saw me. I untied the veil and slipped it over my head. When I walked past and into the lean-to, he took a step back and I thought he might shove me inside, but instead he slammed the door shut after I'd entered. Then I heard a lock clicking into place, and I was once again a prisoner.

But this time I had Jeremia's scent on my hands, and even though I felt alone in this place, I wasn't. My family would always be with me, watching me through the secret windows between the leaves.

Ten

The next day I heard the lock unclick on the outside of the door, and a fist pounded on the wood.

"Breakfast," Belen said.

I made breakfast, washed the dirty clothes and returned to the house for my next attempt at baking the bread. The batch of yogurt culture I'd made after my failed attempt and after buying fresh milk warmed at the back of the stove. I checked and double-checked the ingredients, kneaded the dough until it stretched and bounced, placed the bowl in a sheltered, sunny area and waited.

I scrubbed the plastic kitchen floor on my hands and knees, weeks of grime dirtying my pail of water, the floor almost as filthy as the packed-dirt floor of our hut. I checked on the bread. I wiped down the walls in the kitchen where greasy splatters and drips of milk had obscured the color—dark blue, I discovered, not gray. I checked on the bread, then washed the living room floor again. By the time I was finished, the bread had risen into a rounded mound that pushed at the towel draped over the top of the bowl. A stirring began in my chest, a tingling sensation that pulled up the corners of my lips and made me giddy.

I punched the rounded mound of dough so it sank back into the bowl and then divided it into four, placing the handfuls of dough into greased bread pans and setting them back in the sun to rise. It was then that I dared believe it was working. I finished the floor in the living room while the dough rose in the pans, pushing against the towel much more quickly this time, as though it had perfected the art of rising. I warmed the oven and put the pans inside. The dough matched the description in the book, and I bit at my finger, a squeak escaping my mouth.

While the bread baked, I moved to the boys' bedroom and scrubbed until a warm glow rose from the wood floor, giving the room an aura of health and naturalness. I checked the door, looked out the front window, determined that no one was watching and then lay down on one of the beds, my head on a pillow. These boys had probably never experienced an earache in their lives.

I could hear the laughter of children, the sound of Eva dancing in the sun, and I slid off the bed, adjusting the veil over my face. I looked out into the street from the doorway. The bread was baking, the children were laughing, my smile reached my eyes—until I saw what the children were laughing about.

A group of kids had gathered in a tight circle, and I assumed they would kick the can and run as they had earlier, but this time their excitement was focused on something other than a tin object.

One of the boys I'd met at the tree house stood in the center of the circle—the boy with crutches, who had sped away in the grasses as though he'd been chased often. Fabio. I could see his face just above the children's heads, his lips pulled tight and his eyes wary. A red gash on the right side of his forehead dripped blood down into one eye, yet none of the children helped him. Instead, they laughed and jostled him. It was like my first day in this town, when I'd been chained to the doghouse and put on display.

I glanced to my right, at Djala's chair. She sat watching, rocking, the gun across her knees. She cackled and rocked, cackled and rocked. I crept down the few front steps and walked carefully, quietly, a silent wolf observing the enemy, making my way to the back of the circle. David stood on the other side of the street. We looked at each other, but he did not come to stand beside me, and I did not ask him to.

Mateo stood in front of Fabio and held the boy's crutches in his hand. He held them close to Fabio's outstretched hand and then quickly pulled them away when Fabio reached for them. He laughed like a hyena, a cackle of ill will, a carrion eater waiting for the prey to show weakness and run.

I pushed my way between a girl and a boy, both of whom stood on tiptoe, trying to see into the center of the circle. Sliding between those in the next row, I found myself with only one child between me and Mateo. I stopped, considered a moment and evaluated whether I would become the next target if I disrupted their game. Here in the sun, Fabio looked thin, pale, with hair so black it made his skin seem translucent.

His surliness was gone, but a determination remained that I could see in the set of his jaw. The wound on his head was beginning to form a hard crust, and on the other side of his forehead I saw a thin line, a raised scar, from injuries past. Maybe life was better for those rejected and sent to the camp in the woods than for those who remained.

I calculated the distance between me and Mateo and pushed aside the child in front of me. I reached out, grabbed Mateo under the arms, hoisted him into the air, turned him and slung him over my shoulder. Many times I had done this with Eva. Mateo was a bit heavier but not unbearably so, and he wasn't as muscled as Eva. He felt soft, malleable and puffy around the waist, as though he were made of rising dough. He did not kick as I walked with him back to the house, but he grunted when his stomach pushed into my shoulder. He dropped the crutches.

The children's laughter changed. Now, instead of laughing at Fabio and his futile efforts to regain his crutches, they laughed at Mateo. When he heard their laughter, Mateo became furious and then began to kick, pounding his fists into my back and pulling at the veil over my head. I held his feet together and endured the fists that pummeled my back like acorns shot from a slingshot.

The veil was off now, but I kept my steady pace. I walked across the lumpy ground of our front yard, glanced at Djala, who raised the rifle at me and offered a gummy smile, and climbed the steps to the house, pushing open the door. The smell in the air had changed from the nutty aroma of baking bread to the slightly smoking smell of bread that had been baking too long.

I was angry as I had never been before.

Mateo continued to pound me with his fists, and now I increased my pace and kicked open the door to his room. I walked to his bed and threw him down on it. He landed on his back, grunting, and looked up at me with startled and fearful eyes. His hands were closed into fists, his face was red and puffy, his breath fast and hard.

"I'm telling Dad," he screamed. "He'll chain you up to the doghouse again and pound you until you bleed."

The heat of anger crept up my neck and into my cheeks. I bit my teeth together hard and swallowed.

"Those kids play with you only because they fear you," I said.

"I have lots of friends and you don't have any. I hate you and wish you'd died."

I walked out of his room, slamming the door behind me, and went into the kitchen. I opened the door to the oven and, with towels over my hands, pulled out the loaves of bread. They had baked too long and were more dense and hard than need be. I sat down on the floor right there and put my face against my knees. Tears softened the material of my brown pants, and I could feel the wet fabric rubbing against my cheek, but I couldn't stop. Someone came in the house, propped open the door and opened the windows in the kitchen and living room. He closed the door to the oven and draped the veil over my head and knees.

Mateo screamed from his bedroom.

"David, don't you be nice to her. You saw what she did to me."

David opened and closed the door to the bedroom. I could hear murmuring in there, a soft conversation that became momentarily loud.

"I won't do it," came Mateo's voice, high and whiny now. "I hate you. Why do you side with her?" Something hard and solid hit the wall, and David emerged from the bedroom. He closed the door behind him and sat in the living room, where he picked up one of the books on baking bread and began to turn its pages.

I lifted my head and wiped my face with the veil. I stood up and washed my hands at the sink. I peeled potatoes, cut up vegetables, prepared a pot of water on the stove and began to add ingredients. Nathanael's favorite stew would be our dinner tonight, accompanied by bread that was a bit hard.

As the stew began to cook and I added salt, strips of gingerroot and chunks of turnip, I also warmed a pan of milk at the back of the stove and began to gently cook the yogurt culture for my next attempt.

As soon as Belen arrived home, Mateo yelled from his room and began to sob loudly, which made me wonder for just a minute if perhaps I'd hurt him more than I'd thought. David followed his father into the bedroom and closed the door behind them. The loud sobs quieted and stilled, and then I heard only murmuring. When Belen came out of the bedroom, I stiffened my shoulders and waited. He spoke to my back.

"You will not discipline these children. That is my job, not yours."

The veil rustled slightly from the breeze through the open windows. I stirred the warm milk in the pan and thought about my life in this village so far. Even though I had cooked, cleaned, washed the clothing and made their lives easier, we hadn't had a single day without conflict. My shoulders were tight and sore from the constant tension, and I'd become hesitant in my actions. Around Belen, I felt like the wolf—not wanting to be touched, wary of his presence and as cautious of his movements as I was of fire.

"You will look at me when I speak to you," he said and grabbed my shoulder, his fingers digging in. I stared at the floor because I could, because he did not know where I was looking and couldn't control that, at least.

"Don't touch him again, hear me? Ever." His voice was low and deep and his hands twitched at his sides, wanting to swing and slap at me. "Tomorrow Celso returns, and we will discuss the next step you will take. You've been troublesome and meddlesome. You are more work than your cleaning is worth."

He pushed me aside and sniffed the stew on the stove. He dipped the spoon into the pot, lifted it to his mouth and tasted. He dipped again, tasted once more, then dropped the spoon onto the stove beside the over-baked loaves of bread and strode out the door. David sat down on the couch in the living room and continued to read the book, or pretended to read the book, but Mateo never did come out of his room, even when we sat down to dinner. I sat in Mateo's place, ate at the table with my brother and father and almost felt like I was part of the family. When the bread was dipped into the stew, it tasted quite good and softened nicely. Both David and Belen ate great chunks of it, but neither looked at me and not a word was said.

∞

In the morning I made breakfast and then returned to the lean-to. I wanted to sweep in the daylight, dust the edges of the room before starting this day's bread making. When I returned to the house, David stood in the kitchen, his hands kneading and turning the contents of a large bowl. His hands were coated in flour, his face had a slight dusting, and his shoulders rotated in rhythm with his hands. I dropped the basket for dirty clothes inside the door and stood beside him in the kitchen. As I watched his hands turning and kneading, the muscles in his arms tensing and releasing, I understood that this was not new to him.

"You almost had it," he said. "The last batch would have worked if you'd ignored Mateo."

"You don't need me to bake the bread."

"Yeah, we do. Dad doesn't want anyone to know I'm doing woman's work."

I continued to watch his hands and could see the confidence and enjoyment he found in doing this. It soothed me to watch him, and I leaned against the stove.

"But they'll send you away if you don't do the bread right, and if you don't stop making Dad mad." David's dough was soft and stretchy, matching the pictures next to the recipe.

"Where will they send me?"

"The city. And I like what you did to Mateo yesterday. He deserved it. He needs it. Mom used to keep him in line, but there's no one to do that now. I want you to stay here."

Tense, release. Tense, release. The dough was smooth and malleable, not sticky or flaky. His movements mesmerized me. When a shadow stretched across the square of sunlight from the door, I looked up, blinking, waking from the calming movement of David's kneading. A dark shape stood in the doorway—I couldn't see the person's face with the light behind him, but David stopped his movements, pulled away from the bowl and stood trembling against the refrigerator door. I stood in front of David and waited.

The man took a step into the room, out of the sunlight, and now I could see the heavy brow, thinning hair and deep-set eyes of Celso, Belen's brother. The man who'd chained me to the doghouse. David breathed hard behind me.

"David, David, David," Celso said, his voice singsong, light and teasing. His eyes didn't match the tone, though, and I moved closer to David. "I've told you before, kid, you're not cut out to be anyone's protector, not even your reject sister's. Making the bread for her, were you?"

A squeak entered David's breathing, a high-pitched wheeze that sounded almost like the buzzing of the cicada. The rhythmic squeaks began to increase in speed until there was barely a pause between them. David held my arm, and then he slid to the floor, his other hand against his throat, his breath coming in gasps. Celso pushed me out of the way and stood over David.

"And look at you now. Can't even breathe. Your mother never should have taught you how to bake the bread."

I turned on the cold water at the sink and ran a cloth under the tap. I knelt next to David and wiped at his face, around his eyes, around his mouth. He stared up at Celso, his eyes huge, his breath ragged. The cool water on the cloth didn't seem to help, but I kept wiping at his face while Celso watched, a half smile on his face.

"Like brother, like sister. You two are both damaged, he with asthma, you with ugliness."

I stood then and pushed Celso in the chest so hard I grunted and he fell, landing on his back in the doorway to the house. I bent down again and wiped at David's face. He could no longer see Celso, but as he watched me, his breath began to slow, began to lose its squeak, and the skin around his lips became pink again instead of blue.

When a shadow stretched through the room, sending its darkness like a blackened cloud over us, I leaped to the side and David raised a hand to shield his eyes. Where I had been the moment before, the flash of a blade came down as Celso swept his knife through the air above David. I crouched now, hands out, and he charged at me, but I leaped aside and ran through the kitchen and out the front door.

I could hear him breathing hard, almost growling, but as soon as my feet touched the grass, I knew I could outrun this man. I could run back to the camp in the woods and never see this village again. But then he would use my running away as an excuse to torment my camp family, and he had probably been tormenting David for years. I slowed my feet, turned and faced the man with the knife.

He charged at me with the momentum of a rolling boulder. He was lumpy and slow with his body but quick and sneaky with his hands. When he ran at me with the knife pointed to my chest, I stepped to the side and he pushed past, but his hand reached for me, grasping my arm and pulling me with him down to the earth, where my shoulder hit hard against the ground. His hold loosened, and I stood quickly.

He rolled, lumbered to his feet and switched the knife to the other hand. His chest heaved, like the dying wolf's in our campsite. I bent my knees, held my hands out from my sides and waited. David appeared on the small porch, one hand steadying himself in the doorway, the other hand on his chest.

Celso barreled at me, the knife flashing, and cut a groove in the palm of my hand. I gasped and stumbled over the lumps in the grass, falling hard. He came at me again, his face angry and mottled, his knife pointed at me and glinting in the light of the sun. I should have run, escaped to the woods when I'd had the chance.

I curled into a ball, held my hands over my head and waited. When the gunshot came, Celso stopped. Djala stood at the end of her porch, pointing her rifle between me and Celso.

"My eyesight ain't too good, Celso. Wouldn't want to hit the wrong person."

The tendons in Celso's arms stood out, tense and rigid. He watched Djala, and I stood, tensing my legs for another run or assault or fall.

"Go back to sleep, Djala," Celso said.

"Think I've slept enough today." She didn't look at me, but I was pretty sure she was speaking to me. "Don't know that Belen would appreciate your messing with his little project here."

"She should be chained to the doghouse."

"Well, she ain't."

They stared at each other, both with jaws set and eyes hard. I didn't know if Djala was being nice to me or if she was merely protecting Belen's interests.

I backed up until I felt the steps to the house behind my heels. I looked up at David. His breathing was normal now, his face no longer pinched and blue. Together we went into the house and shut the door. We watched Djala and Celso from the window over the sink in the kitchen. David held out a towel to me, which I wrapped around my right hand. I had been holding my hand up and the blood had dripped from the cut, disappearing into the sleeve of my black sweater. We didn't hear what was said, but Celso walked down the street and then disappeared between two houses. David put the bread dough in a bowl, placed it in the sunny spot and covered it lightly with another towel.

He stood in front of me for a minute, and we looked at each other.

"The loaves mustn't burn this time," he said. Then he left the house, and I watched from the doorway as he dragged his feet in a slow, plodding path through the dust of the road.

When I pulled the loaves from the oven, the top of the bread was a crisp golden brown and the smell in the house breathed of possible success.

Belen walked in the door, followed by Celso, almost tripping over the backs of Belen's shoes. When I saw the two men together, I wondered if they were twins—same heavy brow, same square body shape, same hooded dark brows—but Belen's eyes looked away while Celso's tried to bore holes in my veil. I bit my lower lip while they examined the bread. What had Celso told Belen about the bread? What had Celso told Belen about me, about Djala, about David?

Celso broke one of the loaves of bread open, sniffed the fluffy interior and took a bite. He shrugged his shoulders.

"Not bad. Not as good as Teresa's, but not bad."

He sat at the table and consumed a quarter of the loaf of bread. I saw Belen tuck the other loaves into a bag, which he placed in the refrigerator. Mateo came running into the house, David trailing behind, his hands deep in his pockets and his eyes wary.

"We smelled it all the way down the road," Mateo said. "I want some."

Belen cut a thick slice, spread it with melting butter and handed the first piece to David. He cut another slice and handed this to Mateo. Then he cut one for himself. David did not breathe deeply and consume the smell of the bread but ate with great bites while watching Celso. Mateo hummed to himself, a tune my mother used to sing to me that spoke of happiness and goodness and maybe some innocence somewhere.

Belen sat at the table across from his brother. He ate his slice of bread carefully. His eyes flickered, never holding still. He appeared to be talking to his bread when he spoke.

"You said she'd make how much, again?"

"In one week she could make as much as Teresa made in a month baking the bread and selling it at the market."

Celso watched me then, his lips pulled up at the corners. "Tell her to take off her veil. I want to see her face again."

Belen nodded at me.

I stood against the stove in the kitchen. The room felt hot, sticky, the yeasty smell of the bread causing my stomach to groan. His reasons for wanting me to take off the veil didn't make sense. He'd seen me without the veil when Djala had shot between us.

"Take off the veil," Belen said.

When I still hesitated, he stood, placing both hands on the tabletop. I slipped the veil off my head, trying to still its fluttering by using both hands. The wound on my hand still bled.

Celso raised his eyelids enough to look at me. He examined me up and down, from the top of my head to my toes. I wanted to look where he was looking. I wanted to understand the knowing look on his face, examine myself from outside my body. What did people see when they looked at me? Why did it feel so different to look out of my own eyes, feel who I was, know who I was, when almost everyone else looked at me with shock and revulsion?

"If she doesn't make the money sitting on the corner, she can make the money in other ways. Her body is fine. Men pay a lot for young flesh like that."

Belen jerked his head away from me. Both David and Mateo sat silently, watching this exchange with serious faces and mouths full of bread.

"We never agreed to that," Belen said. "I'll not have her used in that way." He glanced at me, at the two boys, back at Celso, who was watching him. "Begging, yes."

Celso said nothing. Something stirred in me, something dark and deep. The way he looked at my body, the smell of unwashed skin and smoke that emanated from him, how he spoke through Belen as though I weren't worthy of his attention—all of this made me see him as a coyote, skittish and devious.

Maybe he hadn't told Belen about attacking me with a knife, or about David making the bread. Should I say something? Might that make things worse?

"We may not need to go that far. Her face alone should earn you plenty of money," said Celso. "Or she could work at the SWINC factory in the city. They'll hire her type there." He looked at me now with his mouth pulled down at the corners and his eyebrows drawn tight over his eyes, as though I were something filthy, something slippery and rotten. He stood, pushing back his chair and wiping the crumbs from the table onto the floor.

"If you decide to send her, I'll be here before dawn. Dress her in rags, add some dirt to her face, make her bring that violin she is said to play."

I forgot for a minute that the veil was in my hand. My lips quivered, and I blinked my eyes. I'd been here for how long? A week? And already they were sending me away. I was too much trouble, too hideous, too incompetent. When I opened my mouth, my voice wouldn't cooperate. I couldn't even summon a whisper.

Belen tapped one hand against the top of his thigh. His eyes focused somewhere on my knees and I stood very still, hardly daring to breathe, hoping that he'd allow me to stay.

"Next month," he said. "This bread will do for now. We can sell it at the store."

Celso slammed his fist down on the table, the bread popping up and dropping back down. Belen looked at his brother. A froth of white outlined the right side of Celso's mouth, and his nostrils flared like a wild boar's.

"She did not bake the bread."

David sucked in his breath. Would the squeaking begin again, the thrashing about on the floor and the blue lips? We waited, the moment thick and oppressive like the moment before I grabbed the crayfish, when I knew it might erupt, snap at me, hide beneath the rock. Belen looked at David.

"Your mother taught you well, David. Then we don't need the girl."

David pushed back from the table and held his hands in his lap. Mateo's head rotated back and forth, a wary owl, his mouth open slightly. I held the veil in my hand, felt its absence and slipped it back onto my head. They wouldn't see my tears—none of them would see my tears.

"She will make money for us in other ways, then. If that doesn't work, she'll return home, take care of the house, and you will teach her how to make the bread. For now, it will be your job, David, but only for us. You will not sell the bread at the market—that is not a man's work. When her money comes in from the city, we will hire someone to clean the house. For now, this will do." Belen's arm swept out, indicating the cleaned house and all the work I'd done. I should have worked more slowly, made them think they needed me forever. David opened his mouth but did not speak.

Celso crossed his arms above his bulging stomach and tried to smile, but the unused muscles resisted, stretching the corners of his mouth long. "And you, girl, will stay close to me when we travel to the city. You'll not run, you'll not attempt anything, or your handsome little friend from the woods will find his throat slit in the middle of the night." When he said the word *handsome*, his eyelids fluttered.

Celso reached around me, his unwashed smell overpowering the smell of fresh bread. He grasped the remaining chunk of bread in his meaty hand and brushed his arm against my chest. The floor shook as he exited the house.

Tomorrow he would be my master. Just as I'd begun to get my feet underneath me, to make friends and find support, I would again disappear as I had from the camp in the woods, where dragonflies flew and crickets sang. How many more moves were left for me? Probably more than I cared to know.

Eleven

The night passed slowly. I listened to the call of the caracara. I heard the squeak of bats as they swooped by the open door. I waited for a dead skunk, for little boys who run shrieking, terrified but thrilled, into the night. No clouds crossed in front of the stars. Nights were cooler now, the air tingly with the scent of falling leaves. I looked forward to the change in seasons. I loved fall, with its brisk temperatures. I especially loved the smell of earth, leaves and rain.

Nathanael, Jeremia and Eva would be collecting wood now for fires on the colder winter nights. They would be drying the fruits, collecting the berries, trapping rabbits and hunting deer to make into salted winter meat. They would be sitting around the campfire, Nathanael telling stories of the river witch who swam through the creek to villages along it and crept into children's huts in the nighttime, taking away their voices. I knew that I'd lived primitively in our camp in the woods, but I also knew that I'd had a good life, free of cruelty. Nathanael had been to the city; he had seen the cars, the huge buildings, the swarms of people, and he had hated it. He had said that only the desperate went to the city—the desperate, the frantic and the rejected.

So he'd stayed with us in the woods and told us of traveling bands of people who packed up their tents, carried them on their backs, moved to a new place and set up their tents once again.

That was me. A nomad. Only I didn't have a tent to carry with me. I had nothing but the clothes on my back, the few items my mother had given me, a cream slip with a brown stain and the violin that could be my voice. Maybe this was my life—maybe I would never know a permanent home again. I thought of running away, gathering my belongings and slinking through the grasses to follow the creek back to our camp in the woods, but I didn't. I would not let them hurt Jeremia. I would not allow Jeremia's father to forget his shame.

Before the sun rose, the shape of a man appeared in the door of the lean-to, the stars obliterated by his presence. His protruding stomach filled the opening, and his body permeated the little room with the smell of ash and sweat.

I was ready for him. I had dressed in all of my clothing: my pants, my mother's slip made into short pants, my mouse T-shirt and the black sweater. I slipped my feet into my brown shoes, draped the veil over my head, left the lean-to and followed him, slinging the violin case over my shoulder and carrying my small sack. The lean-to was not my home. I would miss only David, but the farther I moved away from our camp in the woods, the more lonely and full of holes I felt.

Celso climbed onto a tethered mule at the edge of our village. The mule began a steady trot down the road and I followed, my heart rubbing against the bones in my chest. As we approached the last houses and prepared to step away from this village and forward to the big city, I heard the pattering of footsteps behind me, and I felt a bit of hope that maybe Belen had changed his mind.

When I turned around, David stopped and bent over, his hands on his knees. His breath made the high squeak when he breathed in. As his breathing calmed, the squeak lessened and soon disappeared.

"Here," he said. He thrust his hand toward me, a lumpy handkerchief tied in a knot hanging heavy in his fist. "May it go well with you."

And that's when the tears dripped from my eyes, down the sides of my nose. The veil covered my face, the night revealed nothing, and David pushed his shoulders back, breathing deep and clean once more.

"And may it go well with you," I said as he walked away.

Celso took the bundle from my hands. With blunt, fat fingers he untied the corners of the cloth and opened the square piece of blue material. Inside were three items: a corner from one of the loaves of bread, a small square of cheese and a slingshot.

Celso took the bread from the cloth sack, broke off a chunk and gave me the remaining portion. He handed the other items back to me and resumed his steady trot.

I rolled up a small piece of the bread, made a sticky dough ball and rolled it around on my tongue. I chewed it slowly as I walked. Fresh and soft, moist and grainy. I hoped as I savored the nutty texture that I would discover ways to be more like my mother and less like my father.

The walk through the woods was peaceful and quiet, but the trees were brown, short and stunted. I missed the tall trunks and feathery leaves of my home and the thick vines full of flowers in the underbrush. Celso didn't speak to me, so I listened to a small owl hooting in the trees, I listened to the creek from the village laughing and giggling, I listened to the call of a wolf, and I wondered how I could play these songs on my violin.

We walked from before the sun rose until after it set.

I was grateful for the bread and cheese. Celso had his own lunch, and I smelled the sausage and fried egg he shoved into his mouth with fat fingers, but I didn't want anything from this man. He watched me with searching looks that made me want to disappear inside my sweater.

When the road became so dark that our shadows disappeared, we crunched through the debris on the forest floor, and Celso built a small fire beneath the stunted trees along the path. He tied my hands together with a piece of rope and looped the rope around a tree. The mule he tethered to the same tree, and then Celso wrapped his coat around himself and lay in front of the fire, falling asleep in seconds. I whispered to the mule and it pushed its nose against me. The animal was warm, soft and smelled of grass. I tried to sleep against the tree, my knees bent, my head against the rough bark, my shoulder pushed into the tree until it ached with a dull throb.

When my body, so tired from walking all day, finally relaxed and I slept, the soft mumbling of words startled me awake and woke the mule. It whinnied and backed away as far as the rope would allow it to go, and then it pulled, its back legs digging into the ground. I whispered to it, but it had had enough of whisperings.

"Cut it then."

"Shh, you'll wake him."

"Hurry up. We'll not have time, at this rate."

The outline of a head appeared around the side of the tree. Celso's fire had died out long ago. I saw nothing but the flash of stars on bright eyes and the glint of light on teeth. The head drew back behind the tree, and a tugging began. The ropes were being unknotted, and my hands tingled as the circulation returned. When the ropes fell away, I stood, my creaking knees stiff and threatening to collapse, my sore shoulder aching.

"Come," the voice said, and a person appeared around the side of the tree. I could make out a shape, loose clothing and bare feet that knew where to walk silently.

I glanced back at Celso, a rounded lump on the ground, and touched the mule's nose. Now that the strangers no longer stood by the tree, the mule ceased its pulling and stood calm, its head hanging low. On feet as silent as theirs, I followed these people into the woods.

The brush became a bit thicker as we moved away from the path, and the sounds of the woods intensified. I could hear tree frogs gulping, snakes creeping and the owl calling. An orange glow flickered against the sickly trees, and I followed my rescuers to the spot of light in the woods.

Two girls looked back at me when we reached the small clearing. Both were smaller than me and dirtier, with matted hair that might have been blond and faces so smeared with dirt that their bodies blended into the brown of the trees. They motioned for me to come and sit down by the fire. On the other side of the fire sat two others: a small girl and a boy with large teeth that stuck out over his bottom lip. The two girls I had followed looked normal, appeared to have no blemishes, but the third was tiny, with hands and feet so small they looked like a doll's. I leaned down to her and slid the veil off my face.

"See? See? Didn't I say?" said one of the girls who had untied me.

"Like Kada," said the other, nodding at me and looking at the tiny girl.

When the tiny girl spoke, her voice was deep, seeming to come from the boy beside her. I looked again and saw shadows under her eyes and lines around her mouth, as though perhaps she hadn't eaten enough or was older than I'd thought.

"Why were you captive?" she said.

I sat on my heels and held the filmy veil in my hands. All of them looked at me, their eyes big, their faces turned to me without fear or disgust. There was no danger here that I could see.

"I must go to the city."

"And work for him?" The tiny girl dug with a tiny hand into the soft ground of the forest and threw bits of leaves, sticks and bark onto the fire. The pieces popped and crackled when they hit the flames.

"To send money to my family."

The two girls I had followed laughed. One nudged the other with her shoulder and then covered her mouth with her hand. The other didn't even bother to cover her mouth.

"That's no father that will tie his daughter to a tree," said Kada.

Nor is it a father who will chain his daughter to a doghouse or kick her in the side or slap her across the head. I knew this. I wasn't traveling to the city for them.

"You may stay with us, with me and my sisters, and with our friend Tollie." When Tollie heard his name, he smiled so big his cheeks squeezed up and his eyes closed. "We are our own family now."

"There are others I must protect," I said, not looking at the two sisters who giggled behind their hands.

"Your responsibility is to yourself," Kada said and looked at me so hard, with such narrow eyes, that I wanted to drape the veil over my head and hide behind its film. What did she know of my life?

"Then why are your sisters with you?"

"They chose to come. They're not rejected, but they wouldn't tolerate my ill treatment, my caging as though I were an animal." The tiny girl trembled as she spoke, a compact ball of defiance, her cheeks pink with heat, her mouth tight with hate. "We take care of each other now, but if something were to happen to me, they would save themselves."

The two girls had stopped their giggling. One of them sat with her head cocked to the side, watching me with one eye, like a macaw. The other looked into the fire with a smile that she never hid. They were about David's age—ten, I would guess. Kada was older.

I stood up and slipped the veil over my head again.

"I will need help with the knots," I said.

The girl tossed long brown hair that almost reached the ground. She looked into the fire and seemed to speak to the flames.

"We help you escape, and your choice is to return. You will never go far in this world if you don't know how to rescue yourself."

I waited, but the group by the fire ignored me now, watching the flames as though they held more sway and power than I ever could. I must rescue myself already, it seemed.

The darkness was beginning to ebb as I tried to follow my path back through the woods. I could see the outlines of the trees more clearly now, and the sounds of waking birds made my hands slick with nervousness. My feet seemed to find every stick, every leaf, and crunched through these straggly trees with as much noise as my father and brothers made tromping through the woods.

When I finally found our camp, the light from the east glowed white in the sky and outlined the trees with the brightness of day. Celso sat by the fire, the thick smell of bacon rising from a black iron pan he gently shook over the flames. When I sat across from him, he did not look up. When he ate his bacon, he offered nothing to me and continued to pretend that I had not returned or perhaps that I had never left.

As he packed his belongings into the bag slung over the mule's back, he said only this to me: "So many children disappear these days and are never found again."

He climbed onto the mule when the sun had risen above the trees, and I followed him, my feet dragging in the dust of the path, my violin bumping a rhythm against my back, my thoughts still in the camp where my family prepared for winter and became accustomed to my absence.

Twelve

The second day was much like the first—we shuffled along the path and met another traveler or two—but on the third day the sounds around me changed. No longer did I hear the song of birds or the chirping of crickets: I heard voices, the shuffling of feet, the creaking of wheels and the hum of machines I could not name. Now and then the roaring of a truck could be heard, and I imagined the word *SWINC* written on the side.

We moved from the path onto a much broader road, which was busy with people. We all trudged along, most of us staring at our feet, ignoring each other, while I wondered what their stories were, where they were going, what their songs might be. Only part of me marched along this road, the part made of muscle, bone and blood. The rest of me lived with Nathanael, Jeremia, Eva and Ranita, and a tiny piece of me, unsure and battered, baked bread with David.

Celso and I reached a farm just as night fell. I was so tired my feet barely lifted from the ground, and my head felt thick. The smell I had first noticed in my father's village, ten times as strong now, grew, swelled, burst from the air around me. The smell was so bad I feared that it was actually part of me, my fear and dread dripping like sweat.

The road we marched on passed huge buildings, great rectangles that could have held fifty houses like Belen's. They grew up into the air, flat, abnormal dwellings that blocked the setting sun and threw a cool, suffocating shadow over the road. A churning noise groaned from these buildings—the sound of animals crowded into enclosed spaces—and on the sides of the buildings in dark lettering were the words *SWINC: SWINE INCORPORATED*. We still followed the creek, the same stream that ran through my camp, through Belen's village, all the way to the city. But here the water was a sluggish swamp covered by a greasy film, three times the width of my creek and barely moving. I shivered as we trudged along.

When darkness fell that third night, we looked past the structures and saw people in a field, stirring a broad lagoon with sticks. Above the lagoon a haze hovered, a fog of thick stench that pushed the oxygen out of the air. This was where the smell was most concentrated, and it was so strong I felt dizzy and swayed from side to side behind the mule.

Once we left the lagoon behind and were beyond the immediate smell and sound, I lifted my head and felt my face pushing through the odor to the cleaner air above. I tried to understand this smell, discern what it reminded me of. But all I could think of was the dead wolf, the rotted body covered with sores.

After passing the enormous buildings, we reached the outskirts of a village called Gloriosa and stopped at the first house, a small wood building with a wide, inviting front porch. Celso placed his hand against my back, and I climbed the steps to the front door. The door was opened by a woman with eye wrinkles that reached out into her cheeks. Her face was as old as Nathanael's, but something about the way she held herself—shoulders back, arms thick with muscle, legs sturdy—made me think she was younger than her face appeared. Her eyes were clouded, but around her mouth were smile creases, and her cheeks had a rosy glow. She peered at my veil with curiosity but not with fear.

"We are traveling to the city," Celso said. "We wondered if you would know of a place where we could stay for the night."

The woman crossed her arms over her chest and looked at Celso. She didn't smile, didn't speak, but simply appraised. She examined him for what seemed a long time and then looked at me. Her face softened, her mouth turned up at the corners into a smile, and the creases around her eyes reached almost to her hair.

"The child needs a place to stay," said the woman, and she opened the door wide.

Celso placed his hand under my elbow and guided me into the house. It appeared that I would not be left outside with the mule this evening but must act the role of a person.

The room was small and warm, with wood floors, wood walls, a wood ceiling. A wood table with benches on either side occupied the middle of the room, and rugs made from strips of bright red and yellow cloth gave the room some cheer. Two pairs of dirt-covered boots and two sets of worn work gloves rested beside the door. I added my brown shoes to the line. On the left side of the room, a fire blazed on the hearth and a weathered man, knobby ankles emerging red and chapped from beneath his canvas pants, sat in a rocking chair, smoking a pipe. He waved us in but didn't get out of the chair.

"We'll be off before dawn," Celso said. He didn't remove his shoes. I saw him glance over to the table, where leftovers from their dinner still emitted delicious smells of butter and pepper that seemed to push the lagoon's odors to the fringes of the room. The woman saw Celso's look and ushered us to the table. She gave us each a fork and instructed us to eat the leftovers from the bowls.

Before I was able to understand where we were and why, I sat at the table with a fork in my hand. My muscles, so tired from marching behind the mule for three days now, didn't want to lift the fork. I could have laid my head on the table and slept right there.

"Ines and Hugo. Don't get many visitors," she said. She slid onto the bench. I could feel her face turned toward me, her watchful eyes examining my veil. She helped me lift the violin off my shoulder and slide it under the table.

"We're going to the city. Her husband waits for us there." Celso stuffed bits of stew and potato into his mouth quickly.

The woman watched me with faintly furrowed eyebrows and eyes so clouded with a white film that I didn't know how much she could see.

"Just a child," she murmured, her breath touching the side of my veil. "So young."

The food was simple, warm and filling, but as it cooled, the smell from the food dissipated and was replaced by the horrid smell surrounding this town. When Celso had eaten his fill, we sat with Hugo and Ines by the fire. I squatted on the floor and Ines knelt next to me, leaving the other chair for Celso. Hugo sat in his chair, rocked back and forth and watched the crackling flames. Ines was like the wind, always touching me, petting my knee, brushing her fingers against the back of my hand. They had lived in Gloriosa all their lives and had worked on the SWINC farm that had been the main employer in Gloriosa for twenty years.

My camp in the woods didn't have a name. Or if it did, I didn't know what it was. The reject place, maybe, or the place of disfiguration. The Hidden Camp.

"Aren't very many children in this town," Ines said, again touching me, her knee against mine.

"Can you play us a song?" Hugo asked, his rocking chair issuing a steady creak. He was worn and weathered, with creases around his eyes and mouth and on his cheeks, but he was like Nathanael—strong, with knotted muscles twisting just beneath his skin. "I haven't heard a violin for years."

My arms were too tired, my head too filled with decay, to liven this room, refresh it from the thick smell that weighed it down, but Celso glowered at me, his face dark and drawn. I pulled the violin out from under the table, unlatched the case and fit the instrument beneath my chin. I eased the bow against the strings and began to play.

I chose to play songs my mother had sung to me, but as I ran out of those tunes, I searched through my own songs, ones I had composed myself, which came to my fingers like treasures. The more I played, the more I wanted to keep playing. Music and stench throbbed for domination of the room.

Hugo smiled in his chair, his lips curved around the mouthpiece of his pipe. I could see sparks from the fire reflecting in his eyes. Ines sat next to me by the fire, her head thrown back and her eyes closed. Whenever I stopped playing a song, they asked for another.

To escape this strange room, I closed my eyes and let my hands hum their language. What would these lonely and empty people have said if I had pulled the veil off my face and showed them my distorted features? They would have been grateful and glad that they'd had no children as hideous as me. There was no place in this world for me, nowhere but with others who looked like I did. I drifted away, feeling the music.

I awoke when my bow clattered to the floor. Ines took the violin from me, laid it in the case and then took a hand-stitched pillow from the other chair and laid it on the floor.

I slept on the floor in front of the fire. Before leaving the room, Celso leaned down and whispered into my ear, "You run, and I'll hunt you down. You leave, and your friends in the camp will suffer because of it."

Then he was taken to a different room, somewhere beyond the light of the fire. Ines asked me if I wanted a bed as well, in the same room as my uncle, but how could I leave the glow of the fire to sleep in the same room as him? Ines brought me a blanket and patted my shoulder.

"Eight," she whispered to me, the glow from the fire painting hollows in her cheeks and shadowing her eyes. "Eight babies. All of them imperfect but so beautiful. I would have loved them, even just one of them, if only they'd lived. Some children live in this town, but not many."

She smiled when she said this. Her eyes shone. She saw all. She saw beyond the veil, beyond our secrecy, beyond Celso's lies. I wanted to pull away from her, but there was nowhere to go, and she'd been nothing but kind to me.

If she had been my mother, she would have kept me, and I would have grown up in a town, accepted and welcome.

Before dawn, Celso came to get me. We did not say goodbye to Ines and Hugo, but Celso placed one small silver coin in the middle of the table.

On the fourth morning, we no longer felt the cool shade of trees, stunted or tall. Our packed dirt road merged with a street coated in a hard black substance from which the heat rose through the soles of my shoes. The plants along the side of the road twisted crooked and thin beneath the sun. I felt exposed here, conspicuous, lost in the wide spaces like an ant without a hill. As the sun grew hotter, people joined us from similar dirt roads. Horses pulled carts, people hunched forward with fruits and vegetables on their backs, cars hummed and buzzed, emitting an odor of burning butter, and the white, growling trucks with the word *SWINC* on them roared past. Too much noise and smell thumped in my head, and I felt confused.

A different vehicle, a small, quiet, two-wheeled one with no smell, rolled by often. I wished I had one. I would use it to propel myself to a place with less noise, fewer people, better smells. My feet hurt, my heels were blistered, my right shoe was falling apart. Now was the time to run back to the woods—a world that felt comfortable and understandable—but under Celso's skin seethed a dark and menacing anger. I knew he would not hesitate to hurt my family.

I stared as we walked, and many of the people stared back. No one else appeared disfigured here or walked beneath the filmy cloud of a veil, but I was not the only one with troubles.

All of the travelers were dirty, all moved forward in unison, but I watched carefully from beneath the veil and saw our differences. A man walking on the other side of the road pulled a cart with wheels. A strap stretched from the front of the cart to his shoulders and chest. He leaned against the band, willing the rattling and banging cart to follow him down the road. A woman wearing a long brown skirt shuffled her feet in the dust of the road. Two children walked beside her, the girl also shuffling her feet, but the boy marched by his mother and sister with his head held high, his eyes flashing, his mouth angry.

Hills pushed from the ground on either side of the road and were dotted with rocks. Where was Jeremia's hill, the one where he'd tucked a broken boy into a hollow and then turned that hollow into a grave? The odor from Gloriosa was lower here, beneath our feet, saturating the ground. Between the hills, as we neared the city, the road grew a border of houses, but these were houses as I'd never seen them before, not even in my books. They were made from cardboard boxes or sometimes wooden slats balanced against each other. The smells from these houses rose pitifully—urine, I thought, and sickness. The children we walked past stared at my veil. I stared at the dirt covering their bodies and at the open sores on their arms.

This couldn't be the city. I found that my hand moved to the carved violin around my neck more and more often with each step that brought us closer to our destination, and I tried to still the twitching of my hands.

We did not stop when darkness shrank the lights to small stars but continued on the road, the houses changing from dilapidated cardboard boxes to houses stacked on top of each other like rocks under a waterfall. The people's voices spilled from the open windows like the din from a flock of starlings. Lines of clothing stretched from the buildings, criss-crossing each other in disorganized spider webs. Here and there in front of the buildings, a few trees jutted through squares cut into hard gray rock, but they looked so forlorn, so lonely and separated, that I wanted to hug one and stay there, our loneliness united. So many people lived here—hoards of people shuffling, pushing, calling to each other. I was just one more.

Celso no longer rode the mule but walked ahead, the rope in his hand. The mule was as tired as I was, its hooves sliding across the hard ground, its head hanging low searching for something to eat, but there was no grass. I kept a hand on its back and leaned slightly, gaining support from its warmth and swaying movements. I tried to look everywhere at once, but I couldn't take it all in. I jumped at noises behind me, at shouts from the windows, at the bump of a stranger's shoulder against mine. My nerves jangled, and I felt flustered and uncertain.

Groups of women, their faces painted vivid colors that blurred their features, stood in clusters where streets came together. Breasts bulged from shirts, naked thighs erupted from short skirts. They moved with big gestures, their strides long, their shoulders rotating. They strode into the streets and leaned into the open windows of cars, where men with square teeth smiled and passed coins from the windows to the hands of the women. My stomach lurched in this place, and my skin tingled the way it did in the moments before a thunderstorm, but no one even glanced at me. It was Celso who didn't fit—a man with a mule who didn't belong in the city.

This was why the rejects from my camp came to the city and stayed. We may not have fit perfectly, but we weren't alone and could, perhaps, get lost in the crowd.

Celso stopped. We stood in front of a building painted a flat gray, like the color of the sky before a torrential rain. The building tilted to the left, almost leaning against its neighbor, and it glowed with swirls, lines and huge swollen words painted on the front. Bars lined windows set high in the walls. No faces appeared at the windows, no singing voices could be heard. This building was cold and lifeless in comparison to the other buildings on the street.

Celso pounded on the door and continued to pound until a light went on in the windows beside the wooden door. The door opened a crack and a woman's face appeared behind the bars.

"What?" she said. I took a step back. She looked rotten, overdone. She was maybe ten years older than my mother, her hair black with a clump of gray right in the front. Her eyes had dark bags beneath them—purple and black bags—and her nose, streaked with red lines, was swollen like her body. Her breath gushed between the bars in front of the door and smelled of rotten fruits.

"I brought another worker," Celso said. Another worker. Celso had intended for me to come here from the moment he came to our camp and pushed me into this new world. He had done this before. This was how he earned his living.

The woman unlocked the barred door with a cluster of keys, then opened the door wide and stood in the opening, one hand holding the door, the other leaning on her hip. Her body, clothed in a tight nightgown, bulged oddly, like it had been squeezed tight in the middle and pushed out at the chest and hips.

"Take off the veil," she said. I slid the veil off my head.

"She'll do. She's young enough to look like a child still. We'll have her sit on the corner until she looks too old for that. Then she can work in the brothel with the others." Her eyes watched me, but she spoke to Celso. "Same as always. Fifty a week for room and board. I take it you want the rest?"

"I will return in a month to be paid." He held out a folded piece of white paper. Her left hand tightened around it, crinkling it. Celso grasped the back of my neck with his hand and squeezed. I hunched up my shoulders.

"I want a hundred from you by the middle of November. Anything less, and we send you to the brothel. Or if you're lucky, you'll work for SWINC."

I knew I didn't want to go to a brothel, a place for girls who were too old for sitting on the corners. When Celso let go of my neck, my shoulders slumped and my bottom lip trembled. Nothing felt like home here—the darkness didn't soothe and calm me like at home. I was jarred by the shrieks and the hum of cars. I would have welcomed the sound of the wolf howling.

Celso turned the mule around and walked back into the street. He didn't look at me and I didn't say goodbye. He looked strange, out of date, as he pulled the mule behind him through the painted women. The mule was silent and calm, shuffling its way beneath the music, shouts and screams of this city. I would not miss Celso, and I didn't want to run after him, but at that moment he was all I knew. I felt sweaty, hot and cold at the same time, and the lid above my left eye twitched.

"Well, come on then, girl," the woman said. "Someone will show you how things work in the morning."

I stepped into the light of the hallway and heard the barred door shut and lock behind me. Light came from a huge lamp hung in the middle of the ceiling. It glowed and glittered, casting shards of light into the hallway like sun reflecting off the spray from a waterfall. Cobwebs stretched from the lamp and shot to all corners of the room. A skittering black bug crossed a patch of oil on the ground that swirled with iridescent purples and greens. The walls were streaked with dirt and patches of rust. I followed the woman and saw a scurrying rat, its nails clicking on the cement floor, leading us down the hallway. It disappeared into a hole in the wall, a natural ending to the crack that started as a thread on the ceiling and became a fissure by the time it reached the floor. My hand moved to Jeremia's carved violin resting against my chest. I squeezed it until my palm throbbed.

Brown doors with gouges hacked out of them like ax wounds on a tree lined the hallway. They were all closed and had only one distinguishing feature—a clear number painted on them in black.

"I'm Ofelia," the woman said. "Your room will be thirteen—unlucky and always vacant. Between five PM and two AM, it's off limits. I lock the doors at night, whether you're in or not."

When she stopped, I bumped into her soft body, which dented and then popped back into shape. She turned, put her hand out and shoved me against the wall.

"Let's get something straight, girl." Her teeth were brown, broken and crooked, with big gaps between them. Deep grooves that might once have been dimples lined her sunken cheeks. "You don't touch me, ever. It's bad enough I have to live with you freaks. I won't be touched by you too. You pay for your room and board, and you'll have a place to stay. As soon as you miss a week of rent, you're on the streets. Understand?"

She unlocked the door to room 13, pushed it open and shoved me inside. She slammed the door behind me. I tried to blink away the darkness.

My eyes burned, my nose tingled, my feet ached. I wanted Nathanael, I wanted Jeremia, I wanted Eva, I wanted Ranita's heart beating against mine. I'd never whine about my mother leaving me, I'd never complain about anything ever again, if I could just go back home. I didn't need a mother, I didn't need a father—I had a family who loved me. I wiped the sleeve of my sweater under my nose.

A slice of moonlight shone onto the floor from a window set high in the wall, and once my eyes adjusted I could make out two mattresses on the floor, on opposite sides of the room. A small table with three legs and stacked bricks for the other leg stood under the window. The cracks in the walls revealed the bones of this building.

Closing my hand around the violin at my neck, I brought it out of my shirt and pressed it against my cheek.

The coolness of the wood soothed my hot face. I removed the real violin from my shoulders and laid it on the ground, and then I slipped my shoes off. The small sack from my mother sat lonely and small on the crooked table.

What else was I to do?

A patter of footsteps, like a child's tiptoeing, came down the hall and stopped. I heard a soft shuffle, and something slid through the crack beneath the door. Then the footsteps retreated and a door softly closed. I picked up the piece of paper and held it up to the white light of the moon. It was a hand-drawn picture of the building, its size exaggerated and swollen between anemic buildings on either side. On the bottom of the picture were two words.

Welcome home.

I slid the picture under a mattress and then lay down, trying to calm my heart and find a way to be quiet, relaxed. I closed my eyes against the sight of the battered room, trying to find a place that soothed, but I heard rodents nibbling at something in the corner, I heard the whoosh of cars passing on the road, and I heard my heart tapping out the pattern of my life against my chest. Was this it? Was this what my life would consist of? I closed my eyes and searched for home inside my head, and slowly the nibbling became the crackle of a warm fire, the whoosh became a soft wind through the trees, and the tapping inside me became the chirp of night crickets. If I could live in my head, I would survive this place.

But this would never be my home.

Part Two

Thirteen

I woke to a pounding on the door.

"Get up," a voice said.

My head felt heavy from lack of sleep, and my body ached from walking for four long days, but I jerked awake because my clothes writhed against my skin. I pulled down my pants and my mother's slip, yanked up my sweater and T-shirt and looked under my clothes. My stomach was speckled with little flat brown bugs that pinched. I slapped and scratched at them, and when the door opened, my pants were around my ankles, and heat rose to my face in a rush.

Ofelia stood in the doorway, her hands on her hips. She looked at me, then uttered a bark of a laugh.

"Bed bugs, girl. Ain't you ever had bed bugs before? Pull your pants up before one of the boys sees you."

I eased my T-shirt and sweater down and my pants up while willing myself not to cry, even though the tears threatened to fall any minute. I tried to breathe deeply, catching the breath that stuck in my throat, but I couldn't find a calm place. I slid the veil over my head, concealing my burning cheeks, and followed Ofelia out the door. The bugs continued to bite, and I couldn't think of a time I'd felt more uncomfortable— maybe chained to the ground in front of a doghouse.

None of the people in the hallway had split lips or exposed gums, nor did they have smooth, perfect features. They chattered, laughed and grumbled at each other. I wandered behind Ofelia, scratched my stomach and tried to hide beneath my veil.

"Show us what you got, girl," said a tiny person beside me. Her head reached to my chest, but she was not a child. Her head was disproportionately big in comparison to her body, and she had breasts and hips. She crossed her arms over her chest and waited. She was the only clean person in the hallway.

I slid the veil off and kept my eyes down, focused on the material in my hands, trying to keep them from fluttering and twitching.

"I've seen your type pass through this place. I give you one month."

"I'll give her six weeks," said a voice near my feet. I looked down and saw a boy pulling himself along on his hands. He dragged his body down the filthy hallway, dirt gathered in drifts and patches across his skin, his pant legs filled to about six inches below his torso but empty and flat where the rest of his legs should have been. "I'm an optimist," he said.

"Don't listen to them, dearie," said someone from the doorway of room 8. The person was probably a woman, but it was difficult to tell, since her skin, bubbled and scarred, was stretched tight from the top of her head all the way down her neck. She was covered in burns, like the patch on Jeremia's arm where he'd bumped into the hot soup cauldron. "I'll bet you surprise us all and only last a night." She merged with the rest of the residents in the hallway.

Where did people who never grew, people with shortened arms and miniature fingers, people so filthy with grime that it was part of their skin, come from? Maybe they were from Astatla, my parents' village—I had seen a few other children there with deformities. Maybe they were the survivors from Gloriosa. Maybe they'd grown up right here, in the cardboard houses around the city where I'd seen the children with sores on their arms.

I didn't need my veil here.

We climbed the stairs at the end of the hallway and entered an enormous common room, the floor almost as grimy as the hallway on the first floor. This room had a kitchen at one end, which consisted of a huge stove, a giant refrigerator and shelves lined with cans and boxes of foods. Lightbulbs shone naked over our heads. Two long wooden tables stretched from one end of the room to the other, and at the head of one of the tables an elderly man with no hair and wrinkled skin served breakfast. When I got closer and heard him talk, I realized that he was young in an old body. I stood in line beside the boy who had pulled himself along on the floor with his hands and picked up a bowl for me and one for him. Oatmeal was ladled into the bowls, and the old-young boy crossed his eyes, stuck out his tongue and hissed when he saw me looking at his wrinkled hands.

The boy from the hallway pulled himself up to the table and sat beside me. He was about my age—maybe a year or two older. He grinned, and big dimples appeared in his cheeks. In the last week I had met more people than I'd met in my first sixteen years of life. I knew none of them yet, but would sit with them, sleep near them, share food with them and pretend to be their friend.

"Don't take the betting personally," the boy said. "We always bet on the new people. I've never seen someone like you stay, though, and I've been here almost my entire life. I'm Oscar. Welcome to Purgatory Palace." He stuck his hand out for me to shake. His lower left lip pulled down when he talked, but the rest of his mouth stayed straight.

"So, you sign up to help with breakfast, lunch and supper once a week. My specialty is pizza. They love it when I cook. We have curfew and wake-up call, but otherwise the rest of the day is yours. We can't go back to our rooms until after two AM because the night shift works until then, but we can come here, to the common room. If you make more money than you need for Ofelia or to send home to your family, you get to keep that money. You should visit my room sometime and see all the stuff I've bought."

I understood the words he said, but nothing made sense to me—the night shift, making money for Ofelia, visiting rooms. I opened my mouth, intending to ask about the night shift, but the tiny woman who'd told me to take off my veil sat down across the table from us. She looked like a child, her arms plump and short, but her face had high cheekbones beneath black, narrow eyes. Her jaw pushed forward.

"There's one rule here," she said, "and you've got to respect that rule. You never, never work someone else's territory. You got me? You find yourself a street corner somewhere, camp out and make sure no one else has claimed that spot before you."

The oatmeal would not go down my throat, even though I'd shoved it to the back so it wouldn't spill out beneath my nose. I swallowed, choked and felt tears come to my eyes. A street corner, making money, staying clear of other people's territory. I still didn't understand what I was supposed to do.

"I'm Candela," the woman said and stuck out her hand.

"Whisper," I said while shaking her hand. Both Candela and Oscar looked at me.

"You don't talk?" asked Candela.

"I do," I said a bit louder.

"You can't just sit out there and whisper. People will ignore you."

And that's when my stomach came up into my mouth and I choked, even though I'd eaten very little. I couldn't do this. All my life I'd tried to do the opposite—be quiet, try not to be noticed, blend in with blackberry bushes and oak trees—and now they wanted me to draw attention to myself. If Candela saw my tears, she pretended not to or didn't care.

"You've got to get attention. How can you make people listen and give you money?"

I didn't know how to answer that. What was required of me? That I shout like everyone else?

"I play the violin," I said. Both Oscar and Candela lowered their shoulders and relaxed their tight mouths.

"You didn't tell us you had a talent."

Tears stung my nose, but I held them in. I swallowed a few bites of the oatmeal and then stood, following Candela, Oscar and the others. At the stairs, Oscar put his hand against the wall and lowered himself from side to side down each step. He pointed to the bathroom, the first door at the bottom of the stairs, and I followed Candela inside: four stalls, none of them with doors, all of them with toilets that flushed, and three sinks. Candela and I sat in the stalls and did what we needed to. I tried to pretend that this was all normal, that I wasn't embarrassed, that I didn't mind when people glanced at me as they walked past, that I didn't care how sticky the toilet seat was. I felt more exposed here than I ever had in the woods, where we had relieved ourselves in a crude outhouse.

At the third sink stood two girls whose shoulders were joined together; between their bodies emerged one arm.

"Hi, Maria, hi, Selene," Candela said to the attached girls while I kept my head down, watching the paths of grime on the floor rather than stare at people who were inseparable. I followed Candela, trying not to collide with anyone in the hallway, trying not to breathe too quickly or to gasp. Oscar met us in front of room 13.

"Bring your violin," he said.

I stepped into the room, slung the violin over my shoulder and took a deep breath. My hands shook against my violin case and felt slick with sweat when I lowered the strap over my shoulder. *Just go along—just do what they do, and everything will work out.* I followed the others into the street. The door to the building closed behind us, the bars clanging like the tolling of bells.

Oscar pulled himself along the street to the right. Candela crossed the street and turned a corner. All the other people from the building wandered off in pairs or by themselves. I stood on a patch of gray cement in front of my new place of residence and watched everyone disappear. My eyes hurt. My stomach itched. I pressed the knuckle of my right hand into my eye and clutched the carved violin with my other hand.

I would not cry. I would not flutter my hands and panic, even though my understanding of the world was winging away from me. Pulling my arms in tight, pushing my elbows against my ribs, I squeezed my eyes closed and tried to imagine the world when it had made sense, when the creek gurgled at night, when the coyotes howled in the hills, when I played rummy with Eva and let her pick out the good cards from the discard stack.

After a few minutes, when I could remember the smell of trees and the sound of larks, I relaxed my arms and opened my eyes. Jeremia's violin was around my neck and my mother's slip warmed my legs. For now, that would have to be enough.

I stepped to the left, then to the right, not sure how to get away from the slanted building that in the daylight looked more like a dwelling for animals than for people. Yet I still would have preferred it to these unknown streets. The city shuffled around me, more noise and bustling than I'd ever experienced before. I could hear babies crying through the open windows, men and women talking to each other and older children yelling.

I trailed behind Oscar, keeping enough distance from his dragging legs that he wouldn't see me but following closely enough that I didn't lose him. I wanted Nathanael back. I wanted something natural—the stream with the crayfish, and the trees with the mangoes. I wanted bats flicking across the moon and Jeremia's predictable unpredictability. It was cold here—there were no trees, no flowers, nothing green. Everything was too frantic and fast-paced. The buildings felt tenuous, as though they might fall down as soon as the people in them left.

After crossing three streets, Oscar stopped. We'd reached a cobblestone town square with a large fountain in the center. Benches, chairs and tables were grouped sociably here and there. I could see a row of chess tables set up beside a short wall against which Oscar seated himself. He didn't rest on a blanket; he didn't give himself any sort of comfort but instead leaned against the short stone wall that surrounded the square. He slumped precariously to the side and changed his face. The grin was gone, the dimples had disappeared, and his shoulders drooped.

Aside from us, few people were in the square. Those who did appear walked quickly across the stones, using it as a shortcut. No cars roared across the bricks. I wanted to look at the fountain, reach my hand into its cold depths, feel the texture of moving water on my skin to remind me of the pond at home, but the water sprayed in bursts, pouring from the hands of angels, and I could not allow myself to touch that beauty, to amble through the open space where people would stare or, worse yet, pretend I didn't exist. I was tempted to untie the veil from around my neck and drape it over my head, but I could tell from Oscar's example that our defects were to be used to our advantage when begging for money.

Four stunted trees in pots occupied the south side of the square. Oscar sat to the west, to my left. I crouched between the four trees, rested my back against one of the pots and watched. It was shaded here, filled with the slight rustling of leaves, and if I closed my eyes, I could pretend I was in the woods. Oscar sat, waiting for someone to notice him. I closed my eyes and tried to imagine Jeremia here—Jeremia filling his time with nothing. He would never have rested against a wall, sat passively and hoped for money. He would have angrily pushed past anyone offering him sympathy, run back to the woods and lived with the foxes. He would have carved his way through the blandness of the stone around him, creating living sculptures of water and wind from dead rock. My fingers moved to the violin around my neck, and I held it in my hand.

A girl my age lurched to the opposite side of the square. Her body curved in a strange manner—her back twisted sideways. When she walked, she used wooden crutches and rocked from side to side. She sat against the wall on the east side of the square and placed a cup on the ground in front of her.

The light grew, became day, but seemed to be filtered through a cloud of dust. People crossed the square in a steady flow now. Most were dressed in pants, skirts and dark straight coats that were not dirty or full of holes. Some of them passed by Oscar or the girl and threw coins into the containers on the ground. Oscar spoke to the people who walked by, his hands reaching out, imploring, but from where I crouched, I couldn't hear what he said.

I understood what I needed to do, and judging from what Oscar and the other girl did, it wouldn't be difficult—if you were able to speak and didn't care that what you said turned you into a carrion eater, a scavenger. I would not make fifty dollars crouched between the pots of four unhealthy trees.

My legs shook as I stood and stepped out from between the pots, joining the walking crowds. I thought the people would avoid me, glare at me, turn up their noses, but they didn't seem to care that I had joined them. I exited the square and stood on a street corner where six roads intersected. The streets angled away from the square, curved around it, bustled with cars and pedestrians or people rolling along on the two-wheeled vehicles. The warmth of the sun began to seep through my black sweater.

No one occupied a corner of one of the streets, so I eased my way between the people and sat against a closed gray door. I kept my head down, not wanting to admit to anyone or to myself that I was about to ask for money. The violin felt good in my hands—heavy, something to occupy my time and attention. The case, a black outer shell with a crimson lining, covered the gray space in front of me, a throbbing heart against the gray stones. The violin was an answer in my hands—the key to something. I fit it beneath my chin and eased the bow over the strings.

The first few attempts to play a song came out scratchy and shaky as my fingers warmed up, but soon the tune smoothed, and I heard the sound of larks singing at dusk. I was able to make my way back to the trees. I played the song of Whisper and closed my eyes to the chaos and confusion around me.

∞

The sun shone high and bright, having consumed half the day when I finally lowered the violin and straightened my shoulders. My neck cracked when I tilted it back, and as I opened my eyes, the canopy of trees from my home in the woods, the song of the crickets and the aroma of the hibiscus faded like a rainbow.

Coins of various shapes, silver and copper, lay on the crimson cloth. I lifted one of these coins between my fingers. It was a thin metal disk with the head of a man on the front and a sheaf of grain on the back. I didn't know what to do with it, what it meant. Was this enough money to pay the rent? Did I have more than the rent—something for Celso? I should have spent more time with Nathanael's money, understanding its value.

I collected the coins and slid them into one of the pockets of my sweater, where they weighed down the material and felt satisfying. I slid my violin into its case, nestling it against the red cloth, and stood. When I raised my head, I looked into the eyes of a man.

He was young and had a thin smile broken by sharp eyeteeth. His face was rough, with hair that grew in uneven bursts. I thought of a skunk with its pointed face and secret weapon.

"Hey, ugly," he said. "We've been watching you." He jerked his head. I looked across the street and saw two more men standing on the corner. Their waxy skin matched the washed-out gray of the stones that made up the buildings and streets—they looked like they'd stepped from the very walls themselves.

Black cars skittered like roaring bugs in the street, but I could see the hunched shoulders and thick necks of the men from where I stood.

"And because you're new to the city and don't know the rules around here, we'll take it easy on you this time."

I covered my sweater pocket with my hand.

"You want to use our street corner, you have to pay for it. If you decide not to pay, we take all of your money and a little something else."

He looked at my body. His eyeteeth settled on his bottom lip, and the whites of his eyes looked bloodied and bruised. The palm of my hand became clammy against the coins. The people who walked by avoided my eyes—they were all busy.

I didn't know how much money weighed down my pocket, but the coins were mine—he would get none of them. I shook my head.

He raised his eyebrows and then whistled a quick, high note. The two men moved away from the gray walls and stepped into the street, walking across without pausing. One was tall, with hunched shoulders and hair that floated in stringy wisps and curls about his head. The other was shorter, with thick arms that he held away from his body. They didn't look to their right or left to avoid the cars but marched across, their strides long and confident, the cars swerving around them and honking like geese.

My back turned hot and cold at the same time. I thought about Belen's hand slapping me across the face and his boot kicking me in the side. I thought of Celso tying me to a tree with a mule.

Just before the men reached us, a man with a long, heavy coat brushed against me. He said, "Excuse me," stepped into the street to get around the eyetooth man and then stepped back onto the walkway. I reached for his wrist and whispered, "Please."

He looked at me, flinched when he saw my face and then glanced at the three men around me. He backed away, yanking his arm from my grasp, and then he ran.

"People know us," said the first man. His smile evaporated, his face more narrow and skunk-like than before. "No one will help you. Now we need all the money, and if you give it to us without argument, we won't make you pay in other ways." The two men stepped closer, their smell caustic and biting, like marsh cabbage.

"I need this," I whispered.

"I don't give a shit," he whispered back and then laughed. The two men behind him laughed with him.

"Let's give this a try," said the man with the thick arms. He stepped around the leader. I held my hand over my pocket and tried to back away, but before I could step beyond his reach, a fist landed in my stomach, knocking the air out of me, and I curled up, gasping.

The first man reached into my pocket and pulled out the coins. I looked at his shoes—black, pointed, the material patterned in diamonds, like snakeskin. Tears leaked from the corners of my eyes and darkened the gray cement in splotches.

"I'll let you keep one as a reminder of what you'll lose if you refuse to pay us." And then they were gone, back across the street, stopping the flow of cars.

I sat down on the cement and tried to catch my breath. Each of my lives seemed to grow shorter and sink lower. How low could a life go? Lower than the earth, lower than the worms, lower than death. When I was able to stand erect and breathe, I didn't feel like crying anymore. I was done crying. Now I would merely exist.

We couldn't return to our rooms until 2:00 AM. I didn't know why I couldn't return until then, I didn't know how to figure out if it was 2:00 AM, and I didn't dare go to the common room in case I was the only one there, so I wandered.

People in the city were always talking to someone, yelling across the street, speaking into cell phones. People in the cars called out of the windows and honked horns, their anger palpable even where I walked. The buildings were all crooked, ragged and cracked, with laundry strung across them and between them. I kept my head down and felt more lonely here than I had when chained to the doghouse. *Sometimes it is worse to be noticed.* Nathanael might have been right in some circumstances, but here I felt like vapor, like smoke, like a shadow that might as well not exist. People brushed against me, bumped into my shoulder, stepped on the heel of my shoe, but no one looked at me or said sorry. The only proof of my existence was the muffled sound of my shoes scuffing against the hard ground.

Everywhere I turned, someone with crooked limbs, distorted features or missing body parts sat with a hat, jar or can in front of them. So many of us. What was wrong with this world that so many human beings were distorted in some way? I stood in the middle of a bridge that rose above the river like a rainbow arch, and on that bridge I saw three beggars, all seated on the cold ground, calling out for money. I returned the way I'd come.

I walked until fewer and fewer people passed me, until the buildings shrank in size, more and more houses appeared and every now and then I passed a square of grass, vibrant and alive. The buildings felt substantial here, rectangular, individual, upright houses painted solid colors. They weren't built on top of each other precariously but stood alone, well cared for.

I stopped at a patch of green that stretched like a surprise meadow in front of me. The open space bustled with shrieking children, benches lined the walkways, and a pond with lily pads rippled with the slight wind. It was as though all the green growth in the city had fled to this one spot, an oasis in the desert of manmade structures. A sign in the middle of the grass said *Hernando Park*.

I walked to the pond as quietly as I could, glancing beside me now and then to see if anyone followed or rushed at me, shouting that I had to leave. It was the first time since coming here that I had smelled green leaves, earth and flowers—it was the first time I could picture my camp in the woods without having to close my eyes and squeeze out a memory. This was where I would collect myself and get rid of the panicked feeling I'd had since arriving in the city.

An elderly woman holding a cane occupied one of the benches next to the pond. Her eyes were closed and her head was leaned back, the hazy sun warming her face.

I sat two benches away. My feet ached from all the walking, and my back groaned with relief when I sat. While orange and white fish flashed through the water in the pond, I pressed my hand where the man had forced the air out of me.

As I closed my eyes, ready to dream myself back home, I heard music—real music, played with fingers and strings, not music squeezed through a radio speaker and interwoven with static. I stood, looked around and hobbled on sore feet to a small grove of trees. Willow trees, the branches long and feathery, guarded the sides of the creek like hunched osprey, the branches dangling over a stream that trickled through the park. Underneath the branches I saw four musicians, three of them seated on folding chairs. One played a violin, one played a larger violin, one played a much larger instrument that he leaned against the ground and held between his legs, and the last played a violin so huge she had to stand up to play it.

The music pulled me back to my camp, to running through the grasses, to a warm fire and laughter. I untied my veil from around my neck and adjusted it over my head. I crept to the other side of the tree and sat on the roots, my back rubbing against the rough bark. I breathed in the beauty of the music—the lightness of the high notes, the sureness of the middle notes, the groans of the lowest notes. There was a wholeness to the music that I never heard when I played by myself.

I dreamed of dark nights by the fire, coyotes creeping just outside our camp circle of warmth, wolves howling up on the hills. Even the smell of this green area seemed right—woods, water, earth. If I had music to warm me, it would be enough.

When the music stopped, I opened my eyes. The musicians shuffled their instruments into cases. They talked and laughed. I didn't belong—not here, in this place where rejects sat on corners and begged for money. I felt self-conscious and unworthy. Someone would come along and command me to leave any minute now. When I'd listened to the music, I had felt like a part of something—a beauty that included even me—but now I was again nothing, and if I disappeared, only Celso would care, because he wouldn't get his money.

As I walked away from the park and back to my new residence, I saw three others like me, one walking with crutches, one limping and one looking down at her feet. All of their shoulders were hunched, trying to conceal the disfiguration that tainted them. I followed them back to the neighborhood where the building with the barred windows leaned toward the dilapidated building next to it. It wasn't dark yet. I wasn't supposed to return to my room, but I didn't know where else to go, and my hands felt stiff and useless as I tucked them under my armpits.

But the doors were open, and I walked inside. I felt a bit of warmth and shook off the cold that had followed me down the street. I walked to room 13, opened the door, closed it softly behind me and then shut my eyes. In the middle of the room I lifted up my arms, raised them so they stretched straight from my body on either side, and tilted my head back. In my head I heard the instruments with their individual melody lines, and I let them ring.

Fourteen

As I stood in my room, my body open to the music, I began to see fireflies against the lids of my eyes. My head resonated with the music from the park, the notes winging through the air. I emptied myself of the last few days, and I began to see the music. The notes were as tangible to me as my own hand. They flitted through the air like hummingbirds and I watched the patterns they made. I saw birds flying in formation, the notes fitting together.

But the pattern began to dissolve when the door to room 13 slammed shut. Candela looked up at me as I stood in the middle of the room with my arms spread wide. She reminded me of Eva, with her watchful eyes, but Eva was quick to laugh, quick to be silly, and I didn't think Candela had been silly for a very long time.

"How much did you make?"

The music in my head dissipated, and all that beauty rushed out of me. I was left with the reality of my life— sitting on a street corner, losing the money I'd earned and living in a house full of rejects. I reached into my pocket and felt the cold metal edge of the one coin.

"Why'd you have your eyes closed when I came in?"

I looked around the room, trying to find a way to describe the music I had seen in my head. I didn't know how to explain that music made me feel real and whole. But maybe I could show her.

"May I play my violin beside you tomorrow?"

"I don't work with other rejects."

"Just one day?" I asked. "One day."

"I thought you were different from Rosa, but you're not, are you?"

I blinked and felt a jolt. Rosa. The idea of Rosa made me feel small again, exposed. I had always been the dumb unrelated sister, the one who wet her bed and cried out for her mother. Rosa had wanted to be beautiful more than any of us. She'd hated her face, hated herself, and I remembered how when we'd looked into the creek together, watching our broken faces appear on the surface of the water, she'd held a handkerchief over the right side of her face, hiding the deep-red discoloration. She'd winked at the image of herself and said, "Buried beauty, but beauty all the same."

"You know Rosa?" I said now.

Candela looked at me with her lips drawn into a tight line. Her hands were still on her hips and she looked like a cat, wary and aloof, ready to flee or pounce.

"Why should I be nice to you? You'll end up selling sex just like she does. My friends never stay."

The words floated in the air between us, hovered and then dropped. When I understood what she'd said, my chest began to squeeze tight. Rosa sold sex. Rosa had been the one who'd told me about sex, about male body parts, about how babies were made. When she had gotten her period, she had declared herself a woman. She said now she could find a husband, someone who didn't care about her raised birthmark, who would see her buried beauty. She would create her own family, one that would never reject her.

So many times I'd woken up in our hut with her hand pushing against my lips, blocking my breath. "You were crying again. Stop it," she would say. But she'd changed my diapers when I was little, and she'd taught me my first word—*wind*. She'd combed and braided my hair when her mood had been right. I looked down at the mattress, envisioning Rosa there, Rosa's limbs entwined with someone else's—someone like Celso, with his unused muscles and sweaty hands.

"One day," Candela said. "That's it, you understand? One day, and then you find your own spot."

I looked at the map of water stains on the walls, at the flaking ceiling, at the exposed boards in the north corner of the room, where I'd heard a rat the night before. How could Rosa stay in this room? No one stayed in this room. Maybe my destiny would match Rosa's. I now knew what a brothel was. I should have known all along.

∞

While the sun still shone, Candela helped me drag the mattresses from room 13 out the front door of the building. She hit them with a flat paddle while I held them up and watched bugs jump into the cracks of the sidewalk. Candela told me this wasn't enough—we'd have to spray the mattresses with poison or the eggs already in the material would hatch, grow and bite.

After sending the bedbugs to a new home, we put the mattresses back along the walls and left the room. Candela showed me a clock on the wall in the common room, one like Nathanael had used back at the camp. When it read 5:00 PM, it was time for us to leave our rooms to the use of others. The front door of the building opened and closed, opened and closed, allowing women with short skirts, tall boots and revealing blouses to enter the building and take their places in the rooms. I walked with my head down and avoided eye contact with any of these ladies, just in case one of them was Rosa. I couldn't face her—not yet.

Candela and I ate dinner, a warm stew thick with vegetables and meat. I was so hungry, I ate two full bowls. The cook, Winston, a boy about ten years old, had two faces, which startled me. He appeared blurred, repeated, like déjà vu. Both faces smiled at me when I complimented him on his delicious stew. I wasn't sure which face to focus on—both sets of eyes looked down when I whispered to him—but I watched him slip extra chunks of meat and large wedges of potato into my bowl. When he handed the bowl back to me and smiled, I felt a little piece of beauty returning to my life.

Two smiles on the same boy—there was nothing ugly about that.

The common room hummed with people. Some slept on the benches, some played games in the corners, some drew pictures or stared at the ceiling. Oscar played cards with the burned woman, a boy with only one arm and another boy whose hooded eyes were too low on his face, his forehead long and empty. There were coins in the middle of the table, and the players shouted, laughed and even yelled occasionally. I sat in the corner, my violin at my feet, and watched. This house wasn't so different from my camp in the woods. Here, too, the people didn't fit with the outside world. Here, too, we became our own family due to necessity rather than choice, but I didn't feel included and didn't know that I ever would.

Too tired to think or attempt socializing, I leaned my head against the wall and after a while drifted into a hazy dream of boys with two faces and girls sharing an arm.

The next day, Candela allowed me to follow her out of the house.

"It's called The Half-Way House, or Purgatory Palace." She waved her arm backward, indicating the building we had exited. "We'll take the sidewalk this way."

I'd followed Oscar to the north yesterday, to the city center, but today Candela walked west. She towed a maroon suitcase on wheels behind her, and when she arrived at a huge hill that slanted away from the morning sun, I helped her pull it up.

"Don't think you're ingratiating yourself with me by pulling my suitcase up the hill. We work one day together and that's it. Got it?"

"I understand," I said, but I didn't. In this city, working together seemed safe.

Before we reached the top of the hill, the buildings began to change. The new structures were covered in a white hard paint that was rough and bumpy. The houses here didn't have words scrawled on them or pictures painted on their fronts. They were pristine, like the houses I'd seen around Hernando Park the day before. Grass appeared in patches, the faded green of winter a welcome relief from the otherwise washed-out colors of the city, and big palm fronds added shade to the house fronts. We passed larger buildings filled with windows, layers and layers of windows that lay flat and opaque beneath statues of leering creatures with horns and fangs. These buildings did not slant to the side or look as though a strong wind could blow them away. They planted their walls firmly into the ground and held the upper levels confidently.

Candela paused, catching her breath for a minute, and then turned to the right. I looked into the windows of shops we passed and saw lamps, furniture carved from marbled wood, toys painted red and purple—there was even a store filled only with angels. Candela tugged at my sleeve when I lingered in front of the stores too long. At a shop where the warming smell of coffee and bread overcame any other street smells, we paused. From her suitcase she pulled a folded stool and an easel, which she set up in the middle of the sidewalk. She placed a pad of paper on the easel and put a flat box filled with thin black rectangles on her knees. She hung a sign from the easel that read *CARICATURES*. $5.00 *each*. Over her left ear she angled a slanted red hat.

"I have an arrangement. I recommend their coffee and pastries, and they let me draw caricatures in front of their store." She leaned in close and whispered to me, "I've done all of their caricatures for free. Look through the window."

When I peered through the window, I didn't see anything beyond the glare of the sun, so I shielded my face with my hands and pressed my nose against the cold glass. There were no customers inside the shop yet, only empty tables, a counter area and maybe fifty pictures lining the walls. The people in the drawings had disproportionately large heads with tiny bodies. One, I realized, was Oscar, his dimples prominent, his mouth wide and warm, his missing legs irrelevant beneath the square jaw and warm grin.

When I looked back at Candela, she picked up one of the black rectangles and drew on the pad of paper with it. Her hands were fast, sure, and beneath the different shades of gray and black, I began to emerge. She made my eyes dark with thick black eyelashes. The eyebrows became prominent, the nose straight, the openings between my nose and mouth mere slits, barely perceivable smudges. The widened nostrils were smooth, softened. I was beautiful.

She gave the picture to me when she was done. I reached into my pocket and tried to give her the coin. She pushed my hand away.

"Play your violin," she said. "Even if you don't make money, you're not getting any of mine." I squatted next to Candela, placing the violin case in front of me and fitting the instrument beneath my chin. I eased the bow over the strings and thought of the music I'd heard in the park the day before. The notes lined up in my mind like the birds flying in formation. I felt the music in my chest, in my head, down my arms and out my fingers. Tucking my chin in close to the instrument, I played the song I'd heard from the four musicians. Then I played it again.

When I finished, I looked at Candela. My head felt a bit woozy. It felt good to play the song, but it didn't have the wholeness, the filled-in melodies, of the music in the park. I felt dissatisfaction now, as though I were trying to make do with a fountain when all my life I'd had waterfalls to splash in, but Candela's eyes were wide, her eyebrows furrowed.

"Where did you learn that song?"

"Hernando Park."

"You heard it in the park? Yesterday? And now you're playing it."

I looked down at the sidewalk and felt uncertain—maybe it wasn't okay. I'd stolen the song and then made it worse.

"Play again," she said, "and make everyone want to hold their arms out and lift their faces to the sun."

I looked up at her. There was an intensity to the way she looked at me that I'd misjudged. Candela wasn't angry or frustrated, she was surprised. Maybe this was how she talked to people—not through smiles or winks but through intensity. It was okay—I hadn't done anything wrong. I closed my eyes, and all around me was the music. I forgot the rest—the bugs in the bed, a lost sister named Rosa, the shocked stares of people around me, the men who'd stolen my money. When I played the violin, I was transported to a different world, a world of sweet smells, tolerance and blue dragonflies in golden fields.

A tap on my shoulder pulled me out of the music. Candela stood in front of me with a mug of hot cocoa in her hands. The steam rose up around her face and made her look unearthly, like a dark-haired angel.

"Time for a break," she said and squatted down on the sidewalk next to me. Coins littered the red lining of my violin case. "Yeah, honey, you're working with me every day. Usually I do three or four caricatures on a good day. Today I've done twice that, and it's not even the afternoon yet. You're good for business."

A girl with a very red nose and watery eyes stood in front of us with two plates. She sniffed and avoided looking at my face.

"That was so beautiful," the girl said. "Here, these are from him."

She nodded toward a table behind me where a customer sat. I looked over, not daring to look up, and saw brown shoes beneath brown slacks. Candela stood and said thank you, but a hand waved at her from above the table, and a voice said, "I would pay far more to hear music like that." The server set the plates on the ground. On them were sandwiches—sandwiches with meat, cheese, lettuce and tomatoes, everything good, crunchy and fresh. Candela took one of the sandwiches and talked to me around a mouthful.

"I don't know, girl. I haven't heard anyone play the violin like that. The guy's right—people would pay good money for this kind of music. How'd you learn to play that thing?"

I thought about the music flying around, waiting to be caught. How do you explain to someone that the music was a part of me, something I'd always known? All I'd needed was the instrument and Nathanael's help with the fingering.

It was like Ranita. No one had taught me to love her—I'd just done it. I felt warmth as I sat there on the cement in front of this café, warmth that refreshed my spirit and helped me feel like maybe there was a place for me in this dilapidated world, even if that place happened to be where others put their feet.

On the way home, Candela and I stepped into a small store with bars across the door and windows. A greasy man was behind the counter, his black hair swiped in sticky strands from the right side of his head over the top to the left. His nose had a large red wart on the bridge. Candela walked to the counter with a can of bedbug repellent and pushed some coins at the man. His gnarled hands took our money, pushed the can at us.

"You filthy people, covered in lice, infested with germs, itching with fleas, scabies, ticks, crawling with worms..."

"Yeah, yeah," Candela said, turning her back on the man. "Ever looked at your own nose?"

I was ready to run, ready to protect my body, ready for a boot to kick me or a fist to land in my stomach, but nothing happened and the man didn't follow us out of his shop. I didn't understand this city. When I didn't expect anger and cruelty, it rose like thorns from the ground, and when I expected it, nothing happened.

We dragged the mattresses from room 13 outside once again and sprayed them with bug repellent. Candela said they needed to air out for a while, and in the meantime we went to the only space available to us, the common room. Already many of the other residents were sitting at the tables, playing games, talking, dozing. I hoped no one would need to use my room tonight. The mattresses were miserable to sleep on, but the floors would be close to unbearable.

Fifteen

I worked with Candela every day after that. I played the violin until my fingers ached and my neck felt like it might never straighten again, but I could feel my songs taking shape, coming alive. I started new songs. I didn't know if the people around me cared that I played only a few songs they might recognize, the rest coming from places inside me where the woods still grew and the breeze rustled the branches. I liked composing my own songs—they felt like something to hold on to in this chaotic place where noises were so piercing and sharp that they buried the undertones of nature.

I began to notice patterns—the same people came to the café where Candela and I sat, and even though I didn't dare look these customers in the eye, I recognized them from their shoes. A pair of brown shoes tapped to the beat of my music, and every day those loafers resided under an outside table, the one closest to me, and they stayed there for a long time, even though the mornings were cold and few others chose to sit outside.

I continued to collect coins and Candela taught me how to count them. The big one with the head of the man and the sheaf of grain on the back was worth five dollars. The smaller, silver one with the pig on the front and the numeral one on the back was worth one dollar. Those were the ones you wanted, the ones that added up to something substantial. The smaller ones were good too but took many more to equal the others. After a week I had enough to pay for two weeks of rent with a bit left over for Celso. Candela said I needed to talk to Ofelia about my documentation. I knew what she meant—the crumpled piece of paper that had been passed from Celso's hands to Ofelia's. It wasn't mine. I didn't really want it. We stood outside Ofelia's door—she lived in room 1—and I tried to stand up straight and look her in the eye, but I'd become used to staring at feet.

"She needs her birth certificate," Candela said to Ofelia slowly, carefully.

"What she need that for?" Ofelia said. Some liquid sloshed out of the glass in her hand and landed at our feet.

"For a bank account," Candela said.

I looked past Ofelia, through the doorway. I'd never seen a room like this. Tapestries covered the walls the way the canopy of leaves had covered parts of my forest home. Beautiful quilts, stitched beadwork, handmade artwork turned her oblong room into a haven, a place where anyone could have been comfortable. Blue rugs covered the floor like a field of cornflowers. Even the cover on her bed was handmade, patched together in squares of dark purple and green. Living in a room like this would keep life gorgeous all the time. Ofelia jabbed her fingers into my chest.

"Whatcha staring at?" she said. "I want my rent."

I opened my hand and offered her fifty dollars in coins. She snatched the money, her fingers jamming into my palm.

"Been making some good money, huh?" she said. "Maybe your ugly face won't have to work the night shift after all, though I wouldn't count on it."

I told myself not to take a step back, not to worry about the splash of liquid on top of my shoe, not to flinch when her breath made my eyes water.

"The birth certificate," Candela said.

Ofelia retreated into her room, shuffled through some papers and returned with a single sheet of crumpled paper.

"Lydia Gane, daughter of Belen and Teresa Gane." Ofelia looked up, her red eyes unfocused. "It should say *rejected daughter of Belen and Teresa Gane.* Here's your reminder of the parents who abandoned you." She flipped the paper at me. I tried to catch it, but it fluttered out of reach and drifted to the floor. I bent down and picked it up carefully, between my thumb and first finger. Ofelia stepped back into her room and slammed the door.

This piece of paper was proof of my existence and meant more to the bank where I hoped to deposit my money than did my physical presence. Ofelia was right—all this paper proved was that I had a name. It said nothing of my life, who cared about me or what I might become in the future. This paper claimed that I had parents, but only I knew it to be a lie.

∞

I liked Candela and her gruff ways. She wasn't hurtful, like Rosa, but told me things straight, honest, with no hidden messages and meanings. I felt comfortable with this, but she didn't tell me everything—at least, not right away. There were times when she hinted at something, when she started to talk about who she was, why she was here, and then she'd stop. It took weeks of working together daily, making money and hanging out in the common room before I heard her story, and then I wondered why I'd wanted to know.

It was late afternoon, and we had about an hour before we needed to make way for the night shift. We sat in Candela's room, which was more comfortable than mine even though the room was the same, a small rectangle with one high window. It contained the same kind of mattress—a flat foam cushion that rested on the floor—and it had the same door placement—right in the middle of the wall. Her drawings adorned the walls. I loved looking at them. I saw Oscar in many of the pictures, and I found myself in two. Ofelia was in a lot of them, but the pictures made her look less drunk, more humane. The pictures flattered all the subjects.

Oscar was with us for a while in Candela's room and we played rummy, a game I had played with Jeremia and Nathanael. Homesickness burned my nose.

"Oscar, are you cheating?" Candela asked as he laid down a set of three aces.

"I don't cheat," he said.

"Right."

I smiled. Jeremia used to stack the deck—put the aces every third card and deal himself an unbeatable hand—but we had all known he was doing it. He would bite the knuckle of his first finger and stop talking. His right knee would bob up and down, up and down, controlled by invisible strings.

Oscar was quiet now. I heard him flipping the cards in his hand. I could almost touch the lines of tension that stretched between the two of them.

"Why do you hate me?" Oscar said to Candela in a whisper.

The anger was gone. This was the real Oscar, without the bravado and the dimples, without the dejection and begging. I wanted to look at him, but I didn't.

"You know why," she whispered.

"We can't be together, Candela," he said. "You know that. Two freaks is one too many. Both of us need someone normal."

"What the hell is normal? If half the people in this city are normal, then I'm glad to be a freak. They're more deformed than we will ever be. At least our problems are right out where people can see them instead of hidden away."

I held my breath. She was talking about Belen, Celso, Ofelia, Jeremia's father. Everyone had deformities, not just those of us who wore them openly. Oscar shuffled the cards in his hands.

"You broke my heart, Oscar, breaking up with me." I could hear a squeak in Candela's voice, a waver that was close to tears. "That's why I hurt you back."

Candela and Oscar sat on opposite ends of the mattress. I sat on the floor, the third point in the triangle. When I looked up, they didn't notice. I eased my breath out slowly.

I saw something I hadn't noticed before as I observed the two of them. Candela was sure of herself, solid and talented. Oscar was unsure, angry, resentful and yet full of charisma. If they were together, Candela would keep Oscar grounded, keep him in the realm of the good, while he could show the world her talent, using his charm. I'd never seen people complement each other like that. Had my mother and father looked like this when they were together? I'd always wondered what my mother had seen in my father, why she'd stood by him when he'd abandoned me and why she chose him over me. There must be something redeemable in Belen if my mother had loved him.

Oscar, too, could be biting and cruel, but when he loved and cared about someone, he did so with such defiance and bravery you couldn't help but like him. And yet, I didn't trust him. Probably never would. His dimples and grins hid an insecurity that could easily become backstabbing.

"You know why we can't be together. I will not be exploited all my life, living in this place, begging. I will be someone."

"You are someone, Oscar. You don't need someone without blemishes to make you whole."

"Yeah, well, you're not going to make me whole either. Two halves do not make a whole when it comes to people." Oscar slid off the bed and out the door.

"Yes, they do," Candela screamed after him. "Two halves always make a whole. Even with people."

I felt like my hair was standing on end. I got up.

"Oh no you don't," she said to me.

I sat back down on the floor and collected the cards. I shuffled them and waited, the tendons in my hands straining as I held the cards too tightly.

Candela took shuddering breaths and then unballed her fists. She squeezed the pillow to her chest and rested her chin on it. Her nose was red, glistening, and her hands shook. She wiped her eyes with the pillowcase, wiped under her nose.

"I've known love. Oscar hasn't. I should try to understand his side, but sometimes it's so hard. Why does he want to be with someone normal so badly? He'll never grow legs." She pushed the pillow against her eyes. She spoke to me through the pillow, her words distant and muffled.

"You know how you grew up? In the woods with friends and people who cared? That's how I grew up. I had a family who loved me. They thought I was so cute, so tiny and adorable. My older sister carried me with her wherever she went and treated me like a doll." Candela pulled her face away from the pillow and rested her chin on top of it. She wiped under her nose with the sleeve of her shirt. "Oscar was left here when he was three days old. The owners of the place, the people before Ofelia, gave him a name and wrote up some papers. He doesn't even know what his parents originally named him."

I'd been abandoned at that age. Why hadn't Belen brought me here, to start a life of begging before I could even walk?

"But I do know what it's like to have family turn on you," Candela continued.

When I glanced up, she was looking at me. I nodded.

"When I turned twelve, I started to grow breasts, like most girls do at that age, but my sister didn't think I was quite so cute when I no longer looked like a miniature child. That's when she became nervous around me and started listening to what other people said about me—I was malformed, a dwarf, and because there was no other dwarfism in my family, I must have done something terrible to deserve this punishment.

"One night, her boyfriend came to our house. He and my sister were going to the dance in town and she was upstairs getting ready. I thought he was so gorgeous, with his black eyes and black hair. I offered him refreshments while he waited for her and we sat together on the couch, drinking lemonade. I think he was fascinated by me. I didn't look like the other girls, and this was disturbing and intriguing to lots of boys. He stared at my body and then he reached out to touch my breasts."

Candela's hands clutched the pillow in her arms. They wrung and twisted the white corners into knots, wrinkled knobs with pointed tips, like albino teardrops.

"I'd never been touched like that before. I'd always been treated like a child, like a doll, but he noticed that I was actually growing up."

She looked at me then, the anger gone.

"I kissed him, Whisper," she said. "I leaned right in and kissed him on the mouth. He pulled me against him, and I could feel his warmth through my clothes. My sister came down the stairs and saw us. She never forgave me. She told everyone at school that I was a slut, that I stole boyfriends, that I couldn't get enough sex and would do it with anyone."

Candela smoothed her thick bangs out of her eyes. She threw the pillow behind her and crossed her legs.

"That's when the guys at school started following me around, calling me names, treating me like a freak. My sister never defended me. She wanted me gone. So I left. And here I am. Eighteen and in love with Oscar. I'm such a moron."

"No," I said.

Her hands reached for mine and squeezed hard until my knuckles cracked beneath the pressure.

"You're not like Rosa," she said to me. "You're not like anyone I know. You are the only person I've ever met who makes me feel good about myself, and I don't even know how you do it."

We sat together in silence for a while, but it felt okay. I could hear the building groan around us. I could hear the mice. I could hear the other Purgatory Palace residents stirring and gathering and heading to the common room. I could hear the honking of car horns and the yelling of people on the street.

"I want to see Rosa," I whispered to Candela.

She let go of my hand, sat up straight and looked past me. "Okay."

A week later, after giving Ofelia the hundred dollars I owed Celso so she could pay him when he arrived, I exited the building with my violin strapped to my back. I turned the corner and stepped into a doorway, the wooden door behind me solid and sure, with bars stretching across the front to ward off possible thieves. After I'd stood still long enough to feel the chill seeping through my torn sweater and into my bones, and when the blurring effects of night had settled around me, I saw two women arrive together. They were laughing, their eyes lined with black, their lips abnormally red, their eyebrows narrowed into thin arches and their coats alive with the fur of dead animals.

Neither of these women was Rosa. I didn't want to meet Rosa inside Purgatory Palace, in one of the rooms where a man might knock on the door and money would change hands. I wanted to meet her here, in the street, in an untainted place, in front of a door that seemed impenetrable.

A bit later, Rosa arrived by herself. I waited in the shadows until I knew for sure that it was her. Her cheeks were no longer puffy and full, her hair had been cropped into short spikes, and her eyes—lined with black—didn't look anywhere but down. It was the raised red birthmark that ran from her forehead down her right cheek to the edge of her jaw that convinced me. She didn't see me even when I stepped out from the doorway. She had almost passed me when I spoke.

"Hello, Rosa," I said.

Her head jerked up, and she looked at me in such a way that I wanted to step back into the shadows and hide. It wasn't hate in her eyes, but something very close to it. And then the look disappeared and Rosa's regular surliness asserted itself, twisting the edges of her eyes down and the corners of her mouth up.

"Well, look who's here." She put one hand on her hip, but the other hand stayed where it was, against her stomach, which bulged beneath her coat. "You're a little young to be here already, aren't you? What are you now, sixteen?"

I shifted from foot to foot and held my hand against my chest where Jeremia's miniature violin rested.

"How'd you end up here? And don't tell me you still aren't talking. If you're going to live in the city with all the other hard-luck cases, you had better make some noise."

I opened my mouth, but nothing came out. She looked at me like she used to—like I was pathetic and small, unwise and unhardened. She used to make me feel so useless, and now I felt that same sensation again. I was that little girl afraid of the dark, sniffling in the night, afraid to make any sound.

And then I heard a squeak, a kitten peep that tittered from Rosa's coat. I looked at the front of her white puffy coat and saw something squirm. Rosa removed her hand from her hip and placed it under the bulge. She jostled the bump up and down, up and down, but when the peeps continued, she unzipped the top of her coat and a tiny head emerged. The eyes met mine and the peeps stopped.

The baby was beautiful. Her lips weren't deformed, her mouth and nose weren't divided by a slit, a birthmark didn't cover half her face in an angry welt. She looked at me with bright eyes that seemed to understand everything at once.

"She's beautiful." My hand reached toward her, to a perfect little Ranita. If she had flaws, they were hidden from view.

Rosa's mouth relaxed, and her hands reached up to adjust the knitted cap on the baby's head. "She is beautiful," she said.

A tiny hand emerged from the coat and stretched out to me, the hand healthy with rolls and dimples. The chubby fingers grasped my thumb and held on with a grip that felt real, as if something substantial and good did exist in this world. Then Rosa took a step back and the tiny hand was pulled away.

"What are you doing here? You're not meant to ever leave that camp. They'll eat you alive here—you'll never survive. Go back to the camp, go live in the woods, hide with the others. Stay good, stay pure." Her voice was so low and biting, it chafed like the brittle snow that cuts in the winter.

"Who is the father?" I asked.

She turned away from me, her feet already pointed in the opposite direction, her black-lined eyes watching the trodden sidewalk.

"Just wait. You'll do the same thing I did. They'll start following you, telling you how beautiful your body is, how sexy you look, and you'll believe them even when you know it isn't true. Then you'll go with them and feel loved like other people are loved. And once you feel that love, there's no turning back. It'll happen to you too."

She walked away, taking the perfect child with her. My right hand was raised. It was level with my shoulder, stretched to Rosa. I lowered my hand and watched her turn the corner where she would enter Purgatory Palace and continue to squelch the defiance that had once kept her eyes level with anyone's.

The nights were thick now, colder and heavy. The painted women began to pace on the sidewalks, their pointed heels like woodpecker beats against the hard ground. I couldn't follow Rosa into the building—I didn't want to see her standing in the doorway of a room, waiting for her customers, earning a living while her baby squeaked and gurgled in the corner.

Instead I trudged west, through the square where Oscar begged, over a bridge where the stream from our village swelled into a black river that smelled of chemicals and latrines, to the blocks of big stores that sold everything from clothes to pots to fishing poles. I had never been here before. These stores occupied entire blocks and stretched above me three or four stories, their shadows silent, solid and sharp, unlike the shadows of trees, which rustle, shift and sway. The windows shone yellow and warm, an *Open* sign flashing in one. My hands were numb with the cold. After watching people push their way into the store or emerge with bags dangling from their hands, I held my shoulders straight and walked into the first store, standing just inside the entryway, watching the people who swarmed like flies around counters and racks of clothing. I adjusted the veil over my head.

I didn't belong here. The city welcomed rejects only on gray street corners. This shiny store belonged to those with money to spend and bellies already full. I stepped back, away from the warmth and unfriendly stares, but stopped when I saw the coat. It was dark green like the forest, thick like the canopy of my home and soft like the feathery arms of the willow. Big wooden clasps the color of cedar held the front of the coat closed, and it had a wide hood that would protect my ears from the winter winds. I touched the dark green material with my fingertips. It would warm me while I stayed on the streets during the day and would remind me of my forest home.

The tag dangled beneath a sleeve—$110.00. More than the price of two weeks' stay at Purgatory Palace or a month of pay for Celso. I touched the sleeve of the coat again and then lifted it to my face, the smell of newness surprising and strange.

While I stretched the fabric across my cheek, a firm hand dug into my shoulder and yanked me back. Almost losing my footing, I flung my arms out, trying to catch myself, and jabbed my fingers into the cheek of a store clerk. The veil slid off my head and drifted to the ground. He screamed. When I recovered my balance and opened my mouth to apologize, he held his hand to his face and shrieked again.

"She attacked me," he said, pointing at me, then stumbling away, gasping in great gulps as he ran.

I glanced from side to side. The people who had ignored me before, who had watched their feet when I stood near them, now stared at me openly, their mouths straight, their eyes narrow. I picked up the veil and backed to the door. I should have left when I'd had the chance, when I'd recognized the exclusion of this place. Before I could make an exit, the man who had grabbed my shoulder came back down the aisle, followed by a short round man wearing spectacles. I turned and ran.

My heart pounded so hard, I thought it might escape through my mouth; the violin on my back banged against me, matching the rhythm of my heart. I turned corners as I rushed past others on the street—right, left, right again, then left, over the bridge, beyond the river. I didn't look behind me, I didn't slow down, I couldn't stop. The veil was still in my hand, and I knew that anyone who saw me would recognize me now and again later.

When my chest began to burn from the cold air and my sides were heaving, I slowed down. I knew where I was. I was in the park where I'd heard the four musicians playing under the willow tree. It was the smell of this place that pulled me back time and again. I looked around, but no one chased me, no one grabbed my shoulder, no one screamed for me to stop. My breath came so fast that I bent over, gasping, and placed my hands on my knees.

The park was dark and empty except for a couple strolling hand in hand. They wore warm coats, gloves and scarves. I shivered in my black sweater with the holes at the elbows. I crept under the willow tree, hiding and panting until my breathing slowed and the panic subsided. Then I sat with my back to the tree and closed my eyes. With my eyes closed and my breath calming, the sounds outside my body became discernible. No pounding feet had followed me into the park, and the honking sounds of the city were quiet here, muted. Up close, I could hear the trickling of the creek, the pip of a bat and the rustle of leaves as the dry branches of the willow rubbed against each other.

Under all this other noise, I heard music. It came from the base of the tree in waves and patterns. The melody floated around me, brushing against my arms and cheeks, but when I opened my eyes, I saw nothing. I closed my eyes again and listened. The song of this jostling city welled up inside me; the sound of my panic stirred beneath the ground. I pulled the violin from around my shoulders, opened the case, fit the instrument under my chin, breathed deeply—my panic finally abating— and began to play. I created a song that sang of my panic, my race through the city and my calming here by the stream.

Until deep into the night, I sat by the tree and felt the music of stars, strays and isolation. The violin fit against my shoulder and became the coat I didn't have, the warmth I didn't feel.

By the time I got back to Purgatory Palace, my hands hurt. I curled my fingers into my armpits and tried to warm some of the ache out of my fingertips. As I approached the house, I stopped and slid into the shadow of a building across the street.

Two men in green uniforms stood outside Purgatory Palace, illuminated by the light from the door. Ofelia, glass in hand, talked to them. She pointed down the street, shook her head and kept the bars of the door between her and the men. A tightness filled my chest, a squeezing that had nothing to do with my arms wrapped around my body. The face of the store clerk—mouth open in fear—appeared in my mind.

The police officers returned to their car, which sent two piercing beams of light into the street, like glowing wolf eyes. Three women with black-lined eyes, short skirts and pointed shoes swayed past the officers.

"Hey, baby," said one of the women. "You looking for me?"

"Not tonight," one replied.

I waited in the dark of the doorway until the police car had merged with the other vehicles in the street, creating a living, changing flow of noise and smog. I crossed the street in spurts, stopping and starting with the sporadic traffic around me. I squeezed into the small space between our building and the one next to it, ignoring the women on the sidewalk as they ignored me. I hadn't noticed how high the windows in our rooms were, but now that I was between the buildings, I saw that I wouldn't be able to reach Candela's window without a stool. Debris littered the ground—newspapers, plastic bags, an old sink. I kicked over a washtub and stood on its upturned bottom. With my fingertips, I reached through the bars to the glass of Candela's window and tapped.

My nerves were strung as tightly as the strings of my violin, and I watched the narrow passage between the buildings, waiting for the officers to return, capture me and lock me away in a world even stranger than this one. I tried to calm myself, convince my sweating palms that they hadn't been here for me—they'd come for someone else—but the fear made my limbs tremble and convinced me otherwise. I'd probably lose my room, lose the one friend I had, lose the warmth of Purgatory Palace. Strange how awful places seem not so awful when a more terrible alternative presents itself. My camp in the woods had been a haven, Belen's house had been bearable, Purgatory Palace was almost tolerable now that I had a friend and a means to make money. Being tossed out into the street felt incomprehensible.

"Whisper." Candela stood in the narrow corridor between the buildings.

"I'm here." I slid between the walls back to the opening.

"Come now, fast. Ofelia's in her room."

Candela turned and ran to the front door. Oscar sat in the entryway, keeping the door open and watching for Ofelia. When I got to the door, Candela took my hand and pulled me into her room. Oscar followed and softly closed the door behind us. Candela rubbed my hands and arms. I was shaking.

"What did you do?"

My knees began to tremble, and I lowered myself to Candela's mattress. "I went into a store on the other side of the river," I said. "Randall and something. I looked at a coat. A clerk grabbed me by the shoulder and pulled me back, and when I tried to catch myself, I scratched his face. They chased me out of the store and I ran."

Candela shook her head. Oscar raised one eyebrow.

"Randall and Burns. Why, of all stores, did you choose that one to go into?" Oscar started to smile. "'Course, when I get my legs, I'm going in there. I'm going to chew gum and tuck wads of it into the pockets of all their expensive coats. I'm going to try on their fancy suits after not bathing for half a year. I'm going to cross that line between them and us, and I'm going to spread rot when I do."

"We'll hide you," Candela said. "You think stuff like this hasn't happened before? A year ago, I had to hide Oscar for two weeks after he got into a fight with a cop."

Candela looked at Oscar. Oscar looked at the ground.

"You can't go back to your room. Ofelia will give you up to the police and throw your stuff out into the street." Candela pointed to the mattress on the other side of her room. "You can stay there."

"Why did you go into a store, anyway?" Oscar asked.

My hands were red and raw. I wondered how much longer I could play the violin in the streets. If it kept getting colder, I wouldn't be able to hold on to the bow, I wouldn't be able to squeeze out the songs, I wouldn't be able to pay Celso and protect my family.

"I need a coat," I whispered.

"Well, that's not where you get one. I'll take you to the thrift store sometime this week. The coats there might not be the prettiest, but they look fine—they're good enough for us beggars."

I was safe, but my mother's gifts were in room 13. I had the violin—the most important gift—but I wanted the scarf that smelled of bread, I wanted the rag doll and the silver spoon. I touched the top of my leg, rubbed my mother's slip against my skin and felt its comforting warmth. I wanted to keep what little I had.

Candela told me I'd get my things back later, when Ofelia wasn't around. But how was I to hide from the police? Anywhere I went, I would be recognized, and if the police were like me, they remembered everything.

Sixteen

Candela was an easy roommate. She didn't snore, she didn't boss or intrude. We spent so little time in the rooms anyway, it hardly seemed to matter that I was sharing hers. Home had become something intangible, foggy and uncertain.

In the mornings, Candela got breakfast while I washed in the basin of water after she did. I used her dirty water; I ate half of her meal. We sneaked out early, before Ofelia was up. We trudged up the hill to the coffee shop. In the afternoons, when we returned, I hid in the alleyway until Candela said it was clear, and then I sneaked into her room. This was our plan, and it worked. For a while.

The city was colder than the forest had been. I didn't know why this would be, as the forest grew on the side of a mountain, but here there was nothing to hold the warmth close and hug it in tightly—no trees, no bushes, no hills. The cement, stone and brick buildings held as much warmth as icicles.

Candela did caricatures. I played the violin. The mornings were cold, but the afternoons warmed up as the sun tried to beat its way through the haze of the city. I had enough rent money for another month, but I couldn't pay Celso on top of that, and I would not resort to begging. I would play my violin until it fell from my frozen fingers.

A few days after the incident at Randall and Burns, while I crouched on the ground and played my third set of songs, Candela nudged me with her foot. Two police officers had parked their car across the street and were walking toward us.

My hands became sweaty, and even though I tried to keep playing, my fingers slipped on the bow and the violin slipped from beneath my chin.

"Run," Candela whispered to me.

My heart began to beat in my left temple.

"Run!"

I didn't bother with the violin case but stood, tucked the instrument and bow under my arm and ran.

"Hey," someone shouted behind me.

My feet slapped against the cement and warmth crept into me, starting in my legs and working up into my chest. As I ran, I heard a strange whistling in my ears. This was the time of year when the earaches started, and I could feel one nesting inside my head like the pinchers of a crayfish. I turned left, then right, then left until I was disoriented.

The footsteps that had chased me down the street seemed to have quieted, although my ears rang so loudly that I wasn't sure. If I had been in the woods, I could have slipped between the trees, crouched in the bushes and camouflaged myself in the vines. I could have disappeared in seconds, but here it felt like hours and I was still pounding down the sidewalks, away from those two police officers.

When I finally slowed down, I was outside the park with the willow tree. I ran to it and crawled underneath its sweeping arms. I placed my back against the tree, pulled my legs up to my chest, balanced my violin on the tops of my knees and tried to slow my breathing. They could find me here—they would—and then what would I do?

The deep breaths started to work, and my gasping slowed. That's when I heard the crashing footsteps that had followed me all the way to this place.

I tried to become part of the tree. I hugged my knees tighter, placed my chin on top of the violin and stopped breathing. Whoever had been chasing me breathed like Celso's mule, ragged fish gasps through his mouth and nose. I didn't dare peek around the tree to see who was there.

The tree shuddered when the pursuer leaned heavily against it. I closed my eyes and tensed my body, ready to leap and begin the chase all over again.

"Whoa…girl…" panted a voice from behind the tree, "you…are…going…to…kill…this…old…man."

I couldn't remember if the police officers had looked old or not. Had one been an old man?

I heard the man slide down the tree and sit heavily on the ground. It was time to run—this was my chance, but I didn't know where to go from here. They would find me no matter where I went. I sat, my muscles taut, and waited.

"Ahhh." His breathing was not quite as fast, not quite as labored. "Whew."

My breath eased out of me slowly, evenly. I was quiet as a bat, still as a butterfly, stealthy as a fox.

"Okay," said the voice. "Maybe I won't have a heart attack. If I'd known you were coming here, I wouldn't have run so hard. There are about ten different ways I could have come to this park, all of them shorter."

Slow as a silent snake in dried leaves, I peeked around the side of the tree as far as my neck would allow. All I saw were feet and ankles. The ankles were clothed in tight black socks, and on the feet were brown shoes. And that's when Rosa's words came back to me.

Just wait. You'll do the same thing I did. They'll start following you…there's no turning back.

I knew what this man wanted, and I would not give it to him. I leaned forward, put my weight on my feet and tucked the violin under my arm. I was about to leap, about to run through the streets again, when he spoke.

"When you listened to us that day under this very same willow tree, I had no idea how well you could play. But when I heard you repeat Bruch's *Concerto no. 1 in G Minor* while you sat in front of the coffee shop, I knew that you were more gifted than all of my other students combined."

He panted for a moment and took a few deep breaths. I was squeezing the violin so tightly, the bridge dug into the underside of my arm.

"I believe that you only heard the piece once. Once! And then repeated it perfectly. Is this true?"

A face appeared around the side of the tree. It was friendly enough, with a fuzzy gray mustache and heavy gray eyebrows, but I knew what he wanted from me and I doubted that it had anything to do with my musical abilities. I stood up and backed away from him.

"Is it true?" he repeated.

I shook my head. I took another step backward while watching him. He didn't get up to follow.

"So you had heard the piece before?" He raised his eyebrows and waited. "Please don't make me run again."

"I don't understand," I whispered.

"Well," he said, "who does? I don't understand where musical gifts like that come from, and yet, here you are. Did you write the other songs yourself?"

I peered through the hanging arms of the tree and nodded. He clapped his hands together. Great creases appeared in his cheeks, creases that had graduated from dimples into caverns and rifts.

"Stupendous," he said. "Marvelous. We must talk more. Come with me to a café and have a bite to eat. I'm tired from the run, and I'm too old to sit on this hard ground."

I took three quick steps away from him. He would grab my arm as tightly as teeth and drag me away. I could not go anywhere with this man. The branches of the willow tree fell around my shoulders like welcome camouflage.

"Right," he said. "Shouldn't talk to strangers, eh?"

My eyes were beginning to hurt, but I was too scared to blink. The throbbing in my right ear reminded me that I needed oil, warm oil, to relieve the ache.

"Okay, then, let's head back to the café where your friend is. She can be our chaperone, eh?" His laugh was deep, melodic. It made me think of waterfalls and swimming holes.

He groaned and pushed himself off the ground. His hands, in fur-lined black gloves, brushed the debris from his pants and coat. When he stood, he was tall, much taller than me, much taller than Nathanael or Jeremia, and heavier, but he leaned away from me and had such a welcoming smile that I didn't step back.

"Now then," he said, holding out his gloved hand. "I am Solomon."

He didn't lower his hand, even though I waited half a minute. I stepped from the branches of the willow tree and touched his fingers with the tips of mine.

"Whisper," I said.

"Wonderful to speak with you at last. I told the police officers that you are my student and that I would speak with you, so I followed you here. They have agreed not to harass you at the café. I can't guarantee that they won't harass you at your place of residence, since they believe you assaulted someone, but the café is safe for now. I'll lead the way. A much shorter way."

With a sweeping arm, Solomon pushed aside the branches of the willow tree and turned his brown shoes back toward the café.

I didn't know what to do. If I followed him and he really did want more than to talk about music, I might become like Rosa. And yet he had seen my face time and again at the coffee shop and he hadn't said anything about being interested in my body. Besides, he had known about me listening to the music under the willow tree.

I watched him until he was halfway across the park. Then I followed, stealthily, silently, as a wolf hunts its prey. I placed a hand over my aching ear.

Never once did he look back.

I followed Solomon all the way to the café. What had seemed like miles when I ran to the park was merely blocks. Candela watched my return, her eyebrows lowered, her mouth a tight, thin line.

Solomon walked into the café, sat at a table near the front window and ordered from the woman who approached his table. I stood with my hand on the door, one push away from entering. Never had the workers or owners asked me to come inside—my place was on the cement, sitting where people walked. I had no right to go in. I had had no right to go into Randall and Burns. I was no longer allowed in room 13 at Purgatory Palace. Who was I to think that I could walk into this café?

Two steaming mugs of cocoa were placed in front of Solomon. Two bowls of piping-hot soup twisted their heat into the air above the table. Solomon saw me standing in the doorway and motioned for me to enter. Would I owe him for the lunch, and if so, what kind of payment would he want?

I thought of Rosa and her beautiful baby. I thought of the money I owed Ofelia, Celso and now, possibly, Solomon. How would I satisfy all these debts?

I stepped into the café.

Keeping my head lowered and my eyes on the floor, I shuffled my way to where Solomon sat. He stood up when I neared the table and pulled my chair back so I could slide in. Somewhere between the police officers arriving and my sitting at this café table, I had become human.

"No coat, no gloves—you'll ruin your hands. Hold them over the soup."

I held my hands palms down over the soup and looked at my fingers, as red and rough as though I had been scrubbing laundry in a filthy river. I turned my hands over and looked at my palms. The steam from the soup warmed even the insides of my fingers, and the smell triggered memories of Nathanael, Jeremia, Eva and me heating up stew over the open fire pit, filling the pot with chunks of potatoes, beets and carrots and throwing in the meat from a rabbit or maybe something bigger if the hunting had been successful.

The server placed a basket of bread on the table in front of us. Solomon unfolded the towel draped over the bread and tore off a piece. The smell of warm dough rose, and I breathed it in, remembering my mother and times when I had felt loved.

I took a sip of the soup. The flavor was even better than the smell. I broke off a piece of the bread and dipped it into the soup. Curling my shoulders, arching my back over the table, I tried to relax, but at any moment this bowl of soup would be taken away from me, the steaming cup of cocoa would be tossed out, and I would be asked to leave or thrown out the door. I hoped he was not watching me eat, watching my careful placement of the food well into my mouth.

When I reached the bottom of the bowl, Solomon slid his bowl in front of me. His generosity increased my hunger— if he would be exacting a price from me, I had better eat as much as I could.

I held my spoon over the bowl, waiting, watching Solomon.

"You said you were hungry," I said.

"I changed my mind."

When I finished the second bowl and felt the weight of warmth and comfort in my stomach, I looked out the window for Candela. She was gone. It was too early for her to be done working. I knew what this meant—she believed I had joined Rosa and now would be working the night shift. She believed I wouldn't need her help anymore. My legs twitched beneath me. I'd had my soup, I was warmed, and now I should leave, save myself, apologize to Candela. But that would be stealing.

I sipped the cup of rich cocoa. My hands wrapped around the cup, and I breathed in the aroma. I could have sat there all day.

"Now," said Solomon, and I jumped in my chair, choking on the cocoa. The drink dribbled out the slits between my nose and mouth and erupted from the holes that were an extension of my nostrils. The towel from the now empty bread basket was close at hand, and I dabbed at my face. My cheeks burned, my chest felt hot, my neck throbbed.

"I'm sorry," he said to me. "I didn't mean to startle you."

I looked down into the cocoa. Solomon's voice was low, soft and careful, as if he were talking to a rabbit, trying to coax it out from beneath a bush.

"I've been listening to your music for weeks. You are astonishing. I don't know where you live, or how you have lived until this point, but I want to offer you a proposition."

My hands started to shake.

"I would like you to be my student. In return, I will find you a room at the university; I will find you a scholarship, and your tuition and housing will be paid for. All I ask is that you allow me to teach you."

I wanted to stare down into my cocoa again, but my eyes betrayed me, showing my vulnerability, and I looked at him. He was watching me, his heavy brows pulled low over his eyes.

"I have gotten ahead of myself. I am Solomon Woodson. I am a professor of stringed instruments at the university, and I would be honored if you would agree to be my pupil."

I looked closely at his face, searching for the truth in this inconceivable offer. Did he really think I would believe this?

"That's not a proposition," I said. "That's a gift."

"The university offers tuition remission to deserving musicians. You are such a pupil."

His smile was so broad that I stared at his teeth. They were straight, white, big. No brown roots, yellow stains, gaping holes. This man had never lived in the forest with other rejects. He didn't know what my life was like. He couldn't possibly be offering me something that only those with unblemished faces received.

"Would I have to..." I paused, licked my lips and glanced around the café. Still no one had come to take away my cup of cocoa. Solomon's brows were no longer down but had jumped up like fuzzy caterpillars, making him appear to be listening intently.

"Would I have to..." I swallowed. "...work the night shift?"

"What does that mean, dear? What does one do when she works the night shift?"

"Give you sex," I said, so low that he leaned forward in his chair to hear me. I instinctively leaned back in mine.

"Come again?" he said.

"Would I have to give you—or someone else—sex?"

He shook his head and then leaned away, his eyes hooded and dark. With one finger, he touched the back of my hand. I pulled my hand away and put it under the table.

"I'm sorry," he said. "I don't know what your life is like, nor do I know what you have been through, but you will never, ever have to work the night shift at the university. You will be given your own room with a lock on the door. You may come and go as you wish. No police officers will chase you down or force you to run away. I am offering you a legitimate proposal and will write it up as such. You owe me nothing but some hard work as my student."

Could this possibly be true? If it was, what would Belen think if I disappeared? What would Celso do when the money he wanted was not there? What would Candela believe? Would Rosa think I'd become like her?

And then I didn't care. I wanted to play the violin—I wanted to live the life he was offering.

"What about this?" I waved my hand in front of my face. Solomon's eyelids fluttered as he glanced at my face, and he quickly looked away.

"I don't care about that, but others might. The first day in the park, you wore something over your head, something light, mysterious." He leaned forward again. This time I didn't back away. "Wear that again. Disguise yourself. Let them guess at the mystery that is Whisper. You are wonderful, a fabulous musician, a great talent. Wow them with your skills so they fall in love with you. Then, who cares?"

His chair creaked and groaned beneath him.

"So what do you say?" he asked.

I considered my options: hiding in Candela's room, going to jail, living on the streets. I didn't have to think long.

"I would like that," I whispered.

"So would I," he said.

And then I allowed myself a small smile—a twitch of the corners of my mouth—and rather than screaming in terror and running away from me, he smiled in return.

Seventeen

The next day I was to meet Solomon at the café and together we would go to the university, where he would show me my new home, introduce me to my classmates and elevate me to a new status—one I probably didn't deserve. I listened to his plans, nodded, inclined my head, but they were words, words, words and I couldn't bring pictures of this new life to my mind. That, in itself, should have been a warning.

When I returned to Purgatory Palace, I squeezed into the alleyway, stood on the overturned bucket and tapped on Candela's window. A few minutes later, the front door to the building opened, and Candela stood in front of me, her eyes watery, her nose red. I followed her into the building, past Ofelia's closed door. Candela didn't look at me. She climbed onto her bed and lay down with her face to the wall. I stood by the door and slowly closed it. My violin case rested in the corner of the room, and when I opened it, the coins I had earned that day still lay on the bottom. I placed my violin on top of the coins and closed the case.

"So, are you going to live with him?" she said. Her voice was low and hoarse.

"He's a professor of music at the university. He wants to teach me."

Candela sat up straight on the bed. I hadn't seen this Candela before. Her face was scrunched around the nose, her mouth pursed tight, her eyes narrowed, her cheeks sucked in. I took a step back.

"And you believe him. I thought you were smarter than Rosa. I thought you had talent and goodness. I thought you would be the one friend who stayed, but you're just as moronic as she is. I hope this life you've chosen makes you miserable. I never want to see you again!" She screamed the words at me. Her fists were tight balls, and her face was the color of the blood stain on my mother's slip. She threw the rest of that day's money at me, the coins rolling around the room.

Panic flittered in my chest.

"It's not like that," I said. "He's writing a contract..."

"Whisper. No one offers opportunities and hope to people like us. No one. We have to make opportunities for ourselves. But you don't have to believe me—find out for yourself. Just don't expect me to be here, waiting to put you back together again when you realize what this guy wants from you." She turned her head away, toward the wall, and wouldn't answer me even when I said her name three times.

I picked up the few coins that had landed by my feet and tucked them into my shoe. I took the picture off the wall that Candela had made for me and slipped it into my violin case along with my birth certificate, the only validation that I existed in this world. Now I had no home, no friends and a promise that might be empty.

I thought of what I could say to her, what I could murmur softly that would fix this, but words were hard for me and I couldn't think of anything. My throat felt closed and tight. I opened the door and shut it behind me.

Ofelia, in a lumpy purple robe and gray slippers, stood at the front door of the building, her back to me. She turned her head when I closed the door to Candela's room.

"Well, speak of the devil," she said with a thin, watery smile.

When Ofelia stepped aside, I could see the two police officers standing outside the door.

"That's her," said one of them. "She matches the description." This officer was skinny, with pointed cheekbones, a pointed chin and a pointed nose—even his eyes looked sharp.

"She's the one," said the other officer. He looked younger than the other, with rosy cheeks and a red-tipped nose. Both men wore green-and-white uniforms that reminded me of lizards and grass snakes.

"Now I've got to fill that damn room again," Ofelia said.

"You're under arrest," the older man said to me.

The police officers stepped aside, a narrow passageway opening between them. I stared at my feet, my brown shoes that would carry me to the next place. My options had disappeared like earthworms, sucked back into the ground where they had come from as if they'd never been there at all.

I walked down the hall and away from Purgatory Palace, a police officer on each side. They led me to the car. The younger man opened the door and waited for me to climb in.

The car smelled of dirty bodies, overripe fruit. A musky odor that reminded me of Astatla upset my stomach. I turned to the side, ready to run. The older police officer pushed against my back, and my head hit the frame of the car right above the door. He pushed me again and I found myself lying on the back seat, my violin beneath me, my belongings scattered on the floor. The two men slid into the front seat so quickly, so fluidly, that the car was rumbling and jerking before I understood that we were moving.

Blood dripped from a gash on my forehead. I wiped it away with the sleeve of my sweater. My insides were twisted into a tight fist, but no tears came to my eyes, no cry came from my throat. I thought about Jeremia's wolf sitting by his dying friend, how silent and forlorn she had seemed, and for the first time I understood that feeling. Nothing was sure in this world. The memorabilia on the floor of the car meant no more than Solomon's offer, a cloud of possibility that had dissipated.

I had cried in embarrassment when the hot cocoa had dripped out my nose, and I felt the sting of tears now as the loss overwhelmed me. But we drove away, and my tears didn't change anything.

We drove past the town square, where the fountain with angels was lit by lights from below. We arrived at the police station in minutes. The police station looked like the twin sister of Purgatory Palace, a low, squat, stone building covered in scrawled words. The older police officer grabbed my arm and pulled me out of the back of the car as if I were about to resist, as if I'd be able to run away and save myself, as if I had anywhere to go. Two women in short skirts and big hair were shouting horrid words through the entryway to the police station. An unwashed man in a sloppy gray coat that hung past his knees was chanting a song under his breath, a tuneless rhythm about a dog bite. These were the people I fit with. These were my new companions.

I blinked at the brightness inside the police station. The front room contained a few desks, people behind these desks and milling people, all ripe with odors that made me hold my breath. The walls were an empty, impersonal gray. Anyone could disappear into walls like that.

"Assault," the older police officer said as he pushed me toward a hard wooden chair by the first desk. The woman behind the desk didn't look up. Her computer screen displayed words, numbers and strange images that disappeared, reappeared, changed and returned like flashes of lightning. She clicked at a row of letters under her fingertips.

The computer hummed, rumbled and emitted beeps and clicking chirps, a living entity with no softness. The woman asked me questions—name, age, date of birth, occupation— and typed my responses into the computer. I swallowed my whisper and spoke over the noises in the room. When I said "musician" for occupation, she coughed a dry laugh, and then her fingers tapped and the word appeared on the screen. When she asked about my address, my home, and I couldn't answer, she looked at me.

"Your mom's been here for a while, a regular attendee. You guys can have a family reunion. You look just like her."

When she laughed loudly, her chin disappeared into her neck. Her hair was the color of the berry from the dogwood tree, and her skin looked flaky and old under a coating of white powder. My mother was not here.

I was being charged with attacking the man in the store who had put his hand on my shoulder and pulled me away from the beautiful coat. My imprisonment would be for a month unless I was able to come up with bail. They told me that someone had to pay two hundred dollars to get me out of jail, the cost of a month's stay at Purgatory Palace, the cost of two months' pay that I owed Celso, the cost of two beautiful green coats that reminded me of forests.

They pressed all my fingers against a black inkpad and then recorded the print my fingertips made on a piece of paper where all my information had been printed in neat, perfect type. They took my picture against a white background, then told me to turn to the side. I had never had my picture taken before—my deformities would now be visible to those who had never even met me.

"I'll take her to her cell," said the younger police officer. I was glad that it would be him—his rounded cheeks were gentle, not angled like the older one's.

He pointed to a door at the back of the room, and I moved toward it. An old woman with no teeth was being asked questions at another desk. When I walked by, she reached out and scratched the back of my hand. I looked at the line of red that appeared on the top of my hand, but I avoided meeting the eyes of this woman I'd done nothing to. The police officer reached around me and opened the door, and I looked down a long flight of stairs. The stairs were made of stone, like the outside of the jail, and twisted and turned downward. The smell of dirt and urine wafted up.

I put my right hand against the wall to steady myself. I wasn't shaking, but I felt tired—very, very tired.

"I'm Officer Nicholas," he said. His footsteps fell heavily on the stairs behind me, spurring me on into the darkness below. Small lights jutted out of the wall—lights that gave off a white glow with no warmth. I'd always thought of the earth as a warm refuge from the chill of the night, but the air in this place grew crisp as we descended.

When we got to the bottom, I stood in front of a row of locked cages with metal bars that reached from the ceiling to the floor. No windows broke the darkness with rays of warm yellow light. I heard a moaning that made the hair on my arms stand up.

The first two cages housed silent, staring men who watched our progress, their clothing so worn and old it fell in strips over their bodies. The moaning was coming from the next cell, from a heap of clothing in the far corner.

"Lizzy, shut up already. You want to scare your new roommate?"

The pile of rags rocked back and forth, but the noise didn't stop. Gray hair, curled and matted like discolored yarn, was all that was visible of the woman inside the heap. Officer Nicholas opened the cell door and waited for me to enter. I took a couple of tentative steps into the cage.

"Oh," he said. "I need that instrument and that sack of stuff."

My hands tightened around the mouth of my small sack. And then my breathing sped up, my heart began to thump, my shoulders hunched. Through all the questions, the giving of my fingerprints, the taking of pictures, I had not felt the tears burn, but now, when he was about to take the last few items that defined who I was and where I'd been, I choked and coughed on my swelling throat and flooding tears.

"I need this," I whispered.

"Sorry. Can't have it. No belongings in the jail cells."

"But there's nothing in here, nothing I could hurt someone with or hurt myself with. The violin was a gift." I could hear the pitch of my voice begin to rise. I felt ashamed—frantic and embarrassed.

Without asking again, Officer Nicholas took the sack away from me and pulled on the violin strap. When he dragged the strap off my shoulder, the violin began to slide down my back. I clung to the strap with my right hand, envisioning the instrument hitting the floor and snapping in half, my life torn in two.

"Got it," he said. His hands were on the violin case, and he lowered it to the floor. I stepped out of the strap and into the cell. When I turned around, Officer Nicholas locked the cell door and walked away with my only possessions. My violin and small sack of belongings would sit on a desk at the bottom of a stone hole. Now all that remained of me was a deformed face, a carved violin around my neck and a stained slip that warmed my legs. The stones seeped cold through my sweater and rough cotton pants, and the floor offered nothing but hardness. There were two benches in the room and a bucket.

A month.

I sat down on the bench nearest to me. It was pushed up against the metal bars of the next cell, a cell with a woman in it.

This woman had red circles painted on her cheeks and blue arches over her eyes. I turned my back to her, pulled my knees up to my chest and curled around myself, wishing I had a blanket to wrap around me. This was it—all I was, all I had left. I was a husk now, an empty nest, and even though I was broken and deformed, no one would rescue me or fit their body against mine. I knew this.

I woke when I felt hands in my hair. Lizzy stood in front of me, layers of tattered clothing hanging from her like vulture feathers.

"Black rain," she said.

I looked into her face, into her toothless mouth. I slid along the bench, and when I got to the end, I stepped off and stumbled to the door of the cage. She watched me. She didn't try to grab me. She didn't run after me with clawing fingers, scratching and tearing. Her crooning had stopped, but the white lights from the stairway threw shadows under her eyes and made her sunken cheeks almost skeletal.

"Don't like what you see?" She put her hands on her hips and offered me a smile of missing teeth and blackened gums. The bars pressed against my back, locking me in as I tried to wedge myself into the corner away from her.

"What you so scared of, lovey? Old Lizzy won't hurt you."

She took plodding, careful steps toward me. I balled my hands into fists. When she was a step away, she smiled and cackled a low, creaking laugh.

"Lizzy knows you, and you know Lizzy."

I shook my head. My breath came fast and shallow. I needed Rosa, someone hard and worn—someone who knew how to protect herself, to lash out and slash. Candela wouldn't have put up with anything from this woman, and here I was, cowering in the corner.

"Lizzy and you are the same."

I shouted so loudly, the echo from my voice, from that one word, bounced back at me, nasal and harsh. The word itself seemed to mock me. "NO."

She cackled loudly, her mouth wide open, an irregular circle. I covered my ears with my hands and squeezed my eyes shut. I screamed over top of her laugh. I screamed until my voice became hoarse. I squeezed my eyes shut tighter and slid down the bars to sit on the floor, crouching there until my arms ached from being held to my ears and until my back developed indentations from the bars behind me. When I couldn't stand to keep my arms wrapped around my head, I dared to open my eyes.

Lizzy was asleep on the bench where I had originally sat, her snores rhythmic and calm. She was not me. That woman was not me. I would never croon in the corner of a jail cell, reek of urine, lose my sanity—she was not me, even though her face looked exactly like mine.

Eighteen

I didn't sleep that night. An earache had come in full force, the throbs and sharp pinches keeping me awake. If I didn't put oil in my ear soon, the eardrum could swell and rupture. I watched Lizzy until I heard footsteps on the stairs above us and the men began to mutter and stir.

"Porridge, my favorite," one of the men said.

"Good thing we're not having bacon and eggs again. I'm so sick of bacon and eggs," said another amid low mirthless chuckles.

"Yeah, yeah," the officer said. "Come up with something new, would ya?"

I needed to go to the bathroom so badly, I was scared to stand up. I wobbled as I rose to my feet, my knees buckling and my back aching. I shakily stood erect and watched Lizzy, wondering when she would rise and remind me again of what could become of me. Even though her eyes were closed, she muttered and twisted her hands in her hair.

An officer I hadn't seen before opened the door to our cell and pushed a tray with two bowls and two spoons inside.

When he left to go back up the stairs, I looked at the bucket. I knew what it was for. I recognized the smell of a homemade latrine, and I was desperate enough to use it, but everyone would see me. Unlike in the bathroom at Purgatory Palace, where the stalls were open and exposed, I felt no camaraderie in this experience.

I crept over to the bucket, imagining Lizzy's clawlike hands stretching out to me, grabbing me as I slid past. I reached the bucket and scooted it against the stone wall. Lowering my pants, lowering my mother's slip, but keeping my sweater pulled down, I looked from Lizzy to the cells where the men were, but they were too busy eating their porridge to notice me.

There was nothing to wipe with. I could feel heat in my cheeks. I sat over the bucket for a few minutes, air drying, and while I did so, Lizzy rose from her bed and took a bowl of porridge. I pulled up my pants and hugged my body with my arms. She did not look up from her intense eating. Her hair fell into and around the bowl while she gobbled—she did not appear to care that some of the food leaked through the slits in her face.

My hands were filthy from the edges of the bucket, but there was nowhere to wash. Every inch of this place felt unclean, from the hard-packed dirt floors to the benches covered with a sticky residue to the bars that looked slick with sweat. I stood in the middle of the cell, wondering how to avoid touching anything. A month I would be here, thirty days, and I could not stand in the middle of the cell for that length of time without touching something.

I took a bowl of porridge and sat on the bench. The porridge smelled of burned pots and sour milk—I could not bring myself to eat it so placed it beside me.

Lizzy shuffled across the room, her back bent, and sat on the bench next to me, picking up my bowl of porridge and quickly shoveling its contents into her mouth. I held my breath and then turned my head away, trying to avoid the smell of body odor, urine and unwashed clothes that contaminated the air around her. My arms were wrapped around my knees, holding them tightly against my chest, but Lizzy's insistent fingers pulled at me, gripping and tugging until I relaxed and allowed her to hold my hand. What did she want from me? I still held my head away, trying to breathe in untainted air.

She began to rock, moving the bench back and forth, and after first trying to resist and hold stiff, I relaxed and moved with her. While she rocked, Lizzy hummed a low song deep in her throat, and my eyes slowly closed. I remembered the tune from when I was a child and my mother used to visit me.

> *Flitting bright macaw dancing in the trees*
> *bring in the sun to shrink away the night*
> *Tookatiel*
> *Tookatiel*
> *The moon is now gone*
> *My soft morning sun.*

One of her hands held mine, and her other brushed over the top of my fingers, gently, lightly, like the touch of dry grasses. My head, so tired from not sleeping, felt clouded and full, and while I rocked I could believe that this was my mother singing to me, holding my hand, keeping me safe. Lizzy turned my hand over so my palm was up, and across it she rolled an object back and forth. The object felt cool and smooth, as though it had been rolled across a hand many times. I opened my eyes and stopped rocking.

"Where did you get this?" I said.

Lizzy hummed her tune again, but the vision of the creek by our house, the grasses in the meadow and the rustle of wind through the trees disappeared and became a mud-packed earth floor, the rancid odor of unburied shit and the sound of discontented men bickering with each other. I held her hands still in mine and shook her arms. "Tell me."

She looked at me then, her clouded eyes focusing on something beyond me, over my shoulder. I shook her arm again and held the object in my hand so tightly that I could feel its grooves beginning to dig into my skin.

"He doesn't know," she said and then giggled as if she were five years old. "I know where they come from, but he doesn't know that I watch him sometimes."

"Who?" I wanted to shout at her and shake her, but instead I gripped the object tighter.

"I took this one without him knowing and I hold it, remembering."

She reached for the wooden piece in my hand, but I stood up from the bench, stepped back and held it behind me.

With my other hand, I pulled the carved violin from around my neck and showed it to Lizzy, waving it in front of her.

"Give it," she said, not seeing the violin.

I stepped back when she reached for me. I held the violin up to her face. She waved it away with her hand and gripped my arm so tightly her fingernails punctured my skin.

"Give it."

"Look," I said and pushed the violin against her cheek. She shook her head, swatting my hand, and finally she saw the small carving. She stopped then, letting go of my arm to hold the carving, her body so close to mine that I could feel her heat.

She turned the small violin over in her hands, looked at all sides and then smiled a warm, understanding smile.

"We are the same," she said, "you and I. You grew up in the camp in the woods. You know Nathanael."

I brought my hand out from behind my back and opened my fist. The cylindrical carving of leaves cascading down from a tree was Jeremia's, and Lizzy had been holding it for so long the wood was worn smooth as a polished stone, and some of the grooves in the wood had lost their depth. We looked at it together, this woman and I. She knew Nathanael. She had watched our camp in the woods—she had stolen a carving made by Jeremia. Was she Nathanael's lost love, the reason he had come searching in the city? She took her carving back, rolled it in her hand and sat on the bench, where she rocked back and forth and hummed lullabies. I watched her sitting there, a woman with a split face, no home and probably no family, and I wondered—would I end up like her someday?

∞

Lizzy slept the rest of the day on the bench. I watched her, trying to piece together her story, which was somehow connected to Nathanael and Jeremia.

Aside from Rosa, Lizzy was the closest tie I had to my home.

The absence of my violin began to weigh on me, pulling me down into the depression that crept along the floors and leached into the skin through the bleakness of this place. The woman in the cell beside me picked her nose; the men in the cells on the other side bickered with each other, stared at me and then offered worn remarks to the police officer who brought us our lunch.

My violin sat on a desk in front of our cells. When I paced to the front of the cell, I could see it, I could sense it. I could feel the tingling in my arms, the need to play. I stood at the bars, not daring to touch their cold hardness, and looked at my case, at that present from my mother that might have cost her a year's worth of baking. I thought about the music I could play with it. Since I had received that violin, I had tried to play it every day—until today.

After our dinner of a stew that had the look and feel of the morning porridge but with bigger lumps, I lay down on the bench and waited for the forgetfulness of sleep. I held Jeremia's carved violin in my hand, felt its curves, the points and angles of its shape, and watched Lizzy do the same with the sculpture in her hand. I closed my eyes and willed my mind to go blank, my thoughts to disappear down my throat to settle in my stomach along with the dense stew, but the ache in my ear had become constant, a festering sliver, and I couldn't forget.

I heard footsteps on the stairs—more than one person—but I felt too cold and too tired to care. The police officer's stick rattled against the bars of the cell, and I slowly opened my eyelids, so heavy after not having slept the night before.

I rushed to the front of the cage. I held the bars in my hands, and when he saw me, he stopped fidgeting, and his warm, large hands eased through the bars and encompassed mine.

"Whisper," he said.

This was what it had felt like when my mother showed up on my birthday.

"Whisper, dear," he said, wiping his nose with a handkerchief he pulled from his coat pocket, "I have had such a time finding you. Are you well? Have you been hurt?"

The mint and coffee smell of him rose up and drifted into the cell, making me want to cry or shout. Rosa's words came back to me for a minute, but I pushed them down, away, under my haze of relief and hoped that he had come to let me out of the cell because he wanted to teach me music and not because he wanted me to work the night shift.

"She's the one, then." The round officer, his neck almost nonexistent, jangled a cluster of keys in his hand and fit one of them into the lock. Lizzy lay folded into her clothing on the hard bench. She didn't move when the door opened to let me out, but she hummed her lullaby and rolled Jeremia's statue around in her hand. I stood beside her for a minute, watching the carving with the falling leaves and tangled vines, and then touched the top of Lizzy's hand with my own.

We were not the same, Lizzy and me, and I would not end up like her. I would control the shape of my future somehow.

"Lizzy," I said. "I'll come back sometime."

She looked up at me, her eyes focused for just a second.

"No," she said. "Don't come back. Be the morning star that becomes the evening sun. Be strong."

Her hand flipped over, and our fingers touched. I could feel energy move into my hand, and I felt it surge within me. Yes. I would be strong. I would be more than this place wanted me to be.

After strapping the violin to my back and tucking the small sack of belongings under my arm, I followed Solomon and the police officer up the stairs while the men in their cells watched me with eyes that reflected the flat white of the stairway lights.

∞

Upstairs, Solomon and the police officer chatted amiably, laughing and shaking hands while Solomon placed a heavy hand on my shoulder and guided me through the maze of desks. This time, no hand reached out to scratch me and no one asked to take my picture.

Solomon handed money to the woman behind the desk, signed a piece of paper and shook the stocky police officer's hand again.

"Her court date is March tenth. She'll need to show up or come back for her month of jail time."

"She'll stand before the judge and prove she's done nothing wrong." Solomon's heavy hand pushed me to the door.

That was it, then. I was free to go until March 10. Maybe that would be enough time to make amends in some way.

Solomon raised a farewell hand to the police officers and then gestured for me to proceed. I walked out of the police station. Solomon unlocked the door to a small black car that was sitting against the curb. He held the door open for me and then got in on the other side.

My emotions felt ready to trickle out my nose, to overflow from the slit in my face and pour out of me. This wasn't happiness—it was something else, something like the touch of ice-cold water against your feet on a hot summer day. My legs eased into the car and I found myself seated in the vehicle. It didn't smell like urine, vomit and deceit like the rear seat of the police car had—it smelled of coffee, cigar smoke and peppermint, just like Solomon's jacket. I held my violin in my lap as we headed to I knew not where, pretending to be someone I wasn't.

And that's when I knew how this would all end. I would go to the university, play my unpolished pieces beside those who played like heavenly beings, and they would see that my musical abilities were nothing, a farce, and they'd take back my opportunity to study music. My shoulders sank into the seat of the car, and I stopped feeling the pressure of expectations, the weight of undeserved grace. I would fail, and that knowledge put me at ease.

We crossed the river and drove past Purgatory Palace. I searched for Rosa, Candela, Oscar, even Ofelia, but I saw only the women with the painted faces, the men with their devouring looks.

"I'd never been in there before—didn't even know it existed," Solomon said when we had passed Purgatory Palace. "So many people with hard lives. I never knew."

"We make our own family," I said. "We fit together because we don't fit anywhere else."

"But that is not the right place for you."

"What is?"

"The university. That is where you should be."

"I won't fit there either."

"Heavens, child. Of course you will."

We drove the route that Candela and I had walked every day. We cruised up the big hill, approached the gray stone buildings filled with turrets, domes and rows of glass windows, and turned onto a street where these buildings lined both sides. This was the National University. I had passed by this street every day and had never known that the huge buildings with the skulking creatures along the roof were part of the university. But it made sense—our coffee shop was just around the corner, which explained why Solomon was always there.

Solomon drove confidently, one hand on the wheel and the other hand waving at people walking on the sidewalk. He turned right and stopped beside one of the beautiful buildings. It must be a church, I thought, although I had never been in a church. It was tall and made of square-cut stones, with brightly lit windows and balconies around the upper level. Solomon turned off the car and smiled at me. I began to shake. New places were never good—that had been the rule of my life so far. I had been a prisoner in Belen's house, a beggar at Purgatory Palace, a criminal at the jail—what would I be here? A freak? An object to be displayed and stared at?

He opened the car door and grunted as he extricated his large frame from the car. I considered staying in the car, refusing to move, but I pulled the handle on the door and followed his example. The door popped open and I stepped out.

For a moment, the world spun around me. Lights lined the streets and walkways like organized stars, and students moved beneath them, coming and going from the buildings. A woman—a professor, perhaps—climbed the stairs to the building, carrying a small leather case in her hand, and amidst all of this I saw myself—small, disfigured, a reject. I grasped the veil around my neck, untied it and slipped it over my head. In the city, near Purgatory Palace, rejects occupied every street corner, like featherless birds, but here I saw no blemishes.

Solomon climbed the front steps to this grand building and I followed, still holding my belongings, my violin strapped to my back.

I tried to take in everything at once, but it was impossible. We walked through a doorway as tall as Purgatory Palace and twice as wide. Inside, the hallways were cavernous and the floors were made from a hard substance that was cold as ice, hard as rock, but beautiful as gold leaves. Our footsteps rang through the hallway, and I shuffled along as quietly as I could, but this was not the forest floor and my steps echoed across the hall, announcing my presence. Students, all older than myself and dressed in expensive clothing, milled about in the doorways to other rooms, laughing with each other. When they saw me under the veil, they grew quiet and watched. I knew they couldn't see my eyes or meet my gaze, but I wanted to look away anyway, down at the floor.

Solomon's office was on the second floor, just past the curving staircase with a stone railing that was as beautiful and polished as Jeremia's statues. We entered a large room with maroon decorations where a tiny man who had been seated behind a desk stood and introduced himself to me. He was the office manager for the music department, he said as he shook my hand vigorously. He came up to my shoulder, and he twittered and fluttered like a cricket, buzzing around the office in such a frenzy I was reminded of Eva jumping with the grasshoppers. "Dorm room number one eleven, Clarence Hall," he said. "A room all to yourself, honey. Here is your meal card. Call me Quincy." He handed me a hard piece of plastic with a blank for my signature.

"We'll need a photo sometime," he said, but when Solomon furrowed his eyebrows and shook his head, he added, "Or not."

His bespectacled eyes looked me up and down, noting the tattered sweater, the threadbare canvas pants and the flat-soled brown shoes that I had been wearing far too long.

"Is the contract ready?" Solomon asked.

Quincy picked up a rolled piece of paper tied with a red string. He handed it to me.

"Well, untie it," Solomon said, his hands twitching as though he would have liked to untie the string himself.

I untied the string and began to read the contract to myself.

"Oh, no. You must read it aloud," Solomon said, seating himself on the front of Quincy's desk.

"I, Solomon Woodson, in agreement with the Music Department at The National University, hereby offer The Watts Scholarship to Whisper _____ for the duration of her studies at the university. She will be given room and board at said school during her education and will also receive a stipend of $100.00 a month.

Terms of agreement for the continuation of her scholarship:

1. Whisper will attend classes and fulfill her obligations as a student.
2. Whisper will attend private lessons with Solomon Woodson while she studies at the university.
3. Whisper will maintain a reasonable GPA and will comport herself in an honorable fashion (in other words, she will absolutely not be allowed to "work the night shift," and if anyone asks her to work this shift, that person will be reported to the university discipline board and punished accordingly).
4. Solomon Woodson will be responsible for Whisper's progress and for aiding her in her acclimation.

Signed,

I, _____, being of sound body and mind, agree to the above terms. This signature has been witnessed by:

Solomon Woodson, PhD _____

Quincy Tell _____"

I looked up at Solomon, and he beamed at me.

"What does this mean?" I asked.

"What does it mean? It means that you will be attending school here, you will stay in the dorm, and I shall be your instructor. It means that you will become a master musician and I will be allowed to have a small part in your musical development. It means, dear girl, that you will have a safe place to stay and will never have to make a living on the street corner again."

The paper shook in my hands. It couldn't possibly be true.

"Well, sign it, then. I didn't know what your last name is, so you'll need to fill that in at the top."

Quincy handed me a pen. I placed the paper on Quincy's desk and slowly, carefully, signed my name. Solomon and Quincy both signed the contract when I was done. Solomon folded the contract, slid it into an envelope and handed it to Quincy. We then did the same for a second contract—this one he handed to me. He grinned at me and patted me on the shoulder. I worried that I would begin to weep uncontrollably if he showed me any more kindness and felt terribly relieved when he stood up from the desk and clapped his huge hands together.

"I will take her to the dorm myself," Solomon said.

"You have class tonight." Quincy looked at Solomon over the top of his glasses.

"Let them know I'll be a bit late. I'll show her the dorm room and the cafeteria. Tomorrow we get clothes from Randall and Burns."

When Solomon said this, he gave me a big wink and a wiggle of his mustache. We would return to the store of my accuser.

I didn't know what to feel. Why not go to Randall and Burns? I'd spent a night in jail and it hadn't killed me—how much worse could a fancy store be?

Solomon handed me the key to my room, which was on the first floor of a massive building about a block away from the music school. He opened the door to the dorm room and turned on all the lights, as though having control over locks and illumination was common and natural. He turned on the tap for the bathroom sink, looked in the closet and declared the room acceptable. It was noisy, located under the stairs where the tramping of feet sounded like tumbling rocks, but it was more than I'd ever had before. As he left, Solomon squeezed my hand, smiled and then quietly closed the door behind him.

Having my own place was odd—lonely, quiet, peaceful and incomprehensible. The bathroom had a shower, something I'd never experienced before. This couldn't be my place to stay, with my own bathroom, a real bed and a closet to hang my clothes in. The closet was empty and waiting for submissions, the desk against the wall had a small lamp that went on with a click of the button, the brown patterned curtains covered a window that looked out over an expanse of green and a walkway that led to the cafeteria. All of this was mine to use.

The mattress was a foam pad, as thick as the width of two hands, that bounced back into shape after I pushed on it. Blankets and pillows covered the bed, and after a shower I crawled beneath the blankets with the key to the door still in my hand. I'd never owned a key, never had the power to keep out whomever I chose. Such power needed to be with me at all times, and I held that key tightly through the dark night—a night without the sounds of the street, the hum of traffic or the friendship of Candela.

I awoke when light shone between the curtains. I listened. I had thought the camp in the woods was isolated, but there I'd had a makeshift family, and here I had only myself.

When I entered the bathroom and saw myself in the mirror, I knew that clean clothes and shampooed hair would not help me fit in. I didn't know what a home was anymore. I had thought it was a place, a place of my own, but it was more than four walls and a roof. Home was belonging.

Nineteen

Only a few lights at the back of Randall and Burns were lit when we arrived the next morning. The clerks were refolding sweaters. The manager, the round fellow who had come after me the last time I was in the store, walked toward us with a large ring of keys in his hand. Solomon, standing outside the door with me behind him, tapped on the glass door with authority, as if he had every right to do so. I adjusted the veil over my head and wished it would stop fluttering and shaking.

"Not open yet," the manager said to Solomon, opening the door just enough to speak through the crack. Solomon pushed his way into the store, crossed his arms over his chest, cleared his throat and placed himself in front of the manager.

"Whisper will be purchasing some new clothes and some other much-needed items. Could you tell me, perchance, if a young man named Swanny is working this morning? I would like to have a few words with him." Solomon was as solid as a tree stump, and his arms remained tightly crossed.

"She can wait until the store opens, along with our other customers."

"No, she can't," said Solomon. "This child was taken to jail, was housed overnight in a cell where ruffians and villains are kept, and she lost twenty-four hours of her life to undeserved and unwarranted incarceration. You owe her not only time but reparation."

The manager looked at me. He pulled at his bottom lip and then spoke to a nearby worker who was straightening a display.

"Get Swanny for me, would you?"

"Go on," Solomon said to me.

I walked past the green coats and let my hand slide across the material. I picked a long brown skirt that reminded me of my mother, and I chose a black sweater with a high neck, long sleeves, wide pockets and no holes at the elbows. I saw a package of underwear and tucked it under my arm, as well as warm black leggings, plain khaki pants and short black boots that looked about my size. As I clutched these items, the prices rolled around in my head like gnats, confusing me. I knew I didn't have enough money, but I didn't know how to say this to Solomon. I didn't know how much reparation he had planned for me. Beneath the veil, I felt my cheeks burning, the flush creeping down my face into my neck.

Solomon waved to me, and I stood next to him, holding the clothing in my sweaty hands. A clerk stood with one foot on top of the other, an unbalanced stork, and chewed on the fingernail of his first finger. When he saw me approaching, his eyes widened, and he held his hands out in front of his face as though warding off the devil.

"Is this the fellow?" Solomon asked.

According to the police report, I had attacked this man with my claws and nails, had used my powers when he was most vulnerable. I examined his cheek, but I detected no bruises or scrapes. He was at least six inches taller than me, and even though he was thin, I was sure he weighed more than I did.

"Stay away," shrieked the man, in a voice so high it sounded like the cry of a crow.

"Come on, man." Solomon's hands twitched as though he wanted to wrap them around Swanny's neck. "This girl wouldn't attack you. Tell us the truth, now. What really happened?"

"She attacked me," Swanny said while taking a step away from me. "She threw her arms at me. She was going to kill me, if not with her hands, then with her spells and her horrid, horrid face."

"What did you do to her?" Solomon let out a long, huffing sigh.

"I touched her shoulder."

I don't know what came over me, how I became so brave, but rather than remain mute, I spoke. It was as though the words were pressed out of me by a squeezing hand.

"He sneaked up and grabbed my shoulder from behind."

"You grabbed her, did you?" Solomon said to Swanny. "Well, you probably scared her half to death."

Swanny had taken two more steps back, and his hands still fluttered around his mouth, but the manager stood behind him.

Swan. Beautiful bird—long-necked, elegant, stylish.

"I wasn't sneaking. I wouldn't have surprised her."

"And where did she bruise you? Where did she attack your face and leave you partially maimed?"

Swanny's right hand moved up past his mouth and touched his cheek with four unsteady fingers. Solomon took two large steps toward Swanny. He peered at Swanny's face, took his chin in his left hand and twisted Swanny's head back and forth, trying to locate the bruises, scratches, telltale marks.

"I don't see a thing," he said.

Swanny glanced at the manager, but the little man shook his head and rolled his eyes. His voice was as low as Swanny's was high. "Swanny, she's only a child."

"She attacked me, I tell you. She flew at me with her sharp talons and tried to scratch out my eyes."

While he said this, I shifted the clothing to my right arm and raised my left hand, examining my fingers. Talons. My nails were chipped and broken but clean. My hands were red and raw but unremarkable. I was a beggar. I had spent a night in jail. I looked like a witch. I almost believed Swanny myself. Without intending to, I lifted my hand and touched my mouth through the veil. This face, this horrid, horrid face. I might play the violin like an angel, but this face would always be how people judged me—what they saw first.

"Didn't you say she was looking at the coat, Swanny?" the manager asked.

He waddled over to the rack of coats, flipped through them to find a size that looked appropriate and glanced back at the now shuddering Swanny. The manager held out the coat for me.

My hand stretched out tentatively to the coat. It would be withdrawn at any moment—I understood that—so I wrapped my left arm around it and then dug through my pockets with my right hand, locating the coins Candela had thrown at me and holding them out to the manager. I knew it wasn't enough—how could it possibly be?—but I wanted that coat as much as I wanted a home. The manager waved the money away and glanced quickly at Solomon, who still stood as though it would take an earthquake to move him. His eyebrows were low and his mustache quivered.

"Keep your money. Swanny gets a discount," the manager said. "And he will withdraw the charges."

Swanny sobbed but kept his hands over his face.

"Right, Swanny?" the manager said.

Swanny nodded.

I held the coat against my cheek, under my nose, all the way back to my room, my very own room with a bed that sat on a frame, a desk that contained two drawers, a closet that would soon hold my old clothing. I tried on the new coat and knew that whenever I wore it, I would think of mangoes, starlit nights, the company of friends and huts in the woods that had been my home.

The impromptu recital, organized to introduce me to Solomon's students, was scheduled for 11:00 AM in the auditorium. A clock with glowing red numbers sat on my desk, announcing the time both day and night. At 10:45 I walked to the building where Solomon taught and looked for the auditorium. I thought the muted colors I had chosen would help me blend in, become part of my surroundings, as they would have in the forest, but here, in the ornate building decorated in white and gold, I stood out like a blemish.

Solomon sat on a stage in an enormous room where rows and rows of seats stretched forward like the cells of a wasp nest. In the rows facing him were about thirty students, scattered haphazardly in the seats. Lights hanging from the ceiling by long narrow cords illuminated the first ten rows of seats, and I slowed my pace, stopping where it was still dark. I tugged at the veil, wishing it would stretch and cover my entire body.

"Whisper," Solomon said and motioned for me to come closer. I slipped one hand into the pocket of my green coat and held Jeremia's violin with the other. My heart pounded in my chest, ready to burst from its cage.

Solomon leaped off the stage and took huge steps up the aisle to where I stood. He put his arm around my shoulders and guided me down the aisle, into the beams of light. All of the heads turned, and thirty pairs of eyes watched me. Some were curious, wondering, questioning, while others were narrow, suspicious, appraising.

"This is Whisper," Solomon said. He guided me to a seat about three rows up and right on the aisle. The girl in the next seat pulled her arm off the shared armrest and turned her head away from me. "She is the recipient of the Watts Scholarship and will be under my tutelage next term."

I concentrated on Solomon, willing everything else to fade away.

"Christmas vacation is in three weeks, and our recital is three weeks after that. When we return from the holidays, we have one week. Stay with the regimen! Now, I want Tomas, Ben, Sara and Rita on stage, front and center. Let's show Whisper what we're all about."

Solomon climbed the far steps to the stage and tapped his foot while four musicians followed, carrying their instruments. They jostled each other, joked, smiled and stood in a rough circle. Solomon placed his feet shoulder-width apart and whispered a beat under his breath while waving his hand in a four-stroke pattern. The musicians readied their instruments, tapped toes to the beat and, when Solomon raised his hands, lifted their bows.

The music moved through me like water—first slow and alluring, gaining speed over the rapids, then sounding like the animals on the shore, the fish in the water, the birds in the air. The low strumming beat spoke of rocks, sand, planted trees. I felt so homesick that a shaky breath whistled from me and puffed the veil.

I wanted it to go on forever.

The musicians drew their bows across the strings one last time and I woke from my dream. If only I could wrap that music up, squeeze it inside me and carry it around, filling that hole of loneliness that wouldn't go away. Why had I only heard the beauty of this music now, sixteen years into my life, when I could have been consuming it all along?

I clasped my hands around the violin case in my lap while Solomon brought all the other students up onstage and had them play. He was showing me something—I understood that—and I could sense that some of these musicians were better than others. When the music stopped, I watched the students whisper and ignore me. The girl beside me spoke only to the person on her other side, as though my veil was a solid barrier between us. The boy in front of me turned around with a big smile that felt false. He looked at the black plastic case that lay in my lap. "What make of violin do you have?" he asked.

Are violins made differently? Maybe I had the wrong version. I shrugged.

"I've got a Doreli," he said, holding up his violin. It was beautiful, with cherry streaks through darker wood and a sheen that reflected the light from the stage.

I opened my case and looked at my violin. In comparison to his, it looked battered and worn. The girl beside me glanced into my case and then laughed. The boy looked as well, then gave me a big grin.

"Not a Stradivarius, then, is it? Someone make that for you?"

The two girls to my right laughed outright, then put their hands to their mouths. I closed the case and looked away. I wished I could ignore them—not care about their whispers, their stares, their appraising glances—but every mutter felt like it was about me and every laugh was at my expense.

My night in the jail came back to me, the night when I had vowed that I would never end up like Lizzy, that I would be proud even when others made me feel like the dirt pushed through an earthworm, but that moment of strength was hard to recapture in this place. I didn't fit in here—I would never belong.

Every day I spent two hours with Solomon and three hours in the tutoring center. The tutor was kind, gentle and patient. When I didn't understand how to take the tests or write an essay, she showed me how. I would be placed in remedial classes soon, she said, to prepare me for university-level instruction. Remedial, remedy, in need of a cure, like I was the disease.

In my private music lessons, Solomon repositioned my fingers on the violin. He showed me sheets with music on them, sheets that I was supposed to read but didn't understand.

"You will learn how to read the music. Don't get so frustrated," he'd say when I threw the sheets of music on the floor and put my face in my hands.

"I'm too far behind. I'll never catch up. I feel so stupid."

"You are not behind, and I will not listen to nonsense. With your talent and natural skill, you sound like a seasoned musician who has played for half a century. Now, let's try again."

He'd pick up the book and I'd look at the notes, trying to make them fit with the sound. Solomon gave me a small round machine, a CD player, that I slid plastic circles into. The music that emerged from the machine was clear and perfect compared to what had come out of the radio back at the camp, and even though I was still lonely, with no one to talk to besides Solomon, the music from the machine filled the empty space. After listening to the songs on my CD player, I would play them on the violin. Aside from my tutoring, I spent most of my days in practice room 303, and there I recreated the sounds as best I could.

The cafeteria hummed with noise and movement, the students like a pack of coyotes, cackling, jostling, gorging themselves and shrieking across the room to their friends. The very first day I went to the cafeteria, I stood at the back of a line that extended out the door of the squat stone building. I waited in the cold, my hands deep in my pockets and my veil draped over my face. Rita and Max, two students from the music program, stood a few people in front of me. They whispered to the other students in their group, and all faces turned to look at me. No one waved or invited me to join the group and no one said hello, even though they were obviously staring. It felt like being chained to a doghouse in a lonely village. After that first day in the line, I waited until the cafeteria was almost closed and then I darted in, sneaking and scavenging, grabbing whatever leftovers were available, and ran out again.

I curled up on my bed, out of the wind and cold, listening to the music of heaven. Gradually, my hands lost their coating of red, rough skin. I hadn't had an earache since my first night at the university, when I'd bought oil at the store on campus. Even though I was physically comfortable and could spend all of my time listening to and playing music, it wasn't enough. I cried more than I'd ever cried before. And a fear that never went away lived in my chest.

I had not paid Celso. Another month had passed, and I was sure he'd come for his payment. He would take it out on me, find me and force me to the brothel, or he would punish my family. I didn't want to think of Jeremia, but sometimes I lay in bed at night, pulled my coat around me and remembered the way his hands made my skin tingle.

∞

On Christmas morning I walked the five blocks from the dormitory to Solomon's house. He lived in a neighborhood with trees—gigantic trees with wide, empty arms and thick, sturdy trunks. I wanted to see them in the summer, fresh with green leaves and arching branches that would shade the street and offer an umbrella of color. Now it was so cold outside, my breath froze in misty clouds when it puffed from my nose. As I walked along the sidewalk here, where the houses were three stories tall with huge windows and supporting columns, I saw a family emerge from a car and rush to a house, where the door was thrown open wide and the people inside the house hugged and kissed the visitors. A yellow warmth glowed from the house. The windows of Solomon's house were the same, bright and yellow like framed campfire lights. When I knocked on the door to his house, a tall thin woman with wide round glasses opened the door. She wore a white apron speckled with little blue flowers.

"You must be Whisper," she said and stepped aside. "I'm Katherine, Solomon's housekeeper. Shall I take your sack?"

I shook my head, hugging the brown paper bag to my chest. This was my gift, and I wouldn't relinquish my hold until it was given. My violin thumped against my back. Shoes were lined up by the door, and I added my new boots to the row. I hung my green forest coat in the hall closet. The veil covered my face, a constant disguise.

Katherine led me down a hallway, past a dining room with a long wide table set with plates, glasses, silverware and candles, a carefully placed arrangement that would soon be cluttered with family—Solomon's son, daughter-in-law and grandchildren were coming for the holidays. Solomon had invited me to Christmas dinner three times, but I couldn't do it. I couldn't sit at a table full of beautiful strangers and try to eat. How would I keep the veil on my face while slipping food into my mouth, how would I keep the children from staring, how would I feel comfortable, as though it were truly Christmas?

We went to the kitchen, where Solomon was sitting on a stool at the counter, drinking a cup of coffee and reading a newspaper. He looked relaxed here, the large, chunky chairs sturdy enough to support his large frame.

"My virtuoso," Solomon said. "I'm honored."

He pushed a chair back from the counter with one of his feet, but I didn't sit. I placed my bag on the countertop. Katherine was quiet, tense in the neck, stirring the contents of a big pot.

"What do you have in the bag?" he asked.

I edged it toward him. Solomon stood, peered into my bag and then looked at me, his eyebrows up. Katherine touched the spoon from the pot to her lips.

"Could I…" I whispered and glanced at Katherine, "use your oven? I would like to bake some bread…"

"I think we can figure out the timing. Katherine is a culinary genius."

She opened the oven door and slid the turkey to the side, proving that there would be room for my bread pans.

I felt like a toad in Solomon's kitchen, short and stumpy in earth-toned clothes that didn't match the peach and purple tiles of the countertops and walls. I was here for only one reason—to make the bread and give it as my gift to those I fit with best. I remembered my mother's recipe word for word, even the lines about the yogurt culture needing to cook for a day, but when I had purchased the recipe items at the store, I had come across something my mother had not known about—yeast, a miracle ingredient that could be added to the bread immediately, making it rise perfectly.

While the dough rose, I played chess with Solomon. I was reminded of Jeremia, who had never been a good chess player. He would furtively make his move and then bite his first knuckle. While playing the game with Solomon, my nose began to drip, my eyes filled up with tears, and my head ached. Would I ever see them again, hold Ranita, play hide-and-seek with Eva, soothe Jeremia's energy or watch the stars with Nathanael? Their absence hurt more every day, a spreading infection like gangrene. Would Celso punish them for my absence?

"Christmas," Solomon said. "I always miss Anna most at Christmas."

I looked up, surprised, although I shouldn't have been. He had children, grandchildren, a housekeeper, but no wife. Maybe that was why he'd invited me to dinner—Solomon knew the loneliness of holidays.

"How long has she been gone?" I asked.

"Six years and three months," he said and looked down at the chess board. After contemplating for a minute, he took my knight with his bishop.

"Do you miss her less or more after six years?"

He looked at me, his eyebrows furrowed. "I don't miss her more or less or the same. I miss her differently each year. This year I miss that I can't talk to her about you. She would know better than I do how to support your inclusion."

I looked down at the chessboard and moved my rook out of his knight's reach. Maybe I didn't want to be included.

"My uncle may come for me," I said. "I didn't pay him in December."

"What will he do?" Solomon asked.

"Hurt me. Hurt my friends."

"We'll pay him now. How much does he want from you?"

I shook my head and looked at my feet. "It's too late."

"We'll alert campus security. They'll keep an eye out for him."

I nodded, but that wouldn't help. How could campus security hold back the wind?

The dough rose perfectly. Between chess games I punched it down, shaped it into loaves and let it rise once more. Katherine seemed to understand that I didn't talk much, so she said very little, showing me where to find the materials I needed for the bread but not demanding that I explain who I was and why I knew how to do this. She was comfortable to be around, quiet and careful like me, not wanting to intrude but also not leaving me alone.

The four loaves were soft and golden when I took them from the oven. Solomon stood at the counter, picked up a loaf of bread, closed his eyes and breathed in deeply.

"Why is the smell of bread so pleasurable?" he asked.

I picked up another loaf of bread and smelled until my lungs were full of the rich, nutty aroma. "It means warmth, comfort and home."

He nodded without opening his eyes and smiled. "Yes," he said. "Home."

I left one loaf with Solomon and wrapped the others in towels as gifts, but as I was preparing to leave, again refusing Solomon's request that I stay for dinner, a chime rang through the house. Solomon glanced at Katherine, moved down the hallway and then returned, almost tiptoeing, with a woman behind him.

She was short and plump, with a soft, lined face. When she saw me, she beamed and stood with her chubby hands wrapped around the handle of her handbag, rocking back and forth on her feet. Even her hair was plump, framing her face in soft white curls. The woman looked like she had been shaped out of a lump of dough and then left to rise.

"Meet Dr. Ruiz, Whisper," Solomon said. He placed a hand on my shoulder, directed me to the high counter and eased me into a chair.

Dr. Ruiz sat in the chair beside me and placed her handbag in her lap. She looked at my veil, and that, at least, I liked, because she didn't glance about the room, looking everywhere but at my face. She met me eye to eye, but she sat too close, the powdery sheen on her face like a dusting of snow. Solomon slipped out of the room as though I wouldn't notice.

"Very nice to meet you, Whisper. I am Dr. Ruiz." She spoke with a slight lisp, a sibilant hushing sound that reminded me of snakes sticking out their tongues. "Solomon has told me about your musical skills and a bit about your unconventional life, but really I am here to see your face, to see if perhaps surgery could be of help to you. May I see your face?"

Surgery. What did I need surgery for?

She pointed to her upper lip. A white line, thin as the vein on a leaf, ran from below her nose to her lip. "I was born with a cleft palate, or an opening at the roof of my mouth, just like you."

I almost laughed. As if her face had ever looked like mine. Her lips were solid, well defined, unsplit, while mine were gaping and unsmooth.

"Do you know what a cleft palate is?"

"No," I said.

She opened her mouth and pointed to the roof with her first finger.

"A cleft palate is when the two shelves at the top of your mouth don't grow together before birth but stay open. It can cause all sorts of problems, like earaches, food and drink up the nose, rattling breath. I would have had all those problems too, but my family had money, and I had three surgeries before I was one year old. And now I've performed operations on many patients with cleft palates, all of which have been successful."

I watched her talk. Her mouth was perfect. Was it possible that she had looked like me at one time? That seemed absurd, dishonest.

"In your case, if you do have a cleft palate, there is a drawback. You are no longer a baby. Most of the surgeries I have performed were done on children under the age of two. In your circumstance, the surgery might be a bit trickier.

But until I can really take a look at your face, I won't know for sure." Dr. Ruiz smiled and all the puffiness in her face pushed up. Her cheeks became big and round, her eyes were almost lost in her cheeks, and even her ears moved back.

"I've had this all my life," I said. "I've learned to adapt."

"Of course you have," she said, "but that doesn't mean we shouldn't consider how your life could improve were the surgery to be done."

How my life would improve. Could the surgery bring my family to me? Could it make my mother live again? Would it change the fact that I'd been ostracized most of my life? Would I be accepted?

"I don't have any money." I slid off the stool and held my paper bag with the wrapped loaves of bread in it against my chest.

Dr. Ruiz hopped down from her stool and stood in front of me.

"My health clinic would pay for the surgery," she said. "There would be no cost to you."

"No."

Dr. Ruiz's smile narrowed and then she suddenly grinned, as though I'd told a joke she hadn't understood at first. "Why don't I give you my card, dear, and you can think about it?"

I made no move to take the card she placed on the countertop. The silence between us became huge, big as the wind through the trees.

"Goodbye, Whisper. I can see that I have made you uncomfortable. That was not my intent." As she brushed past me, I smelled a red flowering camellia.

I waited where I was, rigid in front of my chair until I heard whispering in the hallway and then the front door opening and closing. My shoulders were tight, my teeth clamped together, but almost of its own accord, my hand reached out, snatched Dr. Ruiz's card off the counter and slipped it into my sweater pocket. When I looked back at the granite, at the deep purple counter where the card had been, it was surprisingly bare. When Solomon came into the kitchen and placed his hand on my shoulder, I dipped, and his hand slipped off.

"Won't you at least listen to her?" Solomon said.

"I would listen if I thought it were true."

"It is true," Solomon said. "A cleft palate can be fixed."

"Not for people like me."

Katherine and Solomon watched as I walked down the hallway, pulled on my coat, put on my shoes and opened the door. I didn't wave as I left the house. They stood in the doorway, their mouths tense and their eyebrows lowered. I wanted to walk away, but I turned and made myself speak.

"Thank you for the use of your oven," I said. "I will think about Dr. Ruiz."

My feet moved me through space, my coat wrapped around me, warm and comforting. Surgery. Corrective surgery for my face. I could look like everyone else. Had Nathanael known? Had Belen known? Had my mother known? The card in my pocket crinkled and rubbed. According to Dr. Ruiz's story, if my parents had given me surgery when I was a baby, I could have had a barely discernible scar like the doctor's. All of us could have been normal. All of us—Ranita, Lizzy and Whisper.

Twenty

Few people passed me on the sidewalk, and even though the houses grew on top of each other, the windows to these houses were closed, making the stillness of this city as unnatural as the green calm before a thunderstorm. I removed my hood, adjusted the veil over my face and stood in front of the jail door, counting to thirty before I dared to enter the building. The woman who had asked me the questions was not behind the first desk. Two officers leaned in chairs at the back of the room, their hands behind their heads, their heels on the desk tops.

"Merry rotten Christmas," the older one said, his face red like a cardinal wing. The air in the room smelled like fermented mangoes. The older officer was lean, thin and wiry, with eyes set close together. I unwrapped a loaf of bread. The officer closed his eyes and breathed in deeply.

"That is what it smells like in heaven." His arms dropped from behind his head to his lap, and he slid his feet off the desk. He stood and swayed. "Who's it for?"

"Lizzy," I whispered.

"She your mom?" His eyes narrowed and he examined me intently.

"No. She's a friend."

I felt a little knot form in my stomach. She could have lived a normal life with Nathanael if she had been given the operation. The other police officer moved to stand behind the one at the desk. The two of them watched me, their faces difficult to read, their eyes glassy and unfocused.

"You missed Lizzy by about forty minutes," one of the officers said. His face was kinder, less hardened, still chubby in the cheeks.

"Where did she go?" I asked.

The younger officer shrugged.

"Heaven," he said. "Hell. Wherever people like that go when they die."

I felt a fluttering in my head, a beating of my heart somewhere in my ears. *People like that.*

"It was the weirdest thing. I'd brought their lunch down—I gave her the food. She was standing, looking right at me, her eyes as clear and focused as I've ever seen them. I had to stop and look at her for a minute—she was kind of creepy, you know? With those eyes, messed-up face. She raised her arms to the side and then one of the lights, the one right behind me, popped. Shot out red, yellow and orange sparks. Made me jump out of my skin. I went upstairs to get another lightbulb, and when I came down again, she was gone. Dead. Lying on the floor of her cell, her mouth pulled into a snarl." The young man's hand reached up to his own face and touched his lips. "She was a witch, you know, making that lightbulb pop like that. She had powers, that woman."

My hands were damp against the paper bag. I hadn't known Lizzy well, I hadn't known what her life had been like, but I did know that she could have lived a life outside a jail cell.

"Merry Christmas," I said.

I left the loaf of bread on the desk in front of the men and walked out the door.

Maybe departing this world could be considered a gift in some cases.

I walked through the cold streets, the colorless lanes, and passed only four people even though I looked around every corner. I did see one man lying on the ground, cardboard under him, cardboard over him. I didn't know if he was still alive. Everyone else must have been gathered around warm fires, singing songs, stuffing themselves full of goose. Even the ladies with the high heels, bare skin and made-up faces were gone, taking the day off to celebrate in whatever way suited them best. Nathanael, Jeremia, Ranita and Eva would be stringing necklaces of holly berries for the tree and gathering pecans for the rice dressing. I could have been at Solomon's, feeling warmth and kindness, if not inclusion.

When I knocked on the door of Purgatory Palace, it was flung open by a tall man with a lopsided nose and a very black, swollen eye. I held my breath for a minute, wondering if Celso had taken over the entire building while I was gone, but the man laughed when he saw me. I had prepared myself for Ofelia, for her sneer, her condescension, her rancid breath, but her door was closed.

"Well, if it isn't Whisper," he said. "Merry Christmas!"

"Oscar…?"

I remembered the veil and slipped it off my head and into the sack. Here, I was not different. Here, I could uncover my face. Oscar wore tan shorts over thin metal legs ending on split wooden ovals that clumped in a stuttering beat against the floor.

He steadied himself with his hands and lurched from side to side as he led me down the hall. Residents of Purgatory Palace stood in the hallway, each with a paint roller in hand and a bucket of paint by their feet. Oscar weaved unsteadily past them, waving his arms in big swings, but he was so giddy with laughter that those in the hallway giggled too.

"I'm almost six feet tall," he said. "Whoa."

His legs leaned to the right while his body moved in the opposite direction, but Oscar didn't fall. Instead, he placed both hands on the left wall and pushed himself back toward the legs. Tears leaked from the corners of his eyes.

Candela stood by the doorway to her room and watched Oscar lurch down the hallway toward her. She held a paint roller in one hand, a big splotch of white paint smeared across her black bangs.

"Of course, he fails to mention that he got a little help from a friend." When Oscar reached Candela, he bent down from the waist, picked her up and held her against his chest. The roller waved wildly as Candela shrieked, and a line of white was smeared across the unpainted door. When Oscar put her down, Candela smiled shyly and touched the arm of my coat.

"Glad you came," she said. We both looked down at the freshly scrubbed floor. The weight of unresolved issues hung like fog between us.

"We're getting married," she said. "He decided that we are meant for each other, even if we're both rejected." I looked at her, daring just a glance. Her eyes didn't narrow, her mouth didn't pull down at the corners, she didn't sigh or roll her eyes. This was a Candela I could trust and love.

"Congratulations," I said, but I felt such sadness, such overwhelming loneliness, that I coughed, choking on the word. She spoke slowly and carefully so that no one else in the hallway would overhear.

"That man who came to get you. Do you live with him?" Her words were abrupt.

"He's teaching me music," I said. "At the school. I live in the dorms."

I took off my coat, folded it carefully and slid it behind the door Candela had accidently smeared. I picked up a paintbrush from her tray and eased it over the chipped door, erasing the streaks and flaws. I didn't know if she would believe me, but I wanted Candela back. I painted back and forth. She spoke after a long pause.

"Do you like it?"

"Yes," I said, "and no." When I tried to swallow, I made a sound like the panting of a dying wolf. "I hate it there, but I want to learn music."

Candela dropped her paintbrush and wrapped her arms around me. I held her against me, tightly, like I would have Eva.

I leaned down, placing my cheek against the top of her head.

"Sometimes we have to do what we hate to get what we want," Candela said.

"Yeah," I said and then smeared paint in my hair from the brush when I wiped the tears away.

Surgery wouldn't change Candela. Surgery wouldn't help Oscar. If I had surgery, would they still want me around? With my free hand, I removed a loaf of bread from the sack and handed it to her. She held it against her nose and breathed in.

"You're staying, you know. Aren't you on holidays from school or something? Christmas is big around here—it's not like we have to be anywhere else. And it just so happens that you could stay for a few days in room thirteen."

If she hadn't invited me, I would have gone back outside and curled up on the street beside the man in the cardboard box.

As we stood together in the hallway with paintbrushes in hand, we talked. I told her about the university, the students who watched and whispered, the music that filled my days with a beauty I'd never known before. She talked about Oscar and how he'd told Blaise, the street bully I'd met my first day here, that he wouldn't pay him anymore. She told me about Oscar tripping Blaise, knocking him to the ground where they could at least look each other in the eye. She said Oscar had been beaten so badly he didn't get out of bed for three days. Ofelia, she said, was getting worse—she stumbled and slurred, grabbed them by the hair and screamed into their faces when she came out of her room.

Ofelia cried every night, the sound muffled but heart-wrenching, and she'd told them that they didn't have to pay rent the week of Christmas if they'd use their money to fix the place up. She was selling it. They didn't know if they'd be allowed to stay when the building was sold or if they'd be out on the streets, living in the hills with all the other beggars.

How could I complain about my life—a room to myself, three meals a day, the luxury of education—when they didn't even know where they would live after the sale? I pretended that my life was acceptable by not saying that it wasn't. When Candela and I had finished our spot in the hallway, we went to see the decorations in the common room.

"Oh, incredible," I said. The common room had been transformed. A Christmas tree spread its branches through the middle of the room, the tin star on top brushing the ceiling, the branches loaded with red bows and lit candles.

"Where did you find such an enormous tree?" I asked.

"The dump," she said. "We find a lot of good stuff there." Candela showed me the branches, perfectly formed, bizarrely symmetrical—a plastic tree with hints of dust between the needles. It was almost as beautiful as Christmas in the woods, where nature adorned the real holly trees with blood berries and where the song of the owl joined our carols. As I began to feel comfortable, warm and relaxed, someone tapped me on the shoulder. Sonja, the woman with the burns, spoke through lips that were pulled tight into bloodless lines.

"Little Miss Princess. The Purgatory Palace is for people who understand hell—you've graduated, honey. You no longer meet the resident requirements." Her wrinkled, pinched fingers poked my chest.

"How long do you have to live in hell to know what it's like?"

"All your life, princess, not just the first bit."

"And what would heaven look like in your world?"

"A soft bed, no begging and maybe a man to tuck me in," she said. She might have been sneering, but her face was so stretched and scarred that all her expressions were the same.

"Then I don't have it either."

Sonja pushed her hand against my chest so quickly I fell back against the table, the edge pushing into my side. I glared after her, but she was right. I didn't belong here—or at the university or at Belen's house. I didn't fit. I didn't fit anywhere except the camp in the woods.

But I was learning music—how to hold my violin correctly, what *arco* and *pizzicato* meant, how to use vibrato and how to make a sound so keening and plaintive, wolves on the hill would howl their replies. Maybe I didn't have heaven, but I was closer than anyone here.

The next day, Candela grumbled and muttered as she brought me to Rosa.

"Forget about her, Whisper. She has her own life now— the baby, her career." The words might have tasted of fire, the way she spit them out. I showed Candela my last loaf of bread and she shook her head, put her hands on her hips and narrowed her eyes.

Rosa lived by the river, next to a huge building with smokestacks that spewed thick smog into the air and that had a barbed-wire fence all around it. White trucks with the word *SWINC* in black letters on the sides were parked behind the wire fence. On the front of the building were the words *SWINE INCORPORATED*, written in block letters.

I hadn't been down her street before, and I vowed that I would never come here alone. The people seemed vacant, absent, as though they lived within themselves rather than outside with the rest of us. Candela held on to the sleeve of my coat and pulled me along as I watched two women in an alleyway, crouched together and jabbing something sharp into their arms. I hugged the loaf of bread to me with one hand and held Jeremia's violin with the other.

Parts of the building were falling apart—metal poles showed through the walls like ribs, crumbling bits of stone exposed more metal, and shards of glass poked out from frames where windows should have been. It was as if the building had been turned inside out.

The smell of urine, unwashed skin and rotted food made my eyes water. I pushed a hand against my nose as we stepped around garbage, old toys and sleeping people lying on the walkway outside the rooms.

Rosa lived on the third floor. Candela and I paused at the door and glanced at each other. I held my breath when Candela knocked. A man opened the door. He was stooped, his shoulders rounded as though they had once been strong but now pulled his body toward the ground. The room had a couch, chairs, a refrigerator, and it seemed much more livable than the outside of the building suggested.

"What?" His hand reached up under his shirt and scratched at an enormous stomach thick with hair.

"Where's Rosa?" Candela asked.

"Gone." He crossed his massive arms over his chest. He was built like the cars I saw rumbling through the streets. "She doesn't want to see you freaks anyway."

"Like I want to see her." Candela pointed her thumb at me, and I tried to loosen my arms from where they pressed the bread to my chest. I thrust the loaf toward the man. Even though the bread was a day old, the aroma of yeast and flour wafted between us like a message.

"She went for a walk. The baby was fussy."

Both of us held on to the loaf for just a minute, and he looked at me fully, seeing me.

"You from that camp in the woods?"

"Yes," I said.

"She cried for hours after she saw you."

"I'll watch the baby if she ever needs help."

"She'd like that," he said, then took the bread, stepped back into the room and slammed the door.

Candela looked at me, one eyebrow lowered, creases between her eyes. She put one hand on her hip.

"Jeez, girl, he just said something nice to you. I've met him twice, when he helped Rosa move out of Purgatory Palace, and he never said anything nice to me."

"Is that the baby's father?" I asked.

"Who knows. He's a leech. She works and he lives off her. I don't like you being nice to him."

"Everyone can use kindness."

"Yeah, or a couple nights in jail."

"No one needs jail."

"That's bull," Candela said. She turned and stomped back the way we'd come, around the sleeping people, over the garbage, through smells so dense and horrid they made my eyes water. Maybe when Rosa returned from wherever she was, she would at least smell the bread-scented air and think of me.

When we reached the street, I looked at the factory next door. A haze surrounded the building, as though fog had settled around it and didn't mean to leave anytime soon. Candela pointed to the trucks behind the fence.

"I think their main factory is in Gloriosa."

All I could remember of Gloriosa was the farm where most of the people in the town worked—the huge buildings that blocked the light and created the head-crushing smell.

"What is SWINC, exactly?" I asked.

"Meat-packing plant. If you don't want to beg, if you don't want to work at the brothel, the next best job for us would be there," Candela said.

It looked like the type of building that if you went in, you might never come out.

When we returned to Purgatory Palace, Candela and I joined the others in the common room. I unstrapped my violin from my shoulder, opened the case, fit the instrument under my chin and steadied my hands. It was nice here, warm and inviting, but I couldn't shake a sadness that made my fingers feel heavy or a tension that spoke of surprise visits from men who meant me harm. I played the violin for many hours a day, trying to understand my emotions. If those around me could find happiness, why couldn't I?

I stayed for seven days—the days between Christmas and the New Year—and even though I played games, talked to Candela, laughed with Oscar and felt comfortable and warm, a hollow feeling had lodged itself in my chest, and I knew that the only way to get rid of it was to see Jeremia again, hold Ranita, play with Eva. I wanted to tell them about the surgery, ask for their advice, but I was on my own here and had to live with the decisions I'd make.

After midnight on New Year's Eve, I left Purgatory Palace. I hugged Candela, wrapped my arms around the tall Oscar, avoided Sonja's eyes as I had all week and wished them a happy new year. I rubbed my fingertips across Ofelia's newly painted door and thought about the snuffling I'd heard in the night, about the sadness that even normal people could feel.

It was the middle of the night, but the darkness of the streets had been pushed back by revelers. Shouts, singing and bursts of fireworks shot pinpricks of celebration into the blackness, and people ran by me, giddy with happiness and camaraderie.

The university buildings were dark, most students having gone home for the holidays, but a few dorm windows winked with light—a few students unable to go home, celebrating in their rooms. I approached Clarence Hall, the tall stone building with four rows of dorm windows, and slid my card into the lock. I kept my head down as I walked along the hallway, the hood shadowing my face, but I sensed someone in the hall before I got to my room.

Shuffling and stifled giggles filtered out from the darkened stairwell beside my room. My heart quickened and my hands became sweaty, the key slipping in my fingers as I approached the door.

"Look who's finally here." From beneath the stairwell emerged three figures. They were silhouettes, dark, but I knew who they were before they stepped into the light of the hallway: Tomas, Carla and Ben, Solomon's students. I stood still, the dorm door two strides in front of me but as far away as my camp in the woods. At least it wasn't Celso.

"Hello, Whisper. You go home? Spend Christmas under the bridge?"

Ben giggled. Carla crossed her arms over her chest. I looked down at the floor.

"And what is up with that stupid veil?" Tomas said. He drank from a bottle in his hand and stood crooked, his limbs dangling and disjointed. The three of them smelled like Ofelia, fermented and poisoned. I stepped back.

"Where you going?" Tomas said, closing the distance between us, his black hair a shadow across his face, his eyes red-rimmed and bloodshot. Carla stood beside Tomas. Ben loomed behind them, tall, gangly, red-haired and smirking.

"We want to know what you're hiding, what you've got under there. Solomon thinks you're some kind of miracle. We think you're creepy." I took another step back, my breath coming in short bursts.

The wall was against my back. Tomas stepped closer. Carla and Ben flanked him. My hand reached up to my neck and clasped the violin made by Jeremia, squeezing until the edges poked into my palm.

"Show us what you got." Tomas reached up, pushed back the cowl of my hood, his hand clumsy and hot, and yanked my veil off my head, dropping it on the floor. I squinted from the sudden light in my eyes.

All three of them stepped back.

"Whoa," Tomas said.

I looked at them, not avoiding their gaze, and set my jaw as I'd seen Candela do. My hands no longer shook, and my breath began to slow. Tomas gaped, his nose pulled up in disgust. Carla's hand impulsively moved to her face, where she touched her lips, her nose, her perfect features. Ben stumbled backward, turned and strode down the hallway.

I stepped forward. I felt the power that this face could wield in a dimly lit hallway with no one around. My breath deepened, my jaw tightened, my shoulders tensed, and then I stepped toward them again, my feet moving as though with a will of their own, and I pulled my mouth into a half smile as I watched Tomas and Carla back away from me. I made a final rush at them, my fingers reaching for them but still clamped tightly around Jeremia's carved violin. Too late, I felt the string around my neck stretch taut and snap. I let go, and the hand-carved violin dropped through my coat to the carpet of the hallway and I stepped on it, snapping the carving in two. Tomas and Carla ran, following Ben, and I stumbled, crying out. I knelt and rocked back and forth. Ofelia's shuddering breaths, heard through the thin walls of Purgatory Palace, now became mine, and I sobbed.

Twenty-One

I stopped wearing the veil. I remembered the night in jail with Lizzy, swearing to myself that I would never end up as she had, but I didn't know where that strength had come from. It was not strength that allowed me to get rid of the veil; it was the knowledge that those three students had already told everyone what my face looked like, and if I didn't reveal my true face, soon the rumors would have me looking so hideous that I would lose any credibility I might have had. So I showed my face, but I was not proud to do so.

When and where to wear the veil had been chosen for me this far—Belen made me wear it, Celso made me wear it, playing my violin in the streets forced me to take it off, this school required that I wear it again, the students chose to remove it. When would the decision be mine to make? The only place where I could be who I was without hiding was Purgatory Palace, but even there I felt like an outsider.

I had a scholarship; I went to the university. What did the other residents have? If the building sold, they wouldn't even be able to call themselves residents.

At my first music lesson in January, Solomon watched me closely. I sat in the metal chair and picked at the violin strings with the first finger of my left hand.

"Why did you remove the veil?" he asked.

I didn't think he wanted to hear the answer.

"Well, no matter. Now I can see your beautiful eyes." He placed his fingertips together, his elbows on the arms of his chair, and tapped his first fingers against his lip. "Dr. Ruiz would like to see you again. Have you given that any thought?" The card from Dr. Ruiz was in my pocket always, a constant reminder that a decision should be made. How could I not think about this? How can the lone wolf not always think about protecting itself?

"She told me that you probably suffer from a great many earaches."

"I'm used to them," I said. "And I haven't had one since I've been at the university." I didn't tell him that I would gladly accept them back again if it meant returning to my home in the woods.

"The surgery would alleviate eating difficulties."

"True." Nothing he mentioned was a new thought. But you don't just change the most defining physical characteristic about yourself without repercussions. Oscar's new legs didn't change who he was. He was still a reject, and his friends understood that—he could take those legs off whenever he wanted and fit in with others who were less than whole. If I had surgery, it couldn't be undone. If my deformities disappeared,

Whisper would be gone—Whisper of the forest, the creek, the camp in the woods. I didn't know if I could be Whisper of the greater world.

Solomon clapped his hands together.

"For now we play. Let's hear your recital piece."

I sat up in the chair, lifted the violin to my shoulder, lowered my chin, closed my eyes and played the song of Whisper when she had known who she was and where she belonged.

The auditorium where our final performance would be held was large enough to hold a thousand people—enough for most of the school population to attend, along with their families. More people in one place than I had ever seen. I walked through the side door, found myself on the stage and held my breath. It was bigger than the meadow with the deer and so dim from lack of sunshine that I shivered. The second level also contained seats and boxes, where people could sit, hold binoculars to their eyes and watch the performers on the stage through special lenses that would magnify defects. I felt like a mouse standing on that stage and wanted to crawl back to my dorm room, curl under the covers and clutch the broken violin in my hands.

We would perform that night. Before the performance, we tested the sound in this large, open space. I wondered how anyone would hear me with so much air to dissolve my song, but Solomon said that the music would wing its way to the far corners of the room and fill hearts with beauty.

Perhaps hearts, but certainly not eyes.

The other students were giddy with nervousness. They tried to appear solemn and serious while they tuned their instruments, but they laughed shrilly and then glanced about, listening to their laughter bounce around the room. Tonight much of the school—and more of the world than I cared to acknowledge—would fill this space and watch me. My only hope was that I would be so tiny on the stage, so minuscule in the great open space and oppressive air, they wouldn't even be able to see my distorted features, that I would be as insignificant as the whirr of a hummingbird's wings.

We played bits of our pieces, listened to the acoustics, tuned our instruments and then played again for the people who operated the sound booth. They adjusted this and that and then asked us to play our songs again. My violin felt weak and small. I had always felt its power before, but here in this great space, its power was a thin trickle of smoke dispersed through the air.

Tomas and Carla, along with Max, Sara and Rita, huddled around Solomon after the rehearsal. They gestured with their hands and glanced in my direction. I knelt in the corner of the stage, put my violin into the case, strapped the case to my back and stood. Solomon walked to me, his heavy footsteps echoing through the room. He pulled at his chin with his left hand.

"Whisper," he said.

A tingling started in my nose. I would not cry here, in front of these students who wanted me to be embarrassed and humiliated. Why did they hate me so? I didn't understand what I had done. I tried to summon the strength I had felt in the jail, the desire to change my life, to be different from

Lizzy, to shape for myself a different fate and to choose when I would wear the veil and when I would remove it.

"I'll wear the veil," I whispered.

Solomon placed a finger under my chin and lifted my face so that I looked up into his.

"The choice is yours," he said. "The beauty of your music surpasses any of theirs."

Me or them. Them or me. Always separated and alone. I would play my song. I would lose myself in my own music, but the audience would not see me. They would see a veil, a mystery, a disguise. In some ways I felt relief, but I was embarrassed to admit this even to myself.

∽

When I walked down the dorm hallway and heard shuffling beneath the stairs, my shoulders tensed, and I strained to hear even more. A small whimper worked its way out of my mouth. Either it was Celso or the other students had come to torment me—today, the day of the recital. I couldn't endure the tormenting today.

I heard rustling, whispering. I hurried the last few feet, running past the darkness beneath the stairs, inserted the key, turned it in the lock, opened the door and slammed it shut behind me. The bolt clicked beneath my hand and I stepped back, watching the door as though it might open on its own, even a lock not enough to protect me from tormentors. I heard no sound but my own panting.

I inhaled through my mouth and felt my breath begin to calm. Then I heard a knock on the door. Maybe if I made no sound, whoever was out there would leave, would think I was asleep, would think I had slipped out the window, leapt into the sky and been blown away by the wind.

The knock came again—a timid knock, a gentle knock, a knock that was low, halfway up the door, and not pounding or demanding. I stepped to the door, peeked through the tiny peephole and saw nothing. Whoever was knocking on the door must be short, must be below my eye level, must be Candela. The possibility that it might be someone I wanted to see felt startling and stilled my twisting hands.

I unlocked the bolt, feeling how slick with sweat my hands had become, and pulled the door open.

For a minute I stared at the figure in the hallway, trying to understand what I was seeing. Then I kneeled, wrapped my arms around her and squeezed so tightly I thought maybe she could become part of me.

"Eva."

"We found you," she said. Her round warm cheek pushed against mine.

I heard more shuffling beneath the stairs, looked into the darkness and saw a shape emerge, a larger shape with a missing arm. I stood, lifting Eva into my arms even though she was getting big.

He had changed. He was lanky and thin, his frame inches taller than I remembered it, even though I had only been gone for three months. His face was different too—longer, less babyish, more angular, with a few prickles sprouting from his chin in sparse patches. His eyes were wary, darting, like those of a trapped animal, and he held Ranita tightly against his chest, wrapped in a piece of cloth. The deep, dark circles under his eyes were also new.

We looked hard at each other. Jeremia stepped from foot to foot, tiptoeing, tense, ready to run back to his shelter or wherever he had come from.

"I missed you," I said.

"We've needed you," he replied. He touched my cheek with the tip of his finger and then jerked away when the front door to Clarence Hall clicked open. A group of students, talking and laughing, entered the building. Jeremia shifted his weight to the left, to the right. I pushed the door to my dorm room open and hoped that he would rush inside rather than out into the shadows, an elusive deer that I would again lose. He looked at the people in the hallway and then slipped into the dorm room. I stepped in after him, still holding Eva against me, and shut the door behind us, cocooning us together once again.

I had not felt arms around my neck or the warmth of a body against mine for a very long time. I sat on my bed and held Eva against me, breathing in the dusky, tree-sap smell of her hair. She held me tightly, sniffled against my green coat, smeared the tears around her face with the back of her hand, the webbing between her fingers catching bits of water and reflecting it in the light. I loved everything about her—the webs of skin between her fingers, the unlaced shoes that needed to be stretched wide to comfortably encase her feet and even the little crusty sleepers in the corners of her eyes.

"You get to live in this enormous house?" Eva asked, her eyes wide as she looked around the room.

"I borrow this room," I said, "while I am a student here."

"But everything is so clean and new. The bed is so soft." She bounced up and down on the bed. "And look at this." She opened the drawers of the desk, shut them and opened them again.

Ranita muttered against Jeremia's chest. He jostled her up and down, up and down, and then pulled her from the strip of cloth. He held her high from the wrappings with his one arm, letting the cloth fall from her, and then he turned her around. She gazed out, her eyes large and black, and then suddenly she smiled. The smile stretched from ear to ear and was such a surprise, such a startling flash of light across her face, that I laughed. Jeremia jerked his head, looking at me with furrowed brows. His eyes lost their intensity, and for a minute I thought he might actually sit down, but instead he leaned against the desk, his body bowed, as supple as a new sapling. I didn't know where he planned to go, but he certainly didn't want to stay.

Eva's face was smeared with grime, the kind of dirt that takes time to accumulate. Shadows like half-moons lay under her eyes, her mouth trembled and twisted, and I could see her cheekbones where I should have seen rounded cheeks. I set her down on the bed and went to the cupboard for food—bread, crackers, small bottles of water. I gave the bread to Jeremia, the crackers to Eva and a bottle of water to each.

Before feeding himself, Jeremia pulled off a soft piece of bread and placed it in Ranita's mouth. Her eyes became intense, dark, her mouth pulled tight, and she sucked on the ball of bread. Her hands came out and grabbed at Jeremia's fingers, and he gave her another soft piece. She was barely four months old. I'd missed almost three of those months. Eva shoved crackers into her mouth without chewing them.

"Slow," I said. She crammed another cracker into her mouth and then smiled, bits of cracker falling from between her lips. I shook my head.

"We thought you were dead," Jeremia said. He leaned against the desk, eating great bites of the bread. "Celso said you didn't pay him."

"What happened?" I asked.

Eva's eyes became big, and her cheeks squeezed up. Large drops spilled onto the crackers in her hands. She sobbed once. I slid next to her, put my arm around her and looked at Jeremia.

"They came on Christmas. The middle of the day. Three men this time—your father and mine and your uncle. Your father only watched. The boys weren't there." Ranita's hands stretched before her again, and she opened and closed her fists. Jeremia gave her a small piece of bread. Her fingers squeezed it, smashing it into pulp, and then she shoved it toward her mouth, open like a baby bird's.

Jeremia didn't look at me. He looked somewhere over my shoulder, his eyes examining the wall behind my bed. I watched the top of his left cheek twitch.

"They told us where you were, that you'd gone to the city and were working for them. They told us you had disappeared, that you hadn't held up your side of the deal and now they were coming to fulfill their promise."

Eva watched Jeremia so hard, creases formed between her eyes.

"They poured gasoline on our huts, on our supplies, on our sitting logs, and when I tried to stop them, Nathanael told me to go, to run to the city and find you. Jun wasn't there to destroy the camp—he was there to get rid of the past. My father wanted me dead."

Jeremia focused on my face now. The scared look was gone, the haunted look had disappeared, and what I saw now were liquid-filled eyes so brown and disturbed that I felt my own eyes filling with tears in response. He lifted his chin, where a gash just under his jaw snaked red and inflamed against the brown skin of his neck.

"So I left with the little ones," he whispered. "We hid from Jun and slipped silently through the forest. I left Nathanael. He's dead, and they'll come for us here."

His voice cracked when he said this. I slipped off the bed, took three steps and enclosed both him and Ranita in my arms. He lowered his head to my shoulder, and with my hands on his back, I could feel the rasping of his breath.

"But you saved the little ones, Jeremia. Look how far you've come," I said.

As I held Jeremia, I was not sure what to feel. Nathanael had died in a fire at the hands of Celso and Jun. I felt the horror of it, but I also felt the heat of anger, seeping from my chest to all the parts of my body, and the determination I had felt in the jail cell. My biological family had done this—my own uncle. While my father watched. This was my fault. If I had paid them the money I owed them in mid-December, none of this would have happened. And now they would certainly come for me.

Jeremia's breathing calmed, and he sat down on the chair by the desk. I crouched on the floor beside him, my right arm around Eva, my left hand on Jeremia's arm, his muscles tight with tension.

"We've been looking for you for a long time," Eva said. "We walked through the forest, we walked through the smell, we freed the animals, we came to the city, we asked a boy with no legs where to find you, he told us to go to that hotel, and we asked there about you. This lady who was my size"— Eva stood when she said this and held her hand up to her head—"told us you were up here."

Jeremia leaned his head back. The twitch was gone from his cheek. His arm drooped, and I took Ranita from him. She cooed and babbled. I touched her nose against mine.

"Sleep," I said to Jeremia. He didn't resist.

He was seventeen and the head of the family. He lay down on the bed, rolled toward the wall and within seconds was asleep. Eva curled up against his back and smiled at me as her eyes drooped. Ranita's thumb made its way into her mouth and then she too began to close her eyes.

The camp was gone. I could never return there. I felt no surprise about this nor did I feel fear. I'd already lost that camp, but now that my family was here, I didn't care where I lived. Somehow, together, we would make it work.

Twenty-Two

I woke up and glanced around the room, feeling lost and disoriented. The winter evening held no light, and only a small crack under the door allowed a yellow beam into the room. Eva snored slowly on the bed, Ranita breathed sweet baby breath into the room, and I couldn't hear Jeremia's breathing at all. A tickle, a feeling of unrest, told me I needed to be somewhere.

Standing quickly, I moved to the bathroom with Ranita still in my arms. I gathered three towels, shaped them into a nest, placed them on the floor near the bed where Jeremia and Eva would see her when they awoke, and tucked Ranita into the cozy nest. Then I shut myself in the bathroom and splashed water on my face.

The recital was soon. The reflection of my face in the mirror didn't calm the twitching nerves in my stomach. I considered waking Jeremia, Eva and Ranita, taking them with me, but I knew that walking them into the huge auditorium would only terrify them. They didn't cross between societies. They didn't wear the veil. This was a moment I must face on my own. I considered not showing up, disappearing like the sound of a whisper, but I couldn't do that to Solomon after all he'd done for me.

I dried my cheeks, brushed my hair, straightened my sweater and felt something crinkle beneath my hand. I removed the slip of paper from my pocket. I placed the card on the counter next to the sink and looked at it. It was a plain card, white with blue ink. Dr. Susan Ruiz's name was small and unassuming, but the possibilities behind the card were as weighty as oak.

I opened the door a crack, collected my violin, strapped it to my back and tucked the broken pieces of Jeremia's violin into my sweater pocket. I clipped a note on the mirror and was about to leave when I glanced again at my reflection. My finger moved up to my mouth, pushed at the slit and gaps in my lip, watching as my gums and teeth showed through the gap, revealing the inner workings of the body that were supposed to remain concealed. This was who I was and what I looked like and what I'd always been, but that could change with surgery. And it could change for Ranita.

I loosened the black veil from around my neck and, with it in hand, walked out the door of the dormitory.

The other musicians already stood backstage in crisp white shirts, elegant black dresses and polished shoes. The first to play—Ben, Tomas, Carla and Michelle—were already onstage. When Solomon saw me, he strode toward me and placed an arm around my shoulders.

"Thank God," he said. "You came."

I pushed my face into his tweed coat. He smelled of mint. Solomon held me away, leaned down so our faces were level and looked into my eyes.

"You will be magnificent."

"I won't," I said. "I can't do this."

"Of course you can. If you can do this on a street corner with raw, stiff hands, you can do this here, where everyone came to hear you."

"They didn't come to hear me, they came to hear them." I glanced at Tomas and Carla onstage.

"But you are the one worth listening to."

I slipped the veil over my head. Solomon patted my shoulder, but he didn't smile. His great cheeks sagged, became jowly and heavy.

As the other students played, I listened, the notes like butterflies flitting around the room. I heard the nervousness in Ben's bow—the cello voice fluttering with his hands. I heard the tension in Tomas's violin—the emotion flat. I heard the anxiety in Carla's viola—the notes rushed, ahead of the beat. I breathed deeply and thought of Eva's arm wrapped around my neck. I thought of how it felt to hold Ranita against my chest, and the way Jeremia's body felt when his breathing rasped in him. There was beauty in my life, and that part mattered more than standing on this stage ever would.

When it was my turn, Solomon placed his arm around my shoulders. Together we walked out to the stage, and I felt for a moment as though I had a father. We walked past the grand piano and around the quartet of set-up chairs.

We stood at the front of the stage, only a metal music stand in front of us. I watched my feet as Solomon moved the stand to one side. The shuffling, the soft whispers, the brushing of feet against the floor echoed sporadically through the space like cricket chirps in the night. Solomon spoke loudly.

"Whisper Gane is the newest member of our string section here at the university. She is also our youngest member. She says very little but allows the music she has composed to speak for her. Please welcome her with me."

Solomon stepped away from me. I heard him walk across the stage toward the piano. He stopped there, in the crook of the grand piano, and crossed his arms over his chest.

I stared down at my feet, at my new black boots that clicked when I walked. I looked at the brown skirt from Randall and Burns that reminded me of a lost mother and trees in the forest. I listened to the sound of my breath.

I raised my head and looked out into the auditorium. The lights, brilliant orbs too white for sunlight, were blinding, but the gauzy black veil dampened the effect. I raised my violin to my shoulder, rested my chin against it, fitted my bow to the strings and closed my eyes.

No longer was I standing in front of hundreds of people who wondered why I wore a veil. I was in the woods, under the trees, by the creek and with my family, but the huts were no longer there, the smell of smoke burned through the air, the birds so silent the emptiness hurt. This was my song. The music carried me away once again, and I lived in my head even while I stood on the stage.

The song ended, my eyes opened, and I lowered the violin and bow, my arms trembling. Solomon's arm settled around my shoulder, and my knees shook beneath that weight. Now was when I would faint. Now, when my song was done.

Solomon whispered against my head, spoke into my ear. "Beautiful. Perfect."

But he was all I heard. No longer did I hear shuffling. No longer did I hear echoing coughs. We stood alone.

And then I heard people shifting their weight, and a sound echoed about the room, bouncing off the walls. Applause. It was scattered and sparse but allowed me to relax my shoulders and control my dizziness. There were not nearly as many people as I had imagined—only a smattering of students, some adults who I assumed were parents, relatives and friends of the other students, and a few professors, sitting in clumps throughout the auditorium.

Solomon held me tightly, my shoulder wedged into his chest, and we stood still until the clapping slowed and the people sat. Then we walked off the stage together, and when I stood with the other musicians, I almost felt like one of them. They smiled slightly, inclining their heads. There was an excitement in the air, a giddiness, and I fluttered on the periphery. I hung there for just a minute, and then I remembered what waited for me back at the dorm. I slipped my violin into its case, squeezed Solomon's hand and walked out the side door.

Before going home, I stopped at the little shop on campus and bought bread, cheese, milk, apples, carrots and cloth diapers.

Beside the diapers were plastic pants, little pull-up pants that went over the diaper. I'd never seen these before. I bought two and laughed when they crinkled in my hand like dried leaves.

At the dorm, I gathered a bucket of ice from the machine in the hallway, dumped it into the bathroom sink and cooled the milk and cheese there. I threw my veil on the floor by the door. I snuggled Ranita against my chest, positioned the towels under my head and lay on the floor. They couldn't stay here in this dorm room, even though I wanted them to. Jeremia, with his need for space, would twitch into the corner, become furtive as an animal. Ranita needed care—how would I take her with me to my classes, to my lessons with Solomon? And Eva. Eva was six now. She could do many things on her own but needed education, someone to teach her now that Nathanael was no longer an option.

I wasn't sure what to do, but tonight I had played my song in front of many people and I had survived.

Just as my breathing and heartbeat began to slow, a knock on the door startled me awake. My first thought was that Celso had found us and would jab his sharp knife into Jeremia's throat and sell the rest of us. But I reasoned with myself that it couldn't be him—not now, not in this place. He'd look for us at Purgatory Palace. It must be Tomas, I thought, or Carla or Max. I couldn't decide if I should open the door and stop the pounding, so it wouldn't wake Jeremia, Eva and Ranita, or if I should ignore it and hope whoever it was went away.

"Whisper, it's me, Solomon. I've got to talk to you."

I tiptoed to the door, Ranita still snoring softly against my chest. I shifted the bolt and opened the door just a crack. Solomon stood in the muted light of the hallway. His face was split in a wide grin, a grin that stretched his mustache toward his ears.

"Come, come," he said, gesturing to me.

I opened the door wider and stepped out into the hall. Solomon stretched his hands toward me but then pulled them back when he saw Ranita.

"You have a visitor. Who is this?"

"Ranita," I said.

"I didn't know you had family. Your sister, then? She looks just like you. Do you have a parent here as well? They will all want to hear my news."

Solomon stepped to the door, ready to meet any other members of my family who might be present, but I blocked his way. What would he do if he saw Jeremia and Eva sleeping in my dorm room?

"She's not really my sister."

"No? That's hard to believe. Look at her almond-shaped eyes, her widow's peak, her pointed nose. If you're not sisters, then you must be related in some other way. She's simply lovely, just like you."

That's when the room swirled around me, the light in the hall seemed to grow sharper and my ears rang. Why had I not seen it before? I remembered Belen's snarl, my brothers' shared gasps, the woman by the creek hinting that another had been born with deformities. I had a sister—a real flesh-and-blood relation whom I was responsible for. I clutched her closer to me and breathed her in. Solomon placed his heavy hand on my shoulder.

"Your life is becoming quite full. You must hear my fabulous news. Guess who was at the concert."

I shrugged and kissed the top of my sister's head.

"Ruy Climaco of the City Philharmonic, and guess who he wants to play with the symphony. Whisper Gane. You, my dear. He requested that you play the song from the recital and the orchestra will accompany you. Isn't that simply marvelous?"

Solomon jumped back and did a dance step in the middle of the hallway. His large stomach stretched and bounced against the fabric of his tweed coat. And that was when Ranita woke up. She opened her eyes, widened her mouth into a yawn and then gazed at me. My sister. She could listen to me play with an entire orchestra. I would do this. I would do this for her.

"Monday we practice with the orchestra. Your sister is welcome to join us. I will let the Resident Assistant know that you have visitors staying with you for a time."

"Do you think I can do it?" I asked.

"You?" he said. He wrapped his arms around both Ranita and me, squeezed us against his ample stomach and rubbed his chin on the top of Ranita's head. "You can do anything."

Twenty-Three

I awoke in the morning with the weight of eyes on me, and when I opened mine, I saw Jeremia watching me. Eva was still curled against his chest, her cheek on her hand. I wondered if he saw changes in me like the ones I saw in him.

Ranita's washcloth diaper had leaked—a warm rush, then a sticky residue—and my black sweater stuck to my skin. I repositioned Ranita on the towels, lifting her gently, not wanting to let go, and stood. After weeks of sleeping in a bed, the floor left stiffness in my limbs that reminded me of the jail.

Jeremia watched as I opened the closet door, pulled out the old discarded T-shirt with the big mouse on it and slipped into the bathroom. His eyes were more curious and watchful than I remembered.

The shirt was clean, laundered and dry, but I had not worn it since before Christmas, when I'd purchased my new clothes. Now, when I pulled it down over my chest, it was stretched tight, and I tugged at it so it would cover my stomach. I didn't remember it being so form-fitting.

I peered at myself in the bathroom mirror. My hair, long and black, hung straight down my back. I pulled it away from my face, pretending to secure it behind my head. The split lips became more pronounced, so I dropped my hair back around my face and over my shoulders.

He stepped into the bathroom behind me. I could feel the heat radiating from his body, and I breathed in the richness of his smell. When his hands slipped around my waist and his chin settled on the top of my head, I closed my eyes and leaned against him. He placed his lips against my neck with the lightest of touches, the lift of a dragonfly, and yet my heart pounded in response. His hands tightened around my waist, and I felt his chest muscles move against my back. Closer, I thought, I want you closer. And then I felt Eva's hand against my leg, and Jeremia pulled away.

I showed Eva the shower. She experimented with the hot and cold taps, shrieking in surprise when water spurted over her extended hand, a shockingly warm rain, and then quickly took off her clothes and stepped inside. I handed Eva the soap and a washcloth. She scrubbed her body, dirt streaking in rivulets down her arms, and then I washed her hair.

I felt Jeremia's presence behind me, the smell that made me think of the forest and cool places beneath the trees. He had found the card I'd left beside the bathroom sink.

"What is this?" He tried to hand the card back to me.

I shut the door to the shower and turned to look in the mirror. Our eyes met, but he never once looked at my misshapen lips or crooked teeth. Maybe he didn't see them anymore but saw only me.

"It's called a cleft palate," I said. "This doctor says she can fix them. Ranita's for sure because she's still a baby."

Jeremia's eyebrows drew together. "Nathanael would have told us," he said.

"Nathanael didn't know everything."

I tensed my shoulders, wondering if Jeremia would turn angry and dark. I thought of his arms around my waist, his chest against my back, and I thought of whirling, happy Jeremia at the fire. That Jeremia was not here now.

"Why would this doctor help her?" Jeremia dropped the card back beside the sink.

"Because someone fixed hers."

"Can she give me a new arm?" he said.

"No, but I think you might be able to buy a mechanical one."

His eyes widened, and his shoulders pulled back. I thought for a minute that he might smile or laugh. Instead, I heard Eva begin to sing, adding her sweet voice to the water falling over her head, and even though Jeremia didn't smile, I did.

They slept the whole day, ate a tray of cafeteria food as if they'd never had such a wonderful meal and then slept again. While they slept, I studied in the library and practiced in the practice rooms. I was learning music from the masters now, and even though I didn't read the notes well yet, I could hear a song once and repeat it almost perfectly. I practiced songs by Cavali, Albéniz, Sanz, and I began to learn different approaches, different ways to express the voice inside. I loved my hours of practice and continued them even though my family was now with me. My other classes were still a challenge, but my instructors were pleased and surprised at the improvements I was making, given my lack of formal education.

Jeremia, Eva and Ranita slept fifteen hours a day, took showers and looked out my window with its view of the campus—at the walking paths between stone buildings and the carefully placed trees that had been pruned and trimmed to look like perfect representations of themselves rather than natural forms. When they began to get restless and impatient, I knew it was time. I would take them to see the doctor on Saturday. I didn't know if she would be there, and part of me hoped that she wouldn't, but I could not put off the meeting any longer.

Dr. Ruiz's office was not far from the school. Eva skipped and sang, dancing like a firefly on the sidewalk in her orange coat, her wrists sticking out of the sleeves like chicken legs. She touched the fences we passed, gaped at the large warm houses and pointed, shrieking, when she saw a woman walking a dog. Jeremia shuffled beside me, his eyes down, his hand dug deeply into his pants pocket. He stepped around the people we passed on the sidewalk, not glancing up. It had taken a week of cajoling to convince him that a meeting with Dr. Ruiz wasn't a commitment.

I wondered what we looked like to those who passed us. The woman with the dog smiled at Eva when she saw her skipping, then held a hand to her mouth when Eva twirled on the sidewalk, her hands splayed above her head, the webbing between the fingers pink and thin. Now that I walked with my family, I had no need for the veil. I kept my head up and looked into the faces of those we passed.

Dr. Ruiz's office was not what I had imagined. I had thought it would be a bustling place with formidable glass doors, like Randall and Burns, but it was just a house of two stories with wide steps leading to the porch and a door painted deep green. I straightened my shoulders and marched up the steps, pretending that my heart and Ranita's were not beating in unison. I had to show my family that I was not afraid, that I knew what I was doing, but my hands shook and my mouth felt dry when we stood on the porch.

Eva pushed the button by the door. Then she stood, arm raised, finger pointed, eager to push the button again. Jeremia waited on the sidewalk below. We listened to footsteps moving inside the house. Both Eva and I took a step back when the door opened.

Dr. Ruiz looked different from the last time I'd seen her. She wore a lime-green shirt and pants that encased her doughy body like a cocoon, and when she saw us, she clapped her hands together and laughed. Her cheeks pushed up into soft bulges, and Eva clapped her hands in response, giggling at this caterpillar of a woman.

"Wonderful that you're here," she said. "Come in, come in."

She stepped aside and Eva followed without hesitating, her head turning as she consumed the artwork on the walls, the wood floors, the sculptures placed in the corners of the first room.

The rugs and curtains of the house were a deep burgundy with bright bits of yellow, as though they had been made from the petals of black-eyed Susans.

Jeremia, still standing on the sidewalk, watched Eva enter the house. His fist bulged in the pocket of his grimy jeans, and his shoulders hunched. He looked down the street, tensed, and I wondered if he would run, if this would be the last I would see of him. I watched, ready to chase after him if need be. Instead, a shiver ran through him, and then he stepped forward onto the stairs and entered the house.

"Bilateral cleft palates. Two of you. And the little one with syndactyly and the older with a missing appendage. Simply remarkable. Such an increase in deformities these days."

We followed Dr. Ruiz down a short hallway with two closed doors on the right and large open rooms on our left. I wanted to stand still, touch with my eyes all the beauty in the rooms, but Jeremia marched forward, looking neither left nor right, following the woman down the hallway as though headed to his execution. It was so different now. Before, I'd just worried about my own reception and had kept my face covered, but now that we were all here together, I needed to know how Jeremia was feeling and how Eva responded to the people around her. I had no time for my own emotions.

Jeremia stopped abruptly at the end of the hall. I looked into the corner between the hallway and the kitchen. There was a statue, long and thin, with smooth, separated pieces running from the top to the bottom. It was a sculpture of water, of shadow, of sunshine beams stretching through tree branches.

Dr. Ruiz looked at us from the kitchen, wondering why we'd stopped, and saw us studying the statue in the hallway. She came to stand beside us.

"Oh, I love that piece, but I'm afraid it fell after I bought it at the marketplace."

She leaned forward, turned the piece around and showed us the back. The sculpture was dented and gouged.

"If I keep it in the corner, no one can tell it's damaged," Dr. Ruiz said.

Jeremia dug into the pocket of his jeans. He pulled out a miniature sculpture very similar to the one in the corner.

Dr. Ruiz gasped. "You did these?" She flipped the miniature sculpture around in her hand. "This is exquisite." She looked up, her chubby cheeks sagging. "You are a talented young man. How did you learn to do this?"

"We had a lot of spare time. You can get pretty good with practice."

"But look at the way the wood moves like water. I've always felt that somehow the water was frozen into the wood."

Jeremia ran his finger down one of the flowing pieces of the statue. "I've gotten better. This is crude."

"Crude? I think this is a beautiful sculpture. Is your work that much better now?" She looked again at the piece in her hand. She examined it from all sides, almost smelling it. "Yes, this one is better. You're right. This one is alive." She looked up at Jeremia, her face serious. "Would you make me a new sculpture? One just like this? I'll find the wood."

I held my breath as I watched Jeremia. He ran his hand over the large sculpture in the corner, his long narrow fingers flowing with the movement of the wood.

"Yes, I'll make you a new one."

"Like this one," said Dr. Ruiz, giving the sculpture back to Jeremia.

"Somewhat similar," he said.

She clapped her hands again, grinned and giggled. "Marvelous. Simply marvelous." She skipped into the kitchen.

Dr. Ruiz bustled about, pulling mugs from the cupboard and filling them with cocoa powder and milk. She set the mugs in a microwave. All the while she chatted about her plants in the window, about the mess on the table, about how thrilled she was that we'd come.

She ushered us into chairs around the circular kitchen table. When a fat orange cat strolled into the room, Eva wrapped her arms around the animal, and the two of them curled up on the kitchen floor, the feline purring a deep rumbling murmur and Eva cooing softly to it and stroking its head. Dr. Ruiz clapped her hands and laughed again. Her lime-green clothing lit up the green of her eyes but made her pale skin look almost yellow.

"May I?" she asked.

I carefully extracted Ranita from the cloth wrapped around my chest. She opened her mouth in a wide yawn, blinked and looked at me. Then she smiled. I felt the sting of tears in my nose and impulsively held her close. The doctor's soft hands wrapped around Ranita's middle and she took my sister, holding her out in front of her.

"Look at you, precious." The doctor rubbed her nose against Ranita's. "We can fix you right up." She leaned Ranita against her shoulder and patted her back a couple of times. She didn't hold Ranita with two hands as though she were delicate and about to break, but gently bobbed her against her shoulder and snuggled her close. I realized that my hands were in the air, twitching to receive Ranita back again. I put them under the table, on my lap, where they could twitch without being seen.

"These are pictures of children and adults with the bilateral cleft palate." Dr. Ruiz pushed a large square book with a dark-blue cover into the middle of the table. She flipped open the cover and pointed to a picture encased in a plastic sleeve. It was a picture of me.

When I flipped the page and looked at the next one, the woman from the first page no longer had the splits from her nose to her mouth, nor did she have the holes beneath her nose. Her teeth did not protrude awkwardly. In the second picture, red bumpy seams had taken the place of the holes. On the next page, the seams were not as prominent, and by the fourth page, the seams were still noticeable scars running from her nose to her mouth, but they weren't swollen, and both her nose and mouth looked almost normal. I leaned over the book, examining the picture as closely as I could, wanting to know how this could happen. I wanted to push the book away, shove it across the table at this puffball of a woman who giggled and chattered like a squirrel. But at the same time I wanted to see more.

The next picture was of a baby. Ranita. Again, the splits in the face were prominent, noticeable, disfiguring and irregular. After a few pages, the baby's scars were nothing more than a fuller upper lip and thin white lines. By the last page, the child was maybe four years old and had a huge smile on her face—a perfect smile showing no gums, only clean, even teeth.

Jeremia sat beside me, breathing against my shoulder. I heard his intake of air, the speeding up of his breath as we flipped through the pages. This could be Ranita. This could be me. Eva abandoned the cat and stood between our chairs, watching the transformation as we flipped through the pages.

"Does it hurt?" she asked, looking at Jeremia. "I don't want it done to Ranita if it hurts."

"Yes," Dr. Ruiz said in her soft voice, the final *s* pulled long, "there will be some discomfort. But the baby will no longer have difficulties eating, she will no longer have the chronic earaches, she will no longer have the nasal voice. The surgery will be easiest for the baby and most difficult for Whisper."

I wanted to hold Jeremia's hand, but his fingers were held tightly to the edge of the table, and his knuckles were white. I leaned toward him, wanting to ease my arm through his, but he was as stiff as one of his sculptures. He studied Dr. Ruiz's face, examining the thin line between her nose and lip, searching her eyes to see if she was someone he could trust.

"Why did it happen?" Jeremia's mouth barely moved when he spoke.

"We're not sure. It seems that something occurs in gestation—some developmental step is skipped, and the child is born with a hole in the roof of her mouth. It is nothing anyone did or could have prevented."

Jeremia watched her as she spoke, his lips drawn tight.

"But," she continued, "there have been too many deformities in the past fifteen years—and we don't know why. There are four of you here, four from the same village, and all with various developmental traumas. Something is causing these deformities, some environmental factor, but we have not figured out what it is. Pollution? Chemicals? Contaminants in the food?" Dr. Ruiz shrugged her shoulders and patted Ranita's back.

Jeremia sat at the table, holding the mug of cocoa in his hand while Dr. Ruiz explained the procedure to us. I took quick, careful sips from the mug. My lips didn't fit against the cup, and I didn't know what might froth from my nose. The cat was now curled up against Eva on the seat of the chair. She stroked the cat and watched us, her eyebrows drawn low.

"We need to go. We need to think about this," Jeremia said, suddenly standing.

"Of course, of course. But don't think too long. The longer you wait, the harder it will be. Syndactyly can also be fixed with surgery."

Eva knew the doctor was talking about her, because she held up her fingers and tried to stretch them wide.

When Dr. Ruiz handed Ranita to Jeremia, his shoulders straightened and his arm held tight to the cooing baby. We pulled on our coats and walked to the door, saying nothing.

"We've got maybe two months before we really need to start the process," Dr. Ruiz said as she followed us down the hallway. "For the baby, do it as soon as possible."

We walked down the street slowly. Even Eva was quiet, her fingers cold and curled in mine.

"It's so much bigger than the earaches or the holes in mouths," Jeremia said. "Why would it matter if your face changed? It won't change you or the fact that you were ostracized by your family."

"But it might help Ranita belong. And Eva," I said.

"I don't want to have the surgery," Eva said. "Then I can't swim like a fish. And Ranita doesn't want it either—I can tell."

"This isn't about want," I said. "It's about need and should. Do you need the surgery? Should you have the surgery?"

"I don't need anything but you. I shouldn't have anything I don't need," Eva said, beginning to skip again.

Jeremia looked at me over Eva's head, and for a minute as quiet and fast as a heartbeat, I thought he was going to smile.

Twenty-Four

We made cheese sandwiches in the dorm room, a calming activity, mundane. Ranita lay on her nest of towels and played with her toes. Eva found my notebook and pencils and drew pictures of animals stacked on top of each other, all with large heads, stick legs and spotted bodies. Jeremia and I sat cross-legged on the floor and looked everywhere but at each other. I took the broken pieces of the violin he had carved for me from one of the desk drawers and slipped them into his hand, trying not to touch my fingertips to the palm of his hand, where sparks seemed to jump up whenever I made contact. He curled his fingers around the pieces.

We were so close to each other I could smell him, a scent that kept me leaning forward, wanting more. It was a heavy muskiness, a manness that seemed new to me even though I had smelled it in the past. If I could just sit beside him like this, feel his heat, smell his scent, I could be happy forever.

"We stayed in a barn on the way here." Jeremia pointed to the picture Eva had drawn. "She's had nightmares ever since."

"What are they?" I asked.

"Pigs. Thousands of pigs."

It had been their fourth night away from the camp. It hadn't been safe to follow the path out of the burned camp in the woods, the path that led to the village where we were from, so they had followed the creek.

They slept beneath the trees and ate roots and shriveled apples. By the fourth day they were so hungry, so cold, so tired of sleeping restlessly beneath the trees, so nauseated by the smell that rose from the creek, that when they saw the huge barns, they sneaked inside the closest building, where rows and rows of cages housed pigs—hundreds and hundreds, teeming and shrieking.

The pigs were rotten. The meat was tainted, grown from animals that were kept in enclosures so small they couldn't turn around. The pigs were so obese their legs couldn't hold their weight.

Eva began to gasp as Jeremia told me the story. I looked at her picture, at the animals stacked on top of each other, at the bent legs she had drawn and the obscenely rotund bodies. Eva pulled at her cropped black hair, covered her eyes and let out huge sobs. Jeremia pulled her to him, held her tightly against his chest.

"When we crept to the third barn, keeping to the shadows and avoiding the workers, we found the young ones. The piglets had been taken from their mothers and were fed from a machine. They squealed in a frenzy for the food."

Eva clawed at Jeremia's arm, trying to bury her face even deeper into his chest. Jeremia rocked her back and forth while she shook and uttered shuddering gasps.

"She ran through the barn, pulling open the gates, screaming at the pigs to run, to hide in the forest, to save themselves. They didn't want to leave the food at first, the round metal machine with nozzles, but Eva ran into the pens and chased them through the open gates.

"Hundreds of piglets ran out into the night. The workers ran after them to get them back. Only two workers followed us. I had to carry Eva over my shoulder and back into the forest because she wanted to free all the pigs and didn't see the danger we were in. At the trees, they caught up with us and shone their lights on us." Jeremia smiled now, a grimace that didn't reach his eyes but pulled his mouth straight. "When they saw Ranita's face, Eva's webbed hands and my missing arm, they stopped, then ran away, scared of us—the demon spirits enraging the pigs."

Eva breathed heavily, relaxing against Jeremia's chest now that the story was over. She turned her face to the side, pressing her cheek against his shirt. Her face was streaked, lined with water, and her cheeks were mottled pink and red.

"The stream was rotten there, so full of pig shit and whatever chemicals they use to get rid of the waste that we couldn't drink from it—not until we were past the town, above the barn and its rot."

Eva stood, shivering from head to toe, and returned to her picture. She started a new illustration, drawing piglets running through a field, running into the trees of the forest, and in this new picture, the sun shone brightly and the pigs had smiles on their faces. She wiped the water from her cheeks with the back of her hand.

"The stream," I said. "Could that be the reason for the crayfish with only one claw?"

Jeremia shrugged, and at the same time we looked at his shirt sleeve, which fell loose and partially empty.

Eva, Jeremia and Ranita slept most of that afternoon, as they had done since arriving at the university. Before resting, they handed me their dirty clothes through the barely opened door of the room. I told them to bolt the door until I returned from washing the clothes in the basement.

I sat on the washing machine, my chin in my hands, and tried to understand what I was supposed to do. I must take them to Purgatory Palace, I knew that—I couldn't keep them with me any longer without jeopardizing my standing at the school—but what would they do there? How would they pay for rent? Jeremia wouldn't beg, I wouldn't have Eva begging, and Ranita would not be used in such a way. Somehow, we needed to make money. My stipend from the school was not enough. What would happen when Celso showed up again? I had no doubt that he would, and every time I went outside, I searched for him.

After placing the wet clothes in the dryer and putting the coins into the slot, I walked across the cement floor to the basement bathroom, one hand against my stomach, one hand against my head. I didn't like using the bathroom down here

because it was cold, as cold as going to the bathroom behind
a log on a winter day, and it was a hard cold that crawled
up your legs and into your bones. I locked the door, lifted
my brown skirt and then pulled down the pants I had made
from my mother's slip. I gasped when I saw the stain. Rosa's
words came back to me then, her belief that when she got her
period, she was a woman and would go to the city and find
a man who would love her. And here I was, in the city, my
body becoming a woman's. I put my face in my hands and
let my tears drip between my fingers. So much loss. I wadded
up toilet paper and stuck it in my underwear. I wished my
mother or Candela were here to help me understand the
changes in my body.

It was during my lesson with Solomon the next day that I
remembered why I was attending the school, why I had abandoned my family once again and why I had risked the wrath of
Celso, which was sure to come. I had taken Jeremia, Eva and
Ranita to Purgatory Palace, where they wouldn't be trapped in
a tiny room, but I had returned to the university. I had to keep
coming back to play music. This was my voice and my story.
Without it, I had little to say and no way to say it.

When I had arrived for my lesson, my hands raw, my
eyes watering not only from the cold but from lack of sleep
and the pain of abandoning my loved ones, I had found a
man in the practice room speaking with Solomon, the two
of them filling the tiny space with their loud voices and wide
frames. The other man was younger than Solomon, less gray,

less rotund and two inches shorter. His voice boomed and his wavy graying hair swished and bounced with every turn of his head. Solomon grinned hugely when he saw me and took two large steps toward me.

"Whisper." He put his arm around my shoulders and pulled me into the room. "This is Ruy Climaco, director of the City Philharmonic."

Ruy Climaco hesitated, his smile thin and controlled. He stood in front of the metal chair nearest to the door. I wondered if he would walk out after seeing me without the veil. He tried not to stare at my mouth, but his eyes glanced, looked away, were drawn to my face again. He shook my hand with the tips of his fingers.

"You are a marvelous violinist—and a talented composer." He studied my face. I looked down, then straightened my shoulders and looked him in the eye. This man may have viewed me as mysterious and exotic the night of our recital, when I'd hidden beneath the veil, but this was me and I would not be ashamed.

His eyes faltered before mine did.

"Recording device," Solomon said, picking up a metal box and showing it to me. "Ruy wants to record your song. Then he and the orchestra will piece together the accompaniment. You will be the youngest musician ever to compose for the Philharmonic." I looked at Ruy Climaco, who still watched me surreptitiously, glancing away quickly when our eyes met.

"Can't anything be done about that?" he asked, pointing to his own lips and mouth. He wrinkled his nose and pulled his lips tight. Solomon paused and narrowed his eyes and then boomed his answer.

"Yes, but it should typically be done when the child is still an infant. We are not yet sure what Whisper's decision will be concerning surgery for her cleft palate."

Ruy Climaco and I watched each other. Solomon looked back and forth between us.

"Well, shall we begin?" Solomon said.

I was not sure I wanted to give anything to this man whose mouth twitched when he looked at me and whose pride radiated from him as sharp as the needles on a porcupine. Solomon placed a hand on my back. I would do this for him, because of his kindness, but I did not and would not like this man who could not control the obvious disgust he felt for me. I sat in one of the chairs, unsnapped my violin case, fit the violin under my chin and began to tune the strings. The three of us formed a rough triangle, and I leaned toward Solomon. Solomon prepared the recording device, setting it on his knee.

This man would not get the song of Whisper, the song of my home, the creek, Nathanael and crayfish. No, he would get a different song, because in his presence I felt none of the happiness my camp in the woods deserved. Instead, I played the song of Purgatory Palace, with its discordant notes that spoke of Ofelia, its jerking low to high notes that told the story of the inhabitants, and its unresolved ending that hinted at our unfulfilled lives. My eyes closed, my heart slowed, and the confusion of not belonging entered the room.

When I finished and opened my eyes, both men were watching, Solomon with a smile, Ruy with a frown. Solomon pushed a button on the recording device and the soft *shush* ended.

"That's not the same song," said Ruy Climaco.

I lowered the violin to my lap.

"I expected the song you played at the recital." One of Ruy's legs rested over the knee of the other. The foot of the upper leg rocked with the twitching of the toe. "I had heard that you were a compliant young woman who would be honored and flattered to play with the Philharmonic. What I see here is a stubborn and sullen girl who does not recognize an honor and gift when it is handed to her. Do you even know what I am offering you, child? What it means to play with the Philharmonic? Musicians pray for this chance, and most will never achieve it, and yet you flaunt it in my face as though you, a freakish and defective child, were too good for this opportunity."

Solomon reached over and touched Ruy on the shoulder. Ruy flinched.

"What does it matter which song she plays? They're all astonishing."

Ruy crossed his arms over his chest. His eyes were narrowed, his lips pursed together so tightly that little creases appeared around his undefective mouth.

"That may be so, but I need consistency if my orchestra is to accompany her. I haven't seen consistency here. I also need someone I can work with, not some demented diva." He waved his arm around in the air. His foot twitched.

"Play it again, Whisper," Solomon said. "Just like before."

I raised the violin to my shoulder, rested my chin on it and considered playing a completely different song, but I couldn't do that to Solomon. I played the song of Purgatory Palace once again.

When I finished, Ruy picked up the recording device, stood, swished his hair away from his shoulders and looked down his nose at me. While he appraised me, I met his look and did not turn away.

"You are hardly the child I imagined under that veil."

"And you are not the man I would have envisioned at the head of a great and honorable symphony."

Solomon clapped his hands together loudly, and both Ruy and I jerked away from each other to look at him.

"Then you shall continue to surprise each other as you work together."

"We will see if I can do anything with this disjointed piece," Ruy said. He opened the door to the practice room, and Solomon followed him out. I clutched the violin and bow in my hands. In a way, he was right. I didn't care about standing on a stage in front of an audience of thousands. It meant little to me except that it allowed me to play my songs and might ease my family's hard life. His vision of the music did not match my own, and I would not give away my songs carelessly. The music was my voice, my life. It was mine to share with whom I chose.

Ruy and Solomon talked in whispers outside the door, but their words crept along the floor and into the room. "She can't stand on the stage in front of thousands of upper-class, money-paying patrons without modesty. She will have to cover that face."

"She will do so, Ruy."

"She covers that face or she does not play. Understand?"

My back was tense, rigid, my hands still squeezing the violin, trying to wring blood from my mother's present, when Solomon murmured a slow yes and then returned to the practice room. He entered the room, adjusted his tweed coat and placed his hand on my shoulder.

"Marvelous playing, Whisper, simply marvelous. Ruy found it astonishing."

I placed the bow across my knees and reached up to touch the violin around my neck. It was gone, broken, and instead I touched my veil, which warmed my neck but spoke of secrets and masks. I liked Solomon. I trusted him. He had accepted me as I was, but he was taking Ruy's side in this, which made me feel wary and alone.

I withdrew everything I had from the bank, gave it to Candela to pay for rent and then wondered what I would do to pay for their stay after that. Seven days they could stay—seven days, and then they would be homeless again. I might have to return to the coffee shop with Candela, sit on the corner and keep every penny that came to me.

In the mornings, Ofelia was rarely around, so Jeremia, Eva and Ranita could wander the building at will, play games in the common room, eat the shared food and meet the other inhabitants, but in the afternoons they walked the twenty blocks to the university and came to visit me. I waited, impatient and nervous, until I heard Eva's light step and Jeremia's wary tread. I brought them to my room, fed them food from the cafeteria and kept them safe while I attended my afternoon and evening classes. In this way, they saw a bit of the city, weren't completely trapped in the tiny rooms and avoided Ofelia while also avoiding the campus monitors who sometimes patrolled the university greens at night.

These were not good options and didn't provide solutions to Jeremia's pacing, Eva's twirling or Ranita's crying. I didn't know how long we could manage this arrangement. We were being watched by some of the other students in the dorm. By Friday, when Dr. Ruiz came to my room, we were sniping at each other, our muscles twitching beneath the skin. Jeremia hadn't slid his arms around my waist since that first day.

"Oh my," she said, dropping a large log to the floor in the hallway. She leaned her hand against the door frame and breathed in gulps, her doughy cheeks pink and mottled. "I've got three more in the car." She leaned on Eva's shoulder and dragged herself into the room, sitting heavily on the bed.

Jeremia and I walked to her car and carried the pieces of wood into the dorm room, where Jeremia examined them carefully, scrutinizing their durability and quality. Dr. Ruiz stayed on the edge of my bed, her breath shallow and uneven. She tried to smile at us, but her cheeks sagged and her breath still came in gasps.

Eva stood on the flat end of one of the maple logs, then raised one leg. "Look at me," she said.

"One of these is for my sculpture," Dr. Ruiz said. "The other three, I thought you might be able to use."

Jeremia extracted a jackknife from his pocket, leaned down to one of the logs and whittled into its side. A long sliver fell off the edge, the wood underneath a smooth, deep brown with lighter streaks that pointed like lightning bolts through the grain.

"And what have you decided?" Dr. Ruiz folded her hands together in her lap and squeezed her legs close together, reminding me of an owl—perched, collected, observant.

Jeremia and I looked at each other. His head lowered once, a quick nod, and I returned the gesture. We hadn't talked about it, but we hadn't needed to. There was no question, even though I felt guilt at knowing the answer. Jeremia and I would always walk the line between accepted and not, but that didn't have to be the case for the little ones.

"Ranita," I said.

Dr. Ruiz clasped her hands together and beamed.

"Wonderful. I will secure the funds, and she will stay at the clinic, at my house. You are welcome to stay with her, of course. How old is she?"

"Four months," Jeremia said.

"Then we'll start in three months. That gives me time to prepare."

Dr. Ruiz stood abruptly and marched to the door. She threw it open, startling the two students standing there, Tomas and Carla. They looked over their shoulders at us, both with smirks on their faces, and then turned and ran.

"Huh." Dr. Ruiz placed her hands on her hips. She observed the other students in the hallway, who looked our way but didn't speak or stepped to the other side of the hallway when passing the room.

"Or you may stay with me now, if need be. Please let me know." She clasped her handbag between both hands and took short, quick steps down the hallway, saying "Shoo" to anyone who looked at her or us. I watched her all the way down the hallway and smiled as I shut the door.

"Ranita will have the surgery?" Eva still stood on the top of the log. With the added height, she was taller than me. "Ranita won't have openings between her nose and mouth?

But it will hurt her." Her eyes filled up with tears. I felt my own eyes doing the same, even though I'd been smiling the moment before. What if this was the wrong decision and instead of improving Ranita's life, we ruined it? Who was I to make this decision for another person? Nathanael would have known what to do.

"Remember the porcupine?" I asked, taking Eva's hands in mine and squeezing, watching the extra skin between her fingers wrinkle and fold. "Remember how painful it was to pull out the quills? But afterward, your hand became better, right?" I turned her hand over and looked at her palm. The scars were mere pinpricks of red, like almost-forgotten flea bites. "The surgery will hurt at first, but Ranita will be very brave, and afterward she won't have earaches and she'll be able to eat normally, without food getting stuck in the opening to her palate."

Eva looked at me with her eyes narrowed. She was not ready to believe, but she was considering.

Twenty-Five

There was a tension in the air, and I had a pretty good idea what it was about. Any minute now, Celso would leap out from between the buildings and slice at us with his knife.

When we knocked on the door to Purgatory Palace, it took a long time for anyone to answer, and I wondered if my fears about Celso might be true. Jeremia stood with his back to the door, resting his foot on the log, which he'd carried on his shoulder from the university. We'd come in the early evening, and Ofelia was usually awake and on the prowl by this time of the day. Maybe we wouldn't be able to get in without her catching us. I was about to give up, about to squeeze into the alleyway and knock on Candela's window, when the door opened a crack and Candela peeked out at us.

"Shh," she said, glancing behind her into the hallway.

Candela pulled the door open and we rushed down the hall to room 13, but we were not quick enough.

Ofelia appeared at the top of the stairs, and she saw me pushing Eva through the doorway into the room.

"You," she screamed and rushed down the last few steps. I closed the door behind Eva and stood in front of it. Jeremia was in, Eva was in, Ranita was quiet.

"You are a thief," she said, her face inches from mine. Red blotches stood out from the skin on her face, deep raspberries of color. "How many people are in there? How many? And what are you paying?"

Red and gray wisps of hair flew around her face, scattered and crazed. I could see the pink of her scalp through the strands of hair. She pushed her face so close to mine that the thin red veins running up and down her nose became ribbons of color. She smelled of sickness. I protected Ranita with my arms, wrapping them around her as she snuggled against me in the cloth wrap.

Candela stood next to me, and when Ofelia balled her hands into fists, Candela bumped against me, sliding me out of the way.

"You are all robbing me. I let you live here, all of you, for almost nothing, for less than you would be charged anywhere else, and what do you do to me? You act like you care about me and then abandon me."

She shrieked the last two words, and they screamed through the hallway like unleashed demons. I flattened my back against the door to room 13, wrapped my arms more tightly around Ranita and turned my face to the side.

Ofelia placed her hands in front of her face and cried in loud, shrieking gusts. Candela put her hand on Ofelia's lower back and guided her to room 1. Candela followed her into the room, shutting the door behind both of them. For a while I heard ranting, then murmuring voices, then nothing. My heart calmed in proportion to the noise, and when Candela finally emerged, my eyes had grown droopy and my head had started to nod.

Candela's face was puffy, her eyes red. She leaned beside me and then slumped to the floor. I slid down the door and sat beside her.

"How the hell am I supposed to fix everything around here?" She had a wet patch on her shoulder as though someone had left a stain of tears. "Ofelia's son finally told her that he doesn't want her staying with them. She's been asking to live with them for years. She's been sending him money since she first bought this place. Now he won't take her in. She's not even sure she'll sell Purgatory Palace anymore. She has to find somewhere else to stay first."

I rubbed small circles on Ranita's back through the fabric of my coat. She stirred and gurgled. I thought about that—a family abandoning an adult, someone without a blemish, though I knew that Ofelia was one of those people with blemishes on the inside.

"What will she do?"

"What we all do when we're abandoned by our families. Make new ones. Endure."

Ranita began to squirm, and her muffled cries could be heard from between the buttons of my coat. I opened my coat and she peeked out, her face happy, curious. Candela held her hand out to Ranita, and Ranita grabbed her first finger. She tugged at it, squeezed it tightly.

"You're the luckiest of us all, you know," Candela said to me.

Ranita blew bubbles and gave soft squeals against my chest. I had my family, that was true, but I didn't know for how long.

∽

Candela started an IOU for Jeremia, Eva and Ranita's stay. She said that when Jeremia sold his sculptures, he could pay the bill. I didn't like to owe, but we couldn't pay, and for some reason, I didn't feel right about taking Dr. Ruiz up on her offer of a place to stay. I hardly knew her, and Jeremia would feel just as caged there as anywhere else.

Every day I had to be at Solomon's office by four in the afternoon, when he would drive me downtown to the grand auditorium. On the outside, the building sat low and round like a fossilized hat, hunkering between rectangular buildings that jutted into the sky, but the inside of the auditorium was rich with reds and golds and was layered with ornate seats that leaned out over the stage. I stood to the right of the orchestra and played the song of Purgatory Palace again and again and again.

The violinists of the orchestra wouldn't look at me. The woman in the first chair sighed loudly when I got ahead of the beat and snorted when I forgot that they were keeping pace with me, trying to match my uneven song. Playing with them was much more difficult than I had imagined it would be. I had to hold each note the same number of beats each time, as though I were a trained cricket. I couldn't slow down or speed up to change my interpretation but had to consistently play the song at the same tempo, the timing perfect. It was like catching crayfish in the stream.

"God," the second violin player said to the first, "I can't believe they let people who look like that just walk around."

I stood on the stage, set apart from the others in a way that was meant to honor and emphasize but instead separated me even more than usual, my misshapen features highlighted and further exposed.

"You lead us, Whisper," Ruy Climaco said, "but it is not a stampede. Again." I lifted the violin to my chin and began at the place in my song that spoke of creeping between pots in the town square, but it was difficult to begin there—the music was my story, and how can someone begin halfway through a story? So I paused, stopped and lost the beat. Ruy threw down his baton and raised his hands into the air as though offering up a prayer.

"This is a disaster. She cannot lead us when she forgets the song herself. Why did I think this would work?" He leaped off the stage and stomped down one of the aisles, his hair bouncing. I looked at the orchestra, wondering if they would leave as well, but they remained, some lowering their instruments to the stage.

We waited so long, I sat down as well, crossed my legs and closed my eyes. When I opened them again, Ruy Climaco was walking back down the aisle. He climbed onto the stage and picked up the conductor's stick.

"Again."

He stormed out almost every day, and we would take a break. Then he would rush back in with new instructions and make us do it all over again. In this way, the music took shape, and soon his theatrics mellowed, came less and less often, and every now and then he even smiled.

Sometimes the music sounded beautiful—complete, like the music of my life—but I was so exhausted by the end of each practice session that I returned to my room unable to complete the homework for my remedial classes and unable to do anything with my family but sit, hold Ranita and watch Jeremia as he whittled the wood. Sometimes they walked back to Purgatory Palace without me. I had never been so tired in my life, not even plodding behind a mule on my way to this city.

And I dreamed of the music all night, seeing the notes piled up in layers. Each day seemed to begin before the one before had ended, and I slept, woke, waited, practiced and then did it all over again. I was ready for the concert to end, for Ranita's surgery to be done, for answers to come so I'd know where my family would be, how we would survive and how we would stay together. It felt as though we were waiting for something, but I didn't know what that something was, and the more we waited, the more unsure I felt.

It was a Thursday, a week before my concert, when I woke up from a horrid dream feeling panicked and shaken, even though I couldn't remember what the dream was about. I had practice that afternoon, a practice I couldn't miss, but I dressed and ran the twenty blocks to Purgatory Palace, only stopping once to catch my breath. The sky was gray and cold, still enclosing the city in winter—fewer people were on the streets these days. Windows were shut, warmth was kept inside, and the women who walked the streets had gone to bed. Only the cars roared, adding their blue smoke to the gray of the sky and making me cough as I ran.

Jeremia, Eva and Ranita were eating breakfast in the common room, and they looked up, surprised, when I sat down next to them. I picked up Ranita, smelled her sweet smell and nodded at her smile. I turned Eva's face to the side, back and forth, examining her for sickness, but nothing seemed out of place, and when I saw Jeremia's raised eyebrow, I began to feel foolish.

"What's wrong with you?" he said.

"I don't know." Trying to ignore the unrest I felt in my chest, the little raised prickles on my arm, the nervous energy that indicated a storm was coming, I glanced around the room and saw nothing out of the ordinary. Winston served the oatmeal, Candela and Oscar leaned close together, whispering and holding hands, Sonja glared, stuck out her tongue and wagged it at me. Nothing seemed wrong, but I felt that at any moment the sky would open up and swallow us whole.

We walked back to the university early because I wanted them with me, even though I couldn't explain why. They settled into my dorm room, Jeremia whittling on the log we'd kept in the dorm room, bits of wood flipping through the air like sparks, Eva taking a long hot shower—her favorite thing to do—and Ranita rolling across the floor, gurgling and shrieking. I couldn't shake my unease but paced the room, determined not to leave even when the time came for practice, but Solomon showed up at the door and convinced me to go downtown.

I practiced with the orchestra, but all through the rehearsal my stomach twisted inside me, and every shadow on the stage felt like a waiting threat. My chest ached as though I'd swallowed something too large, and my hands trembled. I didn't understand. We had two months before Ranita's surgery, I had a week before the concert, my family was healthy and well. What was wrong with me?

It was when we walked back to Purgatory Palace that evening that my premonition became reality. As we arrived at the building, a crowd of people was standing outside, listening to the crashes and shrieks that came from inside. I knew that what we'd dreaded for weeks had finally come to be. A mule stood tethered to a shriveled stump of a tree. The mule stretched his head to the ground as he ignored the people around him and searched for bits of grass.

I waited for a minute with the others on the street, Ranita strapped to my chest, Eva holding Jeremia's hand, but I knew this was about me and that I would have to face whatever tornado whirled through Purgatory Palace. I looked at the people around me and saw Winston, Sonja, Maria and Selene, but I didn't see Candela, Oscar or Ofelia.

I pushed my way through the crowd in front of the door and ran up the two steps to enter the building, Jeremia just a step behind me. We passed Ofelia's room, where the door, torn off its hinges, lay like a broken arm in front of the doorway. Her room was in disarray—tapestries tattered and ripped, lamps scattered in shards on the floor, her bed off its frame, overturned. Bottles of alcohol were scattered every-where, the glass glittering like a trail of icicles.

The doors to the other rooms had been completely removed and were leaning across the hallway. Whenever we glanced into the rooms, we saw destruction—dismantled beds, broken dressers, tossed clothing. In Candela's room, her beautiful caricatures lay in fragments, our torn and damaged faces peering up at us.

The common room, so huge and wide, so able to house all of us when it needed to, felt closed-in, even though there were only five people in the room.

Celso walked to each table and threw it over. Jeremia's father, Jun, followed behind, pouring Ofelia's alcohol over the wood, splattering it against the walls and floor. Ofelia followed them, pulling at Jun's arm, which he yanked away. Candela followed Ofelia. A body lay in the corner of the room, the legs twisted at such odd angles that I knew they must be broken, that he must be dead, but it was Oscar, his legs come loose from his body. Beside Oscar crouched my brother David, gasping and wheezing, his hands grasping his shirt front.

"You've ruined my life," screamed Ofelia. "You destroy everyone's life."

"Whose fault is that?" yelled Celso. "You should have paid me when I was owed."

"I told you, I don't have the money and that tramp was hauled off to jail. Like I'm responsible for that."

Celso turned abruptly and grabbed Ofelia by the neck. He squeezed, and she clutched at his hands.

"I'm sick of your whining, you old bat. Look what you've done to yourself. I can't stand the sight of you."

She clutched at his hand, gasping, her eyes bulging and scared.

"You think I'm afraid of you just because you live in the city and work in this big building? That's nothing to me. I hate this stinking place."

Candela began to beat against his side with her fists.

"Let her go," she said. "You're killing her. Let her go."

Beside Celso, Jun watched and laughed.

And then Celso saw us. We were grouped together in the doorway, Jeremia beside me, Ranita strapped to me and Eva holding on to my coat with one hand. When he saw us, the room became so still I could feel Ranita's breath against my chest. Celso let go of Ofelia's neck and with a great grunt, lifted another table and threw it to the side. Jun poured alcohol over the wood.

"You're too late," Celso shouted at me. "You should have given me the money when I came weeks ago. Because of you, the old man burned."

It was true. I'd killed Nathanael. It felt as if the floor was shifting beneath my feet. Jeremia squeezed my arm.

"No, Nathanael burned because of you, Celso," said Jeremia. "It's not our fault you're a murderer."

"Rosa still pays me. You know that? She's been paying me every month since she came here. She's such a hardworking little whore."

I was going to be sick. All my wanderings boiled down to this one moment when I had to face the truth. My mentor sister slept with men for money, I had killed Nathanael, and I didn't know how to care for my family. I felt the tears, the sting of guilt, but Jeremia shook my arm hard, and I felt the fury in his grip. Fleet and agile as a deer, Jeremia leapt over the toppled tables and maneuvered his way around the destruction as though none of it existed. I had seen him like this before—climbing the trees, rising above limb and leaf as though they were irrelevant obstacles, as though missing an arm meant nothing. I wanted to look away, not observe the anger that would be unleashed, but at the same time his beauty was most magnificent when he moved with such timing and grace.

Celso crouched, ready, the knife at his side, but Jeremia came with such force, Celso was up against the wall of the common room with Jeremia's forearm against his neck before he had time to slice. Jeremia's father dropped the bottle in his hand and rushed at Jeremia, his hand outstretched. Jeremia's foot landed in his stomach, and with a grunt Jun crashed against the wall.

Before I could think about what I was doing, before I remembered that I had a baby strapped to my chest and a child following behind, I leaped over the tables, stepped over the chairs, jumped over broken bowls—I was back in the forest once again, my footing sure.

With my shoulder down and my arms protecting Ranita, I threw myself at this man who had risen seething with anger, ready to rid himself of a forsaken son who was less than perfect. His hand was aimed at Jeremia, about to thrust a knife into Jeremia's side, when I threw my shoulder into him, right under his arm. The hand with the knife rose into the air, piercing his own face.

I stumbled over a bench at my feet and tried to regain my footing, landing heavily on my side. I remembered the baby at that moment and tore open my coat. Ranita looked at me and then shrieked. I jostled her up and down and moved my hands over her body. She seemed whole—I felt nothing sticky, no blood, no limbs twisted into awkward positions. Jeremia still had Celso pinned to the wall. Celso pushed at Jeremia's face, trying to dislodge Jeremia's arm, but his pushes were weakening, his face a dark red and his eyes bloodshot, bursting. Celso's knife lay at Jeremia's feet.

I pulled myself off the floor and stepped around an overturned table, wondering who was shrieking so loudly. I put my hand on Jeremia's arm. He didn't feel me, didn't see me. When I looked at his face, I saw his mouth twisted, his eyes blackened, the tendons in his neck taut, but he was not screaming. I touched his cheek. He jerked and then saw me.

"Enough," I said.

His eyes refocused on Celso, who was now feebly pulling at his arm with both hands. Jeremia stepped back and Celso fell to the floor, gasping and clutching his neck.

"Did you know?" Jeremia's voice was hoarse, low, as though scraped over rocks. "Did you and Belen know that surgery could correct a cleft palate?"

Celso's face slowly lost its purple color and became blotchy. His eyes no longer swelled from his face, and his cheeks sank back into their place. He gave a dry cough of a laugh.

"Of course," he whispered and then put his finger to his lips. "But what good was she to us if she couldn't make money on the street corners? That's what all the rejects from the forest have done when the time was right."

"Except for me," Jeremia said.

"You're a boy. We didn't know what to do with you."

"Where's Belen?"

"Pah. Jun is twice the man Belen will ever be."

And then we looked at Jeremia's father. The knife, still clutched in Jun's hand, was embedded in his right eye. His screams pulsed with each breath. I held my hands over my ears. Ranita cried against my chest, Jun screamed on the ground, Ofelia moaned and twisted her hands in her hair, David lay on the ground next to Oscar, and Eva curled herself into a tight ball by the door to the common room. I sank slowly to the floor.

I rocked back and forth, my hands over my ears. I had done this to Jeremia's father—I had shoved the knife up and into his eye. These men had come to do harm, to cause violence, and even though I had been defending my family, I was no better than them. I'd sunk to their level. The goodness I'd once had, the innocence I'd brought with me, was gone. I no longer knew who I was, where I belonged and what my song should be.

Twenty-Six

For three days I slept. I lay in room 13 and kept my face to the wall, staring at it so hard I saw all the way back to the forest. Candela sat with me sometimes, rubbing my back, brushing my hair away from my face. Eva lay on top of me, pushed her soft cheek against mine and told me how much she loved me. David stayed with us, sharing room 13 with our surrogate family. He didn't seem disturbed by the people in Purgatory Palace—he had found his way to the common room and had been teaching Winston how to bake bread. Ranita had become Jeremia's responsibility once again. People whispered when they were around me as if my way of speaking had become contagious.

I heard what they said, I understood the situation, but I was so tired. I didn't know how to get rid of the ache in my limbs, the weight that pushed on my shoulders, shoving me into the ground. I wanted to become part of the earth, melt into the soil and feel the roots of trees holding me together. There I could feel whole again and remember the song that had once been my voice.

Jeremia told me that his father, Jun, would recover. Ofelia had called a doctor. The doctor came but couldn't save Jun's eye. He would wear a patch to protect the world from his disfigurement.

Celso was fine. He had a bruise across his neck, but bruises—at least the ones you can see—heal. The residents of Purgatory Palace had cleaned up the spilled alcohol, the tossed furniture, the broken doors. The building was salvageable because the men hadn't set fire to it. Oscar, it seemed, had not been killed but had a concussion. He whispered to me that a concussion a day kept insanity away.

David decided to join us. Celso had demanded that he come with him to the city. He'd wanted to show David how the rejects lived, selling their bodies or begging on street corners. Celso had believed that David would turn away from me then, but instead David found kindred spirits at Purgatory Palace. He cooked with Winston, played cards with Oscar and slept so hard his snores filled the room.

Ofelia was moving into her own apartment, away from us freaks, but had decided not to sell the building. She had placed Oscar and Candela in charge as long as they paid her monthly rent. Candela and Oscar were so excited, had so many plans to turn Purgatory Palace into a haven, that they argued about it constantly. They couldn't agree on anything, not even the new name. Heavenly Haven. The Final Stop. The Last Resort. Home.

"We'll have a restaurant upstairs and Winston will make all the food. We'll divide the common room into an area of shops and we'll sell all kinds of artistic things—we'll sell Jeremia's sculptures, my artwork, your music, David's bread. We'll tell the night workers that they have to go somewhere else. We'll make so much money with our art that we'll never have to beg again!"

I listened, but I didn't turn my face away from the wall. Moving my head was too much work. Who would come to a restaurant run by rejects, and who would eat food cooked by a boy with two faces? And where did I fit into all this? Would I live here again or keep going to school? If I stopped going to school, my lessons would stop, my work with the orchestra would cease, I would lose the wholeness of the music that I'd grown to love.

Solomon came to visit. He had visited Ofelia before but had never seen the rest of the building or all of the inhabitants. He was subdued, speaking to me softly, finally understanding just a bit of my life. Solomon probably thought the orchestra would spur me into action, convince me to rise from this bed and feel well again, but I was just too tired to get up. I felt like my song was gone and I'd been left with nothing to say.

Jeremia sat in the corner of the room and whittled. His sculptures were different here in Purgatory Palace. In our camp, the forms had spoken of water, twisting branches, beams of sunlight. Here they resembled flames, shards of glass, the points of knives. Dr. Ruiz bought the first sculpture from him, paying him enough money for a month's stay at Purgatory Palace. He saw that he could make his living in the city, whether he liked it or not.

When Dr. Ruiz came to buy the sculpture, she clapped her hands and laughed out loud. She refused to whisper.

"There is so much work to be done here. And you have such a wonderful family. But where did all these people come from? Why are they all gathered here?" She sat in my room and listened to the stories of Purgatory Palace.

Winston, the boy with two faces, had been born in a village south of the city. When he was born, the people of his village thought he was a marvel, that he was blessed and could predict the future. But in the years after he was born, the village's water supply completely dried up, the wells became stagnant, the crops failed. Their belief in the miracle of the boy with two faces changed, and they blamed him for the destruction of their village. They left him on the doorstep of Purgatory Palace.

The connected sisters—conjoined twins, Dr. Ruiz called them—were from Gloriosa. Their parents worked on the farm and already had three children before the farm came, before pigs became the main source of income, and then they had the twins. They didn't need more kids—kids who had to do everything together, who couldn't be separated, so they brought them here.

Dr. Ruiz brought bandages with her, skin-colored bits of tape, and she applied them to Ranita's lip.

"See?" she said. "This is what she'll look like after the surgery."

I turned my face away from the wall and opened my eyes. I looked at Ranita, who appeared blurred, misshapen. I lifted my head from the bed and stared at her face. She had no blemish. The tape covered the irregular openings and turned her perfect. This is why I was here—to make a better life for my little sister.

The room swirled around me, brightened, and I felt something in my chest—a small bud that was growing, blooming, spreading to my limbs. Jeremia stopped whittling, the conjoined twins stopped speaking, Eva stopped hopping on one foot, and Dr. Ruiz's cheeks puffed into a smile when I got off the bed. My legs felt shaky and my arms weak as I stood. I brushed off my clothes, opened the case of my violin and fit the instrument to my shoulder, under my chin, and it all came back, everything I had said through my songs. I played the song of Purgatory Palace. It was my first practice in three days—I closed my eyes and felt the music. I pulled the veil from around my neck and draped it over my head. Candela, Dr. Ruiz, David, Jeremia, Eva and Ranita all watched as I pulled my coat on and put the violin back into its case.

"I need to talk to Solomon," I said and walked out the door.

∞

Solomon was in his office at the school. He sat behind a desk littered with newspapers, disposable coffee cups, wrappers. His usually smooth chin was stubbled with growth, and his peppermint scent was muddled by coffee, bad breath and body odor. When I entered his office, he held his hands out to me and spoke in a shaky voice.

"Whisper, can we ever make it work?" His voice was as hoarse as mine. "Have I lost you and the beauty of your song?"

I understood now why I walked between two worlds and why this had become my place. I was the bridge—I was the translator between those who come into this world whole and those who don't. Ranita would join me as a member of both worlds.

"I'm ready to play."

He rubbed his eyes with both hands, stood and walked around the desk, lumbering in heavy strides. He looked at me through eyes so bloodshot I wondered if perhaps he too should lie down on his bed and not move for three days.

"Are you sure?"

I wasn't sure. How could I be? I was about to tell my story to a roomful of people in a huge auditorium, and who knew if my message would come through? But this was the way I spoke and this was my story and these were my friends who needed my help and this was my little sister whose cleft palate would be fixed and whose earaches would disappear.

"I'm sure."

The auditorium was vacant, hollow and dark. We were early. As Solomon and I parked in our usual spot, a car pulled into the space next to ours, and out of it stepped Dr. Ruiz, Jeremia with Ranita and Eva, David, Candela and Oscar.

I couldn't stop the sudden tears. I sniffled, rubbing my nose on the sleeve of my sweater, and tried to smile, but my mouth wobbled and my lower lip drooped. Candela put her arm around my waist on one side and Eva did the same on the other. Jeremia stood in front of me, his eyes dark, his mouth straight.

He reached out and touched my cheek with the tip of his finger. Then he pulled me away from Eva and Candela, slipped his arm around my waist and held me against his chest. I pressed my cheek against his neck and listened to his breathing.

Dr. Ruiz walked beside Solomon and we all made our way to the dark stairs that led from the parking garage to the auditorium. We walked down the aisle, Eva gasping and pointing as we went, touching the ornate gold decorations on the sides of the seats. I'd never been here when the orchestra was absent and most of the lights were turned off. The building felt very hollow, emptied out, and I clutched Eva's hand, glad to have her warmth beside me. Solomon and I sat on the stage and waited.

Ruy Climaco rushed in, flipping his hair from his shoulders and leading his body with his chin. His eyes and mouth were narrow slits in his face and his arms pumped back and forth, the baton gripped like a sword in his right hand.

"Well, miss," he said before he was halfway down the aisle. "Think you're a bit high and mighty, don't you? Think you can come and go as you like—well, young lady, I'm here to tell you that playing with the City Philharmonic is an honor, and you, child, should understand that. You don't miss practices for the Philharmonic even on your deathbed—and you, you especially, should be grateful for the opportunity…"

As he talked, a baby gurgled behind him, and then someone coughed. Ranita shrieked, cooed, blew bubbles. Ruy Climaco slowed his speech and turned around. When he saw the group of people seated in the front row, his hand moved to his face, fluttered and covered his mouth.

"Good God."

The people in the front row smiled, except for Jeremia, and Oscar waved a leg at Ruy. Ruy turned around abruptly, his jaw clenched.

"Let's begin, then, shall we?" Solomon said.

We practiced for two hours. I tried to remember all the advice given to me by Ruy Climaco and by Solomon. Ruy hummed the accompaniment, I kept the beat steady, I counted in my head and played the song of Purgatory Palace.

I was only a small part of the performance, and my piece came in the middle. For the first half of the evening I sat in the front row with my family. Jeremia and I took turns holding Ranita, bouncing her on our laps, feeding her bits of a roll. She gurgled along with the music, but the sound she made was lost in the song of the orchestra. For a time, she seemed to listen, but mostly she slept.

At intermission, Solomon stood up and motioned for me to follow. When I rose from my seat, Jeremia pulled on the sleeve of my sweater. He held his hand out to me, the back of the hand up, the fingers curved around something in his fist. I opened my hand beneath his. His fingers touched my palm, and when they did, energy burst into me, tingled through me, and I was awake as I hadn't been for a long time. Something dropped into my hand. It was my carved violin, complete and whole once again. Jeremia said nothing, but for the first time since he had returned to me, he smiled. I leaned down and pressed my lips against his. He kissed me back, strong, sure, unembarrassed.

I stood beside Solomon at the back of the stage, and he said to me, "You, Whisper, are the strongest person I know."

I had just curled into myself for three days. I had been sad, lonely, lost and abandoned. I slipped the string around my neck and felt the weight of Jeremia's violin against my chest.

Pulling my shoulders back, pulling my stomach in, I stood straight and finished tuning my instrument. My veil had slipped to the side, and I adjusted it over my face. It was time.

The orchestra members took their seats, tuned their instruments, readied themselves. Ruy Climaco climbed the steps to the stage, turned and bowed to the audience. The audience clapped—a few yelled. I allowed myself a slow, careful smile.

"We are honored to have a guest violinist today. Whisper Gane, a sixteen-year-old virtuoso, will be playing a piece that she composed herself. Please give a warm welcome to Whisper Gane."

Ruy's arm swept toward me and his face turned in my direction. He beamed as though he had never been angry. I took a deep breath and tucked my bow under my arm. With my left hand I reached out to Solomon and squeezed his arm.

"Your song is a miracle, Whisper, and your story needs to be heard."

"Thanks for being the first to listen," I said. I walked onto the stage, I bowed to the audience and smiled when the front row of listeners screamed, yelled and whistled.

"Break a leg, Whisper," yelled Oscar, his voice booming through the auditorium, one of his legs held up over his head. Some audience members laughed, others gasped.

Looking out into the audience, the lights from the ceiling blinding me to anything but those in the first few rows,

I listened to my heart—the slow, steady beat of calm. I fitted my violin to my shoulder, rested my chin on it and, at Ruy's signal, began to play.

My hands didn't flutter, my heart didn't race, my knees didn't become slick with sweat. I was transported to Purgatory Palace, to a place where love existed at the edges of torment and loneliness. My song found wings and flew through the auditorium. I kept the beat, I listened to the orchestra, and we played in harmony.

As I drew my bow over the strings of the violin for the final notes, I opened my eyes and saw that in the first row, all my family and friends were on their feet, clapping, screaming and yelling my name. Their enthusiasm leaked from the front row to the back, and soon the entire audience had risen to its feet, clapping, whistling, cheering for me, a reject, a lost member of this world.

When the clapping died down, I continued to stand in the same spot. Silence filled the room after people had shuffled down into their seats. Ruy held his hand out toward me and instructed me to take a bow. Instead, I tucked my violin under my arm, reached up with my left hand and felt the veil whisper against my face as I lifted it from my head.

Gasps rose up like moths from the depths of the audience. Ruy stood in front of the orchestra, his face frozen, his hand stiffly held in front of him.

I stepped foward and looked over the audience. Tonight, almost every seat was full. My friends and family in the front row screamed once again and yelled my name. It was then, as Whisper Gane without the veil, that I took my bow.

Acknowledgments

I would like to thank: Tony Wolk, my thesis advisor, for his patience and unswerving optimism; Michelle McCann, Diana Abu-Jaber and Barbara Ruben for joining the thesis committee; Danielle Schneider, Sasha Sterner, Arianna Strong and Samantha Thompson, my student readers, for their time, feedback and willingness to be guinea pigs; Connie Barr, Kelly Garrett, Marla Bowie LePley, Laura Marshall and Lisa Nowak, my writing group members, who gave me consistent feedback and believed in the big picture; John and Andrea Struyk, Angela Struyk-Huyer, Catrina Huyer and Alana Miner for feedback throughout the writing process; Eric, Quinten and Eli for their patience and unfaltering support. And finally, thank you to Sarah Harvey, my editor at Orca Book Publishers, who believed in the project and whose guidance was invaluable.

Chris Struyk-Bonn previously detassled corn, worked in a small motor-parts factory, framed pictures, served in various and sundry restaurants and sorted eggs in an egg factory. She is currently a high school English teacher in Portland, Oregon, and has at last discovered a job she thoroughly enjoys. *Whisper* is her first book.